I0788547

SHADES OF NIGHT

J.E. Taylor

SHADES OF NIGHT © 2022 J.E. Taylor

Cover Art by Luminescence Covers

SHADES OF NIGHT
PREQUEL
YOUNG BLOOD

Duty and fate collide when a cocky young alpha finds his forbidden mate.

Robby Young never anticipated meeting his true soul mate on the first day at the Monster Defense Academy, especially considering relationships with other members of the agency are strictly prohibited.

When that girl ends up listed as his partner, Robby has to muzzle his wolf to keep her safe.

If he falls prey to his desires and crosses the line his father set, he'll sentence his partner to a position in front of the firing squad.

YOUNG BLOOD 1

A S WE CRESTED THE top of the hill, I caught the first view of my home for the next year. The Monster Defense Academy sprawled out before us, tucked in a valley of the Appalachian Mountains of New York. Dark, squat buildings surrounded the center high-rise that gleamed in the midday sun. The entire footprint of the academy was bigger than most small colleges, but the interconnected buildings made it look like a giant octopus with a huge dick sticking out of its center.

"Do I really have to…" I started, still staring at the buildings with enough disgust that I was sure it bled into my face.

"Yes," my father said from the driver's seat before I could finish my sentence. He glanced at me with the same piercing blue eyes I saw in the mirror on a daily basis. "You're a legacy. You will carry on our tradition. One day, maybe you'll be running the company."

I scoffed. After all the information my father fed me over the years, I didn't want anything to do with the Monster Defense Agency. But my father had grand plans for me, whether I liked it or not. Leading the Allegany pack was one thing, and that I was all for. But walking in his shoes at the MDA? No way. I wanted nothing to do with that.

Unfortunately, I had no goddamn choice.

At least I wouldn't be here alone. The rest of the legacies in the pack would be here with me. We'd be paired with witches and then hunt the vilest creatures out there. That might just be the only thing I looked forward to. Ripping apart vampires had its own sick appeal, especially because a vampire was responsible for the rest of my family's deaths.

The only reason I was breathing today was the fact on that fateful night, I was not home with my mom and my younger brother and sister. I was at my beta's birthday party. Me and a half dozen others watching late-night television, laid out in sleeping bags on the family room floor while a vampire feasted on my family. I still remember my father arriving at Johnson's house before the sun rose the next morning. His eyes had been frantic as he searched the sleeping bags on the floor and when they landed on me, it seemed all that tension turned into something else that made his eyes shine. Relief. Disappointment. I have no idea, but blood streaked his shirt and hands, and he had some in his hair, too.

That night was the only time in my life that I ever recall my father visibly shaken. And dread filled me at the tears shining in his eyes. He took me aside and delivered the news that shattered my world.

I shook the memory away as we pulled up to the grand entrance of the academy. We were the only ones up here on the plateau, looking down at the lower parking lot where the rest of the wolves and witches were being unloaded from buses and cars.

"Why aren't we unloading down there?" I waved to the mass of new recruits.

"We're the elite. This is where I enter."

I hated the superiority in his voice. I glanced at the lower parking lot, wishing I was with them.

A crop of red hair caught my attention and I blinked, with my duffel bag halfway to my shoulder. Even from this distance, I caught her attitude and the ream of swears spilling from her mouth as they hauled her off the bus. Something inside me stirred.

A slap against the back of my head brought me back into the present. "Everyone here is off-limits. You're going to marry the right wolf. You understand?"

"One you deem worthy?" My voice dripped with sarcasm. He was going to marry me off to some alpha's daughter once he found a worthy alliance. It was not my choice. None of this was my choice.

He glared at me.

"Fine. I get it." But my gaze kept drifting to the crowd below. Not only did I wish I was with the rest of my pack, now I wanted to seek out that girl.

"I'm serious. No fucking around here. You keep your nose clean and learn everything you need to do the job right." He shook his finger in my face.

I had to clench my jaw against the urge to bite his digit off. Instead, I hauled the duffel bag over my shoulder and headed inside where a short, bespectacled man led me to my dorm room in silence.

White painted cinderblocks and gray linoleum flooring met my gaze as I stepped into the room the little man waved at. It certainly did not instill any sort of excitement for being here, especially considering the furniture looked too small for my stature. But I guess it was better than sleeping on the hard floor.

A bathroom stood to the right of the entrance door, and the entire thing was about as big as my oversized walk-in shower at home. The scent of antiseptic in the bathroom permeated everything, as if it had just been scrubbed clean. It was enough to sting my nose.

"The assembly starts in twenty minutes in the grand hall." He left me to claim a bed.

I threw my duffel bag on the single bed on the right, assessing the lack of length. Man, if I stretched out on that thing, my lower legs would hang off. I was going to seriously miss my California king at home. I ran my hand over my face, irritated at the prospect of spending a year in this glorified coat closet. I turned and stormed out. I didn't want to be the last person into the assembly, and I wanted to catch that brazen redhead, despite my father's warning.

He wanted me to marry a nice werewolf. Someone subservient. But I liked my women feisty and bold, not meek and mild. And I didn't care what she was. Human, witch, wolf, fae: it didn't matter to me. The only off-limits species was vampire, because those monsters were the walking dead. They even smelled hideous.

I followed my nose, and searching for the assembly hall took less time than I anticipated. It wasn't difficult. I just followed the magical signatures filling the air. Wolves and witches filled the entry leading to the assembly room. Because I had been in the sleeping quarters, I entered the hall on the balcony level and descended the stairs as I scanned the crowd.

Johnson, my beta and the reason I wasn't in a grave with the rest of my family, gave me a wave. I nodded at him but didn't head where he and the rest of my pack stood in a tight circle. My gaze kept moving, past the frown on my father's face, and over the nameless crowd, until it locked with hers.

The reaction was immediate, like a shot to my chest. Her eyes widened as she took me in, and the smile that toyed on her lips had my wolf nearly in a frenzy to claim her. I stepped off the stairs on legs that felt like rubber, and I lost her in the crowd now that I didn't have a clear view.

I cut my way through the mob, catching sight of her as I maneuvered around people. She moved toward me, and when we met in the middle of the gathering, it was as if everyone disappeared. Her chocolate eyes scanned me.

"Hi."

Even her voice made me want to drop to my knees in front of her. Her beauty made the rest of the women in the room seem like hags.

"Hi." I put out my hand. "I'm Robby Young."

"Sarah Stone." She took my hand in a sure grip and pumped once before breaking the contact.

But her touch was enough for me to know.

My father had told me what happens when we meet our true mates. The wolf in me reacted to her, and I had to struggle to keep him in check, despite the crowd surrounding us. He wanted to stake his claim on this wild one right here. I inhaled her citrusy scent as if it were more precious than air. This wasn't just physical, either; it was as if my soul cried out for her, and the glint in her eyes was enough to make me step closer.

A hand landed on my shoulder. I almost didn't turn away from her, but the hand squeezed hard enough to break whatever spell she had on me. I turned, meeting my father's stern gaze.

"The assembly is starting." He didn't remove his hand, either. He pulled me away from Sarah Stone with an iron grip. The scowl on his face screamed disgust, as if my being near her threatened his fucking kingdom.

I glanced over my shoulder and caught the flame of her hair in the crowd as we entered the assembly.

"She is off-limits." His growling voice filled my ear.

I snapped my gaze to his. "What?" I shook his hand off my shoulder. "But she's my true mate." There was no way I was staying away from her.

His step faltered, and his glare homed in on mine. "The MDA will not tolerate interagency relationships."

"It's not like she's my partner." I rolled my eyes at him. "Besides, they made an exception for you and Mom," I pointed out.

Although the agency did have a strict rule against becoming romantically entangled, he and my mother had gotten a pass. I didn't know whether that was because of his legacy standing or because he had become invaluable to the agency, but they didn't crucify either of them. Scolded them, from what I understand, but did not kill them for their transgressions.

Of course, if they had been partners, it would have been a very different story. That's why the agency matched males with males and females with females—it lowered the opportunity for that to happen. The punishment for violating that rule was archaically severe. And not in a job loss way.

It usually meant forfeiting the witch's life, unless they were powerful mages. Then, in that case, the wolf met their end. It was all way too militant for my tastes.

"She was a wolf." He grunted at me, as if that made a difference. "That girl is a witch." He led me up front, where he pointed to the aisle seat before he headed up on stage with the rest of the agency board.

I turned, scanning the auditorium. My gaze landed on her in the back row on the far side of the auditorium. When she looked my way, my lips tilted into a smile. She responded with a grin and a little wave of her fingers.

Man, my wolf was in so much trouble.

I turned back to the stage, to a searing glare from my father. He leaned over to the board members and whispered something I could not pick up. The shock on their faces made me shift in the seat but they nodded at him and took out a bound ledger, marking it up.

When Mr. Simmons, the headmaster of the Monster Defense Academy, stepped up to the podium, the lights dimmed. I stared at the nondescript human as if he wasn't there. I mean, his lips moved and his hands moved in an animated fashion, but I did not hear a word he said.

My mind was focused entirely on the redheaded girl in the back row.

YOUNG BLOOD 2

A S SOON AS WE were excused from the assembly, I stood to leave.

"Robert," my father called as he hustled down the stairs.

I hated when he called me by my formal name. I was Robby to all my friends and everyone else in the family. I never asked to be a junior, and I tried like hell to differentiate myself. Even with my friends, who were loyal because I treated them with respect and not because I instilled fear in them.

I had the capacity to pull the alpha card and force loyalty, but I never used it. I wasn't into the control game that so many other alphas, my father included, were into.

When Robert Young Senior was out for blood, the pack quaked. He had a mean streak that would make any self-respecting wolf run with their tail tucked between their legs. He ruled the pack through fear, and it irked me. Although, I had to admit that even I got a little skittish when he was on a rampage.

"What?" I snapped. I couldn't wait until he left, and I was free to be myself.

"Remember. Learn." His stern finger waggled at me. "Nothing else. Understand?"

"Yes, sir." Arguing never boded well with my father. And I was still a month shy of eighteen, so technically, he was still in charge of my decisions. At least until he left the campus. Then I was on my own.

"And you will stay away from that girl." He pushed his alpha influence on me.

It draped over me like a wet blanket, chilling me, but I just stared back at him, unwilling to cower, especially on this point.

The muscles in his face jumped, as though he ground his teeth. While other wolves in the vicinity nearly folded in on themselves or turned and hurried along to get away from this display of power that my father was attempting to wield over me, it didn't faze me.

I didn't accept his authority on this one.

"Damn it, boy. Do you want to ruin your life?"

"No, sir." I didn't have a choice in the path he set me on. It was expected of the pack to serve up their young to this organization like sacrificial lambs. As such, I wasn't necessarily going to play by their rules of engagement, especially because my wolf demanded I claim that girl, and who was I to ignore my wolf?

"Then do as I demand," he growled, low.

I neither nodded nor shook my head, but I did turn and walk away, leaving him to stew at my non-reaction. I headed straight to my room, like we had been instructed, to unpack before dinner. Then after we ate, we were expected to head back to our rooms for the night.

My father arranged for Johnson to be my roommate. Allegany pack members usually had pre-arranged roommates who were part of the pack, but from what I understood, they usually opted to room with their partners. Even so, I was glad Johnson was my roommate and not some stranger. It was an indication at how fundamentally powerful the pack was to the MDA.

When I got to my room, it was still empty. Johnson hadn't had a chance to bring his stuff to the room like I had as the son of the grand master of the entire Northeast region. By the time I had unpacked my duffel bag, Johnson strolled in with an expression I recognized.

My father had gotten to him.

He threw his bag on the other bed and turned, opening his mouth.

"Don't." I put my hand up. "I do not want to hear whatever the hell he told you to say."

Rick Johnson closed his mouth and ran his hand through his dark hair. "Okay, man, but it's your funeral."

"My dad got them to change the rules. I can, too." It was cocky to think that way, and I knew it, but there was no way on God's green earth that I was going to deny my wolf this.

"Maybe I'll sleep with her."

Before he even finished saying the thought, I had him against the wall. The growl that tore from me was enough to make Johnson wide-eyed. "If you want to see the sunrise, I suggest you kill that urge right now."

"Shit. Fine." He put his hands out, palms forward in submission. "I didn't realize..." He trailed off, eyes still wide with shock.

"She's my true mate, and I'm not letting my father, or the MDA, dictate what I can and cannot do with her."

"Robby, they are serious with their rules. Besides, you don't know if she's into you. She's not a wolf. She wouldn't feel the connection you're feeling."

I nodded, stepping away from him. Her pupils had dilated when we first met, as I'm sure mine had. But did that mean she was into me? I didn't know, but I sure as hell was going to find out.

I spun away from Johnson and stalked out of the room in search of the dining hall in this monstrous academy. When I finally found the dining room, it was still locked, so, I parked my ass on one of the benches in the hallway, waiting. Not for the doors to open, but for my redheaded dream to walk by.

The door to the opposite hallway creaked, and I caught a glimpse of red hair poke through. I had to clamp down on the smile. She liked being first, too. Either that or she was on the same mission I was.

"This is the dining hall." I allowed a small smile at her gasp, and then her wide eyes landed on me.

"Why are you so early?" She looked around at the deserted hallway.

"I'm hungry." I shrugged. "And I hate to wait in line."

She slid into the spot next to me. "I like to be early so the food isn't picked over too much." She stretched her legs out and crossed her ankles and arms, leaning against the wall with the kind of smile on her face that stirred more than my wolf. Her hair was long, with the kind of waves you see on the beach in the summer, but not frizzy, and the color wasn't the scream-in-your-face red that you get with dye. I had seen too many girls back home try to achieve this look, and it always turned out unnatural. Sarah's hair was a subtle auburn that truly turned heads.

My wolf demanded that I claim her right now, but I couldn't just get down to business right here in the hallway, despite how much I wanted to. Plus, I still didn't know whether she was into me or not, and claiming someone who wasn't on the same page was unthinkable. At least in my world it was, but I've seen it happen and the claimed were always resentful. I didn't want to start a life with anyone based on resentment.

"So, are you here by choice or was this forced upon you, too?" She stared at the doors that led to the dining hall.

"It's expected of me." I sighed.

She snorted. "So, you were forced as well."

I debated on how to answer her statement. "I'm the next in line to lead the Allegany pack, so it's my duty to be part of the MDA."

She chuckled and glanced sideways at me. "An alpha? I would have never guessed."

I couldn't tell whether she was being coy or not.

"Why aren't you with your pack?" She nodded toward the opposite door, as if she knew where we were staying.

"Hungry. Remember?" I didn't want to come right out and say I was waiting for her to show up. That would put me in a weird category, and I didn't want her to think I was creepy.

"Mhm." She studied me out of the corner of her eye. "Have you read the handbook yet?"

"No, but I probably could recite the rules of this place to you in my sleep." I offered her a smile while my wolf pushed the boundaries of my control. I leaned forward, putting my elbows on my knees as I picked at a hangnail on my thumb as a diversion.

"Are you one of those who follows the rules religiously?" Hope bled into the lilt of her question, and I turned to meet her gaze.

There was the sign I was waiting for. She licked her lips and the light danced in her dilated eyes, making me smile. But before I could answer her, Johnson slid into the hallway.

"The cafeteria isn't open yet?" Johnson waved at the door and then he looked at his watch before he focused his attention on Sarah. "Well, hello," he said in his silky seduction voice that almost drew a growl from me. He stuck his hand out. "I'm Johnson."

"What, did your mother not like you or something?" Sarah shook his hand.

I pressed my lips together against the smirk that crept onto them. I gave Sarah a sideways glance, and her face had the same half-suppressed smile that I was trying to keep off my face.

Johnson turned red at the comment and shoved his hands in his pockets. "Johnson is my last name."

Sarah's eyebrows shot up and her mouth popped open for a split second. If I hadn't been looking at her, I never would have caught that flash of surprise. "Oh. I'm sorry." Her cheeks turned a rose color that complemented her hair.

The sound of locks releasing had us all turning toward the dining room door. When it swung open, I shot to my feet. Sarah followed and we descended on the newly laid-out buffet, heaping barbequed ribs, potatoes, and corn on the cob onto our plates and finding a seat in the back corner together.

With my back to the wall, I had a view of the entire cafeteria, from the buffet tables to the massive fireplace that had pristine birch logs stacked inside for show. The arched ceiling was broken by stained-glass windows that would paint the room with color at noon when the sun was high. Beyond the buffet setup was a raised platform with a long table waiting for the school staff to enter. I didn't give that area any more than a cursory look.

The rest of the school rushed in moments later, and the quiet solitude we had went straight to hell. I didn't get a chance to talk at any length with Sarah for the rest of the evening, even with her sitting across from me at the table. Not when the rest of the pack had joined us and monopolized the conversation. Every time my leg brushed against hers under the table, a jolt of electricity traveled from the spot we connected, shooting straight to my heart.

All I knew was when she licked the barbeque sauce off her fingers, I had to blink a few times to get myself under control. I wished it was something else she was licking like that. Johnson actually elbowed me to get me to stop staring at her.

"I should go try to get some sleep," Sarah said when her tray was empty and her eyes at half-mast of a food comma. "I want to be awake and aware when I meet my partner tomorrow."

I went to stand and offer to walk her to her room, but Johnson grabbed my knee under the table and gave me a quick shake of his head. He nodded toward the head table. A table I hadn't paid any attention to all night. My father sat near the headmaster, with his arms crossed and a scowl on his face.

Fuck.

I couldn't leave the dining room with her. Not with his complete aggravation radiating over the entire room. I turned back to Sarah, but she had already stepped away.

Double fuck.

I took a breath and gave Johnson a nod of thanks. If I had wandered off with Sarah, she would likely get booted from the school tomorrow. Although, on second thought, that might not be a bad thing. Especially if she was here under duress. If she was let go at this stage of training, there wouldn't be a single thing keeping me from claiming her.

I smacked Johnson's hand away and crossed to the exit. But by the time I pushed the door that she had first come through open, the hallway was empty, and I couldn't rightfully wander around the women's dorm looking for her.

"Shit." I had lost her.

YOUNG BLOOD 3

THE NEXT MORNING STARTED out gray and overcast, with rain in the forecast. Not the best mood-inspiring day to meet partners, but I was just as anxious to learn who would have my back in battle.

I grabbed a quick breakfast and headed to the assembly hall and the corkboard outside the door with the list of names. I stared at the sheets on the wall announcing who our assigned partners were. My finger ran down the list and when I came to my name, my brain stalled.

I stepped back as the rest of the students slid by to read the list.

"What the actual fuck?" Words finally slipped out of my mouth, but my feet wouldn't budge. I stared at the damnation written on the board as a fiery anger filled every cell.

My father did this.

"Seriously?" Her voice rang from the spot next to me. "You're my partner?" She looked up at me. "A fucking alpha wolf?"

I glanced at her, and my gut tightened. My wolf nearly burst forth, but I kept him under wraps. Because now, if I gave in to this blinding need, it meant she would be put under the guillotine. Literally.

"Apparently." I tried to keep the hostility out of my words.

"Someone must really hate me," she muttered under her breath.

I cocked my eyebrow at her. "What's that supposed to mean?"

She squared herself in front of me, crossed her arms, and glared. "I'm not subservient to anyone."

I laughed, because she was such a perfect fit for me. I didn't want a meek bitch underfoot, and it just burned even more that my father had fucked up any chance I had with this girl.

Her eyes narrowed. "I'm serious."

"I'm not laughing at you. I promise." I glanced at the list, wondering who had been misplaced with my father's last-minute change. But there were no other female and male pairings on the list. Which meant a few candidates had been escorted off the property in the dark of night. My gaze sliced back to hers. "And I'd never try to impart my alpha influence on you."

She blinked up at me as if I had just answered whatever prayer she had engaged in the night before.

"I'm not here to control my partner. I'm here to spill a lot of vampire blood." I grinned down at her. "So, if you aren't up for that, then we *will* have a problem."

The slow, sure smile that spread over her lips, along with that insane spark in her eyes, made me curse my father even more.

"I'm totally down with that." She held out her hand. "Partner."

I didn't want to touch her, but I also didn't want to offend her, so I took her hand in a tight grip. "Here's to a lifetime of ridding vampires of their heads." My wolf nearly yanked her to my chest, but I let go of her instead. He balked at me.

Her lower lip sucked between her teeth as she glanced at the list again. "Um. Do they expect us to room together?"

When her gaze came back to mine again, all I could think about was seeing her undressed in my room. That wouldn't end well for either of us.

"My beta is my roommate." For once, I was glad for my status here. It saved me from sentencing her to death, because in that kind of intimate situation, I most certainly would not be able to control my goddamn wolf.

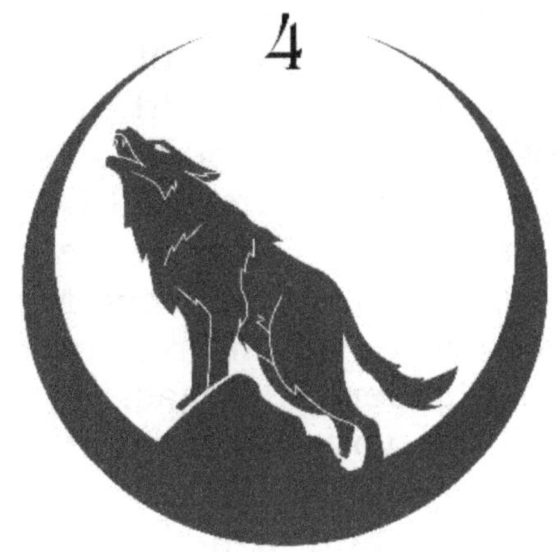

YOUNG BLOOD 4

WHEN WE ENTERED THE assembly room, my father sat on stage with that smug *I know what's better for you than you do* look on his face, and a growl escaped. I maneuvered Sarah into one of the rows in the middle of the theater instead of going to the seat up front that my father no doubt reserved for me.

Sarah raised an eyebrow at me, and I shook my head. Explaining my father to her would open me up to questions I had no intentions of answering. Questions that might open a door that I so very badly wanted to keep closed.

A frown appeared on my father's face as we took a seat; his gaze slashed to the front seats and then back, as if he silently commanded me to move my ass where he wanted me to be. I pointedly sat in the seat, crossed my arms, and stared my father down. It was my declaration that he did not control me like he believed he did. I could relate to Sarah's dislike of being controlled. I hated when others fucked with my life, and my father just crossed me for the last time.

At least when my mother had been alive, she ran interference for me. She let me cultivate my friends, gain their loyalty my way. My father just wanted to beat me down and remind me I'd never be as good of a leader as he was.

"So... you and your father don't get along?" Sarah asked.

I glanced at her and sighed. "I'll never live up to his expectations."

"Sucks to be you." She leaned back in the chair and adopted the same cross-armed pose I had and gave me a curious side eye.

Damn, I wanted to take her back to my room and ravage the hell out of her. That look alone could undo my resolve, and the reality of spending the next however many years at each other's side without acting on this ache in my chest cramped my stomach. I closed my eyes and took a deep breath to get a grip on my libido and my wolf. I wanted years next to this girl. Even if it meant being just her hunting partner.

If I crossed the line, it meant *her* death.

Sudden, almost violent hatred flooded every cell like hot lava. I clenched my fists against the raw flare of rage that brushed over me like a thousand sharp claws shredding my skin. Noise filtered around us as people took their seats. When a hushed silence fell over the auditorium, I opened my eyes.

The lights over the audience dimmed and my gaze locked with my father's. Whatever smug look he entertained flashing at me fell. His expression crossed from irritation into almost alarmed, as if he read the visceral burn filling my veins, but it was gone after a few moments. The fact he needed more than a second to regain his composure pleased me. I rattled the old man.

And until this moment, my attempts at making him uncomfortable had always failed. But tonight, I nailed it. All it took was him ruining my life and my reaction to his fucking meddling to get here.

The seat next to me creaked. "There you are." Johnson slapped my shoulder as he settled in.

I grunted at him.

"Hey," he said around me.

"Hey," Sarah said with a nod of acknowledgment. "Johnson, right?"

He flashed her a smile that I wanted to pummel off his face, but she just rolled her eyes and sat back in the seat.

I sent a glare in his direction, and his smile faded.

Sarah leaned forward and hooked a thumb at me. "Are you his roommate?"

Johnson nodded, and she smirked at him.

"Good luck with Mr. Moody here." She glanced at me and leaned back in her chair.

I cocked my eyebrow at her.

"What?" she asked me. "You've been all kinds of moody since we met. It's like you're on your period or something."

Johnson snorted a laugh.

My lips crept into a smile. "I'm usually not this bad," I grumbled. But she was right. I hadn't exactly been my laid-back self around her. Not

with every single cell in my body screaming at me
to claim her, and knowing doing that would mean
her death.

I wasn't sure I'd ever be myself again.

YOUNG BLOOD 5

I PACED ACROSS THE floor in our room as Johnson droned on.

"Even if you claim her, she'll be executed, and you'll be exiled from the pack."

"I am fully aware of what the consequences are." I knew, but I kept searching for a way around them. Even if I did ascend to the alpha of our pack, it wouldn't mean a thing. If I crossed the line, she'd be sentenced to death. The MDA did not spare witches, and in their eyes, a rogue wolf was just as dangerous. So, if I broke the rules, my life as I knew it would be over.

But that didn't stop the burning desire filling me. That didn't stop my wolf from demanding I take her. "You have no idea what it feels like being near her. It drives my wolf insane." I ran my hand through my hair and threw myself down on the bed.

"Dude, you've got to control your wolf."

Johnson stating the obvious just made my blood boil even more. "My father broke MDA protocol."

"Yeah, but your mom wasn't his partner."

It's as if my father schooled him in every possible answer. Although it was true, it still burned.

"Get some sleep, Robby. Classes start early." Johnson turned off his light and was snoring within minutes.

I stared at the ceiling for what seemed like hours, playing over every option in my head, and they all led to the same place.

Losing my true mate.

"Fuck," I mumbled and rolled onto my side, hating my father even more with every passing second.

❧ ———— •◦•◆◉◆•◦• ———— ❧

A SHRILL RING PENETRATED my head, and I reached out, slamming the snooze button. Morning had come way too fast—but then again, I tossed and turned most of the night.

Today started the living hell I would have to endure for the rest of my life. Or at least until I retired. Then, and only then, could I act on this insane need rampaging through me. It was a bitter pill to swallow.

The alarm rang again, and I swatted it, sitting up and grumbling. Johnson stepped out of the bathroom and gave me a raised eyebrow.

"I know, I'm moving." I grabbed my clothes and towel, and headed into the bathroom to clean up. My stomach rumbled, and I hurried through my morning routine. I was going to need a decent breakfast and a gallon of coffee to get through the day without nodding off.

The cafeteria was full of students, and the buffet had been sufficiently picked over by the time we got there. I surveyed the room and found the crop of red hair in the masses, wondering who her roommate was because everyone else had chosen to pair up with their partners, with the exception of me and my beta.

I piled food on my plate, grabbed the biggest coffee, and headed toward the red hair sitting at the end of one of the tables away from everyone else.

Johnson cleared his throat behind me, and I glanced at him. He nodded toward the table with the rest of my pack.

I huffed. "Go find your partner. We're supposed to be using downtime to bond with them. Or didn't you read the program booklet?" At least I had that going for me. It was expected to spend the time away from class with partners, but they had never before paired a male and female together, until this year. Besides, my wolf was pulling me toward her and right now, in this crowded room, it was the safest place to give in to his needs.

I put my tray down, and she looked up at me with those wide brown eyes that I could get lost in. Her lips morphed from the frown she wore as she stared at her food to that dazzling smile that made my brain stall.

I sat down, feeling my face crack with a smile just as bright as hers. "So, who's your roommate?" I looked around the cafeteria before I dug into my food.

"I have my own room. I guess there isn't any other female who isn't paired up." She shrugged but didn't seem too put out by not having to share her space.

"Does that bother you?" My attention returned to her, and I swear she radiated a citrus scent that made my mouth water and my mind wander.

She leaned forward. "I actually like it, but don't tell anyone because I have a feeling they would change that in a heartbeat if they knew."

I pressed my lips against a smirk. "And you're telling the alpha prick you have as a partner this because?" I raised an eyebrow at her.

She blinked and leaned back in her seat. Her mouth popped open in a little O as if she realized it wasn't prudent to trust me.

That was not my intention. I needed her to trust me, just like she needed me to trust her. If we didn't, we would fail out in the real world. I knew I'd have her back, even if it was to my detriment, but if she didn't feel that same loyalty, then I was screwed. "Don't worry, I won't say a thing," I whispered and couldn't help the grin that formed when her eyebrows lowered into a scowl.

"Asshole," she muttered and picked at her food.

"Yes. But I'm the asshole who has your back." I pointed my fork at her. "You aren't hungry?" I asked after she moved the food around her plate again.

"It's not Starbucks." She shrugged.

I belted out a laugh and almost sprayed my food all over her. "Your parents let you go to Starbucks?" My father never let me go to the fast-food places near our pack lands. He said it was poison to our bodies.

"My parents are dead."

Well, that was a conversation killer. "I'm sorry. I didn't know."

"If they were alive, I wouldn't be here."

Deep down, I cursed the fact they were dead. If she wasn't here, there would be no stopping me from claiming her as my mate.

"But the state saw fit to hand me over to get me off their hands." She continued to pick at her food, stealing glances at me, as if she were gauging my reaction.

"You like to cause trouble?"

A secret smile appeared, and she looked up at me. "If you could have anything in the world right now, what would it be?"

Such a loaded question, and I had to actually bite my tongue to keep from saying what I truly wanted. That would open a dangerous door. "I am unsure how to answer that," I finally said.

"Come on, you must want something. A designer watch, a pair of cowboy boots to go with your high and mighty attitude, a leather coat?" She took a bite of her toast, daring me to say something.

I shrugged, thinking about my motorcycle gear. "Leather sounds good." I started to lean back but froze when a deep-brown leather coat settled on my shoulders. I stared at my arms and then moved my gaze to hers.

"But I prefer a wicked knife." She held her hand out and a blade appeared in her palm. "I conjure things. Pulling them from who knows where." She put her knife down by her plate and smiled.

"So, the answer to my question is yes. You like to stir the pot." I smiled. "What would you have done if I said I wanted a Maserati?"

She shrugged. "I would have told you to look outside." Her smile faded. "The thing is, I'm not sure if I'm creating this stuff out of thin air or if it exists and I'm just pulling it to me."

"So... stealing?" I cringed as I asked, but it certainly was an intriguing ability.

"I'd like to think I'm creating it and not stealing it, but I have no clue." She sent the knife back to wherever it came from but she left the leather on me.

I bit my lip and cocked an eyebrow. "What about a horse?"

She shook her head. "I'm limited to *things*. I can't conjure anything living. Which sucks, because I'd love to have a big-ass dog to play with."

The way she said that turned me on. "Well, you've got yourself a big-ass wolf to hunt vampires with. So, in a way, you got your wish."

Her cheeks reddened, and she preoccupied herself with downing her coffee. Then she grimaced, setting the cup aside. A blink later, a Starbucks coffee sat in her hand. "I can't drink that stuff." She nodded toward her nearly full cup.

God, why the hell did my father curse me like this? I shifted in my seat and focused on my food, finishing my meal before wiping my lips with a napkin like my mother taught me. I looked up to her studying me over the rim of her coffee cup and wished like hell I could read her mind.

"We should get to class." I piled up the garbage on my tray. I reached for hers just as she did. "I got it." I took her tray, too. It gave me a minute to compose myself, and I took a deep breath as I threw away the papers and leftover food from her plate before stacking the trays on the conveyor belt that would take them to the kitchen for cleaning.

I harnessed my wolf and turned back toward Sarah. She stood waiting for me, bathed in a streak of sunlight; her hair looked as if it were on fire and that half smile on her lips nearly cut my legs out from underneath me. As I approached her, Johnson walked in our direction, along with someone I didn't recognize. Behind him, the pack followed with their partners.

Sarah stepped in stride with me as we led the group out of the cafeteria. She glanced over her shoulder and then up at me with a raised eyebrow as my pack followed.

"It's a pack thing," I said quietly as if that explained the weirdness of them all converging on me like I was their king or something equally as special. I wanted to lead, but didn't want to be treated like royalty. I'd have to have a word with them later, because this was an embarrassing display of follow the leader.

Classes went by in a blur, and I was glad to have something else to occupy my mind, even if I was hyper-aware of Sarah next to me the entire time. Learning the history of creatures like Pegasus and the phoenix, which no longer existed, was intriguing. Hell, it could be werewolves or witches or fae on that list someday.

But my life's mission was to put vampires on the extinct list.

YOUNG BLOOD 6

DAY IN AND DAY out, I fought with my wolf as I sat next to Sarah in class or sparred with her in our self-defense classes. During the physical sessions when we were paired up, I never let loose. I never attacked her with my full strength.

"You're holding back," she snarled at me. "How the hell am I supposed to defend myself out there if you won't come at me with all you have?" She wiped the sweat off her brow with the back of her hand and snapped it onto the ground.

My lips tilted into a smile. "If I went full out, I'd rip your head clean off."

"Bullshit!" She swung at me, and I caught her fist in mine, displaying exactly what type of speed I was capable of.

This time, instead of letting her go, I pulled her against me and stared down at her. "Trust me, sweetheart. You do not want me letting loose on you or anyone else here." The growl in my voice was more feral than even I expected.

Her eyes widened as she glanced up at me, and her pupils dilated like being this close to me did the same thing to her. And it wasn't fear I saw in those irises; it was the same heat burning through my veins.

Damn it.

My wolf rose to the surface, and my teeth transformed. I let go of her and stepped back, getting a grip on my wolf before he took over completely.

Johnson barreled into me from the side, taking me to the ground with a roar. It was sudden enough to make me lose my tenuous control. I shifted and turned on him, baring my teeth in a feral growl.

My wolf was ready for a serious beating, and I was going to be the one who drew first blood.

Johnson shifted a moment later, growling with the same ferocity.

Sarah stepped between us, putting her palms on either side of her, one facing me and the other facing Johnson. My growl stalled at her audacity.

You never step between two wolves getting ready to tango. Ever.

"Cut the crap!" She glared at us and then focused on Johnson. "You want a fight?" She slammed her hands on her chest. "Come at me. Let's see what you've got." A pair of wooden swords appeared in her hands, and she stood at the ready like some ninja queen. When Johnson didn't move, she said, "He won't go at me with everything he has. Maybe you're just as much of a wuss."

I bared my teeth at him, wanting to keep her from harm, but Johnson didn't even look my way. He stalked toward her and then launched, but Sarah twirled away, parrying, and slammed the side of her sword into Johnson's shoulder, knocking his trajectory off so he sailed right past her.

Fuck. That just turned on my wolf to a degree I couldn't harness and ignited my need to protect her.

The next time Johnson leapt at her, I launched into his side, knocking him away, and turned on her. If she wanted to play this game, who was I to argue?

"Oh. Now you want to play?" she teased as the rest of the class stopped their own sparring to watch this unfold. Her eyes sparkled and her grin heated me to the core.

I stalked around her, letting a low growl form in my throat. Johnson stalked opposite me, but I wasn't sure whether he was there to test my partner, or keep me in line. Either way the two-on-one seemed to make Sarah thrive. The skin of her chest flushed as if this excited her as much as it revved me up. She held the swords out from her sides, keeping them between us, and she matched our slow maneuvers around her.

Johnson wasn't as patient as I was for an opening, and he launched. Sarah parried, doing the same move as before, but he was ready and he yanked the sword from her grip, opening her up to my attack. I launched, hitting her square in the chest, and knocked her onto her back. I shifted my paws, pinning her upper arms.

Then the tip of her sword pressed between my ribs at my side.

"It might not be a kill shot, but it will scramble your insides, so I suggest you get the fuck off me before I shish-kebab you." She stared up at me with such ferociousness that I had to clamp my mouth closed, or else I was going to lick that look right off her face.

Fuck. I wanted this girl.

I sidestepped and then snatched the sword from her, tossing it away. When I looked back, I was staring down real steel in one hand as her other pointed a sword at Johnson. I traded a glance with my beta and then stepped back. He did the same as she sat up and then, with a quick and very impressive jump, she landed on her feet, still brandishing the steel swords in our direction.

Johnson shifted to human form and some of the ladies in the room gasped at his nakedness. It was part of the deal. When we shifted, it basically shredded our clothing; therefore, when we shift back, we're as naked as the day we were born. We hadn't covered werewolves yet in class, either, so I guess the witches who weren't familiar with us would just have to get used to it.

Sarah raised her eyebrow and then looked at me, expecting a full-Monty view. Well, she wasn't going to get that, not when I was so fucking turned on by her that I'd never be able to mask my desire. Instead, I trotted out of the room and shifted when I got to my locker, where I had stashed extra clothing just for this type of scenario.

I splashed cold water on my face at the sink, getting my libido in order as Johnson stepped into the room.

"What are you doing?" he asked as he retrieved a pair of shorts to cover himself up.

"Cooling myself off," I answered.

"She's going to see you shift back at some point." He waved toward the gym, correctly analyzing my retreat.

"No shit. But not when I'm so fucking hard that I can't hide it," I mumbled through the towel covering my face. I pulled the towel down and closed my eyes.

"You need to get laid," Johnson said.

I snorted a laugh and nodded. "But that's not happening here."

"Some of the guys were already talking about a road trip to the city tomorrow." He glanced at me. "Are you in?"

"Fuck yeah." I needed to get out of this place and as far away from the stress pulling my insides apart as possible.

We headed back into the gym again, and only the instructor, Mr. Martin, and our partners were in attendance. Mr. Martin's face was pinched in irritation and his blond spiked hair was cockeyed, as if he had been running his hand through it in aggravation. He shifted his spectacles at us as we approached; crossing his arms, he scowled.

Sarah stared at the floor with her cheeks the color of crimson wine.

Mr. Martin pointed at the two of us, his finger slashing back and forth like a pendulum. "That was not sanctioned. You could have gotten hurt!"

"Chill, Grandpa," I said. "We wouldn't have harmed her."

His face reddened until I thought steam would pop the top off. "You're a werewolf, and she's just a girl."

I crossed into his personal space and glared down at him. "I'm an alpha. I know the strengths and weaknesses of my pack, *and* my partner. We would not have harmed her."

"She has a bump on the back of her head where she hit the ground," he challenged, puffing out his chest like a cockatoo.

I slashed my gaze to Sarah, and she rolled her eyes like it was no big deal. "Bumps and bruises are part of sparring." I looked back at our instructor. "Aren't they?"

"She could have sliced you with those swords and spilled blood." Mr. Martin still seethed, as if my question annoyed him even more than our actions.

"I'm her partner. She has my back, just like I have hers. And if she inadvertently sliced us, well, we weren't quick enough, and that's our problem, not yours."

"You three are on probation until I see fit to release you."

I shrugged, and Johnson pulled me back a step.

"Does that mean we can't leave campus this weekend?" he asked.

"Correct. You can only go to classes, the library, the gym, and the cafeteria. The rest of the time, you are to stay in your rooms. No joining in on the games in the quad, no running on the paths, nothing. And certainly no leaving campus."

"Fuck," he muttered under his breath and glared at me.

Sarah's face fell. "I had plans."

"Your plans are canceled until I say so," Mr. Martin snarled. "Now go clean up for dinner."

Sarah took a deep breath and marched toward the door. I caught up with her and grabbed her arm. She spun around on me and smacked my bare chest hard enough to sting.

"You should have given me your all during class and not made a fucking spectacle of it." She yanked her arm from my grip and stormed into the girls' showers, leaving me staring after her.

Now I needed to know just what her plans were, and if there was a guy involved. The insidious burn of jealousy caught me off guard. I spun on my heel and headed back to my room with my wolf in an uproar.

"What the fuck were you thinking?" Johnson growled when I stepped into the room.

"You're the one who tackled me out of nowhere." I slammed the door behind me.

"You were stepping over the line," he mumbled.

"I was in control."

"Bull-fucking-shit!" He pointed at me. "Your wolf was already coming out. You were not in control."

My teeth had made an appearance when I slammed her into me. "I was aggravated." But my tone didn't convince even me of that excuse. I clawed my fingers through my hair. "I had control," I finally said, but the skeptical scowl on Johnson's face echoed what I knew in my heart.

This entire situation was out of control. I grabbed clean clothes and headed into the shower without another word. I dialed the knob as cold as it would go, shaking under the icy water as my teeth chattered and the chill bit me bone-deep. I scrubbed my skin and lathered and rinsed my hair, forcing myself to deal with the chilling water.

But the frigid shower didn't even come close to dousing the fire in the center of my soul.

YOUNG BLOOD 7

THE MINUTE I STEPPED into the cafeteria, the whispering stopped. Johnson followed after me. It wasn't until I sat down with the pack that I realized Sarah wasn't here. I scanned the room just to be sure and then sighed, digging into my meal with all the gusto of an inmate on death row.

Sarah still hadn't come when they started to close the food stations. I got up and packed a plate to go. When I returned to the table with a cellophane-wrapped dinner plate, Johnson raised an eyebrow.

I didn't dignify his silent question with an answer. "I'll be back upstairs in a few," I said to him. "And I don't need a shadow. Understand." My gaze bore into him, but I refrained from using my alpha influence. I hated it when my father did that, and I wasn't going to do it to my beta unless I had to.

"Fine. But it's her funeral if you fuck up."

"I know." I turned and headed out of the cafeteria. Instead of heading left to my section, I turned right and wandered through the girls' ward, using my nose to try to find Sarah's room.

A group of girls armed with backpacks sauntered down the hall toward me.

"Do you know which room is Sarah Stone's?" I asked because it was easier than following my nose, especially considering the hallway was filled with everyone's scent. Besides, I wasn't in wolf form, so I couldn't quite pinpoint hers among the rest.

The lead girl pointed behind her. "Last door on your right."

"Thanks." I gave her a nod.

"You could get in trouble for being in this wing," she said as she passed by.

"It's a good thing no one is going to rat me out, right?" This time, I did use my alpha influence, and the girls seemed to fold in on themselves and almost cower at the power I radiated.

"Right," the lead one said in a wince.

The door at the end of the hall opened. "What the hell are you doing?" Sarah asked, as if she could feel my alpha influence all the way down the hall. Her voice was slurred but the glare she gave me was sharp.

The rest of the girls hurried off without so much as a look in our direction. I continued down the hall with the plate in front of me, undeterred by my partner's piercing look. But the closer I got, the more she reeked of alcohol. No wonder I couldn't pick up her scent—it was doused in vodka.

"I don't need food." She started to close her door.

I stopped the wood with my hand. "I beg to differ." I pushed her inside and closed the door behind me, painfully aware of how close she was to me. But below that feisty anger was a deeper pain that I couldn't walk away from now that I saw it. "Where did you get alcohol?" I scanned the room for any evidence of it.

She put her hand out and a half-empty bottle appeared. "I'm a witch. Or did you forget that?"

I crossed and put the plate down on her desk. When I turned, she had the bottle tipped to her lips and was guzzling it like it was water. The shock of seeing her nearly drowning herself in liquor made me reach out and snatch the bottle from her.

"Easy there."

"What the fuck do you know?" She pushed at my chest. "Give me that."

I raised it over my head. "No. Not until you tell me what the hell is wrong enough for you to get hammered in a place where if they caught you, you'd be in a shit ton of trouble."

"It's none of your business," she snarled, still trying to get the bottle.

"What, did I ruin a weekend with your boyfriend?"

"No, you asshole. You ruined my chance to visit my parents' grave."

Her words hit me hard, and I slowly lowered the bottle. Handing it to her, I took a seat on the empty bed. "I'm sorry. I didn't know."

She shook her head and stared at the bottle. "They died in a car crash last year. Today's the anniversary of their death."

Quiet layered over the room.

"Think you can conjure me a glass?"

A moment later, a cup appeared in my hand, and I held it out nodding toward the bottle.

"You could get in trouble," she said.

"Fuck it. This is a valid reason for a drink."

She filled my cup halfway, and I raised my glass. "To your parents. May they be filled with heaven's joy and peace for all eternity." I touched my glass to her bottle in a toast and downed the contents of the cup. The smooth burn of vodka flowed down my throat, hitting my stomach, and sent a rash of heat all the way to my toes and fingertips.

She stared at me as a tear escaped, sliding down her cheek unchecked. "Losing them nearly killed me," she said, searching my eyes.

I nodded. I knew the impact of losing a parent. Especially one you were close to. But this wasn't about me or how I felt when a vampire ripped my mother from this earth. I would be able to purge that anger with every vampire I killed in this job.

"What happened?" I stared into my cup, ignoring my wolf's demands to hold her. If I moved any closer, I'd be in a hell of a lot more trouble than just drinking with my partner.

"A car crash on their date night." She let out a soft laugh. "They still did date nights after almost twenty years of marriage. Can you believe that?" She sniffled and stared into the bottle.

"Sounds like they were still in love." My heart squeezed at the thought. I couldn't imagine that at all. Although my parents cared about each other as fated mates do, they never truly showed it. There were no date nights in my home. Just the alpha bastard demanding all of us be subservient, including my mother. The only times she stood up to him was when she didn't agree with how he was treating me or my siblings.

"Do you have any other family out there?" I asked, knowing it was a long shot.

She shook her head. "Nope. No siblings. No long-lost aunts or uncles. No living grandparents. Nothing. And I've been in state facilities for the last year. Until I turned sixteen and the state decided I was best suited for the Monster Defense Academy." She glared up at me. "So now I have to hunt monsters until I die instead of being a doctor or lawyer and finding someone to settle down and have date nights with."

My lips tilted into a partial smile. "Yeah. Like being a doctor or lawyer is the same as a monster hunter. You can't literally kick ass in those vocations."

She pouted in a way that made my hands clench. I wanted to suck on her lower lip and make her forget all her pain. But that would only make things worse. I took a deep breath.

"Maybe," she finally allowed and glanced at the plate of food. "Thank you." She waved at the dinner I brought her. "You didn't need to do that."

When her brown eyes met mine, I nearly slid off the bed onto my knees and begged her to be mine. But I formed a smile and remained seated across the room. "It wasn't a problem." I shrugged. "It's part of being partners." That was the best crap I could come up with. "You should go easy on the rest of that bottle. You don't need alcohol poisoning on top of everything else."

Her gaze narrowed, and she took a swig. "I can handle it."

I let out a laugh. "I'm not saying you can't, but straight vodka for a woman your size is bound to play hell with your system if you drink too much. And I'd kind of like to see you in action out there. I bet you're one of the fiercest women here." Actually, I knew she was just by watching her sparring matches over the last month and a half.

"I am the fiercest one here." She flipped her hair over her shoulder and straightened her back.

I leaned forward. "Be fierce. Ditch the rest of that bottle," I dared her.

She looked at the vodka and then waved the bottle away. Her chin jutted out at me as if she had done something incredibly fierce.

I couldn't help it; I snorted a laugh and she started to chuckle as well until she fell backward on her bed laughing so hard, I couldn't tell whether she was hysterical with the funnies or hysterical from missing her parents.

She held her stomach, silently shaking with her face buried in her bedding. I stood and took a step closer as concern replaced my jovial mood. She stiffened and glanced up at me, still smiling as she wiped tears from her cheeks.

"I haven't laughed like that since before my parents died." Her voice shook with her continued giggles. "Thank you. For making me laugh. For the food... everything. But if you get any closer, I'm not responsible enough right now *not* to do anything we will both regret in the morning."

I froze in the spot as my mind toggled between "make a damn move" and "get the hell out of this room now." When she hiccupped between chuckles, that seemed to get my legs moving.

"I'll catch you tomorrow," I said over my shoulder and walked out of the room, heading across to my dorm as the need to ravage her screamed in my veins like an incessant echo that would never die.

YOUNG BLOOD 8

"**I** HATE MY FATHER." The words came out with such venom that Johnson's eyes widened from across the room. I slammed the door behind me and crossed, throwing myself face-first on the bed.

"Hate's a strong word, dude."

"You have no fucking clue how much I want to beat him to a bloody pulp right now." I turned my head away before I tore into him for doing my father's bidding.

"If I could denounce him without denouncing the pack, I would," I muttered. At this point, my best bet was becoming the alpha of the pack. Then I wouldn't have to listen to anything the old man said.

"He's still on the board of the Monster Defense Agency," Johnson said.

I turned and glared at him. "He could change the rules if he wanted, but he'll never do that. He'd rather see my true mate hanging from the gallows than in a relationship with me."

"You don't know that."

"Who the fuck do you think arranged for Sarah to be my partner?" I moved up to my elbows, waiting for him to answer. "Who do you think chose to fuck up my entire life?" I raised my eyebrows. "Because it certainly wasn't me."

"I get it. But it is what it is, and you need to move on." He closed the textbook he had been reading when I stormed into the room.

Johnson didn't have a clue. He hadn't met his true mate yet and didn't begin to comprehend the demands my wolf was making. I was surprised my father didn't have any sympathy for me, but then again, Sarah wasn't a wolf. I rolled onto my back. *If she had been a werewolf, would he have moved heaven and earth to interfere?*

I already knew the answer to that question. He wouldn't have interfered.

My father's racism stemmed from the fact Sarah was a witch and not a wolf.

⁂

BREAKFAST THE NEXT MORNING was nearly empty. A whole dozen of us remained at the school—the bad kids or the rejects with nowhere else to go. I piled the food on my plate and started for the table Johnson had chosen.

Sarah walked in with dark sunglasses, her hair braided, and a black leather outfit that nearly had me stumbling. She looked like a killer version of Laura Croft. But her red braid made her look even more badass. I caught myself before my mouth dropped open, and I just raised an eyebrow.

"If you're trying to look the part of troublemaker, you nailed it," I muttered as she approached.

She slid her glasses down her nose as she got closer, showing me her bloodshot eyes. "I'm compensating," she whispered. "And you don't have to yell."

I smirked. "Hangover?"

"From hell." She continued on to the buffet, poured an extra-large cup of coffee, and grabbed a single piece of toast along with a canned ginger ale before she headed to our table.

It wasn't much, but I guess if I had drunk two-thirds of a bottle of vodka on my own, I'd be hurting too. I took a seat next to Johnson and a few minutes later, Sarah sat down opposite me.

Johnson's eyes were just about bugging out of his head at her. Just like the rest of the crew stuck at the school this weekend. Hell, even the lone she-wolf looked at her with a spark of interest.

Ignoring my wolf's rantings was getting harder to do, especially with the citrusy scent drifting off her like a natural elixir. Man, I wanted to lick her just to see whether she tasted as sweet as she smelled. I focused on my food instead.

"Young lady, what the hell are you wearing?" Mr. Martin snarled from behind her.

I looked up at her and then at the teacher seething behind her.

Sarah straightened her back and slowly turned in her chair. "I'm wearing clothing fit for kicking his ass." She pointed at me. "Which I fully intend to do after breakfast."

I choked on the sip of coffee, spitting all over the table. "Excuse me?" I said through my coughs.

"I don't..." the teacher started.

"He owes me." She glared at him. "I had plans that this wolf fucked up. So, with or without your permission, sir, I am going to beat his ass to a pulp. And I'm going to do it in my kick-ass outfit."

She oozed attitude that even I wouldn't fuck with.

Mr. Martin pressed his lips together, and his face reddened as she stared him down through her dark glasses.

Now she was going to get reamed. I waited for the explosive reprimand.

He clenched his teeth and wagged his finger at her. "No sharp weapons."

What the fuck did he just say? My brain didn't think I heard him right.

"No, sir. I won't use sharp weapons." She nodded and turned back to me with the type of grin that made me want another frigid shower.

His glare shot to me. "And no wolf. Save that for the field, understand?"

I was so fucked. "Yes, sir," I hissed while my lungs still burned with the coffee that had slid the wrong way.

He pointed at Johnson. "And no sabotaging their sparring."

Johnson shook his head and held up his hand. "I swear."

Mr. Martin dropped his gaze back on Sarah. "A bit of advice. You should keep your fighting gear for the gym to avoid potential problems."

I cocked my head. "What potential problems? Relationships are off-limits here."

His gaze slashed to mine. "Exactly. And everyone needs to remember that." He scanned the whole dozen of us who remained in the cafeteria with a pointed scowl.

"And what happens if we cross the line?" the female wolf asked, drawing everyone's attention.

Mr. Martin turned to her. "The consequences are swift and severe. We own every one of your asses until you either retire or you die in the field. Get used to living, or dying, by the rules."

She scoffed at him, and Mr. Martin cut his glare at her. That little wolf started clawing at her throat as if she couldn't breathe.

He crossed to stand in front of her. His eyes sparkled with malice. "Dear Miss Carlyle, if you don't learn to respect the rules here, your partner will pay the price. Hunting solo is a deadly endeavor for a witch."

"Leave her be." I pushed my alpha voice over the dining room. It had the desired effect and Miss Carlyle took a hefty breath as tears of fear and disdain cascaded down her face.

Mr. Martin wouldn't look at me, he glared at the floor, though and I felt the brush of his angry magic as he made a beeline out of the room. The only one in the vicinity who wasn't cowering in some fashion was Sarah.

I cocked my head at her, and she pointed a finger at me.

"I'm subservient to no one. Remember that, alpha boy. I'll see you in the gym in ten minutes." She stood and marched out of the room.

"Alpha boy?" Johnson whispered from the spot next to me.

"She's still pissed because I ruined her weekend plans." I stood and scooped up my nearly empty tray. I set it on the rotating cleaning rack and headed to my room to change. A little fiery witch needed to meet the training mat today, and I prayed my wolf would stay in line.

YOUNG BLOOD 9

I STEPPED INTO THE gym in my T-shirt and shorts. She was already doing forms on the mat like a trained ninja. Her leathers didn't seem to prohibit her movement, either. The bo she held whistled through the air with each twirl. I paused and then peeled off my sneakers and socks, lining them up near the door, getting myself mentally ready for close contact.

We weren't the only ones in the gym, either. All the students from the cafeteria were sitting quietly on the edges as if we were the main entertainment for the day.

I stepped into the sparring ring and bowed to Sarah.

She stopped her forms, bowed, and then smiled. "Are you going to give me your all today?"

I stalked forward. "I don't plan on holding back, so get ready for some broken bones, missy."

She slowly twirled the staff in her hands as she countered each of my steps, moving us into a tighter circle. "Me? I think you're going to be the one who breaks. But whether it's your bones or your ego, we'll find out."

Oh, she was cocky. Even with flawless forms, she'd never be able to nail me with that bo. I clenched my fists, tapping into my endless sexual frustration, turning it into fuel. I went after her, and she countered every single one of my moves—parrying, spinning, jumping, and swinging that bo like an ISKA World Champion.

When she went on the offensive, even my speed wasn't enough. She landed her first hit with a swing of the bo into the back of my knee, and I went down with the force of it. I caught myself before my face hit the mat and rolled, coming up on my feet—only to be smacked again, but this time on the back of the other thigh. Pain flared like a nest of bees had stung me where she hit. I spun and ducked before the next swing nearly connected with the side of my head.

"You've been holding out on me," I said through clenched teeth. She had never landed a hit in training class. But then again, I never went after her with the full force of my skills.

"I didn't think your pack would take kindly to me beating the shit out of their alpha." She smiled in such a way that revved my wolf. She swung again, this time going for my shins, and I jumped, but she already calculated my move and brought the stick up, nailing my shins anyway.

I launched forward and tucked, rolling onto my back with legs that I could tell would sport some ugly bruises tomorrow. "You wouldn't get a lick in against my wolf." I stared up at her as she stood just out of range, twirling the bo from hand to hand, leaving no chance for me to jump to my feet and get a hit in.

"Prove it."

"Did you just dare me?" I rolled over onto all fours and glared at her.

She grinned. "I dare you."

That was the last straw. My wolf took over even though Mr. Martin yelled from the sideline. But this time, Johnson had my back. He held Mr. Martin on the sidelines.

I growled at Sarah, watching the bo and not her sparkling eyes. If I looked at her eyes, I would knock her to the floor and mark her as mine. My wolf didn't quite get that would be her end. He would fight to the death defending her, but it wouldn't be enough. Not with the archaic rules of this organization.

My muscles tensed as she twirled her body toward me, her bo spinning at almost an invisible speed. She swung and I reacted, dodging to the side, but it wasn't fast enough. The end of her bo connected with my ribs, knocking a yelp out of me. My wolf took over and went after her with all the fury locked inside me.

She switched to defensive moves, and her eyes widened. The first flare of fear reached the surface, and it smelled sweet. Especially when I caught the bo between my teeth and yanked it from her hands. My wolf launched and my paws connected with her shoulders, knocking her backward with the force.

Time slowed, and I flew with her.

Shit. My partner was going to hit the wood floor. Not the mat. And it would be hard enough to split her skull wide open. I shifted, putting my hand under her head just in time to protect her from the bulk of impact. Her head slammed my hand into the wood and the crack of bone filled the auditorium. I clenched my jaw against the flare of pain that traveled from my hand up my arm as my full weight landed on top of her.

I let out a hiss as her wide eyes met mine. "Fuck," I growled and pulled my hand out from under her head, and rolled off her, curling up on my side as I cradled my broken hand.

Better my hand than her head. That kind of impact could have killed her.

"Robby?" Her warm hand landed on my shoulder, and I looked up at her as a pleasant burn radiated from the point her skin made contact with mine.

Concern painted her face and her gaze seemed to flit over my naked form, as if she didn't understand where my clothes had gone. I had run into the men's locker room as a wolf before, so she hadn't seen me shift back.

"This is what happens when a wolf shifts back to human," I said, still cradling my throbbing hand against my chest. *How many bones had I broken?*

Her lips twitched and that smirk made an appearance as if she enjoyed the view just a little too much. "Is your hand okay?" she asked after a moment.

"At least one of the bones is broken. Your head is pretty damn hard," I said. I couldn't let her think I had softened in any way, regardless of the electrical current flowing from her fingers right to my soul.

"So I've been told." She actually looked remorseful. "You didn't have to do that."

I gave her a genuine smile despite the sharp pains shooting up my arm. She might not be here if I hadn't. "It's what partners do. I'll always have your back. Even when I'm the one who put you in harm's way."

Johnson threw one of the gym tarps over me, interrupting. I didn't know whether to be pissed off or grateful.

"I told you not to shift!" Mr. Martin yelled, wagging his finger at me again as he approached.

"I dared him to," Sarah said, with her hand still on my shoulder.

She squeezed a fraction tighter, as if her nerves were finally getting to her. I don't think she was aware she was doing it either, but the connection of skin against skin stirred my wolf, and I was thankful for the tarp. I adjusted it and sat up, dislodging her touch and making that electric hum assaulting my body stop.

Her declaration silenced the teacher for a moment, and he looked truly shocked. "Do you have a death wish?" He ran a hand through his hair. "You never dare a wolf to come forth. That's just asking for trouble."

She shrugged. "He wasn't giving me his all."

I snorted a laugh. "Actually, I was. You're the one who's been holding back this whole time." I waved my good hand toward the bo. "You're fucking fast with that thing. And I mean like ninja fast."

Her gaze snapped to mine, and her eyebrows rose.

"Where did you learn that?" Mr. Martin's momentary annoyance transitioned to interest just a little too fast for my tastes. It was as if he were looking at his student in a totally new light.

"I've been taking jujitsu since I was old enough to walk. But I'm a little rusty. I haven't been in the dojo for a while." She glanced at me and narrowed her eyes.

I huffed. If this was her in rusty form, then anyone she came across out in the field was as doomed as my heart was. There were some benefits to having a fucking ninja warrior as a partner. Although, I still would much rather have her as my mate.

"Why did you stop?" Mr. Martin asked.

"State care doesn't support it." She stood and offered me her hand. "So, I never got my third-degree black belt."

"I'm good." I waved her off. If I stood with her help, I wouldn't have a hand to keep the blanket in place, which had been more necessary as each moment passed.

"At sixteen?" Mr. Martin scoffed at her.

"I'm almost seventeen. And yes. That's fourteen years of study."

His eyes narrowed. "They usually don't let those under eighteen obtain black belt, never mind degrees in belts."

She crossed her arms and glared at him. "It was my father's dojo."

"And where is your father today?" he asked.

"Dead and buried. Which is why I've been sentenced to this place for the rest of my life." Her venom had all of us leaning away from her, as if her toxic attitude were somehow contagious.

The way Mr. Martin paled made me nearly laugh out loud. He thought she had something to do with her father's death. I could see it in the fear that bloomed in his eyes and the stench he was emitting.

I cleared my throat. "I think we need to get an x-ray on my hand." I held it up for him to see. The back of my hand was noticeably red, and it had swelled enough to confirm what I already knew. At least one of the metacarpal bones had cracked.

"Take him to the infirmary," Mr. Martin spat at Johnson and then turned back to Sarah. "And you and I will need to update your records, so I know your skill level." He pointed toward his office.

Johnson helped me to my feet and held the blanket closed behind me as we headed into the locker room. I caught Sarah's glance just as she and Mr. Martin disappeared into his office.

"She's deadly," Johnson whispered as we stepped up to my locker. He opened it and handed me another set of spare clothing.

The awe in his voice caught me, and I grabbed him with my good hand, slamming him against the metal. "Don't even think it. Understand?" The thought of anyone here at the academy touching her drove me crazy. If they did, it put her in danger, and my protection instinct where she was concerned was obviously stronger than my desire.

He nodded and swallowed hard. "Sure, Robby. I won't even entertain the idea." He put his hands up in surrender, and I let him go.

I dressed and headed to the infirmary and a cast that had my name on it. But my unease at the way both Johnson and Mr. Martin had been gawking at Sarah had my stomach in knots.

Johnson wouldn't do anything. He was bound by my alpha orders, and I gave him a direct order not to even think about getting into Sarah's pants.

But Mr. Martin was a different beast. I didn't know whether he had to follow the same rules we were bound by. *And if he did, would he care about the ramifications?*

The thought chilled me, and I let out a growl, startling the medical tech who was now wrapping my hand in plaster.

YOUNG BLOOD 10

THE BEATDOWN SARAH GAVE me became somewhat of a legend at the academy once the students came back from their weekend furlough. Sarah proved to be one of the best fighters in the class, beating wolves and witches as if they were children play fighting with the adults. And I had to sit on the sidelines watching, like a fucking invalid.

However, seeing her fight with the grace of a dancer and the brutality of a natural killer inspired a sense of awe and pride in me. It was almost as acute as the want in my bones. I was damn glad she was my partner.

"So, when do you get that off?" Sarah asked in that breathless way she had when she had exerted herself. She sat on the bench next to me and pointed at my cast.

Her tone crawled under my skin, scratching at the binds holding my wolf back. Her hair dripped from perspiration and strands stuck to her face. I had to clench my fist so I didn't follow through on the urge to tuck those stray hairs behind her ear. Even as sweaty as she was, she still had that sweet citrusy scent underneath, teasing me to the breaking point.

"Next week." I glanced at the dirty plaster encasing my forearm and hand and, as if on cue, my wrist started to itch. And that itch just kept growing. My finger couldn't reach it either, so I pulled a pen out of my notebook and shoved it into the cast. Even that didn't quite reach it, but that didn't stop me from trying.

Sarah cleared her throat and gave me that look that stopped me cold. It was her *don't do that* expression that I couldn't ignore.

I sighed and slipped the pen back where I pulled it from.

"Then what? Physical therapy?"

"That's what they tell me." I wasn't all too excited about therapy. I just wanted to get back into sparring with two hands. But they insisted, so I was at their mercy.

"PT isn't as bad as you think."

"Mhm." I kept my eyes glued on the next match because I didn't really want to discuss the merits of physical therapy today. I had already heard it from the doctor at the last checkup. "Are you going on furlough this weekend?" I asked, to change the subject. The pack members were headed into the city again and our punishments had been lifted.

I was looking forward to finding someone to let out this pent-up sexual tension with.

"Nah. I got nothing out there." She sighed and leaned against the wall, stretching her legs out in front of her.

"What about your friends?" My gaze moved from the action on the mats to her.

"What friends?" She raised her eyebrows at me. "It's not like I have my pack here with me." She sneered.

I met her gaze, trying to recall any time she was with anyone but me and the pack, and I couldn't. If she wasn't with us, she was alone. My sudden compassion must have shown on my face because she stiffened next to me.

"Don't look at me like you feel sorry for me," she hissed under her breath and crossed her arms.

I reschooled my features and shrugged. "To each his own." I pretended not to care but that sour taste of pity still laced my mouth. I had always been around others and had the pick of who to hang out with if I chose. I couldn't imagine not having the pack.

"Did you have friends before..." I trailed off, still watching the action on the floor.

She sighed. "A couple. But they were so caught up in the social circles at my old high school that we lost touch. The state moved me to the city, where there were more resources for us rejects."

I glanced at her.

"Anyway, your pack seems to be the only ones here who I've gotten to know beyond a nod of acknowledgment." She shrugged. "And it's a bit overwhelming at times."

I chuckled. "You don't like being the center of attention?"

"No. I'd rather kick ass and then fade into the woodwork." She glanced back at the group fighting and the teacher yelling out instructions. "So, a quiet weekend will actually be nice. I can catch up on my work and just chill with a good book."

A very large part of me was torn. I needed to offload some of this stress built up inside me because my lack of being able to spar with anyone to get out the aggression in another manner had been stymied by my broken hand. But knowing she was back here alone left me chilled, as if something bad would happen in my absence.

YOUNG BLOOD 11

I SHIFTED IN THE passenger seat of Johnson's car, trying to get comfortable while I stared out at the passing scenery. The rest of the pack in the back seats of the SUV talked nonstop about what they were going to do once we arrived in the city. Most of it was finding a girl they'd never meet again and doing all the things my wolf wanted to do with Sarah. All the things I needed to do with a stranger, so I didn't break that cardinal rule with my partner.

It was the first weekend Johnson and I were allowed to leave the Monster Defense Academy since we arrived. It was also the first time since I met Sarah that I was farther than a building away, and that did not sit well.

"What's your problem?" Johnson asked under his breath as he glanced at me.

I just shook my head. I couldn't put it into words, but each mile away turned into pins and needles on my nerve endings. The cafeteria had been nearly barren when we grabbed dinner, and Sarah was one of the few left at school this weekend. We had eaten and bid her goodbye on our way out.

When the city came into view, I shifted again as the prickles became almost a siren wail. "I need to go back."

"What?"

"Something's wrong. Either turn around, or stop and I'll get out."

"But..." He waved at the city, probably thinking I was just being fickle because of my feelings for Sarah. Feelings that the rest of the pack were not privy to.

"You can come back. It's only going to eat an hour of your time if you just drop me off at the door."

Silence settled over the car. "What's going on?" Tom asked from the way back.

"I'm not sure. Alarms are going off in my head, like something bad is happening to my partner." I glanced over my shoulder at him and shrugged. "I have to go back."

They all traded glances. It wasn't unheard of for partners to get distress calls from their magical counterparts. They taught us to be aware of those nagging feelings because they were usually on point.

Johnson took a breath and then turned the vehicle into the grass median, narrowly missing a drop-off. He barreled across, and hit the high speed lane on the opposite side of the highway like a seasoned stunt driver, neatly fitting himself between two speeding cars. He weaved in and out of traffic with his foot to the floor and made it back to campus in half the time.

Instead of parking in the student lot, he slid to a stop in front of the school entry and threw the car into park. Taking the keys out, he nodded at the door. I was already halfway out of the car when the rest of the doors opened and the pack piled out, following my lead.

Desperation clawed at my insides as I nearly ripped the front door off its hinges and ran to the nearest stairwell in the girl's dorm. We pounded up the stairs, sounding more like an earthquake than six men.

My heart hammered in my chest, and the noises coming from inside her room sent a rash of fury through me. I didn't even try Sarah's doorknob. Instead, I lifted my foot and slammed it right next to the locking mechanism, shattering it and throwing the door wide.

Three witches had her pinned face-first to the wall. An array of weapons lay on the floor, and at least one of them had blood on the blade. Her shirt hung in tatters. What made me shift into wolf form was the fact her pants were being pulled down by the asshole standing behind her, who already had his down around his ankles.

The clang of the cast preceded my launch into the air. He didn't even finish his turn toward me and was just registering the shock of our entry when I relieved him of his head. It rolled across the floor and his body fell under my weight.

The shock of the decapitated witch left the other two frozen in fear, with their eyes wide enough to nearly pop from their heads.

I turned on them with my teeth bared and the taste of blood filling my mouth. More than my growls filled the room, too, as my pack fanned out in the small space, pinning them in place. Sarah twisted her wrist free from a witch's grip and a wicked-looking knife appeared in her hand. She speared it right through the bastard's throat with a growl equal to mine.

His last gurgling breaths left us with one asshole to contend with.

That remaining witch let go of Sarah and put his hands up, radiating enough fear to make me want to slowly tear him to shreds just to enjoy his screams.

"What's going on here?"

A stern voice from behind us made all eyes swivel to the door, except mine. Mrs. Kemper, the women's dorm supervisor, gasped from the doorway.

I guess it took her brain a moment to recognize two dead bodies. But it didn't dissuade me from the last blubbering witch. That asshole pointed at Sarah as if this had been her fault. I bared my teeth and every muscle clenched as I readied myself to rid the world of another would-be rapist.

Sarah's movement shifted my gaze, and I glanced at her as she pulled her pants back up with hands that trembled. Even her breathing rasped in unsteady pulls of air as if she held back the tears that I knew had to be there.

"They were attempting to rape my alpha's partner when we came in," Johnson's human voice announced with the same feral fury coursing through me. "He felt her distress, and we came back as fast as possible."

Sarah's gaze shot to mine, her eyes widening a little. A tear escaped the corner, sliding down her face.

That tear cut deeper than I expected, and I focused on the last witch. My wolf demanded retribution. I launched, and my jaws clamped down on his throat as my paws hit him in the chest, knocking him into the wall with a bang.

"Stop!" Mrs. Kemper yelled.

"Armor," Sarah commanded at the same time.

My pelt became heavier just as the witch swung a blade at my side. I expected pain, but metal clanged against metal, and I tore to the side, ripping his throat out before jumping away from the fountain of blood pouring out of the wound.

He slowly dropped to his knees. The knife dropped from his grip, and then he fell face-first into the growing puddle of blood. His last breath hissed from his torn throat.

Sarah stood in the middle of what seemed to be the only dry spot now. Her cheek had a black-and-blue mark on it. As she turned, I caught sight of one of her breasts through the torn shirt. A crescent-shaped bloody mark stood out where one of the bastards dug his nail into her skin. There were other scrapes and bruises on her, but that bloody crescent in the side of her breast pushed my wolf beyond reason.

I attacked the dead corpse, shaking it with all the fury filling me. My snarls carried over the room and my pack shifted into human form, staring at my display of wrath.

Even the teacher backed up.

When the rage finally peeled back a notch or two, I dropped the dead carcass and stepped back, panting.

Mrs. Kemper asked, "Is this true? Were they…" She couldn't seem to finish the sentence, as if the thought was so heinous that even she couldn't fathom it.

Sarah nodded. "Yes. If Robby and his pack hadn't come back…" She visibly shuddered and kept her gaze lowered. She paled as her eyes bounced around the gore streaking her floor.

I glanced at my pack. They all stood in human form with their hands shading their privates. I crossed behind them to the bed and shifted; the metal armor that had saved my wolf from the witch's knife clanged on the ground. I grabbed Sarah's throw blanket and wrapped it around my waist, tying the ends together so it wouldn't fall off, before I turned to my shaking partner.

I crossed to her. My stomach turned at the sensation of warm blood sliding between my toes, but I ignored it. She needed me more than I needed physical comforts. I just pulled her into my arms. "I'm sorry we didn't get here sooner," I whispered.

She nodded against my chest. "You're shaking." She glanced up at me.

"I've never killed anything but game before," I said.

"You will need to go before the academy board for this," Mrs. Kemper said.

I turned, and Mrs. Kemper's incessant blinking chilled me. Her gaze wasn't on me. It was on Sarah, as if all this were somehow her fault.

"I'm sure they will understand my actions," I said, owning my murderous rage.

Her gaze bounced to me, still fluttering her eyelids as though she couldn't comprehend what she was seeing. "I, um, I need to lock you both up until, um, until Monday when the chancellor gets back."

"Can we at least clean off the blood and change clothes?" I asked.

She shook her head. "No. And you boys need to go to your dorm rooms. The chancellor will want to speak with you as well." She pointed out to the hallway and her gaze traveled over the room. Her cheeks paled, and she looked up at us. "Come now, until we can figure out what happened here."

I tightened my jaw.

"It's okay," Sarah whispered against me.

"The hell it is," I barked. "You were attacked and overpowered with the intent to do harm. They deserved the death they got." The snarl in my voice was back. "And this wench somehow thinks that is your fault." I glared at Mrs. Kemper. "It isn't right." I pressed my lips together. "And my father is going to hear about this." I hated pulling that card, but it had the desired effect.

Mrs. Kemper recoiled. "I'm just following protocol." She pointed toward the hall. "We need to secure the crime scene." She waved us out of the room. She closed the door behind us and took each of our arms, leading us down to an area of the school we had never ventured. A trio of cells sat side by side; she opened the first door and pushed me inside, clanging the door closed.

I reached out and hissed as my hands touched the bars. "Silver?" I snapped.

She nodded and shoved Sarah a little more roughly than necessary into the cell beside me. She slammed the cell door closed and stepped back, smoothing out her shirt. "I'll have one of the medical staff come down and take a look at you." This time her voice held a small bit of compassion. "I'm sorry. This is protocol," she added and scurried out of here.

Sarah sat down on the barren mattress and hugged herself. Her teeth started to chatter, so I undid her blanket and reached my hand through the bars, careful not to touch the silver.

"Here. Just as long as you promise not to gawk."

She stared at my hand. "Your cast is gone." She took the blanket and looked away, wrapping it around herself before she sat back down.

"It's probably on your dorm room floor." I sat and placed the pillow over my lap before I flexed my hand open and closed. The shift finished the healing process, like it always does. I scratched the dry skin on my wrist and leaned my head on the concrete wall behind me.

My wolf berated me. *If I had marked her, none of this would have happened.*

I huffed at him. *Yeah, none of this would have happened because she would be dead.*

"Are you okay?" she asked softly.

I looked over at her, realizing she'd been studying me. With an offered smile, I nodded. "I'm sure the fact I killed those guys will hit at some point, but as of right now, I don't have a single regret."

"You didn't kill them all." She glanced down at her hands, one of which was still streaked with blood.

"They deserved it."

She raised her gaze, as if maybe they didn't deserve to die for their transgressions.

"You did nothing wrong."

She laughed. "I said hello as I was leaving the library. I guess that's as good as an invite to my room to the graduates."

I shook my head, focusing on them in my mind. They weren't familiar faces. I don't think anyone in our class would fuck with her, knowing how deadly she was in the sparring ring. I slid my gaze at her. "You didn't beat the shit out of them."

She laughed bitterly. "I tried, but their magic had a little more punch than mine." She reached up to her black-and-blue cheek and winced. "Luckily, it didn't work for long on me. I guess their magic usually held down their victims until they exhausted themselves, but it only held me for a few seconds before I broke through it. Unfortunately, those few seconds were enough for them to physically subdue me once they wised up to the fact their magic wouldn't hold me in place." She shuddered. "If I hadn't been able to fight through their charms..."

"I would have walked in on a whole lot more, and your entire room would be painted with bits of them." I gripped the pillow hard enough for my fingernails to tear into the fabric.

She nodded.

I let her words sink in. "So, they've done that before."

"They bragged about what they were going to do. And that they'd done it to enough lower-level witches over the years to have notches all the way down their bedposts." She cleared her throat and spit into the sink near her. Her aim was impressive. When her gaze slashed back to mine, it was filled with that fire I was used to. Her lips tilted into a dark grin. "I was able to weasel out a name of one of their victims, but it wasn't one I recognized. I figured I'd need someone else to validate my story because I had every intention of killing them. I just didn't know if it would be before or after."

"I felt your... anxiety."

"That's a good word for it."

"You know what I mean."

"I'm glad. I wasn't purposely transmitting, though."

I took a deep breath. Usually, partners send out a mental transmission in times of stress. What she didn't know was that fated mates have a stronger connection than MDA partners did, even when they weren't mated. And I was living with those signals every day. I seemed to be able to read her every mood pretty damn accurately because of the bond.

Good Lord, what the hell would this connection be like if I actually claimed her? I slid my gaze to hers and shrugged. "I don't know what to tell you. I felt your unease and when it turned to alarm, I told Johnson to either stop the car or turn around."

"Thank you." She wrapped the blanket tighter around her shoulders.

"You'd do the same if I was in trouble."

She snorted a laugh and met my gaze. "I don't think I'm physically capable of decapitating someone with the snap of my jaws."

I grinned and stared at the floor.

"But yes. I'd kill to protect you."

Her soft admission nearly released my wolf, but I took a deep breath and just nodded my acknowledgment. "Think you could do that magic thing so I'm not sitting here naked?"

"Unfortunately, I can't. I tried already. We're both stuck in what we've got on until someone comes and lets us out."

"Fan-fucking-tastic," I muttered, and stretched out on the cot with the pillow still draped over my lap.

"How much trouble do you think we're in?"

I stared at the ceiling and chewed on my lip before I tilted my head back to look at her. "You have nothing to worry about." I would see to that. What those assholes tried to do and apparently had done to others was no better than any of the monsters they were training us to hunt, and they should get the same capital punishment for their vile deeds.

YOUNG BLOOD 12

TURNED OUT WE HAD to stay in those cells for longer than I cared for without a change of clothes or the opportunity to wash the blood off. Saturday came without so much as a crumb of food or anyone coming down. No medical staff to check out Sarah and no food and not even a jug of clean water.

I didn't even know what time it was, but I knew we had been in these cells for at least twelve hours.

"You'd think they'd at least bring us breakfast," I muttered, glaring at the bright hallway outside of the dim cells.

"Can you look the other way?" she asked.

I raised an eyebrow and looked at the wall instead of at her. The sound of a bladder releasing into a toilet echoed on the walls. Her sigh of relief made me smile. I glanced at the toilet in the corner of my cell. The sink turned on and ran, and then after the water turned off, I waited until the sound of mattress springs creaked before I reacted.

"My turn." I stood, dropping the pillow onto the bed. I wasn't as modest as she was. If she looked, she'd see my bare ass. I relieved myself, washed my hands, and then took a few handfuls of water from the faucet. It left a metallic taste as if these pipes hadn't been used in ages. I forced a couple of breaths before I returned to the mattress. I replaced the pillow over my lap and stretched out.

Saturday blurred as we waited for someone to come by.

"Do you think they forgot about us?" I asked as my stomach groaned again. At least it was just noise right now. I didn't look forward to another day of being incommunicado with my pack. Instead of dwelling on our situation, I sat up and crossed to the sink. At least we had water. I leaned over so my mouth was as close to under the faucet as possible and turned on the cold water, swallowing gulp after gulp to help with the stomach pangs.

"I don't know." Sarah lay curled up on her side on the cot. "But we can go a week or two with just water." She sent me a morbid smile.

Well, no one came Saturday either and by Sunday morning, my stomach growl had dropped into a category that rivaled my feral growl. My face had stubble growing and it itched like hell. The dried blood was flaking in places, and I could tell I smelled less like a man and more like an animal.

Sarah wasn't much better, except she still had that citrusy scent that made her rankness more palatable.

My stomach groaned, and she giggled.

I rolled onto my side and adjusted the pillow, glancing at her through the bars. "You find my stomach growling funny?" I pressed my lips together against a smile.

"It's obnoxious."

"Being locked up here for two nights is obnoxious," I muttered under my breath as my stomach was nearly eating itself.

"Did you get any sleep?" she asked through a yawn.

I nearly laughed out loud. With her this close to me, I couldn't relax enough to sleep, not with her readjusting her position so often that I just wanted to break through the bars and hold her and chase her nightmares away.

"Not really," I answered and glanced back. "You snore."

The hallway door creaked open, and I sat up.

Johnson came into the hall, carrying a stack of my clothes. Mr. Fritz, the men's dorm supervisor who had initially showed me to my room on the first day, flanked Johnson on one side and Mrs. Kemper on the other. Johnson didn't quite meet our gazes. It was as if he had been told not to engage.

My gaze bypassed Johnson's and landed on Mrs. Kemper. "What the hell? You were supposed to send one of the medical techs to check her out. And what's with not sending us food?"

Mr. Fritz sneered at me and then slashed a glare at Sarah. Mrs. Kemper couldn't meet either of our stares.

"I figured you needed clothes and..." Johnson started but Mr. Fritz cleared his throat. Johnson glared at him. "Neither of them did anything wrong," he snapped and the muscles in his arms tightened under his shirt like he were getting ready to take a swing.

If Johnson continued, he'd end up in a cell, too. "Thanks for the clothes." I started to get up.

"Stay where you are," Mr. Fritz snapped.

I sat back down with the pillow over my privates.

Mrs. Kemper unlocked the cell and waved for Johnson to enter with the stash of clothing. "Just put it on the floor and then come out."

"Fine," Johnson muttered under his breath and stepped in far enough to clear the door. He put the clothing down and exited just as quickly. His frustration radiated from him. Even without my heightened senses, it was visible in the scowl on his face and the tenseness in his muscles. As they walked out, he glanced my way and the trepidation in that one look clenched my stomach.

I retrieved the clothes, and as I pulled out the underwear and slid them on, a piece of paper stuck out from between the folds of my jeans. Before I unfolded it, I pulled my jeans on and slipped one of the T-shirts over my head. The fact he had given me an extra shirt struck me as odd.

I unfolded the note and read the first line. "Johnson thought you might like a shirt, too." I held the extra T-shirt out to her, careful not to touch the bars.

"That was nice of him." She took the cloth and turned away from me to slip off her shredded shirt, replacing it with my oversized top.

It took me a second to tear my eyes away from her and back to the note. They were planning to crucify both of us.

I huffed. Their lack of attention to us in any form told me enough, but Johnson's note just compounded the truth that this organization was as evil as the monsters we hunted.

"You have that name, right?" I asked her as I read his assessment of what they were charging us with: She lured those men into her room. I killed them out of some jealous rage, per their write-up. The pack would not be allowed to testify on our behalf. I closed my eyes and nearly crumpled the paper.

"Yes."

"Do you think anyone else at the school has been attacked?" I glanced at her. The entire school would be witness to this farce, and if we had allies in the audience, I needed to know.

She chewed her lip and nodded. "I think at least one has from what they were saying. But I'm not sure. Why?"

I handed her Johnson's note.

As she read it, her cheeks turned red and I swear, for a moment fire blazed in her eyes. "Is he kidding?" Her gaze slashed to mine.

I shook my head. "We're going to need others to validate your story."

She looked at the paper in her hand again. "Isn't your father on the board?"

"Yep," I said. "But I don't think it'll matter unless we can prove they were repeat rapists."

Sarah crumpled the paper and shot it into the toilet, cursing under her breath. She flushed the toilet and then threw herself on the cot.

"Those assholes promised me I'd hang if I said anything," she muttered and met my gaze.

"That's not happening." I would make certain it didn't, because I would spill a whole lot of MDA blood if they tried. And I wouldn't be alone. My pack would back me. It would be an outright war.

Sarah slung her arm over her eyes and sighed.

We went another restless night without food. In the morning, the door creaked open, and Mr. Fritz and Mrs. Kemper approached our cells with frowns of disgust.

Not a word was said. They just opened the doors and waited until we stepped out. Mrs. Kemper led the way, and Mr. Fritz took the position in back of us. It felt like walking the green mile as we were marched through the halls into the cafeteria. No food was present. Only a table with two chairs faced the raised stage. On the raised platform in front of us, the administrators of the academy, along with the teachers, sat. In the center was my father.

I held one of the chairs for Sarah and then took my seat next to her. My father's dark stare was enough to make me want to fidget, but I remained stoic, with my hands folded before me. I didn't break eye contact with him, either. It was my silent challenge to this ludicrous display.

When the students filed in, lining the walls and gathering behind us, my father broke his gaze and surveyed the crowd.

I glanced at Sarah, but she had her hands clenched in her lap; she stared at the table, her face pale enough to give me pause. That was when I felt the force of her terror. I had been so consumed with staring down my father that I blocked everything else. And her terror felt like a swarm of bees attacking me. I took a breath and glared out at those in charge. I would annihilate them if they tried to harm her.

One of the administrators cleared her throat, and her face pinched in distaste as she looked at us. I had only seen her in attendance at orientation, so I didn't have a clue what her name was. The whispering in the auditorium died down to a hush.

"We are gathered today to pass judgment on these two students. One who seduced three graduates and the other who killed them in a jealous rage." She waved at us.

My pack scoffed in unison.

"There will be no interruptions from the crowd!" she snarled.

"So, the academy endorses rape." I projected my voice so it reached every single ear in the room. I leaned back in the seat, crossing my arms, displaying the dried blood still streaking my skin.

She blinked at me and pointed a gnarled finger in my direction. "Silence!"

I slammed my hand on the table and stood. "I will not be silent. Those thugs attacked *my* partner. And they've done this before. She was not the first. And if they had succeeded, she wouldn't be the last. Those bastards deserved a slow and painful death, and not the quick work I made of them."

Her mouth dropped.

Sarah stared up at me with wide eyes, as if my outburst wasn't warranted.

"Son..." my father started.

"You condone what was done?" I snarled, glaring at him. "You condone witches controlling their victims? Making them do vile things just for their twisted enjoyment?" I slung the words like weapons and turned toward the crowd, scanning them. Two female witches looked at the ground, just as pale as Sarah. My anger flared even more, and I glanced back at our judge and jury.

I straightened my spine. "And you would condemn an innocent for this?" I felt power swell inside me as the alpha in my wolf bristled. The wolves around me and on the stage seemed to shrink in on themselves. Even my father had a moment where he seemed to be cowering. "You. Will. Not." The power in my voice rolled over the entire room. Even some of the witches seemed to roll into themselves against the power I projected with those three words.

"You are not in the position to make demands," my father said through clenched teeth, as if denying my alpha order.

I smiled. "I am the alpha here." I stabbed my finger on the table. "I stand for what is right for *my* pack, and my pack includes witches and wolves from all over, standing obediently in attendance behind me. If it was one of your pack members who was assaulted, you wouldn't bat an eye at my swift justice. Well, it was *my* pack member who these three assholes assaulted." I turned and pointed to the two other witches who still shielded their eyes, and then waved at Sarah. "And they did nothing but nod a hello in the library when their partners were not here to protect them."

"But they were strong mages," the pinched-faced woman whined, as if that gave them a pass to violate anyone.

"I don't give a fuck who they were. They used their magic to sexually assault young witches. That makes them a target of this agency that you are training us all for. Dark magic is prohibited." I took a breath and glanced at Sarah. "And if you still choose to condemn her, you condemn me. I will not stand by and let you kill an innocent because of some archaic rules of engagement that do not apply to this situation. In other words, you will have to go through me to get to my partner. And I'll take as many of you down with me as I possibly can." I stared down my father, putting the stakes out on the table.

"She's a witch."

"She's part of *my* pack." I slapped my palm on my chest. "And I protect *my* pack. Had I known this was happening, I would have annihilated the three rapists before last night. They were the abominations, not the women who fell victim to their trickery."

Every eye in the room was on me. Admiration flowed in waves from the student body surrounding us, and animosity charged from the board in front of us, as if I should have remained quiet and subdued like a good student.

"How did you hold them off long enough for your partner to return?" one of the witches behind me asked in a voice that held devastation. Her blonde hair was tucked behind her ears, and she had stepped to the front of the crowd, her eyes imploring Sarah for an answer. She was partner to Hannah, a member of my hometown pack.

Sarah turned and shrugged, speaking for the first time since this farce of a trial began. "It was a struggle, but I was able to break through their bitter magic every time they slung it at me."

Hannah stepped out of the crowd and focused on her partner. "They assaulted you?"

A tear slid down the girl's face, and she nodded.

"Why didn't you tell me?" Hannah asked soft enough that the board didn't hear her, but both Sarah and I did, and we exchanged a glance. The focus and care Hannah showed displayed exactly what partners were supposed to do for each other.

"Because those assholes told her they would see to it that she was executed if she breathed a word to anyone." Sarah swallowed and looked at the board, all passing judgment on us. "It was the same threat they tried to impress on me as I fought them off and mentally sent an SOS to my partner."

"You weren't the only ones." A second witch with dark hair hanging in her face stepped forward; a wolf from another pack snarled at the board and then focused on her emotionally wounded partner.

A third and fourth student stepped forward, adding to our defense. That made one witch assaulted for every weekend since the furloughs started. My stomach clenched. I turned my anger toward the front of the room. How long had they *allowed* this shit to go on?

I leaned forward on the table, reining in my furious wolf. "Are you going to condemn *my* pack?"

In that one growling sentence, I became the leader of the entire school. The shift of emotions in the room altered in our favor. Not only did I have the support of my pack members who had witnessed the atrocity, but the rest of the wolves and witches stood with us.

There would be brutal bloodshed if the board condemned us now.

YOUNG BLOOD 13

MY FATHER'S GAZE SCANNED over the crowd. "Mrs. Wyman, perhaps we should discuss this with the accused in private."

At least the bastard was smart enough to read the room correctly.

The pinched-faced woman glared at him and then looked at me. "And what of the charges of jealousy, Mr. Young?"

I laughed and traded a heated look with my father before meeting her gaze. "I protected my partner. If doing what we're taught at this academy is considered jealousy, then that's truly fucked up. I would have reacted just as violently had I walked in on those assholes abusing *any* of the women in this room, including you." I pointed my finger at her. "My mother taught me right from wrong and ingrained in me a strong sense of swift justice. I act when I witness evil, ma'am."

My father's gaze swept over me as if he saw me for the first time. As if he had just witnessed me level every alpha in the region on the mat. I shocked him with my conviction.

Too bad he didn't think it was real. Granted, Sarah *was* my true mate and seeing what they were trying to do drove my wolf over the brink of reason, but it had nothing to do with jealousy. It had everything to do with rage. Rage regarding the audacity of those assholes to think they had a right to touch Sarah without her consent.

When my father's chest swelled with pride, I narrowed my eyes at him. He wasn't the one who taught me how to respond to evil. All the credit on that went to my mother.

"You have not answered my question. Are you condemning *my* pack?" I asked again. I wasn't backing down, not with our lives in the crosshairs.

Johnson stepped next to me, followed by the rest of my hometown pack. Then the rest of the student body pressed forward, forming a solid line around us, and we severely outnumbered the board.

Sarah slid her chair back and stood up as well, adding to our display of unity.

Mrs. Wyman glanced around at her peers, getting consistent head shakes as she met each member's gaze. She faced forward and folded her hands in front of her as she scanned all of us. She finally looked at me.

"No, Mr. Young. We are not going to condemn your pack today. But we will be watching you and Miss Stone. If there is any more trouble, you two will be facing harsher punishments than just a few nights in lockup.”

“Thank you, ma’am. Now if you would excuse us, we need to go clean up.”

I turned without waiting for any response. The crowd parted, and we marched out of the cafeteria, and separated at the outer doors. Sarah headed back toward her room, and I to mine.

Johnson caught up with me just as I stepped into the room.

“Thanks for the heads-up.” I closed the door behind me.

“No problem. From what I gathered, they were aiming to have Sarah killed. It made no fucking sense to me, and you needed to know.” He stretched out on his bed.

I stripped out of the clothes and headed for the shower to scrub the dried blood off me, but a knock on the door made me pause. I grabbed the towel off the back of the bathroom door, wrapped it around me, and answered the door.

Sarah stood in the hall, looking lost. Her eyes widened as they took in my bare chest, and then she met my gaze.

“Um. My room is still...” She licked her lips and shifted from foot to foot. “Can I use your shower?”

“They haven’t cleaned up your room?” I stepped back, waving her into our quarters.

“No. They haven’t even removed the bodies.” Her face turned a shade paler.

“Jesus.” I grabbed the clothes that Johnson had brought to me in the jail cell and stepped into the bathroom, redressing myself. When I entered the room again, I said, “I’ll clean up my mess.”

After all, I was the one who shredded the shit out of two humans. "You are welcome to use our shower." I nodded toward the bathroom.

She looked at the bathroom and then at me, as if debating. "You weren't the only one who killed." She took a deep breath and let it out slowly. "I'll help you, but I can't guarantee I won't throw up."

I smiled. I was glad I didn't have anything in my stomach. "I might, too," I admitted. The thought of cleaning up human remains left a sour taste in my mouth, but I wasn't going to leave her to do it alone.

"Do you want me there?" Johnson asked.

Sarah looked at him and shook her head. "You don't need to be there."

"More hands to help." He raised his hands, waving his fingers.

That pulled a smile onto Sarah's face. "If you want to clean up blood and guts, then I guess you're welcome to join."

"Not that I want to, but we were all there, so I'm willing to dispose of the garbage, too."

I couldn't tell whether Johnson was flirting with Sarah or not, but the idea of help wasn't one I was going to turn down. We stepped into the hall and headed toward the girl's dorm. When we got to Sarah's floor, the four women who had been assaulted were hanging around the door to Sarah's room. As we approached, they turned to us.

We stopped in front of them.

"I'm sorry for calling you out," I said before any of them could speak.

Hannah's partner gave me an uneasy smile. "Thank you for stopping them."

I extended my hand. "Robby Young."

"Heddie Thompson." She shook my hand.

"I'm sorry that we didn't know to stop them before they attacked you," Sarah said. "We would have filleted their asses sooner had we known." She swung her door open to the carnage.

I might not have been so insensitive, but none of the girls gasped or shied away from the bloody scene. A satisfied smile actually appeared on Heddie's lips as she surveyed the damage.

Then Heddie looked at me and Johnson. "Thank you."

"No problem at all. As I said in that farce of a tribunal, everyone here is part of my pack and as such, it's my duty to protect you from harm." I shuffled my feet and looked in at what I had done in my rage. "I'm sorry I failed you," I added, looking back at the four girls. I really should have known what was going on.

"No one knew. We didn't even know among ourselves." She waved at the other three witches who hadn't been introduced. "If they had assaulted a wolf, you would have known."

"True." I couldn't argue with her. Wolves carried a stronger bond of silent communication.

"I'm still trying to figure out how your partner was able to give you a heads-up that something was wrong," Heddie mumbled under her breath as her gaze jumped between me and Sarah.

"I guess we're on the same...wavelength." Sarah shrugged. "I'm just glad I was able to break their spells."

Heddie's brow creased. "How?"

Sarah glanced in the room and sighed. "Sheer force of will."

"I was terrified. I couldn't even think straight," Heddie said.

"Yeah, well, I was pissed and plotting their deaths." With that, Sarah stepped into the room. "I don't even know where to begin."

"Disposing of the bodies might be a good start," I said from behind her as I surveyed the carnage. "Damn," I whispered at the extent of blood and gore coating the room.

Sarah looked back at me. "You were truly terrifying in action."

I let out a laugh, but it wasn't quite my natural bust-a-gut laugh. This one held the raw nerves now playing across my skin at what was left of the last body. The first two would be easier to pick up. But the last one was in pieces. I glanced up at the ceiling; there were even splatters of blood and bits of skin and bone stuck on the cinderblocks above us.

"Do you have garbage bags and rags and cleaning solution?" I asked.

"A mop and a bucket?" Johnson piped in.

"Cleaning gloves?" Heddie said from behind us.

I turned. The four witches hadn't left. They stood behind us, as if they intended to help.

"You really don't need to help," Sarah echoed my thoughts. "We've got this."

Heddie glanced at Sarah and around the room. "I can't get rid of it, but I can concentrate the mess into a single pile."

We all turned and looked at her. Sarah's eyebrows probably mimicked mine.

"I can control matter," she said.

I did recall things moving at her opponents when she fought in the gym. Even Hannah had to dodge a projected missile coming for her in the ring.

"Telekinetic?" Sarah nodded, as if she recalled the same things. Sarah had fought her, too. But Sarah was unbeatable in the ring, even with magic coming at her in all forms. Which was probably why she was able to break through these assholes' magic. She had proved she had that skill time and time again in sparring matches.

Heddie nodded and looked up at the splatters on the ceiling. A crease appeared between her eyes, and she splayed her hand out, moving it slowly toward the wall, where more splatters of blood covered the concrete blocks. The mess followed her hand, rolling away and leaving the cinderblock clean. It looked like a giant had wiped away the blood and guts in one stroke of a sponge. Heddie continued, pulling the grime from the walls and gathering it all into a pile on the floor.

Sarah's ceiling, walls, and furniture were clean when Heddie finished. But the witch looked as though she hadn't slept in days from the effort.

"Thank you." Sarah marveled at the newly sparkling room. The floor was another story, but the linoleum would clean easily with a mop and bucket once we removed the bodies. "You should go get some rest or something to eat," she added.

Heddie and the others left us to finish cleaning up.

Sarah conjured up large, thick garbage bags like the ones used for construction garbage, along with shovels and three buckets of bleach-smelling liquid with mops.

A throat cleared from behind us, and we turned.

My father stood in the doorway, along with Mrs. Kemper.

"We are here to collect the bodies," Mrs. Kemper said.

I glared at her. "And you couldn't do it before that farce of a trial?" I growled.

"Easy, son." My father tried to appease me.

All it did was aggravate me more. "Fuck you," I snapped. He stood by the rest of the board. He wouldn't have intervened if they had convicted us. He would prefer to keep his station in the agency than support his son.

"Robby," Sarah said sternly.

Johnson actually put his hand on my shoulder and shook his head.

My father glared at Sarah. "I don't need you interjecting in my conversation with my son."

"She can interject her thoughts into any conversation that I'm having," I snarled and pushed with my alpha powers. "She is my partner and as such, you will not disrespect her or anyone else in my pack."

My father growled in response.

"We were not allowed to disrupt the room until a verdict was issued," Mrs. Kemper said while she uncontrollably wrung her hands. "Please step out while we take care of this."

"Fine." I stormed past, brushing my shoulder against his and knocking him back a step on purpose. Sarah and Johnson followed me out. Three men with insignias from the coroner's office stood outside with a cart piled with body bags.

They replaced us in the room.

My father stepped out in the hall and leveled a stare at me that was supposed to make me fidget, but I crossed my arms and pressed my lips together against the flurry of derogatory words that wanted to slip free.

"I wouldn't have let them harm you," he said softly.

"But you sure as shit would have let my partner hang." I nodded toward Sarah as my head pulsed with anger.

His gaze sharpened. "I could not influence the board's decision."

"Bullshit," I snarled and turned, walking away. If I stayed, I'd throw a punch.

A hand caught my shoulder and I tensed, spinning back, thinking it was my father, but Sarah stood there instead. She poked me in the chest hard.

"He's your father, and he's here. He could be gone tomorrow, so you have to give him some slack."

I knew she was coming from a place where neither parent was here, and she saw things differently than I did. *If she knew what he had done, would she still be coming to his defense?* But I wasn't about to spill that secret. Especially if she struggled with the electricity between us as much as I did, because it was always there for me.

"He's a bastard who didn't lift a finger to save us."

She blinked up at me. "He's still your father."

I closed my eyes and hung my head. A moment later, the squeak of the cart drew my eyes open. The coroner staff pushed the cart out the door, loaded with three body bags.

"We'll talk later," my father said from where he stood.

I gave a nod without looking at him. I was sure during winter break I'd hear more than an earful. But for now, we still had the rest of the semester to get through, which wouldn't be easy with the added scrutiny.

YOUNG BLOOD 14

T HE NEXT FEW WEEKS were uneventful. It was as if my declaration in front of the board had elevated me to the untouchable realm. It was irritating, especially because I was back in the sparring ring and no one but Sarah would give me their best. Even Johnson pulled his punches, as if going at me at full capacity was some sort of sin.

"What the fuck, man," I grumbled and slammed the door to our room.

"Dude, you're the alpha. No one wants to challenge you."

"How the hell am I supposed to get better at fighting if no one will actually give me their best?"

"Your partner does. She's fucking fearless."

He nailed it dead-on. Sarah was fearless. And angry. And smart. A challenge to me in every conceivable way. She could outwit and outmaneuver me in the ring unless I turned wolf, and then she still bested me most of the time. But the times I took her to the mat were my favorite. It gave me a second with her underneath me, with her eyes ablaze and her breath heaving. Thankfully, I was in wolf form when that happened, but it still took everything not to claim her in those moments.

"That she is," I muttered. Instead of arguing with Johnson, I stripped and stepped into the shower, letting the warm water wash the sweat off my under-utilized muscles. I was not looking forward to winter break. I had obligations at home with the job I had at the local dive, waiting tables. I planned to give notice before I came back, because in the spring, we'd become full-fledged agents and get assigned to wherever the hell they wanted to place us.

I was hoping for somewhere up north in mountain country, but with my luck lately, it would probably be at headquarters in the city, which didn't thrill me. I liked the countryside, where I could shift and just run until my muscles gave out. Although, the alternative would likely be in my father's office, and that would be worse than death. Having my old man hanging over my shoulder every second of every day would drive me batshit.

Plus, not seeing Sarah on a daily basis was going to be rough. Regardless of the situation, seeing her was the highlight of my day.

My stomach growled as I toweled off and dressed. I figured if I could stretch out the evening somehow, I wouldn't have to pile into Johnson's car afterward and head into the lion's den.

I stepped out of the bathroom and scanned my things. Johnson had his duffel bag stuffed for the trek home, but I was only going to bring my dirty laundry home. I didn't need to carry it back and forth if I didn't have to. I stuffed my duffel with my towels and the clothing in my laundry basket while Johnson cleaned up.

I didn't wait for Johnson. I wanted as much time with Sarah before he carted me off for the winter break, and like the first day, we were both early and the doors hadn't opened yet.

"Hiding from everyone?" she asked as she slid onto the bench.

I sat and nodded. "I'm not looking forward to going home, either."

She snorted a laugh. "Well, I'll be here if you need me."

I raised an eyebrow.

"Where am I going to go?" She leveled a look as though I had actually spoken.

I had forgotten that she was in state care outside of these walls. "If you need me, just text and I'll be here as fast as I can. Or call like you did before." I gave her a halfhearted smile, praying she wouldn't have to send out a mental SOS again. I wouldn't be able to get back here as fast as I had that night.

She paled a fraction and nodded. "Let's hope I don't need to. But I'll text you to death because I'm sure I'm going to be bored senseless here."

Sarah was not one to sit idle. Ever. Even studying in the library, she had to jump up and go find this book or that book to answer her questions. I don't think I've ever seen her sit down for more than ten minutes at a time, unless we were eating. She was worse than I was, with energy to burn.

"If I don't answer, don't think I'm ignoring you. I'm probably working."

"You've still got a job at home?"

"Yes. But I need to give my notice because I won't be going back after break."

"What do you do?"

"Wait tables. The pay is shit, but the tips are pretty good."

She stared at me and shook her head. "I can't see you waiting tables."

I stretched my left arm out. "I can balance more plates on my arm than anyone else in town. And I've never dropped any of them." I grinned. "Ever."

"Well, you just jinxed yourself." She pointed at me just as the locks on the cafeteria doors clicked and the staff pushed the doors open.

"We'll see about that." I stood and waved for her to go first. She made a beeline to the buffet, and we had our plates overflowing before any of the other students stepped into the cafeteria.

The cafeteria filled quickly as we scarfed down our food, sitting in the same end seats we had become accustomed to. The pack and their partners filled up the rest of the table along with the witches who helped us clean Sarah's room.

The seat next to Sarah was now reserved for Hannah, and Johnson always sat to my right no matter where we seemed to be. Everyone nodded at me as they passed, and frankly, outside of the ring, I liked the show of respect. If only I could get them all to understand that their respect should translate into giving me their all when we sparred.

Dinner flew by too fast, and Johnson nudged me with his elbow. I gave him a look, and he tapped his watch.

"I know. I'm just not thrilled at the prospect of going home," I muttered, and Sarah raised her eyebrow from across the table. I stood with my tray and reached for hers.

"I got it. You don't have to clear my tray." She smiled up at me as she held her side of the cheap plastic so I couldn't just swipe it off the table. "I might go for a little more of the apple crisp anyway." She nodded to the dessert section and the abundance of apple crisp still sitting there.

"It doesn't seem like it's that good." I still eyed the dessert, but now I could smell it above all other scents, and it did trigger my mouth to water.

"Stop stalling. Go home and make amends with your dad."

Her tone didn't give me any choice.

I rolled my eyes and headed out, dumping my tray in the tray caddie before Johnson and I went to grab our bags.

I stretched out in the front seat and stared out the window as Johnson drove. This time it was just the two of us, and he had the sense to keep quiet. The closer we came to home, the more my mood worsened.

"It's not going to be as bad as you think," Johnson said.

I scoffed at him. My father was going to beat the crap out of me for my indiscretions. I'd be sporting bruises for weeks from the whupping that was sure to greet me the minute I stepped

through the door. After all, I had challenged the
alpha.

YOUNG BLOOD 15

I WAS NOT WRONG to be wary of home. Johnson stopped in front of the dark mansion I had left four months ago. The hairs on the back of my neck prickled.

"Thanks for the ride." I grabbed my duffel from the back.

"No problem. I'll see you in a couple days. I think we cross shifts next weekend at Joe's."

"I'll see you then." With a nod, I closed the car door and headed toward my house, digging in my pocket for the house key. I slipped inside and set my bag down. Shoes came off next because, regardless of being a wolf, we were not to track mud into the house. It was something my mother pounded into my head and although she had died almost ten years ago, I still respected her rules.

No sounds hung on the heavy air. Not even the echo of a breath in the house. However, I felt the malevolent anger pressing down on me. Instead of heading into the family room, I grabbed my bag and headed up the stairs to my bedroom.

The moment I stepped into the room, I startled at the figure standing at the window. I hadn't even looked up when I got out of the car; otherwise, I would have seen him. I expected my father in his recliner in the family room, not standing sentry at my window.

For a moment, I was my younger self and all I wanted was an ice cream treat, but I hadn't done my chores and my father said no. I snuck a dollar from his wallet and when I returned home from enjoying the ice cream, he had been standing in the same place wearing that same fiery glare.

But this time, he was not justified in his anger.

I threw my duffel on the floor. "What?" I bellowed at him.

"Don't you use that tone with me." He pointed his finger at me. His sharp canines were on display, which meant he was particularly dangerous.

"I will use whatever tone I please."

He was on me in an instant and slammed me into the wall. "You are not the alpha here," he growled in my face.

"No?" I cocked my head and pushed out the alpha influence like I had at that farce of a trial. I narrowed my eyes at him, but I did not strike out like my clenched hands wanted to. I still honored my mother, and beating the shit out of my father wasn't something she'd be proud of. But I could bend him to my will.

He growled at me and landed the first punch right into my left side.

Air rushed out of my lungs, but I refused to curl over. Hell, I had been hit harder sparring with Sarah. "Back off," I warned.

I parried before his next punch connected, catching him off guard as I deflected his fist, sending it into the wall next to me, and then I spun out of his grip. It was something I had never had the guts to do before. Oh, I was capable, but I was still under his influence, whether I liked it or not.

All that fury that I carried inside since he fucked with my entire life surfaced and I growled, baring my teeth, but I didn't shift into wolf form. My wolf was even more furious at the old man; if I set him free, he would fight to the death.

"Isn't fucking up the rest of my life enough of a punishment? Or would you prefer to bury me?" I glared at him.

My words had the same effect a hefty slap would have. My father reeled back a step and his eyes widened as his jaw dropped. "I would never..."

"Yet you are so willing to beat me." I stayed out of reach. "And take away the one thing that would make me complete."

"She's a witch," he hissed, as if she were a leper instead. "She put you under some sort of spell."

I laughed. "Sarah couldn't cast a spell to save her life. Do you know what her magic is?"

"I don't need to know. She is not a werewolf, and she is trouble."

"She is not trouble. She's fiercer than any wolf in this pack. Fiercer than Mom."

"No one was as fierce as your mother. And yet she still was taken by a blood sucker." His teeth slipped back to human. "I did what I did to protect you."

"Protect me, or your status?" I snapped back, with my fangs still on display. I put my hand up, splaying my fingers out. "Don't answer that. I already know." I ran my hand through my hair, trying to rein in my aggravation. "Coming home was a mistake."

"You have obligations here."

I hated the fact he was right. I couldn't just leave. I had to give some sort of notice to the restaurant, but it was going to be a hell of a lot shorter than originally planned. "Get out of my bedroom," I snapped and pointed at the door. "As soon as my obligations are met, I'm out of here."

"I have someone I want you to meet," he had the audacity to say. "She will make a perfect alpha's mate."

"I'm never agreeing to anyone you decide is a proper mate. I already met my true mate and nothing on this earth is going to sway me any other way. And because of what you did, there will be no heritage to hand down beyond me. I'm the end of the line."

He paled at my words and went to open his mouth.

"It's all your doing." I pointed at him. "This is the consequence of *your* actions." Instead of waiting for him to leave my room, I turned and walked out of the house, shifting the moment I hit the sidewalk. I needed to run until this anger dialed back. Otherwise, I was going to do something colossally stupid. Like challenge the current alpha, which would mean only one of us would walk out of that alive. And although I was angry, I did not want to commit patricide.

⚜ ⬥ ⚜

THE NEXT DAY, I walked into Joe's and into the office where Maddy sat at the desk, doing the schedule. She looked up and smiled, but it only held for a moment.

"What's up?" she asked with a voice that bordered on concern.

"I'm giving my notice." I moved my weight nervously from foot to foot. I didn't like disappointing Maddy. Not when she had gone out of her way to give me a job despite my father's initial protests against being a lowly waiter.

She looked at the paper in front of her and then back at me. "How long?"

"What's the minimum?" I cringed as I asked. The longer I was at home, the more likely I was going to take a swing at my father.

"Customarily, it's two weeks." She used her hands to smooth out the paper in front of her, scanning the schedule she was making.

I nodded and sighed. I knew that was the usual. But I couldn't fathom being in the same house as my father for that long. Not with the volatility between us right now.

There had to be a way to shorten that timespan. "You wouldn't bend on that, would you?"

She leaned back in her chair. "You have something better lined up?" She pursed her lips, studying me.

"No. But staying will result in bloodshed," I admitted. She had seen me sporting bruises a time or two before and although I brushed them off, I could see the suspicion in her eyes.

Maddy looked down at the schedule in front of her and chewed on her lip. "Think you can get through three days?" She looked up at me. "If so, I can rearrange things so you have longer shifts over the next three days, and then we can call it even. Would that work?"

"Yeah." I gave her a partial smile, knowing her accommodating me might come back to bite her. After all, I was talking about bloodshed with the pack alpha. And I hadn't been given that role yet. I was no longer sure my father would give me that honor, or whether I would eventually have to fight him to the death for it.

YOUNG BLOOD 16

I ARRIVED HOME FROM my first shift and the house was blissfully empty, so I unwrapped the cheese steak I had brought home from the restaurant and set myself up in front of the television. I found new episodes of a series I had been watching before I went off to the academy and pressed play.

My father came in during the second episode, and it was as if a horde of bees had entered with him. The tension between us ratcheted up so high that the meal I scoffed down started to feel as if I swallowed lead.

Two more full days of work before I could kiss this tension goodbye. Although I was sure it would feel more like years by the time I got on my bike and headed back to school.

"What the hell are you watching?" He glared at me as he settled into his chair with what looked like takeout. Of course, he only had one take out box with him, so if I hadn't brought home my dinner, I would have had to order something from delivery or go without. The cupboards here were pretty barren, as if my father hadn't been hanging out at home much.

"A show." I didn't bother looking over at him either. My phone dinged, and I glanced at it. My first text from Sarah, and I couldn't help the smile that formed. Instead of fishing for how I was dealing with my dad, she jumped right in, telling me about her day.

Apparently, they had her helping out in the kitchen. That's something I couldn't really see her doing, but she promised she'd make us all something when we got back, but to set my expectations, she did make charcoal out of a batch of brownies, so it was an eat-at-your-own-risk situation.

I chuckled under my breath.

"If you're not going to watch this crap, give me the remote," my father growled.

"I am watching it."

"You're texting. That isn't watching the show," he grumbled.

I sent him a look that would have shut anyone else up, but he returned it with the same fierceness.

"I can leave and never come back, you know."

"You aren't eighteen yet."

"Um, yes, I am." I couldn't help the snark in my voice. It happened to be around the same time we got benched at school and I found out about Sarah's parents. My father hadn't even sent a card. But if I really thought about it, he hadn't ever been the one to initiate the celebration. It was always someone else in the pack bringing a cake over.

He blinked and creased his brow, as if he were trying to remember my actual day of birth.

"October, Dad. My birthday was in October." I tossed him the remote and stormed away, making sure my steps were heavy enough to vibrate the floorboards. I walked out into the cold night and pulled out my phone again, rereading Sarah's text, letting the chill of the air cool me down.

Even with anger thrumming in my veins like a high voltage blast, her words soothed the beast inside me, and I took breath after breath, seeing my exhale on the frosty air.

Two days. That's all I needed to endure. That is, if we didn't come to blows.

I started to write a text of the shit going down and deleted it just as fast. I did not want to lay my problems at Sarah's feet. Not when she really had no understanding of the years of constant friction between me and my father. She also had no clue of what the man had done to us. I'm not sure she would be so understanding if she knew he had intentionally sabotaged our future.

I tucked the phone into my pocket and glanced up at the clear, moonless night. The constellations stood out against the black canvas in pins of bright light. This view didn't happen in the city. I circled around the house to our picnic table and stretched out on the cold wooden surface on my back. Every now and then, a satellite would track overhead, crossing the sky in an arc before it disappeared on the horizon.

A shooting star streaked across the sky, and I made a wish. The one wish I knew was impossible now. But someday, maybe the rules could be changed, and I could be with Sarah for real, without putting her life in danger.

I KEPT STARING AT the clock, anxiously awaiting quitting time. I had packed my duffel this morning with all the clean clothing and had it behind my bedroom door, ready to collect and tie down to the back of my motorcycle. At least snow season hadn't started in earnest, so driving to school wouldn't be a game of slip and slide.

I collected the tip from my last table, cleared the dishes, and cleaned the table, getting it ready for the next patron. That was the end of my working career at Joe's Grill. It had served me well through high school. I took one last look around and then headed in back to clock out. My last paycheck would be direct deposited like all the others, and I'd be back in the money again—at least for a little while.

My father was wealthy, but I'd always worked for my keep. Not because he made me, but because I did not want to be indebted to the bastard. Not after the way he had treated me since the rest of our family died. I'm not sure whether he blamed me for their deaths because I was over at Johnson's house, or if he wished it had been me instead of Mom, Carl, and Casey, but after their deaths, he acted as though he were the only one in mourning. The wedge between us prior to that night became an unfixable chasm.

I sighed and pushed the card into the ancient time recorder, waited for the click and pulled it out, putting it back in the slot on the wall. I turned, intending to head to Maddy's office, but she and the gang had gathered behind me. I had been too far into my own thoughts to hear them.

"We wanted to give you a little going away gift." Maddy shoved a box into my hand with a beaming smile.

Heat filled my cheeks. I did not expect this from the staff. I ripped the funky paper off the square box and peeled open the lid. Inside was a mug wrapped in fabric. I pulled both out and laughed at the "You're Dead to Us" mug and one of the Joe's Grill T-shirts.

"Thanks," I said, and Maddy pulled me in for an awkward hug.

"Stay safe out there," she whispered in my ear. She lost her husband to an agency sting gone wrong, so she knew more about what I was walking into than I did, and I knew a fair amount.

"I will," I whispered. "Thanks for giving me this job."

"My pleasure." She gave me a squeeze and then released me, wiping at her eyes.

I gave everyone a nod and then hightailed it out of there before this lump in my throat turned into an embarrassing show of emotion. When I pulled into the driveway on my motorcycle, my father stood in the doorway with his arms crossed like an evil sentry. His gaze penetrated through me. I turned off the motorcycle and took off my helmet, leveling the same impassive gaze that my father regarded me with.

I swung my leg over the seat and hung my helmet on the handlebar. There was a bite to the air, and it smelled like snow was coming, which made the itch to get going settle into my bones.

But the way my father was blocking the doorway, I had a bad feeling that this wasn't going to be as easy an exit as I had hoped. I did not want a showdown. I didn't want this to come to blows.

"I don't want to fight," I said as I approached. "I just want to get my things and go." I slowed when I got close enough to be within arm's reach. He hadn't budged.

"Where do you think you're going?" His voice held a feral warning.

"Does it matter?"

He pressed his lips together and his nostrils flared. "Yes. I do not want you to put yourself in a position that will screw up your future."

I took a deep breath. "I can handle myself with Sarah."

His eyes narrowed. "I saw the way you defended her."

"I would have defended anyone in the same circumstances. It wouldn't matter who it was happening to. Seeing that vile shit turned my stomach, and I would have reacted the same damn way."

"You would have torn them to pieces?"

I opened my mouth to answer but nothing came out at first. "I would have stopped them by any means necessary." That I was sure of. I would have killed them for their transgression. It was my knee-jerk reaction in the presence of evil.

The muscles in my father's arms flexed, making his shirt bulge. "I saw what you did. That was irrational anger. You lost control."

I bit the edge of my lower lip. I had lost control. They were trying to violate my partner. "Yes. I did lose control. But that's because I was witnessing true evil. And that is my response to that shit." Admitting it to him stung. "Your worries about me fucking up with Sarah are unwarranted. Those consequences are not something I'm willing to gamble with."

"And what if she loses control with you?"

"Stop. Neither of us is going to cross the line. But if I stay here, I'm likely to throw a punch at you. And as much as that would feel good with the shit you've pulled on me, it isn't good for the pack." I met his gaze. "And me fucking around with Sarah not only puts her at risk, but it puts the pack at risk. I won't do that. So, please get out of my way so I can get my stuff and get the hell out of here before I lose my temper."

His face reddened and his glare sharpened.

It looked like getting out of here unscathed had just become a futile effort.

17

YOUNG BLOOD 17

"IF YOU EVER HOPE to lead this pack, you'd do well to remember your impact on them. You must think of their needs above your own," my father lectured from the stoop.

"What the hell are you talking about?"

"Leaving someone short-staffed, for instance." He pursed his lips as he looked down his nose at me.

"Maddy said it wasn't a problem." She had rearranged things to accommodate my request, but she didn't indicate that my leaving would provide a hardship to her the way my father insinuated.

"She wouldn't tell you otherwise. But you put your needs over the pack's needs." He reached inside the door and then tossed my duffel bag to me with more force than necessary.

"I would have had to give notice before the end of the break anyway," I argued. But guilt bit at the edges of my skin, making me fidget.

His eyebrow cocked, challenging me to say it wasn't a problem.

I knew better than to take the bait, even though he had gotten under my skin. I'd give the restaurant a call when I arrived at school just to make sure she didn't need me for the rest of the break. If she did, I'd find other sleeping arrangements.

I turned on my heel and headed to my bike, securing the duffel bag before I grabbed my helmet. "Let Johnson know I won't need a ride back to school."

"That's your responsibility," my father barked. Irritation laced every syllable.

"Fine," I muttered as I put on my helmet, and then situated myself on the bike so I'd be comfortable for the more than two-hour ride. With a kick of the starter, my hog rumbled to life. Without another look, I turned around and headed away from the house and the nightmare that was my father.

Halfway to the academy, the sky decided to dump an angry snow squall that matched my mood. My back tire slipped, and I caught myself, slowing the bike down to a reasonable speed for the conditions and not the breakneck speed I had been going. I didn't need to end up as roadkill.

The rest of the ride was very much a white-knuckle trip. The snow followed me as if I had my own dark cloud overhead. Truthfully, winter roads were not the best for a motorcycle, but I needed to get away from home, so I took the risk.

By the time I reached the academy, my muscles ached from the stress.

I unhooked the duffel bag, praying my clothes weren't soaked through, but with the heavier weight of the bag, they probably were. I didn't know whether I had enough surfaces in the room to hang my clothes to dry or not. It gave me another reason to be angry with my father. If he wasn't such a dick, I wouldn't have had to drive my motorcycle in a snowstorm.

With a sigh, I pulled my motorcycle cover out of the storage space under the seat and stowed my helmet in its place before I covered the bike, securing it with straps that went under the body of the machine so it wouldn't blow off in a windstorm.

I tucked the front tire in the bike rack that would be enough of a stabilizer to keep my motorcycle upright for the duration of the winter and then hiked up the hill from the student parking lot. I filtered through my keys until I found the one for the outer doors of the academy. Underneath the front door awning, I shook off the snow that had accumulated on my shoulders and in my hair just from the walk up the hill before I stepped in the building. I went straight to my room and peeled out of my soaked jeans and leather riding coat.

And then I checked out my duffel bag. Half the clothes were damp, and the other half soaked enough to be able to wring out water. At least they were clean. But it would take a day to dry all this shit. I took the time to hang things on everything I could find. When I finished, my room looked like a dry cleaner's back room.

I still had a pair of sweats and a couple T-shirts in my bureau, and I pulled them on before I fished out my phone from the inside pocket of my coat.

What are you up to? I texted Sarah.

Just hanging in the library. How'd work go?

I tucked the phone into my pocket and left my room, jogging barefoot down the hallway, and snuck into the library. She had her back to me, and I padded across the floor soundlessly. She jumped when I slid into the chair next to her.

"Work went fine." I grinned at her. "But I couldn't deal with the home situation, so I'm back for the rest of break."

She blinked at me. "How the hell did you get permission to stay? I had to jump through hoops to get them to let me hang here for winter break."

I glanced around and shrugged. No one else was in the library. "How many of you are here?"

"Just a couple of us." Her cheeks reddened. "And I couldn't tell you their names because they aren't in our classes." She leaned back in the seat and sighed as she pointed at me. "You are going to get in a shit ton of trouble."

"I'm a legacy and apparently the alpha here." I gave her my winning smile, as if that made all the difference in the world. But I would have to talk with someone about staying, and I hoped my actions wouldn't backfire on me.

"Well, then you'll be my guinea pig for the rest of the break." She beamed as if there were great rewards awaiting me.

"Doing what?" I shifted in the seat at the glint in her eye. My wolf fought for dominance but I kept him leashed and in control.

"You will be my taste tester with whatever concoction I put together in the kitchen." She waved at me as she spoke, as if I were royalty and going to be treated like it. It was damn cute.

I smirked at the grin playing on her lips. "So, I'll be eating a lot of charcoal?"

She swatted my arm with a laugh. "No. I only burned the first batch. I haven't made charcoal bricks since." Her chin jutted out with pride.

"Well, then I think I can do that, especially if you've already mastered brownies. There's nothing better than a warm brownie with a glass of cold milk."

"Actually, brownies in a bowl of milk is better." She closed the book she was reading and yawned. "You want some?" She didn't wait for an answer. She just grabbed my hand and pulled me out of the seat, dragging me along behind her.

Let's just say, I ate like a king over the rest of the winter break.

YOUNG BLOOD 18

THE NEW SEMESTER SLID in with a blizzard, the likes of which hadn't been seen since the seventies, bringing with it subzero temperatures and intermittent power outages. On the third night without power, the staff brought all the students down to the cafeteria, where they lit the huge hearth for the first time in several years. Smoke belched out of the fireplace until the oversized chimney was hot enough to vanquish the cold air and allow the smoke to rise up the frigid shaft.

Even with all of us in the cafeteria, a roaring fire, and over a hundred wolves in all, we weren't able to get the room temperature beyond the mid-fifties. Sarah was huddled close enough to touch, and she shivered hard enough for her teeth to chatter in a constant click.

"Why don't you go sit near the fire for a little while?" I nodded toward several witches hogging the warmth. Most of whom she knew well enough to intrude upon.

"I'm fine." She stuttered her words between teeth clacking.

I nodded for Johnson to move to her other side. "You are going to get sick if you don't get warm."

She opened her mouth to argue, but I covered it with my hand.

I did not want to hear any of her arguments. "You'll owe me a decent pair of jeans." I pulled my hand away, shifting into my wolf. I glanced at Johnson, and he did the same. I curled up with my back against her side and Johnson shifted and leaned against her opposite side, sandwiching her with our warmth.

Other wolves in the room followed suit, huddling up against the nearest witch to give them some of our inherent warmth without making it inappropriate.

Sarah's chills subsided, and she stretched out between us, still bundled in her blankets. But she threw the edges over us. "Thank you."

I turned my head to look at her. I had to harness every emotion and every urge to claim her in that moment. Especially when her fingers slid over my brow of black fur and then gently scratched my ear. I closed my eyes and sighed before I stretched out on my side, with her weight against me.

By morning, the power was back, the fireplace held only embers, and we were sent back to our rooms so the staff could make breakfast. But it was the best night I've ever had. Sarah had kept her hand on my neck while she slept, and just the feeling of her that near me was more than enough to bring on that bitter taste of loss and regret as I padded my way back to my room with Johnson in tow.

He whined at me as we got closer to the room, but I didn't pay any attention to him. I was too lost in that dark space of knowing I would never get what I truly wanted in this life.

I shifted and opened our dorm room. Chilly air drifted over my naked form, and I held the door open for Johnson. He didn't shift until we were inside the room, where he could at least pull something on as quick as possible in the still frigid air.

After we both dressed, Johnson asked, "Are you okay?"

I huffed. "I will be." Knowing last night was the closest I'd ever get to sleeping with my soul mate stung like a beast.

"All I know is I haven't felt that kind of loss from you since your mother died."

I glanced at him. "You felt my mood?" It was common for the pack to feel their alpha's emotions if they were strong enough, but I wasn't the official alpha, yet.

He nodded. "Quite a few of us did."

Shit. That wasn't good. I didn't even have a viable excuse for it, either. And no one but Johnson and my father knew I had feelings for my partner. I not only had to muzzle my wolf, but I also needed to imprison my emotions from this point forward.

I threw myself facedown on the bed, mentally scolding myself for letting my emotions bleed through to the other wolves in the pack. "Just tell them I got blindsided with my mom and brother and sister's death again. Make up some shit about power outages and my mom cuddling with us to keep us warm."

I glanced over at him, and he actually looked impressed.

"That would be a viable story, but they've been dead a long time."

"It's all I got."

"I could add that all of us huddling together made you remember the good times before and then add your piece." Johnson raised an eyebrow like that was more believable.

I nodded. "Thanks." I closed my eyes. I hadn't gotten much rest last night with her body against mine.

"You coming to get something to eat?"

"I'm not really hungry. I'm going to catch a nap before classes start." I needed the time to also get my emotions in check before facing everyone.

"I'll come grab you after I eat."

I gave him a thumbs-up and the lull of sleep claimed me.

YOUNG BLOOD 19

THE SEMESTER FLEW BY, and our last exam was one that took place in the gymnasium. With the class lined up, they had the first group step into the middle of the room, where thick cushy mats covered the floor. That first set of trainees had no warning before the line of agency officers raised their guns and shot.

The guns let out a *phew*, more like an air gun than bullets, but it still set off my alpha protective instinct. I went to take a step forward, but Sarah grabbed my forearm, defusing me enough to focus on the first line of students.

It wasn't bullets that hit the trainees. It actually looked like a dart. My brain stalled for a moment, trying to connect a memory to my current circumstance.

Tranquilizer. The thought barreled through my mind before the first witch fell unconscious. My father shot a rogue wolf once with one of those things. That rogue fell hard. And the wolves in the midst fell a few seconds after the witches. Now the oversized mats made a whole lot of sense.

The echo of dozens of students falling onto them still rang in the gym.

"Since you have the benefit of a warning, unlike these poor souls..." an instructor who none of us had ever seen in any of our training sessions said. He was short, at something like five six. If Sarah stood next to him, she would tower over him as though he were a dwarf. "Understand how you react when you wake from the tranquilizer will impact your ultimate station in the agency." He smiled, and it reminded me more of a weasel than a man.

I glanced at Sarah, but she was still staring at the others now being dragged off to the side of the gym and deposited on less forgiving mats. Buckets were placed by each person's head, as if they expected everyone who was tranquilized to vomit on waking.

My mouth turned into a bed of aluminum, and I tried to swallow it down. The idea of being that vulnerable bothered me, especially considering I was hiding a golly-whopper of a secret. And I had no idea what was in the tranquilizer.

We were next in line. When they waved us forward, I said, "Is this really necessary?" I had only made it a step or two at most when I felt the sting in my chest and looked down at the dart embedded in my skin.

Sarah faltered next to me, and I tried to catch her, but my muscles decided to stage a mutiny. I went down but didn't even feel the hit of the floor.

"HOLY FUCKING HELL," I whispered as knife shards pierced my brain. Even the light filtering in through my closed eyelids was painful. My stomach did a slow roll, and I clamped my mouth closed, slowly sucking air through my nose, willing myself not to hurl. The sounds of others doing just that filtered in.

I was glad I chose to get a few more minutes of sleep instead of food this morning, but between the headache, the sounds of retching, and the stench, I wasn't sure I'd be able to keep whatever acid was churning in my belly where it was.

Sarah.

The thought broke through the momentary paralysis, and I cracked my eyes open. I slowly moved my head to look around. Sarah was still unconscious next to me, but a few of the wolves in our line had already woken up. The first group all seemed to have their heads stuck in buckets.

The instructor was speaking, but I tuned him out, concentrating on the slow cadence of my breath. It seemed to be the only thing that allowed me not to throw up. And I kept at it until I heard her ungodly moan.

I cracked an eye, and she shot up so fast for the bucket, I thought she was possessed. Her entire body contracted with the heave, and I pulled myself up, gathered her hair and held it in a loose ponytail at her back. I rested my forehead on my hand, with her hair tickling my nose. Despite her horrific sounds, her hair still had that vague citrus scent that steadied my stomach.

After a while, she stopped heaving. "How are you not sick?" she whispered.

"I didn't eat this morning." Exams had drained the hell out of me and my choice to get some extra shut-eye seemed like a gift of fate. I would have been over a bucket, too, had I eaten breakfast. I let go of her hair and gave her some breathing room.

She slowly turned toward me as if moving might trigger her stomach again. The whites of her eyes carried a relief map of red veins as if she came close to blowing a vessel. Her face still held the paleness that everyone else in the room carried. "Thanks for holding my hair."

"I'm sure you'd do the same for me if I needed it."

"Yeah. No. I'd be out of here in a millisecond because if I did what you just did, I'd end up heaving all over you." She put her hand over her mouth and nose. "All this throwing up around us..." She didn't finish her sentence, and her throat bobbed as she held back another torrent.

I handed her my empty bucket and took hers to the men's room, flushing the contents down the toilet, and then I rinsed out the bucket. Before I went back into the gym, I threw cold water on my face and the back of my neck, hoping to make this headache go away. But it did nothing to ease it.

I made my way back into the gym as what looked like the last group went down with tranquilizers, which made me wonder how long we were actually out. Sarah leaned against the wall with a small can of ginger ale that the instructor was handing out to everyone.

"When you can get up, please head into the auditorium," the instructors requested.

I grabbed a soda as I passed the weasel-like man and helped Sarah to her feet.

"You must have a stomach made of iron," she muttered, taking small sips as she walked.

"It was just a stroke of luck." I led her into the auditorium and grabbed one of the seats near the back. Settling in, I cracked open the soda and took a small sip, closing my eyes as the cool fizzle slid down my throat. For a moment, I didn't know whether my stomach would accept it. After a few slow breaths, my belly growled at the lack of contents, and hunger set in. I drained the small can and crushed it in my hand, hoping it would ease the pangs now gripping my belly.

Sarah glanced sideways at me. "Even the sound of the can crunching hurts my head."

"Sorry." I tossed the crumpled metal into the garbage by the door. The aluminum hitting the metal made a loud clang and Sarah winced.

"Did you even get tranquilized?"

Her exasperation nearly made me smile.

"Yes. And I'm not exactly feeling chipper." I leaned my head back and closed my eyes. "It should fade in a couple hours," I added.

"That weaselly guy told me the same before he handed me the soda." The sound of sipping followed before she continued. "He also said it was a half dose. I can't imagine what a full dose would do."

"Probably a lot of the same, just knocked out for longer." I kept my eyes closed even though the assembly room was dark enough to not shoot stinging shards of light into my irises like a thousand tiny needles.

"True." She sighed and shifted in the seat.

I opened the eye closest to her as she scrunched down far enough to lean her head against the back edge of the chair. She had the right idea, but my height didn't allow me to slouch as much as she could. I rolled my neck and crossed my arms, watching as the assembly room filled with pale students sporting the same tranquilizer hangover.

The lights slowly came up and the entire crowd groaned in response, me included.

"My name is Harrison Littleton. I am a senior trainer from the head office in New York City," the weaselly-looking man said from the stage as if he were better than all of us here in the room. He couldn't have been much more than ten years older than we were, but between his superior attitude and the fact he didn't have any scent of magic or wolf on him, that only meant one thing.

"I think he's just human," I whispered to Sarah. I knew there were at least a handful of high-ranking humans on the board of the Monster Defense Agency, because my father always grumbled about them being totally useless.

"How can you tell?"

I glanced at her. Had she not retained anything we learned this last semester? When she looked at me with her bleary brown eyes, I pointed at my nose.

"Oh, yeah," she whispered, and her cheeks reddened. "Sorry. It's hard to think with this headache." She rubbed her temples, still looking a little peaked.

I thought about razzing her, but my headache had just gone from manageable with the dark room to splitting again with the lights. And I woke up before she did. So, I gave her a pass this time.

I glanced back at the stage and Harrison Littleton, who droned on about graduation. The only thing that caught my attention and had Sarah sitting up more was when he started talking about assignments and what would happen next.

By the time this graduation ceremony was finished, all the assignments would be cataloged and printed out and hung on the board outside the auditorium. We would know where we were going as soon as we walked out this door to pack up our things.

That perked a lot of us up. I glanced around and found Johnson staring back at me, as if he needed reassurance that I did indeed make it through the ordeal. I hadn't even looked for the rest of my pack in the gym. I was too concerned with Sarah and that weighed on me. I sent him a halfhearted nod. I needed to be better than that in the future. I scanned the audience and met several sickly looking gazes with the same nod of approval for making it through the academy.

At least, wherever I was going, the Allegany pack would follow—unless my father screwed me even further. After our last encounter, I wouldn't put it past him.

The man kept droning on and then he finally announced the academy's headmaster. Mr. Simmons stepped up to the podium and praised us for being one of the finest classes the academy had ever seen despite some challenging times earlier in the year. Our grades and physical stamina had far outpaced some of the more recent graduates and we were sure to become fine agents in the field.

"The reason we do graduation after the tranquilization test is to assess your ability to focus after. And for the top student in the class, the bar is even higher. You have the honor and privilege of stepping up on stage to say a few words to your fellow students." He smiled and scanned the audience back and forth, and then his gaze pulled back to me before he looked down at the paper before him. "This year's top student has become an exceptional leader. He's the best and brightest we've seen in these halls since his father graduated years ago."

"Fuck," I whispered, because I knew what was coming and I was not prepared for it.

"Mr. Robert Young Junior, will you please join me on stage."

Sarah snickered beside me as I climbed to my feet.

I looked down at her. "I should drag your ass up there with me."

"I wouldn't be caught dead on stage in front of all these people, Junior." She gave me that playful smile, needling me with the one part of my name I hated.

"And bring your spirited partner with you," Mr. Simmons added after looking at the notes handed to him. "Because her scores are just as impressive."

I grinned down at her. "Now you don't have a choice."

She paled as she looked at the stage and then me with pure panic.

I felt her terror in my bones and faltered for a moment. This fierce woman suffered from stage fright? She could kick ass in the gym in front of the entire class, but the idea of standing on stage made her even more sickly looking. I extended my hand, hoping I wouldn't have to do anything drastic to get her moving.

"Come on. I promise, you won't have to talk. You can even hide behind me if you need to," I said softly enough that very few around us heard me.

She tentatively took my hand and followed behind me like a scolded puppy. If I wasn't feeling every nuance of her fear, I would have found it amusing. I climbed up on stage and released her hand, smiling at Mr. Simmons, who waved me to the podium.

"Say a few words to your graduating class," he said.

I stepped up to the microphone and glanced out at the class. "It seems my partner here, while ferocious in the sparring ring, suffers from a bit of stage fright, so I'll speak for the both of us when I say it has been a pleasure and an honor to study beside each of you." I scanned the crowd again, zeroing in on all the Allegany pack members and their partners before moving my gaze over the rest of my classmates.

I glanced back at Sarah and then pulled my focus back to the group. "Being a leader, an alpha, means taking care of your pack. There are plenty of alphas here, and when you get to your destination, make sure you understand who your pack consists of. Here, everyone in this room was part of my pack. Out there, it could be infinitely larger, and you may not be the lead honcho, so show whoever is in that role the respect they deserve." I took a breath. "Remember your purpose. And remember to have a little fun as well."

A few members whooped and then winced, like they had momentarily forgotten they had tranq-hangover. I smiled.

I glanced back at Sarah and saw a hint of a smile appear.

The fact this was the last time I would see most of these people hit. I was going to truly miss this. "So, are you ready to get out there and kick some vampire ass?" I raised my arm.

This time, it seemed my call to celebrate was met with more enthusiasm. Many raised their arms and yelled, "Hell yeah!"

I stepped back and took Sarah's hand, raising it in the air with mine, and the audience started to clap. It was exhilarating.

I gave Mr. Simmons a smile and a partial bow before I stepped to leave the stage.

"Whoa there, you two," he said. "Don't you want to know your assignment?"

We both swung back toward the podium, and my muscles tightened with anticipation.

Mr. Simmons looked at the paper in his hand and grinned. "You two are headed to the Big Apple."

"Headquarters?" I asked. That's where the hot-bed of vampire activity happened on a daily basis and had for years. It was also one of the most dangerous assignments you could get in the agency.

"Yes. Headquarters."

I straightened my back, glanced at Sarah, and then gave a nod. "Sounds about right." I searched the crowd. As much as I wanted a countryside station, the thought of being able to tear through vampires at the rate that the agents at headquarters did made me shiver with anticipation. "I'm all for being in the capital of vampiric activity." I grinned. "And I am looking forward to slaying as many blood suckers as possible."

YOUNG BLOOD 20

SO, NEW YORK CITY was not ideal, but at least it was where most vampires seemed to congregate on the East Coast. Johnson, Hannah, and a few others from the Allegany pack were assigned here with us, but it was by no means the bulk of my pack. The rest had gone home to the backwoods of New York and didn't have to deal with the light pollution or sound pollution that was driving me batty.

The living arrangements were no better than at the academy. The small efficiency apartments were no bigger than the dorm rooms had been and they packed everything in that space: kitchen, bedroom, and bathroom with no real living space. It was claustrophobic as hell. Especially considering we were living in the same building where we worked.

I needed my own space, but I had three years before the trust fund my mother left me activated. Then I would be able to buy almost anything I wanted. I kept my eye on the real estate sales and the different areas I wanted to live in. Brooklyn was by far the best option, and there were some upscale areas that I had my eye on. Sarah wasn't looking down near Brooklyn. She was looking up in the Harlem area, which was more affordable, and the homes were a bit smaller.

She had to wait until she turned eighteen to access her parents' estate, but her birthday was in December. She only had to get through the summer and fall before she was free of this place.

So, we dealt with communal living and learned the rituals we all needed to keep safe, like always having our weapons on us, both blades and guns, as well as wearing our anti-compulsion charms, so vampires couldn't compel us. That was the most dangerous part of dealing with a blood sucker. If you didn't have your charms on, you were dead.

I itched to get out there and slay some vampires, but we weren't cleared for field work yet. Instead, we sparred, studied, ate, and slept until Harrison Littleton thought we were ready. He was militant on the rules, to the point of reaching beyond a boss. He was more like a dictator, and I had to stanch my aggravated alpha wolf any time I dealt with the asshole.

Sarah and I sparred regularly. She was getting even faster now that she had other agents to spar with who did not hold back. Same with me, it was refreshing to be challenged, and stung when I got my ass kicked. At least that was getting rarer these days.

We were sparring when Sarah and I were called into Harrison's office.

He looked frazzled in a way we hadn't seen since we arrived. His hair stood out in spikes, as if he had been running his hands through it and his cheeks wore the blotchy redness of irritation. "I need you two to go to this address." He handed me a piece of paper. "It's a suspected vampire nest, so things might get hairy." He sucked in a breath of air through his nose. "Usually, for a thing like this, I'd send the entire force, but I have been instructed to send you two."

I raised an eyebrow at that. *Why would they choose to send two new recruits instead of seasoned agents?* "Why?"

"Because my more experienced agents are dealing with another, more pressing issue, and I cannot divert them to a suspected nest until they are finished with the job they are on. And of the newbies here, you two are the only ones who seem to be fit for the job. I'm not one to send agents to the slaughter, either, but those higher than me think you two will be fine."

Either that or the higher ups really want us dead. I shook that thought out of my head and focused on the assignment.

"What constitutes a nest?" Sarah asked, seemingly satisfied with Harrison's answer.

"More than half a dozen vampires living in a home."

Sarah put her hand out and a katana sword materialized in her palm. It was the perfect killing weapon to separate the vampire's head from their body, which, outside of dragging them into the sunshine, was the only way to kill a blood sucker for good. Although tearing their hearts out sounded fun, they weren't alive, so it would just leave a hole in their chest, which would heal by the next sunset.

She handed the sword to me with a smile and pulled another one for herself from the ether. Harrison's lips curled into a frown. He did not have high regard for witches. He thought they were as tainted as any of the others, including werewolves. But wolves were far superior in intelligence, speed, and strength enough so that he begrudgingly respected us.

"Just make sure you have your charm on," Harrison said. "And take a cab. Your motorcycle is too noisy. They'll hear you coming from miles away."

I pulled the chain from under my shirt, showing that I had it on. Sarah did the same, and then we changed into street clothes and were off on our first job. My heart pounded as I read the paper. "You might want to hang onto these until we get there." I gave Sarah the sword. "I doubt we'll get a cab holding these."

"You're probably right." The metal in her hands disappeared as if it never had been there. "But the minute we get out of the cab, I'm retrieving them."

"Fine by me." I raised my hand, hailing a cab. It took a couple of minutes before one pulled up to the curb. We piled in the back, and I rattled off the address. I pulled out my wallet and peeled out a twenty for the fare, shoving my wallet into the interior pocket of the worn leather coat that Sarah conjured for me at that first dinner at the academy. When we got out, I didn't want to be shuffling through my wallet. I wanted a clean drop-off, so we had more of an element of surprise.

Vampires would smell us coming, so the longer we lingered on the street, the more prepared for our attack they would be. Assuming they were even awake, considering it was near noon and the sun blazed down. At least it was cool enough to wear the jacket. Spring days in New York City could be a scorcher, but this one had been blessedly cool.

"Drop us off a few houses down, please," I added when we finally turned onto the road.

The driver looked in the rearview mirror with a nod. The minute he pulled over, I shoved the twenty through the slot, even though the fare was a hair less than ten bucks. I nodded for Sarah to go and slid out the passenger door after her. "Keep the change." I slammed the door and took a deep breath as the cab pulled away.

I glanced at the numbers and spotted the one we needed to check out. It was New York City. The doors were likely locked, and the house was in the middle of a bank of row houses. I just hoped the occupants of the homes on either side were at work because this was likely to be a hell of a ruckus.

The shades were all drawn in the unit we were hitting. The ones on either side weren't, so that was another indicator and one of the things we needed to target once we got inside. Sunlight was our friend, and the more shades we were able to open, the safer we would be.

I glanced at Sarah. "Can you conjure the door key?"

She put out her hand; her lips moved as she read off the address from the sheet of paper and a key appeared in her palm.

She really did have the coolest magic.

"Target the shades first," I said. "That way we at least have a safe place if the shit hits the fan."

"Good plan." She handed me the key and then put her palms up. A moment later, the swords appeared. She held onto mine, and we approached quickly. I slid the key into the hole and turned. The click of the lock disengaging made me smile, and we entered the house quickly. I traded the key for a sword and closed the door behind us, enveloping us in darkness.

Sarah reached out, grabbing my arm.

I could see in the dark. She couldn't. We moved toward the living area on the right, where I had seen the shades, but on this side, big panels of wood blocked the entire window, and they were nailed in place.

"Fuck." That's when the stench of death hit me. My heart thundered at the shuffling from the far side of the room. Vampires were uncurling from their positions on the floor and climbing to their feet. The man on the couch curled his lips back, baring teeth as his glare met mine.

There were more in the back rooms; I was sure of it just by the smell.

The only way Sarah would survive this was if she could see what she was swinging at. I had a second to scan the wall. Luck was with us, and I reached out and flipped the light switch right next to where we stood, bathing the room in light.

Now she could see them. Outside of being pale, vampires didn't look that different from humans or witches or werewolves in human form, except for the fangs and the red eyes. Oh, and another difference that rang through the room was the hideous hiss they made. It made me twitch. That hiss hit a pitch that hurt my wolf ears.

My guess was right; that hiss brought forth more from the back rooms. This was a nest all right, but there were more than a dozen vampires in this house. I backed up toward those wooden shutters with Sarah at my side and my grip on the sword tightened.

"Double fuck," Sarah whispered, but there wasn't the fear I expected.

I glanced at her and blinked at the crazy smile on her lips. Although her heart pounded as frantically as mine, it was as if the shot of adrenaline woke up the kick ass side of her. This was my battle queen, and fuck if I didn't want to claim her right now.

We focused on the group of vampires stalking toward us.

"Stay still," the leader who had risen from the couch said in a commanding tone that would have frozen us in place had we not had the charms on.

Sarah stepped far enough away from me so that her swing wouldn't harm me, and she positioned herself at the ready. "I don't think so, motherfuckers." She didn't wait for them to descend on us. I had a brief moment to witness her cunning and skill as she beheaded the lead vampire. Then I jumped into the fray.

Heads rolled, literally. But when Sarah cried out, my wolf took control at the sight of a vampire with their teeth in her arm. The same fury that had captured me in her dorm room rushed through my veins, and I leapt at the vampire accosting her, tearing his torso in two. It was enough to dislodge his teeth, but it also left a bloody gouge in her arm.

She didn't stop fighting, and I turned my sights on the rest of the nest, decapitating as many with my jaws as she was with her katana. One of them dodged my attack and launched at me, hitting my shoulder with teeth as sharp as mine.

I yelped and the whistle of a blade slicing through air followed. Although the teeth were still embedded in my skin, the rest of the body fell to the floor. I met Sarah's gaze with a nod before we took down the remaining vampires.

When there weren't any more attacking, we glanced around at the carnage. Sarah was covered with blood and her open wound still seeped. Thankfully, you couldn't be turned just from vampire blood alone; otherwise we would both be screwed. I limped over to one of the windows and took the bottom edge of the board between my teeth. I yanked and nails creaked. I yanked again and the bottom portion ripped from the wall.

Sarah moved to the corner away from where I was trying to get the window covering off. Anywhere else in the room would be dangerous because when this mother gave way, wood would fly. I kept pulling.

She dialed a number on her phone. "It's clear, but we could use a little medical attention." She glanced at her arm and then at me, where the vamp head was still attached. "We both were bitten. Me on the arm and Robby has a decapitated head still clamped on his shoulder."

The wood creaked some more and then all of a sudden it gave, ripping drywall with the force and spraying white dust into the room. I tossed the wood toward the far corner where there were no bodies and then tore the shade right off with another yank of my teeth. It fluttered to the ground, and the sun bathed me with warmth. The head still attached to my shoulder burst to ashes, leaving only a bloody welt. Any of the bodies in the path of the sunlight did the same, leaving a plume of ash in the air.

"His vamp is now ash, but there still are puncture wounds," she said as I headed her way. "He's in wolf form for now as well."

I limped over to Sarah and licked her wound, cleaning it as best I could before I curled up next to her, putting my head on her leg. Now that the adrenaline had faded to nothing, the reality of what happened hit hard enough to make my wolf form shake. Fear laced my mouth at what could have happened today, and I did not want to shift back to human form so she could see this side of me.

It would be too transparent. Too readable. She would know in an instant that I was in love with her. The slow stroke of her hand on my head and her soft coos of "shhh" were nearly more than my wolf could take.

The minute the cavalry arrived, I shifted back to human form, so I could relay the details of the encounter along with Sarah. And my partner, the goddess that she was, clothed me with a wave of her hand. But the jacket she had given me was in shreds on the floor. I went to it and fished out my wallet, sliding it into my back pocket. I loved this damn coat.

I caught her staring at me, and I shrugged, holding up the coat.

"I'll conjure you another one when we get back," she said as a medic tended to her arm.

"Thanks." I glanced at what I could see of my wound. It still oozed where the vampire had latched on. Even though I had been in wolf form, the wounds didn't heal as fast as they normally would. Something in the vampire's saliva slowed down my healing capabilities.

When the medic finished with Sarah, he took a look at my punctures and put a bandage over it before he loaded us into the agency ambulance.

The adrenaline had fled and all that was left was an exhaustion pummeling my muscles. Sarah looked about the same as I felt. With our first mission came our first injuries. But I also got to see Sarah in action, and she was fierce and strong and relentless.

I wondered how many more times I would get to witness her being such a badass and still be able to control my wolf.

Someday my wolf would win, and he would damn us both.

YOUNG BLOOD 21

FIFTEEN YEARS LATER...
I stepped into the conference room for our daily morning brief and scanned the room for the crop of red hair. But she was absent. I hadn't run into her in the pit either, and my gut clenched.

Over the past year, the connection I had with Sarah seemed wonky. She seemed more closed off, as if she were hiding something, but under that secrecy, she seemed to be truly happy, as though she had met someone. Which was enough to make my wolf rant all the louder. And then, a few weeks ago, it changed into something like grief. I even saw it in her eyes each day, but she still didn't open up to me. Her sudden change unhinged me, and now her being late just scrambled my insides.

Sarah was never late. Me, on the other hand—I wasn't as punctual to a fault as she was. Maybe she was in the restroom. But the growing alarm inside didn't pipe down at that viable excuse.

I took my normal seat and waited, fidgeting in my chair as the seconds ticked by. Harrison walked in and closed the door, sauntering to the front of the room to start the meeting.

The chair remained empty next to me and that sense in the pit of my stomach that something was wrong grew to a nearly unmanageable level. *Where are you?* I texted her.

Overslept. Not feeling very good. Cover for me?

I stared at the reply. If it was anyone else, I might have taken it at face value, but Sarah was never sick. Even if she had a bender the night before, she was in here, looking green and gross. My abdomen knotted.

The moment the meeting ended, I tried to make a quick exit, but Harrison caught me before I could get away.

"Where's Stone?" He nodded toward the now-empty briefing room.

The first excuse that popped into my head, tumbled from my lips. "She said she thinks she may have had some bad food last night. I'm going to head over and check on her. I'm not sure whether to bring coffee or soup." I gave the boss a dubious smile, praying it wouldn't cause too many questions.

"Coffee might be your best bet. And tell her she needs to get her ass into the office as soon as possible. You two need to chase down the last lead we have on the dumpster vampire before the trail disappears. There hasn't been a body in three weeks. Either he has taken a vacation or there's going to be a bloodbath in New York City."

I nodded and headed out to the car, texting as I walked. *Coming over with coffee.*

In the shower, give me a few minutes.

Well, at least she was out of bed. That familiar tingle ran up my spine, and my wolf struggled against the binds I've kept him in for the last fifteen years. Against all odds, I've kept him in line. Although it has made both of us more volatile on the hunt. When I let him loose to kill, he's vicious to a fault.

I stopped at the nearest coffee shop and grabbed her favorite coffee and one for myself, and then headed to her house. That uneasy feeling had bloomed, making my wolf restless.

Pulling into her small driveway did nothing to ease my nerves. The moment she swung the door open, my wolf nearly burst forth at the smell of death radiating from inside. I held onto the coffee cups in my hands, praying that it was something else. But one more sniff told me otherwise.

What the fuck?

"Sarah?" I cocked my head, searching her face.

"It's been a tough morning." She sighed and swung the door wide, waving me inside.

Fuck. Fuck. Fuck. This cannot be happening!

Every muscle burned. My mouth went dry, and I cautiously stepped over the threshold. My knuckles turned white with the strain of not crushing the cups in my hands. I offered her one and was thankful my hand didn't shake.

She reeked like a vampire, but there was an alluring scent competing with the dead stench surrounding her. When she took a sip of coffee, my brain stalled. Vampires didn't drink anything but blood.

I glanced around the entry, looking for another explanation. Nothing presented itself, so I glanced back at her. "You're... You smell different." I closed the door behind me.

"I had this house locked up tight and warded." She turned and headed into the kitchen as her stomach rumbled.

She didn't turn back to look at me. A panic that I couldn't contain slid through me like a tornado, and my wolf whispered to mark her. That was the only logical thing that would keep her safe. I ignored his incessant whining. When she didn't continue, I asked, "And?"

She spun back to face me with eyes that pleaded for me to understand, but she didn't speak. My heart jumped in my chest, and I licked my lips, trying to put the muzzle back on my wolf's rantings.

"And?" I asked with more force. The cup in my grip crushed, spraying coffee everywhere. The sting of hot liquid on my skin gave me a much-needed slap of sanity. But it was short-lived.

Sarah pulled a vial full of coagulated blood out of her pocket and handed it to me. "This was all over my bedroom floor and walls."

I shook the hot coffee from my hand and snatched the vial from her. I didn't want to know what was inside. I rolled it between my fingers, as though I could change the contents just by moving the thick liquid this way and that. "You know I'm obligated to report this," I said with the regret of a thousand missed opportunities in my voice.

"I don't want to be locked up like Manuel." She shifted her stance into ready form, as if she prepared for a fight.

I almost laughed at her. I wasn't going to fight her. We hadn't talked about what happened to Manuel. I already knew her stance, but I couldn't condone having him out on the streets. But this was Sarah. *My Sarah.*

I couldn't fathom locking her up. Hell, I knew I'd never report this, despite what I said. I crossed and towered over her, invading her personal space. Being this close to her set that inferno that had been burning for fifteen years to the unmanageable level. She was already doomed by whatever had happened.

"Do you really think I'd lock you up?" I studied her face and willed my hands not to reach out to cup her cheeks and take her mouth with mine. Logically, I had nothing to lose anymore. But my heart needed convincing. I had been protecting her from my wolf for so long that it was a natural reaction. If I let my wolf have his way, there was no saving either of us.

Her brow creased and her gaze narrowed up at me. "What?"

"I'd tear your throat out before I'd let you rot in a cell for the rest of eternity." But that wasn't going to happen, either. Not with my wolf demanding what he wanted all along.

She swallowed hard and dropped her gaze to my chest. Her fear blanketed me.

I lost the battle and reached out, cupping her chin and forcing her to look at me. "You aren't built for captivity."

I hated that I couldn't speak freely with her. But my point still held. Neither one of us were built to be caged for the rest of our lives.

I got hold of myself and let go, moving back to give her space and clear my head.

"Asshole," she muttered and rubbed her chin.

That was uncalled for, and I realized what nonsense had tumbled out of my mouth. I guess I would have reacted the same way if I stood in her shoes and my partner just told me they'd rather kill me than lock me away for life.

"You would do the same for me," I said, trying to soften the harshness of my original statement. I'm sure she could follow through with a threat like that, too. Sarah was a force. She had always been one. But no matter the threat, I would never harm her or lock her up. Ever.

My heart clenched in my chest. I was doomed.

I glanced at the blood in the tiny container and pressed my lips together, saying a prayer to the gods above that this wasn't hers. I unscrewed the lid and took a sniff. That sweet smell of lemons and caramel coffee drifted out of the vial, and I closed my eyes. "It's your blood."

Two conflicting emotions hit like a Category 5 hurricane making landfall: devastation because Sarah was *other,* and my wolf was doing a fucking jig like this was the best possible situation.

"Just run it through the database," she insisted.

It was enough to send a rash of uncomfortable heat over my skin. Alarm settled into my cells, and I glanced at the blood and then shook my head slowly. "If I do that, it will raise questions."

"But aren't you obligated..."

I put my splayed hand out, silencing her. "If I run this through the database, yes, I'm obligated. So, I am not going to run it through just to confirm what I can already smell. And what any wolf at headquarters will smell the moment you walk in. You are...*other*." I snarled out the last part, fighting my base nature.

Sarah collapsed into the chair at the kitchen table.

"What happened?" I asked but did not venture any closer. I needed distance to think, and my mind had already started thinking of ways for her not to be tracked down like the rest of the vampires we hunted. Those always ended with a dead body, and I couldn't allow that to happen to her.

"I have no clue." She shrugged and pushed away the coffee with a scowl. "I went to sleep and then woke up with my room painted with blood, but there wasn't a drop on the sheets. It only covered the walls and the floor, like my bed itself had been covered by some magic spell to keep it pristine." She lifted her chin and held out her wrists so I could see the unblemished skin. "There isn't a goddamned mark on me, so how could I have bled out like that, and be sitting here talking to you this morning like nothing happened?"

I stepped closer and started to shake with the need welling up inside me. "You need to quit," I said as my gaze darted all around the room at everything but her. It was a stupid statement. I knew there was no quitting. That carried the same death sentence as relationships. But my mouth kept betraying me in the onset of panic. "Tell them you found something less stressful."

She burst out laughing at this whole ludicrous situation. "Quitting is a death sentence. You know that as well as I do. Besides, they won't buy it."

She was right. They knew she was as much of an adrenaline junkie as I was. *Fuck.* Here goes nothing. "Then tell them you need to quit because you want a relationship with me."

Her laughter exploded into that of hysterics, and my panic morphed into a hot anger. "You don't think they'd buy that?"

"Would you?" she sputtered through her laughter.

Irrational irritation gripped me, and I spiked the glass vial onto the kitchen floor. It shattered, bathing the room in the scent of her blood, and my wolf took control. I crossed the distance and pulled her out of the seat, slammed her into the closest wall, and battled with my wolf as she stared directly into my eyes.

"What the—" she started.

My wolf won.

I crushed her lips with mine in a forbidden kiss. Her mouth opened, and I wasn't sure whether it was in surprise or in response to my kissing her, but I took full advantage of it, teasing her tongue with mine.

In that moment, I knew I lost the battle. My wolf was now in control, and I'd never get it back. Not now that I'd tasted her. Other or not, my wolf wanted her.

Then her knee connected with my balls and that moment died with a flare of pain. I dropped her and started to fall to my knees when she pushed me hard enough to fall back on my ass.

"Don't you ever fucking manhandle me," she yelled. "We may be partners, but that is where we have always drawn the line."

Flames leapt from her hair, her hands—even her face—and my eyes widened. *She's on fire!* I glanced at the window as I moved back, still holding my aching balls, but the light was all wrong.

Sarah ran her hand through her hair as if she had no clue, and then she looked toward the reflection in the microwave door. Her eyes ballooned wide and then she raised her hands, looking at the same red flames that I was.

All of the sudden, the flames went out and she was my Sarah again. Except, this was something insane. No vampire we knew of had ever broken out in flame like she just had. Unless they were dragged out into the sunshine, and that was usually accompanied by screams before they turned to ash.

"Sarah?"

She shook her head at the question in my voice. She was just as thrown by all this as I was.

What the hell had attacked her last night?

I got my bearings and crawled to the table, pulling myself up into the chair.

"Do you need some ice?" Sarah asked, but her voice still shook.

"I'll live. But a coffee would be nice, since mine is all over your entry." I hooked my thumb over my shoulder.

She nodded and it was as if she were glad to be doing something normal after that display of whatever the fuck that was. I don't blame her; the sounds of the coffee machine calmed me down enough to think past her lips on mine.

She put a cup in front of me and took the seat opposite me, putting the table between us, as if that solid barrier could keep us from breaking the rules again.

"Do I feel cold to you?" she asked out of the blue and then slid her hand across the table.

I hesitated. Touching her would reignite that inferno, and it was all consuming. But the plea in her eyes had me reaching out to cover her hand. Her warmth seeped into my palm, and I kept my hand in place longer than I should have.

"No. You feel normal."

She rolled her eyes at me and then looked at her wrist. "I'm half tempted to cut myself to see if I bleed."

"Don't," I said. "I'm barely containing my wolf as it is." I waved toward the wall where I had kissed her, hoping she would understand.

"What's that supposed to mean?" She leaned back in her chair and crossed her arms.

Ah, fuck. Another goddamned rabbit hole that I don't need to jump into. I pressed my lips together and shook my head.

"Well?" She stared at me waiting for an explanation that I did not want to get into.

"Sarah—"

She cut me off. "Stop with that tone. I'm not fragile, so don't you dare treat me that way." She pointed at me like one of our instructors at the academy. "Besides, you're the one who brought up your wolf, so just speak your mind like we've always done. *This* shouldn't change that."

I couldn't help the snicker. She really didn't know how I felt about her. "Well, my wolf isn't sure whether to tear you to pieces or..." I trailed off with a shrug, although a dimple made a quick appearance.

"Or what?" She leaned forward, catching my gaze.

"My wolf can't seem to decide between tearing you apart or fucking you. If you spill more of your blood, I'm not sure I can contain him." I met her gaze, a little exasperated for having to spell it out.

"You want to...fuck me?" Her voice cracked, and she leaned back in the chair.

"My wolf." I swallowed and stared at the table. Damn it. She had enough schooling on werewolves to know that my wolf's desires were just a magnification of what was already in my heart.

"And this sudden urge was triggered by my change?"

I just lifted a single shoulder and glanced out the window. I was damning both of us by admitting this to her, but I couldn't lie to her. Not when she asked such a direct question.

"Why wait to tell me this until now?" she asked quietly. The question was filled with something more.

I slowly forced my gaze to meet hers, baring every emotion I had locked inside for all these years. She drew in a breath and her eyes widened as if she finally saw the truth. "We are *supposed* to be partners. They kill witches who cross the line. You *know* that."

She opened her mouth to speak, and her phone rang. She put it to her ear without breaking eye contact with me. "Sarah Stone."

Her face paled at whatever the caller said. Then her hands burst into flame again and she dropped the phone onto the table.

I moved to her side. "Who was that?"

"I, uh. I don't know." She wrapped her arms around herself and shivered. Her hand splayed across her throat in almost a protective reflex.

Seeing her so disturbed broke another piece of that wall surrounding my wolf, and I crouched next to her, touching her arm. The connection shot a jolt of heat through me, and all I wanted to do was take her in my arms and claim her. "You don't know?"

"No. But I suppose we should hunt this bastard down."

Oh, fuck no. "You can't work. You can't go near anyone from the office. Not with how you smell."

"How do I smell?"

"You smell like death already claimed you. Like almost every damn vampire I've killed has. But it is mixed with something sweet and light and tangy that makes my wolf want to claim you right this moment to keep you safe and protected. It's strangely abhorrent and alluring at the same time." Words just tumbled out of me like a damn leaky faucet. I blinked, trying to gain some sense of control.

"Different than before?"

I smiled. "Before, you smelled like caramel coffee with a side of lemon cake."

She narrowed her eyes at me. "That's my daily coffee shop order."

"And it suited you. As sweet as that was to take in daily, this"—I waved at her—"along with the vibes you are transmitting, will set off every single supernatural alarm within blocks of wherever you go." I forced myself to stand, to get a little distance. "Stay here while I take a look around. I'm going to see if I can detect a trace of this bastard."

God, her bedroom smelled like blood and bleach, and I nearly gagged from it. Death was here, and I could almost see her struggle. The fact I could still smell her death over the bleach was a testament to how much had been drained from her body. And it was all over the place. Despite her scrubbing, I could see the traces left behind.

I growled and stopped at the entrance to her reading nook. The chair held the smell of death, and it was strong enough to tell me the vampire who attacked her had been in it for a while. But there was another scent overlaying it, the same way the bleach overlayed the blood, that made me remember a time early in our career when Heddie successfully did a masking spell on Hannah. It smelled like sandalwood and spice then. That's what the overlaying scent was. A fucking masking spell.

The window had the sigil on it, but it was open, making the warded barrier useless.

I went back to the kitchen, deep in concentration, and took my seat across from her. "Are you sure you set up all your wards properly?"

"Yes. Why?" She glanced at me.

"I smelled something with the same dark signature, but it seemed to be masked. Like whoever was here had traces of magic on his being. And he was here long enough for his smell to permeate your sitting chair by the window. And your window is open."

She blinked at me, as if she didn't comprehend what I was saying.

"Could you have left it open?"

"I swear, every window and door was closed and warded. Including that one. Besides, it is not warm enough for me to leave my window open at night." She crossed her arms. "I don't have a built-in heater like you do."

I stared into my empty cup with a nod. "I'll tell the boss you're dealing with food poisoning. You need to stay here until I can find out a little more."

"Bullshit. I need to find this asshole and slice off his head."

My gaze widened at her words, and I shook my head. I couldn't let her do that. If she killed her maker, she would die, too.

YOUNG BLOOD 22

I WALKED INTO THE agency, chewing my lip while deep in thought. *How was I going to get her out of this?*

Harrison cut me off.

"Where's your partner?" he asked with his eyes narrowed in suspicious slits.

"She's got a pretty bad case of food poisoning. I tried to talk her into going to a hospital, but she didn't want to leave the bathroom."

"Are you sure that's it?" He seemed to growl the words.

"Dude, it's coming out both ends, so yes, I'm sure. It's either that or a wicked case of the stomach bug, but she doesn't have a fever." I glanced behind Harrison at the pit. "Didn't Karen have a bug recently?" I asked. Karen was his administrative assistant, and she was out for a few days with a stomach thing.

He muttered under his breath. "Yes. But Sarah's never been sick."

"Yeah, well, you can see for yourself, but if it's contagious, you'll probably get it just by standing outside the door." Harrison was a bit of a germaphobe, and I used that to my advantage. After Karen called in, he scrubbed down his office and her desk with enough bleach so it even stung the noses of the witches in the pit. It was unbearable for us wolves, and we fled the floor until the stench dissipated.

"What do you have for me today?" I asked, making him focus on something other than Sarah, and hoping for something light enough that I could do some research.

"I was going to ask Johnson to divert and gather resources for Manuel, but since you're not with your loudmouth partner, I think you'd be perfect to gather a stock of blood."

As much as I didn't want to do that, at least I'd have a legitimate reason to pilfer blood banks and bring something to Sarah to satiate her needs. I knew Johnson hated doing this as well. It was akin to a Mafia lord leaning on a shop owner for kickbacks. So, it would give him a reprieve.

I grabbed the cooler from the infirmary and headed out in one of the company cars, making a quick stop at my house to grab a secondary cooler. The agency didn't care what blood type was confiscated, but I did. I would only choose the most popular blood type because there was more of an abundance, but I also didn't want to take O negative, which could be used universally. So, my focus was on the O positive and the A positive, unless the bank was falling short on those; then I would take a few of the O negative. It made me feel slimy at best, but the blood banks seemed to be willing to part with enough bags to make it doable to fill my small cooler and still have a good amount in the agency's cooler for Manuel and the infirmary.

I dropped my cooler back at my place and headed to the agency to drop off the rest of the blood and the company car, exchanging it for my own. I headed home, grabbed the cooler, and then headed to Sarah's hoping this wouldn't be a mistake.

I paused at the door and took a breath, trying to get my mind set in the right place, but the way kissing her felt this morning kept clouding my mind and riling up my wolf. I knocked rapidly on the door, shifting my weight with the cooler in my hand. I certainly hoped this would help her fight whatever hunger she had to be feeling by now. I sent a text telling her I was here and inside, I heard her phone ping.

The door swung open, and a blast of sunshine hit her directly in the face. My heart slammed into my ribs, and I quickly stepped close, blocking the sun from hitting her. It took my brain a second to register.

She wasn't even singed by the sun. If she was a full-fledged vampire, that blast of sunshine would have blackened her face and left the stench of burning flesh on the air. I popped my mouth closed as she moved back and waved me inside. I stepped closer and reached out, running my thumb along the perfect skin of her cheek.

The only thing that had ignited was my libido. I wanted to slam her against the wall and kiss every inch of her skin. Instead, I whispered, "You didn't burn."

Her cheeks reddened. "No shit." Her gaze fell to the large cooler in my other hand. "What's that?"

I had almost forgotten the cooler. But in light of the last few minutes, I wasn't sure whether she needed it or not. "It...uh...may be a mistake." I cautiously placed the cooler in front of her and stepped back, putting space between us, as if the heat slithering inside me might actually turn into a blaze I couldn't stop.

She opened the top and stared before her gaze snapped to mine. "What did you do, steal these from a blood bank?"

I let out a nervous laugh. *If she only knew.*

"Jesus, Robby." She slammed the top closed and crossed her arms in that defiant way that reminded me of my mother when she was aggravated with my father.

"You need to eat." I shifted my weight as my own need increased. My wolf was restless and knocking at the cage again.

"Is this what you do for Manuel?" She turned a little green, and I looked away with a shrug.

The air around me changed, and I swallowed hard as my wolf nearly tore free. When I glanced back at Sarah, she was looking at me in a way that blew my resistance to shreds. And she was transmitting it through the air like a mating call in the wild.

"What are you doing?" My wolf's teeth came out. I trembled against his demands and stared at Sarah's amused gaze.

"I'm not doing anything. Why?"

"Because you are tossing out pheromones like dice at a craps table."

God, her gaze felt like a caress as it slid down my body. It was as if she were really seeing me for the first time in years. My pants became constricting against my hard member. *She doesn't understand what losing control means.*

She chuckled and sucked her lower lip between her teeth, slowly raking it as she released it.

"Please, stop," I pleaded. But those pheromones just increased, as if my plea turned her on. Her gaze went lower on my body, and I swear her eyes sparkled at the sight of my desire on display.

That broke me.

"Ah, fuck," I growled. The next thing I knew, I had her pinned to the wall again, but this time, instead of kicking me in the balls, she wrapped her legs around my waist, pulling me against her with the same kind of need accosting me. I searched her brown eyes for a moment. "What are you?" I whispered, but didn't wait for an answer. Instead, my lips descended onto hers with an eternal claim.

This was what my wolf wanted since the day I first saw her. This was what I had denied for fifteen years. This was what I wanted every day for the rest of our lives.

Futures be damned, I was claiming this woman, and nothing on God's green earth was going to stop me. I pressed my hips into hers, and she moved with the motion. Tearing at her clothing, I moaned in her mouth at the sweetness of her.

I forced myself up for air and moved my lips to her jawline, nipping at her skin, teasing her—and my wolf who insisted I claim her now. But I had made him wait fifteen years; I was going to enjoy every fucking inch of her before I claimed her.

She tugged at my shirt, and I moved my hands away from her, using the wall and my hips to keep her in place as I raised my arms. She peeled the T-shirt off me and tossed it aside. Her gaze landed on my throat and a flare of hunger crossed over her eyes before they met mine.

I paused and my breath kept coming in short bursts as I barely contained my wolf. "I'm supposed to be the alpha." I ground my hardness into her in a slow twirl of my hips. "I'm *supposed* to be able to control my wolf."

Her lips twitched into such an evil smile. "Maybe I don't want you to control your wolf. Maybe I want your wolf to ravage me."

Oh, fuck me. She knew just what to say to unleash him. "You have a wicked, wicked heart," I growled and wrapped my arms around her, carrying her to the living room couch.

Too many clothes. I tore what was left of her shirt off and tasted her skin, traveling lower as my member throbbed in my pants and my wolf nearly howled at the need stirring in my belly. I was going to make this a thousand times better than any of my wet dreams.

I nearly creamed my jeans at the thought as I took her breasts in my mouth, one after the other, rolling my tongue over her sensitive nipples. She arched into me and ran her fingers through my hair, whispering my name with such reverence.

I got her jeans unbuttoned and yanked them off her, moving my kisses down her belly while I situated myself between her open legs. The invitation in her eyes was just as much of an elixir as her citrusy scent.

I sucked on the inside of her thigh without losing eye contact with her. "I've dreamed of doing this for years," I admitted. Then I lowered my mouth to her sweet core. And God help me, I couldn't stop licking and teasing her. Not with the way she moaned my name. She was so fucking wet when I finally got my pants off. And she was panting as though I had taken her all the way to heaven.

I was so hard, and my wolf demanded I take her. I pulled away from the sweetness of her pussy, picked her up off the couch and put her on her knees in front of me; then I was inside her in one thrust. I closed my eyes, giving into the carnal need.

She arched into me, her shoulders leaned into my chest. Her breasts bounced with the force of my thrusts. I cupped one breast with my hand, twirling the hard nipple between my fingers as my other hand found her swollen clit and circled it slowly, knowing the dichotomy of movement would bring her over that brink again.

"Wicked woman," I breathed against her neck, playing her, holding on to my own release as it built. Her pussy clenched around me with her next orgasm, milking me, stripping me of any control.

I bit down on her shoulder, piercing her skin with my canines, claiming her as my passion blinded me. She screamed my name and clenched me again and again, as if marking her sent her into a giant wave of simultaneous orgasms.

Her blood coated my mouth, and I pulled my teeth from her as the connection solidified inside me. Her heart pounded in time with my own. Her hips moved just as violently as mine, and then I let out something between a howl and a moan in her name. My release was more like a fifteen-year pent-up explosion, infinitely more intense than anything I had experienced in my life.

I leaned forward so we both were half on and half off the couch. My breath panted in her ear as the fire of her soul blended with mine. A sense of lost time gripped me. I could have had this sensation that first night I met her if I had followed through on my wolf's demands.

I kissed the wounds I made. Wounds that would turn into my personal tattoo of claim on her. The bites would heal, but my mark would never fade.

She turned her head and stared at me. "You marked me."

I traced the cuts with my fingers, staining them with her blood. She was mine now and the MDA would have to understand. They'd have to back off. *Wouldn't they?*

I nodded before I met her incredulous gaze. She didn't look pissed like I expected. After all, I had just claimed her without her consent. "Yes."

I didn't have to hide my desire any longer. I also didn't have to hide the awe she inspired in me, or the love that had built over the last fifteen years. She was my sun. My moon. My everything.

And I would slaughter anyone who tried to take her from me.

The End

Continue Sarah and Robby's story with WICKED HEART - Book 1 of the Shades of Night Series.

SHADES OF NIGHT
BOOK 1
WICKED HEART

Waking up to blood smeared walls certainly does not instill calm. Quite the opposite, considering I had locked my house up tight with deadbolts, sigils, and safety spells to ward away evil.

And I went to bed alone.

With no memory of a struggle and no signs of a dead body, there's only one logical conclusion. One of the demons we hunt at The Monster Defense Agency broke into my home.

My insatiable cravings clue me into exactly what I'm dealing with, and now I need to track the bastard down and fillet his ass.

Otherwise, my life will be forfeited, and I will become the hunted.

1

WICKED HEART 1

SUNLIGHT PIERCED THE ROOM and I stretched, unaware of anything else but the cool comfort of my bed and the taste of sleep in my mouth. My eyes slowly opened, squinting at the warm rays bathing my face. Instead of turning away, I let the warmth spread over me as my eyes adjusted to the brightness.

But the sunlight wasn't piercing like usual. It was streaked in a haze. I blinked at the blood covering the double window just beyond my nightstand, and my heart lurched.

"What the hell?" I clasped the covers tight around me, but my body still shook with the rawness of my nerves. The sheer volume of the gore on the walls next to my bed and at the foot of the bed was enough to set me into a panic and forsake all my years of training with crime scenes.

I sat up with a gasp, taking stock of myself, inspecting my arms and my unblemished torso. I reached for my throat, thinking the worst, that I was somehow dead, but all my fingers felt was smooth, unbroken skin.

I pinched my arm to be sure I wasn't still in some weird nightmare and flinched at the sting of my nails digging into my skin. My mouth dried to the point I thought I'd either throw up or fall into a coughing fit.

I had gone to bed alone last night. The house had been quiet and dark, and I had not woken once I laid my head on the pillow.

Or had I?

I scanned the carnage.

Whose blood painted my walls?

Cringing, I turned toward the other side of my oversized king bed, imagining a dead body. But all that was there was an empty spot where the blanket was still neatly folded over. I let out a partial sigh of relief, eyeing the other blind spots in the room with trepidation. The rest of the room only had stray drops that looked as though they were splattered from whatever fountain had hit these walls.

I didn't know how I would have handled it if something from my job hunting for the Monster Defense Agency, or MDA for short, had been lying dead beside me. I shivered with a litany of horrible images that thought conjured, but it was nowhere near as unsettling as my bedroom right now.

I glanced on the side of my bed and blood marred the floor as if whoever had been cut had turned in a slow circle, leaving behind their life in red streaks.

But there was no body on this side of the bed. And no footprints.

I shivered and brought the blankets closer around me in an effort to stave off the cold now gripping my chest. I forced myself to breathe in and out slowly. This scene wasn't all that unnatural in my line of work, except it was *my* bedroom and not some nameless victim. When my heart stopped galloping as if it wanted free of my chest, I released my grip on the blankets and forced myself to crawl forward. I needed to see what was on the floor beyond the end of the bed.

I needed to see the remains of whatever had splattered my walls, even though my instincts told me to run.

But the floor was just as barren as the side of my bed, and just as blood-ridden. I felt my throat again just to be sure, but all that met my fingertips was unbroken skin and a pulse that was near terror.

I threw the covers back and attempted to get off the bed without stepping on any blood. But that proved to be impossible as my toes depressed into a section of the sticky goo spread on the floor as if someone poured a vat of honey instead of a person's life juice all over the place.

My stomach did an unhappy flip, tightening my throat in the process. The cold tackiness sliding between my toes meant that this kill, whoever it had been, was done early enough in the night for everything to coagulate. The stench of iron overwhelmed me, and I gagged.

I made it into the bathroom and shut the door on the mess while taking deep, cleansing breaths. I glanced around the clean and tidy bathroom for any signs of an intruder, but not a damn thing was out of place.

Closing the lid of the toilet, I sat down, lowering my head between my knees as a high-pitched buzz attacked my ears. My vision swarmed, and I forced myself to breathe slowly. All I needed now was to hyperventilate and pass out.

When I thought I had some control over the panic pummeling my veins, I slowly sat up and focused. I needed to get my mind in the right place to look at this with an objective eye, as if I were on the job.

My bed was pristine, as if nothing nefarious had happened. There was no body and no footprints leading out of the room, outside of mine now that I stepped in the mess. And two of my walls were covered with enough blood for a dead body to be somewhere.

My lack of need to relieve myself struck me. Normally by this time I was racing to pee. Something was not right, and I closed my eyes. I stood abruptly and spun to the mirror with my heart throbbing in my chest. I stared at my reflection. Sleep-matted hair, pale features, ruby-red lips, like I had been sucking on a cherry lollipop, and the kicker—my brown eyes seemed to carry a reddish hue. Of course, it could just be my auburn hair, but still, I do not ever remember my hair casting a red tint on either my eyes or my lips.

"Damn it!" I muttered under my breath. It made no sense. The sunlight hit me in the bed. If I were truly a vampire as my red eyes hinted at, I would have turned into ash the moment the sun touched my skin.

I leaned forward and pulled my lips up, looking for fangs. Nothing was visible in the mirror, and I straightened up, mystified.

"What the hell happened?" I scratched my head, studying my reflection. *How the hell could I have not woken up?* was the more pressing question, besides *What the hell do I do now?*

As if the heavens heard my cursing, my stomach started to rumble in a manner that was unusual. I leaned back against the door and just stared at my reflection, going over every last thing I knew about vampires.

Vampires were not alive, and yet my heart thundered in my ears. There weren't blood donors to satisfy their hunger like so many of the popular fiction books described. Vamps killed. They bled their victims dry to the point the victim's skin was almost concaved, looking more like mummies than humans when the vampires finished with them. That was the reason vampires were at the top of the kill on sight list for MDA. I glanced at my reflection. I certainly wasn't dried out like a damn mummy.

Vampires also had the power to compel and alter memories just by command. I shivered, wondering whether my head had been messed with.

I glanced toward the window and the sun filtering in. Vampires burned in the sunshine. I didn't turn to ash with the morning sun. Even with blood-streaked glass, it would have burned if I was a vampire, wouldn't it?

Had I missed one? After all, it was our business to hunt and kill these things before they infested an area.

I snorted at my image.

"You fucking bet your ass you missed one, and somehow that thing got into your home." My eyes flashed, with the irritation scraping my skin like barbed wire.

Now I'm talking to myself. Stellar.

I closed my eyes and took a cleansing breath. Maybe there was some other logical explanation. I willed my phone into my hand from wherever it was, and the small electronic device appeared in my palm. Thankfully, my retrieval magic hadn't been nullified by whatever happened during the night.

I flipped it open and started to dial my office, but I paused. My reflection stared back at me and the warning in my eyes was clear.

What happened the last time a hunter had been compromised?

"Fuck." I closed the connection and ran my hand through my hair.

The last time someone was turned, MDA locked them up in the high-security wing reserved for only the deadliest monsters. Most cells were empty because we rarely brought in anything we hunted alive.

Hell, I think Manuel was still down there, seething in his perpetual state of blood depravation.

I had almost quit that day, but no one quits the MDA. Retire to the burbs, sure, but quit? Nope, that was a death sentence.

I opened the door to my ruined bedroom and wished I had the type of magic that could make it sparkle. But my magic was limited to retrieval of *things* only.

Even if I had wanted to, I could not retrieve the culprit who did this to me and settle this score with a snap of my fingers. I willed the clothing I reserved for cleaning up crime scenes and slipped them on before I attacked the bloody mess.

WICKED HEART 2

MY STOMACH CONTINUED TO rumble even though my throat tightened closed as I scrubbed the carpet on autopilot. If I thought about it being my blood, I would freak out. Instead, I made cleaning up my sole focus. Thankfully, my bedroom had been painted with glossy, mold-resistant paint and that scrubbed clean without stripping the drywall. If I had chosen flat paint, I would have had to tear down the drywall to get rid of the stains. As it was, the carpet now looked as if there were great pink swirls along with the natural gray tones. It looked horrid enough for me to consider redecorating the entire room.

I sat back on my heels and pulled out the small vial from my pocket. Coagulated blood sat at the bottom of the container like sludge from a clogged drain. I had to figure out how to have this tested. I needed to know whether the owner of the blood was in our database. Or whether it truly was mine. If it was, there would be a hit.

My phone buzzed, and I looked at the display. *Where are you?* Robby, my partner, wrote.

Why did this have to happen on a workday? I glanced at the clock and hung my head. The morning meeting had already started, and I was nowhere near the point I could leave my home. Never mind stand in a room full of hunters and go unnoticed.

I knew in my gut that my life as a vampire hunter was over and now I'd be on the MDA's list, but my mind wasn't ready to accept that. I certainly wasn't going to be locked up. I shivered at the mere thought of being locked in an eight-by-eight cell for eternity.

Overslept. Not feeling very good. Cover for me? I sent back and returned to cleaning.

Robby would cover for me, but he would expect an answer. We'd been partners for fifteen years, since we started at the academy, and in all that time, he had never seen me take a sick day.

MDA usually paired witches with werewolves of the same sex together to avoid romantic entanglements, although that didn't always work. Either way, having a relationship with another member of MDA was prohibited. When the time came to pair me with a partner, either they had run out of female wolves, or, the more likely option, they paired me with an alpha to attempt to keep me in line. Me, a witch with minor magic abilities, paired with an alpha male who was hotter than an inferno in the middle of a desert at high noon.

I had my own opinions, and I never kept them quiet, and in some cases, I pissed off some very high-level members of the organization. I think they had it in their minds that an alpha would be able to control me.

Ha. Not.

That had been a constant source of jokes between Robby and me over the years. Maybe he sensed my volatility, because Robby never once tried to control me. As irritating as his ribbing could be at times, I couldn't imagine anyone else having my back the way he did.

Shaking thoughts of Robby out of my head, I leaned on my heels and scanned my progress. The carpet was considerably frothed with soap. Now, I needed to run a commercial-grade steam cleaner over this mess. Wringing the rag out over the disgusting bucket of dirty water for the last time, I stood and dumped the liquid down the shower drain before throwing the pink rags in the washing machine in the hallway.

With my magic, I called on a commercial carpet cleaner with all the bells and whistles. The machine that appeared before me was a monster fully loaded with cleaning solution, and I plugged it in, connected the hose to my sink, and started cleaning, praying this beast would be enough.

It took me three passes to get the carpet spotless. I had to dump the dirty water from the carpet cleaner out in my shower, and I sighed at the red stains now on my floor tiles. I sent the carpet cleaner back to wherever it came from and got down on my hands and knees with a scrub brush and some bleach. As hunting agents, we knew how to clean up a mess, and I was so thankful for knowing what to do to erase the evidence. Still, if MDA came in and sprayed blood-detecting solution, I'm sure my floor would glow like the Christmas Tree in Rockefeller Center.

When I finished, I stripped my clothing, shoved them into the washing machine, and started the gruesome load. As far as going to the office today, that would be a disaster, especially considering an unnamed need thrummed in my veins, making me want to drink a gallon of something disgusting.

My phone dinged before I stepped into the hot stream of water in my shower, and I glanced at it.

Coming over with coffee.

In the shower, give me a few minutes, I sent back.

I scrubbed up quickly, toweled off, and dressed in a pair of black jeans and a blue T-shirt, brushed out the knots in my hair, and willed a pair of colored contact lenses to hide the red tint in my eyes. I blinked at the brown eyes in the mirror and sighed. There wasn't a thing I could do about my lips, but I'd deal with that somehow.

My heart thundered in my ears as I turned away from my reflection and headed downstairs. The doorbell buzzed just as I reached the ground floor, and I swung the door open.

Robby towered in the entrance with two steaming cups in his hands. Robby Young was a force to be reckoned with. His dark hair fell across his brow and curled at the edges of his coat collar, much shorter these days than it had been when I first met him, but it still was fashionably longer than most of the men in the MDA. And he was built like a bulldozer.

His sharp blue-eyed gaze narrowed at me, and he sniffed the air.

Damn wolves. They can always smell when something is amiss.

"Sarah?" He cocked his head, searching my face.

How did I ever think I could fool Robby?

Robby was loyal to the company and the suspicion in his gaze left me trembling. "It's been a tough morning." I sighed and swung the door wide, waving for him to enter.

He cautiously stepped over the threshold with his knuckles turning white on the paper mugs, as if he strained not to crush them in his grip. He offered me a cup.

When I accepted it and took a sip, his forehead creased. He lifted his nose in the air again as his gaze swept my entryway.

"You're... You smell different." He closed the door behind him and stared at me.

His confirmation of what I knew in my bones still didn't settle well. "I had this house locked up tight and warded." I turned and headed into the kitchen as my stomach rumbled in an obnoxious manner. I stood with my back to him, debating on what to say next. We had been partners since I started in MDA. Fifteen years together hunting demons and vampires and rogues who decided humans were a delicacy, and now I fell into that damned category.

At least I thought I did, but I was not completely sure. I set the coffee on the table, unable to drink any more of the nauseating liquid.

"And?"

I spun back to face him, to meet his soulful gaze. A gaze I dreamt about over the years, but one that was off-limits due to agency rules forbidding agents from becoming romantically involved.

I could hear his heart racing as fast as mine, and he licked his lips before shifting his weight back and forth. "And?" he asked with more force. The cup in his grip crushed, spraying coffee everywhere.

His reaction jolted me, and I refrained from taking a step backward. Instead, I reached into my pocket and pulled out the vial full of coagulated blood, passing it to him. "This was all over my bedroom floor and walls."

I swallowed hard. If Robby thought I was a threat, he'd shift and tear me to pieces. I had seen him do that before, and although it was awe-inspiring as a partner, it was downright terrifying as a potential victim.

He shook the hot coffee from his hand and snatched the vial from my grip. He rolled it between his fingers and then glanced up at me. "You know I'm obligated to report this," he said in a way that screamed regret.

"I don't want to be locked up like Manuel." I shifted my stance and clenched my hands. After Manuel, I made provisions for an event like this. If Robby tried to drag me in, he'd have a fight on his hands. I would hurt him if I had to, even though it went against everything I believed in.

He crossed and towered over me, invading my personal space as he stared down at me. The blood flowing through his system smelled divine, like a four-star steak dinner, and I inhaled the scent before meeting his gaze.

"Do you really think I'd lock you up?" His voice softened as he studied my face. His eyes reflected a storm of emotions: aggravation, devastation, and something underneath it all that made me wary.

It took a moment for his words to sink in, and I blinked up at him. The Robby Young I knew was by the book, to a fault. It was my turn to narrow my eyes. "What?"

"I'd tear your throat out before I'd let you rot in a cell for the rest of eternity."

I swallowed hard and dropped my gaze to his chest mere inches away from me. The urge to turn and bolt filled me, but I refused to run. Not when he could shift and be on me before I could get to the front door.

He reached out and cupped my chin, forcing me to lock gazes with him. "You aren't built for captivity."

His firm touch created a web of heat that enveloped me. I tried to yank my chin from his grip, but it was impossible. My stomach fluttered with panic and something more carnal between groans of hunger pains. Robby finally let go, moving back a step to give me room to breathe.

"Asshole," I muttered and rubbed my chin where his tight grip had nearly bruised my skin.

He raised an eyebrow. "You would do the same for me."

He was right. I would rather take his life than see him chained in captivity. Neither one of us were built for that. Hell, I don't think anyone at the MDA was built for it, and we all cringed when they locked up Manuel. Although, I was much more vocal about the injustice than anyone else, which earned me another reprimand from our boss. He did not like my opinion injected into the already tense situation. Hell, he didn't like my opinion, period.

Robby glanced at the blood in the tiny container. His lips pressed together in a way that I'd never seen, as if he didn't want to confirm what we both already knew. He unscrewed the lid and took a sniff, and then he closed his eyes and hung his head as he capped the vial again. "It's your blood."

"Just run it through the database," I insisted. It was MDA protocol.

He glanced at the blood, rolling the glass between his fingers as if he could change the contents in some way. He shook his head slowly. "If I do that, it will raise questions."

"But aren't you obligated..."

He put his hand up, silencing me. "If I run this through the database, yes, I'm obligated." His gaze slashed to mine. "So, I am not going to run it through just to confirm what I can already smell. And what any wolf at headquarters will smell the moment you walk in. You are...*other*." He snarled out the last part as if fighting his base nature.

We hunted *other*. That was our job. Still, to hear what I expected took the strength out of my legs, and I sat at the table before I crumpled to the floor.

"What happened?" he asked but did not venture any closer, as if getting close to me might make him befall the same disaster.

"I have no clue." I shrugged as I pushed away the coffee. "I went to sleep and then woke up with my room painted with blood, but there wasn't a drop on the sheets. It only covered the walls and the floor, like my bed itself had been covered by some magic spell to keep it pristine." I lifted my chin and held out my wrists so he could see the unblemished skin. "There isn't a goddamned mark on me, so how could I have bled out like that, and be sitting here talking to you this morning like nothing happened?" I dropped my head into my hands, and my stomach made an ungodly noise, demanding sustenance.

He stepped closer and seemed to tremble in my peripheral vision. I glanced up at him before he backed up again, sucking half his lower lip between his teeth like he always did when his mind went into overthinking mode. "You need to quit," he said as his eyes darted all around the room at everything but me.

I blinked at him. There was no quitting. He knew that. That carried the same death sentence as relationships.

"Tell them you found something less stressful."

He was reaching; I could see it in that deep crease between his eyes and the way his eyes darted back and forth. That was the first indication that Robby was not handling this well either.

I burst out laughing at this whole ludicrous situation. "Quitting is a death sentence. You know that as well as I do. Besides, they won't buy it." They knew I thrived on the tension and thrill of the hunt. Hell, Robby knew that better than anyone.

He met my gaze, his eyes pleading, as if there had to be a way out of this god-awful mess that wouldn't land me in a cell or dead. "Then tell them you need to quit because you want a relationship with me."

That did not curtail my laughter one bit; it only increased it. That would be even more absurd. Robby was a player, and everyone knew that. Robby's gaze narrowed in a way that only made it worse. Although I fantasized about the man and all the dirty things I wanted to do to him, it would be a disaster between us if we ever crossed that line. I did not have a submissive bone in my body, and that was expected of an alpha's girlfriend.

He shifted uncomfortably and crossed his arms as I continued to laugh at him and his shitty ideas. "You don't think they'd buy that?"

"Would you?" I sputtered through my laughter.

Robby's expression transitioned from irritation to outright anger, and he spiked the glass vial onto the kitchen floor. It shattered, bathing the room in the scent of blood. Robby crossed the distance and pulled me out of the seat, slamming me into the closest wall. His hands squeezed my upper arms as he stared directly into my eyes.

The intensity in his gaze, along with the fact my legs dangled far from the floor, heated my skin with a fire that I had tried to ignore for fifteen years, along with a rash of panic and anger.

"What the—"

His mouth crushed over mine in a forbidden kiss, and it had all the possessiveness of an alpha male. My mind stalled at the softness of his lips mingled with a hint of mint still present on his tongue, but my body reacted rather violently at the intrusion of my personal space. I kicked out as hard as I could, connecting with Robby's balls.

His breath hitched, and his grip on my arms disappeared.

I dropped the eight inches to the ground and pushed him on his ass, pointing my finger at him with a hiss. "Don't you ever fucking manhandle me," I yelled in his ever-reddening face. "We may be partners, but that is where we have always drawn the line." I ran my hand through my hair, trying to control the rage dancing over my skin like a hot flame.

He moved back, his eyes widening as he held his family jewels. If his expression hadn't transitioned from pain to outright surprise, I never would have glanced away.

I caught a glimpse of my reflection in the tinted microwave door and stalled. Red flames rolled over my exposed skin and hair, making my untamed mane glow. I blinked, trying to right my vision, but the blaze persisted. My mouth dropped open as I raised my hands, staring at the fire coating them. Shock cooled my out-of-control temper, dousing the flames. Tendrils of smoke drifted on the air around me.

"Sarah?" Robby asked from the ground.

I shook my head at the question in his voice. I was just as surprised as he was. No vampire we knew of had ever broken out in flame like I just did. Unless they were dragged out into the sunshine, and that was usually accompanied by screams before they turned to ash.

I glanced around to be sure, but there wasn't any direct sunlight falling on me, and I met Robby's awe-filled gaze.

Just what the hell had attacked me in the wee hours of the night?

WICKED HEART 3

ONE THING WAS FOR sure. I was no longer just the human witch I went to bed as. No matter how hard Robby drilled me on what happened, I couldn't recall a damn thing. I had no idea what the hell happened to me, but there was enough blood painting my walls and coagulated on my floors to tell me whoever had done this had bled me dry before they turned me.

Even so, my heart pounded in my chest, giving me the impression that it was still pumping something through my veins with each beat. So, I could not quite categorize myself as dead.

"Do I feel cold to you?" Vampires always felt cold. At least the ones I had the unfortunate chance to touch. I reached my hand out to him.

He covered my hand with his, and his wolf-warmth seeped into my skin, sending heat all the way to my heart. His hand lingered and when he finally pulled it back to his coffee, it was as if he didn't want to sever that connection that always seemed to flash between us whenever we inadvertently touched. "No. You feel normal."

Normal? I'd never be normal again. I huffed and looked at my wrist. "I'm half tempted to cut myself to see if I bleed." I ran my finger over the blue veins under my skin. My pulse registered in my fingertips.

Robby's gaze shot up from the fresh coffee I brewed him after we both recovered from the aftermath of his sudden smooch attempt and my spontaneous outburst of flame.

"Don't," he said. "I'm barely containing my wolf as it is." He waved toward the wall where he had kissed me, as if that explained that bomb.

This was news to me. I just thought he had reacted to my laughing at him with a macho attempt at showing me it wasn't as ludicrous as my laughter suggested. "What's that supposed to mean?" I leaned back in my chair and crossed my arms.

He pressed his lips together and shook his head like he didn't want to expand on his comment.

He should know better than try to bait me and then switch subjects.

"Well?" I waited and forced myself not to tap my foot in impatience, which he absolutely detested.

"Sarah—"

I cut him off. "Stop with that tone. I'm not fragile, so don't you dare treat me that way." I pointed at him. "Besides, you're the one who brought up your wolf, so just speak your mind like we've always done. *This* shouldn't change that." I waved my hand down my body.

That drew the kind of snicker that made me want to smack him.

"Well, my wolf isn't sure whether to tear you to pieces or…" He trailed off with a shrug, although a dimple made a quick appearance.

"Or what?" I leaned forward, catching his gaze.

"My wolf can't seem to decide between tearing you apart or fucking you. If you spill more of your blood, I'm not sure I can contain him." He met my gaze, a little exasperated for having to spell it out.

I blinked at him and slowly leaned back in the chair. "You want to…fuck me?" My voice cracked. I knew enough about werewolves to know their desires were rooted in the human side, not the wolf side, which only reacted to base instinct.

Tearing me apart made sense because I was apparently no longer human. But sleeping with me? That wasn't a wolf instinct. At least not unless a wolf found their true mate. We had been partners way too long to entertain the latter.

"My wolf." But he wouldn't meet my gaze now.

Holy crap. "And this sudden urge was triggered by my change?" I fished, because now I was damned curious, especially considering I'd wanted to shag him since the day we met. I never once suspected he was into me, though. Not during the long stakeouts or the near-death experiences we faced together. And certainly not when he flaunted his conquests to me. Hell, with the kind of work we did, having an outside relationship was doomed from the get-go.

Frankly, his escapades were as well known in the office as mine.

His shoulder lifted and lowered, and he glanced out the window at the day beyond.

Shit. That wasn't the answer I expected. I expected an unequivocal yes. Not this vague shrug. Robby wasn't a convincing liar. His face revealed every emotion, or so I thought. I didn't know what to do with his discomfort at my line of questioning. "Why wait to tell me this until now?" I asked, truly miffed as my mind started questioning the possibilities.

His eyes slowly moved to meet mine, and what I saw drew my breath in hard.

"We are *supposed* to be partners. They kill witches who cross the line. You *know* that."

Holy shit. My heart skipped a beat, but before I could speak, my phone buzzed. The taboo of work relationships within the MDA had stopped both of us from saying anything, but it was clear in that one glance there had been something more with him as well.

I swiped the Answer button without looking at who the caller was. "Sarah Stone," I said through gritted teeth as fifteen years of missed opportunities flooded my mind.

"You survived."

The deep voice along with the statement captured my total concentration and turned my skin frigid. "Who the hell is this?"

A dark chuckle filled the line just before it went dead. My gaze shot to the number, and I cursed under my breath. Unknown caller, unknown number. *Figures.* My hands burned with frustration and flames ignited on my fingertips. I dropped the electronics as if the mobile device had been the thing to set my skin on fire, but it doused with the bang of the phone hitting the table.

"Who was that?" Robby asked, bringing me back to the issue at hand.

I had been so distracted by the call that I hadn't noticed him get up and round the table to stand close enough for me to hear his blood cruising in his veins. My heart thundered in response, and I moved my chair away because the sudden urge to bite him and draw some of his warm blood into my mouth became overwhelming.

"I, uh. I don't know." I met his gaze and wrapped my arms around myself to stanch the continuous shiver that seemed to take hold at the sound of that voice. My hand splayed across my throat in almost a protective reflex.

Robby crouched next to me and touched my arm. His eyes showed genuine concern, along with that hot temper just simmering beneath the surface. He sometimes felt like a walking, talking tornado. And right now, his sights seemed to be solely on me.

"You don't know?"

"No." I tried to shake his hand loose, but his grip tightened on my arm. "I suppose we should hunt this bastard down, though."

"You can't work. You can't go near anyone from the office. Not with how you smell."

"How do I smell?"

"You smell like death already claimed you. Like almost every damn vampire I've killed has. But it is mixed with something sweet and light and tangy that makes my wolf want to claim you right this moment to keep you safe and protected. It's strangely abhorrent and alluring at the same time."

"Different than before?" I ignored his comment about his wolf. If I concentrated on that, he very well might tear me apart before the sun dipped under the horizon. Because if Robby got too close to me, whatever was driving my thirst would ignite.

His lips tilted in a smile. "Before, you smelled like caramel coffee with a side of lemon cake."

I narrowed my eyes at him. "That's my daily coffee shop order."

"And it suited you." He licked his lips. "As sweet as that was to take in daily, this"—he waved at me—"along with the vibes you are transmitting, will set off every single supernatural alarm within blocks of wherever you go." He straightened his knees, rising to his towering height. "Stay here while I take a look around. I'm going to see if I can detect a trace of this bastard."

I stayed at the kitchen table and stared at the cold cup of coffee mocking me. Normally, by this time of the morning, I would have downed two of those things. But I just couldn't stomach it beyond that first sip when Robby stepped in the house. My mind stayed away from the fact Robby and his wolf had deeper feelings for me than just a partnership. Maybe he was better at covering up his feelings than I ever gave him credit for. I had suspected something the first time we met, but by the next day, we were listed as partners and he never even attempted anything inappropriate. And now that I was like this, I was a danger to him. My heart squeezed tight in my chest.

The longer Robby was here, the more tempted I became to give in to my new base instinct to rid him of his blood.

His wolf would have nothing on this growing need. It burned and made me parched in a way I never fathomed. I was starting to feel sorry for vampires, if this was their constant existence.

Robby's footsteps seemed louder than before as he walked the floors above me. Every now and then, his feral growl would release, as if he smelled every last moment of a struggle I could not recall.

It took him a good ten minutes before his footsteps descended the stairs, and a few more as he searched out this level.

When he finally came back into the kitchen, his eyebrows were low in concentration. He slipped into the seat across from me.

"Are you sure you set up all your wards properly?" he asked.

"Yes. Why?"

He glanced around. "I smelled something with the same dark signature, but it seemed to be masked. Like whoever was here had traces of magic on his being. And he was here long enough for his smell to permeate your sitting chair by the window." His gaze found mine. "And your window is open."

I had been too preoccupied with cleaning the room to even look at my reading nook by the side window, but I was damn sure it was closed when I went to bed. My mouth ran dry.

"Could you have left it open?"

"I swear, every window and door was closed and warded. Including that one. Besides, it is not warm enough for me to leave my window open at night." I crossed my arms. "I don't have a built-in heater like you do." Wolves were notorious for loving the cold, and they could radiate enough heat to drive a room into the low eighty-degree mark, even in subzero temperatures.

He stared into his empty cup with a nod. "I'll tell the boss you're dealing with food poisoning." His gaze rose to meet mine. "You need to stay here until I can find out a little more."

"Bullshit. I need to find this asshole and slice off his head." *Before I give in and feed.* I could not admit that last part to Robby. But I knew that removing the head of the one who turned you killed the curse.

His gaze widened.

It took a moment for the reason why to rear its ugly head. The moment the creator fell, so did the victim. After all, I was no longer alive. Only the vile magic that my maker held kept me animated. I didn't correct my statement because, honestly, I didn't wish to remain alive if this overwhelming craving was a hint of my existence.

4

WICKED HEART 4

I AGREED TO STAY put until Robby called, but I was wearing a path in my carpet from my pacing. *Who the hell did this to me?* And on the heels of that thought: *Robby's into me?*

My brain waffled between the two, and both of them captured every last ounce of anger and confusion pummeling me, leaving me both hot and cold, like some middle-aged woman going through menopause.

I concentrated on the more dire situation. I'd deal with Robby later.

I should at least remember a fight to the death. Shouldn't I?

My phone buzzed and instead of just answering it like I did before, I glanced at the caller. Unknown. It was either a telephone solicitor or the one responsible for what I was now.

I did not want to give the impression to either a telemarketer or the man who called before that I was happy they were interrupting my day or open to a long conversation on the benefits of protecting my Windows from a virus. Once I kept a scammer on the phone for a good half hour, acting innocent and frightened at his description of what could happen to my computer if I did not address the issue by giving him my personal information.

I had traced that call back to the source and when I read off their address when they asked for mine, silence had been the caller's response. I told that annoying con artist that I was coming after him with my wolf in tow, and he hung up so fast, it tickled me. I often wondered whether I should pay that scammer a visit, but it was likely a pimply teenager versus a hardened criminal. Besides, there were others who hunted those types of people. We focused on monsters.

With another scam artist, I told them to repent when they mentioned computers. To repent and kneel down, asking for forgiveness for interfacing with such evil. That was even a faster reaction than rattling off their address had been. After that, I never got a Windows virus call again.

Gritting my teeth in anticipation of irritation, I answered my phone. "What?"

"Tsk, tsk," the smooth, satiny voice purred. "You should be nicer when answering your phone. I could have been someone important."

His toying tone set me off, heating my skin with instant aggravation to the point I thought I would flash over. "Fuck you," I snarled. This was the bastard responsible for the blood covering my walls. I probably should be a little more polite, but I was not in the mood. I started my tracing app with a tap of my screen. "You nearly made me have to redecorate my bedroom, asshole."

"You should show me a little more respect." The words came out in more of a growl this time.

My attitude seemed to push his buttons. That pleased the hell out of me. I wasn't going to be nice to someone who...who what? I still didn't remember what happened, but I wasn't going to ask. Not on the phone. If he was here, that would be a different story. And I would get all my questions answered before I ended his ass.

"Why is that?" I toyed with him despite the ache in my jaw from clenching it too tight.

"Because I made you," the voice said, radiating hostility...or frustration. I couldn't tell which. "And I can *un*make you."

Ah. Hostility. That was the usual reaction to my bitchiness. There was no way I was going to let anyone control me. Even my partner knew I was uncontrollable, and had for the last fifteen years. Robby had been smart enough to never even attempt it. He joked about it all the time, but not once did he try to enforce his alpha powers over me to make me submissive.

This asshole apparently thought he *was* in control. It was time to enlighten him. "I'd like to see you try."

"You made the mistake of not stopping me last night, too." This time his voice was more chilling.

I halted my pacing and stared out the front window, trying to remember exactly what happened, but it was all a big blank. I clamped down on the chill that gripped me. "What the fuck did you do to my memory?"

A chuckle that gave me the willies came through the phone, and I was tempted to throw it across the room.

"I *could* have wiped out every last one of your memories and left you a clueless mess, at the mercy of your partner. I understand he gets off on ripping vampires to shreds."

How did he know about Robby? "Was that your intent? Turn me, so my partner would kill me?"

Silence filled the line. He didn't understand the partnership I had with Robby. If he had, he would have known that Robby would never harm me. I saw it in his eyes this morning. It pained him that I wasn't just a human witch, but he wasn't about to turn me in to the MDA, especially with the bomb he delivered.

A shiver climbed up my spine when the silence continued. "You're a real bastard."

"So I've been told."

"I swear, the next time our paths cross, I will rip your head off." If I continued to grit my teeth this hard, they'd all splinter from the pressure.

"Promises, promises."

The line went dead.

I squashed the temptation to throw my phone. But I needed to get this fury contained, so I reached for Robby's empty coffee cup and chucked it across the room with everything I had.

I've never witnessed a cup shatter into dust, but that's exactly what happened on impact, along with gouging a hole in the drywall.

I was now even more angry at my inhuman strength. I tilted my head back and let loose a guttural roar. Although some might relish the added strength, it meant I was truly *other* now, and would be hunted and either put in a holding cell until I died, or someone like Robby would tear me to pieces.

I wanted to destroy the entire apartment, and my hands burst into flame. I clenched my fists at the suddenness of this fury, but before I gave in to the need to smash more things, I caught myself. I liked my home, even though I felt violated by something I could not remember. I unclenched my fists, shaking my hands to douse the fire. With a few slow, deep breaths, I regained control and stared at the mess I just made with the cup. The dust from it tickled my nose and I wiggled it, trying to head off a sneeze. It didn't work and I sneezed three times in succession.

The mess was small, but I did need to clean it up; otherwise, I'd be sneezing all day. Hell, it could have been worse. I could have burned the entire place down or smashed my furniture to hell. I could deal with a broken coffee cup and went in search of rags to clean up my mess.

As I wiped up the dust and microscopic particles of glass, I forced my breath to slow. I needed some perspective, and this roiling anger wasn't helping. Neither was the thought of being locked up in my own home. That set my teeth on edge.

But I knew as soon as I stepped outside my door, I'd be fair game for the hunters, even with my MDA badge.

Damn that fucking blood sucker.

My hands slowed, and I sat back on my haunches. My gaze traveled to the ceiling and my head cocked to the side as my mind reworked the crime scene with a new angle.

I had not been the vampire's meal.

I covered my face and sighed. I couldn't believe it had taken me this long to connect the dots. Which told me exactly how freaked out I was about this whole thing. Our vampire victims weren't showcased in a bloodbath like what I woke to in my bedroom. Every vampire victim we'd encountered through the MDA was a dead body drained of every last drop of blood. Those situations did not end with walls painted with blood. Those situations had a complete absence of a blood trail.

I blinked and stared out the window as chills danced over my back like a legion of spiders.

This was deliberate. But why?

My mind wandered to Manuel. He had been turned as well, but his situation sounded vastly different than mine. He had an accident with his motorcycle and nearly bled out on a deserted road when a vampire found him; instead of killing him, he turned him out of spite for the MDA. Manny had crawled to a deserted building and found a shaded place to wait out the day.

Then he made the mistake of coming into the office. The moment he stepped inside, every werewolf caught his scent. And poor Manuel's teeth made an appearance. I guess being desperate and hungry had made him not have control over his cravings. But he was aware enough not to attack anyone; otherwise, he would be dead instead of sitting in a cell for eternity. If he had been a werewolf, he might have been able to talk his way out of it, but he was a witch like me. Witches don't have fangs.

I finished cleaning up the miniature shards of glass and threw the dust into the trash compactor. My mind kept going over things. Even though my stomach had growled when Robby was here, my fangs hadn't surfaced.

Was I a vampire?

I opened the refrigerator and then the freezer, looking for anything appetizing, but nothing struck my fancy. My hunger had reached a new level, and all I could think about was sinking my teeth into the soft flesh of someone's neck.

My hungry train of thought slammed home just what I was, but it still didn't quite settle well. I ran my tongue over my teeth. Nothing sharp met my flesh.

I open and closed the cabinets too, but none of the food in my home looked appealing. Not even the basket of fresh fruit on the counter. I picked up an orange and smelled it. The citrusy scent turned my stomach, and I restrained myself from squeezing it in aggravation. I gently placed it back and headed into the living room, stretching out on the couch.

My brain was a mess, jumping from Robby to my situation and back. I studied the spackle pattern on my ceiling as if it had all the answers.

Just how much of my memory did that bastard really wipe out?

I bit my lower lip, trying to figure out what my last true memory was. Closing my eyes, I started to wade through memories as if they were stowed in a file cabinet instead of in my head.

WARMTH WRAPPED ME IN her arms, and I sighed, blinking my eyes. I had dozed off while trying to catalog the last few days. Blinding sunshine from the living room windows blanketed me. Awareness filtered in, and my heart lurched in my chest. Vampires burn in sunlight, even window-filtered sunlight, and these windows were not marred with blood. That same stream of light transitioned to toasty as I shifted, and self-preservation kicked in. I rolled off the couch and into the shadows to get away from it.

I glanced down at my body, expecting to see smoldering skin, but there was no sign of burn marks. Just the tingling sensations where the sun warmed me.

What the hell?

First, fire spouting from my exposed skin earlier today, and now, I withstood direct sunlight without turning into a charbroiled hockey puck.

How long has the sun been on me?

My head spun with the ramifications, and I glanced at my hands. "What the hell am I?"

WICKED HEART 5

THE RAPID KNOCK ON my front door startled me, and I crinkled my nose at the faint wolf scent that wafted underneath the threshold. My phone pinged, and I glanced down at Robby's text telling me to open the door.

I needed to know what he found out, and swiftly crossed to swing open the front door. A blast of sunshine directly hit my face. I squinted and put my hand up to shield my eyes.

Robby's gaze widened and his heartrate tripled as he quickly stepped close enough to block the path of the sun.

Based on his open-mouthed gasp and the way his eyes kept searching my face, I guessed this time the sun did scar me, even though I didn't feel burnt. I self-consciously reached up to see how bad it was, but all my fingers found was smooth skin. My mind stalled again. *Direct sunlight didn't burn me.*

I stepped back, waving him inside before I closed the door on the morning brightness, still confused as to what I was. I mean, I had died, or at least the amount of blood hinted at that. And Robby said I smelled like death. I focused back on him.

His mouth still hung open, and he blinked like a man who had just seen his favorite car squashed under a bulldozer. He reached his hand to my cheek to verify what his eyes were seeing. The light graze of his thumb on my skin brought heat to the surface, but it wasn't because of the sun.

Every last dream I had ever had about him started to filter through my head like a lewd porn flick. I tried to blink it away, but knowing he had at least some of the same feelings I've had just wouldn't erase them completely.

"You didn't burn." His voice held reverence and awe that made me self-conscious.

"No shit." My gaze fell to the large cooler in his other hand. "What's that?" I asked, glad to have something else to focus on except the way Robby was looking at me.

He glanced down at it as if he forgot he had it. "It...uh...may be a mistake." He cautiously placed the cooler in front of me and stepped back, putting space between us, as if the heat between us might actually ignite this time.

I opened the top and stared at the substantial number of bags inside, all carrying thick, red liquid. My gaze snapped to his. "What did you do, steal these from a blood bank?"

Robby let out a nervous laugh.

"Jesus, Robby." I slammed the top closed and crossed my arms as I straightened and sent him a searing glare. But this did the same to my stomach as smelling the orange had. It tightened in disgust.

"You need to eat." His gaze dropped to the floor, and he shifted his weight nervously.

He expects me to be thankful. "Is this what you do for Manuel?" My stomach turned at the thought of biting into the cold bags of blood.

His lips pressed together, and he looked away with what I could only categorize as a halfhearted shrug shrouded by guilt.

Truthfully, before today, I would have done the same thing if the tables were turned. But he had no clue what the cravings demanded. It wasn't just a need for blood. My veins burned with a hunger he would never comprehend. My gums ached above my canines, as if I were cutting new teeth. And since Robby stepped into the house, my need to bite him had become nearly uncontrollable.

I wondered what he would taste like, and I licked my lips, thinking of more than just blood. I almost laughed because I couldn't figure out whether this sudden fixation on him was due to my need for fresh blood or the heightened longing that accosted me now that I knew he had similar desires.

His gaze returned to mine, but instead of the guilty look he wore a moment ago, that hunger he had just before he kissed me this morning was back, and it looked as though it was on the verge of detonating.

"What are you doing?"

His cautious question, along with the appearance of his canines, only increased whatever had taken hold of me. His form trembled but he didn't move toward me like I wished.

He didn't bolt either.

"I'm not doing anything," I said. But I wasn't so sure now that desire to ravage him ruled my veins and because I was already damned by whatever I was, there were no more imaginary lines that we couldn't cross. Thoughts of undressing Robby and feeling him on me...inside me...stirred this carnal hunger. "Why?"

"Because you are tossing out pheromones like dice at a craps table."

I chuckled and sucked my lower lip between my teeth, slowly raking it as I released it. There were several places on him that I wanted to bite, not just his throat. I wondered what sex with him would be like, and certainty filled me. He would be the best I ever had by far.

I took him in, from his dark hair and brighter than normal blue eyes. His face was chiseled with sharp cheekbones, a strong jaw, and a nose that fit perfectly in the middle above supple lips that were soft, and I would expect demanding in true action. His canines poked out, denting his lower lip with their sharp points. Whatever I was doing was pulling his wolf to the surface and it thrilled me.

"Please, stop," he pleaded with a breathless quality that I had never heard from my partner, and damn did it turn me on even more.

My gaze moved lower, to his broad chest that reminded me of Thor from the movies. Even underneath the tight shirt, I could see the muscles quiver as if my gaze actually caressed him. His broad torso slimmed to a finely cut waist. His jeans hugged his form, and I could see the results of whatever I was emitting in the hardness of his member outlined in the fabric.

"Ah, fuck," he growled and the next thing I knew, he had me pinned to the wall again, but this time, instead of kicking him in the balls, I wrapped my legs around his waist, pulling him against me. "What are you?" he asked, but did not wait for an answer. Instead, his lips descended onto mine like an eternal claim.

I let the kiss consume me, along with the feel of him grinding his hips into mine. Fabric ripped and then his hands were on me, making every dream I ever had pale in comparison to the reality of him. His hands were softer than I imagined as his rough calluses glided over my skin. He moaned in my mouth as if he had dreamed of this for as many years as I had.

He broke the kiss and moved his mouth to my jawline, nipping as he moved lower, sending shivering heat through to my core. I tugged at his shirt, and he lifted his arms so I could pull it off. At the sight of his bare chest, my hunger sparked, but I refrained from tearing into the throbbing vein in his neck. I needed this more than blood.

He paused, and I met his gaze. His chest rose and fell as he attempted to corral the frantic need making his eyes wild. "I'm supposed to be the alpha." He circled his hips. "I'm *supposed* to be able to control my wolf."

My lips twitched into a smile. "Maybe I don't want you to control your wolf. Maybe I want your wolf to ravage me."

"You have a wicked, wicked heart," he growled and wrapped his arms around me, carrying me to the living room as he kissed my throat. He placed me on my back on the shaded side of the couch and worked his way from my throat to my chest, creating a growing heat inside me. He toyed with my breasts while he worked on the buttons of my pants. I ran my hands into his thick, silky hair, enjoying his attentions more than I ever dreamed. He undid my pants and with a yank, my jeans slid off. He tossed them aside and continued working his way down my body.

Each of his kisses left a warm spot before air brushed over it, leaving a relief map of bumps in his wake. "I've dreamed of doing this for years," he said against the skin of my inner thigh as he met my gaze.

Then his mouth was there at the juncture between my legs, and all logical thought left me. His tongue created a warm magic through me that left all my wet dreams of Robby in the dust. He kept going long after I came. By the time he stopped, I was panting his name and every muscle in my body quivered with the blinding intensity.

My brain registered the sudden swell of air when he pulled away and before I could adjust my position, he flipped me onto my knees on the floor in front of him. The jolt sent a web of chills through me. Before I could ask what the hell he was doing, Robby's hard member entered me from behind with a brutal thrust that made me arch into his chest and let out a yelp of surprise.

"Wicked woman," he breathed against my neck as one hand moved up to my breast and the other found my clit, circling it with such slow circles that contradicted the speed and power of his thrusts as his hips pounded into me.

He seemed to know exactly what to do to bring me right to the brink. And just as I was starting my release, pain exploded in my shoulder. Robby's canines tore into my flesh, marking me as his. I cried out as pain and pleasure pummeled me, sending me tumbling through my blinding release.

A moment later, he howled with his release, nearly lifting me off the floor with the strength of it. His thrusts slowed and we fell forward onto the couch. My shoulder throbbed, but it wasn't exactly painful. Warmth traced from the bite, encompassing me in one of Robby's warm hugs. Robby kissed my skin, running his tongue over the wounds he inflicted. His labored breath blasted in my ear like a hurricane.

With my body satiated, and the smell of blood in the air, my hunger flared. I turned and met his exhausted gaze, and then looked at the bite on my shoulder. "You marked me."

He traced the cuts with his fingers, staining his digits with my blood. He nodded before he met my gaze. "Yes." There was no apology in his statement and his eyes held almost a defiant look, as if he expected me to be furious.

The smell of fresh spilled blood flipped a switch inside me, and I pivoted in his grasp, pushing him to the floor. He looked up at me in surprise until I straddled him. Hunger gripped me but it was still eclipsed by desire, and I circled my hips while staring at my blood on his lips.

His eyes sparkled up at me as he took me in. In all the years we had been partners, he had never once looked at me as if I were the sun and the moon. But he was now, and my heart revved into overdrive.

It was as if I finally saw a side of Robby that he had kept hidden from me. I leaned forward, crushing his mouth with mine, tasting the sweet tang of iron on his lips and his tongue as it tangled with mine.

I could fall into this bliss forever.

He reached for me, but I grabbed his wrists, pinning them to the floor. I wanted the control. I wanted him begging me instead of the other way around. It was my turn to rule his body the way he had mine.

"My turn," I purred and readjusted so his hardened member slipped inside my aching path.

He closed his eyes and tilted his head back, whispering my name. His open mouth was enough to pull me back to his lips, and he groaned softly as I sucked his lower lip between my teeth. Then I moved my tongue down his jawline to his throat as I ground my hips to his.

Heat filled every pore and as my lips brushed over the vein in his throat, the need for blood overrode my desire. In a blink, my fangs elongated, and I tore into his artery.

Oh my God. The sweet tang of his blood filled my mouth. He tasted like the sweetest dessert paired with fine wine. I never wanted this to end. Even when the spice of his panic filled my mouth,

I still held on. His hip thrusts became violent as I kept hold of his wrists. His arms strained against my hold but the sweetness of him filled me.

"Sarah, you're killing me!"

Robby's voice penetrated the haze surrounding me, and it wasn't in that sexual tone that revved my pulse. It held panic mixed with pain, and it slapped me back into reality from whatever blood spell I was under.

I yanked my teeth from his flesh and sat up with my eyes wide and the taste of blood satiating every need my body demanded.

Blood spurted from his neck where I had bitten him, and I covered it with my hand, pressing hard enough to slow the flow as my own panic surfaced.

He yanked away from my hand with a hiss. "Ouch."

A burn mark in the shape of my palm covered the bite marks and no more blood came from the wounds, as if my flesh cauterized the holes in his flesh. Shock filtered through me, and I snapped my gaze to his.

"You bit me," he said indignantly, his fingers testing the burnt skin.

I licked my lips, still tasting his wolf essence. His hips still circled below me, maintaining the friction between us. Obviously, biting him hadn't dampened his mood for sex. In fact, I think it made him even more horny, based on the redness still present in his cheeks and the darkness in his eyes, as if his pupils had almost entirely taken over the blue of his eyes.

I let a small smile form. It certainly made my engine fully engaged. I no longer had hunger pulling at my stomach, but my drive to ravage him was fully engaged.

Something about this bite-for-bite thing lit a fire inside me. "You bit me first."

"You're a fucking vampire." He gripped my hips now that his hands were free.

I wasn't sure whether he intended to uncouple us, but I squeezed my thighs tight enough for him to hitch a breath.

Now that I drank blood, I couldn't argue that I wasn't a vampire. But I withstood the sun, so I didn't actually know what I was, just that I was more.

"I'm more than a vampire, if you hadn't noticed."

"True." All his irritation morphed into an intense stare and that crooked smile of his that always made me feel like putty in his hands.

I twirled my hips slowly, taking advantage of my position on top of him.

His eyes rolled back into his head as a soft groan escaped his lips. "You feel so fucking incredible." The slow motion continued, and then his eyes snapped open wide, and his gaze shot to my face. "You...stopped."

My hips still twirled, stroking him with each gyration. "I beg your pardon?"

He licked his lips while keeping eye contact. "I don't mean you stopped this." He thrust his hips to make his point. "You stopped feeding."

Now my hips did still.

A crease appeared between his eyes. "Please don't stop *that*." He gripped my thighs and guided me into a faster rhythm as his mouth opened in something between an exhale and a groan. "I'd like my brain to be completely fucked, if you don't mind."

He smiled up at me with normal human teeth. I had somehow tamed his wolf, and now all that was below me was this god-like man, and damn he felt good. I rode him until he called out my name and we both collapsed in ecstasy.

WICKED HEART 6

THE WARM WATER OF the shower pulsed on the back of my head, washing away the cobwebs of the after-sex euphoria, along with the crusted blood from my shoulder. My brain still could not wrap around the last few hours. We christened almost every room in my house in a mad frenzy to make up for fifteen years of pent-up sexual tension. It was as if we had unleashed two nymphomaniacs who just couldn't stop until something broke.

That something had been the guest bed. A smile formed on my lips just thinking about it. His expression of absolute shock when the mattresses fell through the frame had been hilarious. We both roared with laughter, but that hadn't stopped either of us from finishing what we started.

The entire day felt surreal, and I could almost believe it was a dream until Robby stepped to the entry of the stall. "Mind if I join?" His voice held a timid, unsure tone that did not belong to an alpha wolf.

I debated as he stood there, looking a bit lost, as if having earth-shattering sex with me had stripped him of his alpha status. I finally nodded when he shifted his weight between his feet. Relief filled his face, and he stepped under the spray, pulling me against his chest.

"I'm sorry. I, um."

I pulled away, glancing up at him as irritation bloomed under my skin, turning the water into a hissing steam as it met with my overheated skin. I had just had the best sex of my life, and I did not want a fucking apology from Robby. "Why are you apologizing?"

"I, um." He lightly traced the bite mark he made during our first round in the living room. "I shouldn't have presumed." He met my gaze with a sheepish smile.

I relaxed. "I thought you were apologizing for ravaging me."

His genuine smile bloomed, and he laughed. "No. I don't regret a moment of that. Especially since I've been dreaming of this since the day we met at the academy."

I cocked an eyebrow up at him. "Since the academy? You mean we could have been shagging like this for fifteen years?" I waved toward the bathroom door and the house beyond, teasing him.

His dimples appeared and he shrugged as his fingers lingered on the bite marks that claimed me as his. "They would have killed you." His smile faded as he tucked my wet red locks behind my ears. "But if I hadn't been so stubbornly by the book, perhaps this would never have happened to you." True regret slid into his eyes.

"Stop. You don't know that. For all you know, I could have been killed by something else at any time over the past fifteen years. Without you having my back, there are at least a dozen times where I never would have made it out alive."

He didn't seem convinced, and he pulled me closer, planting a kiss on my forehead. I hugged him back.

"You might not be here either, because for all the times you saved my ass, I've saved yours as well," I added, looking up at him.

"Mhm," he said.

Whether it was in agreement or just acknowledging I spoke, I wasn't sure.

"But if I had marked you earlier and we somehow got around the MDA's archaic rules, no sane monster would have messed with an alpha's mate."

"Who said the bastard that did this was sane?" I glanced up at him. "He *knew* who I was." I sighed and pressed my head against his chest. I didn't want to revisit the minimal information I had at my fingertips. I just wished I could blast through the barrier holding my memories hostage.

He maneuvered us so he was under the full spray of the water and tilted his head back, running a hand through his hair before he glanced at the array of body washes lining the shelf. A single eyebrow cocked up as he looked down at me.

"What? I choose the body wash of the day based on my mood."

He studied the lineup and broke out in a laugh at the last two. "Seriously? Wake the F*ck Up and Calm the F*ck Down?" He took a deep inhale. "I like whatever you just used. It's not flowery."

I handed him the Wake the F*ck Up body wash and his dimple deepened.

"Figures."

"I'm more of a citrus girl. I hate smelling like a gardenia."

He took a handful of the body wash and smeared it across his chest, foaming it up until the scent of wolf and sex faded and that of citrus and eucalyptus filled the space. I stepped out of the shower to let him clean up without me taking up half the space.

I pulled out a clean towel and left it on the closed toilet lid for him before wrapping my soaking hair in another. Then I grabbed the terrycloth bathrobe off the hook on the back of the door and covered myself before heading into my bedroom to find something to wear.

The shower went off as I pulled a sweater over my head. With my discarded towel and bathrobe in hand, I stepped back into the bathroom to hang them up.

Robby had wiped a path across the steamed mirror and was inspecting the burn I had left on his neck. His blue eyes swiveled to mine in the reflection. He chewed on his bottom lip and then turned.

"I need to figure out how to keep you out of lockup." His eyes held the seriousness of my situation, along with an underlying desire as his gaze traveled down my form and back, as if he were memorizing every detail.

The fact he didn't say "we" set a searing burn beneath my skin. I reached around him and grabbed my brush, tearing into the knots with as much aggression as his words sparked. I didn't even have to voice my aggravation. I guess my face transmitted every ounce of it.

He rolled his eyes at me. "You know what I mean." Robby skirted around me and left me to my knotted hair. He came back a few minutes later with his jeans on and a shredded shirt in his hand.

I took the last stroke of the brush and set it down on the sink. "Before you ask, no, I don't have any shirts that would fit you." I spun to face him.

"Can you pull one from my closet?" He raised an eyebrow.

I was not in the mood to use my magic. "I rather like your bare chest and I'm not inclined to cover it." I flipped my hair back and smiled at him, pushing down the irritation that had welled up from his comment.

He dumped the ruined shirt into the garbage can next to the sink without a word and then stood, towering over me as he studied my face. "Are you wearing contacts?" He cocked his head like a questioning puppy.

I reached up and plucked the contacts out in answer and he recoiled. "I've been wearing them all day." I flicked them from my fingers into the garbage can without looking at my reflection. From Robby's reaction, my eyes still had that red ring around my irises like they had this morning.

"I'd definitely keep using those contacts. Especially if you decide to leave the house, which I highly advise against. But I know you. And frankly, I am surprised you stayed in all day." He reached out and tucked a stray hair behind my ear.

His touch sent a tingle down my spine, and I shivered from it in the most delicious way. Robby pursed his lips and a single eyebrow cocked up in question. He inhaled and took an unsteady step back, as if he was afraid he'd get burned if he was too close to me.

"You're doing it again," he said in that low, husky voice.

I grinned, amused. "So, any time I feel at all...horny, you're going to act like a teenage boy in the back seat of a car on prom night?"

His eyes sparkled and dimples appeared in his cheeks, but he took another step back instead of closer. "I can't think when you do whatever this is. So, the answer is probably yes." Another step of retreat. "And I can't spend another who knows how long here." He pulled his phone from his pocket, showing me the multiple texts from our boss. "Your phone probably looks the same, so if one of us doesn't get their ass into the office soon, he's going to send out the cavalry." He waved at me. "And you definitely can't go into the office."

I closed the distance and put my palm on his chest, right over his heart. His heart knocked so strong that I licked my lips as my libido flared. I stared at the pulsing artery in his throat a moment too long before I forced myself to look into his eyes.

A feral lust reflected in his irises, promising me all sorts of decadent activities. But he took another very deep breath before he stepped backward, right into the side of my wall.

Damn. The boy had one hell of a lot of control. I would have been tearing fabric within seconds had he not retreated.

I toyed with the idea of cornering him, but I also knew our boss. I didn't know what would piss him off more: me turned into whatever I was, or Robby and I sleeping together. Either way, our situation was dire enough for me to back off.

He started out of the room.

"Do you think whatever I'm emitting will affect others the way it affects you?"

The muscles in his back stiffened and he stopped in the doorway, sending an alarmed gaze over his shoulder at me. "I hope not. Otherwise, I'll end up at the top of the most wanted list."

My jaw dropped, and his lips twitched into a smile.

"I'll tear anyone to pieces if they so much as brush by you in an inappropriate manner."

The growl in his voice chilled whatever heat I had been stoking, and my hand went to the mark on my shoulder.

"That's what being marked by an alpha wolf means. If someone decides to make a move on you, it will be the last thing they ever do." With that, he stalked out of the room and a few moments later, the front door slammed closed.

I fell into the reading chair by my window and watched as Robby slid into the front seat of his car. He sat for a moment and ran his hands into his hair. I could almost read his mind. That was his *What the hell have I done* expression. I'd seen it enough to know. When his eyes found mine, his hands dropped to the steering wheel. He sent me a nod and then pulled out of my driveway without another glance.

Absently, I rubbed the spot where he bit me, and warmth encompassed me as if he were still here with his arms around me. The sensation didn't lessen as the sun dipped below the horizon. As the full moon snuck into the sky, that warmth transitioned to worry.

I didn't want to go to sleep. The last time I did, I woke to a bloody mess. I didn't want to wake to another disaster.

WICKED HEART 7

THE SHRILL RING OF my phone brought me out of the stupor I had fallen into. I blinked and glanced around the room. But the ringing was not within my bedroom. When I reached the living room, my phone stopped. I crossed and swiped it off the table, annoyed.

I should have just willed the thing into my hand, but no, I got up from my comfortable spot and climbed all the way down to my dark living room. I glanced around, blinking. It was dark, but I could see everything as if it were day. The fact I wasn't navigating shadows made me a little giddy and a little sick at the same time, confirming that I truly was *other*.

No number displayed in the recent call list, and I ground my teeth together. *Had that bastard decided to toy with me again?* I refrained from squeezing my hand around the phone for fear I'd turn it to a crumpled piece of metal. I didn't know whether it had been the asshole or not, but the feeling in my stomach left me almost certain it had been my nameless nemesis.

I took a soothing breath, and then scrolled to Robby's number and pushed the phone icon next to his name.

"What's up?" Robby asked with the sounds of the station in the background. But his voice wasn't his normal upbeat self. He seemed as strained as I felt right now.

"You're still at work?" I paced to get the increasing aggravation out of my bones.

He grunted. "I got the lecture from hell and have been relegated to desk duty." His grumpiness came through the phone line.

My mouth went dry, and I stilled. "Why?"

A sigh filled the line. "Harrison didn't buy the food poisoning thing. Not with the number of missed calls, and I had to come up with a viable explanation, especially with the burn on my neck. So, I told Harrison we slept together."

He told our boss? What the hell was he thinking? The way his voice lingered on the last syllable told me there was more. I wasn't sure I wanted to know the details, but I asked anyway. "And?"

"And that I marked you."

His quiet admission made my heart drop. *For the love of all things sacred, why would he do that?* I closed my eyes. *He had no choice. And maybe being marked by the alpha of the Allegany pack might just save my life.* I should have checked into the office this morning and told them I was sick; then he wouldn't have been in this situation. "Shit," I muttered.

But he wasn't done. "And that you smacked me with a hot pan after I bit you," he continued.

I snorted a laugh. Robby was quite resourceful with that fib. I was surprised they bought any of it. His ability to fake facts was akin to an infant navigating a busy highway. It always ended with disaster.

"He said that seemed more your style than the normal subservient reaction. He's just glad you didn't kill me with it." He let out a soft chuckle that faded away. "And now I'm on the bench until he can get things sorted."

I went to sling a sarcastic remark but paused as my brain caught onto the nuance in his tone. "What's going to happen to me?" I knew the MDA did not react well when partners crossed the line. It was as bad as quitting.

"That's the kicker," he grumbled. "I've been ordered to fire you."

I must have heard that wrong. "Excuse me?"

"We violated company protocol—what the hell did you expect? One of us has to be let go. And because you're my mate, they are willing to spare your life." His exasperation came through in the clip of his voice, but it was better than being relegated to a body bag.

Bunch of macho jackasses. My aggravation bloomed hotter. "And because I'm a weak human woman, I'm the one who gets cut?"

"You said it, not me."

I could almost see him putting his arms up in the "whoa, it wasn't my idea" posture. I ground my teeth together. "I am not weak or useless," I growled into the phone.

Silence filled the line, and there were so many words hidden in that absence of sound that I wanted to scream. I probably had said more than enough at this point, but I didn't care. I had a mission, and with or without MDA, I was going to accomplish it.

"I'll be over as soon as he lets me leave." He sighed into the phone. I imagined him pinching the bridge of his nose like he did whenever he was aggravated.

I blinked. I didn't need him to console or coddle me. I needed to hunt down the bastard who ruined my life. "That's pretty fucking presumptuous of you." It was out before I could stop the words.

"I may bite you again just for your snarky tone," he growled. "You're my mate. Start acting like it."

I let out a laugh. "Maybe this time, I'll bite you back," I said, knowing he wouldn't out me on a company line, and that my warning had more of a threat to it than his. Besides, he never asserted his alpha status on me before, and if he thought he could do it now, he was sorely mistaken.

"You wouldn't dare," he said in that low, sexy voice of his.

The one that started my engine as if I were a grand prix driver. Damn this man for making me no better than a horny teenager.

Conflicting emotions ran through me: aggravation and this unmanageable lust that his low, sultry voice triggered. It was a wonder that the frustration hadn't resulted in fire spurting from my tightly fisted hand.

"You can sling pheromones through the phone, you know," he said in an even lower tone. "Stop doing that."

The image of Robby sitting at his desk, sporting a hard-on, brought some levity to the situation. "That is very good to know," I said in an equally sexy voice.

He let out a low groan. "Damn your wicked heart," he whispered.

This conversation was sliding down the sexual slope, and I did not want to continue it with ears I was sure were listening. I chuckled in response and disconnected the line.

My phone immediately rang, and I swiped without looking. "Did you forget to whisper sweet nothings in my ear?"

That dark snicker filtered through the line, making every hair on my body stand on end. "I didn't realize that's your thing, but I'd be happy to oblige."

I needed to remember to look at my damn phone before answering. The taunting bastard kept chuckling. "What do you want?"

"I'm curious. Have you fed yet?"

I growled low, unwilling to answer this prick. "None of your goddamned business."

"Why don't you come on upstairs and we can play some more? Perhaps engage in a little oral fun tonight?" His purr chilled me.

The squeak of a floorboards upstairs drew my attention. My heart dropped at the certainty that the bastard was in my house. I spun and moved like a bolt of lightning, climbing the stairs two by two. I slid into my bedroom to a shadow in the sitting alcove.

My chair turned and the man sitting in it pulled a derisive growl from my lips. I had the weird feeling that I had seen him before, even though he remained in the shadows. I just couldn't recall where. His teeth flashed in a wide smile of triumph, but it faltered as soon as he got a good look at me.

He hissed and shot to his feet, baring his fangs. "What have you done?" He stepped toward me. Half his face illuminated in the light. He was shockingly attractive, with dirty-blond hair, a chiseled chin, and an aristocratic nose. He looked almost like a Norse god, but his eyes held murderous rage, as if I had somehow betrayed him.

Burning anger ran rampant inside me, and my free hand engulfed in flame. I wanted to see this bastard lit up like a vampire torch.

His eyes dropped to my hand and widened, and then he turned and fled out the window as if he understood my intention to snuff out his monstrous ass.

The phone at my ear clicked, and by the time I got to the open window, the intruder was gone. I shook my hand, dousing the flames even though my own fury had grown almost unmanageable.

"I will find you and drag you out into the sunshine! You hear me?" I yelled out the window through clenched teeth. I didn't know whether the asshole could hear me or not. But now at least I had a partial description.

And his lingering scent was enough to track.

WICKED HEART 8

AFTER THAT ENCOUNTER, SLEEP was not a possibility. I paced instead, tempted just to go out and hunt on my own, but I knew how dangerous that was, especially without Robby. We never went on a hunt alone. It was a good way to get killed.

It was well past midnight when I heard the tentative knock on the door. As I closed the distance, Robby's distinct wolf smell wafted in, and I swung the door open, staring at the nervous energy filling Robby. He refused to look at me.

Before he could even speak, I said, "He was here."

Robby's head snapped up, and his gaze turned feral as it scanned the darkness behind me as though the intruder was in his territory. His growl came next, and he nearly shoved me out of the way to get inside to make sure it was safe. He bound up the stairs and into my room as I closed the door and followed him.

His lips curled back at the scent filling the room, and then he looked at the ward still on the glass of the open window. His gaze jumped to mine. "That was closed when I left."

I nodded. My gaze went to the sigil and then back to Robby. A new horror dawned on me at the same time Robby tilted his head. There were only two explanations as to how that bastard got through. Either he was one hell of a powerful mage in addition to being a blood sucker, or I had let him into this house willingly at one time or another.

A chill captured me, and my arms broke out in gooseflesh.

Robby's gaze narrowed. "You know him?" The words spit out in a snarl.

"I have no fucking clue," I snapped back. My gaze dropped to the floor as I searched my memories and only came up with gaps. "He wiped my mind clean of any memory of him." And that was one of the more dangerous powers of a vampire. But I would have known what he was just by his scent.

I blinked again and my eyes closed tight. I didn't have this acute sense of smell before I became what I am now. But I should have known. I should have picked up some sort of magical signature. It was my job to hunt those things down, so if I did know this bastard, why didn't I know what he was?

The memory of him half in the shadows and half in the light slammed home. What I saw looked nothing like a hungry blood sucker. Even his eyes were the wrong color. They weren't outlined in red like mine, and outside of the scent of death clinging to him, his demeanor was different than any other vampire I had ever slaughtered. He was...playful when his chair turned before he caught sight of me. And then his entire demeanor changed to one that radiated hostility.

The fact he looked like a Norse god didn't help my case, either. He was exactly the type of guy I would pick up in a bar as my next conquest, with the intention that maybe he could wipe out my inappropriate thoughts of my partner. None had succeeded so far, but this guy had the look that could distract me, especially with Robby being taboo.

Robby stared at me while my brain filtered through all the possibilities, and the longer I took, the redder his face got. His canines remained out, as if he were attempting to control his baser instincts.

"Did you fuck him?" he growled in that same accusatory tone.

I met his gaze. "What part of I have no fucking clue don't you get?" My irritation bloomed, and it was all I could say because there was nothing in my brain that would help. There were blank spots in my memory—lost time—but I didn't know how many occurrences there were. I looked at that damned window again and shuddered.

Robby ran his hand through his hair and then crossed to the window, closing it. "Whatever happened in the past is moot. You're *my* mate now."

This macho bullshit crawled under my skin. "No one owns me."

His head snapped in my direction, and his eyes bore into me. "You are bound to me, Sarah."

"That does not mean you own me." My aggravation level just ratcheted up a few notches, and I pointed a fiery finger at him. Alpha shifters were possessive as hell. I had seen it in our department, but there was no way I was going to be his docile woman. "Do not expect me to be submissive."

He crossed to me and slapped a pair of cuffs on my wrists before I could react. Then he pushed me into the wall, staring me down with a ferocious glare. "I never expected you to be submissive," he growled low, and then leaned forward and kissed my neck before his head dropped to my shoulder.

He had me pinned to the wall, and I couldn't move my hands. *Is Robby getting kinky with me?* My libido roared to life at the thought. We hadn't played with handcuffs earlier. I glanced at his exposed neck and a deeper hunger stirred.

Robby stiffened against me, as if he could sense my mood shift. "And I never expected to have to lock you up for your own fucking safety." His words came out rough and then he looked up at me with eyes that pleaded for me to understand. "They brought in a seer."

I stared at him as shock filtered through my bones, bringing with it the kind of betrayal that cooked me from the inside out.

A seer.

That meant Harrison thought there was more to Robby marking me than he said. That meant they didn't trust him to tell the truth, and a seer would have busted the truth right out of his mind. *Damn the MDA.* And damn Robby for intending to bring me in.

I'd be locked in their cells until I either went insane and they had to put me down like a rabid dog, or, a more morbid thought, until I died of old age, which as a vampire could be centuries.

"You promised me," I snarled and kicked his shin as hard as I could. "You promised you wouldn't let me waste away in a cell." I pushed him hard.

He winced and took a step back. "I had no choice. I either bring you in or they will put you down." His face scrunched in aggravation. "They wouldn't even listen to me when I told them you were my mate and not some rogue that would endanger the public." He ran his hand through his hair as his eyes glossed over with a sheen of tears. His frustration bled through. A derisive growl slipped out from deep in his throat.

I pulled at the cuffs, but they were charmed so that monsters like me couldn't break them open. "Let me out of these." I lifted my arms up for him to do just that. "You owe me that much." I had no intention of letting them lock me up. I had made provisions, and it was time to activate them. But I couldn't do that locked in these handcuffs.

His jaw tightened, and he shook his head. "I don't have the fucking keys." His hands fisted and opened repeatedly. I could see him slipping, fighting his sensibilities, as if he were thinking of doing something terribly stupid that would likely get us both killed. "There's nowhere to run. The house is surrounded." His voice broke.

"And if I go quietly, you can keep your damn job." The sarcasm leapt out before I could button it up.

His face crumpled in a way that surprised me. He shook his head. "No. I'm just as cooked as you are. But at least I'll be alive until they can sort out what to do about my pack."

A crackle came through the bud in his ear. "You have five minutes to bring her out." The hard voice of our boss resounded from the speaker in his ear.

"Seriously, you're wired?" I yanked at the cuffs again, but no amount of strength would break the enchantments.

He ripped the earbud out of his ear and spiked it on the ground, slamming his boot on the thing before he grabbed my face, planting a kiss that was both passionate and desperate. "I can't do this," he whispered against my lips. "I can't lock you up, and I can't kill you like I said I would." His kiss deepened and his body pressed against mine in a way that we did not have time for.

I pushed him away. "Bring me to the closet under the stairs."

"Why?"

I made a calculated bet on my partner. "Emergency escape," I said so low only he could hear me.

His eyebrow rose, and with it came a spark of hope. He hauled me over his shoulder and made his way downstairs, keeping to the shadows. He slowly opened the closet door and stepped inside the crowded space, putting me back on my feet.

"You never—"

I clamped my hand over his mouth. I remembered precisely why I built this escape hatch. I never told a soul about it, but it was imperative after what MDA did to Manuel. They turned on their own. There was no loyalty in MDA and seeing that, especially after my spirited arguments against locking him away had failed, had made me start this endeavor.

The day after they locked him up, I had come home and started my research. This escape hatch hadn't been easy to build. Nor was disposing of the earth I dug up underneath the house. It had taken me weeks of long evenings to do this, but I was so glad I had. The only drawback was we would have to crawl through the storm drain systems under the city. But at least that was better than the sewer lines, which had been a second option that I dismissed. Those all led to the sewage plant. At least the storm drains opened to the river.

I just hoped the storm drains hadn't overflowed and wiped out my exit. It had been months since I checked. And the last time I did, I had to remove a thick layer of mud that caked the escape hatch that I blasted in the drain. Thankfully, the drains were big enough for Robby to crawl in and there hadn't been a ton of rain this month; otherwise, we'd run the risk of drowning.

When I removed my hand from his mouth, I raised up the cuffs. I needed them off because the MDA could track these things. Robby shrugged and shook his head. He had nothing in the way of getting them off. So, they had fully stripped him of even his pocketknife. Bastards knew he was as much of a flight risk as I was.

I turned my back on Robby, leaning against him in the close confines as my mind rushed through options. My newly found strength wasn't enough to break the cuffs, which meant Robby also didn't have a chance in hell of breaking them either. I stared at the metal glinting in the sliver of light coming between the door and the entranceway to my house.

If I didn't do something fast, they'd be in the house and all over us in a matter of minutes. Anger and aggravation mixed into what was dangerously close to panic, and that bloomed the hot power inside me. My hands ignited.

I put my hands out, far away from my body, as the metal of the cuffs turned a molten orange. I pulled on the source of power in my belly, targeting my wrists with this unwieldy power.

Behind me, Robby audibly sucked air between his teeth and stepped away from me, as if I were as hot as my wrists. A chunk of the metal dripped onto the floor, making the wood below it hiss. The smell of burning wood filled the tight space. Hope flared, and I knew time was at a premium, so I yanked my hands to either side. The cuffs fell as if they were made of paper and the floor smoldered under the discarded hot metal.

Instead of letting my fascination with what I had done rule my head, I focused on the wall in front of me. I whispered an incantation and ran my finger along the panel in front of me in a proper entry sigil. The wall disappeared, and I stepped over the smoldering cuffs, reaching to pull Robby through with me.

The minute we slipped through my magic portal, the space we passed through shimmered, and the secret door closed, becoming solid once again. But not before flames had sprouted on my closet floor. Darkness doused us, but I didn't have time for a spell that would provide us light. I knew the distance, and I pulled Robby along fast. That fire put both of us at risk. If we didn't hurry, we could be overcome with smoke in this tight space. I could feel the tickle in my throat already.

The gradual drop ended, and I pulled up to a stop.

"Ladder," I whispered. A ladder tall enough to reach down to the sub-terranean tunnel I built appeared before me. The magic I just expended would be trackable, but without the ladder, the fall alone would break legs. "Climb down." I put Robby's hand on the metal, and he swung around me and started the descent into the increasingly dark pit without question.

I followed him and the minute I touched the rough dirt, I sent the ladder back to wherever it came. The air down here was cleaner, but that wouldn't last long. Just a few more steps and we were at the drainage pipe.

I moved around him and muttered the same incantation that opened the door above, and the metal covering the pipe disappeared. I pulled Robby forward and pointed to the hole, knowing his wolf sight could see just as well as my new vampire sight. "Go to the right."

Robby raised an eyebrow at me.

"Go. There's a way out. I promise."

He sighed and crawled into the hole. I followed, and this time I closed the panel behind me and whispered a second incantation. One meant to destroy the path leading to my house. I brought down the dirt since all I could do was retrieve things with my core magic. The incantations took me months to perfect for the doors. It wasn't in my normal arsenal of magic, so I had to compromise in a way that my magic could utilize.

"Move!" I snarled from behind him as the world around us thundered. The hole we just climbed down crumbled above, blocking the entrance.

Robby crawled fast, and it was all I could do to keep up with him. When he slowed ahead of me, he whispered, "Which way?"

"Left."

There were a couple more switchbacks before the grate that dumped the water into the river came into view.

"I need to be in front," I said.

Robby stopped and laid flat so I could climb over him. He didn't say anything, but he did smirk and glanced over his shoulder at me as I passed over him. I knew that look. It was a combination of *We need to talk*, and *I want to shag you right now*.

For the last time, I said an incantation and traced the metal. The door swung wide. "Dive shallow," I said and then launched into the river. He followed and then I turned, pulling my magic back. The solid grate reappeared.

Darkness cloaked us as we swam to the edge of the river and hauled ourselves out. I glanced back toward my house. In the distance, flames licked the sky. I didn't know whether that was a good thing or a bad one. Had they assumed we perished in the fire? If not, we were outlaws.

Robby followed my gaze, and his eyebrows rose.

"I guess that fire took hold faster than I thought." I glanced down at my wrists, and the angry red marks where the steel had bit my skin stood out.

"I have never seen a supernatural being burn through charmed handcuffs," Robby said almost reverently. He took my hand and inspected the burns before he looked at me. "I'm not sure what you are besides vampire and witch, but I'm damn glad to not be locked up beside you for the next fifty years."

I let out a near hysterical laugh. "Fifty years?"

He shrugged. "I don't know how long we'd survive in captivity. It certainly isn't a normal lifetime."

My brain just caught up to his words. "Why would they lock you up?"

He waved to his throat. "It's what they do." His distaste for the company we formerly worked for bled through in his words. "Either that or they'd execute one or both of us. I made a calculated bet they wouldn't kill you if they knew I marked you." He glanced back at the drainage gate. "When did you do that?"

I squeezed the water from my hair and followed his gaze. "After they locked up Manuel. I wasn't going to bet on MDA being humane if something went wrong, especially after what they did to him."

He quietly studied me. "You never said anything." Hurt flared in his gaze and he looked away.

I laughed. "You work for MDA."

"I was your partner." His glare told me more than any words could. "I kept you safe for fifteen years. Why would you think I wouldn't continue doing that until one of us died?"

"You're loyal to the agency."

Fury filled his gaze. "I was loyal to you. Not the goddamned agency," he muttered. "And it's past tense. I *worked* for MDA." He ran his hand through his hair and stood, offering me a wet palm. "Now I'm a rogue alpha with a fucking powerful mate who's on the wrong side of the law."

"Regrets already?" I teased, trying to break the tension between us.

Dimples appeared in his cheeks as his gaze went from the sewer grate to me. "The only regret I have is not marking you the first day we met."

WICKED HEART 9

WE FOLLOWED THE RIVER until the light started to break the horizon. Robby walked at my side with my hand clasped in his. We tracked north and west, away from the city and the shoreline. The outlet that dumped us into the river was a mile from my house and we had walked at least another twenty-four miles over the last six hours.

My muscles hurt and all I wanted was to curl up in a warm bed and sleep for another two days. But until we had put hundreds of miles between us and MDA headquarters, we were not safe.

"Where are we going?" Robby finally asked as he eyed the horizon.

I honestly didn't know. I had no family and no friends outside of MDA. They made sure their recruits were loners, or entire packs in Robby's case. He was a legacy member of MDA, so we had no one to turn to who would help us. I shrugged. "Away."

If we turned to the outlaws, the monsters we routinely hunted, they would tear us apart. We knew of a few locations where they hung out, but that was a different kind of death from what MDA offered.

"Would Mickey be a safe bet?" I asked. Mickey was one of our informants who we trusted for information.

"No. He'd turn us in for whatever reward money they are offering." Mickey was definitely one who would serve his own self-interest above ours.

"I've got no other ideas." I sighed as the cramps in my tired muscles continued to spasm. "But I need to find some shelter and catch a little sleep. I am exhausted."

He chewed on his bottom lip. "There may be a place we can go, but I'm not sure we'd be welcome." He shuffled his feet and stared at the ground.

"Where?" Just by his demeanor, I knew I wasn't going to like his suggestion.

"Do you remember Rosalyn?" He flinched as he slid his gaze to mine.

The name sparked a flurry of contradictory feelings. Rosalyn had been one of his more serious relationships, despite not being a werewolf. If I recalled correctly, she wasn't a supernatural, nor was she aware of the supernatural world, including knowing what Robby truly was. He kept his daily world from her.

"Did you ever tell her what you were?" I tried to leave my judgment aside, but it still burned deep, leaving me a little unsettled. *What if we went there and he decided I wasn't enough?*

He shook his head, still avoiding my gaze. "No. She got a job offer out this way." He let out a soft laugh, glancing around. "Did I ever tell you she asked me to come with her?" He finally looked at me.

I nodded. Robby told me everything. And I knew his decision weighed on him, but I didn't tell him it would be a disaster. I didn't tell him not to go, even though at the time my stomach dropped at the idea of losing him as a partner and the only real true friend I had.

"I couldn't go. Not with the pack. Besides, MDA would never have let me go, and I wasn't about to bring this world into hers." He scanned the woods and then met my gaze. "Plus, it meant leaving you. And while losing her had been tough, my wolf would have never let me leave you."

I cocked my head and narrowed my gaze. "What is it with your wolf and me?"

He laughed, but it still carried the sharpness of nerves. "I will tell you *that* story some other time. I'm just as tired as you are, and I think this is our only choice. Otherwise, we find a big enough bush to curl up under. But that doesn't guarantee our safety like her place will."

I just grunted. Anything would be better than falling asleep out in the wild, where we were exposed. It's funny how when you get a few miles outside the city, everything thins out to open country.

"She lives out this way." He glanced at the landscape surrounding us.

I stopped and stared at him as the heat of jealousy burned in my veins. "You kept tabs?" I hated this feeling of insecurity.

He looked away and shrugged. "She reaches out from time to time, but I keep my distance. She has no idea about anything to do with the supernatural world. She thinks I'm a bounty hunter." He laughed, but it wasn't at all natural.

"So just looking at me will blow her fucking mind." I glanced at him because I was sure my eyes still burned red, which was as far from normal as it got.

"Think you could manifest those contacts?" He winced as he asked.

"You know better than to ask that. My magical signature is trackable."

Robby ran his hand down his face. "It's the only option I can think of, but with you as you are, it puts her in mortal danger."

It took a moment and then I understood his hesitation, and it just compounded my feelings of inadequacy. Theoretically, if my hunger flared, a defenseless human would pay the price. But I was more in control than he thought. "I'll be fine. I haven't had a twinge of hunger since we..." I searched for the words but couldn't articulate them, so instead I waved at his burnt throat. "If needed, you could always fill a wine glass for me."

His eyes narrowed. "I'm not your feed bag."

"Apparently, you are," I snapped back at him as my exhaustion and insecurity got the better of me.

He gnashed his teeth and let out a growl. "Fine. It's better than taking the chance of you roasting in the sunshine or killing a human." He took my hand and started to move away from the river.

"I didn't burn in direct sunlight." I hesitated, uncomfortable with moving back into civilization. But he was right; we needed a place to rest.

He glanced over his shoulder at me. "True, but we haven't tempted long exposure in direct sun, and I'd kind of like to enjoy my mate for a little more than a day before she dies, especially after waiting so damn long." His playful grin swept away my insecurity.

Although I believed a full day of sun probably wouldn't leave me crispy, he was right. *Why take the chance?*

"It's all I got." He looked back at me with pleading eyes.

"I know." I begrudgingly followed him.

WICKED HEART 10

HE WOVE THROUGH THE little town and on the far side, we approached a small bungalow in the middle of nowhere, like a desert oasis. The lights burned bright, and I caught movement inside.

"What does she do?"

"She's a special needs teacher."

That explained why she was up at this ungodly hour. I never caught the sunrise in the morning even on my best days. The only times I did was our all-night stakeouts; otherwise, it was bright and sunny when I finally crawled out of bed.

We approached cautiously, and the lights started to systematically go out room by room. By the time we passed the little convertible in the driveway and reached the beginning of the walkway, the last of the lights inside doused and the front door opened.

Rosalyn, a pretty, petite blonde, stepped outside and pulled up short at the sight of us. Her eyes widened and her mouth made a little O of surprise. Her gaze locked with Robby's and then dropped to our clasped hands.

Whatever dreams had made that flare of hope run across her face at Robby standing on her walkway died. Hurt flashed briefly in her eyes and then her face hardened. She pressed her lips tightly together as she adjusted the purse on her shoulder.

"I'm just heading to work," she said in a tone clipped with irritation.

"I need a very large favor." Robby let go of my hand, approaching her without me at his side. He stared at the ground, grappling for the right words before glancing at me and continuing. "My sister has gotten herself in a bit of trouble." He wiped his face and looked away from me, right into Rosalyn's gray eyes. "And we need a place to lay low for the day. I promise we will be out of your hair before you get home."

Sister? What the hell?

She eyed me suspiciously and then glared at Robby. "I'm not a fool," she said with a hard edge to her voice.

"She's my half-sister," he said with an exasperated eye roll. "And she got into a little trouble gambling." He cleared his throat and shifted his weight from foot to foot with a nervous laugh. "Actually, she's gotten herself into a lot of trouble, and I need to hide her somewhere while I figure out our next step."

I bit my lower lip and painted a look of guilt on my face, following his lead. I wrung my hands nervously to add to the ruse. At least I still had the red marks on my wrists as if I had been brutally bound, so that added to Robby's story.

"And if I don't help you?" Her gaze traveled to me and then back to Robby.

Robby sucked in a breath and looked at the sky with a wince on his face. "When they find us, she'll probably end up as a sex slave in a trafficking ring and I'll likely be executed for trying to hide her. She owes some very bad men a lot of money." The last part he said with a growl and an angry glare in my direction.

I opened my mouth, and he put his hand up.

"I don't want to hear your excuses," he snapped.

I pressed my lips together and looked at the ground. This was truly the first time I had ever seen Robby do a convincing song and dance out of lies. I was quite impressed with his improv skills. I just wished he had this level of conviction at the office earlier today; otherwise, we wouldn't be out here in the middle of nowhere trying to score a safe house.

Rosalyn recoiled when he mentioned trafficking, which made me wonder what kind of past she had that made her have that visceral of a reaction. Horror etched into her features, and her gaze shot to Robby. "Are you sure they won't find you here?" she asked, her voice now layered with trepidation. She looked around, as if some bad mob members were going to crawl out from behind the sparse trees on her land.

He raised an eyebrow at her. "Why would they even know we were here?"

She opened her mouth and closed it just as quickly, letting out a quiet laugh as she softened. "Fine." She turned, unlocking the house. "But don't eat all my food, okay?" This last bit she directed at Robby, as if she knew just how much of a food whore he really was. "And don't go before I get a chance to catch up with you, okay?" she added softly to Robby.

"We won't touch anything but water until you get home." He offered her a disarming smile, and she bought the whole thing.

Who the hell was this man?

She nodded and held the door open for us to enter.

Robby slipped inside, and I trekked the last few steps to the door with my head lowered as if I shouldered a world of guilt. "Thank you," I mumbled as I slipped by her, into her small but immaculate house.

One step inside, and I became super aware of the filth covering me. I stopped and took my shoes off on the welcome mat so I wouldn't leave a muddy trail throughout her home.

When I bent to pick them up, she said, "You can put those either in the closet or on the back porch if that makes you more comfortable." She gave me a smile that screamed thank-you, and I nodded in return.

I could see why Robby had liked this woman. She had a big heart as well as a neat streak that rivaled my own.

"Robby, don't be an ass. Take off your shoes," I said before he could traipse all over the house.

"Thank you. I'll see you both later." She shut the front door behind her.

We waited until we could no longer hear her car, and then I went out to the back porch and banged my shoes together to get the dried mud off. Robby stepped out next to me and followed my lead, banging his shoes together without a word. He must have known my mood had swung a far cry into sour land.

"Sister?" I swatted his arm with my nearly clean shoes.

"If I told her you were my girlfriend, we'd never have gotten in the door." He glanced at me.

He had a point.

"When the hell did you learn to act like that?" I glared over at him. I had never seen him bullshit so effortlessly or so convincingly.

He side-eyed me with a smile. "Every day of my life has been a goddamned act since I saw your name listed next to mine at the academy."

My mouth dropped open, and I stared at him.

"You never knew what I truly felt. You never knew the fucking agony of being with you every day and *not* being able to do all the things that constantly played in my head." He leaned close to me and scraped his lips on my cheek. "I not only protected you from the monsters out there, but I protected you from me." He pulled away and banged the last of the mud off his shoes.

"Why?" Logically I knew the answer, but emotionally, it didn't compute.

"If I acted on what I really wanted, it would have been your death sentence." He shook his head. "That thought was even worse than muzzling my wolf." He glanced at me and then back at the house. "Besides, with Rosalyn, I had time to formulate what story I was going to throw at her. That usually helps." He grinned at me.

I glanced down at my mud-ridden clothes, ignoring the pull of my heart. There was nothing I could do about all the lost years with Robby, so I focused on the current situation instead. "I need a shower and to find a washing machine. You could use some clean stuff, too." I waved at his dirt-clad jeans and smeared shirt. We both looked as if we had crawled through a mud field.

I wandered through the house, opening doors and closets until I found a set of stairs leading into a basement. There sat a washer and dryer, and I stripped, dropping my clothing into the drum along with a healthy dose of liquid cleaner. I turned, and Robby handed me his clothing.

His naked form woke my libido, but he shook his head before I could even step toward him.

"Not here. It does not feel right."

I guess if we were in one of my ex's homes, I'd feel the same. "Okay. Let's find a shower while the washer runs and then a bed to get some shut-eye."

He nodded, and we took turns in the little shower in the main bathroom. When we were finished cleaning up, I grabbed the towels and brought them downstairs. The washer had finished, and I transferred the clean clothing to the dryer and dumped the towels in the washer. I'd add the sheets to the wash after I got a couple hours of sleep.

By the time I climbed up to the guest room, Robby was already under the sheets of the queen-size bed, snoring away. I slid in next to him and pressed my back against his to ward off the chill in my bones. This house wasn't the warmest when wandering around it without a stitch of clothing on. I set the clock on the nightstand to wake us up at noon because I didn't want Rosalyn to come home to find us naked in the same bed. That shit couldn't be explained. Plus, it would give me time to do the sheets, remake the bed, and put the towels away before our host returned home.

Despite my swarming thoughts about how long Robby had been hiding his feelings, once my head hit the pillow, the lights went out.

WICKED HEART 11

THE DOOR BANGED OPEN, and we both shot up to sitting positions. Thankfully, I had the sheet tucked under my arm; otherwise, my entire bare torso would be visible like Robby's next to me.

"What the hell?" I blurted with a mouth pasty with sleep.

Rosalyn stood at the door, waving a paper in one hand and a gun in the other. Her eyes were wilder than I imagined she'd ever looked in her life. They darted between us, and she threw the paper at Robby. "You lied to me." The gun waved from Robby to me and back in chaotic jerks.

Her heart pounded so hard it set off a reaction in me. One that made Robby clamp down on my arm with one hand and reach for the paper slowly with the other.

"I already called the police," Rosalyn screamed.

"When?" Robby asked calmly.

I knew he was anything but calm based on his pulse alone.

"As I was driving here. I told the police that the murderers on the front page of the paper were in my house."

I tried to break Robby's grip, but he clamped down harder. "We did not kill anyone, Rosalyn."

"She isn't your sister, is she?" The gun went from him to me.

"No. She's been my partner at MDA for fifteen years."

"Another lie! She doesn't look like a bounty hunter at all. Do you take me for a fool?" Her rising anger needed to be extinguished; otherwise, one of us was going to get shot.

"No. It isn't a lie. I hunt vampires," I said, considering Robby had already mentioned MDA.

"There are no such things as vampires!" Rosalyn's hands shook more than they had been, making her more volatile. "*You* are the monster, according to that story." She pointed the gun at the paper.

Shit. She's losing it. My fangs clawed at my gums as my patience thinned to nothing. I chose to smile at that moment, flashing my new teeth in all their pointy glory.

"Stop it." Robby glared at me before I could speak and confirm there were worse things than murderers in the world.

I closed my mouth, willing my teeth back. My insides were roiling. If we didn't get up and get dressed and get out of here, the police were going to show up and attempt to throw us in jail. Or worse, MDA would show up. Either way, blood would be spilled.

"No." I glared at Robby and then stared back at Rosalyn, gaining her full attention. My power expanded inside me, and I harnessed it, directing it at Rosalyn with a mental shove. "You will not remember that we were here. You spiked a fever at work and must have been hallucinating when you called the police. Go to bed and for the love of all that is holy, put that damn gun back in your nightstand where it belongs. Now." I pushed the command out with my voice and my fangs grazed against my tongue.

She swallowed hard and then her face went slack, and the gun lowered to the floor.

"Go. To. Bed." My skin crawled at the empty expression she now wore. *Had I looked like that when the bastard stole my memories?*

Rosalyn turned away like a windup doll and marched down the hall to her bedroom.

Robby was no longer paying attention to me or to Rosalyn. His gaze was locked on the paper she had thrown onto the bed. I leaned over and sighed. Our pictures were splashed across the front with some made-up crime.

We didn't have time to deal with that. "Get out of bed and bring the paper with you," I ordered, taking charge of the situation.

I stripped the sheets off the bed and remade it as though no one had been there, and then took a quick glance around the room to make sure there was no trace of us. In the basement, I shoved the sheets in the washer with the towels, and started the machine.

I ripped open the dryer and tossed Robby's clothes to him before dressing myself. He dressed while he read the front page of the paper. In the corner next to the washing machine was a backpack. I threw it at him. "Go find some food." And then I was out of the basement, looking for something to make myself less noticeable.

In the bathroom on the first floor, I found an elastic and braided my hair. It was the best I could do to tame my mane into a lower profile. If I had a hat, that would even be better, but we didn't have time to search the house. The clock was ticking, and Robby was taking food from the cabinets when I came out of the bathroom.

"That's going to have to do." I headed toward the back porch where our shoes were. I paused at the door, my eyes widening at the full sun. *Shit.* A hat would be so much better, and I scanned the room. On the wall near the garage door sat a coatrack, and on it was a baseball cap. I ran over and grabbed that, plopping it on my head while Robby was already outside, slipping on his shoes.

On impulse, I grabbed the windbreaker that hung by the hat and slid it on, covering my arms completely, and then joined Robby on the porch, putting on my shoes just as quickly as I could.

We were sprinting into the woods when the sound of squealing tires reached us. Robby traded a glance with me.

"Maybe I should shift. We could cover more ground if you're on my back."

"We don't have time to stop, and you don't have any more clothing."

"These clothes are splashed all over the front page." He tossed me the backpack.

I caught it and put it on my back, clicking the front strap together as he shifted, shredding his clothing. He trotted beside me. I turned the baseball hat backward, knowing that I would lose it otherwise, and then I dove onto his back, wrapping my arms around his neck and my legs around his torso. His sprint turned into something like the wind, and I buried my face into his fur, holding on for dear life as he navigated the thickening woods away from Rosalyn's house.

Hours and miles flew by until Robby became winded. He had to slow to a jog to catch his breath. He stopped when we were deep in the forest. The moment I climbed off him, he shifted back to human form. His hard body glistened with sweat as he paced to cool down.

This was a view of Robby that I was used to in my job, but this time I took more notice of the way his muscles contracted and relaxed as he paced. His ass was an exquisite piece of art that I did not turn away from like I normally did.

"Really?" he asked, his breath still labored.

"What? Have you seen your ass? It's perfection in the flesh." I waved at him.

He grinned. "I'll never catch my breath at this rate."

I blew him a kiss and then took the backpack off, zipped it open, and dumped out the contents. Pop-Tarts, mini cereal boxes, an unopened package of Twizzlers, crackers, nuts, and the little plastic cups of mixed fruit tumbled onto the ground, along with what looked like oversized gym clothes.

Robby's eyebrow rose, and he grabbed the drawstring shorts that looked to be at least four sizes too large for Rosalyn. His lips twitched into a smile, and he slid them on. The shirt wasn't large enough for him to wear, but at least his privates weren't on display and distracting me anymore.

"Were those yours?" I waved at the faded gray shorts.

"They certainly weren't Rosalyn's." He took a seat next to me, digging through the array of snacks he snagged. He picked a pair of strawberry Pop-Tarts and devoured them in a few bites, downing it with one of the small fruit cups. "Aren't you going to eat?"

Although my stomach was growling up a storm, the snacks he had packed didn't light my appetite the way Robby did. I wanted some more of his blood, and some more of his carnal appetite. I licked my lips, meeting his gaze with a suggestive grin.

"No way. The last time, you almost didn't stop." He shook his head.

"I can't eat that food." I had a dark feeling that this hunger would eat away at my mind until it made me insane.

"We need to find somewhere to hole up for the night. I haven't slept more than an hour in nearly thirty hours now. And I expended most of my energy yesterday with you." He cocked his eyebrow at me. "On a reduced blood load, no less."

The least I could do was not drain him of the rest of his blood today after he rocked my world all over my house. "Fine. Then tell me about your wolf?" I crossed my arms, challenging him with something equally as uncomfortable as being a living donor.

He blinked as if he had no idea what I was talking about, and then the conversation we had before going to Rosalyn's surfaced and his eyes reflected understanding.

He packed the contents back in the bag, slung it over his shoulder, and took my hand. "Walk while I talk," he said, and we continued north, looking for a suitable cabin in the woods or something equally as remote and deserted close by.

"My wolf is the reason we are partners." He sighed and glanced at me. "He knew the minute we saw you that you were my true mate."

His words impacted me like a brick to the head. "I felt an immediate connection to you, but you never acknowledged it after that first meeting." I slowed and tried to pull my hand away, questioning everything I had learned about werewolves and true mates. They weren't supposed to be able to deny their mates, but Robby certainly denied me for the last fifteen years.

His brow creased as he searched my gaze. "Witches aren't supposed to feel the connection until marked."

"Well, I fucking felt it, and I thought you did, too, at the time. But then you backed off and I figured it was just a physical thing with me because I had never seen anyone as gorgeous as you in my life." I wiped my face and tried to pull my hand out of his again but he held fast. "You aren't supposed to be able to deny your true mate."

He blushed and a smile toyed on his lips for a brief second; then it soured with a bitter laugh. "I made the mistake of telling my father after he hauled me away from you. He did not approve of me mating with anyone other than a wolf and tainting the blood pool." His grip on my hand tightened with his frustration.

"My old man made damned sure I wouldn't act on my instincts, too. He was the one who made sure you were my partner and he explained what they did to partners who crossed the line." He took a deep breath. "So, I locked down my fucking wolf, and dedicated my life to a company that would rather kill their employees than see them happy. All because they believe there's a massive risk for disloyalty when you're in love with your partner."

I barked a laugh and met his pointed gaze. "There's a massive disloyalty to the company because they are a bunch of militant dicks who think fear is the right way to create obedience."

"There is no quitting the MDA, especially for a legacy. Only retirement or death."

"Or being locked up in a cage for the rest of your life."

"That's the same as death," he said, and I didn't disagree.

"You could have told me, you know," I said as we started to walk again.

"And what exactly would you have done?" He didn't look at me, and I could tell by the tightness of his jaw that he still held a world of bitterness inside him.

"I probably would have gotten myself killed," I muttered, remembering that connection I felt when our eyes met from across the room.

Robby gave my hand a squeeze. "Then I made the right call."

We fell into silence as we searched for a place to get some rest.

# WICKED HEART 12

TURNS OUT THE ONLY place we could find was a dilapidated shack at the back of a farm that had already been tilled for the next season. Once in the cramped space, Robby stripped and shoved the shorts into the backpack. He pushed me against the door and then stepped into the center of the small shack, shifting. Once in wolf form, he laid on the floor, leaving me room to curl up next to him, and he wrapped himself around me, radiating warmth in a way that nothing but an electric blanket could.

I used one of his paws as a pillow and he rested his massive head on my shoulder, sighing. His eyes slipped closed before mine did. I studied his wolf form. He was as black as night, with those mesmerizing blue eyes. And his fur was soft and silky against my skin. He was as gorgeous a wolf as he was in human form.

One eye opened and stared at me for a moment. I could almost hear the command of *Sleep!* resounding in my head. His eye closed, and I followed suit. Sleep was harder this time because the hunger pangs pulled at me, but I wasn't about to sink my teeth into a wolf. I had a little more self-respect than that.

I wondered whether the asshole who turned me had returned to the house. If he had, I hoped like hell MDA was still there and had dispatched him. But a sinking feeling in my stomach told me he was hunting me just as aggressively as MDA. And this time he didn't want to toy with me. No, I had the distinct feeling he wanted me to feel regret and pain.

I shivered and Robby's paws pulled me closer, as if he knew I had a dark thought that chilled me to the core. With Robby's heat, I finally was able to slip into darkness and let my exhausted body rest.

THE AIR SMELLED DIFFERENT. I covered my nose and curled tighter. A low growl filled the space and whatever warmth was seeping into my back shifted. My eyes snapped open. Robby stood over me, staring at the door. The stench of wet dogs surrounded us, buffered only by the rickety wood of the shack we had taken refuge in.

I climbed to my feet and secured the backpack on, blinking at the wedges of light filtering inside the shack. We had slept clean through the night. I put my hand on Robby's back, but his focus was still on the door and his lips were pulled back in a menacing snarl.

This space was not big enough to maneuver in if we had to fight, and my heart thrummed in my head like a fluttering hummingbird. I glanced at the walls surrounding us and then up to the ceiling, but there was nowhere to hide. I stepped forward, reaching for the door, but Robby shifted and grabbed my arm, shaking his head. He unzipped the backpack and retrieved his shorts, slipping them on.

"Stay in the shadows," he whispered in my ear.

"Bull—"

He kissed me hard. I guess it was his way of overriding my wishes. When he pulled back, his eyes were sharp and serious, and he physically moved me to the side.

He opened the door, squinting in the sun. The *pew pew* of a dart gun reached my ears just as Robby stumbled back. In the center of his chest was one of those industrial darts used to take down an elephant in the wild. He stumbled and then his gaze found mine, with his eyes wide and frantic. Then they closed, and I caught him before he fell.

Gently, I laid Robby on the ground and yanked the tranquilizer out of his chest, tossing it away as the burn of anger started in the center of my heart. My protective instincts flared, and I stood in the shadows, glaring at the open door.

"We know you're in there, Stone. We know what you are." Our boss's voice came through the partly opened door. "And we know the sun will kill you if you aren't properly covered."

They didn't know shit about me, and I reached for the door, ripping it off the hinges before I tossed it to the side of the shack. Sunshine flooded in, blanketing me with heat. My eyes blazed, and I stepped over Robby and out of the shack into the sun, proving that I was not what they thought I was. Although I was unsure where the source of all this chaotic power inside me came from, I was glad it broke every rule there was about vampires.

"The sun does not harm me." The fury and hunger riding my veins ignited my hands.

A few of my coworkers gasped.

I turned my palms toward the dozen members of MDA surrounding us, holding them out to the sides. Thankfully, the flames remained in my palms as I willed, instead of encompassing my entire form.

The *pew pew* of the air gun sounded again, and I reacted, catching the dart before it touched my skin. Now my fire flared, sending flames from every exposed surface of my skin. It melted the tranquilizer in my hand. I dropped the puddle of metal and boiling liquid at my feet.

I reined in the flame, fighting against the need to engulf the contingent surrounding me. The fire subsided, and I tapped into that mass of power and turned it on my ability to persuade, the same way I did with Rosalyn, harnessing it in my core.

I scanned the group, recognizing half a dozen members of Robby's pack all adorned with anti-compelling charms. If I couldn't compel them, I would have to kill them because there was no way I'd let them lock us up. But I really didn't want to do that to any members of Robby's pack, especially Robby's beta.

With a mighty mental shove, I projected my words. "I suggest you all holster your weapons."

They all holstered their weapons, looking just as shocked as I felt.

Damn. I can compel them even with their charms on. Holy crap, what exactly was I?

My heart thundered, and I breathed a sigh of relief. "Keep the weapons holstered," I added when Harrison reached for his again.

His weasel-like face scrunched in anger.

"Robby's *our* alpha," Johnson, Robby's beta, said, as if he had a claim on him. He stared at me with a crease between his narrowed eyes. "You haven't done anything to him, have you?" His voice carried an ugly accusation.

My gaze shot to him. We went way back, to the days of the academy. He was Robby's beta then, too, and always seemed to be hanging around. I cocked my head at him as more questions surfaced. "I am his mate."

"Bullshit," he said.

I pulled my shirt aside, showing them all Robby's mark, and Johnson's face fell.

He sniffed the air before shooting his gaze at Harrison. It seemed no one told the pack what was going on.

"Did you know?"

Johnson shook his head.

"Obviously you didn't know Robby marked me." I rolled my eyes. "What I'm asking is did you know he felt the way he did for all these years?" I glared at him.

"I've been his beta all my life. Who do you think talked him off the ledge every week?" he snapped.

"I don't know whether to thank you or kick your ass," I said, and he had the decency to lower his eyes. "Do you still have Robby's cowboy boots in your trunk?" Robby would need some shoes and clothing, and Johnson had borrowed Robby's extra pair of shoes more than once after shifting because he always seemed to forget to pack his. And he rarely returned anything. "And a backup bag of clothing?"

He nodded.

"Give them to me," I ordered.

Everyone watched as he pulled out boots and a bag and crossed, dropping them to my side. He stood, waiting for the next order like a blank page.

"Go. All of you except Harrison," I snapped the order, and yet again, they were compelled to follow. "And this never happened," I added before they could turn and trot off.

I kept my gaze on Harrison Littleton. Our boss. The one who locked up Manuel. Who would have locked me up in a cell and thrown away the key. He would understand just what I had become soon enough.

When everyone had gone far enough that their engines were a low whine on the wind, I focused on Harrison. "Put your weapons on the ground and come here." I pointed to the spot in front of me.

He dropped his gun and the knives on his belt on the ground, and started forward. Each motion was stilted, as though he tried to ignore my compelling spell. Harrison was a weasel of a man with a pinched face, a receding hairline, and beady eyes the color of filthy mud.

"You shouldn't be able to do this. What are you?" he asked as he came to a stop in front of me.

I smiled, revealing my fangs. "Do not move a muscle," I ordered, reveling in the power thrumming through my veins. "As to what I am? I'm a new breed of vampire, and I'm damned hungry."

His eyes didn't have a chance to fully widen before my teeth dug into his neck. Hot blood rolled over my tongue and down my throat, satiating the parched feeling accosting me. I actually felt my cells hydrating from the flow, and I pulled greedily at the punctures, draining Harrison of his life's blood a torrent at a time. All while Harrison remained still, as if he were a statue.

He made a pleading noise, as if he knew the end was near. It was enough to break the bloodlust that had overcome me. I did not want to be a killer of humans. I didn't want to be at the top of the most wanted list. I wanted them to back off, and killing Harrison would make that impossible.

I pulled my fangs from his skin and met his wide-eyed gaze as blood slid down his neck. I lifted my finger, willed my flame into existence, and then cauterized the wounds, stopping the flow of blood.

He winced and glared at me as if I had just sacrificed his first born.

"I'm not a complete monster." I blew the flame on my finger out. "But I am a new breed of nightmare. So, you would do well to stay the fuck out of my way while Robby and I hunt down the bastard who did this to me. Understand?"

"You are an abomination," Harrison hissed, his eyes slits of venom.

If looks could kill, I'd be dead ten times over.

I leaned closer, and he recoiled. "I could have easily killed you, but I *chose* not to. Remember that." I tapped his nose and stepped back, giving him some breathing room.

"You should be put down," Harrison said through clenched teeth.

Harrison would never give up the hunt. Not now that I had gotten the best of him. I should end him, make him disappear, but I was not the monster he thought I was. I needed to give him something more to think about. Something that could somehow benefit him. "Here is something you should consider before you just condemn me. Imagine the kind of damage I could do to the bastards who truly got off on hurting humans."

Just for a moment, I saw the spark of possibility fill his eyes, as if I just opened a door he hadn't even considered. But the minute he tried to move, that spark disappeared and the anger at being controlled returned.

My window had passed. Even though I had Johnson's clothing for Robby, I nodded toward Harrison's car. "Give me Robby's sweatpants and sweatshirt you have in your trunk." I put my hand out, waiting.

Harrison growled under his breath. "I don't know what the hell you are, but we will find out and take you down," he muttered as he marched to his trunk and pulled out clothing with Robby's name on them at my bidding. He slammed them into my hand.

"If you decide to continue hunting us, it will not end well for you. Now go, before I change my mind and slaughter you."

He did an about-face and marched to his car. I waited until he was out of sight before I reached down and collected the backpack and boots and returned to Robby's side.

Regret slid through me like a slippery snake. I really should have wiped away Harrison's memory, but I wanted our boss to know what he was up against if he decided to continue his hunt.

WICKED HEART 13

ROBBY SLOWLY CAME TO just after the sun dipped below the horizon. He moaned and grabbed his head. In our training as newbies, we had to be tranquilized to know the effects. The headache coming out of it was as hellish as a particularly nasty migraine.

I ran my hands through his hair and whispered, "Shh."

"What happened?" He opened an eye for a moment to look up at me, but even that motion made him turn a shade of green and he stilled, taking long, slow breaths like we had been taught.

I continued to run my fingers through his hair in a steady, methodical flow.

"Tranquilizer." I had enough time to replay the entire ordeal to the point I was probably more uncomfortable with what I was than Harrison had been. "Did you know I can compel agency members even when they are wearing their charms?"

This time both his eyes opened, and he stared up at me, forgetting that his head might split in two at any moment. His gaze moved around the shed as if he was really seeing where we were.

"We're not in a cell." It wasn't a question, and then his gaze jumped back to me.

"No. We're still in that god-awful shack." I gave him a soft smile, and he searched my eyes, which I was sure held every ounce of regret flowing through me.

"How?"

"I compelled them to sheathe their weapons, and I commanded the pack members to leave after I announced I was your mate." I bit my lower lip and nodded toward the boots, backpack, and sweats I procured in my standoff. "But I got you some clothing before they left, and they won't remember a thing."

His gaze moved slowly to the pile and back.

"And I decided Harrison was my human feed bag."

"You killed Harrison?"

I shook my head. "No, I stopped feeding before he was too far gone. But I'm sure he felt the full force of blood loss once his adrenaline faded. And I'm second-guessing my kindness where he's concerned." I took a deep breath. "Letting him go without wiping his memory of me might come back and bite us."

"You stopped?" Robby sat up with a wince and turned toward me. His cheeks paled, and he froze, sucking air through his teeth.

"Yes." I glanced down at my hands now folded in my lap. "He made a noise of protest and that yanked me out of my bloodlust." I picked at my nail. Although I had told Harrison that I chose not to kill him, that was not completely true. Had he not made the noise, I might have sucked him dry before sanity kicked in.

Robby reached out and cupped my cheek, tilting my head so I would look at him. "The key thing for you to remember is you stopped." He wiped his face, taking those long breaths to get himself under control from the effects of the tranquilizer.

I reached into the backpack, pulling out one of those little fruit cups and offering it to him.

"Not yet." He closed his eyes, keeping his head as still as possible.

I flashed back to my training experience with tranquilizers. I had thrown up everything, heaving until only a trace of stomach acid was left, so Robby either had an iron stomach or some serious self-control.

Thinking about the way he ravaged me back at the house, my bet was on serious self-control because that kind of passion said worlds about how much he kept his wolf in check. It had been truly explosive. I couldn't believe he suppressed his wolf for fifteen years.

His lips twitched into a smile. "You're slinging those pheromones again."

My cheeks heated, and I glanced at the open doorway. "We're a little exposed right now."

Although screwing around seemed like a good idea, anyone could walk in, and if I was preoccupied, we could be taken be by surprise. Which would be a disaster.

He glanced over his shoulder and a light laugh escaped. "I wish I could have seen their faces." The humorous light danced in his eyes despite him still being a bit peaked.

"Johnson was a bit thrown by me being your mate." Actually, he had looked downright flabbergasted when I said it. As if he almost didn't believe me. But I guess the mark on my shoulder along with something in my scent must have given him confirmation because his mouth closed pretty quickly.

"He shouldn't have been. He knew what happened. And he knew what my father's wishes were. He talked me off that ledge at least a thousand times over the years."

"So he said. I guess he was surprised you let your wolf win."

"I'm sure he was," Robby said. "No one underestimated my feelings more, except maybe you." He reached for the sweats and slipped them on, and then slid the boots on. "I think I can walk now without throwing up."

I stood and offered my hand, helping him to his feet, then strapped the backpack with food in it on my back. Robby slung the other pack over his shoulder and then picked up the fruit cup I had left on the ground. He opened it and downed the sugary syrup along with the sweet fruit. He tossed the empty container into a bucket that sat in the corner and then froze in place, closing his eyes. That slow, steady breathing resumed.

I didn't speak. Either he was going to win the battle with his stomach, or he was going to hurl. Nothing I said or did would help either way, so I remained silent and skirted around him to step outside.

One minute, I was breathing the night in and the next, I was slammed into the side of the shack. A hand squeezed my throat and the angriest green eyes I had ever seen stared back at me. With his grip still clamped on my neck, he spun me, so my back was pressed against him.

"Call off your dog," he snarled in my ear.

Robby, in wolf form, leapt out the door. His hard eyes glared at the man holding me.

When I didn't speak, he said to Robby, "Stand down. Or would you like to see me tear her head clean off?" His grip on my neck moved to under my jaw, and his nails dug into my flesh. "I made her. I can unmake her, too."

Robby froze in place as his growl slipped. Concern and aggravation crossed his gaze and then his teeth reappeared.

"She's mine." The man dragged me a step backward.

Robby's gaze went feral, and his snarl echoed off the wood of the shack. He took a step forward, keeping the distance between us steady.

The bastard's scent filled me, seeming familiar, yet I could not recall who the hell he was. I took another whiff and recognized death underneath the sweet glamour. "When you didn't pick up your phone, I knew something was amiss. Imagine my surprise when I found your house reduced to ashes. Then I heard the news reports."

He stepped backward again, dragging me with him.

Robby matched him step for step.

"Give me my memories," I commanded.

He laughed in my ear, his breath tickling me. "You cannot compel your master."

Damn it. "You are not my master." The thought of it left me physically ill.

"No? I was more than that before you stupidly pledged your allegiance to a fucking dog." His grip on my throat tightened.

Robby hated to be called a dog. He was an alpha wolf, not a measly dog. Fury filled his eyes as he stared at us.

"What are you?" I asked as the man dragged me another step away.

"You know what I am."

"A filthy vampire." I spat out the words.

"You didn't think I was filthy when I was in your bed," he said in such a teasing tone that it pulled a vicious growl from Robby.

I blinked and aggravation bloomed. I couldn't remember and I didn't know whether this bastard was baiting Robby, or whether he was telling the truth. How the hell could *I* have ever been romantically associated with a vampire? I shook my head. "I don't believe you."

His hand tightened even more on my jaw, limiting my ability to breathe. "Maybe I'll just erase *him* from your memory," he whispered in my ear. "Then it won't matter when I rip him to shreds."

I stiffened. That kind of venom only bled through when it was personal. My fire stirred, swirling inside me. *Protect my mate,* it whispered, as violently as a hurricane. I stared at Robby. He was a man I could never allow to be forgotten.

I screamed, letting the fire engulf me. It flared bright, and a yell sounded from behind me as the bastard's hands released me. I spun on my heel and growled at him as he patted his clothing down, putting out the flames I had set, his eyes wider than they had been in the bedroom the other night.

I gathered up the energy inside, intending to smite the bastard, and just before I hurled it toward the asshole, he disappeared into smoke.

Robby took off with a snarl.

"Robby, come back here!" I didn't yell as a plea. I yelled as a command, and Robby was back in seconds, growling at me. "I don't care what you think. Going after him is suicide. We don't have backup."

Robby transitioned back to his human form. "I don't care that we don't have backup," he snarled as he crossed the distance. He lifted my head to inspect my throat. He ran his fingers over a tender spot, and I winced.

"*I* will be the one doing the tearing apart." His conviction was total, and it was hard to argue with a naked werewolf.

WICKED HEART 14

ROBBY WALKED WITH PURPOSE, putting as much distance between us and that shack as possible. He didn't say much, which was good because I was turning over everything again and again in my head and banging against that wall between me and my memories like a bull in a cage.

"Why?" he finally said. His tone was one of hurt, and I wasn't sure where it was coming from.

"Why what?"

"Why would you sleep with a vampire?" He didn't even look over at me.

"Who said I did?" I snapped. I couldn't accept that I would have done it knowingly. Of course, his physique matched my personal preference. Good-looking, built, and a voice that sounded like honey. It was more a reflection of Robby than I cared to admit. The only variation was this was a blond, not a brunette. And the only thing out of character was he was a vampire. "Maybe he was just trying to get a rise out of you." My words sounded hollow even to my ears and the glare Robby sent chilled me to the core.

"That was personal, Sarah."

He was right. Everything about my encounters with that vampire echoed a personal connection. From the initial playfulness in my house to the fury in his eyes today. "Maybe I killed his mate," I mumbled, knowing in my gut that wasn't the case. But I still could not come to terms that I had any relationship with such a vile creature.

But if I had killed his mate, he would have just sucked me dry and left a dead husk on the bed for MDA to find. Instead, he bled me to the point of death and then turned me. That wasn't the action of vengeance, was it?

God. Why couldn't I break down this barrier in my mind?

"He would have slayed you himself if you had done that," Robby said, echoing my thoughts. He chewed on his lower lip. "Why the memory black out?" He glanced at me, looking at me with a scrutiny he hadn't before. He slowly shook his head. "Besides, if you had been sleeping with him, I would have smelled him on you."

I always showered first thing in the morning. I didn't know whether Robby would be that observant when we were just partners, despite his wolf's obsession with me. "Did you ever smell anyone else?" I prayed the answer was yes, but the longer he thought about the question, the more my heart dropped.

"Not that I can remember," he muttered and took a deep breath. He knew my reputation. He knew I bedded more than my fair share of men, just like he slept with dozens of women. We both had tried to ignore what was between us by finding solace elsewhere.

We walked in silence, both stewing over the situation. The gaps in my memory made it impossible for me to say either way. Frustration left me on the verge of catching fire, and I took a breath, calming the snaking heat inside me.

"You were a little more preoccupied over the last couple weeks," he said after a few minutes went by.

"When did that start?" If I could pinpoint the timing, maybe I could find the gaps in my memory and catalog them all, tracing them back to where I may have met that bastard.

He chewed on his lower lip and narrowed his eyes as he inspected his memories. "It was just the last three weeks. One day, you were fine and the next, everything made you jumpy. Before that, you were merely vague about what you did in the evenings when we had off, which wasn't all that unusual." He glanced at me. "I was vocal about my conquests. You weren't unless something embarrassing or funny happened, and then I wanted to duct-tape you."

I let out a small laugh. I did remember the flashes of annoyance on his face when I talked about my dates. "Up until a couple months ago, I was finishing up the escape tunnel. That's why I was vague. I didn't want to slip and get in trouble for building a contingency plan."

"You could have told me about that," he grumbled.

I met his gaze. "If I had, we'd be locked up right now." The seer would have pulled it out of him, and that would have been the end of our freedom and possibly our lives.

"Touché," he said with no emotion. "When you started acting off, I got worried. It wasn't like you to clam up when something was bothering you. Which is why I came over after the morning meeting yesterday. I knew something was going on. You were never out sick."

"I figured." I sighed. "Maybe we can match up our memories and that will help me figure out where my memory gaps started."

He slowed his pace as he stared at me. "You figure if you can pinpoint it, you can piece together what happened?"

I nodded. "I don't like being in the dark like this."

"And what if you find that you were willingly sleeping with that asshole?" The flare of anger radiated in his voice.

"Then I somehow missed that he was a vampire."

"And what if you didn't?"

I stopped walking. "I..." I closed my mouth because I couldn't say I would never sleep with a vampire. I had dug a hole in the ground under my house in the event I had made a mistake in my job and underestimated someone. I had an escape route for just that reason. Although I would like to think I would not, with the gaps in my memories, I couldn't be sure. "Why would he wipe my memories if that was the case?"

"Because what he did was horrific. He slit your throat and coated your walls and floor with your blood. You had to have struggled to have your blood fly that far, and he wanted to spare you that memory." He glanced away. "It's what I would have done for someone I cared about. Especially if I was turning them to claim them for myself." He slid his glance back to me.

I shivered at the thought and wrapped my arms around my midsection. "Then why taunt me? Why play with my emotions the way he did on those phone calls?"

"Testing your memories?" he said, but even he sounded like he was reaching.

"I'd much rather think he turned me to control me and not because we were lovers." Even saying the words made my stomach clench.

I started to walk again, but Robby grabbed my arm, stopping me.

"What if..." He searched my gaze.

Insecurity did not look good on Robby, and right now there was a large gap in my memory that was playing with his alpha status, bringing forth doubts a mile wide. I could see it in his eyes and in the way his grip around my arm tightened. He had given in to everything he felt for me, and it wasn't just lust between us.

Could I have something that matched this intensity? Something that made me not wish it was Robby holding me?

That thought scared me as much as it did Robby.

I stepped closer, placing my palms on his chest. We both had slept with countless others and none of them captured our attentions for more than a few months at best. Rosalyn was one of his serious diversions. *Could this vampire have been one for me?* Even if he had been, that was all he ever would be—a diversion from Robby.

I tiptoed and planted a soft kiss. "Even if I did sleep with him, he was only a distraction, like everyone before. With the fire you created in me even before we admitted it to each other, no one could replicate that."

His gaze softened, morphing into one full of carnal desire, and he glanced around us at the empty road cutting through the thick forest on either side. We hadn't hidden our path like before and perhaps that was my arrogance or his mind being elsewhere. Now he did move us into the thick woods, but he had a purpose. His head swung from side to side, looking for an opportunity.

My heart leapt into my throat. *What if the vampire had followed us?* We were out in the open. Unprotected. I slowed, pulling against Robby's drag as my gaze darted all around us. It felt like a thousand eyes watching.

"Let's find a hotel," I said when I couldn't shake the feeling of being watched or the certainty that if Robby made love to me out in the open, one of us would not see the sunrise. "I feel too...exposed out here."

He slowed to a stop. "Fine. If we are going out into public again, I need a real meal."

I nodded my agreement. He needed it. Especially if he followed through on that look shining in his eyes. Food, sex, sleep. Sounded like a plan to me.

15

WICKED HEART 15

WELL, AS THE SAYING goes, even the best laid plans can go to hell in an instant. They weren't kidding.

We sat in the restaurant across from a little roadside motel, waiting for our food. It was late enough to be close to closing time, so the place was nearly empty. I decided on just a coffee, hoping to be able to nurse it enough that it didn't turn my stomach. Robby chose a hungry man's breakfast, which was what we were waiting for when the door chimed.

I glanced outside at the eighteen-wheeler in the parking lot. I assumed that was who came in, but a square column blocked our view of the entry. This section was the only one that was open in the restaurant.

A sting bit the side of my neck, and Robby's eyes widened. He stood and a dart stuck out of his chest a moment later. I started to turn, but then a curtain of black fell across my vision.

<hr>

MOVEMENT PULLED ME OUT of the dark. I shook my head and was rewarded with the type of headache that only a tranquilizer could inflict. I went to lift my hand to move my hair out of my face, but neither of my hands would move. I flipped my hair behind me, gritting my teeth against the slow flop of my stomach. Lights flooded the space, illuminating the inside of a large container.

The damned eighteen-wheeler.

I blinked the haze out of my eyes and looked directly at Harrison Littleton's smug smile. My gaze traveled over the crew in the trailer and landed on Robby, still out cold on the ground. They put him in a silver collar and silver shackles. I could see the blackened skin of his wrists from where I sat. Thankfully, he was still unconscious, because that was going to hurt like a bitch when he woke, even more than a tranquilizer headache.

I also noted that not one of Robby's pack was present in the back of the container. Looking at the crew, I didn't think any werewolf was in attendance. If there had been, they would have never let Harrison collar Robby with silver.

"You bastard," I growled and looked at Harrison. "Unlock him," I commanded, and my voice resounded back at me. That was when I realized I was truly screwed.

"You cannot compel us through this soundproof glass," he said into an intercom and tapped on the glass wall in front of me.

I smiled, revealing my fangs. "You think you can lock me up?" I closed my eyes and let the fury fill me. The injustice of hurting Robby in the way they had sent me to the edge of reason.

"You broke protocol. You broke the rules, and he aided you. You are no better than the monsters we hunt." Harrison's voice blasted through the room.

"I should have killed you," I growled, letting the inferno inside me grow. My hands had already engulfed in flames.

"If you attempt to escape, I will see to it that he is doused in silver." He pointed at Robby. "If you are a good girl, I will let him live."

"You will let him free?" I asked as my gaze traveled between Robby and Harrison.

He laughed and shook his head. "No. He's going to be locked up indefinitely, just like you. But he will be alive."

I glared at him. The silver option was reserved for the most heinous of werewolf crimes. There were packs that outlawed that punishment because it was an inhumane death, but it seemed MDA wasn't aligned to werewolf law, and they certainly weren't opposed to blackmail. My stomach knotted.

"I swear, if you harm him any more than you have already, I will tear you apart piece by piece and I will relish your screams. You will be begging me to die and when you are without arms and without legs and without eyes, I will fucking turn you and let you live forever as a fucking freak."

He glanced at the person next to him, who seemed to be reading my lips and conveying what I was saying to him. "I'll compel you to suck my dick." He smiled, pleased with himself.

"You cannot compel your master. And who says I'll let you keep your junk?" I tilted my head and narrowed my eyes.

His smile faded, and he shifted his weight.

"To show me you will follow through on your end of the bargain, take him out of the silver cuffs and collar, and put him into the charmed cuffs, please."

Harrison looked at his translator and then over at Robby. He nodded and mouthed the order.

I watched and waited while they removed the silver. I winced at the blackened skin under the cuffs, and nearly cried when I saw the burns from the collar. They switched out the tether that kept him attached to the side of the truck and clasped the wrist restraints to it.

"You really are a bastard." I glared at Harrison.

"And you really care about your partner," he said.

I wanted to wipe that smug smile off his face. I wouldn't have let them do that to Robby, even if we hadn't crossed the line and landed in bed and mated. I would have walked through the fires of hell for him, and I hated that Harrison knew that.

He pointed a finger at me, and his eyes blazed. "This is why we don't condone what you two have done," he yelled. "It makes you vulnerable."

"And you don't think platonic partners who have worked together as long as we have aren't subject to the same vulnerabilities?" He was a fool if he didn't think partners would take a bullet for each other, regardless of their gender.

"They put MDA first. Love complicates that."

"Bullshit!" I struggled against my bonds and a little voice inside my head told me I could melt it away. I could melt this entire truck into oblivion. But that would include Robby, and I wasn't going to toast the good with the bad.

I hung my head in defeat.

"You were such a cocky bitch," he said low into the microphone. "The little witch who could pull whatever she needed from the ether. Well, now you're under my control for the rest of your miserable life."

I gripped the arms of the chair I was chained to, wishing there was a viable way out of this that didn't end with Robby dead.

The truck lurched to the right as if it had been sideswiped, and then tires squealed. Panic replaced the calm look on everyone's face, and they grabbed for supports. I was chained in a chair that was drilled into the floor surrounded by soundproof plexiglass. I wasn't going anywhere.

The chair jerked to the side and people flew into the wall Robby was chained to. His body pressed against the panel. Then the sound ended and the canister we were in tumbled like a child's toy. The chains held Robby relatively in place, the same way the chair I was chained to kept me unharmed. Blood splattered on the plexiglass when someone was hurled into it. But it didn't give.

Then the side panels of the truck started to rip off in random strips. My heart lurched. One minute, Robby was in the truck and the next, he wasn't.

"No!" I screamed as the truck skidded to a halt on its side. I let myself go and I blasted the chair and the plexiglass walls surrounding me, eviscerating both. I didn't even bother looking to see whether anyone in the truck had survived the crash. I fell to the side panel, landing on my feet, and bolted toward the back doors that hung open uselessly, hurdling over bodies as I went.

I found Robby close to a hundred yards away from where the truck came to a stop. My chest squeezed at the sight of him, bruised and broken to an almost unrecognizable mess.

"No!" I bellowed into the night. The mark on my shoulder ached as if it mourned the loss of my mate as much as I did. I grabbed the cuffs around each wrist and ripped them apart with my bare hands, tossing them aside. Anger and despair mixed in my blood, creating a need to wipe out the world around me. But that wouldn't bring him back.

I glanced at my unmarred wrists and then at Robby's slack mouth. *I could bring him back.* But I knew he would never forgive me if I made him into a monster. With a heart as crushed as his body, I straightened him out, setting bones that weren't aligned. I wiped the hair off his brow and kissed his forehead and each cheek, one just turning the gray of death and the other a mass of crushed bone and ripped skin. I pressed my lips to his cold ones, sobbing.

My tears fell on his face and his chest when I pressed my ear to his heart. Nothing sounded inside him. I held my sobs, held my breath to see whether there was life in him. But there was none. My mark already knew he was lost to me, but it took until that moment for my mind to catch up.

My heart shattered in my chest. Ugly sobs echoed on the rocks around me. Everything I loved had just been destroyed in an instant by MDA. I pressed my lips to his again as tears dropped unchecked from my eyes, bathing his slack face.

"I'm so sorry, Robby. I'm so, so sorry," I kept repeating, crying in that ugly way that loss brings.

My only consolation was that Robby hadn't felt death claim him. He was still unconscious when the panel gave and when the truck crushed him as it flipped over.

A throat clearing in the distance stopped me mid-sob. I turned toward the truck. Vengeance reared her merciless head as my gaze landed on the reason for my mate's death. A lone man stood, holding a blubbering Harrison by his hair.

I rose up to my feet slowly. The bastard who turned me held the man who would have caged and enslaved me. Oh, this was a trifecta of revenge waiting to be delivered. And I was primed to unleash hell.

I took a cautious step toward them, acutely aware of the vicious snake coiled up inside me. My hands engulfed in flame despite my trying to rein in the chaos pummeling my every muscle.

"A peace offering." The vampire pushed Harrison toward me.

I narrowed my eyes at him. "You orchestrated this," I snarled, waving at the truck.

His lips twitched into a smile, and he shrugged. It wasn't a denial, and my wrath ratcheted up a notch.

"You are just as responsible for his death as Harrison is." I pointed behind me toward Robby's still form, shaking with the rawness of his loss.

"You can take your anger out on me later. For now, he is my peace offering. The rest are dead, but he is still breathing, and I believe you want to rectify that. Do you not?" He cocked an eyebrow at me.

Oh, I did. I wanted him to suffer by my hand. I slunk forward like a cat on the prowl, wishing I had claws to match this unwieldy fury. "I told you not to hunt us," I growled, sounding more feral than Robby ever had. I moved in front of him, baring my fangs. I tore at his throat, drinking, but then I pulled away, sealing the cuts before Harrison bled out or lost consciousness.

A vampire's death was too easy.

He stared at me with horror painted on his face, shaking as if it were below zero out here on this deserted highway.

I realized my threat I issued in the truck must be flitting through his mind right now. But that wasn't nearly enough. Not with Robby dead from being attached to that truck panel and this asshole was responsible for where Robby had been inside the truck.

My shoulder tingled with approval. My mark demanded retribution just as clearly as my heart. "You think I'm going to dismember you and turn you into a vampire." I chuckled at him and shook my head. "That doesn't seem like a just punishment." I tapped my lips with my finger, staring at the inside of the truck as my mind filtered through all his vile threats. "You threatened to douse Robby with silver." I glared at Harrison and straightened, moving a step back. My lips stretched into a savage smile.

The acrid stench of urine filled the air, and a wet spot spread over the front of Harrison's pants. He understood the venom in my eyes. He understood where I was going with this enough for terror to wash him almost ashen. And I delighted in the smell of fear radiating from him. It was more potent than blood.

"And since I'm the cocky bitch who can pull what I need from thin air..." I snapped my fingers and willed a vat of boiling silver to spill over Harrison.

I thought the smell of piss was bad, but human skin being boiled was worse. Harrison didn't scream long, but it was enough to satisfy the vengeance burning my veins. I waved and the silver vat disappeared. Harrison was now just a dead lump under a layer of boiling silver on the asphalt.

But he wasn't the only one who I needed to dole out justice to. My glare moved from him to the being who had presented Harrison as a peace offering. Peace was the last thing on my mind right now.

The vampire who turned me looked a little green as he stared at the dead man. The fact he didn't have the stomach for something so vile nearly made me laugh. This was the asshole who coated my walls with *my* blood.

I willed a blade into my hand. The glint of metal brought his gaze to mine. "I don't just want to drag your ass into the sun anymore. Now I want to cut out your fucking heart.”

“You already did.” He opened his arms wide. “Might as well take the shot with a knife, too. I doubt it would hurt any less.”

His tired voice accompanying the words hit like a lightning bolt, making me pause. He didn’t even step away in defense, like any sane being would do when facing down their death.

“What the fuck are you talking about?”

He moved fast and before I could stick him with the blade, he torqued my wrist, sending the knife clattering on the pavement. He slammed me into the truck, pressing his body against mine as he ensnared both wrists in his hands and stretched my arms out to the sides. He was strong, perhaps stronger than I was physically, but it was the sadness in his eyes that made me not ignite on the spot and burn him to a crisp with the fire raging in my veins.

“Get the hell away from me,” I screamed, trying to yank my wrists from his grip.

He leaned against me with his full weight. The feeling of it suggested something sexual, even though his lips pressed into a thin line. There was no mirth in his expression. Just anger and deep hurt, as if I had killed his best friend.

“You are infuriating.” He slammed my wrists again to make his point. “I am your master. You *will* do as I say.”

“Bullshit! No one owns me. Not you. Not Robby. Not MDA. No one!” I growled, surprised by my outburst. Usually, masters could command their children. But I was not the least bit compelled by this vampire.

He slowly shook his head as if he were waging a war inside himself. "Fuck it," he muttered, and then his lips crushed mine. "Remember everything," he whispered against them.

I gasped, and his tongue entered my mouth, exploring as though he knew exactly how I liked to be kissed. His tongue tangled with mine as the barrier in my mind blew to pieces in a blinding flash that flooded me with memories.

Cassius Chase. His name is Cassius Chase.

Months ago. I met him at Hawks Bar. Months. Fucking months. I've known him for more than six months.

My knees went weak, and Cassius held me in place, deepening the kiss and pressing his hard form against me.

Cassius sat in the corner of the bar, minding his own business and looking tragic, as though his entire world had been shattered. Seeing him with that deep frown as he studied his drink had tugged on my heart in a way that only Robby could.

My coworkers had left, and I dreaded another night digging my escape route, so I lingered, nursing my drink. He hadn't moved from his spot, and he hadn't looked around the bar, so when I finished my drink, I moved to the seat next to him.

"Why do you look so sad?" I asked, a little braver with the vodka warming my blood. The minute he turned his seafoam-green eyes in my direction, my mind stalled. Bam. It was as if he put a spell on me. If he asked me to sleep with him, I would be hard-pressed to say no.

His lips twitched into a soft smile. The kind you just wanted to kiss. "Who said I was sad?"

That deep voice toyed with me, striking strings inside that made me want to do dirty things to him. Curiously, it was the same playful tone that Robby had used on me a time or two after some long stakeouts where we were punch-drunk tired and it always lit my fire. But Robby never followed through on the promise of that tone. Lord, this guy better follow through, because that tone had the same effect on me.

I blinked, trying to think of a comeback, but I was too lost in my own dirty thoughts to come up with something appropriate.

He chuckled softly. "Perhaps I was just deep in contemplation."

"About what?"

"Life in general. What lies beyond." His eyes flashed to my lips before glancing behind me and then back at my face.

"Deep thoughts for a weeknight." I glanced over my shoulder at another group leaving the bar and then back at the mysterious stranger.

He nodded and waved the bartender over. "Another whiskey for me and..." He looked at me expectantly.

"Screwdriver," I said.

"And a screwdriver for the lady, please." He relayed our order, and a few minutes later, drinks were put on the wood counter.

I took a sip and went to ask him what he did for a living when the band started up in the lounge.

He closed his eyes, as if it were the most annoying noise on earth. Truthfully, it wasn't my deal either. I was usually home by this time of night. "Feel like taking a stroll?" I pointed toward the door.

He leaned closer. "You sure? I could be a serial killer."

He smelled like a masculine mix of hickory and musk. Sexy and forbidden, and his words chilled me. I leaned back enough to look him in the eye. "I lock up serial killers." I smiled and opened my jacket, showing him my agency badge.

He laughed as if it were the funniest thing he had heard all day. "Well then, my fierce little lady, you can protect me out there." He slipped from the seat, offering me his arm.

Sliding my hand through his elbow felt weirdly right and my nerves bloomed. But the moment we stepped out of the bar, the quiet of the night descended and my momentary jitters faded away.

"Where would you like to walk?"

"We could take a stroll through the park." I waved toward the park uptown. "Or we could go where there's a lot of people." I tested him. If he said park, I would surmise he had nefarious intent, even though I was the one who invited him on this stroll.

He glanced at his watch. "There's always people at the skating rink," he said, offering a different option that was populated.

"Eh. The music there is just as loud. I need a little calm."

He smiled down at me. "Calm is good. I know this little coffee shop a few blocks down that's open twenty-four hours. Feel like a coffee?"

I turned my head to the side, breaking the kiss and breaking whatever spell he seemed to have on me. He still held my hands flush against the truck. "How were *you* in a bar and none of my coworkers picked up on it?"

He tilted his head and cocked an eyebrow. "I had a magic sachet that I carried to mask my scent."

Which meant he had access to a witch or mage of some kind. I wondered whether that was in my memories. Memories that went back six months, not a month like Robby thought. I closed my eyes, trying to block it all out. "You are still responsible for Robby's death."

His lips thinned. "If I hadn't intervened, you would have been locked away, where I could not reach you."

I stared into his stormy eyes. There was anger and something deeper reflecting in his endless green eyes. But my heart was still morning the loss of my true mate and my shoulder throbbed, demanding retribution. "Did Robby ever have a chance?"

Cassius's eyes flashed, giving me a glimpse of twisted fury before his face smoothed over and he shook his head. "I would have eventually killed him for touching what was mine." His gaze lowered to my chest with such a possessive fervor that my fire flared.

No one owned me. *No one.* I slammed my knee into his balls with all my strength and shoved him away from me, ignoring my fire's demand to destroy him. I bolted down the pavement, past Robby, past the debris of the accident, putting as much distance between Cassius and me as I could.

"You know where to find me," Cassius yelled with a strained voice. "I'll be waiting."

He'd be waiting a hell of a long time, if I had any say.

But no matter how fast I ran, I couldn't outrun the onslaught of memories. Flashes of our history accosted me with every step, squeezing my chest tighter until I couldn't draw a full breath.

WICKED HEART 16

THE SUN HADN'T RISEN yet, but a spitting rain had started and that slowed me down. I had sobbed for most of my wild sprint and now that the sky had noticeably lightened, I needed to find a hotel. If MDA came and arrested me at this point, I wouldn't care.

The magnitude of memories kept hitting me, and I couldn't deal with them. Not with Robby dead and my heart shattered from more than one man.

I took the next exit ramp and found a small-town motel. When I walked into the lobby, the desk clerk straightened. I crossed. "I need the room on the far corner."

He nodded and went to the computer.

"Do you have a credit card?" He smiled at me, as if seeing a strange woman dripping water on his lobby floor was normal.

I almost got snarky and asked whether I looked like I had a credit card. But instead, I tapped into my new vampiric power. "Give me the key, and then you will forget you ever saw me. The only thing you know is that room is out of order, so there is no need for housekeeping or renting it to anyone else. Understand?"

His face went slack. "Yes, ma'am." He pulled the room key from the pegs with a nod. It was as if he were looking right through me when he handed it to me.

I left the office and went to the room, locking the door behind me before I closed the curtains and fell face-first on the bed.

Now that I wasn't moving, the memories swarmed, weighing down on me.

Conversations. Laughter. Sex. All of it overwhelmed me.

Cassius was more than just a fling, too. That burned more than the sun, because Robby's fears were warranted. I was truly in love with Cassius. But I hadn't broached the subject with anyone at work. I hadn't even told Robby about him. I kept him close to the vest and avoided all the normal spots that the crew at MDA frequented. I did not want that bubble to bust wide open and leave me devastated.

Oh. But it still had. And that event coincided with the same timeframe Robby mentioned. That was when I found out exactly what Cassius was.

The memory overloaded me. I scrunched my eyes closed against it, but it still seeped through.

I had gotten off early and wanted to surprise Cassius. I rarely had this type of time free, and I didn't want to wait until dinner, so I stopped by his house. I went to knock, but I really wanted to surprise him, so I tried the front door. If it had been locked, then I would have wished for a key. But the door swung open.

I would have to talk to him about his lack of security. He shouldn't be leaving his door open like that in the city. There were too many nefarious characters around to be so lax.

Once I was inside, the fact that all the drapes were drawn struck me as odd. I crossed the entry and stepped into the hallway that led to his bedroom. Noises were coming from within the dark room and my heart jumped in my chest.

Either he was working out, or... My mind wouldn't let me finish that thought. We had never discussed being exclusive. I had just assumed. At that moment, I almost turned around and left, but curiosity got the best of me. I pushed the door wide.

I froze. He was not working out.

Cassius was riding a bound woman whose glassy eyes stared at the ceiling. He had his face buried in the crook of her neck, as if he were giving her the mother of all hickeys and groaning while doing so.

I gasped and he sat up, turning toward the door. Blood dripped from fangs coming out of his mouth, and his eyes widened when he saw me. The woman below him did not move and the wound in her neck barely dribbled.

That was when I recognized death and what the man I thought I loved truly was. My heart dropped, and my mind screamed for me to run.

"I can explain," he said, but I was already sprinting toward the door.

I could deal with the kink if that was all it was. But he was a fucking vampire. And the signature of bound, sexed-up, and drained was what we had been hunting for months at work. That victim would likely be found in a dumpster tomorrow, miles from this house.

How the hell had I missed that?

How could he have been at that bar without any of the wolves from MDA knowing it? God damn it—that stupid sachet he carried.

How fucking stupid could I get?

I was so preoccupied with my thoughts that I didn't even feel Cassius pass me, but he had. Either that, or he had the ability to be in more places than one, which was frightening as hell.

Either way, Cassius blocked my exit. His teeth were still on full display, but he had been aware enough to pull on some sweats. But they still tented with his unquenched desire. He was lucky he didn't try to stop me fully naked. That would not have gone well for him.

"Please, Sarah. Don't go."

His plea struck me like a lightning bolt, and I ground my teeth, ignoring the compel he was trying to lay on me thanks to the anti-compelling medallion still around my neck. A barrel of feelings accosted me. Betrayal and confusion clouded my mind, but underneath that, my heart felt as though someone had stuck a blade clean through it.

"Get the fuck out of my way, you cheating bastard." I surprised myself with what tumbled out of my mouth. It wasn't that he was a vampire, but that he was having sex with that woman while he drained her of blood. Hell, she was long dead based on the lack of blood coming from her severed artery. That sickened me.

"I..." He closed his eyes and wiped his face. "I can't just kill," he said. "I want to make sure they feel pleasure when they die."

"You are a sick fuck." My heart exploded into a million tiny pieces that I had no hope of ever repairing.

"Would you rather I tear their throats out and have their last moments be of horror and fear?" He crossed his arms over his chest as if killing them wasn't a choice and I should forgive him for his transgressions because he thought his rationale was rational.

"I would rather you not fuck anyone else." Really, that's where your head is at? I balked at my own focus. "Actually, I would rather you not KILL anyone," I amended my statement, refocusing on the right priority of the moment.

"That is not possible. I need to feed at least once a week. Otherwise, I might attack you in a state of blood lust."

"Oh. So, you're fucking other women for me?"

His face scrunched in frustration. "No. It's part of my feeding ritual."

"What am I to you? Just a meal that you've been romancing?"

He met my gaze. "You are everything to me."

The soft way he said the words made me step back. My heart squeezed in an entirely *inappropriate manner. This was a killer standing before me. A killer we were hunting. One I should put down. But my heart was too wrapped up in him to end him.*

"I can't do this. Not with everything so fresh." I splayed my fingers out, palms toward him. "So, please move."

He hung his head and opened the door, letting me leave. He didn't even ask me whether I would be the one hunting him down.

That woman's body was found the next day.

How many women could I have saved? It was the same mantra that rang through my head every day since that night. And every time, it chilled me to the bone. That coincided with when I started acting squirrelly like Robby mentioned.

He noticed my fidgeting. He noticed my unease, but never said a word. Robby's loss hit me again, and I sobbed in the bed, unable to stop the flow of tears. Had I been honest with him the night I found out about Cassius, we wouldn't be in this horrifying situation. He would be alive, and I wouldn't be this hunted monster with a thirst for blood.

WICKED HEART 17

I TOSSED AND TURNED, and my shoulder tingled ruthlessly, as if Robby were calling for me from the great beyond. I finally fell into the black around noon and still the memories accosted me. I had six months of memories to scour and the only one I did not want to see was the night I was turned.

Although my conscious hadn't allowed me a glimpse of that night, my subconscious put it all on its full and gory display in a dream.

That particular night, I had gone home after drinks with the crew. I had more than my fair share, and Johnson drove me home. Robby hadn't gone out with us. He had stayed at the office to look at some earlier cases. We hadn't had another dead dumpster body in almost three weeks.

I didn't know whether Cassius was feeding and dumping elsewhere or what he was doing. But I had not taken one call from his unknown caller ID since that fateful night, and I missed him despite what he was.

I stumbled up to the bedroom in the dark and the minute I stepped into my room, I knew something was different. My sitting chair faced the window, and that window was cracked. I didn't remember opening it.

Then the chair slowly swiveled around, and Cassius stared out from the shadows. He tilted his head and his eyes blazed red. He hadn't been hiding the bodies. He had not eaten.

His hands gripped the arms of the chair as he stared at me. He took a deep inhale and smiled. "I always did love the way you smelled."

His voice slurred just enough for me to get the idea Cassius was just as drunk as I was. And for a vampire, that was quite the feat.

My hand fell to the belt that held my knives, and he stiffened until I unlatched it and they fell to the floor.

He was on me in an instant, his lips ravaging mine as though I were his life blood. His hands tore at my clothing; seams ripped and cloth fell, and he kissed my throat, my breasts, my stomach, and then he knelt before me and licked my clit. When he put my leg over his shoulder, I stiffened, thinking about the bite marks on his victims. But all he did was kiss the tender flesh before focusing back on my core, creating a need inside me that surpassed my wariness of what he was.

I ran my hands through his silky hair, moaning my pleasure to the dark surrounding me. He brought me to heights I never had reached before and then, when he was damn good and ready, he deposited me on my bed, on my hands and knees, and situated himself behind me.

The minute he plunged into me, my back arched. The bed didn't feel right under my palms, but his long, hard punishing strokes kept my attention on him. He pulled me up, so my back rested against his chest, and fondled me as he continued to slam his hips to my ass. I lost track of how many orgasms I had as he rode me. His kisses on my neck and shoulder were so soft that the dichotomy of his punishing thrusts and his gentle kisses turned the heat up even more.

"Sarah," he moaned, embracing me tight enough to trap my arms to my side. "Oh, my sweet Sarah. I love you and you will be mine forever," he whispered in my ear.

"Cass," I moaned and tilted my head back onto his shoulder, enjoying this punishment. But in my heart, I knew this was the end of it. I couldn't condone letting him kill innocents. So, I was going to enjoy this last hurrah with him before I did what was right.

"You will not remember me," he commanded just as my orgasm exploded through my body. He raked a blade across my throat.

My heart was already racing and the jet of blood that exploded out of my severed artery covered the wall across from the bed. I tried to turn in his grip and all I did was paint the side wall and window with my blood.

Cassius held onto me, riding me through my death, moaning my name as his release exploded inside me. When my vision faded, I felt something press to my lips. Something warm slid down my tongue into my ruined throat, burning its way to my stomach.

Then nothing but blackness surrounded me, and an all-consuming heat burned, as if I had been dropped into the fires of hell.

I sat up with a scream coming out of my throat. My hands flew to where Cassius had sliced me, but there was nothing. I stood and ran to the bathroom, vomiting what little was in my stomach and then just rested my head on the cold porcelain as tears threatened again. I wasn't sure how much of that dream was fact and how much was my brain being squirrelly. But it certainly fell into Cassius's modus operandi of pleasuring while he killed. Except he didn't drink my blood. Instead, he turned me so he could have a subservient companion for the rest of his days.

Bastard.

I flushed the toilet and walked on rubbery legs into the bedroom. Cold air filtered in from the open door, and I drew up short at the large figure backlit by the sun. My hands immediately ignited and then the figure closed the door behind him.

"Sarah?"

I fell back against the bathroom door at the sound of that voice, and my hands squeezed shut, dousing the flame. My heart thundered and stuttered at the same time. I blinked out the sunspots from my eyes, but I still didn't believe what I was seeing.

He stepped closer, and I rubbed my eyes and then pinched my arm because this could not be. But his soulful blue eyes said differently.

"Robby?" I asked. *He had been dead.* I checked his heart, his pulse, everything. And his bones were...crushed.

How was he alive? Could I trust this, or was it just another heartbreaking dream?

His lips tilted into his signature smile, and my legs gave out. I crumpled to the ground, still staring at him.

He moved swiftly across the room to my side. "Are you hurt?" He frantically checked my arms and then searched my eyes. "I was so worried when I saw what was left of that mess on the highway. And I could smell that bastard among the dead. That's when I caught your scent and followed you here."

I lifted my hand to his cheek. Solid, warm skin met my palm. "You're alive," I whispered, and the tear faucet turned on. I threw myself into his arms, sobbing.

He held me tight and then pulled me back where he could see me. "What happened?"

I laughed at such a high pitch he winced. "We were ambushed by MDA at that restaurant. They were taking us to home base to lock me up and that asshole Harrison threatened to douse you in silver if I didn't behave." I picked up his wrist and turned it this way and that, and then hooked my finger under his chin, tilting it up. There were no signs of the silver burns left on him. My stomach dropped.

Had Cassius done this?

I had woken without a scratch. But Robby's eyes were still blue and not the red of a hungry vampire.

Tears threatened again. "He had you bound in silver cuffs." I traced his unmarked skin. "And a silver collar."

Robby glanced down at his wrists and then back at me. "I don't have any silver burns. Maybe you were mistaken." The way he looked at me was as if I had been hallucinating.

I shook my head. "No. I am not mistaken, and it gets worse. He did switch out to steel when I told him I would behave. And you were chained to one of the truck wall panels." I wiped the tears that had leaked out and created hot paths on my face. "There was an accident. The truck was pulled apart and the panel you were on let go. I don't know if it was the truck itself that crushed you, or if hitting the road with such force did it, but Robby, you were broken. When I say broken, I mean half of you was almost unrecognizably crushed. I tried to straighten you out and align your bones, but it wasn't enough. You weren't breathing and you were already cold when I found you. No pulse, nothing." I hitched in a breath, trying not to relive the emotions, but they were there, burning just below the surface. "You were dead, and I cried over you for a good ten minutes before he showed up."

He glanced down at my hands and turned them up. "You didn't feed me your blood, did you?"

His voice had the chill I expected with that question.

I shook my head. "No." I let out a near hysterical laugh. "I did think about it, though, but you would have never forgiven me."

He nodded. "You're right. I wouldn't have."

I sniffled. "The only thing I did was cry on you."
I wiped my nose on my sleeve. "You could have
bathed in the number of tears I cried on you. And
last I knew, tears don't bring back the dead."

Robby jerked back and looked at his hands
and then at me. "I remember warm rain hitting
me and fanning out in prisms of light, heating me
from the inside out. It was like walking through
heaven with God's grace at my side and his light
seeping into every last cell. And then I opened my
eyes to the sun and the area was a god-awful
mess of death, with police crawling all over the
accident scene." His brow creased, and he studied
me. His forehead smoothed out and he started to
laugh. "Oh my God. It makes perfect sense."

I sniffled and scrunched my forehead. "Are you
going to clue me in on what makes perfect sense?"

"You. It makes perfect sense. You've got to be
a phoenix. That's the only species whose tears
can bring back the dead." An eyebrow cocked.
"The only other explanation is a necromancer,
and I've seen you kill plants on a weekly basis.
You aren't a necromancer." He grinned. "A
phoenix explains so damn much."

"What does it explain?" I argued. We learned
about phoenixes in training, but they didn't
spend very much time on them because
phoenixes hadn't been recorded anywhere since
the thirteenth century. Just like the unicorn and
Pegasus, they were extinct.

"The fact that you spontaneously break out in
flame when your emotions are high. The fact you
are a vampire, but you can walk in the sun
without turning to ash. The fact you can stop

feeding. Your bloodlust does not control you because you contain light to the vampire's dark."

Although his descriptions rang true, I still didn't buy it. "There hasn't been a sighting of a phoenix in centuries," I balked.

"Well, I think I'm looking at one right now."

He was convinced. He had studied the extinct species much more intently than I had, so he was probably right. Still, I wasn't convinced. "Where the hell would it have come from? Neither my mother nor father had any abilities. My magic seemed like an anomaly to them and everyone else in the family. There is no family history to support this. Besides, my parents died in a car crash, and they didn't magically resurrect from the dead."

"Look, it is the only logical explanation as to why I'm alive. Unless you fed me your vampire blood." His eyes darkened as he stared at me.

"I didn't. But maybe *he* turned you," I said.

His bright eyes dulled a fraction, and he looked at the floor before shaking his head. "I was out in the sun."

Cassius couldn't withstand the sun. All our dates started when the sun went down and ended before it rose in the morning. Mostly because I wanted to catch a shower before going into the office, but even when he was at my place, he would leave early enough to miss the sunrise.

Robby was right. It couldn't have been him. Otherwise, Robby would be dead for the second time in a way that my tears could not resurrect.

"It also explains why you were clean of the blood when you woke. A phoenix burns away death to be reborn." He looked down at himself.

"And it would explain the fact I have no signs of injuries."

Although it could explain how I woke up without a spot of blood on me or my bed, my mind went back to the memory. The feeling of smoothness under my hand and not the soft down of my comforter.

"Damnit, he put plastic down on my bed. That's why it wasn't a mess. Fucking freak." Cassius had played with me the same way he played with his food, getting off on my death before he tried to revive me.

"Did you remember something?" Robby's eyes sparkled with hope.

I looked at him and then slumped into the door. *How did I begin to explain Cassius to Robby?* "Um...he willed me to remember everything after I killed Harrison. He's the vampire who was responsible for those women we found in dumpsters."

Robby studied my face, and his turned cold as he read me correctly. He sat back on his haunches. "You knew him."

I traced the pattern in the carpet between my knees and nodded, afraid to meet his gaze when I could feel the frustration gathering around him like static electricity.

"How long did you know him?" A hardness crawled into his voice.

"A little over six months." I cleared my throat and forced myself to look at him.

Deep hurt reflected in his eyes, and my stomach clenched.

"You knew he was a vampire for six months and said nothing?" His voice came out in an accusatory growl.

"No. I didn't know what he was until I interrupted his feeding ritual a little less than a month ago. That's why I was acting weird." I shook my head frantically. That would have been unforgiveable; as it was, knowing what he was for almost a month before he attacked me was bad enough.

"How the hell did you not know?"

Fair question and exactly what I asked Cassius back at the crash site. "He carried a charm sachet that disguised his scent and magical signature. He told me he carried it for protection from evil." He had said as much at the accident scene, but I now remembered finding one in his coat and him telling me it protected him from evil. *God, how blind I was to all his tells.* I hadn't even questioned his motives back then. I just took it at face value and never even thought twice about it. That wasn't like me. Cassius had me so wrapped around his finger that I was blind to what he was.

Robby digested my words, his eyes narrowing before they shot back to me. "You found out before he attacked you, and you still let him into your house."

I chewed my lower lip and shook my head. "I didn't let him in that night. He was waiting for me in my reading chair when I got home. I hadn't seen him since the evening I caught him in action. And I hadn't stayed to hear his side. And believe me, he pleaded for me not to go that day."

Robby crossed his arms. "You saw him feeding and you did not kill him?" The red blotches in his cheek announced his building anger.

I just shook my head, knowing how lame that truly was in light of all that had happened. I had been so thrown by what I saw that I clammed up. I couldn't face the fact he had duped me for six months while I was trying to solve his victims' murders.

"And you didn't turn him in either?" His tone was clipped into the danger zone.

If I hadn't been his mate, he would have shifted and taken care of me in a fit of anger.

Another shake of my head.

His silence filled the room, and I thought I'd scream.

"And you didn't tell me about him." He stood and retreated to take a seat at the table by the door, far enough for me to feel the yank of my heart. He glared at me. "You loved him."

I swallowed and stared at the carpet before forcing my gaze up to meet his. "At the time, yeah. I thought I did." I didn't want any secrets between us. "I was lost and confused, and I felt betrayed and naïve and all the things I should not be in this line of work. There are so many things I should have done but didn't and they've all led me here."

"I thought I was your best friend." His hurt bled through in his words.

"You are. And now you're my mate." I touched my shoulder where his mark was. He watched the movement, but he didn't react. I let out a low chuckle. "You know, he said you never stood a chance. That he would have eventually killed you for touching what was his."

Robby burst out laughing, but there was no humor in it. In fact, it chilled me to the core. He stood and started to pace like a caged lion. When he stopped, he pointed at me. "I will be the one doing the killing. He deserves nothing less than being torn limb from limb." His low, growling voice filled the room.

Robby never claimed ownership over me, and the fact he didn't go on a rant about how I was his compounded the differences between him and Cassius. Robby considered me his equal. That was clear in all our partnership ventures. He didn't see me as subservient. And if he had, I had certainly shattered that idea.

He finally stopped pacing and stared out the crack between the hotel room curtains. "You didn't trust me."

"No." I hadn't trusted him with my relationship, with the escape tunnel, and finally with the fact that the guy I had been falling for hard had turned out to be a vampire. "But I trusted you with my life."

"But not your secrets." He was quick to come back but he didn't look at me.

"No." I could have offered a dozen excuses, but it wouldn't matter. My not trusting him hurt him more than me falling for someone else. It hurt him more than my keeping Cassius a secret even after I knew what he was.

"Are there any more secrets?" He glanced over his shoulder.

I sucked in my lower lip. "I slept with him." This was hard. Admitting that I willingly slept with him the night he killed me wasn't a proud moment.

He stared at me as his mind worked through those words. He knew my reputation, and it took him longer than I thought to garner my meaning, but when it slammed home, his gaze narrowed into angry slits. "The night you died."

I nodded.

"Willingly?"

I winced but nodded. "He killed me during…"

He put up his hand, gesturing for me to stop. "I need to go." He started toward the door, and I was up and across the room faster than a blink, blocking his exit.

Panic flushed my cheeks. I knew why he was mad. It was the same reason I was so disappointed in myself. "I was drunk," I started, knowing it wasn't much of an excuse. I should have hauled him in and locked him away for being a vampire.

The muscle in his jaw jumped.

"Don't. Go." I stepped closer and placed my palm on his chest. "Please, Robby. You eclipse everyone who has ever come before. Please stay."

His desire went to war with his principles, and it all reflected on his face as he stared down at me. I could have slung pheromones at him to sway his decision, or commanded him to stay, but I wanted him to come to terms with everything and choose me on his own and not through coercion.

"No more secrets," he warned. "Otherwise, mate or not, I am gone."

"No more secrets," I agreed.

Robby pressed his lips together and glanced at the door behind me before his savage stare dropped back to mine. With a feral snarl, he swept me into his arms, brought me to the bed, and proceeded to show me just how intent he was on never letting me forget I was *his* mate.

WICKED HEART 18

ROBBY STARED AT THE ceiling as I studied his profile. His uncertainty blanketed me like a cold shower, and I shivered next to him, pulling his gaze to mine.

"I'm still angry with you," he said.

I had to bite down on the *No shit* that almost tumbled from my lips. Right now was not the time to razz him about his mood; otherwise, he might actually bolt out the door like he tried to earlier. "I know. Great sex doesn't make it go away."

His dimple appeared and was gone just as quick. "Yeah, but it sure does make you think twice about walking out."

There. He said what I feared the most. Even more than his death. That I wasn't enough, especially after betraying our friendship the way I had. I bit my lip and glanced away as shame heated my face.

"I'm sorry," I said softly.

He hooked his finger under my chin, forcing me to look at him. "I know no one owns you," he started and kept my gaze. "But just so we are clear, I will not be so kind if you betray me like that again."

I gulped at the intensity in his gaze and nodded just as my heart warmed with his words. He wasn't running out on me. This was why Robby was *the one*. Even though he claimed me as his mate, he still didn't feel he owned me; he did not feel entitled, which I could not say the same for Cassius. "I understand."

"Not a single secret. Ever. Not even if you get the notion of surprising me with a gift or something equally as innocent. It's still a damned secret." His voice carried his feral anger.

I leaned away from him. "So, I can't keep anything from you." I didn't phrase it as a question; I just wanted to be sure I was crystal-clear on what he was saying. I did not want to fuck up based on a miscommunication.

"No. Nothing from the inconsequential to the important. You cannot fuck with my loyalty like that again and expect me to remain at your side."

I agreed with a nod. Honestly, I'm not sure I could just sweep away the level of dishonesty if I had been the one on the receiving end. Hell, I hadn't been able to turn the other cheek with Cassius when his duplicity was revealed. "You're a better person than I am." I ran my fingers over his bare chest. "But I expect the same. You kept a hell of a secret for all these years." Even though his secret was one that could have done us both harm. He did have good reasoning for keeping it, but it still crawled under my skin.

"You know the reasons why I didn't act on that."

"Mhm." I kept his gaze.

"Fine. I promise no secrets. Ever." He sighed and closed his eyes. "You didn't even tell me you were seeing anyone. I can forgive most of it, but why in God's name did you keep your relationship a secret? I mean, I told you about Rosalyn when we were dating."

He had told me about Rosalyn when he first met her. I remember the twinge of jealousy that zapped me when he told me she might be the one. He had been open with me on his relationships, regardless of whether I wanted to hear it or not. "I didn't want MDA ruining whatever we had before it had a chance to grow, and I wasn't saying anything until I knew it was solid. This wasn't just another conquest."

His jaw tightened as I spoke. "I guessed that much."

"Look. I didn't want to have you poking at my feelings, especially after trying to find someone for the last fifteen years who made me forget about you." I jabbed him in the chest. "And still, there were a few times I almost let it slip, but I held back. And before I could actually come clean and tell you I finally thought I found the one, the shit hit the fan."

A flash darkened his eyes. "Where does he live?"

I swallowed hard, slicing my gaze to his. "What?" Just looking at him, I knew his intention. He was going after Cassius. My heart dropped.

Robby looked at me in that feral manner that froze my center. "You heard me."

"In the city," I said slowly, trying to figure out a way to stop him. He could not go after Cassius alone. Not with Cassius admitting to me that he intended to kill Robby. Not when we had just started to give this connection a true run. "Robby, you can't..."

He sat up, giving me his back, which had muscles so taut I thought they'd snap. "What is the address?" he snarled and reached for his jeans.

I grabbed his arm. "You can't go after him alone. It's inviting disaster."

He glared at me. "The. Address."

There was no reasoning with him right now. Although I wanted Cassius to pay for what he did to me, sacrificing Robby was not the way.

"You don't have your wards. He can compel you. If you go after him, you will die."

"I'm going to tear his head off with my bare hands," he said through clenched teeth.

"What will killing him do to me?" I asked as a stall tactic. But as soon as the words were out, I understood my hesitation at divulging the address. It wasn't just to protect Robby. Usually when the master was slaughtered, his children died, too, which was why Robby hadn't wanted me to go after the vampire myself.

It was *my* death sentence.

Robby stared at me as his anger transitioned to something else equally as unmanageable.

"That mother fucker," he growled and fisted his hands. "If I kill him, I kill you." He slammed himself back down onto the bed and ran both hands through his hair. "Crafty bastard." He glanced at me. "He made it impossible for me to retaliate or for me to let MDA retaliate." He looked back at the ceiling. "He protected you in a way that was fucking genius."

"Why would he do that?" I asked, but I already knew.

"He's in love with you." He closed his eyes. "And he knew partners in the MDA are loyal to each other. He just didn't know my feelings were far deeper than that."

19

WICKED HEART 19

"**H**OW LONG ARE WE going to just lounge in bed?" Robby asked after we grabbed a couple hours of solid rest. He glanced at me as he ran his fingers over the healed mark on my shoulder. It now looked more like a tattoo than a crusted bite.

I covered his hand, stilling it because it was distracting my ability to form coherent thoughts. The mark he made was warm all the time, like a little piece of Robby had been left in me when he bit me. Instead of answering him, I asked, "Am I supposed to feel you through this?" I touched the mark.

He nodded. "You're supposed to be able to, but if it didn't react to my death—"

"Oh, it reacted." I cut him off, and he cocked an eyebrow. "It reacted as badly as I did."

"Did you know I was alive?"

"Not to my knowledge," I started, but I stopped and tilted my head. "At least not consciously. The mark started tingling before I fell asleep." I met his gaze.

"And what does it feel like now?"

"Warm and safe. Like a piece of you is with me."

He smiled. "So. What was your plan?" He waved at the hotel room. "How long were you planning on staying here?"

"I was planning on staying here indefinitely. But that was when I thought you were dead."

He sighed. "You were really that devastated, that you'd let yourself waste away on account of me?" His eyebrow cocked, challenging me.

I kept his gaze. "I couldn't fathom surviving the weight of your loss pressing down on my chest. It was like losing my parents all over again."

He knew how devastating my parents' death had been. That one car accident changed my life. Had they not died, I don't know whether they would have sent me to MDA academy. But the state certainly didn't have a problem with sending a sixteen-year-old into the lion's den. The only good thing about being inducted into the Monster Defense Agency was meeting Robby. We had become fast friends early on, and one drunken night I had unloaded just how lost I was after my folks died. Every year, he brought me a drink and gave a heartfelt toast to my parents on the anniversary of their death, without fail.

He leaned forward and pressed a soft kiss to my lips. "I'm flattered," he whispered. "I did not realize I had that big of an impact on you."

"You weren't the only one pining away in silence for all those years," I mumbled under my breath, but apparently not low enough.

His dimples appeared.

I glanced at him. "What would you have done if it had been me?"

"I would have gone on a rampage, a bender, and then slept with whatever I could get my hands on."

"You are such a lying ass," I grumbled and sat up, reaching for what was left of my clothes. "You wouldn't turn around and sleep with anyone." I stared at my shredded shirt. He had been in such a frantic hurry to show me who was truly the boss that he made my only shirt into something unwearable. "Why do you do this?" I held the shirt out for him to see.

He offered a lame shrug. "There are times that taking clothes off properly just isn't fast enough."

I rolled my eyes. With Harrison dead, I figured what the hell and wished for clothing choices for both of us. Two piles magically appeared on the end of the bed.

Robby sat up and looked at his clothes, then his gaze jumped to mine with pure panic in his eyes. "Why did you do that?"

I held up my ruined shirt. "Which do you think would call more attention to us? Me in public topless, or my magical signature?" I glanced at the clothes. "Besides, I chose your favorites."

He sighed. "We will have to hightail it out of here pretty quick. Otherwise, Harrison is bound to find us."

"Um. Harrison is dead." I shifted my stance and pulled on a shirt. "Did you see that silver blob on the road?" I straightened my shirt, avoiding his eyes.

"Yes." He drew out the word. His hand stalled over his clothing.

"I. Um. I did that." I met his horrified stare. "I wasn't exactly in my right mind. I had just tried to piece what was left of you together and lost my shit. He had threatened to do that to you, so I retaliated." I shrugged a shoulder.

"You killed Harrison." He ran his hand through his hair.

"He threatened you, and the fact we were in that truck was his doing. Basically, in my opinion, he killed you. So, yes. I fucking toasted his ass in the same horrifying way he had threatened you with to get me to comply." I crossed my arms. I was not going to apologize for killing that asshole.

Robby laughed. "I just wish I could have seen his face," he said and finished reaching for his clothes. "He was a royal dick."

"Well, he did piss his pants."

"I bet." He slid his shirt on. "But he wasn't the biggest one at the MDA. The higher-ups really have a thing for brutality, and they will be coming after us now." He pulled his pants on and stood, buttoning them. "I wouldn't be surprised if they send my pack."

"There wasn't a single member of your pack in that truck," I said. "If there had been, they would have never allowed you to be chained in silver."

"Don't be so sure. At this point, they'll consider me an outlaw. An alpha who chose to betray his pack. They'll come after me as if I slaughtered everyone on that truck."

"So, I will need to compel them." I sighed. It hadn't been difficult the first time, but I was sure they'd be charmed to the hilt the next time we encountered them. Just like with Cassius, it wasn't a matter of if; it was just a matter of when, and I just sent out a big red flag with my magic.

"Well, since I already screwed us..." I willed backpacks with changes of clothes and cash so we could get along without having to scrape by or coerce anyone else.

Robby gave me his *Really?* look but didn't say anything. Instead, he put on the backpack and headed toward the door.

I left one hundred dollars on the nightstand and slipped out into the new night with him.

"Where to?" he asked.

I thought about going deeper into the countryside, but that would mean we would stand out more and more. "Back to the city."

"That is probably the dumbest idea you've ever come up with." Robby truly looked exasperated. "Why?" he asked when I didn't back down.

"Because there are more *other* in the city than out here in the country."

"Right. Hundreds of *other* who would like nothing more than seeing a former member of MDA ripped to pieces."

I sucked my lower lip between my teeth, seeing his point clearly. "True, but maybe we can bring Cassius in and have him locked up like Manuel. Wouldn't that exonerate us in the eyes of MDA?"

He stepped close. "You are so naïve," he whispered down at me. "We could bring in every vampire in existence and that still wouldn't clear our names. Not with the MDA."

Shit. I gnawed on my lip, mulling it over as I scanned the empty motel parking lot before glancing back up at Robby. "So, we're basically dead men walking?"

"That about sums it up." He did the same scan and tilted his nose higher in the air as the wind shifted. He seemed to relax a fraction as he glanced down at me.

I narrowed my eyes. "How do you know all this about MDA?"

He raised his hand and then pointed to his own chest. "Legacy, remember?"

That's right. Robby was a legacy at the agency. He knew more about it than most because he took the alpha station when his father stepped down. Generations of the wolves in his family served the MDA. He knew more dirty secrets through his alpha connections than I'd ever kept. "So where do you suggest?" I asked after studying him.

"The farther away from the city, the better. It puts distance between us and our enemies and will stop me from doing something incredibly stupid." Again, he sniffed the wind as it ruffled his hair.

"By doing something stupid, you mean going after Cassius."

"Yes. Every fiber of my being demands revenge. I want his head toasting in the morning sunshine. And if I end up in proximity to where he is, I'll be more likely to follow through on my baser instincts."

"We can't hide from Cassius forever. He'll eventually come looking for me. He has no clue that you are alive, and if he did, he'd quickly try to rectify that. He's not fond of competition." I didn't add that Cassius believed I was his; that would only serve to aggravate the wolf in Robby.

"I'd like to see him try." Robby sent a cold glare at me.

"Without our charms, it would be a disaster of epic proportion." I put my hand out, willing our charms against coercion from any being into my hand. I tossed one to Robby and smiled as we took off away from the hotel, where my magical signature would lead a team of MDA agents, but all that would be left was just that.

My signature.

WICKED HEART 20

RUNNING THROUGH THE WOODS was getting tiring. I would have preferred a car and the open road instead. But stealing wasn't anything either one of us wanted to do. We were already in serious trouble. We didn't need to do anything to aggravate our situation any further, and using my magic was a strict no-no. The magic needed to pull a car to me would be a hell of a large beacon, and we needed to distance ourselves from the MDA as much as possible.

Robby's stomach growled, sounding more like an earthquake than hunger.

"You need food."

He glanced at me. "Not until I'm sure we've been able to lose them."

The only thing that might make that truly the case would be a river crossing, and there wasn't anything big enough to mask our scent until we got to the Delaware River. And that still was miles away on foot if we kept going north and west of the city.

"Seriously, you need food, and I could use a drink."

He slowed to a jog and glanced at me. "Your eyes have that red tint. You aren't safe around people."

Irritation bloomed. "Did you see me bite Rosalyn?"

"No. But we've been going for hours, and I don't know when the last time you…" He waved at me.

"I had a drink from Harrison before I killed him with the silver vat."

He braked to a walk and ran his hand down his face. "You really do have a wicked heart." His dimples appeared. "I'm glad I'm on your side."

I kept pace next to him, and he clasped my hand in his.

"You know, there were at least a dozen times that I nearly crossed the line with you over the years and it was always after you did something insanely violent."

"Really?" I sent a sideways glance his way.

"Yup. Something about a woman who can truly kick ass and wield a weapon like a kung fu master is so damned sexy."

"So, you're a fan of the Bride?"

He laughed and his eyes twinkled. "Pretty much. But she wasn't a redhead, and she was not as skilled as you are."

Comparing me to the character of the Bride in the *Kill Bill* movies really was the highest honor anyone could bestow on me, but to say I was more skilled than that sword-wielding femme fatale was ludicrous. "What are you buttering me up for?" Robby usually didn't dole out compliments without a reason.

"I'm not buttering you up for anything. I'm just being honest with you, and with myself. Whatever life *we* have together from here on out is going to be difficult, so capturing special moments between running from the law is important." He sighed. "And I really don't want to end up with anything unsaid."

"Oh my God. You really are a soft-hearted romantic, aren't you?" I stared wide-eyed at him, stopping so he'd turn and look at me.

He squared himself in front of me and planted his hands on my arms, running them down the length until his hands clasped both of mine. "I do normally wine and dine my women." He delivered his quirky smile that just about cut me at the knees.

"Well, in a way, you met those qualifications." I glanced at where my bite marks had been on his neck. They were gone now by whatever mojo resurrected him, but his throat did look appetizing. Just not in the food-type way at the moment.

He barked laughter and then he lifted his wrist to my lips. "Care for a drink?" He waggled his eyebrows at me.

I scraped my teeth against his skin and then planted a kiss. "No. A drink is not what I want. But you need sustenance before I drain you of strength."

His eyebrow cocked suggestively, as did the corner of his mouth. "What did you have in mind?"

I grinned. "I don't know. Something challenging that we did not do in my house."

Good Lord, the smile Robby gave me made my legs feel like jelly. I had seen that smile dozens of times, but never so bright or intense as it was now, and it did the same thing it always did: turned my insides into molten lava. My hands even ignited.

His eyebrows shot up as he yanked his hands from mine. "Damn, I guess I *can* bring on the heat."

This was the Robby I dealt with for at least eight hours a day, five to six days a week for fifteen years. The light humor and that dazzling smile, except now, I got to do all the things I dreamed of with him. Being on the run wasn't so bad with him by my side.

He pulled me into his arms and turned me in to the nearest tree. His mouth covered mine with a deep and tender kiss.

"Why did we ignore this?" I whispered under his lips.

"Because MDA would put out contracts on us," he said as he trailed his lips down my neck.

Growls surrounded us. Talk about being caught in a compromising position. At least we had clothes on. But if they had waited five minutes to pounce, his pants would have been around his ankles and my legs would have been wrapped around his waist. Damn the MDA.

Robby slowly straightened and met my gaze. I smelled it, too. How he could be so dead-on about things I would never know, but MDA did send his own pack to tear us to pieces. The muscle in his jaw jumped and he slowly turned. Making any sudden movements would launch a vicious attack.

I stood on my tiptoes and glanced over his shoulder at six large wolves, all with their teeth bared.

"Look. I really have no desire to hurt you," Robby said with his hands out, where they could see them.

The gray wolf of the pack shifted, and Johnson stood where the wolf had been. The rest of the pack remained in wolf form, with their teeth bared and their growls announcing that they weren't here for a friendly pack meeting.

"You should have thought about that before you ran with a vampire." Johnson shot his chin toward me. He had a charm, similar to the ones around our necks, hanging against his bare chest.

On closer inspection, they all had anti-compelling charms. I wondered whether I had the capacity to override them just like I had overridden them before or whether Harrison had them figure out what a fire-wielding, day-walking vampire could be nullified by. *Could I still compel them?*

Robby let a low growl form in the back of his throat. If he had been in wolf form, the hairs on his neck would be standing on end like the pack surrounding us. "She's my mate, so her…species means nothing. And I'm your alpha, so back the fuck off."

Johnson sniffed the air. "Did she turn you?" His voice held dark accusations, as if Robby were somehow more than a wolf now.

I couldn't smell anything different. If anything, he smelled sweeter, more alluring to me, and his wolf scent was less noticeable.

Robby glanced back at me and shook his head. "No. Why?"

"Because you smell different." Johnson sniffed again and bared his canine teeth. The mood in the circle darkened.

Robby took a step forward and shifted.

My eyes widened and the growls stopped at the sight of him in wolf form. My breath locked in my chest for a moment. I wasn't the only one stunned by Robby's appearance.

Robby was at least twice the size he had been the last time he shifted. And more noticeable than his incredible size was the transformation of his midnight-black coat. Dear Lord, it looked as though someone had hand-painted golden tips on the end of every last piece of fur.

He was dazzling.

Johnson's gaze shot to mine. "What did you do to him?"

"Nothing," I said, just as awed as he was.

"This is not a manifestation of nothing," he snarled at me but did not dare take a step forward. The others remained fixed in their spots, just staring at Robby as though he had somehow attained godhood.

"He died in that truck accident," I started, but Robby cut a glare in my direction, silencing me.

"So, you turned him," Johnson growled. His eyes flashed with an anger so bright I felt it.

My heart pounded in my chest and my mouth dried. "No. He has not had a drop of my blood, outside of when he claimed me as his mate. And you know that doesn't turn a wolf." My voice rose as the hostilities ratcheted up with his feral accusation.

"If he died, then how the hell is he here?" Johnson's eyes narrowed.

"I cried on him. Okay? Somehow that resurrected his ass. It wasn't blood, it was tears," I snapped, getting more than a little angry at the situation. I did not want to hurt Johnson or any of the others, but if they launched an attack, it would be their last. That protective reflex that surfaced at the shack started to roil in my belly.

Robby growled at me as if I should not have revealed that.

Something in the way Robby reacted made Johnson blink at me, transforming his glare to something like surprise.

"What?" He thinks I turned you." My panic manifested, and I waved toward Johnson with a hand that was fully engulfed in flame.

Johnson looked at the sky as if the sun somehow hadn't fully set, but only the fading blue of twilight dotted with the first signs of stars speckled the heavens. His eyes fell to my engulfed hand.

"Damn it!" I shook my hand and tendrils of smoke drifted off my fingers as the flames doused.

He stared at me, his mouth open enough to be comical, but I didn't laugh. When the truth clicked in his mind, his eyes widened even more. "She's a goddamned phoenix?" His voice cracked and his gaze sliced to Robby's.

Robby's wolf bared his teeth, growling. The pack reacted in kind.

"Sit!" I yelled. Every single wolf, including Robby and Johnson, sat, and all the growls ceased as all eyes turned to me. I guess I still did have the power to override the damn charms. I stepped next to Robby and reached out to touch his soft fur. "Not you, honey." I amended my command to exclude Robby.

My teeth poked out as I stared at Johnson. "I don't know what I am. Vampire, phoenix, witch." I shrugged. "I guess I'm some hybrid combination now, but I do know daylight doesn't harm me." I stepped forward and took Johnson's hand, bringing his wrist to my mouth, sniffing it. I licked my lips and dropped his hand even though I really wanted to sink my teeth into his flesh and steal a drink. "And I can control my thirst even when tempted. But most important of all, I can stop feeding before I kill the host."

He scoffed. No one had heard of a vampire stopping before. The ones we caught in the act were easy to subdue because they didn't stop feeding. Cassius had stopped, but the woman he had been drinking from had already died. He just hadn't gotten off yet.

Telling him I stopped with Robby wouldn't be enough. I could see it in his eyes. "Stay," I commanded, and then reached down and grabbed his wrist again. But this time, I sunk my teeth into his flesh, drawing a single mouthful of blood before I made my teeth retract despite the burning need to continue to drain his blood. I ran my finger across the holes in his wrist, cauterizing them before I dropped his hand and met his gaze. "I'm just more dangerous to the assholes we hunt now."

He let out a high-pitched laugh and stared at his wrist as I stepped back by Robby. The rest of the pack stared as if they had seen a miracle, mouths open and eyes wide.

Robby shifted back to his human form. "She is not a danger, and she is my mate. I will protect her with my life." He glanced at me. "And I'm still the alpha of our pack, but I cannot continue to work for MDA with all I know. They will ruthlessly hunt her down or worse, cage her. I cannot condone either. So, you have a choice. Accept this, and work with us, or face your death. If Sarah has to enlist her powers, there is no chance for any of you." He hooked his thumb in my direction.

None of them moved from their seated position, and I remembered I had commanded them all to sit. They were still stuck in place. "Oh. Yeah. As you were." I waved at them, pulling back my control.

Johnson climbed to his feet and glanced down at his wrist before he looked beyond Robby to me. "You brought him back to life by crying on him?"

I let out a soft laugh. "Who knew tears could raise the dead?"

"So, what is it going to be?" Robby crossed his arms, interrupting our conversation like he always did any time Johnson showed interest in anything I said. It was as if he were blocking Johnson off from his territory.

I glanced at Robby. "Do you mind? I was talking to Johnson."

Robby glanced at me and pressed his lips together. "I do mind. He still works for the MDA."

I sighed and crossed my arms. "But he's part of *your* pack."

Robby closed his eyes. "I know. But I'm not going in with them and neither are you." He turned back toward the group of wolves. "You have to make the call," he said to Johnson.

"You know we are obligated to report this," Johnson said. But at least his voice was laced with regret and not the angry disgust it had been when he first approached us.

At his unspoken concession, the rest of the pack shifted into human form. I was used to seeing wolves do this, but all these naked men in the woods made me nervous.

"Shorts?" I asked and a stack appeared in the neutral place between us and the pack. Everyone grabbed a pair, including Robby.

"Before you decide to report this to the MDA, consider what will happen to you for letting us go. You know as well as I do just how spiteful the MDA management is. They will turn on all of you if you tell them you let us go."

"Lying won't do any good either. Not with the seers," I said, reminding Robby why we were in such dire straits. It wasn't because of what happened to me; it was because Harrison didn't think Robby was telling the truth.

Robby glanced at me and sighed.

"You need to do what is right for you. If it lands you in trouble, I guess you know how to find us. You're always welcome wherever we are," I said. This was Robby's family, and I would never turn them away if they were in trouble, despite the fact they had been hunting us for the MDA.

That garnered a whole lot of raised eyebrows.

"As long as you wear those charms, MDA will know where you are," Johnson said.

My heart thundered, and Robby and I traded a glance before we tore the chains from our neck and tossed them to the ground as though they were poison. "Have they always tracked us through those things?" I asked, horrified. I had worn those charms when I was at Cassius's place. At least the last time, when I caught him. He had tried to coerce me to stay and that medallion saved my ass.

Crap, that could screw me if they ever found out he was the vampire who turned me.

"Probably." Johnson's gaze bounced between Robby and me. "Maybe we could say you outsmarted us, because when it comes right down to it, you did. Only with logic and not evasive action."

"That may be just enough of the truth not to get caught. But there's one issue." Robby pointed to Johnson's wrist. "The same one that got me busted."

He stared at his wrist for a couple of minutes. "Perhaps we can just say we toasted your asses. Dragged you both out into the sun and that did it."

"Wrong. Harrison knew sunlight didn't affect me." I glanced at the ground. "You would have known that, too, if I hadn't wiped your memory of the last time we had an...encounter." I finally met Johnson's gaze.

"When was that?" Johnson's jaw tightened.

"You surrounded us in a shack and someone tranquilized Robby." I shuffled my feet. "I fed on Harrison before I sent him packing."

He huffed and kicked at the ground with his bare foot. "So that's why Harrison blocked us from his next ambush."

"Considering everyone on that truck died except me, I'd say that was a stroke of luck for all of you. Especially since that bastard locked Robby in silver cuffs and collar, and then threatened me with dousing him in silver just to keep me in line."

No one spoke, but all eyes pivoted to Robby's throat and then back to me, as if the lack of evidence made my statement total bullshit.

"How did you survive that crash?" Johnson asked with a skeptical tone that ruffled my feathers again.

I took a breath. "He had me locked in a chair, anchored to the floor with a soundproof plexiglass wall between us. You know, the kind we lock up vampires in so they can't compel us?" I challenged them with a raised eyebrow.

Most of the pack avoided my gaze. They knew what I was talking about. Although none of those vampires ended up in the cages down below our buildings. A shiver rolled down my spine. All of those setups had a hatch above to allow daylight in after MDA got what they needed from the caged vampires.

"I couldn't compel him, and I couldn't use my fire to get out of the binds before the accident because of the threats Harrison issued. I wouldn't put it past him to kill Robby just to spite me. And after the panel that Robby was tied to ripped out, all bets were off. I got to him as soon as I physically could, but it was too late.”

“You killed all the men in that truck.”

I shook my head. “I didn’t touch anyone but Harrison. Truthfully, some of those guys died in the accident. I think that truck must have rolled at least a dozen times. They weren’t strapped in like I was.” I met their gazes. “Harrison is a different story. He wouldn’t leave it alone, even with my prior warning, and Robby was dead because of his single focus.”

“You dumped silver on him?” Johnson’s voice took on the shiver that visibly coursed through his body.

I nodded. “He threatened to do that to Robby, so...”

“Do you have any idea how hard that was to scrape off the road?” one of the others who I rarely encountered said. His name was Daniel or Donald or something that started with a D. He had always been relegated to the cleanup crew and was a quiet one by nature. As a werewolf, he was not bad to look at physically, but his face was forgettable in a crowd of beautiful men. Unlike Robby or Johnson, who could be fashion models or Hollywood stars if they desired.

Robby let out a laugh. “Harrison was always a big pile of dick anyway,” he said, and the pack laughed with him.

“So, what do I say?” Johnson asked, bringing us back to the burning issue at hand.

Robby glanced at me. “Tell the truth. That we’re both some sort of *other* that you can’t peg, but we didn’t threaten you or any human we’ve been in contact with, so you felt it was prudent to let us be. We're better serving MDA than against them."

Johnson rolled his eyes. "That will go over well."

"It's better than them finding bodies and no explanation." I couldn't help it. I needed to paint the picture for them. If they came at us again, it would end in the same devastating loss as the truck incident. I wouldn't allow them to harm Robby ever again. And even if they had the right charms, I was reasonably sure my fire could wipe them all out in a millisecond if I chose.

At least that was what the textbooks we studied at the academy had said about the phoenix.

"Besides, I can compel you even when you have your charms, so saying we are some kind of new breed of *other* is a better explanation than vampire, since you don't have a defense against me unless you threaten your alpha." I glanced at Robby. "And understand this—I will never let MDA get the drop on us again. So, any threat to Robby will not end well for whoever is stupid enough to issue it."

"I dislike that your partner is so fucking logical." Johnson waved the pack away. Five men shifted into wolves and took off, heading back the way we had come. He waited a moment and then glanced at Robby. "Fifteen years, man. You went fifteen years without giving in. Why now?"

"Simple. It was either kill her, which my wolf would not abide, or let him have what he's been wanting all this time." He glanced at me and smiled. "Besides, you of all people know just how damn hard it was for me to resist her."

Johnson let out a low chuckle. "Yeah, man. At least once a week I had to talk you off that ledge. And if you had come to me before you made this rash decision, I would have done it again."

Robby's smile faded away. "It wouldn't have worked this time, and you know it. I couldn't allow her to be caged for the rest of her life. And if I was going to break protocol, I might as well do it all the way. Go big or go home." A grin toyed on his lips.

"Yeah, well, it could be your death sentence." Johnson glanced at me. "And yours, despite your heritage." His gaze returned to Robby. "I'll do my best to keep that under wraps as well, but if they find out, there will be no hiding from MDA."

Robby gave him a nod. "Which is why I didn't want her to spill that secret." His glare at me pounded that issue home. "Now get going." He waved Johnson away. "I was in the middle of ravaging her, and I don't think she wants an audience."

He shifted and bolted the way the rest of the wolves went. It just seemed way too easy. Not a drop of blood was spilled, unlike the last MDA confrontation.

WICKED HEART 21

ROBBY'S STOMACH GROWLED AS he kissed my throat. The moment he had been sure the pack was out of range, he had pushed me against the tree again.

"You need food first." I pushed at him, but that only made him press more of his magnificent, scantily clad body against me.

"Sarah, I'm not interested in food at the moment. In case you hadn't noticed, I'm interested in you."

Oh, I noticed. How could I not, with his hips pressed into mine and him only in flimsy gym shorts? "You'll last a hell of a lot longer with me if you have food. Besides, I'm not looking for a one-minute wonder."

He guffawed to the point he snorted and pulled away so he could look me in the eye. "I've never been a one-minute wonder."

I raised a single eyebrow, challenging him.

The growl in his stomach persisted, and he rolled his eyes. "Fine." He picked up our backpacks, handing me mine before he pulled out another pair of boots from his.

He needed to be more judicious of when and where he shifted because those were the last shoes he had, and I couldn't keep using my magical signature to manifest things and draw MDA's attention to where we were.

"Besides, we should put some distance between us and those charms." I pointed at the discarded necklaces.

"True." He finished tying his boots and hauled the pack over his shoulder before he took my hand.

We moved deeper into the woods, heading north and west. Away from the Eastern Seaboard and the city where all our enemies laid in wait.

We still had a few solid hours before the sun broke the horizon and anything would be open that offered the kind of hearty breakfast Robby needed, but it allowed us to put more miles between us and those charms. For each step away, the tension between my shoulders lessened.

"Are we far enough away yet?" Robby asked in a teasing tone.

"No." I wagged my free finger at him. "Food first, then we can find a motel room and you can ravage me all you want."

He engaged his puppy dog eyes. The ones he usually reserved when he wanted me to go out in the cold to pick up coffee, and it always set an irritation switch on inside me because I was fucking helpless to say no to him when he gave me that begging look. "Stop that," I snapped and yanked my hand from his. "You need to behave until then."

"What if I don't want to?" He caught me in his arms and planted a heated kiss, even though he kept moving.

I discovered the moment his lips were on mine that I had no motivation to stop him. His persuasion skills were legendary, and I found myself melting into him. The fog he created in my mind cleared, and I pulled away from his lips.

A flurry of flying fur caught my gaze just as a gray wolf clamped his teeth on Robby's arm. I wasn't sure whether the beast had meant to bite Robby or me, but Robby dropped me and pushed me to the side as he shook the beast free.

Blood ran down his forearm where the wolf had torn Robby's skin.

"Do not move!" a voice commanded from the shadows.

Robby stopped, freezing in place as his eyes widened. The wolf growled at him, baring its teeth.

I stepped next to him and stared at the wolf.

"Not a shifter," Robby whispered without moving his head, his arms, or even a muscle beyond his lips.

Before I could pull my fire to the surface, a man stepped into view. He was ancient and he smiled at us, revealing sharp teeth. "Good boy."

He snapped his fingers. The wolf backed up to stand by his side. His red eyes took us in as though we were a fine steak meal.

Robby growled in his throat, and the ancient vampire chuckled and licked his lips. The vampire moved quick and before I could blink, he had his teeth embedded in Robby's bloody arm.

"You really shouldn't have done that." I willed my hand to engulf in flame and grabbed a handful of the vampire's hair, yanking him away from what he thought was an easy feast.

The moment his fangs were free, whatever spell he had over Robby dissolved. Robby shifted into his wolf form and when the vampire's dog launched at me, Robby batted it out of the air with his paw.

I let my fire grow.

The vampire screamed and glared at me in horror as I smiled, showing him that he wasn't the only vampire in the woods.

"You bit *my* mate," I snarled and latched onto his throat. I needed sustenance, too, but drinking from the vampire was like feasting on the dead. I pushed him away in disgust, spitting his blood on the ground between us.

His eyes were wide and frightened as he took me in. Robby kept the wolf from attacking me, but the feral growls still made me glance at their dance.

The vampire took the opportunity and launched at me, hooking his teeth into the side of my throat. My shot nerves exploded, and before the bastard could draw too much blood, I let my fire erupt from every cell. It engulfed the ancient vampire and he screamed, but didn't dislodge, even though he had ignited.

Now I was angry. My fire flared white, blinding me. When my vision finally cleared, the forest in front of me was on fire and the vampire was gone. Just a swirl of ash. I turned, and Robby was far enough away from me to make me gulp. The vampire's pet lay smoldering on the ground nearby.

Robby stared at me, his eyes wide and blue like the afternoon sky. His wolf mouth opened in surprise, and then he whined as he stared at the forest fire. I didn't wait to analyze what just happened; I ran and hopped onto Robby's back. He took off like the wind, racing as fast as he could so we weren't swallowed by the fire greedily eating the dry tinder all around us. The wind swirled, fueling the flames. I coughed and hung onto him as he darted from clear forest patch to clear forest patch, his golden tips reflecting the growing danger.

The wind shifted, pushing the flames away from us and back in the direction we came from, but it wasn't until we crossed a wet steam and hauled ass for another couple of miles before Robby slowed to a walk, panting to catch his breath. He glanced over his shoulder beyond me and the panic in his eyes subsided. He stopped; I slid off his back and he shifted.

"Jesus, what the hell happened back there?" He ran his hand through his hair as he paced in his birthday suit.

A chill skittered down my spine, and I wrapped my hands around me, noticing my total lack of clothing for the first time.

"You went off like a damn firebomb."

I ignored him and reached for his arm. His arm had healed enough to just show scabs where both the wolf bite had been and where the vampire bit him. We had had enough bites throughout our career but thankfully none of them had been close to fatal because we had each other's back.

Just not like that. Exploding fire was a whole new paradigm, and it rattled him just as much as it rattled me. Especially the part where I protected him as if my base instinct to protect my mate had manifested in my fire.

"I'm fine." He pulled his arm away. He checked my neck. "So are you." Now his gaze roamed down my body, as if his brain were just catching up. "You didn't burn me." He met my gaze and pulled me close with a nervous laugh. He ran his hands down my back until they cupped my ass. He leaned forward, nuzzling in the crook of my neck, nipping playfully. "The fire just went around me as if I was in a glass bubble and pushed me to the edge of the blast radius." His tongue traced my jaw and then his lips crushed down on mine.

This time I did not stop him. Energy be damned; we were both still high on the crazy adrenaline of outrunning a forest fire, and I really didn't care what was underneath me as long as Robby was draped over me. He didn't rush either, and by the time the moon shone high in the night sky, I was panting and begging for him to satisfy this deep ache he created in my core.

Robby finally gave in and climbed on top of me, making love to me slowly in the soft leaves. He traced my face with his fingers and looked at me as if I were the eighth wonder of the world.

"I love the way you look at me," he said, echoing my thoughts before he caught a soft kiss.

I smiled, enjoying the languid motion of his hips slowly stroking me. "No one has ever looked at me the way you are right now."

He grinned and touched his nose to mine so he was nearly crossing his eyes and I couldn't help it; I started laughing. So did he, in such a full and carefree way that melted my heart and stirred the heat inside me.

He tilted his head and captured my mouth with a kiss that started as slow as his hips. But soon, his tongue and his motion quickened, igniting both of us in rapture that transcended the chaotic lovemaking at my house. This intimacy had been missing from everything before, and I thanked the gods above that we finally gave in to this bliss.

He tensed, groaning my name softly in my ear before he caught my earlobe in a nibble that sent heat tendrils through my already satisfied form.

Instead of collapsing on top of me, he rolled off and pulled me onto his shoulder. We stared at the star-filled sky above as we both slowly came down from the sexual high.

"Can we just build a cabin here in the woods and live off the grid?" he asked. "Create a pack of our own?" He raised his eyebrow and glanced at me.

The smile that had been on my lips faded. "I don't know if I will be able to have children."

His head turned and he stared at me, blinking as if he had forgotten what I was.

"I don't know that I'm technically alive," I said to his deep stare.

"Oh, you're alive." But his eyes still held an ounce of doubt.

"I'm a vampire."

He shook his head. "You're more than that." He drew his lower lip between his teeth and then looked back at the sky, as if weighing what that really meant. "I still want to live with you off the grid, whether you can conceive or not."

"But you're an alpha." I knew what the expectations of an alpha were in the pack. Not only to be a leader, but breed leaders.

He nodded. "Yes. I am." He glanced at me. "And you are my mate. For better or worse, in sickness and in health. Till death do us part."

I sat up and glanced down at him in surprise. "Those are wedding vows."

His lips tilted into that half smile that made me feel like melted putty. He picked leaves out of my hair and then propped himself up on his elbow. "What did you think being mated means?"

"I guess I never equated mates to marriage."

"You might want to start thinking about that, because as soon as this shit storm settles, I'm putting a ring on your finger to make it official to the world."

"I don't need a ring or a ceremony." I placed my hand on his shoulder, leaning forward to capture his mouth with mine.

"Mhm." He tasted me and then pulled away. "Don't you want to marry me?"

I sighed. "I just never considered marriage a viable option for me even before all this and now..."

He sat up. All the humor and softness of the moment vanished. "You don't want to marry me."

"That is not what I'm saying." I threw my hands in the air and stood. "I want to be with you."

"But?" He climbed to his feet and stared down at me.

"We haven't even said we love each other," I blurted.

"Sarah, I've loved you since the academy. As a friend, as a partner, and now as my mate. So what is the real issue?"

I wished I had clothes on so I could put my hands in my pockets. No sooner had the thought passed through my head, clothing drifted onto my skin. And my boots appeared on my feet. I met Robby's annoyed gaze. "What? I didn't know what to do with my hands," I said in defense.

"Can you at least conjure me something to wear, too?" He waved at his magnificently naked form. "Then you can explain what the real issue is about marrying me."

I wished for clothing for him and manifested jeans, work boots, and a button-up shirt, but I left it unbuttoned. I stepped closer, pressing my palms to his bare chest. "The issue is marriage is a human institution. We are not human." I met his gaze.

"To the world we are."

"I don't give a flying shit about the world. I just care about us. I am committed to you with everything I am and everything I will become. I'll never betray your trust again, and I will hold you dear for however long we have together."

He smiled down at me. "I still want a big wedding with my entire pack in attendance, so they understand this isn't just another notch on my bedpost. I want to dance with you under the full moon and smash cake in your face and get drunk with our friends before I take you to some swanky upscale hotel suite and proceed to ruin every piece of furniture in the hotel room while consummating the marriage."

I grinned at his description and the impish light dancing in his eyes. "So, no private island ceremony with just the two of us?"

He laughed. "Nope. A ceremony fit for a queen."

I crinkled my nose. "That is so not my style, and you know it."

He laughed. "Yes. I know what I'm describing is as far from your style as humanly possible." His dimples played in his cheeks. "I just like to see that hint of panic in your eyes when you think about anything formal. You got it every time we had to go to the annual awards ceremony for the MDA."

"You can be such an ass, Robby Young." I swatted his chest. But he was dead-on accurate. I tried to make sure we had a stakeout that night, or had to follow up on a critical lead to get out of it. Most of the time it worked, but the times I had to show up dressed up like a debutant, I was as uncomfortable as any introvert in a crowd.

"And you are so easy to rile up, Sarah Stone," he teased, with a tickle to both my sides.

My smile faded as I studied his face. "I am sorry I kept Cassius from you."

His good humor faded. He nodded and traced my lower lip with his thumb. "No secrets ever again."

"No secrets, ever," I agreed.

WICKED HEART 22

WE CROSSED OUT OF the forest onto a quiet stretch of road. Robby's hunger pangs rumbled like a thunder cloud, but there was nothing in sight in either direction. Just how far from civilization had we wandered?

We padded on the dew-stained grass as the moon started its descent in the west. To the north, we could see gray smoke drifting against the night. Both of us turned south, sticking to the gravel on the side of the road. It crunched under our boots and every now and then when the wind shifted, I could smell the forest burning.

"Do you think they'll be able to put it out?" I asked after we had walked a few miles.

"I certainly hope so. It's been drier than normal this year, though."

"I hate the fact I did that." I sighed and peeked over my shoulder. The smoke stood out clearly against the dark sky, but now it seemed whiter than before.

Robby looked back. "White is good. It usually signifies steam, so maybe they're getting a grip on it." He glanced at me, catching the worry in my frown. "You were defending yourself," he said. "And if you hadn't been a vampire, you would have been just as compelled to stay still and we would both be dead right now."

I shivered at the thought.

He slid a sideways glance at me. "We've seen vampires compel each other before."

I nodded. "What's your point?"

"I think I made my point. You are more. I don't remember enough about what a phoenix brings to the table, but I think that is responsible for the major differences in you."

"A new breed of nightmare," I said with all the excitement of a fly stuck in glue. "And you want to have children with me?" I sent a questioning glare his way.

"Actually, I do." He slung his arm around my shoulder and squeezed lightly. "They would be perfect little nightmares, just like their mother."

I knew enough about Robby's family roots to understand his desire, and at some base level, I shared that same dream. But it was a pipe dream. Something we would never attain. It was just another raw deal delivered by Cassius.

The rumble of a car caught our attention, and we turned to see a pickup truck flying down the road. Seventies rock music blared out the open window, and it slowed as it approached us.

"You all are a long way from civilization," the driver said as his cigarette bobbed up and down between his lips with each word.

"We got a little turned around, trying to get out of the way of that fire." Robby hooked his thumb over his shoulder. "How far is it to a local diner?" His stomach rumbled loud enough to raise the driver's eyebrows.

"The nearest town is about thirty miles down the road. I'm actually heading that way for a construction job." He glanced at his passenger seat and then back at us. "The cab is a little tight, but if you don't mind a little wind, you can hop in the truck bed." He pointed toward the truck bed behind him.

I shrugged. The cab of the truck was full of tools, enough so that there would only be room for maybe half a passenger in the space, if that, and that was only if they were really tiny.

We came from the city where people minded their own business and never went out of their way for strangers. Suspicion bloomed in my stomach, and I glanced at Robby.

He took a whiff of the air and gazed in the direction we were heading before he glanced at the driver and smiled. "That's mighty kind of you. We will take you up on that." Robby stepped to the back, and hopped onto the bumper and over the tailgate before he reached his hand out to me.

"Are you sure?" I whispered as unease settled in my belly.

"He's just a normal human," he whispered back.

I took his hand, and he hauled me in the back of the truck as if I were made of fabric instead of flesh and bone. Robby's natural strength always made me feel less than I was, even now when I was his true equal. Well, I had held him down on my floor, so maybe I was the stronger one now.

We lined ourselves up against the cab near the window that opened at the back of the driver's head, and I gave Robby a sideways look. That feeling of unease had turned up a notch, and I almost said let's just walk.

Robby must have read my hesitation, because he whispered, "He's good."

But that didn't settle my nerves.

"Hang on!" the man yelled and then hit the gas.

We nearly slid all the way to the tailgate with his acceleration. We shuffled back as the seventies rock music blanketed us, loud enough for us not to be able to speak to each other without shouting.

The truck vaulted at the same breakneck speed it had approached us at and I smirked at Robby. "At least he has good taste in music."

Robby smiled and nodded. "Time for a little catnap." He pulled me close, draping me with his warmth. His eyes were already drooping from the lull of the truck, and he leaned his cheek on the top of my head while I snuggled in against his shoulder.

Robby's heat, along with the motion of the truck and the music filling my head, lulled me as well. Just as I was drifting to sleep, something buzzed near me and bit me on the back of my shoulder. I went to swipe it away and sleep sucked me down into the black.

WICKED HEART 23

MY EYES SNAPPED OPEN, and I gasped for air in the dark room. My head pounded in time with my heartbeat. My arms and legs were splayed wide and bound at the wrists and ankles. My back was against soft fabric. The familiarity with the situation made my heart squeeze.

"Robby?" I asked the dark, because the last thing I remembered was drifting to sleep against his shoulder in the back of that damn truck. I couldn't move and no matter how hard I tried to pull the fire from within to burn through the bindings holding me, nothing happened.

Lights flared on, and I squinted against the blinding brightness.

"Good, she's awake." Cassius entered the room and yanked a chain.

Robby stumbled in behind him, collared in silver with his hands bound behind his back. His chest was bare, but covered in black and blue marks. His face was barely any better.

My gaze shot to Cassius. "What the hell do you think you are doing?" I snarled. My voice shook with both the anger buzzing through me as well as a hint of fear. I hated that little twinge. I couldn't let Cassius know I was afraid; otherwise, he would think he had the upper hand.

"Teaching your dog a lesson." He yanked the chain again, making Robby nearly lose his balance. Cassius clasped the end of the chain to a fastener in the floor. "Kneel," he commanded, and Robby dropped to his knees with a growl. Cassius yanked his head back. "Mind your manners while you are in my home."

"Fuck. You." Robby growled.

Cassius backhanded him, and Robby's head jerked to the side with the power of the blow. Cassius smiled and slid his gaze to me.

Everything inside me went frigid with that look. It promised pain and death, and I struggled against the bonds holding me in place, unable to push my fright down. It was front and center and making me shake.

He let go of Robby's hair and stepped closer to the bed. He reached out and yanked the sheet covering me off.

Cold air licked my skin, and my eyes widened at my lack of clothing. The bastard had stripped me before he bound me, and my mind raced back to the figure tied to his bed when I walked in on him feeding. My gaze darted to Robby.

"I swear, if you touch her..." Robby growled, his eyes just as wild as the panic filling me.

Cassius put his hand on my breast and squeezed hard enough to pull a wince out of me. "I will touch whatever the fuck I want. I have been searching for her for centuries. The lost phoenix. The one destined to be my bride." He ran his fingers along my skin, gently, as if revering me.

Gooseflesh formed and I shivered, shaking my head. "I am Robby's, not yours," I snarled, and my thoughts jumped to Robby and my conversation in the woods. We had said our vows to each other, and I had meant every word. A part of me wished the MDA had locked us up, because what was in Cassius's eyes was darker than being in a cell until we died.

"Oh, but you were promised to me." He challenged. "And when they hid you away, I annihilated every last one of your kind in my effort to find you. And then I went after the witches who hid you." He shook his head, and a scowl marred his pretty face. "You are mine, not some filthy alpha's, regardless of how the hell you brought him back to life."

He shot a glare at Robby. "Before I burn away every memory of you from her mind, I need to put you in your place."

He pointed at my mate, and my heart lurched.

"You will never be able to erase him from my mind," I vowed. "I won't *allow* you to wipe him from my memory. If you even try, all I'll remember of you is that you're a green-eyed demon." I struggled against the bonds holding me in place. I called on my fire again as Cassius glanced in my direction. Nothing happened. No fire, no snap of the leather. Nothing.

"You can't burn your way out of those bonds," he said. "The bed is warded against *all* of your unique powers. You are at my mercy. And when I am done with him, I will attend to your needs."

"You bastard. Leave him alone!" No matter how much I struggled, I couldn't break the restraints. Silently, I begged the gods not to let this vile creature kill Robby. The smile he sent made my skin crawl. There was bottomless cruelty in it.

"I'm not going to be the one who sucks him dry. That, my dear, will be reserved for you." He pointed at me.

He expected me to kill Robby. My struggles stopped, and I glared at him, slowly shaking my head. "You cannot compel me to do your bidding."

"Who said I was going to compel you? You'll do it willingly."

I wanted to wipe his pompous grin off his damn face. "That is never gonna happen."

"Oh, I promise that is how his life will end. But you won't know who the hell he is." And with that, he focused on Robby, circling him with his eyes in tight slits and lips pursed. "What horrors can I inflict on you? What exactly would break an alpha?" He tapped his lips. "Besides fucking your mate in front of you. That's coming, but I'm not sure it's enough. Especially after you claimed what was mine."

"She was mine long before you ever walked into her life." Robby glared at Cassius, but under the anger, I saw a desperation in him. He was at this vampire's mercy too. Obliged to follow every order and watch what Cassius had in store for me.

"Leave him alone, you bastard!" I yelled, but Cassius ignored my outburst. He ignored the chains rattling with my effort to get loose and cook him to a fucking crisp.

"She was your partner. Not your lover. Besides, she was promised to *me* centuries ago, and she has laid in my bed willingly, and I have had her in every conceivable way." He glanced at me with a heat that left my mouth dry. "And she will again soon enough."

"I will never willingly give myself to you," I promised.

He chuckled at my declaration, as if it were a child's tantrum that would pass. "You will. And you will beg me to fuck you." He focused back on Robby, and his glare promised the worst. Robby growled at him but didn't move from his position.

Beating him to within an inch of his life wasn't going to break an alpha male, and he looked as if Cassius had already taken liberties with his fists.

He grinned down at Robby. "Making you my bitch might break you." He glanced at me. "In all the centuries I've been alive, I've never *had* an alpha wolf."

Robby's eyes widened at the statement. It would mess with his head big-time to be violated by a vampire in such a way.

"Sick fuck," I snarled. I never thought Cassius was that diabolical, but the way he grinned and the fact his hardness was evident enough for me to see the outline of it in his pants turned my stomach. I could deal with him taking what he thought he deserved from me, but this was horrifying.

"While tempting as that may be, especially with such a pretty dog..." He ran the back of his knuckles across Robby's cheek. "It wouldn't be enough to break this bastard." He pulled back and punched Robby's cheek. "Humiliate him, yes, but break him?" He shook his head. "No."

Blood splattered from Robby's mouth and the scent of it drifted on the air, igniting my hunger. Seeing him draw blood from my mate set my rage indicator to overdrive.

I screamed my rage, straining against the bonds.

Cassius laughed as he kept circling Robby. "Physical violence focused *on him* will not break this alpha. But just for giggles, pull your pants down and bend over for me."

Robby glared up at him; his muscles strained to disobey, but he did as commanded.

Cassius slid behind him and stepped close to Robby. He stared at me with an evil smile.

"I will kill you," I vowed with a voice that shook with the anger burning in my blood. "I swear to God, I will rip your fucking cock off." Oh, how I hated Cassius. If I had my way, he'd be dickless in a matter of seconds.

He clucked his tongue. "Promises, promises." He stepped away from Robby. "Pull your pants up and sit on your heels like a good dog." He patted Robby's head. "Maybe later," he whispered to Robby.

The insinuation left me cold.

"While fucking your dog might humiliate him, I don't think it would shatter his mind. But I imagine taking my frustration out on you is a different story," Cassius said, and his gaze cut to mine. "You betrayed me, and that demands a reckoning."

"You ruined my life," I growled, trying to stall whatever horrors he had in mind. "You made me into a hunted freak. Haven't you done enough?"

"Oh, sweetheart, that isn't even close to enough." He glared at me and approached the bed. "I am going to break that dog, and then you are going to plunge those fangs of yours into his neck and suck every last drop of blood from him."

"Never," I snarled through clenched teeth.

"I promise you, by the time I am finished with you, he will be erased completely from that pretty little head of yours." He tapped my nose lightly, and I snapped at him. He pulled his hand away from my exposed fangs just in time.

"Do your worst, mother fucker, because no matter what you do to me, you will not erase him from my heart. I will not allow it. Ever."

His eyes flashed a twisted anger so dark that I gulped. "You know what is more dangerous than a woman scorned?" He reached out and took my index finger in his hand. "A vampire betrayed." He crushed my finger, snapping the bones.

I gasped at my shattered bone and then my nerves recognized the pain, sending sharp stabs up my arm.

"Don't you dare hurt her!" Robby growled, every muscle strained against whatever compelling spell Cassius had put him under.

"You mean like this?" He snapped my thumb, nearly severing it from my hand.

I screamed as hot agony flared up my arm.

"Do you know how many bones are in the human body?" he asked with a mean smile.

The kind of smile I envisioned on a serial killer's face.

"You are fucking insane!" I groaned and glared through eyes blurred by tears.

Robby shook with rage. His eyes jumped to mine, and there was panic alongside the fury.

Oh, God. This was how he intended to break Robby. Not just fucking me in front of my mate, but making Robby see me in agony while he could do nothing but helplessly watch.

I couldn't stop him either.

"I intend to break almost every one of them while you watch." Cassius nodded toward Robby, confirming my worst nightmare. Cassius leaned forward and licked my throat. "You will be begging me to take you and to take every last memory of yours before I am done with you."

"Robby is my soulmate. You will never erase him from my memories," I vowed, glaring at Cassius through my tears. "And I will never beg you to fuck me. Ever."

"Oh, I will erase him from your memories. And you will beg me to fuck you. And you will kill him." He snapped the bones in my forearm with a sickening crunch. "I promise you will do all those things and so much more."

Hot agony burned in my arm, and my breath locked in my chest. I forced an inhale and screamed my pain to the ceiling. Tears flowed and pooled in my ears. The way he had me stretched out aided in my pain as bone scraped against bone with every motion I made.

"Goddammit, why don't you just do that to me instead?" Robby bellowed, frozen in his kneeling form with his arms straining against the silver binding his wrists behind him.

Cassius glared at Robby with a hideous smile spread across his face. "Because breaking your bones won't do a goddamn thing to your mind." He cocked his head. "Butt-fucking you might, and that may still be on the table for when I'm done with this deceiving bitch." He snapped the bone in my upper arm.

I shrieked, arching my back at the level of pain accosting me. Sobs ripped from my chest. This was only one of my limbs. My mind balked at the thought of all my bones crushed to a pulp, one by one, by this hideous beast.

"Care for a little pleasure with that pain?" Cassius whispered in my ear, and then took my breast in his mouth, sucking it gently like he had done when we were dating. His hand traveled between my legs, fondling me with such gentleness, as if I were his lover, not his vehicle for vengeance.

"No," I hissed as my right arm throbbed in time with my pulse. The pain had dulled a fraction, but it still ruled my mind.

Robby continued to growl as if the man were stripping him of everything he loved.

"Okay. Pain it is." Cassius stood and slammed the heel of his hand into my right clavicle. The snap of bone filled the room.

I choked with the flaring agony. I couldn't even turn in on myself. White spots filled my vision, and my sobs sounded far away.

He smiled down at me as he rounded the bed to my left arm. "You won't pass out, my dear." He reached onto the table, picked something up, and snapped it under my nose.

I turned my head away from the awful stench of smelling salts, creating a web of pain on my right side. I gagged on it as he followed my movements until I glared up at him.

"You bastard."

"You will feel every horrifying crunch and the acute pain that follows." He caressed my stomach and then squeezed my breast.

"Please, stop," Robby pled, but Cassius ignored him.

Cassius wanted me to beg for him to end this. To wipe my mind. To give in to him. To be his. That would never happen, no matter what horrors he had in mind. I could scream until I blew out my vocal cords, but I would not give him what he wanted.

"I know I usually like my victims to feel pleasure." He dipped his finger inside me with that gentleness I was used to from him. "But the fact you allowed a dog to claim you as his mate makes you an exception." He reached up with his other hand and crushed my entire left hand in his. "Pleasure and pain are bound. Just like we are." He removed his hand from between my legs, focusing on my forearm.

I started to blubber, and I hated myself for it.

"Would you rather I fuck you into oblivion like I did when I turned you?" He raised his eyebrow.

The memory of that night swirled alongside the pain, and I hesitated a moment too long.

Robby bellowed loud enough to rattle the bed.

I shook my head. I couldn't willingly, even under duress, give myself to Cassius. That would crush Robby. "No." The word came out on a shaky voice I almost didn't recognize.

He snapped my left forearm. "You will be mine. Wouldn't it be less painful to give in to me, than to keep this ruse up? You do remember how good I was in bed, don't you?"

Tears streaked my face, pooling in my ears as unwanted flashes of our history together played in my mind. But he still wasn't as all-consuming as Robby. "I will never be yours."

His face transformed into a furious mask, and he snapped my upper arm and left clavicle in a one-two punch that locked the air in my chest.

Robby yelled through his own sobs.

I finally drew a breath, and the scream that followed hurt my ears and made my throat raw. *How many more bones were there? Ribs, hips, legs. Dear God, I couldn't do this.*

"Please," I sobbed as he climbed up on the bed and straddled my hips.

His hand went behind him to play with me, stroking and flicking me in a way that nearly had me vomiting. He plunged his finger inside me and smiled.

I shook my head. "Please stop," I said through my tears.

He stilled, and his eyes flashed dangerously.

He didn't understand; there was no amount of pleasure that he could deliver that would wipe out this debilitating pain. I didn't even think Robby could bring me to a release. My gaze moved past Cassius to Robby's devastated face. His stare was at the juncture between my legs. He must have sensed me looking at him because his blue eyes found mine.

Tears cascaded down his face freely and there was so much anguish in his eyes.

Cassius splayed out both hands across my ribs. "Last chance?"

Anger flared at the injustice of his offer. I couldn't beg him to take me. "Fuck. You." I gasped, baring my teeth at him and letting the anger dictate me and not the pain peeling away my sanity.

"No!" Robby screamed.

Cassius pressed down hard and quick, and the snapping sound of multiple bones echoed in my ears. He released the pressure and moved to the space between my legs. The movement of the bed aided the agony racing through my chest. Breathing hurt as each inhale stretched broken bones and each exhale scraped them back together. I couldn't even scream.

My eyesight faded into spots and a high-pitched buzz captured my hearing. And he put another damn smelling salt under my nose, bringing me back into full agony mode.

"I do not enjoy this," Cassius said as he fondled me again.

"Could. Have. Fooled. Me." I struggled to speak, but now I was more intent than ever to deny this bastard anything. "You. Will. Never. Win."

Fury blazed in his eyes. "I will fucking win. And he will not even be a distant memory when you wake up. He will be just another source of food for you." He slammed the heels of both palms in the middle of my thighs.

Another bout of sickening snaps filled the room, and I found the air to scream.

I guess my refusal to bend pushed Cassius too far, and he undid his pants, crawled up my body, and lined himself up with me.

My eyes widened, horrified.

"You are mine," he snarled and slammed his full length into me. The pain of every broken bone being jarred by his thrust pulled another gagging scream from me.

Robby yanked on the chain holding him in place, bellowing as loud as I was. But his cry was out of pure fury; mine was blinding pain. I met his frantic gaze, memorizing his blue eyes as best I could.

Cassius yanked my head to the side away from Robby and whispered, "You will not remember him," before he sunk his teeth into my throat as he continued his assault. This was his modus operandi. This was the end of my pain and the beginning of pure hell.

"Robby!" Panic overrode the pain pummeling every bone as this bastard pulled my life out a gulp at a time. This was how he intended to wipe out my memory, and I knew from experience how successful he had been in doing so the first time. I would not die for long, though. As a phoenix, I would be reborn, but I wasn't sure my memories would survive the transition.

"Sarah," he cried. "I love you!" His voice carried the same desperation crashing through me.

"Please don't do this," I whispered with the last of my strength.

But Cassius kept pulling the blood from my veins as he relentlessly pounded his hips into mine.

He groaned, speeding up his assault until his body stiffened with his release. He sucked harder, pulling out the last drops of blood still coating my veins. He kept sucking even after cold caressed my skin and all pain disappeared, dropping me into blackness.

MY EYES BLINKED OPEN, and my chest arched as I pulled air deep into my lungs. I ached everywhere, but my attempt to curl in on myself was thwarted by leather binds around my wrists and ankles.

"What the hell?" My brain balked. I had no memory of being chained to a bed before I woke up.

I lifted my head and a smiling face at the end of the bed greeted me. His blond hair was slicked back neatly, and his green eyes were familiar. Then everything I knew about Cassius Chase barreled back and my internal alarms blared.

"How are you feeling?" He cocked his head to the side.

"How the fuck do you think I'm feeling? Get me out of these things." I rattled the chains holding me in place. "Why in God's name am I chained to your bed, Cassius?"

He grinned and stepped aside. "I brought you a gift." He waved to a shirtless man kneeling on the ground, who had that haunted look of a disaster victim.

The man's blue eyes warmed my soul.

"What the hell am I supposed to do with him?" Anger started to burn in my veins.

Cassius's smile faltered, and the man on the floor actually smirked but didn't speak.

"Let me out of these things!" I demanded and yanked on the bindings again. "Did you kidnap me because of what I saw?" I growled at him.

"I turned you. And you need to eat."

"You fucking turned me? You mother-fucking green-eyed demon. Let me out of here!" I spat out the words, glaring at Cassius as if I could kill him just with a look. I wanted to rip his dick off and shove it down his throat until he choked. "I am not drinking that man's blood. I do not kill humans. I kill vampires like you."

"He isn't human. He's a wolf."

"Oh, great. Now you're going to have a pack hunting us down for killing one of their own. You are a damn moron!"

The man behind Cassius started to laugh.

And God, the sound of his laugh turned me on something fierce. His humor-filled, slightly crazed gaze found mine.

"I told you to be silent," Cassius snarled, and the man went silent. Cassius's furious gaze slashed back to mine. He yanked the sheet covering me away and he climbed between my bare legs.

"You will forget everything you know about vampires and the Monster Defense Agency," he growled, and then his teeth buried into my inner thigh.

"Cassius, what the fuck?"

He didn't respond; he just kept sucking blood from my thigh.

"You're going to kill me." I tried to wiggle my thigh loose and then my gaze moved to the man chained to the floor. He gave me a useless shrug, but his eye blazed in a way that felt personal, as though this hurt him as much as it hurt me.

He mouthed something that looked an awful lot like "Love you," and I shivered. *Did I know this man? Is that why my shoulder tingled with heat, and I felt warm and comfortable when our eyes met?*

Blackness descended before I could ask.

MY EYES SNAPPED OPEN, and utter terror filled me. My stomach growled, and I stared at the darkness surrounding me. Movement wasn't possible, and I squinted to see whether I could make out anything of my surroundings.

Something moved in my peripheral vision, but my eyes couldn't seem to focus on anything but general forms, as if I suffered from a concussion. I had no idea where I was.

"Hello?" I asked.

Lights switched on, blinding me. I blinked away the bright spots and a man stood from a chair on my right, passing in front of a lump on the ground. The man's hands were bruised, as if he had been punching a wall. Or another person. My gaze jumped to the form on the ground before returning to his sharp green eyes. Nerves bit in warning.

"Hello, love. Are you going to behave now?"

The form on the ground looked up, pulling my attention to him. One blue eye looked out at me, the other swollen shut. Blood dripped from his mouth and the smell of it made my mouth water.

My gaze moved back to the green-eyed demon standing at the foot of my bed.

"Do you know who I am?" he asked with a cocked eyebrow.

I tried to recall, but there was nothing but a blank slate in my head. "Was I in an accident?" I asked instead of answering him. I had no idea who he was, but he did not instill calm in me the way that peculiar blue eye did.

Green-eyes pursed his lips. "You could say that," he finally said. "Are you hungry?"

My stomach made a hideous noise in answer, and he waved a hand at the beaten man. "I brought him as a gift to satisfy your hunger."

I cocked my head. "I don't understand."

His grin widened. He walked over, untied my wrist and ankle restraints, and helped me out of bed.

I glanced down at myself. "I'm naked."

"Yes, my little vampire, you are. And you need to feed," he said to me and then looked at the man. "On your knees."

The man pushed himself onto his knees and met my inquisitive gaze. Pain marred his beautiful features. Black and blue tattooed his chest, and I glanced at the green-eyed demon's hands.

"You beat him?"

He shrugged as if it wasn't a big deal and then reached for the silver collar, unclipping it.

I gasped. Underneath the collar was blackened skin, as if burned. I reached out and touched it.

He winced but kept his good eye on mine. I could get lost in this man's eyes, and his lips were supple even when marred by blood.

I wiped the blood off his lower lip and stared at my fingers. I slipped my stained fingertips into my mouth, and my stomach clenched. My teeth nearly ripped through my skin, but that little bit of blood ignited my hunger.

I leaned forward and captured the man's mouth in a kiss, sucking his lower lip between my teeth. His tongue slipped into my mouth and the kiss nearly melted me.

The green-eyed demon yanked me away from him. "No," he growled. "Bite his throat and drink." He moved the man's head to the side, exposing the man's throbbing vein.

I palmed his cheek and then leaned in. Just the smell of him was enough to drive me wild. In an instant, my teeth punctured his vein, and I was rewarded with a flood of blood. *Lord, it tasted like the sweetest wine.* I drank greedily, as though I hadn't fed in years. His pulse slowed.

"Sarah," he whispered in my ear. "You're killing me."

His voice coated me with love, and my eyes snapped open. I pulled away in horror. The man dropped to the floor, and he smiled at me before his eyelid closed.

"Finish him," the green-eyed demon growled and pointed at the man.

I backed away, certain that I did the right thing, especially when the man on the floor chuckled softly.

The green-eyed bastard brought his foot back to kick the man, but that was as far as he got. Anger flared, and I turned my teeth on him, catching his arm before he could follow through on that kick. I tore a chunk of skin off his forearm, knocking him off-balance.

He reacted, and his palm hit my chest like a wrecking ball, sending me sailing across the room. Damn, it hurt. And then I slammed into the wall hard enough to knock the lights out.

WICKED HEART 24

SIX MONTHS LATER...
Consciousness ebbed in as stealth as a nightmare, and I blinked my eyes open. I ached and tried to curl into myself, but I was not able to move either my arms or legs. The ceiling above looked familiar, but I couldn't place it. My mind was as foggy as my memory.

"Are you going to be a good little vampire?" a deep voice asked from the shadows.

A figure dropped the drapes shielding the room from the outside world and turned. He was handsome, but I couldn't place him. I didn't even know who I was. Crushing panic hit when his green eyes became visible. I struggled in the bonds that held me to the bed.

"Are you going to behave?"

I screamed as he approached. *Green-eyed demon!* The thought barreled through my head and with it came both fear and fury.

"I have a gift for you." He put up his finger and then stepped to the door and pulled out a whistle.

A moment later, a man with a silver collar and arms bound behind him stepped into the room. He glared at the stranger, but when his eyes fell on me, he stumbled, as if seeing me physically hurt him. His blue eyes held such pain. He opened his mouth but the green-eyed demon who called him clicked his tongue.

"Silence," he said in a commanding tone that even made me want to hush. "And do not move unless I tell you." He reached behind the man and unclipped the collar around his throat. "Good dog," he said in a condescending tone. "Now, kneel."

The dark-haired man dropped to his knees and winced.

The green-eyed demon came closer, and I tensed. But my gaze kept going to his captive and those soulful blue eyes. Those eyes calmed the storm inside and gave me a sense of sadness so deep that it was impossible to escape. Something inside me broke at the sight of him, creating a web of pain through every cell. Dread filled me, and I looked at the green-eyed devil as he leaned over and untied my feet. Then he untied my hands.

"I brought you a hot meal." He waved at the prisoner.

I licked my lips and looked between the two men as competing emotions hammered me.

"He is yours to devour, my dear." The green-eyed demon helped me from the bed. "I want him to experience the true horror of what you are."

Hunger raked my cells, and I could hear his heartbeat. It sounded like a thousand galloping horses. He smelled divine, like a sweet, decadent dessert with an underlying animal scent.

"What is he?" I asked, unsure those were the right words to ask the question that was in my mind.

"A wolf."

The way he whispered those words thrilled me. Somehow, I understood what he meant, and I approached the blue-eyed man, staring at the burn marks on his throat. Those blue eyes pleaded.

"Let him speak." I wanted to hear the timbre of his voice and what plea was behind those eyes.

"Alas, I cannot."

The blue-eyed man was pleasing to look at, and my body responded to him. Oh, how I wanted those arms around me. But somehow, I knew if I revealed that desire, the green-eyed devil would not be pleased, and pain would follow.

"Mine?" I whispered and looked to the green-eyed devil for confirmation.

"Yours." He smiled, but there was something sinister in that look, as if perhaps I had used the wrong word. "Now feed."

The blue-eyed man moved his head ever so slightly as if he was saying no, but being this close to him, hearing his heart thunder and seeing the vein in his neck pulse, was too much.

"Tilt your head up," the green-eyed devil said. "Offer her your throat."

The man slowly lifted his chin, fully exposing his neck to me. He shook as if the effort was too great.

I put my hand on his bare chest, and the muscles underneath my palm constricted. He closed his eyes, mouthing a word that I didn't know.

Being this close to him was like being plugged into an electrical socket. I felt alive, and longing set in. I pressed my mouth to his throat, and his pulse quickened, along with his rasping breath.

My teeth pierced his flesh, and his blood flowed into my mouth. The taste of him was exquisite, and I pulled mouthful after mouthful, tugging him closer with each suck. His heartbeat under my palm slowed and his skin chilled as I pulled his life blood from the far reaches of his body.

"Sarah. Killing me."

His strained whisper was like a punch to the gut, and I pulled away from him in horror.

Those blue eyes flashed at me before they closed, and the man crumpled to the ground. Blood trickled from the wounds I inflicted, and I fought the need to latch on again until there was no more of that sweet-smelling nectar.

"Finish what you started," the green-eyed devil growled.

"No." I had no idea why that word slipped from my mouth but it did, and along with it came the certainty that it was the right choice.

The green-eyed devil growled and grabbed the silver collar off the floor. He slapped it around the man's throat. The stench of burning flesh filled my senses and then the blue-eyed man was dragged from the room. But not before a dimple appeared in his cheek as if he had won another victory.

Then he was gone from view.

I stepped toward the open door, but before I could blink, the green-eyed devil was back, and he looked angry, as if I had betrayed him.

"You will obey."

"No."

"I made you. I can un-fucking make you." He prowled forward with his hands in fists. "All you will remember is the love you had for *me*," he shouted in my face and then brought me close.

Fangs pierced my neck, and I stiffened. Pain filled my head, blinding me, and then I fell into a void where only agony and terror gripped me. A scar on my shoulder throbbed in time with my heart, reminding me there was more than this void. More than the misery, and if I persevered, I would be rewarded.

WICKED HEART 25

ROBBY YOUNG
She still couldn't kill me. Six months of this bloody game, and she still has sense enough to stop. Even if she doesn't know why.

I smiled and then a shiver coursed through me hard enough to make my teeth chatter as my body fought to refuel. One of these days, she would kill me. I could not continue to donate my blood at the pace that bastard demanded.

My mind drifted back to that first time he killed her. I had truly lost my mind watching him break her bones and then when he mounted her, I felt myself fracture. He got what he wanted: a broken alpha, more broken than her dead body splayed out on the bed.

Logically, I knew she was a phoenix. But seeing her dead, broken, and defiled form on the bed had destroyed a part of me.

When she ignited like a funeral pyre, I had lost it and just bellowed wordlessly until my vocal cords shattered. I expected her to be nothing but a blackened skeleton. Her fire burned pure white, like it had in the forest. It felt as though I had been transported into the landscape of hell. No one could withstand that type of heat.

But the fire burned out almost as quickly as it started. I blinked at the pristine sheets and at her rosy cheeks and the cadence of her chest moving. None of her limbs were angled wrong with the broken bones like they had been before that bastard killed her.

My God, seeing her transform from the dead and broken husk I was so used to seeing in our investigations, back to the embodiment of life, silenced my sobs.

Awe at the power she held blanketed me. And when she woke a few minutes later, she was my Sarah, all spunk and anger, and I loved her even more than I thought possible. But after he stripped her of life again, he beat me, whaling his anger on me in punch after punch. I blacked out and didn't see Sarah's miracle that time, nor any time since.

Her reincarnations seemed to take longer each time. And although that might be the thing that has kept me alive this long, God help me, there were days when I wished she wouldn't stop feeding on me, and I could end this crippling pain. Seeing her bound on that bed and knowing he was taking full advantage of her whenever he damned well pleased drove me batshit crazy.

The air shifted, and I looked up. For a moment, I could have sworn I felt her near me. I scanned the room and then dropped my head onto the small mattress in the center of my silver cell. I must be losing it. Hell, if a miracle occurred and we escaped this madness, I'm not quite sure I'd ever be able to fully restore my sanity.

I knew I wasn't sane anymore. I had lost my grip on reality because I craved her teeth in my flesh. I craved her that close to me. When her hair fanned over me and her breath tickled my throat, it was a moment in heaven. Sometimes her hand landed over my heart and sometimes it cradled my head, but it was *her* touch, even if she was using it to gage my death.

My eyes closed. All I had to do to end this was keep my mouth shut as she pulled my life out in mouthfuls of blood. Yet I clung to life, to that desperate hope that she would come back to me. It took everything I had to break Cassius's silence command, and when I did, it triggered her to stop. The day I couldn't break his compelling command to remain silent was the day I would die.

Well, theoretically speaking. If she didn't kill me, the silver bindings eventually would. They sapped my strength, leaving me little energy to fight back. And this damned collar had been on long enough that silver poisoning was a sure bet. And at this point, I wasn't sure it was something I could come back from anyway.

The door to the room opened, and Cassius walked in, whistling. He dropped something on the floor in front of the cage, and I stared at them in horror.

Good lord, those are Sarah's eyeballs.

"If she can't see you, she can't react to you."

What the fuck kind of monster was this asshole? A low growl escaped but it wasn't feral enough to encompass all the fury and fear that filled me. "You are a crazy fuck," I whispered, because that's all I could muster at the moment.

He twirled the dog whistle on the cord around his finger. "We'll see." He almost skipped out of the room, as if he had figured out a sure way to win this battle of the minds.

That fucking whistle. Someday, I was going to shove that thing down his fucking throat. He programmed me to come to him when he blows it, as if I were a damn domesticated dog.

My gaze landed on the beautiful brown eyes, so very out of place on the barren floor in front of my silver cage. My heart slowly fell into my stomach. *What if he was right? What if he had figured out a way to wipe the fight out of her?*

I looked away as despair layered over me like a cold blanket, and I fought to keep warm. With the last of my strength, I sent a prayer to whoever in heaven would take pity on us.

Please, Lord, let Sarah find herself again, and if it is your will to let me be a part of it, so be it. If not, please don't let her blame herself for my death. She is not aware of the levels of psychological warfare that bastard has waged against her for months on end. It's in your name I pray. Amen.

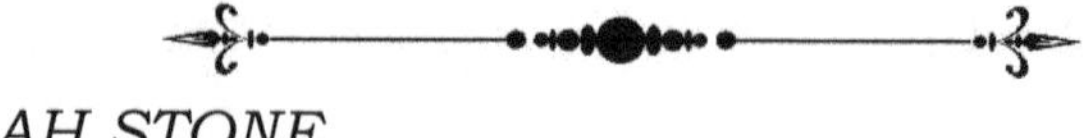

SARAH STONE

Darkness surrounded me, and my body felt weightless in the void. I was no one. I had no memory, no identity, and no emotion. Until a light shined in the distance. As it crept closer, awe enveloped me.

An ornate flaming bird approached and then circled around me. When it landed, it shifted into a beautiful woman with flames in her red hair. She smiled at me, and warmth bathed every cell.

"You must stop this, my child."

I cocked my head. "Stop what?"

"Stop letting that vile vampire rule your mind." She reached out and took my hand. "And protect your mate. He is the reason I am here. You tell him his prayers were answered."

"My...mate?"

"Your wolf with fur as black as night, painted with golden tips. He has been abused for months by that vile beast, and will not survive another episode. So, you need to claim your memories." She gently pulled me forward into an unfamiliar room where a silver cell sat, and a man lay curled on a barren mattress, with hands behind his back bound in silver and a silver collar around his throat. "You need to get that vampire to remove his bonds. Not only has your feeding weakened him, but the silver is slowly poisoning him."

A gasp escaped my lips as the hard truths of our situation ebbed in and sadness enveloped me. His eyes opened, searching the space as if he felt me near, and his pained expression crushed a part of my soul.

"I did that to him?"

"No." She led me back into a dark bedroom, where a form lay bound to a bed.

A man paced, muttering under his breath. His hands ran through his hair, leaving it in a spiked mess. He looked completely insane. "You will be mine," he growled and paced. Then he pounced on the woman, shaking her still form.

I caught a glimpse of her face. "That's me," I whispered.

"You will be mine, you hear me!" the man bellowed. "If you can't see him, you can't react to that filthy fucking wolf."

My insides turned frigid with fear as the man peeled open my eyelids and ripped my eyeballs out. He left the room with them, and I shivered, repulsed at the barren caves where my eyes used to be.

"Do not worry. He did not steal your eyesight. When a phoenix is reborn, she becomes whole. And this time, you will be whole not just physically, but with every last memory intact, including this conversation we are having. You need a full understanding of what you're dealing with. His last command was for you to only feel the love you once felt for him." She grimaced as she looked at me. "So, you must play along. You must get that silver off your mate, and you must end this today while the sun is high enough to spill into this room." She cupped my cheek. "I can only do so much to help, but I can break the binds he has around your memories. But if you falter, your mate will die, and you will forever be at that man's mercy. I would not wish that on my worst enemy."

I stared at my dead and eyeless form on the bed and nodded. When she wrapped her arms around me in a warm hug, flames enveloped us.

One by one, the walls Cassius put up in my mind shattered, letting the events of my entire life flood in. If she hadn't been holding me, I would have collapsed to the ground with despair.

How could Robby possibly be alive? The thought crushed my insides as I relived each moment of our captivity. Each demon act that Cassius inflicted on both of us. I sobbed against this woman's shoulder, and she held me tight, shushing me softly as she combed my hair with her fingers.

When my sobs subsided, she continued, "You are a mighty phoenix and a crafty witch. And even though vampire blood taints a human soul, you are not tainted by it, and you are not bound to your maker. You *will* survive his death."

"Will killing him burn away this vampire curse?" I asked through the assault of memories.

"No, child. You've tasted human blood and therefore the curse cannot be lifted. But you control the darkness within you. It is bound to your light and that is a much stronger force."

"Who are you?" I wiped my tears and pulled away from this magical savior.

The softness of her smile warmed me the same way Robby did. It bathed me with unmistakable love. "I am your mother. I was not spared in the slaughter of our kind, but I made sure you were well hidden before I was caught and slayed."

I narrowed my eyes at her. "There hasn't been a phoenix since the thirteenth century."

She nodded. "Yes."

"I've been alive since the thirteenth century?" Cassius's claims flowed back into my memories.

She chuckled. "No. Not in the human sense that you are used to. You were born in this century. The witch who safeguarded your soul for me passed it from generation to generation until the world had all but forgotten about the phoenix. That was when she implanted you in your human mother's womb." She gently kissed my cheek.

"Cassius said I was promised to him." I stared at her as that thought chilled me enough to shiver.

She pressed her lips together and glanced away. "Your father made that promise. A trade for eternal life. Your life for his self-gratification." Her tone turned dark, and the light surrounding her faded. "I did not agree to give my child to a vampire." Her gaze snapped back to mine. "And certainly not one who wishes to build an army and take over the world like that vile creature." Her features transitioned to a scowl. "He slaughtered every last one of us to find you."

"What can kill a phoenix?" I asked as her words sunk in. I needed to know what my weakness was.

"We have a finite number of rebirths, my dear. You are dangerously close to nearing yours, and your ward knows it."

"Is that why you came?"

She shook her head. "Your mate's prayers convinced the father to send me. He did not pray for himself. He prayed for you to be spared any pain that his death would cause."

My throat closed, and I pressed my lips together against another sudden wave of tears blurring my vision.

"I must be going, but before I do, you need to remember these words and utter them when that vampire scum is not present. It will break all that bastard's charms and set you and your mate free of his control."

I blinked back my tears, sniffled, and nodded, waiting.

"Frange vincula."

"Frange vincula?" I repeated, burning the words to memory.

"Yes. And remember, you must convince him that his memory control worked, which means you will need to convince him that you are in love with him, and only him."

I shuddered at the thought, but I would do anything to free Robby.

She turned to go.

"Mother?"

She stopped and glanced over her shoulder. "I love you, child. Now steel your nerves." She shifted back into that beautiful phoenix and flew away, dropping me back into the darkness as her fire burned through my soul.

I INHALED AS IF I had been underwater for ages, my mind sharp for the first time in months. I took breath after breath as my eyes adjusted to the room. I blinked, surprised I could see after his desecration of my dead body.

Movement drew my eyes, and I steeled my reaction. My mother's words echoed in my head, and I let my gaze fall on Cassius as he approached the side of the bed.

He smiled down at me. "Do you know who I am?" he asked softly, but his eyes reflected the dangerous storm brewing underneath.

If I answered wrong, he would eviscerate me.

I slowly smiled. "My love," I whispered. The only way I could make my eyes reflect that feeling was thinking about Robby and his soulful blue eyes.

Cassius brightened, as if he had finally won a long and bloody war. "Yes, my dear." He grinned and stepped forward, undoing the cuffs around my wrists and ankles. As soon as he untied me, I sat up and wrapped my arms around him, pressing my lips to his.

He jerked in surprise, and then kissed me in earnest, burying his hands in my hair as he groaned with a longing that sickened me. Then he pulled away. "I have a gift for you, if you'll indulge me for a moment."

"Of course." I remained seated on the edge of the bed with a dreamy smile as I watched him hurry out of the room. At least he didn't use the whistle. If he had, I would be up shit's creek.

"Frange vincula," I whispered the moment I was sure he was out of hearing range. A hiss traveled through the room, and I felt the charms disintegrate. If I wanted to pull my fire, I was now free to do so.

A moment later, he stepped into the room, practically dragging Robby behind him. Cassius's expression was one of triumph, and I had to keep my eyes on him in order to keep this ruse going. If I looked at Robby, I would blow it. I needed to play this game for both of us, no matter how much Cassius made my skin crawl.

He clasped the end of the chain to the floor. "I've brought you dinner."

I cocked my head, feigning innocence. Every command he had given before he drained me compounded would have left me with the mind of an innocent child who knew nothing of the kind of monster he was. "Dinner? I...I don't understand."

"You are a vampire, my dear. We drink blood from the veins of live beings."

"Oh." I sniffed the air and tilted my head to the side. "It doesn't smell like you do." I stood, keeping my gaze glued on Cassius, as if I couldn't tear my eyes away. I focused with rapt attention, on purpose.

"Well, no. It wouldn't. I'm a vampire like you, and this is a wolf."

"A wolf." I tested out the word as if it were the first time I had ever said it, and then furrowed my brow at him.

"A dog. You know, a furry companion."

I took a quick glance, avoiding Robby's eyes. "But he looks like you do." Actually, he looked a hell of a lot skinnier than he had six months ago, and his pallor was sickly enough to almost make me forget to keep in character.

Cassius took a breath and ran a hand through his hair. "He is a wolf shifter. You remember wolves, don't you?" he asked.

I felt the wave of information flow from him. If I had been the stupid mindless drone he thought he created, it would hit like a flurry of pictures.

I widened my eyes accordingly and clapped. "Oh, can I see? Can I see it in wolf form?" I nearly jumped up and down like an excited child.

Annoyance passed over his features, and he took another breath.

I kept in character, begging him with wide eyes. "Please, my love. I want to see a wolf."

"I don't think that's a good idea," he finally said when he reschooled his own face into the patient lover gaze.

Regretting wiping my mind already? I pushed the thought away. Now was not the time to gloat. I was still walking through a bed of hot coals that could ignite at any moment.

"Please." I crossed to him and tiptoed, pressing my lips to his.

Robby growled, and I ignored him.

"I want to feed on a wild animal. I want my face buried in soft fur while I taste his blood. Please?" I kissed Cassius again, letting it linger while I pulled him closer to my fully naked form. The thought of burying my face in Robby's fur was revving my engine more than I cared to admit, but with how I was acting, Cassius took it as a sign that he was the one affecting me this way.

I broke the kiss, and Cassius's eyes sparkled with triumph. His gloating smile was meant for Robby, not me.

When his eyes flicked toward my mate, I followed his gaze, glancing warily in Robby's direction. "You can control him, right?" I looked back at Cassius, searching his evil green eyes. Eyes I wanted to pluck out of his head and stomp on with my own bare heel.

"Of course I can control him." He rolled his eyes as he peeled me off him. He did not seem to like this clinging thing I was projecting, which thrilled me. He reached down and unclasped Robby's wrist restraints.

I kept my gaze on Cassius and displayed excitement, as if I were a child in a candy store. He thought it was because I was going to feed on the wolf, but it really was him freeing Robby that made my blood run hot.

"Stay," Cassius growled and unclasped Robby's collar. Despite the command, he stepped behind me, pulling me back a few steps to where he felt was a safe distance.

I glanced over my shoulder and smiled at him, and then turned back to Robby.

Robby shook and the devastation painting his face nearly drew a gasp from me. I put my hand over Cassius's on my shoulder and squeezed it lightly, as if showing my appreciation for his actions. But it was really as compensation for the shock of Robby's desolate expression. I forced myself to meet Robby's gaze.

"Why isn't he shifting, love?" I asked Cassius, and then sent a wink at Robby.

If he comprehended my wink, he didn't show any signs of it, but the growl that came from him was menacing as he looked beyond me to Cassius. In a blink, the massive black wolf with golden-tipped fur stood before us with his teeth bared.

Cassius pulled me back a couple of steps, gasping. His eyes were wide in a way I had never seen from the vampire. He hadn't seen Robby's wolf since before I pulled him from death with my tears. Cassius gripped my arms and took another step backward, still reeling at the giant wolf in front of us.

Excitement flooded my senses.

"Sit!" Cassius hissed from behind me, and Robby obeyed. "And do not move a muscle."

I don't think Robby caught my wink. His eyes still carried a crushing hopelessness, as if Cassius had finally won. I turned and gave Cassius a hug because I couldn't stand to see Robby so lost. I squealed with delight before I peeled out of his arms and approached my mate, studying him like one would a lab rat. I ran my hand down the fur of his chest, and he shuddered from the touch.

"What an exquisite animal." I circled around him, trailing my fingers through his fur. "Oh, my." Just touching him warmed my soul, and I sent a playful glance at Cassius, licking my lips suggestively, conveying that I was turned on. I moved away from Robby, toward the far window, praying it was the right time of day, that opening those curtains would bathe my wolf in sunlight and keep him safe from Cassius's fury.

"What are you doing?" Cassius asked, alarm rising in his voice.

I reached for the curtains and smiled over my shoulder. "I want to see the wolf in the moonlight." I slung the curtains wide.

"Don't!" Cassius yelled. He moved toward me with eyes wide with fear, but it was too late. Sunshine split the room, and he jumped back into the shadows, gasping.

I turned, keeping that same innocent and excited smile on my face. I stared at Robby. His fur glistened in the sunshine, and his gaze split between me and the vampire in the shadows. I could see the gears in his mind moving and his confusion overshadowed his despair.

"How are you not burned?" Cassius gasped. His eyes were even wider with shock at me standing in direct sunlight than they had been when he saw Robby's wolf.

That's right. He didn't know about my day-walking abilities. I circled back to Robby, burying my face into the fur of his neck, nuzzling it and purring.

I glanced back at Cassius with a grin. "Oh, Cassius, this is delightful." I turned and crossed to him. "But before I address the needs of my stomach, I seem to have a different kind of hunger that demands to be satisfied." I reached up and started unbuttoning his shirt, pushing him toward the other set of curtains.

The look on his face was priceless and before I even got to his belt, he was tearing at his clothing. "Stay," he commanded at Robby, and then he was stripping faster than I could keep up with.

He started navigating me toward the bed, but I stopped him by skirting under his arm and positioning myself behind him. I kissed his shoulder and ran my tongue down the line of his neck.

"What—

His voice cut off when I wrapped my hand around him and started to stroke. It took everything I had to not dig my nails into him. Soon enough I'd take his manhood, but right now, I needed him preoccupied with flaunting my willingness to get him off to Robby.

Cassius started to turn toward me.

"No, I want the wolf to see what a wicked heart I have and what kind of magic my mouth can do before I tear his throat open," I whispered and licked the line of Cassius's neck.

Robby growled, and Cassius glanced over his shoulder at me. I smiled at him and licked my lips. "But if you'd prefer..." I glanced toward the bed, hoping my bet was the right one. Otherwise, I would lose the element of surprise.

"Oh, no. This is perfect." He turned back to Robby with a smug smile.

I stroked Cassius slowly, switching hand to hand as he sprang to life in my palms. My back-and-forth movements ran my breasts against his back, and I kissed his neck, running my tongue over his shoulder, biting down on my gag reflex. I would have to scrub my mouth clean after this.

"Sarah. Oh God, Sarah. I need you to suck my cock." Cassius tilted his head back and groaned as I continued my calculated strokes.

He turned his face towards me, and I captured a kiss, wishing for a knife in my free hand. The cool metal handle fit snug in my grip and with a flick of my wrist, I castrated the bastard.

Robby's eyes widened.

Cassius hadn't registered that I cut off his dick yet, but that was going to change in seconds. I turned, spinning out of his grip, and threw open the curtains behind me, shielding the severed member still in my palm.

His breath hitched and his eyes widened as blood cascaded down his legs. He turned and screamed like a little girl. "You bitch!" His hands covered the bloody stump where his cock used to be as his face turned crimson. He dropped to his knees in the only sliver of shade left in the room.

I held the still hard thing in my hand. Disgust coursed through me, and I met Cassius's gaze before reaching my hand out so the sun could hit his severed penis. It burst into flame, and ash sifted between my fingers. "That is for every single depraved act imprinted on my brain, from what you did to all your victims through the centuries that you walked this earth, to what you did to me in my bedroom, and most of all, for the vile acts you did here to both of us." I nodded toward Robby and righteous anger flared. My hands burst into flame, and I pointed a fiery finger at Cassius. "You asked how I can withstand the sun? I'm a fucking phoenix, you filthy moron." I had to grit my teeth against dousing him in my flame.

I glanced up at Robby, finally meeting his gaze. "Frange vincula," I said and the last of the charms holding him in place evaporated with a hiss. "While I would love to cook you to a fucking crisp, Robby has a score to settle."

"Stay," Cassius yelled in a strangled voice, but his commands fell flat.

Robby stood and his growl became feral as he moved toward the injured vampire.

"You once told me a vampire betrayed was more dangerous than a scorned woman. Well, you've never encountered a wolf who you've mind-fucked for months."

Robby launched and in one move, he tore Cassius's arm clean off and flung it into the sunlight.

I moved to the window and watched as he tore Cassius apart piece by piece, tossing the bits into the sun, where they turned to ash. Cassius's scream hurt my ears, but I delighted in Robby's brutality. When all that was left was Cassius's head on his gutted torso, and the vampire's screams had become whimpers, Robby decapitated him and made sure the rest of the vile vampire landed in the path of the fiery sun.

When the last piece was ash, Robby's gaze fell on me. Gore covered his snout, and he seemed to smile at me in that canine way that I used to love. Tears brimmed, blurring his slow advance as my pain came through my anger. What that bastard had done all these months was worthy of his end.

"I don't know how you survived," I sobbed and took a shaky step toward him.

His wolf stepped close and licked my cheeks, whining, and then he transitioned, and his lips captured my tears in featherlight kisses before he claimed my mouth in a kiss that seared my soul to his for the rest of time.

He kissed me so fiercely that he pulled the air right out of my lungs. "You didn't die when he did," he said against my lips and then his arms wrapped around me, tightening like a vise as he shook, letting his own relief loose. "How?"

When I had control, I pulled back enough to meet his gaze. "I am a badass phoenix with a wicked fucking heart."

He smiled and pressed his forehead to mine. "Thank the Lord."

"By the way, my mother told me to tell you your prayers worked."

His chin quivered and he hugged me before kissing me gently. "I...I need to get out of this place," he whispered, breaking this moment. He shivered uncontrollably in my arms.

His need to escape the place where he should have died, and I should have been Cassius's plaything for the rest of eternity, burned as acutely in my veins as it did in his plea.

I closed my eyes and wished clothing on our bodies. The hushed whisper of fabric filled my ears, and then I took Robby's hand and led him out of this house and into the busy city streets.

WICKED HEART 26

ROBBY STUMBLED, AND I wrapped my arm around him as we weaved through the streets. Sirens sounded as we shuffled away from the upscale Brooklyn brownstone. I guess when I whispered the incantation that my mother had given me, all the charms Cassius had protecting his house broke, and someone must have heard him screaming, and called the cops.

"Where are we headed?" Robby asked with a voice that was too weak, and my heart knotted in my chest at how sickly he looked in the sunshine.

"Home," I said because, ironically, Robby's place wasn't that far from Cassius's house. It was our only option because my house had long since burned to ash.

"We don't have a home," he mumbled.

"Your mortgage was paid up. It's the best we have until you gain your strength back." One glance told me he needed real rest and not the pain-laden stupor he'd likely been in for the last six months.

"I'm fine," he muttered before I even finished my sentence.

"You look like shit," I responded, as quickly as he did. "And I need to scrub my fucking mouth and hands clean." I shuddered under his weight.

He glanced at me and even his eyes looked dull and nearly absent of life with the exception of the spark of anger that lingered. "You touched him," he said with a low growl. "Willingly."

"I cut off his dick." I slashed a glare in his direction.

"Still."

Robby did not have all the facts, and he needed them. He wasn't in the room the last time Cassius killed me. He didn't hear his memory command. "The last time he killed me, he commanded that I only remember the love I had for him," I explained. "And I did what was necessary to get that silver off you."

"Were you playing him this whole time?" He glanced at me.

"No," I admitted. "If you hadn't prayed for me…" I pressed my lips together at the horror and pain that statement brought me. Taking a breath to steady my voice, I continued, "If you hadn't said that prayer, neither of us would be here, free of that bastard. You're the one who convinced our heavenly maker to let my mother talk to me."

"You saw your mom?" His eyes softened.

"Not the one who raised me and died in the car crash." I met Robby's gaze. "She wasn't the one who originally conceived me and who died safeguarding my soul from Cassius. She never agreed to give her child to a vampire." I turned left down an alley as the sirens got closer, skirting through the maze of side streets until we came out a few blocks away. I turned right and then left again at the next intersection, and Robby's place came into view. "She's the one who burned down all of Cassius's memory barriers and gave me the phrase that destroyed his hold on both of us."

"Frange vincula?" he asked.

"Yes." I was impressed that he remembered, even down to the right pronunciation.

"It's not something I'm apt to forget, especially since those words made the binds of his commands feel like a bomb disintegrated them."

His feet moved with the speed of someone stuck in wet concrete. I needed to keep him alert and walking because I couldn't carry Robby. Even at his reduced weight, he was still heavy and carrying him would bring unwanted attention. As it was, we didn't look natural. It was clear I was holding him up but thankfully, we didn't run into anyone by taking the narrow alleyways between buildings. "You know how a cat has nine lives?" I asked as we turned onto the small walkway that led to his modest brownstone.

"Mhm."

The stairs proved to be more difficult for him, as if his body was breaking down from either the silver poisoning or the lack of blood. It took all my concentration to help him up without us tumbling down.

"Well, a phoenix has a finite number of lives, too." I put my hand out and willed his house keys into my hand. I didn't care about the Monster Defense Agency right now. We had been totally off the grid for six months, and if they came, I'd let my power go like I had done in the woods. Burn down everything except Robby that was within a few hundred yards. The lock twisted, and I pushed the door open, nearly dragging Robby inside.

"Is that why she came to you?"

"No. Your prayer did that. You saved us by praying for me." I leaned him against the wall and shut the door, locking up behind me.

He found his dusty couch and collapsed on it. When I took a seat next to him, he dropped his head into my lap, curling up on the couch as if his entire form hurt.

He needed a real meal, something that would give him a fragment of strength. "What do you want to eat?"

"Steak," he said without hesitation, and I conjured up the biggest, heartiest, rarest-cooked steak, along with a tall glass of milk. He picked up the meat with his fingers and took a nibble, chewing slowly with his eyes closed, as if eating took too much energy.

The bastard had locked Robby up in a silver cage for six months and made me nearly drain

him of blood at least forty times. That amounted
to a little less than twice a week since we were
captured, and Robby was still alive. Which
meant that asshole had to have given him some
food so he wouldn't starve to death between
donating blood to me because he wanted me and
nothing else to kill my mate. "What did he feed
you?"

He opened his eyes and glanced up at me.
"Rats he caught in his attic." Grimacing, he
stared at the steak in his hand and took another
bite, this one bigger.

I shuddered at the thought. I'm sure the rats
were raw and, in some cases, long dead. It made
me hate Cassius even more. I would conjure up
steaks every five minutes if that's what it took to
get Robby back on his feet. I ran my hand
through his hair as he ate. When he finished, he
tossed the picked clean T-bone onto the plate
and then licked his fingers.

He rolled onto his back and stared up at me.
"Did I die?" he whispered.

My vision blurred, and I tried to blink back
my tears. But one escaped and slid down my
cheek, splashing onto his forehead. "No. We got
out of there."

His chin quivered and tears escaped the
corner of his eyes. "I lost my fucking mind,
Sarah. And I'm not sure I can get it back." He
slung his arm over his eyes. The burn marks on
his wrist were deep into the layers of his skin.

His muffled sniffles cut deep, and just the
sight of his blackened wrist and neck turned on
the waterworks. "I nearly killed you so many
times." The words came out strangled in a sob,

and he moved his arm back so he could look at me.

"But you didn't." He slowly sat up and I turned, wrapping my arms around him. When I put my head on his shoulder, he stiffened. A flash of fear crossed his face, like I was going to bite him again.

The tears just kept coming, and I pressed my face against his neck as the sobs racked my body. He trembled, but kept his arms around me and his hands flat on my back, feeling the solid mass of me underneath his palms as if he didn't quite believe this was real.

I kissed the side of his neck and he flinched, but when I moved my lips to the edge of his clenched jaw, he looked down at me as if the kiss broke him out of whatever terror he was reliving.

I claimed his mouth with mine, moving myself to straddle his lap. No matter what I did, I could not get close enough to him to steady my pounding heart. When I pulled away, he stared at me and the doubt in his gaze kept the tears flowing.

Tentatively, he reached up, cupping my cheek. He ran his thumb through the warm tracks streaming down my face. His lashes shined with his own tears as he caressed my cheek with his thumb. "God help me if this isn't real..."

How could I get him to understand that it was? I pinched his bicep, hard.

"Ouch." He flinched and looked at where I had pinched him. Then his gaze snapped back to mine, and he glanced around at our surroundings, as if waking from a nightmare. "This...is real?" He searched my eyes and then pulled me into a tight hug. "Thank you, Lord," he whispered and laid his head on my shoulder.

Robby's hands trailed over me, as if he were memorizing every curve with his fingertips and convincing himself that this was indeed happening. "I thought I had lost you," he whispered as his blue-eyed gaze locked with mine.

"I would die a thousand deaths and still come back to you." I crushed his lips in a kiss that promised a lifetime of unbridled passion.

The End

Continue Sarah and Robby's story with CROOKED SOUL - Book 2 of the Shades of Night Series.

SHADES OF NIGHT
BOOK 2
CROOKED SOUL

Escaping from captivity brings its own special challenges. Like dealing with PTSD, along with major trust issues.

When an ancient vampire arrives from overseas, she comes with baggage from a past long before I was born. And she is hell-bent on revenge.

Not only are we trying to dodge the monsters, but we are back on the radar of the Monster Defense Agency, and they are pissed.

If Robby and I can't get our shit together, either the MDA or the master of the vampire who nearly destroyed us will finish the job.

1

CROOKED SOUL 1

ROBBY'S ARMS AND LEGS curled around me in his bed with a grip that was almost painful as he held on tight enough to nearly crush me. His eyelashes laid on his cheeks like a fan of black against the paleness he still carried from our ordeal. His dark hair had dried in matted clumps along with random spikes from nuzzling into the pillow.

Still, he was beautiful to behold, bed head and all, even with his drop in weight from six months of eating just rats provided to him whenever Cassius had thought of it. It had been just enough food to sustain life, but nowhere near what Robby needed to remain healthy. His huge alpha werewolf form had thinned enough to make him look like a prisoner of war.

I traced the lines of his jaw gently, marveling that he was still alive. By all rights, he shouldn't have survived. He should have died in my arms, and my heart ached with the pain of my participation in his suffering. I had been watching him sleep because whenever my eyes closed, the bad dreams came alive, and I couldn't deal with my trauma right now. I needed to focus on Robby, on getting him back to health both physically and mentally.

He was deep enough in sleep not to stir at my touch, and his breathing remained steady. He hadn't been willing to talk to me about what happened beyond what I remembered. Even though only a couple of days had passed since our escape, I still had to keep reminding him that this was real. Much like when I woke from my own nightmares and my heart plummeted for a moment, thinking I was still tied to that goddamned bed.

Both of us needed reminders that we were at Robby's place and not still locked away in Cassius's house.

Cassius Chase fractured Robby's mind, just like he threatened. But he was never able to erase the warmth of Robby's mark tingling in my shoulder. He hadn't been able to wipe away the pull in my heart whenever I was near my mate. If he had, neither of us would be here, safely tucked in his bed.

I sighed, and Robby's eyes fluttered open. His gaze landed on my face and his pupils dilated even before he smiled. Every now and then, I'd get a glimpse of the old Robby, like right now, but then it would pass, and my heart would drop as if I had taken a step off the balcony of the Empire State Building.

His post-traumatic stress disorder presented in flinches whenever I came near his throat. But his grip on me most of the time belied his skittishness, as if his heart knew more than his mind.

But for now, my Robby smiled at me from inches away. His gaze made me feel like another wonder of the world, and it warmed me from my core all the way to my fingers and toes. My mark tingled in response.

The side of his throat that I had cried on when we arrived home healed completely. That was also the side I tore into when Cassius made me drink his blood. But Robby's whispering of my name stopped me every single time, sparking raw fury from the vampire who wanted to control me. However, Robby's wrists and the opposite side of his neck were still burnt from the silver collar and shackles. Although, this morning, they didn't look as angry as they had yesterday.

"Hey," Robby said with his rough morning voice. He stretched, uncurling his legs from around me.

"Hey." I smiled, still cuddling in the crook of his arm.

His gaze landed on his visible wrist and all that lightness surrounding him evaporated. That haunted look slid back into his eyes, and he dropped his hand onto the bed and stared at his ceiling. "It wasn't just a nightmare."

"I wish it *had* been just a nightmare." Neither of us could shake the effects of what happened to us for long. It sucked.

Robby moved his gaze to me. He studied my face while his finger lightly traced my lips. "I craved your bite," he said. "Sometimes I think I still do."

Every time he revealed a piece of his pain, it squeezed my chest, like a noose tightening around me. I pulled myself on top of him and kissed him hard. "I will never puncture your skin with my teeth again," I whispered against his lips. "I would rather starve to death."

His hands landed on my bare hips, and he caressed my lower back and ass, squeezing my butt cheeks as he sighed under my lips.

That sigh always preceded him pulling away, and this time was no different. He rolled me off him and sat up on the side of the bed with his back to me like I was a one-night stand and not his true mate.

"Robby," I whispered as another layer of fear wrapped around my soul. What if he never came back to me?

His shoulders rounded and he hung his head before glancing back at me. "He made me kill you."

I reached out and ran my fingers across his back gently. Cassius had made Robby kill me once. I had woken and just screamed and struggled against the bindings, calling Cassius a dirty demon. I guess I held onto most of my promises that I had made to that bastard. In an effort to smash Robby's hold on my heart, Cassius called him in and ordered him to choke me until my face was blue and my neck crushed. The bastard thought that would be enough to psychologically fuck with me so I would drain Robby dry the next time I sank my teeth into his throat, whether he spoke or not.

Robby had sobbed as he strangled me to death. He pleaded and begged for Cassius to stop. I had never seen him so desperate, but his hands just kept squeezing, no matter how hard I bucked against my bindings.

"He fucking fondled you while I choked you to death." He stared at his trembling hands. He met my gaze. "I couldn't stop. Not even after you died. My hands kept squeezing even after your spine shattered." He wiped his hands on the sheet, trying to absolve himself of that horror.

"He compelled you to do it."

"He also compelled me to be silent while you fed." His gaze slid to mine. "I was able to break that every time. So why couldn't I do the same then?"

I didn't have an answer for him, and his pain echoed in my shoulder like a deep wound that would never heal. "He coerced me to nearly kill you so many times." I reached for him, and he knocked my hand away with a flare of anger.

"You stopped. Every fucking time. I couldn't."

I sat up. I didn't know what he needed but my heart ached for him. "I forgive you."

"Well, I don't fucking forgive myself. I couldn't do a goddamn thing when he was hurting you. I still hear your screams when I close my eyes. And I was helpless. Fucking helpless when he killed you over and over again. Just as fucking helpless as I was when he ordered me to choke you to death.”

I took a slow breath. There was something I could do, but I wasn’t just going to steal his memories without his consent. I had been there, and it nearly doomed both of us. “Do you want me to make you forget what happened?”

His angry features transitioned to abject horror, as if I had suggested an even more hideous thing than anything Cassius had done to us. “Why the fuck would you even suggest that?” He stood and stepped away from the bed as though I might spontaneously combust and blow us both up.

“Because I hate seeing you hurting like this, and I don’t know what to do.” Tears sprang, blurring my vision, and I swallowed hard, forcing the lump that had formed in my throat down into my roiling belly.

He raked his hand through his hair and then splayed his hands out at me. “I just...I just need time to deal with this.”

My breath locked in my chest, and I couldn’t pull air in for a moment. This was where he was going to reject me. Still, I forced out the words I dreaded an answer to. “Do you want me to go?”

His eyebrows shot up into arches of surprise. “No. That’s the last thing I want.” The strain in his voice lessened with those words, and my tight chest eased.

“Then what can I do to help?” I needed to have a plan. A way to mitigate this helplessness accosting me.

He ran his hand down his face as his eyes darted around the room at the shadows before

they finally settled on me again. "Be…patient."
He leaned on the edge of the bed and gave me a
soft kiss. "It may be awhile before I can get my
shit together."

I nodded. "I can be patient." I lied. I didn't
have a patient bone in my body.

He smirked and that glimpse of the old Robby
flashed across his face. "Liar. You've never been
patient a day in your life." He turned and headed
into the bathroom, giving me a full view of his
backside.

His ass was still perfect, even with the drop
in weight.

The shower turned on, and I crawled out
from under the covers. I made the bed nice and
neat like it had been before we messed it up with
our fitful sleep, and then headed into the
shower.

Robby stood under the water with his eyes
closed, letting it cascade over him as his chin
nearly touched his chest. Standing there, he
looked fully defeated, which sparked irrational
anger within me.

This was what Cassius had hoped for. That
he would carve a chasm between us that was too
deep to overcome. Well, I was damned if I was
going to allow that.

I stepped into the shower, and he stiffened
and glanced up at me.

"Cassius can't win." I stared at him and
stepped closer; he backed up a step. "You have
to promise me you will not let him win."

Robby blinked, as if all the synapses in his
brain were misfiring. His hands trembled at his

sides, and he held the panic of being cornered in his eyes.

"You are a bloody alpha wolf. Don't *ever* fucking forget that." I poked his chest. "And I'm your goddamn mate." I leveled a glare at him. "And there will never be any secrets between us. Ever."

He scoffed at me and looked away. I reacted, stepping close as my hands ignited with the frustration scraping my skin. Steam hissed around us. I shook my fire out and reached for him. He flinched and then grabbed my hand, yanking me to him. He claimed my mouth in a rough kiss and then spun me around, so I was pressed face-first against the wall, with him pressing his entire form against my back.

"There are some things that are better left in the dark," he whispered in my ear and then nipped my neck as his hands truly began to wander for the first time since we got back to his apartment. This wasn't the frantic touching to make sure I was real. This was Robby exploring my skin with his hands.

"No secrets," I stressed.

His exploration abruptly halted, and his head came to rest on mine. "There are worse things than killing your mate with your bare hands."

His tone chilled me, despite the steamy shower. I turned to face him. "What did that bastard do?" Everything Cassius had threatened ran through my mind, and my stomach knotted.

Robby shook his head slowly and ran his knuckles over my cheek. His gaze laid bare the horror he experienced, and I swallowed hard.

"He didn't just mind-fuck me." He glanced away. "He made me..." He pressed his lips together and shuddered. "Fuck your dead corpse," he finished and slashed his gaze back to me. "I can't shake that shit."

My stomach slowly turned, and I put my hand over my mouth, unsure whether it was from the gruesome image he painted in my head, or the raw disgust of what Cassius did. Either way, I was glad that bastard met such a violent end.

"The next time I was dragged into that room, I was sure you'd kill me. I almost didn't fight it either. But I did manage to say your name, and that was all it took for you to refuse to finish me off. His grand plan failed again." His lips tilted into a ghastly smile.

I remembered Robby's look of disbelief when I pulled away from his throat. I hadn't understood it then, but I certainly did when my mother gave me my memories back. That was one of my quicker deaths. "Cassius snapped my neck that time."

Robby nodded. "Yes." He shivered and seemed to shrink in on himself. "And then he beat your dead body before turning his fists on me."

I couldn't let him close the world out. I moved closer and wrapped my arms around him in a hug.

He hesitated and then slowly wrapped his arms around me.

"I will be patient as long as you don't shut me out."

Robby kissed the top of my head. "I'll try my best not to."

2

CROOKED SOUL 2

I STEPPED OUT OF the bathroom, wrapped in a towel. I was half a step away from the bed when the bedroom door swung open, crashing into the wall with a bang, making me jump. Johnson's wide-eyed stare fell on me, along with the business end of his gun aimed directly at my chest. I froze and my mouth ran dry. I didn't want to kill our oldest friend, but if he pulled the trigger, I would incinerate the bullet and him along with it.

Behind Johnson stood a woman I had never seen. Her wide eyes narrowed when they took me in, and then her glare moved to Johnson, as if it were his fault I was in Robby's bedroom, scantily dressed. That look screamed jealousy.

I glanced sideways without moving a muscle. Robby stood with the towel wrapped around his waist, but his complexion had turned almost gray with the fear radiating from him. The hand holding his towel clasped trembled.

"What are you doing here?" I asked, refocusing on Johnson.

"This is my place," he said.

Johnson's voice seemed to knock Robby out of whatever terror gripped him, and he stepped into view. "Since when?"

The gun moved toward Robby for a moment and then Johnson slowly lowered it, blinking as he stared at his alpha. It took him a moment to get his composure back. "Since you dropped off the fucking planet. Someone needed to step in and run the pack." He holstered his gun without me making him as his gaze traveled over the two of us. When it landed on Robby's neck, his brow creased and the muscles in his jaw twitched.

"Rick, who are these people?" the woman behind him asked.

I had never heard anyone call Johnson by his first name. Not even back when we were in the academy. I traded a glance with Robby.

But Johnson's gaze had already narrowed into slits of anger as they slashed to me. "What the fuck did you do to him?"

"She didn't do this to me. The dumpster vamp did." He crossed his arms over his chest, and his gaze jumped from Johnson to the woman. A single eyebrow rose. "You finally mated?"

Johnson glanced over his shoulder at the woman, and then smiled back at us like a kid showing his parents a prized trophy. It was the quintessential alpha claiming his mate smile. "Mated, married, and are just returning home from our honeymoon." He puffed his chest out.

She blushed and glanced shyly at the floor.

It was enough to irritate me, and I willed clothing on both Robby and me. Fabric shifted under the towels, and I peeled the cloth from around me and stepped by Robby, pulling his off as well now that he was fully dressed, too. I hung the towels on the hooks on the bathroom door and took a deep breath before stepping back out into the bedroom.

"Technically, she was supposed to be your mate," Johnson said. "But then, when none of us could reach you or feel the alpha connection anymore, your father named me alpha and insisted on this union."

"So, you just agreed." The sarcasm in Robby's voice bled through.

Johnson grinned and shook his head. "It wasn't that simple." He glanced at the woman, and her cheeks reddened. "Dude, if this is what you ignored for fifteen years, I give you props," he finished and met Robby's gaze.

I started to laugh. "You mean to tell me that the woman Robby's father has been trying to marry him off to for the past few years is your true mate?"

"As fucked up as that sounds, yes." He put his arm around his woman. "Judy, this is Sarah Stone. She's Robby's true mate."

Her gaze jumped between us. Her mind didn't work nearly as fast as ours and her mouth opened then closed again before her eyes narrowed. "Hi," she managed to squeak out as her gaze landed back on Robby. Her eyes went from confused to fearful as she clung to Johnson.

Robby gave her a nod. "No offense, but you're not my type." He stepped closer to me and slung his arm around my shoulder.

I gave him a sideways glance.

He leaned close. "She thinks I might still claim her since I'm the rightful alpha of the Allegany pack. My father made an alliance with her pack when he married her to the alpha he handpicked." He met Johnson's gaze. "I'm not taking your station."

Johnson's shoulders relaxed.

"But I bought and paid for this house with my hard-earned money. It's mine, not yours," Robby added with force in his tone. "It was not my father's to give."

Johnson blinked and glanced around, as if Robby had just torn a limb from his body instead of claiming what was rightfully his. "What are we supposed to do?"

"There is a guest room." His offer was better than I would have given. "And the agency *and* my father are not to get a whiff that we are alive. Understand?"

Johnson glared at Robby. "I can't do that. It will fuck with my career if I keep this from them."

"I spent six months in a fucking silver collar while that bastard killed Sarah over and over. I am not spending the rest of my life in a cell because you found some goddamned loyalty to such a fucked-up organization." Robby trembled with the fury filling him.

I put my hand on his forearm to try to calm him down but he shook it off. The malice radiated outward, and Judy had the sense to cower. But Johnson stood firm. He still believed Robby wouldn't hurt him. But the man he knew had been substantially changed by Cassius, to the point I couldn't even predict how he would react.

"You better run," I said to Johnson, because if there was such a thing as steam coming from ears, Robby would be sending out plumes of it.

Robby snarled and took a step forward.

"Don't shift," I commanded before he had a chance to let his wolf loose.

He spun on me with his teeth bared and his fists clenched, and then he grabbed me by the arms, shaking me. "Don't you ever try to control me again!" he screamed in my face.

I put my hand out toward Johnson, because out of the corner of my eye, I saw he foolishly stepped closer, but I didn't dare break eye contact with Robby. Not until I had my say.

"I *will* fucking control you when you're about to tear your best friend to pieces just because he feels he has to do his job," I snapped back. "You wouldn't get over *that* shit either once your head cleared." I poked my finger into his chest hard.

Robby continued to growl low in his throat. His grip on my arms was punishing and would leave bruises, but it was better than having him decapitate Johnson in a fit of anger.

I chanced a glance at Johnson. "Just go down to the kitchen. We'll be there in a few minutes."

Johnson had his hand on his gun, and I saw the doubt in his eyes.

"I'll be fine. Just do *not* call in the cavalry. Otherwise, I swear, I'll turn this place, and everyone within a hundred yards, to dust. Understand?" I put enough venom into my voice that he paled.

Robby still snarled at me, as if he were an inch away from snapping my neck.

"Go," I hissed when he didn't budge, and Judy grabbed Johnson's arm, practically dragging him from the room.

I met Robby's gaze. "I know you hate it. I know *why* you hate it. But you would have never forgiven yourself if you hurt Johnson. And you would never forgive me if I didn't intervene." I put my hands on his waist and squeezed, even though the action hurt where he was constricting my biceps.

His growl subsided and his grip loosened, but he did not let go. Robby inhaled and closed his eyes. He dropped his hands and stepped back, distancing himself. "I can't be caged again."

No kidding. By some miracle, I kept those words locked up. He didn't need my sarcasm right now, but he did need my assurances. "I will wipe out all of New York before I let that happen."

He smiled in a way that warmed my soul. He knew I was capable of turning New York City to ash if I so desired.

"You may have to if he runs to the agency." His blue eyes opened and found mine.

I nodded. "I know. So, we need to convince him not to, like we did before." I reached out and took his hands. This time, he let me.

"I'm all sorts of fucked up, aren't I?" He searched my eyes, as if I had all the answers.

"Yeah. So am I. I just bury it deeper."

He blinked and then pulled me into a hug, as though he hadn't considered just how much Cassius may have messed me up.

Dying that many times and that many ways haunts my dreams, but I didn't say anything. Not with Robby being so fragile.

"I'm sorry, babe." He kissed the top of my head. "I've been so wrapped up in my own shit that I never even considered what you went through."

"It's okay. You were nearly knocking on death's door a couple days ago. I didn't want to burden you with my issues while I was trying to help you get some strength back."

He tilted my chin up and planted a soft kiss. "Let's go see where we can get with Johnson using reason. If we can't get him to comply, you're going to have to compel him."

I really didn't want to do that to our oldest friend, but I would if it meant keeping us safe. I led Robby out of the bedroom and down the stairs, hoping they hadn't just bolted.

CROOKED SOUL 3

JOHNSON AND HIS MATE sat in the kitchenette with freshly brewed coffee in front of them. Their whispers weren't on the same page. She wanted him to call the agency, but he wanted to hear us out before all hell broke loose.

He wasn't an idiot. He knew I could compel him just as effectively as I had Robby upstairs. He also knew I could make them forget us. That I could make them forget they lived here. And if I wanted to be a royal dick, I could make them forget he was the alpha of the Allegany pack.

I slid into the chair across from them while Robby retrieved a cup of coffee. I didn't speak, and Johnson's wife just glared at me as if I were the problem here.

Robby took the seat next to me, set his coffee down on the table, and put his hands out flat on the wooden surface next to it, where the silver burns were on full display. His gaze flashed to me before he focused on Johnson.

"I apologize for my behavior upstairs." He pressed his lips together. "I was caged for six months, so the idea of being caged again…" He shuddered and his hands curled into fists. "Makes me lose it."

"How could someone kill her multiple times?" Johnson's wife spat out and waved at me.

"Because she's *other,*" Johnson answered, as if he had that part memorized.

I leaned back and studied her. "Judy, right?"

She nodded, eyeing me suspiciously.

"Are you aligned with your mate or are you aligned with the agency?"

She recoiled as if I had slapped her. "I'm loyal to Rick," she snapped. "What the hell kind of question is that? How would you like me to ask you the same?"

I smiled, revealing my sharp canines. "I'd burn down the city and everyone in it for my mate. I'd drain every last drop of blood in your veins if that meant he was safe." I covered Robby's fisted hand.

The click of a hammer being pulled back made both our gazes dart to Johnson.

"Put that away," I commanded in a growl.

Johnson's upper lip pulled back in a snarl as he reset the hammer on the gun he had under the table and then set the hunk of metal on the edge, still within reach. "You threatened my mate."

I nodded and leaned forward. "And you threatened mine."

He blinked and glanced at Robby, as if he were slowly understanding his militant loyalty to me as opposed to anyone or anything else.

"Locking you up is not the same as murder." His gaze snapped back to mine.

"And being locked up for any of us is worse than taking our lives. Or do you think you could live if you were separated from her forever? Locked in a cage like an animal?" I challenged.

Robby sat stoic, letting me handle the conversation. The way his hand trembled underneath mine had me worried. He cleared his throat.

"Like I said upstairs, you will not enlighten the agency or my father that I am alive." He glanced at me. "That *we* are alive."

"Her magic has a signature." Johnson crossed his arms. "What the hell am I supposed to do when they discover there is magical breaches surfacing in my home?"

Robby's lips tilted in a smile. "This place is warded."

My gaze snapped to his. That was a new piece of information.

He side-eyed me and shrugged.

"I made my provisions when I bought this place." He glanced around the kitchen. "Otherwise, they would have already broken the door down. You've been whipping up steaks like a Kansas City chef since we got here." His dimples appeared.

I had wondered why they hadn't descended on us like maggots on a dead bird. Now I knew.

He turned back to Johnson. "I will let her burn the entire world before I allow the agency to put us in cages. If you have any doubts about her ability to do that, I suggest you remember that forest fire near where we last met." He cocked an eyebrow at Johnson.

Johnson's mouth popped open, and then he seemed to recompose himself. "What happened?"

"A vampire with a wolf attacked us. If she hadn't been *other*, we would have both been sucked dry by that bastard, and our meat left for the wolf." Robby pulled his hand out from under mine and crossed his arms.

He chewed on the edge of his lower lip and his eyes narrowed. "Did anyone at the agency know where you were heading when you came after us?"

"Your father knew. I don't know if Terrance did, but since the two of them run that agency like a tight military unit, I'm sure he must have known."

In all the years I worked at the Monster Defense Agency, I had never once met the elusive head, Terrance Winters. I had met Robby's father, and that man was as cold as they come. The board wasn't any warmer. They showed up every year to speak with the new recruits and attended the welcome dinners.

When Robby took the elite spot of alpha for his pack, there had been a formal dinner. Most of the agency attended, as well as the entire pack. It was an affair that would have made the rich and famous envious. And I hated every minute of it.

But it was Robby's induction into the role his father had groomed him for. Yet, Terrance hadn't been at that event, either.

"Have either of you met Terrance?" I asked as I noodled on why Robby was digging at this particular bone.

Robby shook his head. "Nope."

Johnson glanced at his girl. "Terrance is Judy's uncle." He met my gaze before it bounced to Robby's.

Holy hell. That meant Terrance Winters was not only in bed with the Allegany pack, he also had the nation's largest pack in his pocket. Although, he did have a tough mountain to climb after his father fell from grace and the werewolf council reformed under new leadership. The new regime outlawed being doused in silver. However, the agency still carried that heinous punishment out. So, maybe Terrance had taken a few of his father's bad habits along with him.

It was why the agency was so feared by all supernatural beings. We were ruthless in our deliverance of justice. Well, at least the leaders' idea of what justice was, albeit one with a very skewed lens now that we were no longer insiders. And to think, we used to be part of their network of intimidating muscle.

I shook my meandering thoughts away and focused on Johnson. The family ties meant our existence would no longer be secret. I glanced at Robby, and his gaze was fixed on a point on the table in front of him. He had that *analyze the shit out of the situation* expression that I was intimately familiar with.

"Our time here is limited," I said softly. "She'll run to her uncle as soon as we are out of sight."

Her eyes widened, and her face paled.

"If she hasn't already," Robby added.

"Tell me the truth. Did you already alert your uncle to our presence here?" I asked the question with the force of my coercion. She wouldn't be able to lie under my command.

"N-n-no," she stuttered and blinked rapidly. "Rick asked me n-not to."

I sat back and slashed my gaze to Johnson, giving him a nod of thanks. "Neither of you will be able to tell anyone about us. Understand?" I narrowed my gaze, forcing my will on both of them.

They winced and nodded.

"If you try, you will be crippled with an unimaginable pain that renders you silent and unable to communicate in any manner."

Robby glanced at me, raising his eyebrow.

I shrugged at him. "It's better than wiping their memories."

Johnson's face reddened, and his glare just got more intense. His girl's eyes looked as if they'd pop out of her head at any moment.

"Robby was kind enough to offer the guest room to you. But I think you'd be much happier living elsewhere. Don't you agree?" I asked.

"Afraid I might kill you in the wee hours of the night?" Johnson said through clenched teeth. His eyes blazed with righteous anger.

I smiled at him and leaned forward.

He leaned back in response.

"Are you afraid I will drain you and your pretty little bride of blood?"

"Stop it!" Robby snapped. "Both of you." He glanced at me. "As you so eloquently put it before, Johnson is my closest friend. Probably the only one left besides you." His gaze slashed to Johnson. "And you've known Sarah as long as I have. Hell, you've had her back all that time, too. So, both of you just stop being assholes."

I glanced down at the table and took a deep breath. What Robby said was true, as much as I hated to admit it. Johnson had kept me alive by thwarting Robby's wolf. I met Johnson's gaze. "As much as it aggravates me, I do have to admit, you kept me as safe as he has." I hooked my thumb at Robby. "So, I'm sorry if I seem overprotective and territorial."

"You're not sorry." Johnson's lips tilted in a smirk. "You've always been as militant as I am in protecting Robby. Even before you became *other* or his mate." He pressed his lips together. "You didn't need to compel us not to say anything, either."

I laughed. "Yes. I did. Family bonds and all, it's the only prudent thing I could do without wiping out your memories. And no. I don't think *you'll* sneak in and try to kill us. But I don't know your mate. She may very likely try because of what I am and because of the gag order you're both now compelled to follow."

"What are you?" Judy interrupted.

"She's a phoenix," Robby said.

"A...what?" She blinked.

"A phoenix," Johnson repeated, glancing at her.

"Like rising from the ashes?"

I laughed. "Yeah." I held my hand out and willed flames to dance across my fingers and then closed my fist, dousing them. "That's how Cassius could kill me multiple times." I shrugged.

Johnson's gaze widened, as if the information we were saying now was new. Robby had said as much upstairs, but the reality of what we went through was just now sinking in his best friend's mind. I could see the gears moving, the horror of it all settling in.

"Wait. You had to watch him kill her?" Judy asked before Johnson could.

Robby noticeably paled and the shake returned to his hands. He nodded as his gaze focused on the table. "Multiple times." His voice trembled, as if he had just stepped back into the memories again.

I reached out and took his hand. He stiffened and blinked, coming back to us from whatever momentary hell he was reliving.

"Shit, man." Johnson ran his hand down his face.

Robby let out a laugh that sounded as stressed as he was. "I'm not sure I'll ever get my shit together."

His admission dropped Johnson's jaw for a moment, but then Johnson said, "I think I'd go crazy, too, if anyone made me watch Judy getting hurt."

Robby twitched and tried on a smile, but it transmitted just how broken he really was.

CROOKED SOUL 4

AFTER ROBBY FINALLY FELL asleep, I slipped out of bed and went downstairs to curl up on the couch and watch a light comedy. I stepped onto the landing and froze at the whispers coming from the kitchen.

"But she is a vampire." Judy's whispered hiss came around the corner.

"Yes. She's that, too."

"They why don't you do your job and kill her?" Judy whispered. "I can't stand the idea of staying under the same roof as a vampire."

I took a slow breath, waiting. Johnson's answer would dictate what I did next.

"Look. I've known Sarah as long as Robby has. She's got a good heart, and she and Robby were the best damn hunting partners that the agency ever had."

"But—"

"But nothing." He cut her off with an annoyed hiss. "If I even attempted to hurt her, Robby would tear me to pieces. He has always protected that girl. Besides, I can't do that to him. Or to her. She's had my back out there. And there's something you should know. We went after them before they disappeared. Cornered them in the woods, and they didn't fight. They reasoned with us after she commanded us to stand down. They could have just as easily wiped us from existence. Neither of them wanted to hurt us, but they weren't willing to be locked up."

"So?" She didn't sound convinced.

"Judy, they let us walk out of those woods unharmed. How many vampires do you know would do that?"

A beat of silence went by.

"None. No vampire we have ever encountered in all the years I've been at the agency just let us walk away. They attack. They kill. But *she* didn't."

"She is still a vampire."

I stepped into the kitchen, squaring my shoulders. "Yes. I am a vampire."

Judy spun around to face me, her eyes wide and filled with trepidation. Johnson's eyes widened as well. Fear radiated from both of them.

I couldn't blame them for their skittishness, either. "And I feel the same way you do." I met Judy's frightened stare. "I couldn't fathom having a blood sucker under my roof. But here's the thing. I am not *just* a vampire. And therein lies the really important distinction, one your mate has more of an understanding of than you do. While I am *other*, my phoenix combats the darkness, giving me control over every aspect of the vampire curse."

"That's supposed to make me feel better?" she asked while reaching for the knives on the counter.

Johnson might not be willing to attempt to kill me, but his mate was not on the same page.

I raised an eyebrow. "Really?" I said when she grabbed the butcher knife and pointed it at me. I looked beyond her at Johnson.

"Judy." He sighed. "She'll just break your wrist."

"How do you know?" She stepped closer, as though this conversation gave her some balls that she wouldn't otherwise have.

"Because she's disarmed both Robby and me before, along with countless vampires. I wouldn't fuck with her. But if you insist, I won't stop you, and I won't stop her when she defends herself."

Her steps faltered, and she glanced back at Johnson. "You'd let her hurt me?"

"No. But this isn't her attacking you. It's you assaulting her. She has a right to defend herself, and if she breaks your wrist disarming you, it's on you, honey."

"Are you serious?" she screeched and pitched the knife at me.

I pivoted and a hiss behind me had me spinning toward the entryway. Robby stood there with the knife sticking out of his shoulder, just staring at the weapon. His snarl echoed in the small space as he glared at Judy and ripped the knife from his flesh.

The smell of his blood filled the room, clouding my mind and sparking my hunger. But the look in his eyes was enough to stanch my sudden need. "She didn't mean it." I put my hands out toward him.

"She tried to kill you," he snarled with his feral gaze still pinned on Judy.

"No. She didn't." I stepped closer, putting my hands on his chest, knowing the contact would calm him, or at least distract him enough to de-escalate the situation. "She's angry and rightfully so. We've turned their lives upside down."

Robby lowered his gaze to me. "Why are you defending her?"

I glanced over my shoulder at her now cowering behind Johnson. "Because she's Johnson's mate, and he is our only friend." I turned back to Robby. "She's scared," I whispered. That seemed to break through his irrational fury.

"Why the fuck is she scared?"

I rolled my eyes and willed my teeth to appear. He stiffened, and I willed them back into hiding. But I made my point.

He blinked down at me and then glanced at his shoulder. Blood ran down his arm and his torso in a steady stream. The rate of blood sliding down from the wound told me the blade had hit something vital. This wasn't just a flesh wound.

My stomach clenched, and I had to stomp out the need to lick him clean. I hadn't fed in days and the smell of freshly spilled blood knotted my insides now that he had calmed enough for my panic to abate, leaving me salivating instead. I reached up and covered the wound with my palm, concentrating on healing him before I broke my promise never to bite him.

My hand ignited.

Robby winced and pulled his shoulder away, but my cauterization skills worked. The blood flow stopped, but it did leave a burn mark in the shape of my hand.

I shook the fire from my fingers. "Can you get me a wet cloth, please?" I asked over my shoulder and led Robby to a kitchen chair. His pallor had turned a shade of pale I wasn't happy with.

Johnson moved, leaving Judy to just stare at us. If a stiff wind blew through the kitchen, she would fall right over.

"Take a seat," I said to her and pointed my blood-covered finger at the far chair.

She obediently sat, still looking at me as if I could either smite her or drain her in an instant. Her sullen eyes darted between Robby and me and the puddle of blood on the floor and back. Clearly, she was not registering what happened.

Johnson came back with a few wet towels, handing a couple to me before he stepped to the puddle on the floor. He started to clean the tile as I worked on cleaning the blood off Robby.

Silence settled over us, with only the swish of cloth filling the space.

"I...I'm sorry," Judy finally said.

"It's okay," I said, and Robby scoffed, glaring at me.

"It is not okay," he said.

"She didn't kill either of us. It's okay." I insisted, and then gathered up the dirty towels, including the ones Johnson cleaned the floor with, and headed down the hall to the laundry room. I hesitated over the washer, staring at the bloody towels. I could just suck a little out and I'd be fine. Instead, I dropped them in the machine and turned to the sink. Before I washed my hands, I succumbed to the need accosting me and licked Robby's blood from my fingers, relishing the sweet taste of my mate before I shook myself out of the building bloodlust and soaped up my hands, cleaning off the remainder of blood. I glanced in the mirror at my eyes ringed with the vampire red and cursed Cassius Chase yet again.

When I returned, the same tense air still hovered in the room. Robby's glare still pinpointed on Judy, despite how pale he now looked from losing blood.

I conjured three steak dinners at the table and sat down next to Robby. "Eat." I pointed. "You lost blood. You need to refuel."

He glanced at the three dinners and sent me a questioning glare.

"It sucks to eat alone." I pointed at the meal. "Now eat."

"I'm not hungry." Judy pushed her plate to the middle of the table.

"Fine." I pulled the plate toward Robby, and the smell of the steak caught my attention, making me salivate the way Robby's blood had. It was the first food that had caught my attention since I had been turned a little over six months ago.

Robby tore into his and so did Johnson.

"Are you sure you don't want the steak?" I tore my eyes from the succulent meat to look at Judy.

"It's good," Johnson said through a mouthful.

"I'm sure. I don't like to eat this late." She waved toward the clock.

It was a little before eleven at night, so I could understand. I hated to eat this late when I was fully human. It always gave me nightmares and restless sleep. Men didn't seem to have that affliction or, if they did, they didn't readily admit to it.

I had a strange urge to pull the plate in front of me and dig in, but I resisted. I hadn't eaten anything solid since I woke the morning I had been turned, and did not know whether it would make me sick or not. I didn't want to end up in a compromising position with a possible death threat living under the same roof.

CROOKED SOUL 5

"WHY'D YOU GET UP?" Robby asked quietly as we slipped under the covers.

I sighed. "I was going to chill with a sitcom." I glanced at him in the dark, and his concern lines were deeper than normal.

"Are you okay?" He studied me as if he hadn't seen the haunted quality of my eyes every day since we escaped.

I hesitated, choking on my standard response. *Was I okay?* The impact hit like a force of a wrecking ball, and I shook my head. That knife could have killed him, and it was only now sinking in. Although I could bring him back with my tears, the pain of losing him once was enough. I never wanted to feel that agony again.

It seemed like days ago that I promised to be patient with him. But it hadn't even been a full twelve hours. Right now, all I wanted was him to hold me and make love to me. I needed him to show me he still loved me after all that had happened with Cassius. I didn't want to lose any more time to this gaping chasm that seemed to have been built overnight.

Sure, he clung to me in his sleep when his fear of losing me manifested the greatest. But the closest he came to anything sexual had been in the shower this morning, but that was more out of self-loathing than any display of tenderness.

A glimpse of the Robby I knew at the academy surfaced in his eyes, and warmth filled me as he pulled me into his arms and kissed my forehead.

"You're shaking," he said softly.

I had no idea I was trembling, but the aftereffects of turning on the autopilot to stop his bleeding in the kitchen never let any other thoughts enter my mind. But now, in the confines of his bedroom, all the awful what-if scenarios looped through my head like a horror flick.

"You could have died," I whispered against him.

He ran his hands through my hair with a gentleness that he hadn't shown since we returned, and when he tilted my chin up to stare into my eyes, heat filled my belly. His gaze dropped to my lips and then slowly raised back with both heat and a flutter of fear.

I didn't give Robby a chance to let that fear make him pull away. I planted a soft but insistent kiss on his lips. His arms tightened around me and just when I didn't think he'd allow me to explore his mouth, his lips opened, and the kiss transitioned from a sweet peck into an exotic tongue dance.

He buried his hands in my hair and deepened the kiss, making a sweet noise at the back of his throat, like something between a whine and a growl. He pushed me down onto the bed, stretching out over me as the kiss continued. I ground my hips into him and every muscle in his body stiffened.

He broke the kiss and pressed his forehead against mine before rolling onto his back next to me, nearly panting as he stared at the ceiling.

Instead of getting angry and allowing him to disengage, I rolled on top of him, straddling him. I needed him, and tonight I wasn't going to let him deny me.

"Sarah," he whispered and reached for me. "You promised."

I could see his intent reflected in his eyes, and I captured his wrists and pressed them into the pillow on either side of his head. "No. You could have died tonight. I am not wasting another moment together because of the ghost of Cassius Chase." I took a deep breath at his wide eyes and pale cheeks but forged ahead, kissing him again. I held his wrists in place, feeling his pounding pulse in my palms and the erratic rise and fall of his chest under me.

"Sarah," he whispered, this time his voice threaded with need.

I moved my kiss from his lips to his jaw and down the line of his throat. His breath hitched in and didn't release until my mouth had moved beyond his pulse point. I kissed his chest, running my tongue from nipple to nipple—tasting his skin, his essence. Goose flesh appeared in the path my tongue left.

He shivered, but it wasn't the teeth-chattering kind of shiver. It was a shiver of sexual anticipation. I released his wrists, running my hands down his arms, praying he wouldn't stop my oral exploration of him.

His gaze locked on me as I moved lower, taking liberties with him that I hadn't since we arrived here. By the time I got to his boxers, they were tented with his desire. And instead of being cordial about it and trying to slip them off nicely, I shredded the fabric in one quick tear.

Robby's eyebrows rose.

"There are times when taking clothes off properly just isn't fast enough." I repeated the words he had said to me back in the hotel after he had ravaged me. That was before all hell broke loose.

A ghost of a smile appeared, as if my words triggered the same memory.

When I took him in my mouth, slowly licking him like a sweet Popsicle, his eyes rolled back in his head and a whisper of a groan escaped. He hiked up on one elbow so he could watch me play with him. I sucked and rolled my tongue around his slit, tasting his salty precum.

Robby threaded his hand in my hair and guided me to take in more of him with each stroke of my lips. The rumbling in his throat thrilled me, and I obliged, taking nearly all of him in my mouth, humming in response to my gag reflex. I had learned that trick a long time ago.

He held me in place, using his hips to pulse farther down my throat. His eyes hooded with pleasure as I choked on the length of him. I started to pull away, but his hand tightened in my hair, forcing me to wince at the pull against my scalp.

"You started this," he said with a crooked smile. But there was no warmth in his eyes, just a frantic need for release. "So just keep sucking," he growled out between his canines with his alpha force behind his words.

Irritation bloomed, and I glared up at him as his unwanted command weaseled its way into my muscles. My lips pressed against his throbbing cock, and I drew him in even deeper in my throat, humming because he wasn't going to let go of me until I complied with his alpha authority. I could see it in his eyes and feel it in the painful grip he had on my hair.

He rose to his knees and held my head with both hands as he moved himself between my lips. "Suck harder," he demanded. "And faster."

This wasn't the Robby who had ravaged me back in my home. This wasn't the man who made love to me under the moonlight. This was a demanding, punishing partner I was not used to. Although his attempt at using his alpha power irritated me, the way he was taking control heated me from the inside, turning my nipples as hard as his.

I resisted his demand for me to stroke him faster, slowing my motion down, but I did suck harder at his request. His reaction was a low groan and more pressure on my head, trying to push me all the way down his hard shaft. I pulled back until only the tip of his cock was in my mouth.

His eyes sparkled at the slow roll of my tongue. I forced my head against the grip of his hands, letting his cock slip from my mouth.

He stared down at me in pained disbelief that I stopped.

I blew lightly on his slick shaft, triggering him to shiver before I took him between my lips again. I claimed control as I moved my mouth in a painful crawl. He dropped so his ass sat on his heels as I continued to tease him in slow motion, caressing his balls and his thighs with my hands and his hard member with my mouth.

"God, Sarah," he whispered with his hands still tangled in my hair.

This time, I set the pace and the depth of each stroke. When I sped up, it wasn't at his insistence, although his hips matched my movement and his breathing got heavier with each stroke of mine.

The mark on my shoulder flared with the intensity of his emotions as I kept up my gentle ministrations. His groans became less reserved as I sped up, sucking, flicking, taking him in deeper against my cheeks and into my throat.

At the height of my control and his exalted whispers of my name, I relinquished it, by tying my hair into a messy bun and then clasping my hands behind my back. I smiled up at him, gently stroking with my lips, sucking him like a sweet lollipop.

A crease appeared between his eyes and then it smoothed as he grasped the fact that the pace, whether gentle or punishing, as well as the depth of his thrusts, was all his prerogative. A wicked smile formed, and he moved just as slowly as I had been, but with each roll of his hips, his cock went farther down my throat.

"Swallow all of me," he whispered with a rasping voice shaking with need. Then he forced his thumbs in the space between my back teeth, widening my jaws. The next plunge left my nose buried against his flesh and tickled by his pubic hair.

I resisted pushing away, humming as he pulsed in my mouth. Breathing wasn't an option with his entire length between my lips, even through my nose. He stared down at me, pushing the last few centimeters into my throat. And then he eased up enough for me to take a deep breath of air through my nose before he went deep again.

"Please suck me."

He continued to roll his hips in a punishingly slow manner. Stealing my breath for longer periods until I became lightheaded from the lack of oxygen and the strength of my sucking. Just when I thought I'd pass out, his pace quickened.

"Fuck," he growled. His cock thickened in my mouth, and he plunged deep, groaning as his hot release filled my mouth and throat in a flood. He pulled back, still spurting hot cum over my tongue as I swallowed. He plunged again with another blast. I couldn't keep up with the torrent, and his seed dribbled from the corners of my mouth as I gulped and fought for air.

He pulled out and dropped onto his back with his breath laboring in shaky pulls. I wiped my mouth on the back of my hand, trying to catch my breath as every nerve of my body craved the same type of release he just experienced. But I knew better. This was a step, and if I pushed it further than I already had, it might backfire.

I stretched out next to him, and he kept his gaze on the ceiling, as if trying to decide what had just happened.

"You promised," he said.

"Yeah, well, when you became my partner, I promised never to cross the line with you either," I said.

He rolled his head toward me. "And look how that turned out."

With his essence still coating my tongue, I sat up and stared down at him. "What the hell is that supposed to mean?"

He stared at me for a moment too long.

My irritation ratcheted up as flames broke out on my fingertips. I quickly clenched my hands. It wouldn't be good form to burn down the only place we had to hide right now.

He ran his hand over his face and shook his head. "It just means I wasn't ready for that kind of intensity."

He sounded so defeated that my heart actually squeezed in my chest, sending tendrils of pain through my entire form. My shoulder ached with a deep sorrow that I couldn't name.

What if we couldn't find our way back to what we had for those brief few days between me being turned and Cassius getting his grubby paws on us?

6

CROOKED SOUL 6

ROBBY SIGHED AND STARED up at the ceiling, still deliciously naked but in that somber mood that left me chilled to the bone.

Thick tension settled between us, increasing my unease. I curled up on my side, swallowing hard. This was it. This was the rejection I expected.

"But I needed it," he finally said and glanced sideways at me. "And it pisses me off that you figured out exactly what I needed before I did."

"You needed a blow job?" I blinked at him, unable to follow his logic.

A dimple briefly appeared. "No. Well, yeah, but that's not the point. What I needed was to feel like

I was in control of something. You completely surrendered to me. I didn't know I needed that." He spoke in a broken flow, like it was difficult to admit. "But it broke through whatever..." He pressed his lips together and then ran his hand into his hair.

I waited for him to say more. He met my gaze.

"Up until tonight, every time I reached for you, I flashed back to the moment your spine shattered in my hands." He stared at me with those soulful eyes of his. "You just replaced that with something incredible." The corner of his lips tilted into a playful smile.

It took me by surprise, swinging my emotions back to center, and the heat of desire filled my skin.

Dimples appeared in his cheeks. "You're slinging those pheromones, honey."

I lifted my shoulder, allowing my lips to move into a Mona Lisa smirk. I wanted a release bad, and I knew if I said anything, it would crush the possibility of him making a move.

"I'm exhausted." He rolled onto his side to face me. He cupped my cheek and pulled me in for a soft kiss. Then he pulled away and snuggled into his pillow like he was getting ready to go to sleep.

He had lost blood, but not enough to suck the wind out of his sails. At least, not in my mind. Especially with how he responded the first time we crossed the line at my house after I drained him of just about double the blood he lost today. He just didn't want the ghosts to come back.

If he wasn't going to take care of my needs, I most certainly would, because tonight, I was not going to sleep frustrated. I moved my hand between my legs and began to stimulate my clit through my underwear with small, circular strokes of my fingers.

His gaze moved to where my hand was and shot back to my face. "What are you doing?"

"What does it look like?" I cocked an eyebrow. "I need the same kind of release you had. And you're obviously too exhausted to do anything about it." I didn't mean for the bitterness to seep into my words, but it did, which made it nearly impossible to feel the pleasure I was trying to create on my own. But I was going to have an orgasm tonight. Period. He had one. I needed one.

His lips tilted into a traitorous smile. "Did you do this often before?" His eyes sparkled with interest.

I narrowed my eyes at him. Although we had been partners for fifteen years, we only were romantically entangled for less than a week, and it was while we were on the run. "Did you?" The heat from my fingers was starting to work its magic.

"I cannot tell you how many times I jerked off to fantasies of making love to you. It was the only way to keep my wolf in line." He didn't look away at the admission. "Show me what you did when you had fantasies of me."

There was a decadence to this. A vulnerability that I did not like. Admitting I came to fantasies of him more times than I could count over the years was opening myself up for being hurt, but my hand kept manipulating that sensitive spot, sending tingles of heat to my belly. "I would much rather have your tongue on me than my fingers," I whispered.

"Show me and maybe I'll oblige," he said as his hand slid down to his own shaft, slowly stroking himself.

I did not expect this keen interest, but it sparked an intense heat that went straight to my nipples, hardening them.

Robby noticed. "Take your clothes off," he said. "I want to see everything."

I sat up and peeled my shirt off, tossing it aside, and went back to stroking myself through my panties.

He clucked his tongue and shook his head. "Everything."

I stripped my panties and continued to manipulate my clit.

"Face me so I can see you come," he said, a hint of a shake in his voice.

I moved my pillow to the side of the bed and faced him, widening my legs enough so I could see his face, and began the slow manipulation again. Each time he made me stop was torture. And now that he was watching and stroking himself back to life, it was even hotter.

It didn't take me long to get to the point of ignition; it never did. And my body tightened with the rush of heat. I moaned Robby's name as my orgasm rang through my form. I needed him inside me, and I moved faster than he did, pushing him onto his back before I deposited myself onto his hard length, taking him all in in one quick motion. He stretched me, triggering another orgasm, and I arched into it, bowing and tilting my head back, but I had the sense not to scream.

He sat up, taking one of my breasts in his mouth and then the other before he kissed his way to my lips. His arms encircled me, and his hips thrust into me with the same ferocity as mine pounding into his. My heart nearly burst from my chest with the intensity of the emotions running through me and the echo of his in the mark on my shoulder.

His tongue played with mine in the same frantic swipes. He held me so tight I didn't know where his heartbeat ended and mine began. He groaned in my mouth, and I felt his release, and moaned along with him as mine ripped through me right on the heels of his.

He ended the kiss and pressed his forehead to mine, his breathing as labored as mine.

"You sure know how to crush a promise." He laughed, ran his hands into my hair, and kissed me softly. "And now I need at least twelve hours of sleep." He met my gaze, and he did look fucking wrecked.

"I'm sorry," I said, and in a way I felt like crap for not honoring his wishes. But I needed this the same way he needed to feel like he was in control.

He tilted his head and studied my face. "Funny. You don't look one bit sorry."

"Oh, I'm not sorry for the sex. I needed this more than you could imagine, but I am sorry that I made a promise I knew damn well I wouldn't be able to keep." I smiled and slowly moved my hips.

"I'm serious. I need sleep. Now." His hands dropped to my hips, stilling my movement. "I don't have the stamina." He palmed my cheek and slowly ran his thumb over my lips. "I wish I did, but six months on the brink of death will do that to a man."

I nodded and uncoupled from him, and he pulled me into his arms as he stretched out on the bed, spooning me. I hadn't gotten comfortable yet and he was already snoring in my ear. I wrapped my arms around his and kissed his wrist.

It was the first time since we escaped from Cassius's that I thought things might go our way for a change. But deep down, I knew better. We'd never live a normal life. Not with the Monster Defense Agency gunning for me.

CROOKED SOUL 7

A SOFT KNOCK DREW me out of my stupor. I weaseled my way out of Robby's arms and covered him with the blanket, and then wished for a bathrobe as I crossed the room. Soft terrycloth slid onto my skin, and I cinched the tie at my waist before I opened the door.

Judy stood on the other side of the door, shifting from foot to foot. "Is he okay?" She nodded toward Robby still sleeping in the bed.

I glanced back at him and nodded. "Yes. Why?"

She looked at her hands, which were wrestling against each other. "I thought I heard him cry out."

I rubbed the crust from my eyes. I hadn't heard anything, but I had been so soundly sleeping that he could have, and I probably wouldn't have reacted for just one of his night terror cries.

"If he did, I didn't hear him." I bit my lower lip.

"I swear, I heard something. I'm sorry if I woke you."

She turned to leave but I reached out and touched her arm, closing the bedroom door behind me.

"Did you hear anything last night?" The rose color that crept into her cheeks told me we were not as quiet as I had hoped. I glanced away, trying to school the smirk off my face.

She shrugged and then nodded.

"Then he probably did yell out in his sleep. He does that a lot since we got away. And I'm sure I've had my moments, too." I gave her an apologetic smile. I glanced around. "Where's Johnson?"

"He left for work early this morning. I guess they had a situation that he and his partner had to attend to." She glanced down the stairs, and a flash of worry passed over her features.

"Johnson will be just fine. He's one of the best."

"He said you two were the best."

Heat filled my cheeks at the compliment. "Well, he held his own, so the worrying you got going there is going to produce nothing but wrinkles."

She chuckled. "It's easier said than done," she said. "Did you want some coffee?" She hooked her thumb over her shoulder toward the stairs.

I didn't have the heart to tell her I couldn't drink coffee or eat food the way she could. The vampire's curse still affected me despite that steak last night smelling like its own piece of heaven. "I'll come down and talk with you while you have a cup, if you'd like."

She shifted her feet again and then nodded. "I don't have many people to talk to here in the city."

I could totally identify with that. "Neither do I." I let her lead the way and as she sat sipping her coffee in the kitchen, I could see all the questions flitting around in her head.

She finally looked up. "What happened?" She waved at me.

I leaned back in the seat. "Honestly? I got duped." It was tough to admit, but that's exactly what Cassius had done. And the feelings I carried around for Robby all these years had chipped away at my judgment. I sighed and looked at the ceiling. "I've been in love with Robby since the academy," I said. "Because he was my partner, any relationship was banned, but that didn't stop me from my feelings." I shifted in the chair. "So, when Cassius came along and swept me off my feet in ways that were so parallel to Robby, I fell for him. I had no clue he was a vampire." I let out a soft laugh. "I should have known."

She digested my words. "Why does the agency ban relationships? I never quite understood that."

"They think it makes us more vulnerable." After what happened with Cassius, I would agree. Loving someone the way I loved Robby left a large target on his back. But it also made us more ferocious when our loved ones were targeted.

There was no room for mercy when that happened.

"And what do you think?"

"I think it's more complicated than that." I chewed on the inside of my cheek as I formulated my thoughts. "Anyone who has a mate is vulnerable." I met her gaze. "We would do anything for the ones we love, so I'm not sure how being partners makes it worse. If the monsters know about your vulnerabilities, they will use it against you. Cassius used me to break Robby out of spite."

"Why would he do that?" She sipped her coffee.

"Because he was under the mistaken impression that he owned me. If Robby and I never..." I closed my eyes and took a breath. If we never crossed the line, Cassius would have killed him without so much as a second thought. I was sure of that. "If Robby hadn't claimed me, I am not sure what would have happened to either of us." I shivered.

"He probably would have killed me because I wouldn't have stopped looking for you."

I spun to Robby in the doorway. He had sweats on but no shirt, leaning casually against the wall. I had no idea how long he had been standing there, but this morning, he looked much more like himself instead of the haunted prisoner of war expression he had sported since we escaped. Even as thin as he was, he still projected that same charisma he had when I first met him.

He glanced at me with a crooked smile. "Since the academy, huh?" He teased as he passed by me and captured a quick peck.

I swatted him as he walked away, headed for the freshly brewed coffee. "He can be a bit of an ass sometimes," I said to Judy while stifling a grin. "But yeah. He made an impression on me from the moment we met."

Judy glanced at Robby. "How did you deny your wolf? I mean, I'm not sure I could have if it felt the same as when I met Rick."

Robby shrugged. "My father made it impossible by making her my partner. I don't know who was slated in that spot to begin with or who her partner was supposed to be, but he made damn sure I wouldn't follow through on my feelings." Bitterness over what his father had done still laced his words.

"Why would he do that?" Judy asked.

"Because he didn't want me tainting his fucking gene pool. I suppose if my brother hadn't been killed, he might not have been as militant." He poured creamer into his coffee and took a seat next to me. "If she hadn't been assigned as my partner, I would have found a way around the rule. After all, my parents found a way to get around it." He shrugged and stared into his coffee for a moment. "As her partner, I got to see her every day, so it wasn't all bad."

"How did you deal?" She leaned forward, as if she couldn't understand denying his greatest urges.

"I fucked anything in a skirt."

His crassness made Judy recoil in the seat, but it was right on the money, and I wasn't all that different.

"Don't look so shocked. I slept with a lot of guys, too. I was desperately trying to run from what I really wanted."

"And you're okay with that?" Her eyes blinked fast as she looked at Robby.

He glanced at me and smiled. "Yeah," he said. "We were both trying to find what we already had but were forbidden to pursue." He took another sip of coffee.

She glanced at us and slowly nodded. "I'm sure Rick had flings before we met, too."

I kept the smirk off my face, but Robby wasn't so successful. At least he had the sense to look away.

I studied her for a moment. She was younger than the three of us were, and from the shine of pink in her cheeks, perhaps Johnson truly was her first. Packs were more militant about that where the females were concerned. It was such a backward notion. The men could screw around, but the women would be ostracized for it. Even Hannah had saved herself for her mate.

"If I had been a wolf instead of a witch, I don't think his father would have meddled with us." I shifted in the chair, unsure whether I really meant it.

Robby snorted. "You weren't his handpicked patsy. I'd bet a million bucks that my father probably would still have been a merciless dick."

I put my hand on his arm, and he covered it with his. There had never been any love lost between them and God knew I didn't receive anything but animosity from the man, but it was not worth holding on to. Not when he was the only family Robby had.

"Let it go," I said. "For you. Not him." If he could find it in himself to forgive his father, then he would be more likely to finally find some peace. "He was only doing what he thought was best for you."

He gawked at me and then his gaze shot to Judy. "What do you think? Because my father was actively trying to hook us up. If all this shit hadn't gone down and our parents decided you were to marry me, assuming I got hit in the head and somehow agreed to that madness, what would you have done?"

She looked between us a little frantically. "I guess I would have honored the commitment my parents made."

Just like a good little alpha's daughter.

"And deny Johnson?" He leaned forward, his eyes narrowed.

A squeak came from the back of her throat at the thought, but she begrudgingly nodded. Her family honor meant more to her than her own happiness.

"You would have been just as bitter and angry as I have been all these years." He leaned back and crossed his arms, glancing my way. "It's not easy to let that go."

"It never is. But you still should try." I gave him a pat on the shoulder. "Why don't you go clean up so we can continue having some girl talk?"

"Trying to get rid of me so soon?"

"Yes. You've made the woman uncomfortable, and I'd kind of like to have a friend who's a woman. It's been awhile," I admitted. My closest girlfriends from the academy had been Hannah and her partner Heddie. Hannah was one of Robby's pack members like Johnson, and thankfully they were stationed here in New York with us. The six of us routinely went out drinking after a hard week at the agency. And I confided a lot in Hannah and Heddie, but not enough to tell them how I felt about my partner. But even so, we had grown close, and I had been devastated when they were killed in the line of duty. After that, I pretty much kept to myself, only going out with the crew occasionally.

Hell, if they had been alive when I met Cassius, they would have known about him. Or more likely, I never would have gone over to him at that bar and engaged in conversation. I likely would have left with them that night and none of this shit would have gone down.

Robby squeezed my thigh and stood. "Sorry for making you uncomfortable," he said to Judy and headed upstairs.

"You want to be my friend?" Judy asked.

I knew it was a vulnerable move, but I nodded anyway. "It would be nice. I mean, I love Robby and all, and we've been each other's sounding board for a long time, but I miss shooting the shit with my girlfriends."

Judy laughed. "Back home, I have a few close friends, and I miss them so much. We used to go to the salon to get manicures and pedicures together and gossip about the latest, hottest trends." She looked at her hands and held them up, showing me chipped and peeling nail polish, as if it were the most horrible thing in the world. Then looked around at the apartment. "I don't have a job or people I can call and just hang with here. It's quite lonely when Johnson is at work."

"Did you live here before you got married?" I leaned my elbows on the table and propped my chin on my hands, giving her my full attention now that Robby had let us be.

She shook her head. "I stayed at a hotel, but after my friends went home, even with room service and a day spa at my disposal, it was boring."

Just in the last few sentences, I could tell we didn't have a lot in common except for our gender. She seemed to be more of a prima donna than any of us were. I maybe had one pedicure in my lifetime and my nails didn't look as good as hers did. She was what Hannah used to refer to as high maintenance.

"Have you thought about getting a job?" I couldn't imagine being cooped up in a house all day with nothing more to do than clean, cook, and watch soap operas. It would drive me batshit.

She leaned forward. "Don't tell Johnson, but I've thought about it."

I cocked my head. "Why would that bother Johnson?"

"Oh, you know. Alphas and their dominance. They want their women serving them at home." She rolled her eyes.

I snorted a laugh. I couldn't imagine the friend I knew being such a jackass. "Johnson has said that?"

"Oh no. He just wants me to be happy. My parents have told me that alphas expect their women at home, making sure the household is taken care of and that when children come, it's the woman's job to raise those children right."

Her parents must be as archaic as the agency itself. Although the agency did put stock in women since we held the more powerful witch gene than men. But there was the occasional male witch that could leave us in the dust from a power spell perspective. Thankfully, those were few and far between; otherwise, the female agent would be as endangered as the phoenix.

"Girl, what do you want?" I cut through all the bullshit I was hearing and went straight to the matter at heart.

"I'd love to work at one of those fancy hotels, helping people plan activities and social events. I'm great at planning celebrations." She seemed to cower a little as she admitted to her dreams, and it was maddening to me to see any woman think they weren't worthy.

"Why don't you apply? What's the worst they can say?"

"Oh, I'd die if they said no." She gripped her coffee cup with both hands, bringing it to her lips in a dainty sip.

"Really?" It just popped out, and her face fell. I regretted letting that out, but maybe I could somehow build this girl up a little. "You don't believe in yourself?"

She shrugged, and I wanted to pound some self-confidence into her.

I took a deep breath, remembering some of the things my parents told me. "You know, a no from someone just means that door wasn't meant for you. It does not mean you are not good enough."

She blinked at me as if her brain could not come to terms with those words. I guess being an alpha's daughter might have much more expectations than I ever had put on me. Thank the gods that I didn't have those kinds of constraints growing up.

"But it means rejection," she finally said, as if that were the worst thing that could happen to someone out in the real world.

This girl had been detrimentally sheltered.

"True. But rejection isn't the end of the world. It just means you need to learn from what you may have done wrong, and it's okay to ask if there was a specific reason or something that you can improve on for the next time."

"Have you ever been rejected?"

The way her eyebrows arched made me smile. Had I ever been rejected? Ha. "Yes. I went job hunting when I was almost sixteen and was turned down at nearly all of them. But I had no experience, and I was shooting for more than what I was qualified for." I shrugged. "But I just kept learning what I did wrong and kept plugging away."

"So, what happened? Did you find a job?"

I let out a laugh. "I did. I actually got hired as a hostess, but before I could start, my parents died. The state swooped in and put me in state care, found out I had magical abilities, and shipped me off to the Monster Defense Academy." I took a breath. "So, my current career was thrust upon me. Despite that, I'm actually surprisingly good at it."

"Until you were turned."

"I'm still exceptional at killing vampires." I smiled. I had fond memories of decapitating dozens of them. "If I could wipe them off the planet, I would."

"But you're a vampire." She blinked at me with a face filled with confusion.

She didn't comprehend how much I loathed those beasts. I nodded. "Yes. But that was by force. It's not who *I am*."

She rubbed her arm and then rolled up the sleeve, showing me a tattoo near the inside junction of her elbow that I immediately recognized. It was a replica of the anti-compelling charm the agency had us wear. She ran her fingers over it. "Rick said it would protect me against being compelled, but you were able to compel both of us. How?"

I stared at the tattoo, not hearing a thing she said after she showed it to me. "Robby!" I yelled over my shoulder. The sound of him rapidly descending the stairs filled the kitchen.

"What?" His eyes darted from corner to corner, as if something waited to spring at us.

I pointed to Judy's arm.

He looked at the tattoo, and his eyes widened. His gaze snapped to me and then back at the exact replica of the charm.

"Where did you get that?" we both said at the same time. It was the perfect solution for Robby to never be compelled by a normal vampire again.

She looked between the two of us and covered the mark up. "It clearly doesn't work. She can still compel me even with the tattoo."

Robby laughed. "The charms don't work on Sarah. But they most certainly do on a regular vampire." He licked his lips. "Does Johnson have one as well?"

"Yes. He said he didn't want his every move tracked by the agency, not when there were times he wasn't sure they could be trusted, so he had one of the artists come to the house the night we were married and we got matching tattoos. Except his isn't on his arm." Her cheeks reddened.

"Where's his?" I asked out of sheer curiosity. If Johnson ever shifted on duty and shifted back, it would have to be pretty well hidden, so his partner didn't see it.

"It's on the inside of his thigh near his groin," she said.

I looked up at Robby and shrugged. We both knew vampires could not compel me, but he was still vulnerable. "Do you think you can have the same tattoo artist come and do one on Robby?"

"What about you?" she asked.

"I seem to be immune to being compelled. At least by vampires." I glanced at Robby. He had used his alpha powers to compel me last night and it had worked to a point, to my chagrin. "But I might want a different tattoo."

"What's that?" He cocked an eyebrow with interest.

"I think it would be neat to have a wolf on my ass cheek." I grinned up at him.

His eyes sparkled and the dimple in his reddened cheek appeared. "I'm going back upstairs." He turned and sauntered away like the old Robby.

Judy leaned forward. "I think he liked that idea," she whispered with a grin of her own. "Do you think Johnson would find that sexy?"

Maybe she wasn't so prim and proper after all.

"There's only one way to find out."

8

CROOKED SOUL 8

JUDY PICKED UP THE phone and dialed. "Rick, do you remember that special wedding gift you gave me before we left for our honeymoon?"

"Yes," he said slowly.

"Well, do you think I can have the number of that painter? I'm thinking there's something else I'd like to have done."

Silence filtered over the line. "Can I get you that when I get home?"

Overhearing the conversation, I got the distinct impression that he did not want the agency to have any inkling that they had the tattoos. I could understand it. They wanted to control every aspect of their agent's lives, and having the charms that transmitted their whereabouts topped the list. So if Johnson didn't trust the agency, then he'd have to have some other form of protection and the tattoo fit the bill.

"I wanted to surprise you," she whined.

I turned away, cringing. Her saccharine voice set my teeth on edge.

"I'm sure it will keep," he said. "I don't have the number here, though."

"Oh. Okay. We can talk about it when you get home to see if you agree." Disappointment laced every syllable, as though he just ruined an amazing surprise.

"Sure. Love you," he said, and the call clicked off.

A few minutes later, a text came through from an unknown number with the name Phillip, a phone number, and a message to tell Phillip to treat it the same way he treated the last favor.

I tilted my head. Johnson had a burner. That wasn't even something I would have thought of. It gave me pause. I wondered what the hell Johnson was doing that would warrant a burner, but I was also thankful. Thankful for both their discretion.

Judy dialed the number. "Is this Phillip?" She paused. "Yes. This is Judy Johnson. My husband Rick contracted you to come to our house on our wedding night." She smiled. "Yes, the charm tattoos. Well, we need you to come again and do one more of those, along with doing a howling wolf on my ass cheek and a friend's as well. My husband said to treat this the same way as the last favor." She listened. "That would be great. We'll be here." She disconnected the call and smiled. "He's going to bring a sample book of wolf tattoos for us to choose from while he does the charm."

"When's he coming?"

"He should be here within the half hour."

Johnson had that much power? Wow. Okay.

"Hey Robby, you might want to shave the inside of your thigh with my razor right now."

"Oh, he takes care of that," Judy said.

Robby poked his head into the kitchen. "Can you at least conjure me up a speedo or something so I'm not going all full monty with you girls watching?" he asked me.

I waved my fingers and a gold speedo appeared in his hand.

"Gold?"

I smiled back at him. "I need a sample of the color I want him to tip the black fur with on my tattoo."

The tilt of his smile was endearing. "You're putting *me* on your ass?"

"I want the world's most gorgeous wolf on my butt cheek, so yes."

"Wait, he has gold-tipped fur?" Judy looked between us.

"It's something relatively new," Robby said. "But apparently I do."

"Oh, I have got to see that." Judy waved for him to shift.

Robby glanced around the room. "Shifting inside here isn't a good idea."

"Oh, come on. Rick has done it."

I chuckled and glanced at the height of the ceiling. Robby's house only had an eight-foot ceiling, which was a far cry from Cassius's cathedral ceilings throughout his home. "Robby would do damage to the structure. He won't fit in this kitchen. I mean, he's always been a big wolf, but now, he's fucking huge. Larger than any wolf you've ever seen."

Her eyes widened. "How?"

"Phoenix tears."

"Excuse me?" She cocked her head like a lost puppy.

"He died and was brought back to life by my tears." I glanced at him. "And that somehow made him extraordinary. Not that he wasn't before," I added with a smile.

She glanced between us and then crossed her arms. "You're shitting me, right?"

"No. You can ask your husband when he gets home. He's seen my juiced-up wolf." Robby smiled and ducked away before Judy could hammer him for any more details.

She looked at me with new interest. "Your tears did that?"

I could see the wheels turning in her head, as if I had a use in her life beyond just being friends. It made me fidget in the chair. "These are things that do not leave this room. They don't leave your mouth." I raised my eyebrows as my commanding tone layered over the room.

Annoyance flashed and her eyes narrowed. "You didn't have to do that," she hissed.

"Are you going to tell me you weren't getting ideas?" I raised an eyebrow, challenging her.

She opened her mouth, and then shut it and looked down at the table. "Fine, I was thinking. I'm sorry."

I gave her a nod. "You're forgiven." Truthfully, if I had been fed this type of information before I was turned, I would be thinking about how to capitalize on it, too.

The doorbell rang, and Judy got up to answer it. She looked through the peephole first and then opened the door with a big grin.

"Phillip, how wonderful to see you again." She waved him in, and he entered with a thick duffel bag and what looked like a large thin suitcase and a smaller attaché case.

"Hello, love. What can I do for you today?"

The way his eyes sparkled made me curious.

"Well, as I said on the phone, one of our friends needs the exact replica of the sigil you did on my arm. And my other friend and I are looking to get tattoos on our ass cheek, if you have time," Judy said.

I only caught a quick hint of his scent when he stepped farther into the living room. This was not a human. But I couldn't quite pin what type of *other* he was. I stepped to the doorway between the kitchen and living room, and glanced up the stairs.

Robby was already descending, and he gave me a warning look that all was not copesetic with this tattoo artist. I racked my brain as to what it could be. I had never seen him before, so it had to be someone Robby and Johnson knew from before the academy.

Why else would he be doing favors for Johnson?

He was setting up his table with his back to us when we stepped farther into the room. Phillip stiffened and gasped.

"Are you okay?" Judy asked from beside him.

He turned slowly, as if any sudden movement would mean a quick death.

I nearly rolled my eyes, but it wasn't me who triggered the fear to radiate from his skin. His gaze locked on Robby.

He slowly put his hands up, palms out, like he was trying to appease Robby. "Look, I mean no harm." His voice squeaked as Judy and I looked on—her with surprise, and me with amusement. Most people who knew Robby didn't act like he was going to tear their head off.

"What are you doing in New York City?" Robby growled.

"I opened a tattoo parlor," he said with both indignance and fear.

"And what exactly do you get paid with? Souls?" Robby growled and then glanced at Judy. "Is that what you and Johnson did, sold your souls for magical tattoos?"

Judy blinked madly, and her mouth popped open and closed as she shook her head.

"Johnson gave me a second chance when he could have easily killed me. I owe him my life, so I've done a few favors like this when he has asked." Words tumbled from his trembling lips, as if Robby would take matters into his own hands.

I stepped next to Robby, and Phillip's nervous pallor went another shade paler. "You know this..." I waved at Phillip. "Soul eater?"

Robby nodded and his teeth made an appearance, as if there were a real threat in the room. "He came through our town once. We ran him out before he had a chance to feast, but once he left pack lands, we didn't pursue him." His eyes narrowed. "Perhaps we should have."

"I don't take much," he whispered, now visibly shaking from head to toe.

"So, you did take from them," Robby growled, pointing at Judy.

Phillip vehemently shook his head, making his hair flop back and forth and then fall into his eyes. He brushed it away. "No, only in my parlor. They sign a waiver for payment that includes a minute fraction of their essence. Just enough to slide under the radar of the MDA."

"But Johnson knew." Robby crossed his arms. His arms barely made a dent in the terry bathrobe. If he had been at his healthiest, a show like that would have split the seams.

Phillip nodded emphatically. "Yes."

"How long?"

Phillip shifted his feet. "Just a couple of months." His gaze kept jumping to me and back, and a crease appeared between his eyes. "You gave a vampire a pass, why are you giving me shit?" He waved at me, seeming to grow a pair since Robby hadn't attacked yet.

"You did that tattoo?" Robby pointed at Judy's arm. "Without payment from her?"

"Y-yes," he stuttered.

"And you're willing to do the same for me without a piece of my essence?" He took a step forward, crowding the soul eater.

He nodded but didn't verbally assent.

Robby growled.

"Yes!" he yelled out, and backed into his table.

"And whatever the girls want? No cost to that either?"

"Yes. As long as you promise to leave me be in my business once I leave here." Phillip's palms were up again, making him look like a criminal giving up to the police.

"Fine. I won't relieve you of your head." Robby stepped back, giving him some breathing room.

I cleared my throat. "And Phillip, you will not say a word to anyone about being here today, and the minute you step back in your shop, you will forget you ever saw us." I pointed between Robby and me, and pushed my compelling power outward.

He looked at me and then through me with a sluggish nod. It only passed over him for a second before he shook his head and patted his table. "Who's first?"

Robby dropped the robe and hopped up on the table with his skimpy gold speedo on.

Phillip's eyebrows went up and he unloaded his bag, setting up a smaller table with ink. He unfolded a piece of paper with a detailed drawing of the charm with all the sigils placed accurately. I'd be willing to bet Johnson drew that for him the first time he had Phillip tattoo Judy and himself.

I glanced over Phillip's shoulder, making him flinch. "Don't worry, I'm not hungry enough to devour a soul eater." I pat him on the shoulder.

He gave me the side-eye and then glanced at Judy. She gave him a reassuring smile that seemed to relax him. "In the attaché are samples of wolf tattoos. Feel free to peruse while I do this." Phillip looked at Robby. "I gather you want the tattoo in a similar location as Johnson?"

"I don't wear gold speedos for my health," Robby said.

I snorted a laugh. "He doesn't. I conjured that for him to make sure you understood what color I want my wolf fur in my tattoo tipped with."

Phillip raised an eyebrow but didn't look my way. Any nerves he might have been feeling disappeared as he got down to business, situating Robby. He pulled out a razor and cleaned up the inner thigh area that Robby had attempted to shave, but my razor obviously wasn't as effective as Phillip's. He plugged in his tattoo gun and hooked it up. "Black ink?" he asked.

Robby nodded and winked at me. "I am partial to red, but black will do just fine."

"The tattoo remains on the skin, even when they shift, right?" I asked.

Phillip glanced at me with a nod. "This charm is embedded into his skin and his very essence. So, he will never be compelled by a vampire, whether he has the agency charm or not." He grinned at me, as if it were my loss.

Judy went to open her mouth, and I shook my head, shutting her down before she spilled that it didn't work with my commands. Hell, I bet Phillip had one of those little tattoos somewhere on his form. My bet was on his leg somewhere, or maybe even his foot. But his stylish high-top sneakers kept it from view.

Judy took the portfolio and opened it on the coffee table. I took a seat next to her on the couch. We looked at the array of wolf tattoos, from tribal ones to more realistic ones. Most were actual pictures of tattoos on skin with the date and a Smashing Tattoos logo in the corner. Judy zeroed in on the ornate tribal tattoos. But the more realistic ones were my jam.

There were a few growling wolves, full faces only, and full body prowling or howling. But the one that struck my fancy was a black wolf, sitting at an angle and staring straight out, as if looking directly at me with that unyielding stare. It held that *I dare you* feel, and with Robby's blue eyes and gold-tipped fur, it would be perfect.

Robby lounged in an awkward position that would surely leave him with an aching back. One leg was bent with his knee pointing toward the ceiling and his bottom leg was folded so the inside of his thigh faced the ceiling, as he leaned back on his elbow. Phillip worked with his tattoo gun on Robby's inner thigh, and Robby stared intently as the needle marked his shaved skin.

The aroma of his blood mixed with ink filled the air, and my mouth watered. I would need to eat sometime soon. Otherwise I might end up biting Robby, and that was a promise I could not break.

Phillip worked inhumanly fast, but he was *other*, and a hint of magic mixed with the blood and ink scents. His scribing needles moved effortlessly, and it only took him an hour to draw the charm into Robby's skin. When he finished and started to clean the area, he mumbled an incantation. With every swipe of the towel, the scent of magic increased, layering over us like a soft rain.

Robby met my gaze, his forehead creased in confusion.

"Did he do that with you and Johnson?" I whispered to Judy.

Judy nodded. "That's part of what makes the tattoo work, just like the necklaces at the agency. At least that's what Rick told me."

Robby's confusion cleared as soon as Judy spoke. The tattoo on his leg glowed as Phillip continued the mantra. When he went silent, the glow magnified before it faded away, seeping into Robby's leg like magic moisturizer. Phillip slathered gel on the tattoo before he put a protective film over it.

"Normally, my human clients keep the tattoo wrapped for five days, but since you aren't human, I would say just keep the patch on for twenty-four hours." He glanced at Judy. "That's about how long you and Johnson kept yours on, right?"

She nodded. "Yes. They were totally healed by then, but we still used the antibiotic moisturizer you gave us for the full five days just in case."

"Who's next?" he asked as he wiped his hands.

Judy and I exchanged a glance.

"Why don't you go?" she said. "Mine won't take as long as yours."

Robby slid off the table and grabbed his robe, putting it on as he crossed to me. I showed him my choice, and he bit the side of his lip, nearly sucking it into his mouth.

"You don't like it?" I asked, hesitating at the doubt painting his expression.

"It's a pretty close likeness." He studied the photo.

"It's fierce but not feral." I grinned. "It will be a perfect representation with your eye color and gold-tipped fur."

He nodded and let out a chuckle. "Then go for it." He handed the paper back to me, and I headed toward the table.

I handed the photograph to Phillip. "The eyes need to be blue like Robby's, and I need you to put gold accents on the tip of the fur like someone meticulously hand painted it on each strand."

"You want a gold wolf?" He raised his eyebrows.

"No. A black wolf with gold-tipped fur. Gold like his speedo." I pointed at Robby. "With blue eyes."

"The eyes are the easy part. This is going to take a little time." He glanced at Robby and then Judy. "I don't think I'll be able to do yours today," he said to her.

She pouted.

"I can't blow off all my customers today. A man's got to eat." His gaze shot to Robby and then to me. "You understand."

The shit thing is I did understand. I was there right now. "If you did hers first, would you have time for mine?"

Judy turned the picture she held his way with her eyes in puppy-dog mode.

Phillip glanced at mine and then sighed. "Fine," he said. "But Johnson owes me this time."

I gave him a nod and went back to the couch with Robby as Judy squealed and gave me a hug before she headed to the table, dropping her drawers with no sense of modesty. She hopped up on the table, and Phillip cleaned her right cheek and went to work.

This time, the magic was more prevalent, and his hand moved faster than it had on Robby, but the details in Robby's tattoo were much more ornate than the tribal wolf that he painted on her ass. The way he moved on this one was quick and sure, as if he had done this tattoo a thousand times.

He finished in half the time and washed the area before he did the same protective film over her art that he had on Robby's.

Judy climbed off the table and showed us her ink.

"Nice work," I said to Phillip as he wiped down the table.

9

CROOKED SOUL 9

AFTER PHILLIP CLEANED UP the table and reset his tools, he looked at me expectantly. I was a bit more modest than Judy, leaving my bathrobe on as I climbed up on the table, only hiking up the back to reveal my ass. And I faced the living room so I could see Robby and Judy.

Phillip didn't say a word, but he cleaned my butt cheek with what looked a little like distaste. When he started the ink machine, he put his hand on me and paused, cocking his head. He glanced at the photo and then at Robby before starting. After a few minutes of inking my ass, he stopped and wiped.

"Look, I usually don't ask any questions of my customers, but you have triggered my curiosity." He met my gaze. "You're warm and you bleed. Those are two things that a vampire usually doesn't have going for them. At least when I've tattooed them, they have never bled." He looked between us all.

"I'm a hybrid." It's all I was willing to concede. No one but my closest friends needed to know what I really was.

The way his eyebrow rose left me smirking. He sighed and continued the tattoo.

"Anyone want food?" Judy asked. "I can make some eggs or pancakes or something." She stood, waiting for Robby and Phillip to pipe in.

My mouth watered at the thought. A pancake sounded truly divine. "I'll try a pancake with strawberries and whipped cream, please." A platter piled with pancakes, dripping with strawberry sauce and a healthy application of whipped cream, appeared at the end of the tattoo table as if I had consciously wished for it. There was enough for all four of us, with extra to spare.

I blinked at the plate and then up at Robby, as if he had been the one to conjure the food. Even my statement took them by surprise. Just like the steak last night, the pancakes smelled like heaven, and I went to reach for them.

"Don't move." Phillip's stern warning halted any motion from me. "If you want to eat, he will need to feed you." He nodded at Robby.

My stomach made an ungodly noise. "There's enough for all of us. Just grab some forks," I said to Judy as she stared at the pancakes with the same hungry interest that Robby did. "Hon, do you mind feeding me?" I asked Robby.

His gaze shot to my face as Judy went into the kitchen. "Will it be all right?"

I started to shrug but thought twice about that; it would move my muscles and I couldn't move from the position I had chosen on my elbows, facing them in some half-modified upward dog. "I think so. It smells as good as you all do."

Judy came back with four forks. "Let me know if you'd like some," she said to Phillip.

The tattoo gun paused and then restarted. "It does look good," he said. "But I need to concentrate."

"I can conjure you up a plate after you finish," I said.

"That would be nice." The tattoo gun resumed.

Robby and Judy pulled up chairs to the end of the padded table I laid on. They dug in, and with the first bite, Robby closed his eyes.

"Damn, these are good." He cut a small piece, dipped it in sauce and cream, and then offered it to me.

Of course, it was half the size of his bite, but his cautiousness was appreciated. It had been over six months since I ate anything, and I had no clue how my body would react. But I wanted the sweet confection.

The moment I closed my mouth on the bite, my taste buds sighed. Sweet and tangy syrup played along my tongue, mixed with the milkiness of the whipped cream. Sinfully delicious. I swallowed and it slid down easily. My stomach made another horrid noise, but it accepted the gift without much strife. I wanted more but I closed my eyes, savoring the strawberry aftertaste. Hell, I could devour the entire plate, but I held back.

"Are you okay?" Robby asked through another mouthful.

I nodded, opening my eyes to meet his gaze, and my mouth for another bite.

He gave me a little larger portion and smiled as I slowly chewed it and swallowed. Two bites were enough to make me feel full, and I waved him and the plate away. He took it to the couch, where Judy and he devoured it completely within a matter of seconds.

I sent the plate back to wherever I had retrieved it from before I put my head on my folded arms and closed my eyes. Lulled by the hum of the tattoo gun—the sting of the needle barely registered—I slipped off into a hypnotized stupor, trusting that Robby would keep me safe.

After a couple of hours, Phillip stopped. "I have everything but the accents." He started mixing colors until he had what looked like liquid gold.

I conjured a mirror large enough for me to see the tattoo. To say I was impressed was an understatement. I waved the mirror away. "The gold should only be on the tips of the fur, so it doesn't lose the black component."

"Conjure that mirror again. I may need some direction." He filled the gun with the new color and rolled his neck before he leaned over.

I did as he asked and watched in my mirror as he added a tiny bit of gold to a few hairs of fur on the drawing.

"Like that?"

It was enough to see the gold, but not enough to make it really stand out like it did when Robby shifted.

"Just a little more. Like an additional half of what you just did."

He leaned in and adjusted the gold to cover more of the tip of the fur.

"Perfect!" I waved the mirror away.

Another hour passed before Phillip pulled away and wiped the tattoo again. "How's that?"

I conjured the mirror and just stared at the masterpiece on my left cheek. It was almost an exact replica of what Robby looked like in wolf form. I sighed, waving the mirror away before I turned to look at Phillip. "You are extremely talented. It is beyond perfect."

He grinned, waved me back down, and washed and covered the area like he did with Robby and Judy.

"Do you mind if I take a picture of this?" he asked.

"Yes. I mind." I did not want anyone else in the world to have this tattoo. "Please don't."

He blinked and nodded, but the disappointment was clear. After all, it was a work of art. He cleared his throat. "You're not a werewolf, so I would suggest you leave this on for the five days. If it seeps, I'll leave a couple of protective films for you to use to recover the tattoo after you clean it. And I'll leave you some antibacterial soap to wash the area before covering it again."

"Thanks." I hopped off the table and took the items from him, putting them on the side table as I stretched my back to get the ache out. "Did you want those pancakes?" I didn't wait for an answer. I conjured another plate similar to the first, along with a fork, and handed it to him.

He finished wiping the table and then took the pancakes before he packed up the rest of the items. With a grin, he nearly inhaled the ample breakfast and then burped. His face reddened.

"Sorry." He covered his mouth a little too late for a second satisfied belch. "That is almost as good as the essence of a soul."

"Thank you," I said when he handed me back the plate. With a wave of my hand, it went back into the ether.

"That really is a handy talent," he said as he packed his tattoo guns and paints. "Do you have a garbage?" He held out a plastic bag full of bloody rags.

I stared at the offered garbage and took it, stanching the need to put it to my lips and suck the blood from the material. I turned and handed it to Robby as quickly as possible, so I didn't give in to the need for blood that suddenly welled.

I shifted my stance and gave Phillip a tight smile as Robby headed for the kitchen.

Phillip studied me. "I still don't understand what exactly you are. Most vampires, whether they were witches before or not, become vampires when they are turned."

I willed my fangs to come out and smiled. "Who said I'm not afflicted with the vampire's curse?"

He laughed. "You're not normal."

I willed my teeth away. "I've never been normal. And that's a good thing."

"Man, I'd give anything for a taste of you," he muttered as Robby walked back into the room.

"Don't even think about it," he growled.

Phillip stiffened, and the poor man's face paled.

"I am hungry." I put my hand up for Robby to chill, but that didn't make Phillip's pallor any better. "If I can have a taste of you, I'll allow you a small taste of my essence like you take from your clients."

Phillip laughed. "News flash. Vampires kill."

"I don't. It's part of that not normal thing I have going on."

"Sarah," Robby warned. "He takes time away from you," he said, explaining exactly what a soul eater does. But unlike vampires, soul eaters rarely kill.

I still had lives left. Not many, but enough so I could sacrifice a little time. "How much time do you take?"

Phillip took a breath. "Days, weeks, months, depending on how much energy I expend. But I try not to drain more than a couple months at the most. Anything more and that seems to ping the MDA's radar, which is how Johnson found me."

Johnson had used his discretion where Phillip was concerned. I'm sure the MDA had no clue because there wouldn't be any way he would do work for free if he was forced to be an informant. Which meant, Johnson wasn't operating at one-hundred percent loyalty to the agency, and he had seen something in this guy that made him skirt the rules.

Interesting.

"A pint for a week," I blurted, needing something to smooth out the craving, and real food did nothing to deter my growing hunger for blood. I would gladly give up a week of time, so I didn't end up biting Robby. "And I go first." I smiled.

He shifted the bag on his shoulder and folded up his table before he looked at me again as if weighing some of the same things I had before I blurted out the deal. He set the bag and the table down. "My curiosity has gotten the best of me." He stepped forward and lifted his chin, offering me his throat.

"Don't, Sarah." Robby grabbed my arm. "It's a trick."

I studied Phillip. The fact he offered me his throat was a large wager on his part. "I don't think so. And I need to feed. I don't see Judy or Johnson offering up their blood."

Robby offered me his wrist.

"I intend to keep *that* promise." I pushed his hand down and met his gaze. "Trust me, and trust that he won't screw me over. If he does, I'll let you tear him to pieces."

Phillip's eyes widened at that, but he remained still with his head up, offering me his neck.

I wasn't going to feed from his throat. That was reserved for intimacy and for enemies. "Not your neck." I took his hand and pushed back his sleeve. Without warning, I dug my teeth into his flesh and was rewarded with a flow of blood. He winced but didn't try to pull away. The soul eater's blood tasted like strong, smoky bourbon, almost like the combination of thousands of souls. I pulled swallow after swallow, satiating my need, keeping my mind in the present instead of getting lost in his life essence.

When I guessed I had taken a pint's worth of blood, I pulled away and swiped my finger across the punctures, sealing the cuts before I lifted up and stared him in the eye. A hazy smoke that looked like spun sunshine surrounded us, leaving a satisfied smile on his face. His eyes glazed over as if he had taken some hard-core drugs.

He blinked and the smoke around us pulled into his mouth as he took a deep inhale. His eyes cleared up, and he stared at me with awe.

"I still don't know what you are, but that small infusion felt like swallowing the sun. I don't think I'll need to eat again for a very long time."

"You already fed?" I hadn't felt anything. No siphoning of energy or life force. It was as if nothing had happened at all. That made me wonder how his feeding triggered MDA at all.

He grinned. "I had no guarantee that you would stop or follow through on your end when you finished."

I stepped back, staring at him. His trust wavered, and I really couldn't blame him; that was why I insisted on going first. "How much did you take?"

"I stopped at a week, as we agreed." He stared at his wrist. "How did you...cauterize the wounds?"

"I conjured fire," I lied. I wasn't going to tell him that was part of my makeup. He had seen me conjure things today, so it wasn't that far-fetched.

He seemed satisfied with my lie and picked up his things. Before he left, he pulled out his card. "If you need any more tattoos, please contact me.

I'd be happy to help you, for a fair trade." He grinned and handed me the card.

"Thank you." I looked at the card in my hand. "Now, do not forget—not a word, and as soon as you enter your shop, you will forget Robby and I were here." I pushed my influence out and that faraway look appeared.

Phillip nodded and left without another word. After he was out of sight, I closed the front door.

"He won't remember us." I handed the card to Judy. "So, if you want his card, be my guest."

I lifted my bathrobe. "Do you like it?" I asked Robby.

He nodded. "It's as exquisite as the ass it's on."

"It is stunning," Judy said from behind us. "Is that what he looks like?" She met my gaze.

I nodded and dropped the hem of the robe. "Yes. And honestly, I hope you never have to see him like that here. If you do, it means all hell has broken loose."

CROOKED SOUL 10

THE THREE OF US chatted for a bit, and then I excused myself and went to clean myself up and get into some clothes. Although the bathrobe was comfortable, I needed something more sensible on when Johnson came home. I wasn't comfortable being half naked around anyone but Robby. Especially after being tied to a bed for six months without a stitch of clothing on.

I opted for a nice warm shower, too. The sensation of the hot water pelting my skin relaxed the knotted muscles that had formed in my neck and shoulders from staying in that position for so long. I rolled my head from side to side to try to loosen some of the kinks.

The air shifted, and I glanced over my shoulder at Robby stepping into the shower.

"Are you okay?" he asked.

"My neck and shoulders are stiff."

"I meant eating. You've been in the shower long enough for me to think maybe something was wrong." He slid behind me underneath the spray, blocking the heat. Before I could turn and berate him, he started massaging my shoulders and upper back, working the knots like a professional masseuse.

"Eating didn't affect me at all," I said, almost groaning when he hit a sensitive cluster of muscles near my shoulder blade. I certainly winced away from his touch, but his fingers followed, working the cluster until it finally gave in a painful release.

He continued to work my muscles until I thought I'd just fall to the floor like a piece of putty. Then his hands surrounded my neck, and he stalled with his thumbs next to my spine, like he was going to work the muscles there. And they so desperately needed it.

But his fingers froze, and I felt the pressure of a squeeze starting, and then his hands were gone.

I turned and he was staring at his hands in horror, and they visibly shook. His wide eyes rose to mine. He spun and put his forehead on the back of the shower wall.

"What is it?" I ran my hand over his back, feeling as if we just went back to square one based on the haunted look he had.

He shook his head. "I had the urge to choke you," he whispered. "It's like he slipped into my head and ordered me to."

I rubbed his back until he stopped shaking, trying not to break out in my own shivers. "You have the tattoo now. Besides, he can't compel you from the grave."

"You aren't safe with me," he finally said and glanced over his shoulder at me.

"Bullshit." I wouldn't ever believe that I wasn't safe with Robby. He'd die for me if he had to, so I wasn't buying this.

He turned toward me and gently took me by the shoulders. "I'm having flashbacks, nightmares." He took a breath and closed his eyes. "Sometimes I don't know what's real, and I feel like that bastard is still pulling the strings."

I stepped closer and wrapped my arms around him. I could totally relate. There were times when I wondered whether all this was a dream and that reality still waited for me to awake. "You aren't the only one. I just don't manifest my setbacks as vividly as you do."

He pushed me far enough away so he could meet my gaze. "I keep forgetting that you were just as fucked as I was." His lips tilted into a ghost of a smile, but the haunted look didn't leave his eyes.

"I was unconscious through most of it." I minimized my ordeal. It wasn't as if I were aware of what was happening, and I couldn't imagine if the tables were turned how I would have survived seeing him slaughtered over and over again. I would have lost my mind.

He scoffed at me. "That's not exactly true."

I rolled my eyes at him. "Dead. Unconscious. Same deal." I wasn't there to witness most of his suffering, and my torment was fleeting in comparison.

He cupped my cheek. "It isn't the same. I wasn't murdered time and time again."

I lifted my shoulder in a shrug.

"Don't brush that off. And don't brush off the fact there are times you may be in danger around me. As much as I hate it when you control me, you may have to do that if I lose it." He wiped his hand down his face. "I love you and God knows I don't mean to hurt you, but I might. And admitting this sucks, but you need to be prepared to defend yourself. Understand?"

I nodded. My flashbacks were more in the form of nightmares, not lashing out at those around me like Robby seemed to do when he felt trapped. He was more of a wild card, but I knew he would never intentionally harm me. His mark on my shoulder ached, and his emotions layered over me. His love, his confusion, and his anger all wrapped up together in a potent cocktail.

I hugged him and left him in the shower while I dried off and willed some loose sweatpants and a T-shirt on my body. I did not want anything tight on my ass. Not with the discomfort of the healing tattoo. I left a pile of loose, comfortable clothing for Robby on the closed toilet seat and took a brush to my long locks. By the time I had all the knots out, Robby stepped out and dressed after toweling off.

"Thanks for the clothing."

"How's your tattoo feeling?"

He shrugged. "It itches a little, but it's not that bad. How's yours?" His gaze lowered to my ass and then back.

"I'm going to have to figure out a comfortable way to sit for the next few days."

"So…no spanking?"

I laughed and shook my head. "No. No spanking."

The minute I opened the bedroom door, the scent of beef stroganoff drifted on the air. That had been one of my favorite meals to cook since the days of the academy when I basically learned how to make it from the staff over winter break. My mouth watered, and my stomach made a horrid noise.

Robby raised an eyebrow. My stomach had made that same noise when I conjured the pancakes this morning. "Hungry again?"

I was, but not for blood. I ran my hand through my hair, pulling it back from my face. Maybe all those deaths and rebirths had somehow changed the makeup of the vampire cravings. The thought of food didn't sicken me the way it had those first few days we were on the run. "Yeah."

He didn't say a word, but that crevice between his eyes gave me a clue that he was deep in thought. When his gaze met mine before we entered the kitchen, he had a million questions in that single glance, just like I had.

My mother said I wasn't able to break the vampire curse, but I could control it with the magic the phoenix inherently has. Maybe this was that control manifesting itself.

I stepped through the entry. "That smells divine."

Judy turned from the stove and beamed. "Rick said he'd be home in a few minutes. Just in time for a nice hearty meal for all of us." She stirred the dish slowly.

Instead of just watching her cook, I busied myself with setting the table for the four of us. I wasn't passing on it. Not when my mouth was nearly dripping with saliva.

Judy glanced at the place settings and looked up at me with a grin. "You want some?"

"I'm not made to pass up beef stroganoff." I folded the napkins and slid them under each fork. "Although, sitting might be a little uncomfortable."

Her eyes widened in commiseration. "I know. Right? I didn't think about the healing time until after you all went upstairs, and I came in here and tried to sit to chop up the onions and garlic. A big nope to that. It took me by surprise because we were hanging out on the couch in the living room before you went upstairs. But I was leaning to the side, and I think you were too."

I had been leaning on my right side with no real weight on my left cheek and she was on the other couch arm. "You're right. Maybe we should eat in the living room." I glanced toward the more comfortable furniture.

She looked at the stroganoff and chewed her bottom lip as she weighed her comfort against eating in here. "I think we'll be okay. We'll just have to lean to the side a little."

"Or balance on the edge of the chair on our good cheek."

She snorted a laugh. "Or that."

The front door opened, and a moment later, Johnson came into view. "It smells damn good in here." He dropped a duffel bag in the corner. He put his hands on his hips and stared at Judy. "Are you going to show me or what?" He raised an eyebrow.

Judy put the spoon down and lowered her drawers, just like that, with a grin as wide as I had ever seen on her and a glint in her eye.

Johnson nodded his approval and then looked at us, expectantly. "I figure he had to have done something on you two since you wiped his memory." He looked pointedly at me. "So, let's see yours."

"I'm not dropping my drawers." Robby crossed his arms. "But apparently mine looks identical to yours." He stared Johnson down.

Johnson moved his gaze away from Robby with a nod. His eyebrow cocked.

"Oh, you have to show him," Judy said.

My face heated. It was one thing showing another woman my ass, but dropping my pants for anyone else but Robby was a problem. It left me vulnerable in a way I wasn't able to allow. "I'm not comfortable with that," I said, shuffling my feet. No stance I adopted felt natural. I finally crossed my arms and looked at the floor.

"Show him," Judy whined from the stove. "It's amazing," she added.

Johnson took a breath and traded a glance with Robby. "It's okay. You don't need to," he said, as if he read my discomfort as acutely as Robby did.

"He's my beta," Robby started and then stopped like it didn't truly matter who Johnson was. "He'd never harm you," he added after a moment. "But if you aren't comfortable, he won't press to see your tattoo." He glanced at Johnson. "Right?"

"Yes." He didn't hesitate. "I'm sorry if I made you uncomfortable." He approached me, sending Judy a shut-up look. "Tell me about it," he said softly, as if he knew just how precarious a ledge I was standing on.

It was ludicrous that I couldn't seem to show him when I had no qualms climbing on the table and baring my butt to a total stranger. Maybe Cassius had fucked with my head more than I thought. I once trusted him the way I had trusted Johnson and Robby, but he betrayed me. So, my trusting of people as a whole had been warped by Cassius's torment.

"It's Robby," I mumbled and looked down at the floor as I grappled with this new hurdle that jumped up in front of me.

"With or without the gold?"

I smiled and glanced up at him. "With."

He nodded. "Nice." He took my hand and squeezed before he slid by me and went to his wife, wrapping his arms around her, kissing the back of her neck to sooth the irritated look on her face.

Judy did not understand my hang-up. I could tell by the way her gaze slashed to mine. The questions in her eyes left me feeling as if I slighted her somehow.

Robby slung his arm across my shoulders. "It's okay. I like that it's just for my viewing," he whispered in my ear.

Judy shook Johnson off and served the stroganoff from the pan, piling it on all four plates. Robby and I sat down as she dropped the empty pan in the sink. I waved my hand and four full wine glasses appeared on the table, filled to the brim with red wine.

Vampires did drink. I learned that much from Cassius.

"You're eating?" Johnson's voice cracked as he looked between my plate and my face.

"Yes. This is one of my favorites. Did you tell her?" I pointed my fork at Judy.

He shook his head. Johnson's confusion made the three of us chuckle.

"That's not normal," Johnson muttered.

I tilted my head. "When have I ever been normal?"

That pulled a bark of a laugh from him, and he dug into the food. "No, I didn't mention it to Judy. This happens to be one of her favorites, too," he said through a mouthful.

I took my first bite, and an explosion of savory flavors played on my tongue. Just like the sweet confection this morning, this nearly had me moaning from the taste. It was as if my taste buds had increased in sensitivity the way my sight and hearing had when I was turned. But instead of being too much, it was like I was tasting the different levels of food combinations both individually and then layered together.

However, just like the pancakes, I could only stomach a few bites. But it was enough to satisfy whatever drove me to eat. "Judy, this is wonderful, but that's all I can eat." I pushed my plate toward Robby. "Why don't you split mine with Johnson?" I said to him.

There was no hesitation; he took half the contents of my plate and handed the rest to Johnson.

But I downed the wine, cleansing my palate with my first taste of alcohol since the night I was turned.

"Did you want any?" he asked Judy.

"I have more than enough. You go ahead," she said.

He piled the rest on his plate and put my dish in the sink before he finished the feast.

Judy reached out and covered my hand with hers. "I'm sorry I pushed you."

Heat filled my face again. "It's okay. I just..." I shrugged, unable to really articulate my hesitation. It's not like Johnson hadn't seen that part of me before. I mean, he had been there the night I was sexually assaulted at the academy. He had seen my bare ass. But I just couldn't bring myself to willingly bare any skin in front of him.

She squeezed and then went back to eating.

I itched to move because my butt ached, and the conversation had brought forth a lot more discomfort than I anticipated. The kitchen was small enough that I could still be part of the conversation and not seem rude, so I got up and crossed to the sink.

"What are you doing?" Judy asked.

I turned. "Cleaning up. You cooked, so I figured I would start cleaning."

"I usually do that as well." Judy glanced at Johnson. "He's worked all day, so I'm just used to doing the cooking and cleaning."

The shock of her statement left me cold. I guess that was what was normally expected from an alpha, and it made me thank the heavens that Robby wasn't a normal macho asshole like most alphas.

"She's not one for sitting idle," Robby said with a grin. "Just don't let her take your plate before you're done. She's famous for trying to do that." He winked at me.

"I don't do that," I mumbled as I scrubbed the pot clean and put it in the drying rack with a clang, trying to control the rising irritation. I never figured Johnson for this alpha macho bullshit either.

"You've done it to me since we've been back." Robby shoveled another mouthful in his maw. The light in his eyes needled me, like he was intentionally goading me.

"I've taken picked bones that only had gristle left from you." I glared over my shoulder at him.

His playful grin almost had me turning the spray faucet on him. He was trying to get a rise out of me, and it was working. I finished what was in the sink and refrained from gathering the plates from the table. It was harder than I expected because that restless part of me just wanted to finish this and get onto relaxing for the night.

I dried my hands on a towel. "So, you don't help her in the kitchen at all?" I challenged Johnson. I couldn't help it.

"Oh no, it's my choice," Judy said before Johnson could swallow his food and answer.

I stared Johnson down.

"You are an alpha's mate. You know what's expected." He leaned back in the chair.

Robby chuckled and glanced at me. "I never expected her to be subservient. As a matter of fact, she made it clear that she would never be that way." He winked at me. "I love her feisty tattooed ass just the way she is, and I always have." He glanced at Judy. "No offense, but I need a woman who challenges the hell out of me, and I never expected her to be a slave to my needs." His gaze slashed to Johnson in such a pointed way that his beta shifted under it.

"And that's why he's a natural-born leader." Johnson waved at Robby with both admiration and irritation. "He never expected any of us to follow him. Yet we all did and would have followed him into the bowels of hell."

Robby laughed but there was no humor in it. It was as if he had stepped back to that moment in the forest when his pack had surrounded us. If he had been in wolf form, his neck would be bristling. "You all were ready to kill me in those woods."

"But we didn't," Johnson said, equally as tense.

"That's because of her." Robby nodded toward me. "She is the only one who stood up for me and stood by me through all this shit. You only backed down out of a sense of self-preservation." He leaned forward with a growl on his voice.

Johnson looked down at his empty plate, his cheeks a bright crimson at being called out.

I needed to defuse Robby. His aggravation pounded in the mark he made on my shoulder. It would be very easy for him to snap. I reached over and cleared Johnson's empty plate as well as Robby's.

Judy was still picking at hers, almost cowering at the heightened testosterone filling the room. Her lips pressed together in thought as she moved the food around.

"Judy cooked a wonderful meal. Don't spoil it by bickering, boys." I gave them both warning looks before I turned my back on them to finish the dishes.

Silence fell on the room for a moment as my gentle scolding settled on them.

"The dinner was outstanding," Johnson said in a soft tone.

I smiled. Maybe he had promise after all. I just prayed he'd learn to be more like Robby and not be an alpha dick like Robby's dad.

"It wasn't anything special," Judy mumbled.

I turned and pointed at her. "Don't do that."

Her gaze jumped to mine, and her perfectly manicured eyebrows arched.

"You prepared a meal. It is special, and don't you ever let anyone tell you otherwise. Making food, keeping the house clean, and making your man feel special when he gets home is just as much work as being out there with a paying job." I pointed the fork I was cleaning toward the window and the world outside. "If you decided to go out and get a job, all that you currently do would have to be shared." I glanced at Johnson. "Marriage is a partnership. Are you that much of a dick that you'd make her carry the entire load?"

Johnson opened his mouth like he was going to launch into an argument with me. I narrowed my eyes at him. Whatever point he made would be wrong, and I think he knew it because he closed his mouth and lowered his gaze to the empty spot on the table where his plate had been.

I believed in the life I grew up in. My parents were partners in everything, from raising me, to the housework, even the cooking. And they still had date nights. The magic never left their relationship and that was the way it should be.

"Oh, but I'm not his equal." Judy pointed at Johnson.

My brain blanked before the burn of aggravation slid along my skin.

"Who said?" Robby asked before I could compose my thoughts enough to speak, and I couldn't have been more proud of my mate.

Judy blinked, as if she didn't understand his question. "I'm not an alpha."

"Well, I am an alpha, but that does not make me better than anyone else despite this archaic view of pack hierarchy. It does not make me entitled to be treated better, either," Robby argued. "There are alphas out there who think they're the shit because of their label. They use fear and bullying to lead. My father is an example of a truly awful alpha leader. He protected his own interests instead of doing what was best for the pack. Hell, he even put the MDA before the pack." Robby wiped his face and took a breath. "A true leader is one who puts their pack's needs above their own and treats every wolf as their equal even though the hierarchy says otherwise." He glanced at Johnson and then over at me. "I've never put the pack first."

Johnson had quietly been listening to all this, processing it. Until Robby announced he had never put the pack first. He slammed his palm on the table. "Yes, you did. You put us first for most of your life. Otherwise, you would have sought her out that first night at the academy and made her yours before your father shuffled the deck on you." He took a breath. "You never put yourself first. Ever. That is why we followed you. Why every student at the school would have gone to battle alongside you." He pressed his lips together. "We did not want to hunt you, but there was no other choice. And that fire Sarah started made it easier for us to say you outmaneuvered us and have it not be questioned." He glanced at me. "I'm not sure I'd be sitting here otherwise."

"You lied?" Judy asked with a tone that bordered on indignant.

Johnson winced. "Just a little." He looked at her. "Just like I did with Phillip." He shrugged. "Sometimes a death sentence is *not* warranted."

CROOKED SOUL 11

ONCE JUDY AND JOHNSON headed to bed, Robby glanced at me. "I need to get out of here for a little bit. Want to take a walk?"

I shifted on the seat and winced as I put pressure on my tattoo. "Do you think that's wise?" I stood up, because sitting was starting to irritate my ass. I wasn't going to be comfortable doing anything, and I wished Phillip had mentioned that tattooing my ass was going to make me uncomfortable for a few days. I might have chosen to get ink elsewhere.

"I don't know. But if I don't get out of here, I'm likely to snap again like I did at the dinner table. Besides, it's dark out and we can head over to

Prospect Park, walk the paths, and just chill for a while."

I needed some fresh air too. It had been over a week that we had been locked in this house, recuperating. Robby had gained a few pounds back and he no longer looked like a POW. "Won't walking aggravate your tattoo?" After all, it was on the inside of his thigh.

He shook his head. "If it does, we can take a cab back. Same if yours starts bothering you."

It wasn't like walking through the forest in the areas west of the city, either. The likelihood of running into trouble was low here, but it still was a risk. However, I just nodded, because I couldn't rightfully say no to the way he was begging with his eyes. It was like having a puppy who was begging for a bite of your steak. I could never resist that look, and he knew it.

He grinned and grabbed my hand, and like an over-exuberant child, he dragged me outside and turned right, toward the direction of Cassius's place and the park beyond. When he took the side street that I nearly carried him down, I hesitated and pulled my hand from his. Going this way would bring us by the place we were both meant to be destroyed.

Robby skidded to a stop and turned, meeting my gaze. He stepped closer. "What is it?"

"You don't remember?"

His eyes locked with mine and now that he was facing his brownstone, he looked beyond me at the street. Robby paled and swung his gaze the other way. "He really lived this close?"

"Yeah." I couldn't make my feet move from where I stood. It wasn't like me to freeze like this, either.

"We can take a cab." He started back toward his place.

My chest tightened, and I could hardly draw a breath with the pressure. I still couldn't move. It was as if this piece of pavement had been painted with superglue and I had stepped in it before it solidified. Every nerve felt raw, as if my body remembered each and every death delivered by that bastard.

Robby came back and positioned himself in front of me. He tilted my chin up so I would be forced to look at him. The concern I saw there was as if the tables had turned between us, and he was here to soothe me versus the daily struggle I had to keep him sane.

"It is okay. I ripped that fucker to pieces. He can't hurt you again."

Heat leaked from the corner of my eye and cut a hot path down my cheek. This crippling dread flowed through my veins like liquid lava, making me shiver it was so uncomfortably hot, and not in the way I liked my heat. This was irrational fear.

"I know," I whispered. "But I can't seem to move." Even my voice sounded constrained.

"Do you want me to carry you back home?"

I nodded. I wasn't ready for the outside world, and it burned. Robby picked me up with one arm behind my back and the other under my knees.

"You should have told me you weren't ready." He kissed my temple.

"I didn't know I wasn't."

He huffed a small laugh. "Yeah. It kind of sneaks up on you when you least expect it. Doesn't it?" He trotted across the street and up the steps, unlocking the door with me still in his grip. "We'll try again some other night."

"Thank you," I whispered against his neck. I guess I wasn't as immune to post-traumatic stress as I thought I was.

He locked the door behind him before he set me on my feet. "No problem. We'll take a cab next time I want fresh air."

That was such an oxymoron that I started to laugh. He cracked a grin as he took my hand and led me upstairs.

I stretched out on the bed on my right side, still in my warm sweats, while he went into the bathroom to get ready for bed. My abdomen cramped and I groaned, curling up into a ball.

Robby opened the door with his toothbrush still in his mouth. "You okay?"

"Cramps," I muttered. My lower abdomen felt as if it were on fire.

He spit out his toothpaste in the sink and stepped back into the room. Climbing on the bed, he put his palm on my lower belly. It groaned in response. Then a smirk formed on his lips.

"You might need to use the bathroom." He hooked his thumb over his shoulder.

I gawked at him. I hadn't peed or pooped since I was turned. That was one of the benefits of being a vampire.

"You ate food. It doesn't just ferment in your stomach, hon."

I blinked at him and then followed his advice. I closed the door and sat on the commode, leaning more to the right so I didn't aggravate my tattoo. It was as if my body remembered what to do after so long, but it was incredibly painful, almost like passing a kidney stone. A large burst of air came out and was followed by my first bowel movement in over six months.

I let out a shaky laugh. This was not one of the things I missed. Not by a long shot. However, the pain was worth the taste of the food today. If this was the side effect of enjoying food, I would just have to deal with it.

I wiped and then flushed the toilet, brushed my teeth, and headed back into the bedroom with a scowl.

Robby grinned at me. "Welcome back to the land of the living."

"Fuck you. I would have preferred that part to stay gone." I climbed back in bed and snuggled next to him despite my foul mood.

Robby wrapped his arm around me and pulled me to his chest. "I'm just glad that didn't happen in a cab." He chuckled against my neck.

"Or while walking in the park." I smirked at him.

He actually snorted against my shoulder, and I joined him in his laughter. It was actually pretty funny when I thought about it.

"If that happened, we would know the answer to the timeless question—does a vampire shit in the woods?" Robby snickered against my shoulder and tightened his grip on me.

I let out a burst of laughter that was loud enough to wake the entire house. "That was bad," I said through gales of laughter.

He couldn't stop laughing against me. As juvenile as this entire conversation was, it provided both of us much-needed levity that we hadn't had for a very long time.

"Man, I needed that," he finally whispered as his chuckles faded away.

"I feel you. I don't think I've laughed that hard since the academy." I wiped the tears from the corners of my eyes. "All because I took a dump."

He started that snort-like laugh again, like he was trying not to fall into the sillies. But it was useless; he just kept shaking the bed, which only made it worse for both of us.

I rolled out of his grip onto my stomach and stared at him, trying to school my features to be neutral. He actually guffawed at that and rolled onto his back. I pressed my lips together, refusing the laughter that bubbled up in my chest.

I put my forehead on my arm and just let it rip. At least the bedspread muffled my laughter. His rang through the room as loud as my initial blast. He rolled onto his side again and ran his hand over my back gently as he wound down again.

"Just don't utter any more bad puns." He snickered as he continued running his fingers over my T-shirt.

I couldn't bring myself to look at him, because if I did, I'd start laughing again.

He let out a long sigh. "So, are you going to tell me what happened out there?" he asked after we both got control of ourselves.

I turned my head so I could look at him. "I just froze." The jovial mood dampened. "I don't think I'm capable of walking past his house."

"Considering the timing, you probably saved our asses."

I blinked and then reality settled. The MDA probably had surveillance on the place. Most psychopaths visited the scene of the crime at some point within a few weeks of a deadly event, even with the inherent dangers.

That's how we caught a few of our more prolific vampires in the past. They couldn't stay away from their favorite feeding spots. And it was one of the reasons we never caught Cassius. He never left the bodies anywhere near where he fed. He trashed them miles away from where he killed them.

Cassius Chase was a smart motherfucker. But then again, he had been around longer than the existence of the good old US of A, so he knew how to play the long game. Too bad he hadn't factored in my bond with Robby. That's what he severely underestimated. And because of that, he was dead.

CROOKED SOUL 12

THE NEXT MORNING CAME faster than I expected. By the time we got our lazy asses out of bed, Johnson had already left for work and Judy was just getting ready to head to the grocery store.

"Is there anything I can get you guys?" Her pen stalled on the paper as she looked up at us.

"I'm good." I smiled. If there was something I wanted, I could just conjure it right to me.

"Ditto." Robby wore shorts and a T-shirt, as if he were going to work out somewhere. He went to a door toward the back of the hall that I assumed was a closet and opened it, disappearing inside.

I had only been in Robby's house a handful of times over the years. And most of the time it was for a Super Bowl party or some serious team-building binge watching. So, I only knew what was on the main floor.

"I'll see you later," I said to Judy and followed Robby's path. The door led to a lower set of stairs and a musty-smelling basement that was covered with mats, benches, and weight machines. The equipment here was better than the gym at headquarters, and I let out a whistle.

"I figured it was time to get my strength back." He curled weights as he spoke, huffing through the words. His arms bulged with the exertion.

"Maybe I'll join you later." My ass was bothering me and working out just didn't sound fun. I headed back upstairs and tried to find a comfortable spot on the couch, but I gave up on that. In the laundry room, I found a mop and some floor cleaner, and I went to work cleaning the kitchen and the living area up. Then I dusted and by the time I stowed away the cleaning stuff, Robby showed his sweaty face. He smiled and glanced around the living area.

"Couldn't sit still?"

"No. My butt hurts."

"Well, come on upstairs and let's make sure the tattoo isn't seeping."

"How's yours?"

He lifted his shorts and showed me. He must have taken off the film before heading down, but it looked like Judy's. No scabs, no blood, just ink in his skin. For a moment, I envied his ability to heal in a snap.

I followed him up the stairs just as Judy stepped in with an armful of groceries. I hesitated on the landing at the top. "Do you need a hand?"

"I'm fine." She looked around the living area. "You didn't need to clean."

I grinned. "It's the least I can do, considering."

She waved me off, and I slid into the bedroom, crossing to the bathroom where Robby already had the shower running and was stripping his clothes.

"Let's see the damage." He made a twirling motion with his finger.

I turned, dropped my sweats, and glanced over my shoulder. His head cocked to the side but there was no alarm in his eyes. Just a curious stare.

"It probably could use a wash," he finally said, and grabbed the antibacterial soap Phillip had given me and nodded to the running shower. "Come on."

"I'll wait until you're done cleaning up before we attack this." I waved to my derriere.

He stripped the last of his clothing and stepped into the shower, soaping up with my Calm the F*CK Down body wash this time. Personally, I would have used the Wake the F*CK Up instead, but the one he used had a trace of lavender, and that did seem to calm him down more effectively than a tranquilizer would.

He poked his head out and shook the antibacterial soap at me. "You ready?"

"Yep." I peeled my shirt off. "I'll let you take this film off, if you don't mind." The angle was such that I'd likely scrape some of the tattoo. I did not want to do that. Not with it being so uncomfortable already. I twirled my hair into a messy bun so it wouldn't get soaked and stepped into the shower.

"You can't have the water hit your tattoo directly, so I'll wash and rinse it, okay?" He poured a healthy amount of cleaner in his hand and waited for me to step inside. He tossed a handful of water on the tattoo and then covered it with the soap in his palm, rubbing in small, tight circles. "I wish you could heal as quick as I can."

"I do too." Whatever underlying itch that had started disappeared with Robby's gentle touch. Having him do it was much better than me trying to contort myself enough to see and scrub.

He straightened and took a few handfuls of water, rinsing before he waved me into the shower. "Clean up and I'll do that again after, so it's completely clean with the antibacterial stuff."

I stepped under the spray, keeping most of my left side away from the water, and reached for my liquid soap. I cleaned the remainder of my body and then let him do a second cleaning of my tattoo before we turned off the water.

He patted me down with the towel and then reapplied another film over the tattoo to keep it clean. He swatted my right cheek and then gave me a morning kiss that lingered enough for me to push away from him.

"Thank you for helping me, but I'm not in the mood for that quite yet."

He smirked and nodded. "This is a first. You not in the mood."

"Yeah, well, I'd like to see you try to get all hot and bothered while your ass stings."

He didn't laugh. "Maybe you need to feed to heal quicker." He offered me his wrist.

I pushed it away, taking hold of his hand. "Robby, I'm never going to feed from you again. That's one promise I intend to keep."

His lips tilted into that soft smile that was so damn kissable. "And what other promise do you intend to keep?"

"No sccrcts."

He nodded. "No secrets." He leaned in and planted another kiss, but it was quick, as if he knew anything more would rev his engine past the point of walking away.

"Come on. Let's go see what Judy brought home and whether she wants help with dinner or not."

We dressed and then headed downstairs to find Judy lounging on the couch with a tray of cheese and crackers on the table. "Johnson's coming home early today, so..." She waved at the hors d'oeuvres with a smile.

"Did you need help with dinner?" Robby asked.

"No. He said not to bother with a big dinner. He's bringing takeout home." She grinned. "You really made an impression on him last night. And while it makes me a bit uncomfortable to be treated as his equal, it also feels nice."

"It is nice to feel like you are partners in a relationship and it's not just one-sided." I glanced at Robby and reached for his hand, giving it a squeeze before I let go and found the corner of the couch where I could lean just so and be comfortable for a while.

"It still hurts?" She nodded at me.

"Yeah. And now it's itching, too." I clasped my hands together so I wouldn't scratch and tried to smile, but it was forced, and Judy knew it.

"Well, thank you for cleaning. It gave me a chance to relax and watch a few shows that I hadn't seen in ages." She stretched like a lazy cat. "Is there anything you want to watch?" She held out the remote.

Robby plucked it out of her hand. "Sure."

Judy stared at him. "I meant her." She pointed at me. "I'm not in the mood for sports."

"Oh, you underestimate me." He flipped through the channels before he found a show he had been watching when the bottom dropped out from our world. He selected it and went back to the beginning of the season. "It's a little violent."

"I know. I binged it all after the season ended." Judy didn't move from her spot on the couch. "Rick wasn't much of a fan, though. He's more sports and reality show oriented."

I snickered under my breath. Although Robby did watch major sporting events, he didn't religiously watch sports. If there was nothing on, he'd settle on a football game or hockey. But for the most part, he just bypassed them altogether and went for the spooky thriller shows and the superhero shows like this one. Although this was more antihero and violent as sin.

Since we escaped, he had been choosing more benign shows that didn't have many triggers, so this was the first time he chose something so violent. It was as if he were testing the waters of what he could deal with. After ten minutes, the character on the screen was locked in a room and the only thing he had to eat to survive were rats.

That was, if he could catch them. Robby switched the program off and tossed the remote on the table.

"Sorry, I just can't take that much stress right now." He sighed and ran his hand down his face. "That episode hit a little too close." He got up and went into the kitchen.

Judy glanced at me with a raised eyebrow.

"That's what he lived off of for six months." I waved at the television.

"Rats?" She peeled her lips back in horror.

"Yes." I trembled with a chill that raced up my spine like a mouse trying to flee a flood.

"Good Lord. No wonder he's so skinny."

"He's actually looking much better than he had when we first got here. Thanks to your cooking." I still couldn't shake that image from my mind. His hands had been bound behind his back. That meant he had to catch, kill, and eat the rats with only his human teeth. My throat tightened, and I shivered.

CROOKED SOUL 13

A S IF ON CUE, Johnson entered the house with several bags that wafted a Chinese food scent over the room.

Robby came out of the kitchen with plates and silverware in case any of us were inept at using chopsticks.

Despite the recent conversation about rats, I found my stomach growling at the prospect of General Tso's chicken over fried rice. A part of me balked because eating real food would result in the same pains I encountered last night, but a stubborn part of me that enjoyed food fought back and won that small battle.

I grabbed a plate and instead of piling on the food like I would have before I was turned into this nightmare, I put two spoonfuls of rice on my plate and just a couple pieces of chicken and a thoroughly coated broccoli head from the box of the spicy dish, and returned to my seat with one of the forks.

"No chopsticks?" Robby said through a mouthful, as if I were committing a major sin.

"Nah." I didn't feel like working that hard, even though it was me who taught him how to use chopsticks in our younger days in the agency.

"You feeling okay?" His eyebrow cocked and he studied me closer, looking for breaks in my psyche, like I might fall apart at any moment.

"Yes. I just am not feeling the chopsticks." I shrugged.

Before he could launch into one of my own famous tirades about how it was sacrilege to eat Chinese with a fork, Judy's phone rang.

She answered and excused herself into the kitchen with a "Hello, Mom," before she disappeared.

She stepped back into the doorway and the vibes she emitted pulled all our attention back to her as she ended the call. The panic in her eyes made me suddenly stressed, as though whatever she was about to say would change our circumstances again.

"What is it?" Johnson asked as he stood.

Judy's frantic gaze jumped from him to us and then back as she swallowed hard. "My parents are on their way over."

"You couldn't meet them somewhere?" I asked as her panic seemed to spread through all of us. I hadn't even finished my measly meal.

She shook her head. "They want to see the place." Her voice cracked. She glanced around, as if the place were in severe disarray. She crossed and started closing boxes and handing them to Johnson. "Put these in the refrigerator," she barked.

Robby grabbed the General Tso's box before she could snag it. "I need food."

"Fine," Judy said in the tone that made it absolutely not fine. Her frantic attempt to clean up put me more on edge, too.

I took Robby's hand. "We'll chill in our bedroom." I pulled him toward the stairs.

"That's the main bedroom," she squeaked with wide eyes.

"And?" Robby asked with chopsticks stuck in the paper carton in his hand and the scent of spicy chicken wrapping around us.

"And they are going to expect that to be our bedroom." She ran her free hand through her hair as her gaze darted between the two of us.

"With our scents on everything in there?" I asked, drawing a gasp in response.

"Jesus. They are going to smell her," she said to Johnson. That only proved to fluster her even more and she turned, marching off with the rest of the food.

Johnson cleared the dishes just as quickly, and we followed them to the kitchen doorway.

"The Chinese food does a good job of masking scents," Johnson said to soothe her as he rinsed the dishes and dropped them in the dishwasher.

"You're going to have to make something up," Robby said. "Like Johnson wasn't comfortable getting it on in his old alpha's bedroom, so you chose the guest room."

"What if they want to stay here?" Her hands shook as they ran through her hair, messing up her perfect hairdo.

"Take a breath," I said calmly, and she did. "That's right, and another." When she seemed calmer, I added, "They can't stay here."

She nodded. At least that wasn't an argument.

"How long are you two going to stay here, anyway?" Johnson crossed his arms. "It's been a couple weeks. Shouldn't you be moving on?"

Robby's eyes narrowed, and his cheeks flared red. "This is my home. Not yours. I am allowing you to remain here. I'm allowing you to remain the alpha of our pack. Isn't that enough?" He radiated with his alpha vibes and both Judy and Johnson cowered from it.

Johnson forced his gaze to Robby's. "I was named alpha of the pack."

Robby leaned forward with a growl as his teeth made an appearance. "Are you challenging me?"

Johnson paused and looked at the floor. He shook his head.

"Fine. We are going to our bedroom. You do whatever it takes to keep your parents away from that room. Understand?" Robby's glare pierced into Judy. He didn't wait for an answer. Instead, he dragged me upstairs and into the bedroom, closing the door behind him.

He took a seat on the end of the bed with the food container grasped in his hand tight enough to nearly crush the box.

"You need to breathe, too." I pointed at him. "Otherwise, that shit is going to go everywhere. And you're still throwing out your alpha vibes. That's a surefire way to set off alarms with her parents." I crossed to him and rubbed his shoulders.

He closed his eyes. "You'd think I'd be better by now," he muttered under his breath.

"You can't undo six months of psychological warfare in a blink."

He opened his eyes and met my gaze. "You've seemed to be able to do that." His lips tilted in a smirk. "With the exception of last night, you seem to be handling all that shit fine."

He had no idea. He slept nights; even though he tossed and yelled out from his own nightmares, he still remained ensnared in the depths of sleep. Not me. I stared at the ceiling, waiting for his outbursts because I couldn't find it in me to fall into my own horrid dreams where Robby no longer existed and the world burned with my fury.

What seemed like ages ago, I had made a promise to never keep a secret from Robby. "I don't sleep much."

His eyebrow rose and before he could speak, the doorbell rang. Judy's parents were here, and it was time to keep quiet.

I pointed to the chairs in the corner by his bookcase. He nodded and we crossed. I chose a book to try to get lost in while Robby finished what was left in the box in record time.

The creak of the stairs caught our attention, and we both froze. I glanced at Robby in horror. We should have locked the damn door.

The handle on the door started to move.

"Don't go in there!" Judy's shrill voice rang out at the top of the stairs, making me jump.

"Why not?" a male voice asked.

"Because we...don't go in there." Judy's voice strained against the words falling from her lips. She wasn't a good liar, and her pitch left even me wondering what had crawled up her ass.

"Isn't this the master bedroom?" the same voice asked.

I could only deduce this was Judy's father because it certainly wasn't Johnson.

"Our room is down here." She left the question unanswered.

"Can we see this room before we head down the hall?" her mother asked.

Judy's reaction would have had me wanting to see what was behind the door, too. I stiffened in the chair and traded a glance with Robby. He still stared at the empty container in his hand, but his head had tilted, as though he waited for the door to open and was formulating some sort of excuse.

"It's not in any condition to be seen. Besides, Johnson tries to avoid going in there unless he absolutely has to," Judy said in a string of fast words.

A pause fell on the group.

"It was my alpha's bedroom," Johnson mumbled. "I'm having issues renovating, and I'd rather you not see my colossal mess until it's done."

"I might be able to help," Judy's father said, and the handle started to turn.

"I'd rather not." Johnson's voice gathered a sharper edge.

"You need to get over yourself, man." A male voice scoffed, and the handle continued to turn.

"No. This is my home, and you will honor my rules. I will show you our bedroom once I have finished my renovations." Johnson's voice boomed outside the door, and the handle stopped moving. "I'm sorry. It's just I couldn't stay in the room with my alpha's essence so embedded in everything, so...I started tearing down the walls and it just got overwhelming."

I could almost hear his apologetic shrug and see his eyes begging for understanding.

"I was his beta, so it's a matter of respect," he finally said, which made zero sense in the scheme of the conversation, but it seemed to appease the in-laws.

"You must have been so upset," her mother said. "Dying at the hands of that vampire bitch must make you want to see her filleted in the sunshine," Judy's mother said. Her voice held such disdain. "It was such a sad ending for someone you couldn't speak more highly of."

Robby and I traded a glance. What had everyone been told? And where the hell did they get their information?

"His death threw the entire pack, and I'm still mourning him. But let's talk about more pleasant things, like what you're doing in the city." His voice drifted farther away from the bedroom.

I looked back at Robby and mouthed, "What the fuck?"

That wasn't what he had said before. He had said they lost the alpha connection, and they assumed he was dead. But for Judy's folks to hear such concrete specifics left me irritated. It was as if the way Cassius had intended for Robby to die was somehow leaked.

And now my curiosity made my skin itch. I wanted to know when they were fed that bullshit.

Robby shrugged. He didn't seem surprised, but a dull anger bloomed in his eyes, as if he were coming to some sort of conclusion that left him just as cold as the look on his face.

The timing mattered.

Their voices got louder again, as if they had finished their tour of the upstairs.

"...been told to stand down while the ancients are here, but I'm not so sure we should." Johnson's voice carried as they got closer.

Robby and I traded another glance, and we both leaned toward the door.

"Vampires should be put down," Judy's father said, and I could only imagine the sneer on his face. "No matter where they are from. They are still cold-blooded killers."

In all our years at the agency, no one had ever told us to stand down. It didn't matter whether the offending monsters were dignitaries or even heads of state from other countries. If they sustained life by draining others of theirs, and had the balls to step into our city, they were a target. So, hearing that someone in the agency had altered the rules of engagement bordered on insanity.

The creak of the stairs followed, and their voices moved farther away, but that didn't settle the itch to barge out and question them until they spilled everything they knew. After all, if the information came from the agency, that meant there was someone compromised near the top echelon, and it would explain Johnson's lack of loyalty to the agency.

If they were compromised, what the hell did that mean for us?

CROOKED SOUL 14

ROBBY TOSSED THE EMPTY carton in the garbage and stared at me. My mark tingled with his frustration. I couldn't blame him. If the agency had been compromised, then who could we truly trust?

Johnson had let another monster go and lied to the agency about it. He had let us go in those woods without so much as a scratch.

Was that self-preservation or was that actually his plan?

Was there a bigger picture that we were missing? A game where we were just someone else's pawns?

I did not like that idea, and I stood from my seat, wanting to pace out my irritation. But I didn't know whether footsteps up here resounded downstairs. Damn it. I sat back down and winced, shifting so my tattoo didn't have pressure on it. I really should just lay down on the bed with the book I put down on the table.

"Can't sit still?" Robby whispered with a smile.

I shook my head as the sound of the front door closing drifted up the stairs. We waited, just staring at each other. It took a few minutes before a soft knock sounded on the door.

"It's clear," Johnson's voice called from the hallway.

Robby was up and to the door, yanking it open within seconds. "You are going to tell me everything that the agency told you about my death." It wasn't a request. It came with the force of his alpha. And if he hadn't demanded the details, I would have.

Johnson glanced between us. "It was pure bullshit. I knew Sarah would never harm you, so to hear she was the one who killed you was ludicrous."

"What did they say, exactly? Word for fucking word."

Robby's hands fisted and my mark went haywire with the sudden flash of fury. I crossed to him and put my hand on his arm before he did something he'd regret. He sent a sideways glare at me before refocusing on Johnson.

"They said she drained you dry."

"When did they tell you this?"

He inhaled sharply and looked at the ground. "A couple days after we intercepted you in the woods."

Judy climbed up the stairs, apprehensively looking at the three of us.

"Who told you?" Robby growled.

This time, I squeezed his arm and shook my head when he looked at me. He was a hair away from losing it.

"Your father," Johnson answered, almost with a wince.

Robby ground his teeth and took a step back, collecting all the anger rising inside him. "How soon after did he name you alpha?" He glared at Johnson, and his teeth had formed.

"Don't shift," I said, sending out the command to everyone in the house.

Robby growled at me, baring his teeth, and I ignored him, turning to Johnson. "Tell me the truth. Did you have anything to do with or any knowledge of our disappearance?" I pushed the question at Johnson, and he reared back as though I had slapped him.

"God, no."

His gasp and wide eyes were enough to convince me. Especially considering my question was fueled with a demand for the truth.

"But I knew it was a lie. I know you. I've known you since we were eighteen. You would rather rip your own throat out than harm him." He waved at Robby. He glanced over his shoulder at Judy and then down at the ground. "And as for your question, your father gave me the title of alpha a couple days later." He pressed his lips together. "And then he introduced me to Judy."

"He didn't even have proof that I died," Robby said slowly and glanced at me, as though I had answers.

"Cassius was so sure after he wiped my memory that I'd dance like a good little puppet." I met his gaze. "So, someone higher up than your father had to be in league with him in some way to get that specific information." It was the only thing that made any sense. Either that, or Cassius was in cahoots with Robby's father, but I just couldn't see the man setting his son up to die.

"Is that why your loyalties to the agency have wavered enough to blow off your orders?" Robby crossed his arms.

Johnson pressed his lips together. "I was never loyal to the agency," he said. "I am loyal to you and to the pack." He glared at Robby. "I never understood their rules. I watched you two drown yourselves in alcohol and sex, trying to deny yourselves what looked to be a match made by the fucking gods. My loyalty to the agency was shot to shit back at the academy."

His gaze pierced into both of us, and I knew the exact moment all our illusions had shattered. The day I was attacked changed a lot of things for us, and our loyalty to the agency was one of the casualties.

Robby's fury seemed to soothe at that answer. "Ancients are in town?" He raised an eyebrow.

Johnson took a deep breath and nodded. "Something's drastically wrong. This latest order to stand down for some fucking ancient race of blood suckers is ludicrous. But it seems the higher-ups made a deal. Those assholes came to find out what happened to one of their own." He glanced between us. "From the information I gathered, they are looking for the freak who killed your friend." He looked straight at me.

"You're looking at the wolf who tore Cassius Chase to shreds," Robby said with a growl.

"And neither of you can spill that to anyone," I reminded them.

Johnson looked directly at me and rolled his eyes. "Like I would ever do that."

"You were ready to turn us in when you came back from your honeymoon." Robby still stood stoically, like if he moved, he might just start tearing into both of them with the renewed anger roiling in his blood.

"That's because when I saw her here alone, I thought the worst. And then I saw you looking like a geriatric reject." He blinked. "I reacted badly." He moved from foot to foot and stared at the floor, as if looking at his alpha would incite a reaction. "I don't react well to shock."

Robby snorted a laugh that had Johnson snapping his gaze up. "You don't say," he said with enough snark to load a gun.

"Neither of us deal well with surprises, as you saw tonight," Judy said from behind Johnson. "Even I've had reservations on some of the orders they've given Rick."

He turned to her. "You have?"

She nodded. "But it's not my place to say anything."

"Why not?" I interjected.

"Because he has a difficult enough job without having me adding my opinion to the mix. I don't work for the agency. I'm not fierce enough or mentally able to grasp a kill order." She shuffled her feet. "I can hunt game, but the idea of hunting people..." She shook her head.

"They aren't people. They're monsters," Robby said.

"That look just like us." She waved at me as her example. "They are people with feelings, with lives, with loves..." She pressed her lips together again and shook her head. "Most of them, like Phillip for example, don't need to die. He's not harming anyone, especially if there is a deal in writing for services. But the agency deemed him deadly." She looked at me. "And you are at the top of their kill list. But you haven't killed anyone."

My mind jumped to our old boss after the truck broke apart and killed Robby, and I traded a glance with Johnson, wincing at Judy's statement.

"He doesn't count," Johnson said, as if reading my mind.

"Why not?"

"Harrison was a royal dick, and from what you told me, he deserved to die."

Judy glanced between us.

"Our old boss chained Robby in silver cuffs and threatened to pour silver over him. He's the one who caused Robby's death, so I poured a vat of boiling silver on him." I met her gaze with a shrug.

She paled and pulled Johnson closer.

"But the guy was militant about hunting them down. He wasn't going to let her walk away. He wanted to cage her like he did to Manuel, another agent who had been turned, and because Robby marked her, he wanted both of them either locked up or dead. And so did the higher-ups." He sighed. "She's never killed an innocent," he amended.

"Yet she's on the top of the kill list," Robby scoffed.

"They believe she killed you. That's why she's on the top of the list."

"The agency was the one that killed me. She brought me back." He ran a hand through his hair in aggravation. "I need some fresh air." He scooted around Johnson and Judy, heading down the stairs.

"It's not dark yet," Judy called after me as I followed him down the stairs and out the door.

"The sun doesn't affect me." I grabbed a baseball cap off the rack near the door and headed out with him. To hell with the fear suddenly lacing the back of my throat. If he needed to walk his frustration off, I'd walk with him.

He stayed on the road his brownstone was on, his hands shoved into his pockets and his head down. I caught up with him and then matched him stride for stride. When we got to the next intersection, he turned left, crossing the road and taking another side street.

"Do you want me to try to get a cab?" he asked as he glanced at me.

Stretching my legs felt good and he had chosen a different path, not the one that would bring us by Cassius's place. "I'm good. If my tattoo starts bothering me, I'll let you know."

With a nod, he kept up his pace, which had me nearly trotting next to him. When my breathing became heavy, he slowed his pace with an apologetic smile.

"Sorry."

"No problem," I said, but the warmth of gratefulness swept through me at his realization his aggressive stride was tiring me out. He may have been working out in the basement, but I haven't been, and I noticed my muscles were already straining after just a few blocks. "I'm severely out of shape," I muttered. This type of walk six months ago wouldn't have affected me this way.

"As soon as that tattoo heals, you can start working out and sparring with me." He slid his hand into mine, as if it were normal for us to walk hand in hand.

My throat tightened at the small, intimate gesture. I shook my head to try to get the sudden wave of emotions to go away. This wasn't like me. I did not get sappy. I blinked the mist out of my eyes and kept my head down. Even with the hat, I was still not inconspicuous. Most redheads weren't.

But the sky was slowly darkening so that by the time we walked the few miles to the park, the sun had set and only a dim ambient light graced the horizon. There weren't many people walking the paths, either.

I cocked an eyebrow at him at the emptiness.

"Just like Central Park, people clear out after dark." He answered my silent question. "It's barren by nine at night. Except for those who shouldn't be hanging around in the park."

"So, monsters and drug dealers."

"Exactly." The way he smiled gave me a chilling thrill.

He wanted to exercise more than his legs tonight. He wanted to take down some monsters. I had only dispatched one since I was turned, and that was because I basically exploded.

As we walked farther into the heart of the forest in the center of Brooklyn, the pathways narrowed, and the woods crowded the sidewalk like arms reaching for us from beyond.

Robby slowed and lifted his nose when the breeze shifted for a moment. He cocked his head and flashed a concerned look in my direction. Scents wafted on the light breeze, dancing around us before the wind shifted again.

Cold bit at my heart.

Vampires were in the park.

And we were upwind.

15

CROOKED SOUL 15

ROBBY'S TEETH APPEARED, BUT he didn't shift as he pulled me closer. We'd see just how effective his tattoo was in a matter of minutes. I conjured a pair of katanas and handed him one. He smiled down at me with the same glint he always had in his eyes when we stepped into battle.

We stepped out of the path into a larger intersection where multiple sidewalks merged, but neither of us were prepared for the nightmare that stepped out onto the path in front of us. She looked as though she were made of alabaster stone. Her features were more like that of an Egyptian goddess than a human, and her black hair lay straight with such precision that I thought it was a wig. Her eyes glowed red, like the taillights on a car.

She smiled with teeth whiter than her skin. "Stay still while my children feed," she said with a voice as cloying as honey.

"I don't think so, bitch," Robby growled and raised the katana to his shoulder, giving me his back.

I adopted the same position, pressing against him while a grin formed with the adrenaline pumping through my veins.

She sneered at us in a way that clearly conveyed annoyance. "You are not supposed to be in these woods. Your agency made it clear we would be given full rein of the parks."

"I assume you are talking about the Monster Defense Agency?" I asked with my hands tight around the hilt of my sword and prayed Robby would follow my lead.

She put her hands up and the advancing vampires halted.

A whisper of a command brushed by my ear, but her lips did not move. It was as if she were communicating with them silently.

"Yes." She narrowed her eyes. "You are defying orders."

I shrugged. "We were never very good at following rules."

"Color me curious," Robby said. "I mean, it isn't every day that an ancient vampire visits our city." His voice was steady, but his body trembled against mine as if trying to contain his wolf. "Why risk it?"

She tilted her head and stepped closer. He growled in response, and she halted. "If you think you can take thirty vampires, shift and see how long you last. I will personally enjoy draining you of blood."

Robby's back tightened.

"Stand down," I said softly and lowered my katana, glancing back at Robby.

He met my gaze with a fiery rage in his eyes, but he lowered his blade.

The ancient being looked me up and down. "Since when do witches call the shots?"

I formed a fireball in my hand and tossed it in the air as if it were a baseball, catching it as I stared her down. "I'm a fire witch." I smiled. "And if you threaten him again, I'll burn every last one of you." I batted my eyes, feigning innocence as I delivered my own potent threat. Fire was almost as effective as sunlight in destroying vampires.

She warily eyed the fireball I kept tossing, and stepped back.

"Why come to our city?" I asked, still playing with my fire in a way that had it growing inside me, itching to be let loose. But I kept it in check. The perimeter of the park was closer than I was comfortable with. If I went off, innocents would die, too.

"I'm looking for someone, and I was informed they were within this metropolis." Her eyes narrowed in such a way that I suppressed a smile.

"And who would that be?" Robby asked. His voice still held a feral quality to it.

I wasn't sure what to expect, but her answer startled me.

"The last phoenix." She grinned. "The one who will allow me to reap my revenge."

She knew about me, and I thought it was Cassius who wanted to use me to rule the world. But he was only doing this bitch's bidding.

"The phoenix is a myth." Robby repeated what we had been taught so many years ago, bringing me out of my momentary reverie. "By all accounts extinct."

She scoffed at him.

"What revenge?" I asked, still holding my fireball as though I contemplated throwing it again. The vampires on my side of the circle backed up another step as I sent a side-eye their way.

"I am the mother of all vampires. I know when one of my children is murdered. My revenge will be very sweet." She smiled in a dark manner that chilled me. "Go." She pointed her scrawny finger in the direction we came. "Before I break my promise to your boss and deliver a bloody war to this city."

Robby growled in a way that I knew he wasn't going to just leave these vampires. He shifted and the entire circle of vampires reared back, including the ancient one.

All eyes surrounding us were wide enough to see the whites around their red eyes. And they were all glued to the massive werewolf by my side. The tables were surely turned, but we would likely be hurt if we took them on. And I could not let my fire go in the middle of the city. I could vaporize blocks of innocents if I did that.

As tempting as this opportunity was, the risk of collateral damage was too damned great.

I jumped onto his back and tossed the ball of fire high into the air.

"Take me home." I whispered the command in his ear and pulled his fur as if it were a rein. "I wouldn't be standing around when that fireball lands," I called over my shoulder as the group moved away from the golden-tipped wolf.

Robby let out a feral growl as he barreled through the line like a bat straight out of hell.

My hat flew off and my hair cascaded down my back, flying behind me like my own red cape as Robby ran. His growl filled the air until the end of the forest came into view. He skidded to a halt and shifted back to human form. He wasn't as conspicuous as a dog anymore, and walking down the city street in wolf form would call unwanted attention to us. Same with him walking in the buff. That would almost get more notice than a massive wolf. Still, he let out a feral growl at me.

I waved clothing onto his naked form and grabbed his hand, pulling him into the street with me as I hailed for a cab. One pulled up, and I just about pushed him inside, rattling off an address on the road behind his home in case the vampires had followed and were listening.

With my heart still wildly beating in my chest, I swallowed the dryness in my mouth as Robby seethed next to me. I conjured money and threw it at the cab driver as he let us out, and I took Robby's hand, leading him down another maze of side streets that eventually came out on his road a couple of blocks from his brownstone.

The minute we were inside, Robby turned on me.

"What the actual fuck?" he growled. "You could have wiped them all out with a wave of your fucking hand. Why didn't you?" His voice rattled the walls around us.

I took a breath. "How many acres did I destroy in the forest?"

He snarled. "What the hell does that have to do with it?"

"There are apartment buildings surrounding the park."

His eyes blinked rapidly, and his fisted hands slowly uncurled.

"How many acres?" I asked again, much more quietly as Johnson and Judy descended the stairs.

"Nearly a square mile of woods burned that day," Johnson said.

"That's more than the footprint of Prospect Park." I pointed at Robby and raised my brow, making my point.

"You went to the park?" Johnson's eyes widened, and considering the directive that the mother of vampires stated, his expression didn't surprise either of us.

"Yes," we both said and glared at him.

He paled. "And?"

"And we ran into a boatload of vampires," Robby snarled. "Who the hell at the agency is working with those dicks?"

Johnson looked at the ground. "I don't know," he said. "But the pack and our partners do not agree with this ludicrous stand down order. The agency said all parks in the metropolitan area are off-limits at night. Don't wander because that could be construed as breaking the temporary truce." He glanced out the window with an expression as though he just bit into a lemon gone bad.

"Killing the ancient will kill all vampires," I said. "Just like killing a master will annihilate all their children."

Robby's glare slashed to me. "You should have taken her out," he snarled. "That bitch wants to use you to enact her revenge."

"Revenge on who?" Johnson said.

He shook his head. "I don't know."

"Oh, yes you do." I stomped my foot to make my point. "She wants to kill *us* for killing Cassius. She's never set foot in New York before. His death had to be what triggered this." I glanced at Johnson. "Did any of you tell the MDA about Robby's larger, more ornate wolf?"

"No. Not to my knowledge. Why?"

"Because he shifted in the park, and if the MDA knew he had golden-tipped fur, they would know he was alive." I took a breath. I didn't know whether that was good or bad. If they were truly in league with the mother of all vampires, then it would be very bad for Robby. But if they weren't, his father would possibly be less inclined to want to hunt me down. Either way, the news was likely to get back to the agency that there was a very large gold-tipped wolf on the loose who fucked with the truce.

With the mother of vampire's assumption that we were MDA agents, they were likely to tear their contact a new one and start a very nasty reaction within the agency. Their agents ignored a command.

No one ignored a direct command and lived to tell about it.

Well, no one except Johnson and the Allegany pack members, it seemed.

16

CROOKED SOUL 16

IN ALL OF THE excitement, my body hadn't remembered I ate earlier, but now it decided to make that ungodly noise, followed by the heartless cramp signaling I needed a bathroom now.

"Excuse me," I blurted and bolted up the stairs with everyone's eyes on my back.

"What's with her?" Johnson asked just before I slammed the bedroom door.

The mad dash across the bedroom was on and made all the more difficult as I attempted to unbutton my pants as I moved. I made it to the commode and started chuckling. If this had

happened in the park, I would have been shit
out of luck.

I snorted laughter even as the cramp
escalated, bending me over with it until I purged
the culprit causing my insides to go crazy.
Maybe I wouldn't eat real food anymore. Because
this side effect sucked.

I cleaned myself up, buttoned my pants, and
headed back downstairs. The minute I stepped
into the living room, three smirking faces
glanced my way. I ignored them and made my
way to the far side of the couch that had been
left open for me.

"So, what is going on at the agency?" I stared
at Johnson. "What changed?" I leaned on my
right side so my tattoo wouldn't get more
uncomfortable. I'd have to have Robby clean it
again before bed. All the excitement of this
evening had irritated me enough to warrant
another cleaning.

Johnson sighed and glanced at Judy before
he moved his gaze to mine. "Manny changed my
perception of the agency, and then you changed
my perception of who fell into the true category
of monsters." He wiped his face. "I knew they
had archaic rules, but locking up Manny instead
of putting him out of his misery...that fucked
with my head."

"What are they doing with him, anyway?"
Robby asked.

"Studying him, I guess." Johnson gave a
shrug. "But every time I have to deliver blood to
him, it gives me the creeps. He begs me to let
him out. I don't think he's sane anymore."

"I would imagine not," I said. "I wouldn't do well locked up like that for over a year."

"You survived," Judy said, as if she knew the details of what went down at Cassius's place.

Robby laughed and glared at her, leaning forward in that feral way that made me tense up. "Barely," he growled.

Judy recoiled into the couch, like the soft cushions could protect her from Robby's wrath.

"Ease up, boss." Johnson put his hand out like a stop sign, calling Robby's attention to him.

"Excuse me?" he snapped. "You allow those things to roam around the city without so much as a leash on them, and you're telling me to ease up?" He pointed out the window. "You casually remark how awful it is to see Manny caged and then have the audacity to wave aside the mind-fuck we went through with a 'oh well, you survived' statement?"

I reached out and put my hand on Robby's knee. He knocked it away.

"I'm not going to lose it. I'm just angry right now. Angry that you didn't let me rip those vampires to shreds. Angry that you didn't fucking toast them to ash. Angry that I ate rats for six months. Angry that I had to watch you die countless times and couldn't do a goddamned thing about it. And I'm angry that my father gave my place away without so much as taking a memento of some kind to remember me by!" He drew in a breath and closed his eyes, along with his fists. "I'm just fucking angry!" he bellowed at the ceiling.

By the time he finished his rant, we were all leaning back away from him. I didn't dare reach out to touch him, not with how quickly he knocked my hand away before. His visible tremors had the three of us trading glances. Robby kept his eyes closed and drew in slow, deep breaths like he used to whenever he was close to getting sick to his stomach.

Soon his hands uncurled.

"I'm sorry I upset you," Judy said, and both my gaze and Johnson's swiveled to her and darted back to Robby.

His piercing blue eyes zeroed in on her and his jaw tightened. "You didn't piss me off. The whole situation tonight has." He stood and nearly toppled over the chair. He grabbed it before it lost its teetering to gravity, and righted it, before he started pacing the room.

I tracked his movement and kept silent. I had an opportunity to kill the mother of the vampires and did not take it. Despite the consequences, I was a little irritated as well. "Robby, if I had taken them out..." I closed my eyes and clenched my teeth against the anger welling up inside me. "I would have killed far more than they will. Plus, there is no guarantee that I would survive."

He stopped halfway across the floor and glared at me. He chewed on his lower lip as he mulled over my words.

"But you survived your master's death," Johnson said.

Robby waved at him and raised both eyebrows in a silent challenge.

"I know I survived his death, but I'm still a vampire. If killing her destroys all vampires, won't that include me?"

"I'm not playing that game again," he said with enough venom to shake my nerves. "I should have killed Cassius when I had the chance."

I tilted my head. "We didn't have the charms on. He would have killed you in an instant had I not forced you to come back."

Robby growled at me. A deep and terrifying growl, like he would tear me to pieces if I continued. Both Johnson and Judy seemed affected by it as they rolled their shoulders in and dropped their gaze to the floor.

But I wasn't having it. I stood and gave him an equally dark stare. "You want a piece of me?" I stepped outside the small ring of furniture and adopted my fighting posture with narrowed eyes. "Come and get it, alpha boy."

I hadn't called him that in years, but it seemed to break through the fury filling him to the point of not being able to contain it. It gave him a target to aim his frustrations.

"No, no, no, no. Not in the living room. You'll break...everything," Judy gasped as Robby stepped within arm's reach of me.

I tuned out both Johnson and Judy's emphatic pleas and circled Robby, both of us adopting fighting stances. This used to be our morning routine after the daily meeting when we were first in the agency. Hell, when was the last time we fought? The reality hit, bringing with it a fiery aggravation. When I met Cassius, I was too preoccupied to get in the sparring ring.

Damn that vampire.

Robby sensed my change in mood and threw the first punch. I parried and grabbed his arm just above the elbow, and yanked, using his momentum to throw him off-balance. Then I swept his feet out from under him.

He landed facedown on the floor with a "oof" of getting the wind knocked out of him. He rolled onto his back and before I could dance out of the way, he swept my feet from under me.

I landed square on my butt and let out a yelp at the pain now radiating from my tattoo. It only made me angrier.

"Stop!" Johnson yelled. "You haven't destroyed anything yet, and I don't want to deal with blood or stitches tonight!"

I climbed to my feet, rubbing my bum to get the sting out of it. Robby noticed and closed his eyes, as if he were mentally scolding himself.

"I'm fine," I snapped, even though I wasn't. That fall hurt enough for me to question whether I had broken the scabs on the tattoo or not. "And I'm not done kicking his ass." I pointed.

"You are under my roof," Johnson said, trying to exude authority.

"It isn't your fucking roof," Robby growled and stepped closer to me. "Let's see what damage I did this time," he said softer to me and reached for the back of my pants.

I swatted his hand away. "Who said I was done?"

Robby looked me straight in the eye. "I say." He crossed his arms and crowded me in such a way as to almost be a silent dare.

I went to strike him, but he grabbed my hand and my opposite arm, turned and slammed me into the wall hard enough to rattle my teeth.

"Stop."

His voice came out in that alpha command that I had no intention of following.

I lifted my leg, aiming for his balls, but he anticipated my move; his thighs clamped down on my knee, keeping me from nailing him. He tilted his head and raised an eyebrow.

"Are you finished?"

I glared up at him. "How come you get to rant and rave and throw a fucking hissy fit and I don't?" I struggled in his grip, but he just leaned his body against me, which not only infuriated me, but it started revving my engine in a whole different manner.

"Because."

I stopped struggling and looked up at him. "Because why?"

"Because I'm fucked up worse than you are."

I balked up at him and started to struggle again. I almost called on my fire, but although I wanted to kick his ass, I didn't really want to hurt Robby.

He stayed still, staring down at me. "Plus, we really don't want to start breaking furniture, do we?"

"Fuck you for being so goddamned levelheaded," I spat up at him.

Robby grinned down at me and then glanced over his shoulder at Johnson. "Sorry." He stepped away from me, far enough to be out of reach of a swing because he knew me well enough to know I might take a shot at him despite his disengagement.

I still huffed, with the heat riding my veins like a feral fire.

Robby met my gaze again. "Seriously, let's go look at your tattoo to make sure I didn't fuck it all up."

"Fine." I stomped up the stairs, sounding more like a mad elephant than I intended, especially because each step sent a web of irritation through my left ass cheek.

17

CROOKED SOUL 17

ROBBY STEPPED INTO THE bathroom with his face schooled into a neutral position, but my mark felt his volatility. That effect of standing too close to a tornado gripped me, and I tensed. He rolled his hand in an indication for me to drop my pants so he could inspect the damage.

"You're still aggravated with me." I kicked off my shoes and dropped my pants, stepping out of them and turning so he could look at my covered tattoo.

"I still think you should have taken them out." He crossed, and peeled off the breathable plastic sheet and dropped it into the garbage.

"You're going to need to get in the shower, so..." He cocked his eye at me and stripped his own shirt.

"Is it that bad?" I tried to arch my back so I could see it, but I could only make out the top part of the tattoo.

"Eh, but it should be cleaned again." He took off his shoes and socks, and then his pants followed.

"I should have gotten this on my hip instead," I muttered as I turned my backside toward the mirror. There were clear scabs on the tattoo and one of them had split and oozed milky-white. Although the skin around the tattoo looked a little inflamed, the only really gross part was the oozing scab. "It's not fair that you don't have the same issues." I waved at him, and he rolled his thigh so I could see his perfectly healed tattoo.

"Wolves heal fast."

I stripped my shirt and bra, and stepped into the shower. He followed, turning the water on and waiting until the temperature was warm enough to not make our teeth chatter, but cool enough not to impede my healing skin. He turned me in to the water and then moved me out of the spray just as fast before he took the antibiotic soap, knelt behind me, and started the gentle cleaning of my butt cheek.

"I would have killed far more people than those vampires will had I let my phoenix loose."

His hand paused and he looked up at me. "There's always collateral damage." He shrugged and went back to work gently soaping up my tattoo.

"That would make me no better than the monsters we hunt."

He pressed his head against my hip. "You know just as well as I do there will always be innocents who are harmed by our inaction."

His blue eyes rose to mine. "If I had followed you to your room that first night, none of this would have happened. I would have claimed you then, and that would have set us on a different path."

I huffed down at him. "Claimed or not, Cassius would still have found me, and he would have killed you without a second thought. And who's to say the academy wouldn't have executed me anyway?"

He bit his lower lip. "I wouldn't have let them."

"You wouldn't have had a choice." I ran my hand through his hair. "I should have told you about Cassius the moment I found out. All this is on me. Not you."

He rinsed off my ass and stood, towering over me. "That's my point. Inaction always seems to bite us. What are we going to lose by not acting when we had the opportunity?" He cupped my cheek as he chewed his bottom lip with worry.

I stepped close and hugged him. "We aren't going to lose a thing." But even as the words tumbled from my lips, my stomach tightened. His words wormed their way under my skin, leaving an itch more pressing than that of my healing tattoo.

He lifted my chin and for the first time since we returned, he leaned down and delivered a kiss as if his libido won out over his fears.

I was not prepared for the searing heat that accompanied the kiss or his wandering hands as they caressed my breasts in a teasingly light touch. His hardness pressed against my stomach, and I pulled away from his mouth.

He pushed me against the wall and dropped to his knees again. But this time, he took my breasts in his mouth before driving lower. I don't know whether it was the shower or the physical fight downstairs that revved him up, but I wasn't going to argue. He lifted my leg over his shoulder and attacked my pussy like a parched man attacks a bottle of water.

I ran my hand into his damp hair and closed my eyes at the sensation, and was immediately taken back to a similar situation against my bedroom wall. I gasped and my eyes snapped open. I blinked, trying to get myself back into the here and now with Robby and not the memory of Cassius doing the same thing before he turned me.

Robby paused and looked up at me with his bright-blue eyes filled with a question I did not want to answer. I did not want him knowing I had a flashback of Cassius—that would be an instant mood killer for him.

I shifted so more of my right cheek was against the wall, using my tattoo to explain the sudden flare of discomfort.

"Sorry," he said with that tilted smile, but he went right back to his ministrations, but using a much gentler touch as he caressed my ass and ran his knuckles along my opening.

I kept my eyes open and on Robby, vowing not to go back to the past. This was now, and

Robby had initiated this. He deserved my full attention and oh, he got it, especially when his fingers joined in on the fun, filling me with a deep ache for more. The buildup was slow and maddening, like he wanted to control my every sensation. My hand tightened on his hair as I tumbled over the crest with a soft moan.

His finger dipped in deep, and my body shuddered with the release. A moment later, he was in me and on his feet, holding my thighs as he rode me against the wall. The taut muscles in his arms glistened with the drops from the shower spray, and he grinned at me in a way that told me this was going to be punishing and satisfying at the same time.

And he lived up to it, keeping his eyes on mine as his hips pounded into me. There was no closing eyes and tilting heads back to moan our satisfaction. This was an intense stare down, as if we were both breaking barriers that Cassius tried to build between us. Just as the vein in his temple started to stand out, Robby captured my mouth in a kiss that muffled his groan. He didn't stop pounding me against the wall until his breath became ragged and his tongue slowed the dance with mine.

He broke the kiss. "Fuck," he whispered and pressed his forehead against mine.

"We just did," I teased.

He smiled the way the old Robby used to, with that impish light dancing in his eyes. He still hadn't let me down, and I crossed my ankles behind him, twirling my hips. I was not ready for him to leave me.

"I am not sure my legs will hold for another round," he said.

That was when I became aware that he was trembling. "But I am comfortable." I pouted and batted my eyes.

He snorted a laugh and shifted his grip. Pain flared in my ass cheek. "Not so comfortable now, are you?"

"Ouch," I whined, but didn't let go. Instead, I pushed him inside me farther, grinding hip to hip.

"You want to go again?" He pursed his lips. "On your hands and knees, and I'll oblige." He lifted his hands away from my ass.

I clung to him, using my legs around his waist and my arms around his neck to keep my hold. Something about that glint in his eyes made me hang on. Although that was the way he had made love to me the first time and marked me, the memory of Cassius burned through that sweetness, souring me to the position. Plus, Robby didn't know. He didn't know that was how Cassius had painted my walls with my blood.

I forced myself to unclasp my legs.

Robby uncoupled from me and stepped under the water stream as he gently stroked himself, waiting for me to comply.

"It's a dominant-submissive position." I sucked on my lower lip as I watched him stroke himself back to life.

"Yes."

His single-word answer had me raising my gaze to his. "You want me to submit to you?" My voice cracked as all sorts of emotions welled up inside me.

He nodded slowly with his head tilted to the side, as if gauging my reaction.

"I submit to no one." I steeled my back as my anger flared.

"Oh, you'll submit to me." He just kept stroking as he stood under the warm water.

"And if I don't?" I slammed my fists into my hips, glaring at his audacity.

"Then you're cut off for the night, and your itch still needs scratching." He grinned. "You're slinging those pheromones, in case you're wondering how I know you're still horny as hell."

Damn him, standing there flaunting his desires in such a way that my body responded.

Still, I hesitated.

His grin faded as he studied me, and his hand slowed to a stop.

"That's how Cassius..." I couldn't finish the sentence.

"I know."

The chill in his tone caught me off guard.

"You forced me to face my ghosts. It's your turn to do the same."

"How..." I couldn't spit the words out of a mouth that had become an absolute desert.

He cocked an eyebrow and resumed stroking himself.

Oh. Cassius must have expanded on our escapades to needle him while he had him locked up. I shook at the thought.

"Hands. And. Knees." Robby wasn't relenting. In fact, he seemed to be hardening more by the minute, as if the idea of dominating over me was what was turning him on.

Slowly, I surrendered because deep down, I knew Robby would never harm me. I stepped in front of him, meeting his gaze, and bit my tongue from begging him not to do this to me. I forced myself to put my trust in him and turned, sinking to my knees and then my hands.

He pushed my knees farther apart with his foot and then knelt between my legs and gently massaged my ass, soaping it up again. But this time, he slid his soapy finger inside my anus with slow and deliberate strokes and his other hand explored my pussy with the same deliberateness.

I glanced over my shoulder at him, and he smiled at me.

"I won't hurt you," he assured me. "But I am claiming you as mine in every way that you let him." His voice went from smooth to growling, and his teeth appeared.

My heart lurched in my chest as two of his fingers stretched me wider. I had let Cassius do things that were considered taboo. Although Robby and I had explored all sorts of positions in my house, he had not breached my ass with more than a finger. And he was huge in comparison.

He pushed his fingers deeper as he played my clit, as if he were strumming strings of a guitar. The heat of the shower played with his movements, and my body responded in more ways than just the warmth spreading through me. Robby was much more patient and kind than Cassius had been. Robby waited until I was panting and dripping wet before he lined himself up to my anus. His fingers never stopped playing, either, and his slow entry had me coming.

He took his time, riding me slowly in and out, as if anything harder would break me. "God, you feel so fucking good," he groaned.

When he slipped his fingers into my pussy, the sensation of being full tripped off another set of orgasms.

"That's it, baby. Keep coming until you scream my name."

I glanced back at him, and his head was tilted up and his eyes closed, with an expression of absolute ecstasy plastered on his face. His canines were still on display, as if his wolf had taken over. His eyelids fluttered open, and that piercing blue shot right to mine with a ferocity that promised a lifetime of fiery lovemaking.

"Harder," I whispered. I wanted all of him.

He smiled and nearly pulled out, but just when I started to whine at the sensation, he slammed into me, balls deep, making me gasp. He paused. "Like that?"

"Yes," I breathed out in barely a whisper. He made this experience incredible. Everything Robby did to me surpassed Cassius. Every nuance of movement and the promise of satiation from Robby was excessive. His love for me throbbed in my shoulder, echoing his heartbeat.

His thumb passed over my clit as he slowly pulled back again. His eyes nearly glowed. His grip on my right hip reached near pain, but he held me in place so I wouldn't chase his exit. "Finger yourself," he commanded and pulled his hand away from my pussy.

I did as he asked, sliding two of my fingers inside me while I pressed my wrist to my clit, applying pressure.

"Can you feel me?" He resumed a slow cadence with his hips.

"Yes." He filled me, and I stroked the outer wall of my vagina with my knuckles, heightening the sensations triggering my body to grip him and my own fingers.

"Oh my fucking God," Robby gasped and sped up his movement. "Whatever you are doing, do not stop."

I was basically fucking myself with my hand in time with his thrusts and the sensation of being filled to capacity made every nerve ending even more sensitive. A low, keening moan of his name started in the back of my throat as heat engulfed me.

Robby went faster, rocking my body with the force of his thrusts.

"Fuck!" he cried, arching so as much of him was inside me as possible. The power of his orgasm set off mine, squeezing all my muscles around him and my hand.

Hot cum dripped down my wrist, and he groaned, pumping the last of his release into me as I shuddered through my own aftershocks.

Robby gently pulled out of me and sat directly under the shower spray. "I think you actually stopped my heart." He let out a soft laugh.

I curled up on the shower floor and glanced at him. My entire body had somehow turned into a wet noodle. I couldn't get up even if the house were on fire.

Satiation turned to worry on his face. "Are you okay?"

"Yes. I just don't want to move now."

He reached up and flipped a switch, and the water went from the pulsing shower head, to a rain shower head above most of the shower. Warm water fell on us, washing away our sweat. "We can sleep here if you want."

I glanced at his tired eyes.

"Sleeping in a shower while it is on is not the smartest move, especially if we are coma-bound." I lifted my head and looked at my left hip. "Besides, I think you need to put another sheet thing over my tattoo." I met his gaze.

He nodded. "But we can just relax for a little while until I'm sure my legs will hold my weight. Okay?"

I smiled and laid my cheek on my folded arm. "I'm good with that."

"Are you sure I didn't hurt you?"

"Yes. I am sure. You just drained me of all my strength."

He chewed on his lower lip, as if something weighed on his mind. My mark burned, making me shift. When I met his gaze, I knew what the questions were behind those suffering eyes.

"What is bothering you?" I propped my head on my hand.

He looked at his hands and then back. "It's ludicrous." He glanced at the ceiling with a sharp chuckle. "I can feel the love you have for me, and I'm still doubting it."

"Because of Cassius."

He nodded.

I forced myself back onto my hands and knees, and crawled over to where he sat, situating myself in his lap. I wrapped my arms around his neck and kissed his cheek. "I'll put it in terms maybe you can understand. If someone else had kidnapped me and Cassius when we were dating and did what he had done to me, wiped my memory and ordered me to drain Cassius, he would have died at my hands. You know why?"

Robby shook his head.

"Because he never had a piece of my soul like you do. You've had it since the day we met." I laughed. "Actually, maybe even longer than that, because when I met you, that ache inside me that I had always had went away. You made me whole." I cupped his cheek, making him look at me. "And your touch is more amazing than anything I've ever experienced. The way you love me...there is nothing that could ever compare to that. Nothing on Earth or in Heaven." I took a breath. "You are my world." I shrugged a shoulder and snuggled against the side of his throat.

For the first time since we escaped from Cassius's, Robby did not flinch away from me.

"I love you down to the very essence of my soul," I whispered.

"You are my soul," he replied and kissed my cheek.

18

CROOKED SOUL 18

THE NEXT MORNING, THE house was quiet
when we got up. I took a quick shower and
pat myself dry. Robby hadn't put a film over my
tattoo last night because by the time we tumbled
to bed, we just fell on top of the covers.
Honestly, I don't remember my head hitting the
pillow.

I hadn't slept that soundly in a very long
time. If Judy or Johnson wanted to drag our
asses into a cell, last night would have been the
perfect opportunity. We would have never known
we were moved until we woke up. Thankfully,
neither of them were of the mindset of locking us
away.

I climbed down the stairs still in somewhat of a stupor to find Robby sitting on the couch with a cup of coffee and the clicker.

"Finally got your fine ass out of bed." He waggled his eyebrows at me.

"Where's..."

Judy stepped out of the kitchen with a tray filled with pancakes, sausage, toast, and eggs along with three plates, assorted jelly spreads, strawberries, whipped cream, and syrup. She winked at me.

"I figured you all could use some sustenance."

"That's enough for a small army." I pointed at the platter as she set it down.

"I'm pretty hungry." Robby glanced up at me. "Did you want anything?" He waved a fork at the spread.

I thought twice about feeding my body, but my stomach responded with a loud enough growl that I couldn't ignore it. Plus, I didn't want to be rude, considering Judy went to the trouble to cook all this. I took a plate and a single pancake and proceeded to stack strawberries and whipped cream on top of the sweet confection until it resembled something a child would have made. I took a seat next to Robby and smiled as I took my first bite.

I was met with another explosion of taste, as if my taste buds were on overdrive. It was just as heavenly as the plate I concocted for them when we had our tattoos done.

"How's your bum?" Judy nodded toward my backside.

"It looked better this morning after a night uncovered," Robby said around his mouthful of food. "Did you put another covering on it this morning?"

I nodded. I had managed to do that without scraping the tattoo. "I think clothes would bother me. Give it a few more days and it should be fine."

"What did you want for dinner?" Judy asked as she piled food on her own plate.

"I can take care of that if you want." I waved toward the kitchen, as if I'd spend any time actually cooking a meal. I knew how to cook because of my days at the academy and sometimes I even enjoyed it, but most of the time I just waved my hand and whatever I desired would be plated before me. That, or I would go out with my friends and have a liquid dinner.

"I love to cook. It relaxes me." Judy took a bite off her plate, savoring the taste of her pancake. "Besides, it keeps me away from the trash television on in the afternoons." She waved her fork toward the box hanging on the wall.

"Not a soap opera fan?" I hadn't watched one of those since before my parents died. State care frowned upon those things and then, at the academy, there wasn't time for soaps.

"Oh, I love them, but just sitting in front of the television all day just makes me feel lazy in comparison to what Rick does every day. So, I clean and cook and do the shopping before I allow myself to sit and relax."

I gave her a nod and focused on finishing what was on my plate. I was able to get half of it eaten before I stopped. It was more than the last couple of tries. I put the plate down and leaned back into the couch, feeling as though I had just eaten a five-course meal and dessert to top it off.

"I can't eat any more."

She glanced at my plate and raised her eyebrows. "That's more than you've had in the last couple days combined." Her shoulders straightened, and she radiated with the smile that formed on her face.

"It was really good." I wiped my lips with a napkin. "Have you talked to Johnson about getting a job?" She had mentioned that the other day and then we got tattoos and hadn't spoken about her pursuing a career again.

Judy's cheeks reddened, and she glanced at Robby. But the man was concentrating on shoveling food into his mouth as fast as possible, as if this were his last meal and he was going to eat until he popped.

"No," she said after a moment, as if she waited for admonishment from the alpha in the house.

Robby glanced up at me and then at Judy. "You want a job?" His words mumbled through a mouthful were almost understandable.

Judy stared at me.

"He asked if you wanted a job." I turned to him. "She'd love to work at one of the major hotels as a planner."

"She should be the cook because this is fantastic." He pointed his fork at his nearly decimated plate.

"I'd love to help people plan their days or evenings or plan events at the hotels."

"You mean being a hotel concierge." Robby nodded. "I could see that."

"But I'm the alpha's wife. I'm expected to stay home."

"Pfft," Robby scoffed and waved his hand at her, as if that were the most ridiculous statement he'd ever heard. "You should go out there and make your own way if that's what will make you happy."

"I don't think Johnson feels that way." Her hands wrestled in her lap as she fidgeted in place.

"Well, then I'll just have to give him an attitude adjustment," Robby said. "You are his equal. Just like she is *my* equal." He pointed at me. "Don't you ever forget that."

Judy smirked. "She did take you down awfully hard yesterday."

"She's a fucking badass. You should see her with a bo." He cleaned off his plate and leaned back in the seat. "As soon as this food settles, we're going downstairs to work out. Did you want to join?"

Judy blinked in confusion.

"Strength training, and maybe a little sparring." He looked pointedly at me and then back at her.

"I've never used the machines downstairs, and the thought of sparring scares me." She looked down at her hands.

"Johnson hasn't trained you to fight?" Robby leaned forward as he shook his head. "Shame on him." He stood and started to clear the plates.

"I've got that." Judy started to scramble to help.

"Chill. You cooked. Relax with Sarah. I'll clean up."

She froze in place and just stared at Robby as if he were committing a grave sin.

Robby laughed. "Sit and relax." He nodded toward the couch.

She obeyed and sat, but her muscles were so tense that a tic in her cheek started as she watched him balance the plates and platters on his arm.

Robby sent me a wink and disappeared into the kitchen. When the water started, Judy looked at me and hooked her thumb toward the kitchen.

I nodded. "He's always been this way. Unassuming, but damn, I'd follow him through the fires of hell." I sighed.

"I'm beginning to understand why Rick has so much respect for him. He doesn't treat anyone as inferior to him. He's nothing like his father. I always cowered a little in his presence, like he exuded superiority. My dad can be the same way. But him...he makes me feel special." She sighed. "Rick doesn't have the same type of gifts as your man does. But he has a good heart and wants to do what is right for the pack."

"Johnson is a good man. I have to admit, I've never met another wolf quite like Robby. He carries himself like an alpha, but he doesn't exercise that power very often. He hates being controlled, so he doesn't do it to others unless it is absolutely necessary."

"But you control him."

"And he hates it. But I do it to keep him safe or keep those he cares about from harm when he loses it." I sighed. "And we both are more prone to losing it since our captivity. It scarred us both deeply." I glanced at her. "More than either one of us want to admit."

She looked at the kitchen. "I can't imagine. If I had gone through what you two had, I'm not sure I could make myself get out of bed and face the world." She glanced my way. "I admire that in both of you."

I shrugged. "All I did was die and rise again. He's the one who was beaten and starved and nearly bled dry multiple times."

The water went off, and Robby appeared in the doorway with a towel as he dried his hands. "You were murdered in some really heinous ways. Don't toss that off like it was nothing." His eyes blazed with anger.

"What he did to you was worse." I kept eye contact with him.

"What he did to both of us was fucked up. Just because you can rise from the ashes doesn't make it any less horrifying." He turned and marched back into the kitchen.

"He has a point," Judy said, raising her eyebrows.

Robby always was on point, but I still didn't categorize what happened to me as awful as what happened to him. Although, I was beginning to realize that he saw things in the same manner. His torture, as much as it fucked him up, was nothing compared to what he witnessed happening to me.

The scraping of dishes being stacked came from the kitchen and then silence. Robby came back in the living room and took a recliner across from the couch. His lips turned down in irritation as he stared at me.

"Let's not do this," I said softly. "Let's not play the *who was fucked up more* game, okay?"

He blinked rapidly and then dropped his gaze with a nod. "Sorry. It just pisses me off when you make it sound like I was the only one tortured." He looked at me and cocked his head. "He broke every bone in your body, hon. Before he..." Robby closed his eyes and shook his head, as if shaking the images away. "Before he killed you," he finished and opened his eyes. "And that was just the first time you died." He raised an eyebrow, then looked at his own hands. Hands that had squeezed the life out of me at Cassius's command.

Judy stared at me in awe.

"Stop looking at me like I'm special. I couldn't stop him until my mother intervened between the planes of life and death. She gave me the magic words to break the spells keeping me from my magic and my memories."

"Fringe vancula?" Robby said, mispronouncing the words.

"Frange vincula," I corrected, and the air crackled. "It broke through the wards holding us hostage. It even broke through Cassius's vampiric hold on Robby." I smiled at the memory of my wolf tearing that vampire to shreds. "It also broke whatever charms he had on the house." I blinked and my eyes widened as I looked around the flat.

"Shit, did we just break my charms?" Robby said as he looked around as well. His gaze snapped to mine. "You can't do magic here anymore." He pointed at me.

Judy looked between us. "That's a strong spell," she said, slowly blinking as if just waking for the first time. She glanced at us and then around the room with a crease between her eyes. "What just happened?"

"What do you mean?" I asked.

"I don't feel…compelled anymore." She looked at me and then glanced at her phone on the table. "Like I could call the MDA on you right now." Her eyes narrowed. "But what's more concerning, I don't feel an ache in the center of my chest that I've felt since I was introduced to Rick." She rubbed her chest. "I mean, I still feel the connection through his mark, but that all-consuming dependence on him isn't there anymore." Her gaze snapped to Robby, as if he would be able to explain the absence of that feeling.

"I'm not sure I understand what you're telling us." Robby glanced at me. "The words just break magical spells." His eyes widened, and he looked down at his thigh and back up at me with fresh fear in his eyes.

"I don't feel…" Judy struggled to articulate. "That spark."

I leaned back into the couch cushions. I still felt the connection with Robby, and that need to be near him still gripped me like it always had since day one. I turned to Robby as well. "Can the feeling of meeting your true mate be manufactured with a spell?"

He shrugged. "Possibly. But to what end?"

I didn't have an answer for him, but the look of horror spreading on Judy's face was like a punch to the gut. She had been somehow coerced into thinking Johnson was her true mate, and if we had never uttered those words, she would have never known.

Her hands covered her mouth. "Could Rick have done this?" she asked through splayed fingers.

Robby shook his head. "No. He doesn't have that kind of underhanded trickery in him. But my father? Well, that's an entirely different story. And if that's what he needed to control his new alpha, then I wouldn't put it past him."

"You think your father would do that?"

"He put Johnson in charge, and then immediately introduced him to the daughter of one of the most prestigious packs in the Northeast." He started nodding. "It's an indirect way of controlling his own interests."

"He's that much of a bastard?" Judy asked.

"Yes," we both said at the same time. Knowing what he did to Robby, to us, I could agree that he was the ultimate bastard, but he was trying to protect his legacy. And people do crazy things when they think their legacy is at risk, especially those in power.

"What does this mean?" Judy rubbed her shoulder as though she were trying to wipe off the mark. Her voice rose to the high pitch of panic.

"You care for him, correct?"

It took her a moment to sort out her thoughts and then she nodded. "Yes. I do."

"Then it shouldn't impact the relationship you've built."

"Even if that was based on a lie?"

"Would you have given him the time of day otherwise?" I was curious to see what her answer was, because Johnson was our friend.

"Have you seen him?" She raised her eyebrows.

I smirked and glanced at Robby. If I hadn't been thunderstruck by *my* wolf, I think I could have been persuaded to start something with Johnson just on the looks department alone. They both were attractive men, so her point was valid. "Yes, I've seen him." I didn't add that I've seen him naked probably more times than she has over the years. After all, when they shift back to human form, it's in the buff.

"And he is a sweet guy." She stared at the ring on her finger. "But I'm not sure I would have just up and married him without believing he was my true mate." She closed her fist. "Damnit." Anger bloomed in red patches in her cheeks, and it radiated from her. "My parents must have known. They didn't even bat an eye. No questions, nothing, and the alliance with the Allegany pack would bring them to an entirely new level of prestige."

"Your parents didn't seem like the kind of people who would do that."

Her glare shut Robby up. "They hammered me for years to marry you. I had no intention of marrying anyone who wasn't my true mate. Even if I didn't meet him until I was ninety and on my deathbed, it was fine by me. So yes. They would do this to get an heir, and they were desperate because I'm an only child."

Robby smiled at her admission, and I cocked an eyebrow at her. "So, you wouldn't marry for the pack?" I asked.

"No. I wasn't willing to do that before. Then I met Rick, and that moment changed my entire view of the future." She stood up and crossed to the door, looking out the side window with a sigh. "Damn it all to hell."

19

CROOKED SOUL 19

INSTEAD OF LETTING JUDY stew the morning away, we forced her downstairs with us and taught her how to use the weight machines. She particularly liked the leg press and the ab crunch machines Robby had. And then we took turns sparring.

I taught her the basics of using a bo, and Judy was an exceptional student. She even got a hit on Robby during their sparring session, but Robby wasn't in top form yet, either. However, she didn't get a hit in on me at all, and I held back; I didn't want to discourage her on her first match.

Soaking in sweat, she wiped her forehead and leaned against the wall as Robby and I engaged in some sparring matches. He met the mat more times than I did, and he did his best not to let me land on my left ass cheek. But I was sure I'd still need a thorough tattoo cleaning when we were through.

"Think you can call Phillip and see if there are any spells that would break the protections in his tattoos?" I casually asked as we made our way up the stairs. I needed to know whether we just nullified their vampire protections along with breaking whatever spell had been cast over Judy.

Judy nodded and grabbed her phone off the table. "I'd like to know that, too." She dialed. "Phillip, hi, it's Judy again." She smiled and blushed. "No. Nothing is wrong with my wolf tattoo. But I have a question about the other one. Is there any spell that can make that magic void that you are aware of?" She flipped the phone to speaker.

"Not unless there's a spell that can change someone's DNA. The protections are not just embedded in your skin; it's now entangled with your essence. Your physical makeup. It is permanent." He paused. "Why do you ask?"

"Because I inadvertently ran into a spell breaker, and I was concerned that it nullified my protections like it did to my house."

He chuckled. "Protections on a physical property can be broken with the easiest of spells. This can't. Not even the most ancient of spell breakers can destroy the bond the tattoo has with you. Even if you had it removed, the essence cannot be unbound without destroying the host."

That was some fucking strong magic.

"Thank you, Phillip." She went to hang up.

"I'm tattooing a vampire later this evening, and we can test it out if you're still unsure. But it's dangerous."

Judy paused and met my gaze. I shook my head.

"What time?" she asked, ignoring me.

"You have to promise not to send in the cavalry," Phillip said cautiously. "I don't need my business destroyed by the MDA."

"I won't. But I need assurances from you that if the protections fail, you will protect me from the vampire."

There was no hesitation in his answer. "I will protect you with my life. I would have the full force of the agency brought down on me if anything happened to you."

"What time?" she asked again.

"Midnight."

Of course they would rendezvous at midnight. It was the witching hour, and everything in the area around his shop would be closed by that time. I wondered what his normal business hours were and glanced over Judy's shoulder as she whipped out his card from the table drawer where she had stowed it. His hours were normal nine to five plus "on demand," according to the card.

"And it's the address on your card?" Judy asked.

"Yes, my dear. The front door is always open."

"Thank you. I'll see you at midnight." She hung up the phone and turned toward me. "You both are coming with me, right?"

"We aren't letting you go alone." I glanced at Robby. The fear in his eyes told me enough, but we had to know whether his tattoo worked or not.

He swallowed and then nodded.

"The tricky part will be getting out of here without Johnson knowing," he said.

I smiled. "I can compel him to sleep soundly."

"You are wicked," Robby said, but that spark in his eye told me he loved the idea.

Judy smiled. "So, we have a plan."

"Speaking of Johnson, are you going to tell him about the spell?" I asked.

"We have to," Judy said. "He has to know about this duplicity." She glanced between the two of us with eyes that seemed to beg for approval.

"Agreed," Robby said. "He needs to know, and we need to be prepared for him to blow a gasket." He glanced at me. "And he can't ever know we took her to that tattoo shop while a vampire was there." He pointed at Judy. "Otherwise, he'll have my head."

JOHNSON CAME IN THE house around six with a crease between his eyes and a vague hello as he took a seat at the kitchen table. Robby pushed a glass of Scotch his way while Judy and I finished preparing dinner.

He took the glass and downed it without a word. It was enough for all of us to pause and stare at him.

"I know where the ancients are staying," he said. "But I've been told to stand the fuck down." His glass slammed on the tabletop, making us jump. His gaze rose to meet mine, and the muscles in his jaw jumped.

"What are you planning?" I knew that look on his face. I had seen it a thousand times in the situation room. Johnson was a good planner, whereas Robby was an exceptional leader in executing the tactical plans that were dreamt up in that room.

"We're going in to annihilate them tomorrow."

"Who?" Robby asked.

"The pack. We aren't going to sit back and allow them to take over the city, even with direct orders. It isn't right. There have already been bodies discovered, but they don't want us to intervene."

"Wouldn't it be better to find out why they don't want you taking them down?" I asked. Going after the number of ancients we saw in the park was high risk, even for the amount of training we had as agents.

He blinked at me. "This from the woman who singlehandedly took down a nest of over twenty vampires?" He cocked his eyebrow. "There are ten of us willing to break the rules to put those bastards on the extinction list."

"I didn't take that nest down alone. I had Robby with me."

"Whatever. There's ten of us going after them." He sneered at me, as if five wolves and five witches were more than enough to get the job done.

Robby glanced at me. There was a gamble that I might be lost if they did kill the mother of vampires, but he didn't argue against taking that risk.

However, I had reservations about him risking his neck along with the members of the pack who fought by our sides in some pretty dicey situations. Johnson was my oldest friend, and I didn't want to see him hurt or worse, a prisoner in a cell next to Manuel. "I still think you should reconsider. There were a lot of really old vampires in the park the other night. And you said all the parks were off-limits at night. You could get hurt, or worse."

"I don't think you should go against orders," Judy said, finally piping into this debate. She chewed on her lip and then quickly dropped the phrase, "Frange vincula."

The air crackled around Johnson, and he blinked, shivered, and then looked around like Judy had done when the spell was expelled. "What the fuck was that?" He glared at Judy as though she had done something to him.

"It's a spell breaker." Robby leaned back in the chair. "The house is no longer charmed, by the way," he added after a moment. "And if you hadn't crackled like a firecracker, you'd be getting a serious beatdown from all three of us."

"What the hell are you babbling about?" he asked with a confusion-creased brow.

"Apparently someone decided to put a spell on the two of you." Robby waved a finger between Johnson and Judy.

Johnson glanced at his wife and tilted his head, narrowing his eyes. "Did you know about this?"

She was already shaking her head. "I thought you had done it, but they assured me that you would never deceive someone in this way."

His gaze moved to Robby and then hardened to the point I thought he'd just burst into either flame or fur. "Your father."

"And possibly my parents," Judy added, as if she didn't want the crowned king of the pack to be taken down alone. "They were desperate for an heir, and I wasn't in any hurry to settle with just anyone."

He glanced at his hand, at the wedding ring. "How did we not know?" He looked up at her, searching her eyes before he ran his hand through his hair and then pushed his glass for a refill.

Robby stood and grabbed the bottle off the refrigerator as we plated spaghetti, salad, and bread, putting it down on the table as Robby topped off Johnson's glass.

Johnson stared at the liquid in front of him and then up at Judy. There was a fondness in his gaze, just like hers, but it wasn't like the fiery glances they exchanged every time they looked at each other until today. "What do you want to do?" he asked softly.

She rubbed the mark on her shoulder. "Being your mate hasn't been a hardship, but whatever they gave us made me much more accommodating than I normally would be. I want a job. I don't want to be locked up in this house playing homemaker and housewife like I have been."

She had more backbone than I gave her credit for, and it made me love her just a little bit more now that we had forged a friendship.

Johnson nodded with a crooked smile. "Oddly, that works for me."

I don't think Judy expected him to react that way. She smiled and straightened her back. "And I want these two to teach me how to fight." Her finger waggled between Robby and me.

Johnson actually pouted. "You don't want me to teach you?"

Now she blinked, and her mouth dropped open. "I, I just assumed."

He smirked in that good-humored way I remembered, which had been absent since they arrived home from their honeymoon. "I've always had the same mindset as Robby has where a mate is concerned. They need to know how to defend themselves. So, I can't think of anyone more qualified to teach you to kick ass than Sarah."

There was the Johnson I knew, and Judy smiled in response.

"But that still didn't answer my question. We were coerced into this marriage by a fucking spell." He pointed at his ring. "Do you want to see if we can make it work, or do you want to call it a day?"

She glanced down at her food. "Calling it quits would make a lot of waves in both our packs." She met his gaze, and I swear there was a flash of melancholy there.

"I don't particularly care about our packs at the moment. What I do care about is what you want. Do you want to break up?"

She rubbed her shoulder, and he glanced at the motion, as if trying to figure out what her physical cues were saying.

I looked across the table at Robby, feeling as if we were infringing upon our friends. He lifted his shoulder and focused on his food. I did the same, not wanting to interject my opinion in the matter. Personally, I thought they were good together. More so now that I was seeing the real side of her.

She laughed nervously and twirled a strand of hair around her finger as she shook her head. "No. Do you?"

Johnson let a breath out and his body seemed to relax with her answer. "No. I kind of like this." He smiled and nibbled on a piece of bread, but his brow was still creased in thought. "But what happens if one of us meets our fated mate?"

"Then we'll have to have another conversation at that time." She pushed her food around a little. "I guess what I'm saying is I'd kind of like to get to know the real you." She snuck a glance at him as she spoke.

"Same here." He raised his glass. "To new beginnings."

"To new beginnings." She took her glass and toasted him. After she took a sip, she said, "Now, how do we get back at those rat bastards?"

"Oh, I like this version of Judy," I said to Robby.

He chuckled at me. "She certainly has a bit more spunk than the one cast under that spell."

"I'm right here." She glanced at us.

"We know. I guess our sparring lesson gave you more balls than I thought," I said, eliciting a laugh from everyone.

"I've always had a mouth, but I've never been accused of having balls." She grinned at me.

Laughing, Johnson asked, "How'd she do sparring?"

"She's a quick study," Robby said. "Tagged me with the bo once."

"You must be rusty," he said to Robby.

"Hey," Judy said, setting her fork down in disgust.

"The only one who has ever tagged him with a bo is Sarah, and she's better than anyone I've ever seen."

"I am rusty," Robby mumbled through a mouthful. "But she's good for someone without formal training." He nodded toward Judy.

"Thank you," she said to Robby. "I had an excellent teacher." She nodded to me.

I had to admit, it was fun teaching someone. Maybe if we could find our way out from under the MDA, I'd open up my own dojo and teach martial arts. That seemed like an impossible goal, but one I would absolutely cherish.

CROOKED SOUL 20

I STEPPED OUT OF the apartment to join Robby and Judy on the sidewalk. "For the record, that felt completely wrong," I muttered. Putting Johnson to sleep until he needed to be at work just seemed sleazy, even though I had been the one to initially offer it.

"I know." Robby put his arm around me. "But we have to make sure these tattoos work, especially if Johnson is planning on storming the castle tomorrow." Robby held his hand up for a taxi.

"If they don't work, what are we going to do?"

Robby took a deep breath and a taxi pulled over before he could speak. He opened the back door. "Then we wake him up and tell him about our dumb little field trip." He waved us into the back seat. As soon as he closed the door, he nodded to Judy.

Judy rattled off the address, and we sat in the cramped back seat of the cab that smelled like stale cigarettes and coffee. None of us spoke, but Judy looked at the watch on her wrist and the clock on the dashboard. Both blinked 12:02 at us. We were going to be a few minutes later than midnight, which might work out in our favor, especially if the vampire was already in the tattoo chair.

The cab pulled up to the address, and Judy pulled the fare out of her pocketbook, handing it to the cab driver as we stepped onto the sidewalk.

I glanced up at the dark windows of the tattoo shop. The only thing visible were banks of tattoo samples like the portfolio he brought to the house. No light filtered from within. The air was eerily still. Not a hint of wind stirred the trash on the street like it normally would. It was as if we had stepped into a void.

Robby went to step forward, and I grabbed his arm. That feeling that I trusted implicitly stirred inside me, shouting warnings like a siren. I almost suggested trying to do this another way. I didn't get my hand out to grab Judy quick enough, though. She had already reached the door.

The jangle of the bell rang, breaking the silence pressing down on me. My feet moved, along with Robby's because neither of us wanted her to walk into the lion's den alone.

"Have a seat. I'll be with you in a moment!" Phillip's voice carried from the back room.

Whispering followed and then a voice I didn't recognize called out. "Come here so I can see you." The voice sounded like liquid honey, smooth and deep and sweet.

I glanced at Robby and Judy, and they both traded glances with me, shaking their heads. I wasn't the least bit compelled, and it seemed both of them were the same. I nodded toward the back room.

Judy waved me forward.

I headed toward the voice, and my hands itched for a blade. I guess my subconscious was more in tune with my magic than I was because the chill of leather handles caressed my palms. I glanced at the snake-like blades, and with steel in my hands, my confidence skyrocketed. I sauntered into the well-lit tattoo room with Robby at my heel.

Phillip's head turned so fast that I thought he'd snap his own neck. His eyes widened at the sight of Robby. The same fear he registered at our home came through in waves, and he pulled the tattoo gun away from the vampire's skin. When his gaze landed on Judy, he sneered.

"You promised."

"They aren't MDA," she said with the sweetest smile as she took in the shirtless vampire in the seat.

"Three meals." The vampire licked his lips. "Just stay where you are." He started to get up.

I handed one knife to Robby and the other to Judy. "Why do they always say that?" I smirked at them and then smiled as I stepped closer. "I

think not, you piece of shit." I let my hands
engulf in flames.

The vampire's eyes widened, and he hopped
to his feet, hissing at me with his teeth bared.

Phillip took a step toward me with a
menacing look on his face.

"Stay where you are, Phillip."

He froze in place with eyes as wide as
saucers. "How do you know my name?"

We ignored Phillip. I focused on the vampire.
Dark hair, red eyes, with a strong jaw. He might
have been good-looking once without the neon
eyes and sharp canines, but now he was just a
target for my anger.

The vampire's eyes narrowed, and he sniffed
the air and startled, taking a step backward
right into the chair. His eyelids fluttered as he
stared at me. He licked his lips and cleared his
throat, getting his composure back, and then he
spoke. "You even smell like your mother. I used
to love that sweet citrus tang until Amara
showed me a new life." He crinkled his nose.
"Now it just smells like rotten fruit."

"Who the fuck are you?" My uneasiness grew,
and I knew whatever came out of his lips was
going to break a piece of me.

"Your father." He grinned, with his vampire
fangs on display. "And I have finally found you,
my missing phoenix child." He spread his arms
wide, but the look in his eyes was deadly.

The memory of all that my mother had told
me between the planes of life and death
slammed home. "You're the bastard who sold my
soul to Cassius?" The words hissed out of me

like poison on the air. My hand flared brighter
as my agitation grew.

He must have thought his declaration would
bring me running into his arms, but I knew his
intentions were not fatherly in the least. He
wanted me dead just as much as that vampire in
the park did. A low growl started in my throat,
and my vision slowly bled red.

The bastard must have sensed my need to
ignite the entire room because he turned and
bolted out of the parlor.

I took a step to follow, and Robby grabbed my
shoulder, stopping me. He hissed, and I turned,
extinguishing my fire. Judy's mouth hung open
as she stared at me, and Robby shook his singed
hand.

"The tattoos work. We need to go." Robby
glanced at where my father took off and then
looked at Phillip still standing like a statue, just
staring at us. His expression mimicked Judy's.

"We were never here," I said to Phillip,
pushing my influence on him to erase the last
few minutes of his life. I grabbed both Robby's
and Judy's wrists, dragging them out of the
tattoo shop onto the deserted street as my
intuition went haywire. Urgency gripped me. "We
need to get out of here."

I conjured a cab and pushed both Robby and
Judy inside before I took the driver's seat. "Shit."
I closed my eyes and willed for the keys. A
moment later, the clank of a keyring settled into
my palm. I started the car and took off like a
Formula One driver. Reggae music blared from
the radio loud enough to make me wince, and I
turned it down. One glance in the back seat told

me I had one very freaked-out passenger in the back who looked as though she had seen a whole posse of ghosts.

"You conjured a cab," Robby said.

"Yeah." I glanced at him and then Judy. "We needed to get the fuck out of there before the rest of the vampires showed up and overwhelmed us."

Robby nodded. "I'm not sure which one of our fathers is worse."

"I think Sarah's father takes the title of king of the bastards," Judy said, finding her ability to speak again.

I snorted out a laugh, still reeling from meeting the vampire who set this whole thing into motion. I took another corner, turning onto the road that would eventually take us to Robby's place. But I didn't want to lead the world directly to me, so I turned onto a side street and then took another turn onto the road that Cassius lived on. I stopped a few blocks from his place and killed the engine as I glanced back at Robby.

I thought about wiping it down so my prints weren't on the steering wheel, but time was of the essence, and I threw that thought away as I climbed out of the car. When we were all on the sidewalk, I willed the cab back to where it came from, praying it didn't just appear on the road somewhere and cause an accident. And instead of following the road down past Cassius's house, I backtracked down the side street I just pulled out from.

Robby and Judy followed, catching up easily.

My heart hammered in my chest in an almost painful beat. Having that asshole's house between where we were and where we needed to be really messed with my brain, especially after the situation at the tattoo parlor. I mean, how often does one meet their three-hundred-plus-year-old father who tried to sell you to a vampire, for what? Eternity?

"Your hands are on fire," Robby said softly.

My gaze jumped from the path before us to my hands, which were indeed flaming. I shook them and then fisted my hands so it wouldn't happen again.

"Do you want to talk about it?" Judy asked with a face filled with concern that I didn't want aimed at me.

"I'm fine." I just kept plowing ahead. When we got back to the road Robby's house was on, I hung a right and continued to make my way to the house. This was not the place to discuss my state of mind, especially considering I wasn't even in the realm of fine.

Out of the corner of my eye, I saw Robby give her a headshake. I almost spun and let some of this bottled fury out, but I kept it under wraps. I couldn't lash out at him when I was mad at the man who claimed to be my father. I could not comprehend a parent doing what he did, just like I never understood why Robby's father was such a self-serving bastard.

When we got to Robby's place, Judy stepped to the door and slid her key in the lock. Johnson ripped the door open, his eyes frantic.

"Where the hell have you been?" he snapped as we shuffled into the house.

"I needed to see if the tattoos still worked after the spell breaker was cast here," Robby said.

Johnson growled at him. "So, you dragged Judy with you?"

"It was my idea," Judy said, snapping Johnson's gaze to her. "And Phillip promised to keep me safe."

Johnson dragged his hand through his hair. "Well, whatever the fuck happened set off alarms at the MDA. I was called out of a sound sleep to get my ass to the office, and you weren't in the bed with me. You weren't anywhere in the house." His exasperation came out in a derisive growl.

"You weren't supposed to wake up," she muttered and sent a questioning look my way.

"I didn't think about a call from work. I said to sleep until he needed to go to work, so technically, he did." I shrugged and received the scathing glare I was expecting from Johnson.

"What the fuck did you do out there?"

I shuffled my feet. "I conjured a cab."

"Oh. Well color me surprised that *that* put you on the fucking radar. And right outside the tattoo parlor that was supposed to be shut down. Thanks so much for putting that shit on their scope, too."

I blinked at him. "Phillip won't remember that we were there."

"Phillip is supposed to be dead." The words hissed out of his mouth.

My eyes widened. Fuck. I turned to Judy. "Tell him to get out of there, tell him you got wind of a sting." I didn't want to be responsible for the soul sucker's demise, especially because he had helped us.

Judy slipped out her phone, and Johnson grabbed it out of her hand. "You can't warn him now. It will be traced back to you. I'm already in a shit ton of trouble—this would make it worse." His gaze slashed to me. "And you're on their radar now."

He pulled a burner from his pocket and handed it to me. "Warn him with that and then destroy the thing."

Judy rifled through her purse and then handed me his card.

I dialed on the antiquated flip phone and put it to my ear. One ring, two, three, and then a quick "Hello," came through the line.

"Phillip?"

A beat of silence. "Who is this?"

"It does not matter. You need to get out of your shop, now. The MDA is coming, and this call may already be too late," I commanded and closed the phone before he could ask any questions. My hand ignited, and the plastic and electronic pieces that made up the phone became a puddle in my palm. I closed my fist on what was left, sending my fire into it. When I opened my hand, only ash remained.

I hoped it was enough.

Robby let out a huff of a laugh and met my gaze. Outside of cauterizing wounds and tossing fireballs, whenever I deliberately used my flame, it came out in a flash of destruction. This was a new level of phoenix control, and it was a heady experience.

Johnson pulled on his coat. "I have to go."

I went to open my mouth and order him not to say a thing about us, but he put his hand up as if anticipating my move.

"I know. I've had your back since the first day of the academy, and I'm not going to fail you now. I just hope Phillip gets out, because if he's not there, then there is plausible deniability on my part."

He gave Judy a peck on the cheek. "We'll discuss this later." His tone was enough to announce that whenever that conversation happened, it wasn't going to be pleasant.

I LAID AWAKE IN bed, unable to settle my restless mind. Robby had tried to open the door to conversation, but I wasn't ready to voice the storm inside me. He gave up and was now snoring lightly in my ear. Having his arm across my waist left me feeling protected, even though I knew if hell rained down on us, it wouldn't be enough. That foreboding feeling gripped me and left me to stare out at the darkness, wondering when the next axe would fall...and whose neck it would sever.

CROOKED SOUL 21

MORNING LIGHT PAINTED THE sky outside Robby's bedroom, and Johnson hadn't come home yet. My mind kept bouncing around at all the different outcomes, making me jittery. I almost got up to pace, but Robby's grip on me tightened, and he sucked in air.

Down the hall, Judy cried out.

Robby sat up next to me, looking around as if a ghost had walked into our room. "Fuck," he whispered and pulled on a pair of sweats along with one of my favorite blue T-shirts. His eyes looked haunted, as if he just witnessed another one of my deaths.

I dressed in comfortable clothes as an ominous pressure radiated from him. When he left the room, I followed.

Judy was in the hallway with a look I recognized. I had seen it enough throughout the years. It was the echo of their mates being harmed. I just never felt it radiating from Robby before.

"He's dead, isn't he?" she asked.

"We don't know that," Robby said, but his eyes were haunted enough for me to know he was lying through his teeth.

I stepped forward and wrapped my arms around my newest friend. It was all I could think of doing. If Johnson was indeed dead, things went very wrong last night.

"I know." She clung to me. "My mark knows." Tears tracked down her cheeks in a slow cadence of sorrow.

She didn't wail or sob uncontrollably like I had when Robby died, but it was enough to hurt her heart, even after finding out about the spell that brought them together.

Wet heat rolled down my own cheeks. I adored Johnson like a brother. If I could get access to his body, I might be able to bring him back. "Catch my tears in a jar." I stepped back and looked at her.

Robby turned back to his room and came back with a little shot glass, handing it to me. He understood what I meant.

Judy stared at me as I attempted to capture my sorrow in a bottle for her to use on Johnson. There wasn't a great deal of liquid when I handed the glass to her. I didn't know if it would be enough.

"Here. Cover it and when you see his body…" I sniffled. "Dump it on his forehead." I wiped my face. "I don't know if it will work or not."

She stared at it and then up at me. "What if they don't let me see him?"

"Make them." It was all I could muster. I turned to Robby. "We have to go."

He nodded. "Let me pack a couple things for us." He turned and stepped into his room just as a knock on the door sounded.

They got there awfully goddamned fast.

Judy sent us a frightened look and then nodded toward the bedroom. "I've got this." She headed downstairs and set the cup on the side table behind a knickknack.

I closed the bedroom door, with my heart slamming the walls of my chest. We were cornered until she made whoever came to tell her what had happened left to take her to his body.

I threw a couple of my shirts and a pair of jeans at Robby and then slipped on my boots.

Robby pulled on his shoes and attended to the backpack, trading a glance with me. A world of conflicting emotions played in his gaze—that haunted look of being trapped and the underlying sorrow for losing his best friend.

I had the same disaster rolling through my emotional bandwidth. We stilled as a throat cleared downstairs.

"Judy," a familiar baritone rang out, and Robby and I looked at each other.

Robby's jaw tightened as the front door closed. He straightened, with a few shirts hanging out of his backpack. He tucked them in and zipped the bag before stilling so we could eavesdrop on the conversation below.

"I'm sorry to have to tell you this," he started.

"Rick is dead." Her voice shook with the emotion she had caged with us—or had been too shocked at the sudden feeling of loss that accosted her to express.

I knew it all too well and never wanted to feel that fatal tug again.

"Yes."

"Take me to him," she demanded, sniffling.

I barely heard the sigh. "It's not a sight you should be subject to."

"I need to see him."

My heart squeezed, and I clenched my hands.

"We think the same person who killed Robby killed your husband, and she left him in pieces. You do not need to remember him that way."

What followed was a beat of silence in time with my thumping heart.

My gaze snapped to Robby's. *What the hell happened, and why the hell were they trying to pin it on me?* My heart stalled and my eyes widened as the truth melted in. It was a goddamned trick.

Judy's fury radiated from a floor away, and I wanted to shout down to her to keep quiet. I wished I had the psychic ability to project thoughts, but I was stuck here while the entire disaster unfolded. I couldn't do a damn thing about it, either. By the time I looked up, Robby was already moving, and he nearly ripped the door off the hinges and barreled downstairs to face his father.

"Sarah didn't kill me like you told everyone." He snarled in a way that unstuck my feet. "And she certainly didn't kill Johnson," he added.

Robby's father stared up the stairwell as if he had expected someone else to barrel down from the second floor, and not his dead son. He blinked and actually stepped back.

"You're a fucking liar." Robby's entire form shook, as if he were trying to contain his wolf. "I bet those ancient asshole vampires killed Johnson." Robby stopped at the bottom of the stairs, his gaze locked on his father. His head tilted. "Unless you killed him yourself."

There wasn't a drop of Johnson's blood on Robby's father. I would have smelled it. He hadn't killed Johnson himself. But that didn't mean he didn't give the order.

"How do you know it wasn't that vampire bitch of yours?" his father sneered. "She didn't have an issue killing her own master—why wouldn't she kill your beta?" He waved at his son.

"I killed that bastard," Robby snarled at the same time I barreled out of the bedroom.

His father's accusations were enough to set my blood on boil. "Because I've been here with Judy and Robby the entire night." I descended the stairs calmly, but every alarm inside me clanged. I just solidified whatever that bastard had been fishing for. The way the man grinned at me left me cold to the core.

"Thank you for confirming Johnson's duplicity." He went to grab Judy.

"Don't touch her," Robby growled. His fangs appeared.

"Stop," I commanded and everyone in the room froze in place. "Not you two." I touched Judy and Robby before focusing on his father again. "I didn't give them a choice," I said to his father. "I took away their ability to tell you." I glared at Robby's father, debating what to do about him. He had just ordered the kill on Johnson; however it happened, it couldn't have been pleasant. Which also meant that Phillip might have been a casualty, too. "So, you just murdered an innocent man." My internal alarms rang louder. They had to know he was coming here, and I knew enough about what the agency did to accomplices to know there was no way Judy was going to be spared. "Robert Senior, turn your ass around and get out of here before I kill you myself." I put my hand on Robby's arm, keeping him in place and grounded.

His jaw tightened but before he could leave, Judy shifted and jumped on his back, digging her teeth into his shoulder. I guess she truly loved Johnson enough to become vengeance personified.

I didn't stop her either, but I certainly was going to stop his father from fighting back.

"Don't you dare shift," I said to Robby's father.

He growled at me as he pried apart Judy's jaws with his bare hands and tossed her to the floor.

"And you won't remember us being here. As far as you remember, she was devastated, and no one was here. Johnson was loyal to the agency. You made a grave miscalculation where Johnson was concerned." I put my hand out, stopping Judy from launching at him again.

The glare I received promised he would get me someday, but today was not that day. He stormed out of the house, slamming the door behind him.

Judy shifted back to human form and glared at me. "Why did you let him go?" Judy let out a harsh growl.

"Because you would have been given the same death sentence as Johnson. It doesn't matter who your parents are. You violated protocol," Robby said with a sour expression and an equally disdaining tone. "She saved your life." He glanced at me. "And we have to get the hell out of here."

I nodded, and he ran up the stairs and grabbed the backpack.

"I don't know how long those tears have a chance of working. So, if you can get to where he is, at least try." I really had no idea whether it would bring parts back together, but my tears resurrected Robby's crushed bones, so if she had the opportunity, it might work.

She nodded, her chin quivering.

Leaving her felt wrong, but we had such a small window to get out of here before we compromised her. At least with my command, it gave her time to get out too. "You might want to go to your folks." I hoped that would be safe for her, but it depended upon how far in bed they were with the agency. If they were anything like Robby's dad, she was screwed no matter what she did.

I stepped out on the front stoop first. I got to the sidewalk with Robby's hand in mine before I felt a sting on my arm and my leg. I glanced at the darts sticking out from my skin and tried to swivel my head to Robby, but blackness rained down on me before my head got halfway around.

I should have known.

CROOKED SOUL 22

MY HEAD FELT AS if I had been slammed with a sledgehammer. I moaned and rolled, falling a short distance to meet cold concrete with my hands and knees. Pain bloomed through my cranium, and my vision fractured in the ambient light surrounding me. My stomach rolled, and I put my forehead on the concrete, welcoming the chill.

"Sarah?"

His voice struck a warmth in my soul, but he was too far away.

"Mhm," I mumbled. It was all I could produce.

"You okay?" Robby asked softly.

"No," I whispered. I had an idea of where we were; if I was right, we'd never see the light of day again, never mind hold each other. And my stomach wasn't cooperating. God, how I hated the tranquilizer hangover, but this time, it was a much harsher awakening than it had been the last time.

I forced my eyes open and scanned my surroundings. Concrete, with only a metal cot, a toilet, and a sink. Not even a shower to properly clean up with. I squinted, forcing my eyes to focus. Robby sat cross-legged in front of a row of bars across the hall from my cell. His expression echoed the same hopelessness that crushed down on me.

My stomach lurched, and I clamped my lips together, crawling to the toilet. The sound of my retching echoed off the walls, making my headache worse. When there was nothing left, I spit and flushed before pulling myself up to the sink to rinse out my mouth. There was nothing worse than vomit taste. I shivered from it, gagging again, but this time nothing came up. I rinsed out a second time and then made my way to the front of my cell.

"Sorry," I whispered and plunked myself down on the floor, stretching out so I could have the cold concrete against my cheek.

"Who's there?" A voice echoed in the hallway to my right, and I moved closer to the bars. On the right, next to Robby's cell, a bearded face pressed against the bars and a wild eye scanned the area.

"Hi, Manny," I said from my spot on the floor. I stuck my hand through the bars and waved my fingers.

The hissing sound that came from the cell had me drawing my hand back.

Robby just shook his head.

"I smell your blood. Please, please just give me some. Just a taste!" His voice echoed in almost a shrill scream.

"Shut up," I snarled, pushing my will, and all went silent. I stared at Robby. "Not you, hon." I wiped my face. "What happened?"

Robby shrugged and stretched out on the floor, too. He reached through the bars carefully, but he couldn't even reach halfway across the hallway. Without a word, he stared at me before he pulled his hand back inside. The hiss of silver against skin filled the air, followed by the stench of burnt skin. "We're going to die in here."

I reached out with the intention of melting the fucking bars. A zap of electricity snapped my hand in the opposite direction. The sting followed, and I shook my hand. "They fucking electrocuted my bars?"

"Mine are silver."

"I could vaporize the entire fucking building," I growled low, meeting his gaze as I started to gather my fire in the center of my being.

Robby stared at his ceiling and slowly shook his head, as if there were something there that I couldn't see from my angle.

"I doubt you'd be quick enough to incinerate the vat of boiling silver that's above my son's cell." Robert Young Sr. stepped into view.

"You'd sacrifice your son to keep me behind bars?" I snapped at the man who could have been Robby's twin except for the gray at the edge of his temples. He held what looked like a smartphone in his hand and kept glancing between it and me.

"He forfeited his life the moment he broke protocol. The same with your friends when they chose to harbor fugitives." He glared at me and dropped a bag of blood on the floor in front of my cage, and pushed it with his toe through the small space that usually accommodated trays of food.

"I'd prefer a nice, rare steak if you don't mind." I pushed it back into the hall, careful not to touch the bars. "And you *are* aware of what I did to the last asshole who threatened to douse my mate with liquid silver." I climbed to my feet and stared him down with a cocked eyebrow, ignoring the sudden vertigo that took hold of me. "You remember Harrison, right? That was my handiwork."

He paled.

"Let us out of here," I commanded.

He turned and glanced at Robby, and that's when I saw the ear plugs and words typing on the screen in his hand. Words on a screen had no impact to compel.

"Fuck," I muttered and looked past him right into Robby's glare. But at least my mate wasn't looking at me with murder in his eyes. I had only seen that level of hatred from him once, and that did not end well for the recipient.

His father glanced back at me with a smirk. "You really didn't think I'd come down here without safeguards, did you?" He waved at his ear. "You are a vampire, after all, and from the intel I received, our anti-compelling medallions don't seem to work on you."

Fury filled every cell, and I screamed my frustration despite the pounding in my head. I wanted to pummel the man into a bloody pulp.

Manny joined me with his insane screech. Robby covered his ears, wincing at the pitch I hit.

His father just grinned. "Don't worry, you'll get used to the cage, just like your friend here." He nodded toward Manny.

Robby's anger crumbled into despair, as if someone flipped a switch inside him.

My mark tingled with the darkness pulling him down into an abyss.

He reached out, grabbing hold of the silver bars. Flesh sizzled, but he kept his hands in place. "Please, Dad, just let us out. Please."

"Robby, let go of the bars," I commanded as the stench of burning flesh tickled my nose.

His hands dropped and his gaze flicked to mine as irritation ran over his features. But that didn't stop him from continuing to grovel. "I'll do whatever you want me to do. Please don't leave us to rot down here. Please."

Robert Senior frowned with disgust at the words scrolling across the screen. "You would be willing to kill her?" He hooked his thumb at me.

Robby startled with tears in his eyes and stepped back away from his father. That haunted look passed over his face. He had already killed me once against his will. Robby's refusal to follow through on that order reflected in his eyes. He wasn't keen on doing that again, even if it meant his freedom. He shook his head. "No."

"Then you'll remain locked up."

"At least put us in the same cell. Don't fucking torture me with her just out of reach. Please, Dad."

Robby's plea fell on deaf ears. Robert Senior glared at his son. "You ceased being my son the moment you chose her over the pack. You shouldn't even be alive right now."

"How the hell do you figure that?" Robby snarled, giving up the pleading that was going nowhere and letting the anger rule him again.

Robby's father looked at his handheld translator. "I was told it was the price *I* had to pay for allowing you to mark her." He looked up at Robby and gnashed his teeth. "What the fuck were you thinking?"

Robby opened his mouth to answer, and then closed it as his father's words sunk in. His eyes narrowed. "You knew?"

He pressed his lips together. "I did not know you were still alive. I was misled." He inhaled and pointed at me. "And I vowed to kill you if I ever had the chance."

"I tore apart the last person who had the audacity to harm *my* mate," Robby said with a voice as cold as steel.

Neither his father nor I acknowledged Robby's words.

I cocked my head at his father. "Why didn't you go after Cassius?"

"It was not in my best interest to go after him." He glared at his son before he pulled a tranquilizer gun from his hip and shot.

Robby's yell followed me into the dark.

CROOKED SOUL 23

MY HEAD POUNDED AND my arms ached. I found my feet and stood, gagging on something in my mouth. Thankfully I didn't have anything in my stomach; otherwise, I would have hurled all down the front of me from the hellish headache throbbing behind my closed eyes, from yet another tranquilizer. Standing relieved the pressure in my arms, but they were still stretched over my head.

I slowly blinked my eyes open and stared into a stoic face in front of me. His red eyes studied me, and he sighed, crinkling his nose.

"Now that you're not in the shadows, you look exactly like your mother."

"What the hell are you doing?" I mumbled through the mouth gag, trying to clear the fog in my head. Then the face slammed home. This was the bastard in the tattoo chair. This was my father.

He tilted his head as if I were a bug and not his flesh and blood. "And your mother's duplicity nearly cost me everything."

I snorted at him because I couldn't laugh in his face with my mouth gagged. Beyond him, a large, nearly empty room stood. The walls and floors were all polished rock of some sort. I didn't know whether it was marble or granite, but it had a sheen that screamed opulence.

"Today, your soul will finally be bound to Amara's like it should have been hundreds of years ago when Cassius was finished with you."

I drew my eyebrows together and cocked my head.

"Then we will take the rest of the lives you have left so your powers can transfer to Amara, and she can rule the world."

I struggled to free myself, and he chuckled, looking up at the hook above me.

"You won't escape. This place is warded to keep you from accessing your fire." He smiled, but the sight of it chilled me. "And if you are thinking the agency you worked for will help you, think again. How do you think you got here?" He waved at the room. "They handed you over, as if it would save them in the end. Fools."

I narrowed my eyes at him. I wouldn't put it past Robby's father. He wanted me dead and out of his son's life. He made that crystal clear.

Robby wasn't here, so hopefully he was still locked up at the agency. I knew he'd never forgive his father for selling me out, but it was better than being turned or killed by these ancients.

"I'll be back. Amara should be here presently." He tapped my nose and exited through the side door, leaving me to mull over an end that I was sure would be painful.

Footsteps echoed and then the tall, alabaster-looking woman with jet-black hair who we had seen in the park stepped into the room—in a white suit, of all things. Talk about a fashion faux pas. When you couldn't clearly tell where the clothing ended and the skin began, there was a problem.

But that wasn't what made my heart stutter.

Every fiber inside me screamed when Amara dragged Robby into the room by hands bound in front of him with the same charmed cuffs MDA used. At least it wasn't silver, but it was enough to keep him from shifting. His eyes blazed with the same level of anger that burned through my blood.

His father sold him to the enemy, too.

When his gaze landed on me, his eyes widened, as if he hadn't realized I was here with him. But that surprise quickly transitioned to a feral growl.

She clucked her tongue at him and waved her finger back and forth. "I understand you were the one who murdered my child." She waved toward me. "An eye for an eye. Your child will die when she does."

Wait. What?

Robby's gaze slashed to mine and then dropped to my abdomen. His cheeks paled. "What are you talking about?" he snapped.

"You cannot smell the change in your mate?" She gave him a sad look. "She carries your wolfling." She grabbed a handful of his hair and tilted his head back. "As soon as she is dead and her soul is bound with mine, I will turn you into one of my mindless soldiers."

I was still stuck on the fact I was pregnant, but those words struck a coldness in me that had my flame snaking through my form, trying to find a way out of the charms snuffing my fire.

Captivity didn't sit well with either of us, especially since the MDA had handed us both over to the enemy. If she turned him, he still had the anti-compel tattoo on his thigh, so she couldn't make him do anything he didn't want to, even in a master-submissive situation. Even so, Robby would be more likely to step out into the sun of his own volition to end himself after he enacted his revenge on the MDA.

Our current situation was a billion times worse than it had been with Cassius. If Amara bound my soul to hers, she would inherit all the powers I held, and with them, she could make the human world tremble—or worse, burn.

I was bound with the same MDA cuffs that were around Robby's wrists. I guess Amara hadn't been apprised that these things didn't hold me when I had access to my power, but she knew enough to have charmed the room so I couldn't burn my way out of this. And she had to have some inkling that I had enough magic of my own to break the charms. Thus, the gag. She didn't want me casting spells or saying the key phrase my mother gave me in the land between life and death.

God, please let Robby know the right pronunciation. Let him remember what had released him from Cassius's hold and what burned through the charms at his house. He wasn't gagged. He had the power to undo the hold on me this time, and then I could fry these motherfuckers.

And once we did that, we had an even more pressing settle to score. The MDA needed to be taken down for their duplicity.

My father came out of the side room, pushing a medical table with scalpels and bone saws. He smiled at me but there was no warmth in it.

I struggled against the bonds holding me, trying to say the words. But all that came out was muffled and not articulate enough to break the magic keeping my fire in check.

A crease appeared between Robby's eyes, as if he were trying to understand me. Then, just as my father stepped in front of me, his forehead smoothed out.

My father tore my shirt and then picked up the scalpel. "You'll have to excuse me while I deliver your heart to Amara."

"Frange vincula," Robby said, and the air crackled with the counter magic those words released.

The blade pierced through my skin, and I tilted my head back with a scream. I ignited like I had when I annihilated that vampire in the woods. White fire shot from every cell, sending my fire out like a tidal wave to annihilate every last vampire in the vicinity, and protect my mate.

When the smoke faded, Robby was on the ground, covering his head. The cuffs still bound his wrists and his wolf. Amara stood near him, except she was charred. Well, everything but her angry red eyes that looked at me with such hatred that I swallowed hard.

My father was gone. Just part of the many who had been in the vicinity torched by my fire. His ashes mingled with the rest like forgotten memories.

She moved her shoulders as if struggling out of a straitjacket. Blackened skin cracked and drifted off her body, shedding and leaving reddened skin exposed. Her gaze darted around the empty room and then she tilted her head back and screamed a wordless bellow of anger.

I detected loss in that scream, too.

The rest of the charred skin burst off her in an explosion.

Robby looked up at her in shock and then glanced at me with wide eyes. The vampire should not have withstood my fire. The rest of them didn't.

Her scream faded, and her gaze landed on Robby. Fury contorted her face, and she reached for him.

I tapped my magic and willed a blade into his hand. The moment the cool handle appeared in his palm, he gripped it and plunged it into her stomach.

But it did nothing to stop her from grasping either side of his head. "An eye for an eye!" she screamed and torqued his head.

The sickening snap of bone filled the room. He crumpled to the ground, with his head looking backward.

Everything inside me shattered, and I willed a sword into my hand. Flames danced across the blade as I charged. The need to kill overrode all my senses. Robby's mark on my shoulder cried out, demanding vengeance.

I didn't even see her pull the blade from her abdomen. As I swung, a sharp pain filled my chest, but that didn't stop me from completing my swing like a grand slam batter. My wrath was too big to let me die before I had my revenge.

The blade sliced neatly through her throat, forever preserving her smug smile of victory. A thin red line separated her head from her body right across the middle of her neck. Rage still ruled my blood, and with a warrior's cry, I sent the hilt of the sword into the middle of her face, satisfied with the crunch of bones. Her head flew across the room at high velocity; when it hit the charred wall, it burst into ash.

I spun and slammed my elbow into the center of her headless chest as the last of my bellow faded. Her body followed the path of her head, but instead of turning to ash, it burst into flames.

I took a struggling breath and staggered, dropping the sword on the ground. It clattered on the hard floor. My gaze dropped to my chest, where the hilt of the knife I had conjured for Robby sat embedded in my heart. My gaze moved beyond my mortal wound to Robby's dead body on the floor.

I fell to my knees, feeling every ounce of despair now that my adrenaline had faded away.

Crawling, I made my way to him, rolled him so he was facing upward and straightened his head, grinding my teeth at the sound of scraping bone. I wailed my sorrow at his loss. Tears blurred my vision, dropping onto him.

My ugly cry echoed off the soot surrounding us because I didn't know whether my tears would be enough to save him this time. My tears surely weren't enough to save our baby either.

I prayed that I could walk in death with both him and our child instead of being resurrected to live out my days, bitter and alone.

I gripped the knife and yanked it from my chest. The metal clanged on the marble floor as I fell forward, collapsing on top of Robby. Tears pooled on his cool skin below me.

I took one breath, and then a second, but the third never came.

Blackness descended.

CROOKED SOUL 24

THE SLOW CADENCE OF breathing brought me from the blackness of nothing. I kept my eyes closed, almost believing the warmth radiating below me. But I knew better than to trust the hope that flared in my chest.

The steady heartbeat echoing in my ear was a mirage of the worst kind. Hot tears leaked out of my eyes, sliding across the bridge of my nose.

Fingers combed through my hair, and I shot to my hands and knees, hissing. I blinked at the blue eyes staring at me.

I glanced around, half expecting some clouds and angels playing harps or something equally as heavenly. But all I saw was ash floating on the air around us.

Robby reached up and cupped my cheek. "She snapped my neck, didn't she?"

"Yes." I choked on a sob and laid back down on top of him. "I didn't know if my tears would be enough this time." I let the sorrow purge in a painful ugly cry. He held me tight, kissing my temple as he whispered "shhh" in my ear. My shoulder tingled with his essence, and that only brought forth more tears. His fingers moved over my naked form and then tilted my chin so I would look at him.

"You died, too." It wasn't stated as a question, either. He had seen my transformations enough to know my phoenix burned all traces of death away.

I nodded and sniffled.

"How?"

"She stabbed me in the chest with the knife, but it didn't stop me from decapitating the bitch."

The right corner of his lips tilted into a sad excuse for a smile at the image I painted for him. His eyes glossed over with tears. He knew what I had sacrificed. What they had stolen from us. His chin quivered and a tear escaped the corner of his eye.

"They signed our death warrants," I whispered. "And murdered our child."

He nodded, and the fury that replaced the sadness in his eyes burned hot. "I don't care if you torch the entire city, so long as you wipe the MDA out of existence." His fingers ran through my hair in gentle flows, belying the venom in his voice.

"But your father..." As much as I wanted the man dead, it was Robby's blood.

"He sold us out." The muscles in his jaw tightened. "And I'm split on whether I want to tear him apart piece by piece or if I want you to pour a giant vat of boiling silver on him. Either way, I want to see him suffer. I want him to understand he doesn't fuck with me like that and live." He inhaled deeply, closing his eyes, reining in all his rage. He glanced at the charred, headless body near the wall. "Wasn't she the original vampire?"

"Apparently."

He blinked and glanced at me. "If she was the original, that means all vampires are her creations, right?"

It took me a moment to boil down his thoughts. When the creator dies, the creations die. I blinked, wondering whether my darker half had been extinguished with her death. I willed my teeth to form into the sharp incisors I was used to. The sharpness of my fangs sliced a thin line in my tongue, debunking the theory, at least where I was concerned. "I'm still a vampire."

He studied me. "Your eyes don't have that red hue anymore."

I smiled, showing him my teeth, but the hunger that always seemed to be present below the surface was absent. I wondered whether I could still compel or manipulate memories. I sighed. I'd have to find out when we got out of here. "Still can produce fangs, so I'd say that part didn't die this time."

"You realize you might be the only one left in existence."

I let out a laugh. "The only phoenix. The only vampire. It doesn't matter. They will still try to hunt us down because I'm capable of razing the earth to dust." They'd never stop so long as those who ran the agency behind the scenes still breathed.

"They fear what they don't understand."

"They should fucking fear me, because now they are at the top of *my* kill list. And I'm not waiting for them to get their shit together. I'm hunting them, starting now." I wiped my face and stood, offering Robby my hand.

I didn't care whether they detected my magical signature or not. As soon as he was on his feet, I manifested clothing and weapons that we both sheathed at our hips.

We headed through the soot-stained room, emerged into an equally charred hallway, and found our way out into the dark night to dole out some revenge.

The End

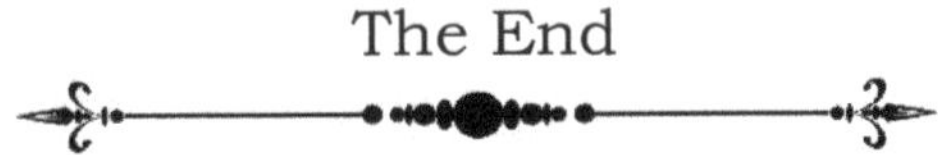

Continue Sarah and Robby's story with
TAINTED MIND - Book 3 of the Shades of Night
Series

SHADES OF NIGHT
BOOK 3
TAINTED MIND

No one in the agency is safe from our wrath.

I am the last of my kind, deemed a monster by the Monster Defense Agency. But the MDA does not understand the hell their duplicity has unleashed.

Robby and I are now on our own hunting expedition.

Our target: the head of the MDA.

Although, it isn't just one man pulling the strings. It's a highly complex network that is more like a damn hydra. When you extinguish one, another pops out of the woodwork.

Two against an ancient organization that trains monster-killers and that knows all our tricks is even harder than it sounds. It's going to take all our skill and intelligence to kill this beast.

And being caught is not an option.

TAINTED MIND
PROLOGUE

*R*OBERT YOUNG SENIOR
I paced outside her cell, waiting, as she screeched in that high-pitched tone that made me wince. It had been a long twenty-five years since that fateful night when everything I knew, everything I trusted, fell to shit.

I let out a soft laugh at how fucking naïve I had been. My wife of thirty-five years, Eve Young, no longer looked like the beautiful woman I married. She had long since turned into a feral husk. She threw herself against the bars, reaching for me and hissing as the silver burned her. Her vampire fangs were on display today. Sometimes her shifter teeth appeared and when they were out, she seemed less in the grip of blood thirst. But it had been years since the shifter side of her surfaced. The vampire's curse had somehow won the fight for dominance and left her batshit crazy.

Her eyes glowed like taillights, giving the hallway a reddish hue.

I guess if I had been starving for blood for months, I'd be just as unintelligible as Eve. It broke my heart every time I visited, but this time would be the last if that vampire hybrid does what she was made for. Of course, Robby will never forgive me for handing them over, especially considering she will likely perish along with my Eve when she takes down the mother of vampires.

But it was the only way to end this nightmare I'd been living in for close to thirty years.

At least that has been my working theory for as long as I've been with the agency, and we've seen it happen. Whenever we killed a vampire, anyone they sired died, too. And the mother of vampires started the entire vampire chain of derelicts. But Robby's girl isn't normal. She's never been normal.

I wiped my face.

That hybrid should have died when her sire died, but she didn't. So, my theory might have a million holes in it. I know I'm grasping, but it's been long enough. If killing the mother of vampires doesn't kill Eve, then the silver bullet I have loaded into the gun at my hip will.

Although the thought of Eve dying pains me, the idea that the agency will be vulnerable enough to take down without their league of vampires protecting them gives me a sense of excitement I haven't felt in years.

And after what they did to my family, I will delight in their ruin.

But for Terrance Winters, just being relieved of his life was not enough. He ordered my family's slaughter. Killing his niece had been a small token of my vengeance for all he has done, and I hope like hell he finds out about her duplicity where the agency is concerned. After all, she aided and abetted a known agency criminal.

That would burn as much as her death.

Terrance made a fatal choice when he chose to punish Eve and me for the choices we made. We defied the rules. Alpha or not, it wasn't a sanctioned relationship. When I had announced I was taking her as my mate, despite her role in the agency, I hadn't been met with friction.

I had actually been embraced and been told it was bold and brave to take that kind of stand. And all the while, the bastard plotted out how he was going to make me suffer.

And the irony of it all: the same vampire bastard who accompanied the mother of vampires to the city this week and issued stand down orders to the agency was the one who turned my wife and compelled her to kill my children. When I walked into the house that evening and saw the carnage, I nearly shot him dead on the spot. The only reason he still exists was that he was quick to remind me that if I killed him, I'd also kill my wife.

I shot that motherfucker with my tranquilizer and then I shot her. Then I called in the cavalry, thinking they'd lock him up along with her.

What a damn fool I was.

Terrance had other plans. He had my wife locked in one of the subterranean cells, ones that only the top agents were allowed to access. It took me years to gain his trust, and all it took was fucking up my son's future to get there.

He told me this was my penance. To be his fucking lackey. And if I decided to retaliate, he would make sure my surviving son suffered for my mistake.

He schooled me with what to say, and I followed the rules. I fed the story to my son that a vampire we had been hunting came and slaughtered the rest of the family, and that I killed him. I sold that story to my only remaining child while my wife screamed in a cell for years.

In desperation, I cornered a seer who was not affiliated with the agency and forced her to read my future to see whether I would ever get my vengeance. She saw two paths and in both, I would lose the one thing that I vowed to save at all costs.

But I had a choice.

An impossible choice.

One that would forever alienate my son, but it meant that when he finally bucked against the system, it would be at the time when his mate found her true powers. Powers strong enough to destroy all the monsters haunting my dreams.

If I did not stop it early on, death would claim all I cared about, from my son to my pack, and I would never feel the satisfying bite of revenge.

Eve's sudden inhale yanked me from my reverie, and my gaze snapped in her direction. The red in her eyes faded as she stared at me.

"Rob," she whispered as her skin started to flake away.

I looked at the woman I had fallen in love with, and not the raving maniac that the vampire curse had made her into. "Evie," I whispered with a raspy voice, choking on my own tears.

When she reached through the bars, I didn't hesitate. I took her hand, not caring if she pulled me against the silver. I wanted to hold onto her as long as possible. It only took a few seconds, but it was enough to wrench my heart.

And then all that remained was ash on the air.

The hybrid witch actually beat the mother of vampires.

And now I'd have to deal with my son's wrath.

1

TAINTED MIND 1

SARAH STONE

I marched toward the last place on earth Robby's father would expect us: the Monster Defense Agency headquarters and the likelihood of a legion of agents just waiting for us to arrive. Anger turned into a lethal snake inside my belly, roiling, churning until I thought I'd explode.

That bastard would pay for handing us over to the vampires. And I would make it as slow as my patience would allow. I wanted him to suffer.

Robby slowed and grabbed my arm. "What's the plan?"

"Annihilate everything in our way until I get my hands on your father." I turned back toward the agency, but Robby's grip on my arm tightened. I whipped around to face him and glared at the hold he had on my arm before pushing my unruly red hair out of my face. My irritation with him bloomed.

"There's a better place to get that bastard."

I tucked my windblown hair behind my ear and stared at him. I don't know what I expected. After all, I was talking about murdering his father, not just stopping him. But from the darkness settling in Robby's eyes, he was in the same headspace as I was. But his blue eyes also screamed caution, making me hesitate.

"If we go barreling into headquarters, we'll be taken down in seconds."

I disagreed and shook my head. "I'll put up a fire shield and blast through anything that comes near us."

He dropped his grip and crossed his arms. His challenging eyebrow sent a flash of irritating heat through me.

"Even a tranquilizer from behind?" He scoffed.

"I've stopped them before."

"When?"

He still carried that look that I wanted to wipe off his face. But he wasn't the enemy.

"When you were out cold in that shed. I knew it was coming." I didn't disclose that it was from one direction, but I was sure if I had my guard up, nothing could get to us.

"Why the fuck didn't you do that when we left my house?"

Point taken. "I wasn't thinking clearly." I ran my hand through my hair, conceding to just how off I had been that night. If I had been thinking clearly, I think half the block would have been burned down by my aggravated blast.

"And you are now?"

I stared into his concerned blue eyes and sighed. I was letting my fury drive me, which was a good way to get both of us killed. Again. But hadn't he been the one to tell me any hesitation on our part always brings about some sort of loss? I glanced back in the direction of headquarters, and that itch to take them all out scratched in the center of my soul.

"You want my father? This will be expected. Let's do the unexpected."

That got my full attention but when he stepped out into the road and whistled for a cab, I cocked my eyebrow at him. Before he could open his mouth to explain, a cab pulled up.

He opened the door and waved for me to get inside. As soon as he shuffled in and closed the door, Robby rattled off an address and the cab driver punched it in the display.

I gave him a side-eye. The address was hours away. His hometown.

The display beeped with the time to destination and estimated fare. The driver turned in his seat, gawking at us. "Are you nuts? That's nearly six hours away."

Robby smiled. "Drive," he insisted.

"I can't. That's, that's out of my zone."

"Drive," I said with a mental push, praying my powers of coercion were still in play.

The driver stared at me and then his eyes glossed over, and he turned and put the car in gear. "My wife is not going to be happy about this," he muttered under his breath.

I exhaled with relief. I still could make people do my bidding if I really wanted to. "We will make it worth your while."

"How the hell can you make up for an entirely lost night of fares?" He glared in his rearview mirror.

"How does ten thousand dollars for this ride sound?"

The car swerved a little, and his eyes widened.

I willed a large pocketbook filled with neat stacks of one-hundred-dollar bills into my lap, along with a change of clothing for Robby and me in a second bag at our feet. I started counting out a thousand at a time, handing Robby stacks of ten until I had ten thousand dollars.

"You don't have to report your tips, do you?" I smiled sweetly at him.

"Um. No." His eyes sparkled. "But I will also need the return fare."

"So, you pocket eight thousand."

"Plus gas." He haggled like he had a choice.

"Fine. I'll throw an extra hundred in for gas." I pulled another bill from my purse and handed it to Robby to hold on to for the ride. He shoved the wad into his pocket and leaned back in the seat.

The driver's demeanor changed from annoyed to amenable, and he turned up the radio. Country music blared through the cab. "I hope you don't mind the music."

Although I would have preferred good old-fashioned rock music, the country playing was the more modern tunes and not the old twangy stuff that made me hostile.

"When was the last time you were home?" I asked softly.

"The night I was inducted as alpha." Robby glanced at me and shrugged.

He had been named alpha a couple of years after we graduated, despite our location in the city. His father's beta helped oversee the day-to-day when they were both in the city. Even though Robby had the alpha title, he had not been back home for over ten years. He conducted pack business via phone and email. The network his father had built made it easy to carry on without him being present.

"Maybe when all this is over, we'll settle down out this way." I glanced out at the changing scenery as we got farther and farther away from the city with each mile. The knots in my back seemed to relax, too. But I knew better than to let my guard down, even with a random taxi driver.

They had to know something happened by now. Especially considering all the vampires ceased to exist. At least, that was the theory. I wasn't sure whether it had been the mother of vampires' death that turned the vampires in the building to ash or whether it was my fire blast.

2

TAINTED MIND 2

ROBBY REMAINED QUIET AS WE got closer to his hometown. The vibes he transmitted weren't of pleasant childhood memories. He seemed far more tense as we got closer to our destination.

"I need gas," the driver said as he pulled off the highway and followed the signs to the nearest gas station.

I handed him a bill through the pay slot, and he pocketed it.

We remained in the back seat as he pumped the gas.

My mark ached from his escalating emotions. "Are you okay?"

Robby turned to me and shook his head. "I never thought my father would sell me out." His voice was low and filled with the pain reflected in his eyes. "I knew he..." He shook his head and stared at his hands. "I never lived up to his expectations."

"That's no excuse for the way he treated you, Robby. I know I said to forgive him, but I'm starting to understand why you can't." That familiar anger flared. If I had my way, his father would be begging for mercy. I would only give it if Robby asked me to, but I don't think that mercy would ever come.

He pressed his lips together and nodded, eyeing the cab driver. "There's no coming back from this." He slashed his gaze to mine.

I didn't know whether he meant killing his father wasn't something we could come back from or what his father had done. Before I could ask, the cab driver put the handle back on the pump, screwed in the gas cap, and slid back into the cab.

We were off again.

The cab pulled up to a late-night diner that looked deserted. I sent a questioning glance at Robby but he ignored me. Instead, he pulled out the money and slid it through the opening before he reached for the bags at our feet.

We climbed out of the car, but before I closed the door, I leaned in. "Enjoy the ride back. And the passengers you took out to the countryside were a single mother and her young son who had their car stolen in the city." I pushed the words as I said them.

The driver looked at the money in his hand and then pocketed it. "I hope they find your car, ma'am." He then pulled out of the parking lot, leaving Robby and me alone with my bag of money and our clothes.

"Why here?" I nodded toward what looked like a closed diner.

"The owner is probably the last friend I have left." He turned and stalked across the parking lot.

I quickly followed. When the door easily opened, a bell announcing us rang from above the door. I glanced up at one of those ancient bells that rang when the door swung into it. It actually made me smile at how antiquated it looked. The restaurant had the usual diner décor: booth seating along the outer walls and little round stools at the counter with what looked like red vinyl covering.

"Be with you in a moment!" A female voice rang out from the back.

Robby smiled in such a warm way at that voice you would have thought it was family who had called out. When she stepped out of the back, I thought she was no older than we were until she looked up and the age lines surrounding her eyes showed. But her hair was as dark as the night and her eyes a bright hazel that bordered more on brown than green. Her smile made her cheeks crinkle.

"Robby Young. What are you doing here?" Her eyes sparkled but her gaze carried caution. When she looked at me, her smile soured. She sniffed the air and cocked her head, looking back at him with a thousand questions in her eyes. "I heard you were dead." Her gaze moved back to him, and she took another sniff before she stiffened, as if she smelled the true *other* clinging to both of us.

"You heard wrong." Robby tensed next to me as he transferred the bag to one hand.

"You don't smell the same as I remember." Her eyes hooded with mistrust.

"If you press that button under the counter, people will die." Robby's voice remained even, but his mark burned with disappointment. He had expected her to blindly accept him. "I don't want to hurt anyone but my father today. So please don't call in the cavalry," Robby added. His voice carried even more defeat than it had when he was in the cell, begging his father for our freedom. "My father gave us up to the vampires."

"Is that what you are now?" Her sharp canines appeared, and she moved into a defensive position, pulling a blade out from under the counter.

I couldn't let her think he had been turned, not with the flare of fear radiating from her. "He isn't a vampire. He's just been resurrected with phoenix tears." I put my hand out and let the fire dance from my fingers before I closed my fist, dousing the flame. "That's why he smells different. I'm the last of my kind."

Robby pulled me close and glanced at me before returning his gaze to the woman. "Sarah, this is Maddy. I used to work for her before the academy, and I thought she was my only remaining friend. But now I'm not so sure." He licked his lips and tried to smile. "Maddy, this is Sarah, my true mate."

Her eyebrows rose at the introduction, and she lowered the knife. Her teeth retracted. "The same

Sarah you texted nonstop the last winter you were here?”

The fact he told her about me gave me the depth of trust he placed in her and the fact his cheeks turned red at the question and a more natural smile formed on his lips gave me more of a warmth in my shoulder. Like he was fondly remembering those days, which was a far cry from why we were here now.

“Yes. This would be her.” He side-eyed me for a quick moment and then looked at Maddy. “Sarah killed the mother of vampires.” His chest puffed out with pride. “And in doing so, she wiped them all off the face of the earth.”

Maddy blinked at us and then leaned against the back counter, as if that fact relieved her of her tension more than anything else Robby said.

“I thought it was odd that your father showed up earlier tonight. We hadn’t planned for anything until the end of the month. But he did mention he was going to the cemetery, in case anyone came by looking for him.” She let out a nervous laugh. “I would have never guessed that someone was you.”

It was all a little too convenient, which meant it was probably a trap.

“You want a little something to eat before you confront your dad?” Maddy put the knife back under the counter for the next intruder.

Robby glanced at the array of pie slices under glass domes on the counter. “I’d love a slice of your apple pie.” He crossed to sit at the counter.

My mouth watered at the prospect. I took the seat next to him. “You can make that two.” I reached into the bag and pulled out another hundred-dollar bill and placed it on the counter.

At first, she just stared at me, but then she seemed to recover and waved at me. "Put your money away, girl. This is on me." She crossed to the pie display and lifted the glass top housing the apple pie.

The scent of fresh apples filled the room, making my mouth water.

She set two plates in front of us and then studied Robby. "You sure you want to do what you're thinking?" she asked after a moment.

Robby focused on the apple pie and didn't respond.

As angry as I was, the turmoil inside him kept trying to pull me under with the force of its undertow. A potent mixture of anguish and fury boiled under his calm exterior.

She didn't press him, but she didn't take her eyes off him either.

When he finished his pie, he met her gaze. "He needs to be stopped."

Maddy looked out at the darkness for a moment and then nodded in a way that told me she knew more of Robby's life at home than I did. "Still. He's your father." Her gaze cut back to him.

Robby's sarcastic laugh filled the room. "You were more of a parent to me than he's ever been."

Maddy gave him a sad smile. "He's been very different since..." She pressed her lips together. "Since he thought you died."

Robby glared at her. "He didn't mourn me. He didn't even take anything from my home in New York as a memento of me before he handed it over to someone else." Bitterness raked his voice. "And then he just handed me over to that vampire bitch, like I was nothing to him."

She bit her lip as she searched his face. "I think you mean more to him than you realize."

"Bullshit!" Robby slapped the counter, and it shook under the power radiating from him.

Maddy's eyes narrowed, but she didn't cower. "Don't throw that alpha bullshit at me, young man," she snapped and pointed her finger at him. "I've never let your father do it, and I certainly am not going to let you bully me into submission, either."

I immediately liked this woman. She had nerve and a backbone that I rarely saw in female werewolves. She caught my smile of approval and her lip tilted for a moment as she met my gaze.

Her laser focus returned to Robby. "Talk to him. I don't know if he has answers to your questions or not, but if you just go out there with the intent to kill the man, you'll never know the why behind his actions. And let me tell you, there is always a why. And sometimes it makes a difference."

"His actions killed my child," Robby growled.

Her eyes softened. "Make sure he knows that as well. I know there is something big and bitter between the two of you, but maybe there is hope for common ground. His treatment of you as a young one was abhorrent for most of us in the pack, but that wasn't always the way your father was. Some of us remember what he was like before he lost everything else."

Robby opened his mouth to argue, but Maddy just held up her hand.

"I know. He was always hard on you. I get it. But you didn't know your father before the agency got their claws into him. He used to be just like you. Full of heart and soul and looked for the good in others. He didn't have to command loyalty from the pack. At one time, we gave him our loyalty freely, just the way we do with you. But loss does nasty things to the best of people. Remember that before you pass your judgments on the man."

"It didn't ruin you," Robby said as he stood to leave.

She gave him a sad smile. "It ruined me in a different way." She glanced around the restaurant. "This place became my sanctuary."

He stared at her and then sighed. With a nod, he turned to go.

"Just promise me you'll hear him out before you deliver your version of justice?"

I glanced between the two of them, Robby with his back to her and Maddy staring at his broad shoulders, as if she could sway his actions. "I'll make sure we hear him out, but if this is a trap of some kind, I'm afraid most of this town will go up in flames. I will not let anyone cage us again." I needed her to know if there was a sting operation happening in the cemetery, it wouldn't end well for this town. Hell, I was prepared to go off like a megaton of explosives and would probably leave a crater the size of Manhattan behind if they cornered us.

"It's not a trap. It could be a way for that boy to finally find some peace." She nodded at Robby.

Robby glanced over his shoulder at her. "I'm not a boy, and right now, I'm waging war."

TAINTED MIND 3

I LEFT OUR BAGS IN the care of Maddy, and followed Robby out the door, catching up to him at the far side of the parking lot. I stepped into stride with him with a heart that thundered nearly as loud as the clanging in his chest. We walked in silence at a clip that made it hard for me to really get a good look at his hometown.

"She knows more than she's saying," Robby said as he slowed to a normal gait instead of the fury-fueled stride he had been using.

"You think it's a trap?"

He shook his head. "She wouldn't send me into a firefight." But even as he said the words, doubt layered over his certainty.

Being fucked over by the last person you'd expect plays havoc with your ability to trust in people. I knew that just as well as he did, and right now the only one who had my back one hundred percent of the time was Robby.

"I don't think she would either."

He cocked an eyebrow at me. I was usually the doubter of the two of us. But my gut told me she had the same aversion to seeing Robby hurt that I had. I had a feeling if given the chance, Maddy and I would become very close.

It took us a half hour of walking the winding streets to catch a glimpse of the rolling Allegany town cemetery. I scanned the mammoth green canvas dotted with concrete and spit-shined marble headstones that I was sure had some sweet epitaphs carved into them, and sighed, thinking of my parents' simple state-carved stone.

"My mother, sister, and brother are buried here." He pointed at the farthest hill. "Just over the crest of alpha hill over there."

"Alpha hill?"

He nodded. "All the alphas and their kin are buried there. My grandparents and great-grandparents are there, too." He glanced around us and then focused on the hill. "Don't be surprised if there's an empty grave already dug."

I stared at him. "That's fucking morbid."

We crested the hill and stopped. Neither of us were prepared for the sight before us. There indeed was a newly dug grave, but it was in a spot where there already was a headstone. I couldn't read it from this distance, but with the sorrow that shot through the mark, it had to be Robby's family's grave. His father sat next to the hole with an old cassette tape player next to him. In his arms, he held a shoebox to his chest, and he slowly rocked with it. Next to him sat the shovel he had used to dig the grave and still farther away was a revolver.

I must have made a noise, because he looked up in our direction with tears cutting paths down his dirt-laden cheeks. He reached out and pressed the play button on the player.

Whining came through the line and then a low chuckle, unlike either Robby or his father. I shivered at that vaguely familiar voice.

"Evie, what the hell are you doing?" rang out over the cemetery. It was so close to what Robby sounded like today that gooseflesh crawled up my arms.

"She's feeding, or have you never seen our kind feed?"

My gaze dropped to the box. I knew that voice, and it chilled me even more. That was the voice of the vampire who had professed to be my father. I nearly let out a crazy cackle at the irony of this particular moment.

"I suggest you think twice about that," the voice said. "I die. She dies." Those words were said with a smile, as if it were an impossible choice, and the bastard knew it would disarm Robby's father. "Besides, this is your penance for shacking up with her. The agency frowns upon that. Or were you so arrogant that you thought you'd get away with breaking the rules?"

"The agency kills vampires." His father's younger voice shook.

"Only those that the mother deems unworthy."

The *pew pew* of a tranquilizer gun sounded, and I stiffened, thinking we were indeed set up. A thud echoed, but Robby hadn't gone down and I hadn't felt the bite of a tranquilizer. I realized it had been on the recorder.

Another *pew pew* sound echoed and then the thud of a body hitting the ground sounded, followed by garbled sobs.

Robby's emotions slammed into me like a bulldozer. His confusion. His anger. His sorrow. All mixed in a dangerous cocktail.

Robby's father hit the off button. "The bastard taped it all. I don't think he ever told that to the agency, or if he did, they didn't give a damn. I listened to it all that night as I drove your mother to a facility. They took her to one of the secure floors that I didn't have access to for years. And they let that bastard go." He looked up at Robby. "I didn't think you'd want to hear your mother being turned or your brother or sister dying."

Robby didn't move or speak. It was almost as if he were in shock.

His father waved at the gun. "It's loaded with silver bullets. Do what you need to." His arm returned to cradle the shoebox as if it were a precious gift.

"What's in the shoebox?" I had to stifle the urge to giggle as the same line from one of Robby's favorite movies barreled through my brain, nearly short-circuiting the moment.

"What I could gather of her ashes today." He looked down at it and then at me, his gaze narrowing as it moved between the two of us. "How are you not dead?"

"I'm the last phoenix." I didn't feel compelled to lie to him or to keep my true identity hidden. I'm not sure whether it was the brokenness he radiated or what, but something in me shifted during the playing of that tape. Maddy had been right. There was a reason, and if we gave his father a chance, maybe we'd get the full picture. And maybe, as she said, it would make all the difference in the world.

Robby took a step forward, focused on the gun. It was my turn to keep him from doing something foolish. I grabbed his arm, and his head snapped toward me, surprised that I'd stop him.

He looked down at my hand and back. "Let go."

"No. There's more to the why than just that tape." My gaze bore into him. "And for me, that tape is enough to alter my perception. It should be enough for you as well."

"Bullshit."

He tried to yank his arm out of my grip, but I clamped down. "Why the fuck did he stay?" I cocked an eyebrow at him.

"They threatened to kill Robby," his father said to my hissed question. "If I ran, they'd find us. But if I remained and showed my loyalty to the agency, they'd let him live and eventually, they'd let me see my mate." He let out a harsh laugh. "What a fucking joke that turned out to be."

"What do you mean?" Robby asked.

"They didn't just want me to remain and be loyal. They wanted the pack, including you, under their control. They claimed legacy." He looked down at the box in his hand, petting it gently. "That's when I sought out a seer who refused to work with the agency." He glanced in the distance. "She was why I was so hard on you. She said you needed to be strong. Stronger than I ever was, because that was the only way you would survive. Only then would I be able to get retribution for the horrors that had been dealt to me. I had to thwart the union of you and your mate. Otherwise, all would be lost. If I was successful, the vampires would fall." He ground his teeth. "So, I robbed you of a true childhood and of true happiness to destroy a species." He shrugged. "And free my mate from the curse that turned her into something I didn't even recognize."

Robby stalked forward and picked up the gun. "You killed my beta."

"No. He's at the tattoo shop, drugged up until either you or I show up to free him."

"Phillip is alive?" I asked, shocked.

Robby's father nodded. "He's harmless, but he wasn't always honest in his dealings. The vampires wanted him taken care of, and if you hadn't shown up, I think Phillip would have been someone's meal."

"And Judy?"

His face hardened. "Judy was payback for what Terrance did to my family."

"She's dead?" My hands burst into flames.

"Afraid so." There wasn't an ounce of remorse in his voice, or his gaze, and Robby raised the gun, taking aim.

"So, every time you hit me, it was to make me stronger to further your cause?" Robby growled.

"Put the gun down," I commanded.

He roared at me, but put the gun on the ground. He shifted the moment the metal left his hands.

His father scrambled back at the sight of the massive golden-tipped black wolf. He was even bigger than he had been before his last resurrection in the city. One snap of his jaws could cut a grown man in half.

"What the hell?" His father squeezed the ash box against his chest.

"Robby, stand down." I hated giving that order. I knew that would slam a wedge between us, but if he killed his father, he would be no better than the man he hated.

His shift back to human form was instantaneous. "Fuck you," he yelled at me. "He killed our child. How the fuck can you forgive him?"

"He didn't know I was pregnant. But clearly, he expected me to protect you. He expected you to survive whatever went down." I waved at the spectacle before us and then conjured clothing back on Robby's bare ass. "Put your pain aside, and really look at your father. Listen to what he is trying to say."

His father's chin quivered as he looked at me. "I used you," he said to me.

"No shit, Sherlock," I snapped at him. "Did you know what I was?"

He shook his head. "I knew you had a unique power that would become known." He rolled his eyes and used finger quotes on one hand.

It reminded me so much of Robby that my brain stalled for a moment.

"But I didn't know you were a phoenix. But that makes perfect sense, with the endless search of the vampires for their unicorn."

"Harrison didn't say anything?" Robby asked.

"Not to me. That little shit reported directly to Terrance." He looked between the two of us. "If you're not going to kill me, I'd like to bury what's left of your mother in her empty casket."

Robby looked at the box. "That's really Mom?"

"Yes. And just for a moment before she turned to ash, she was your mother again." Another tear breached the corner of his eye. "She was my Evie."

My mark throbbed with loss.

"Did it hurt?" Robby asked with a voice rough from emotion.

Robby's father shook his head. "No, she looked relieved. Like her nightmare was finally over."

Robby nodded and pointed his chin toward the open grave.

His father jumped in and opened the head piece of the casket. He gently dumped the ash from the box onto the satin pillow. "I'll love you always," he whispered and then closed the casket. He climbed out and picked up the shovel.

I conjured two more shovels and handed one to Robby before I stepped forward to help his father. We worked in silence, with only the sound of shifting earth as we moved it from the pile back into the ground. When we finished, his father rolled the sod back over the grave, stomping it in where he cut so it didn't look quite as disturbed.

Then he did something that left me speechless. He dropped the shovel and pulled Robby into a hug.

"I love you, boy. I'm sorry I was never able to show it."

It took Robby a moment but then he hugged his father back. But that wasn't what caught us off guard. When they pulled away from each other, his father approached me and hugged me.

"I'm sorry I couldn't accept you before. That would have been a death sentence to you both." He kissed my cheek. "And thank you for keeping him safe." He pulled back and for the first time ever, I saw underneath the façade. I saw such a resemblance to Robby that my vision blurred behind a sudden sheen of tears.

He stepped away and picked up the tape machine, handing it to Robby. "They're going to be coming for me. So, you two need to get the hell out of here."

"Why would they come for you?" Robby looked at the cassette player.

His father's smile turned dark. "Because I left Terrance a gift. His niece's head on his desk."

TAINTED MIND 4

I SHUDDERED FROM THE VISUAL he painted. We couldn't leave him to the agency. They'd kill him in a New York minute. "We want to destroy the agency." I met his father's gaze.

"You've fulfilled your destiny. Go find a nice corner of the world and settle down. Start a family where it's safe." His eyes held the sadness as they dropped to my belly and then met my gaze.

It was an appealing thought, but I knew better. I pursed my lips and glanced at Robby. "Nowhere is safe as long as the agency exists."

"You know as long as we're alive, they'll hunt us," Robby added. "Just tell us where Terrance is, and we'll take care of this."

Robby's father laughed in a way that left me cold. "Terrance isn't the only one pulling the strings. Even though you took a big chunk of their benefactors out, there are still others making the puppets dance. It's not as easy as eliminating Terrance. If it were, he'd have been dead a long time ago—by my hand."

I glanced at Robby, and he met my gaze. I saw the same hesitation in him that coursed through me. We couldn't let the agency get hold of his father. That was as good as killing him ourselves. Robby had lost enough. Losing his father after finding out the man had sacrificed everything to protect him wasn't in his makeup. Yes, his father had been a bastard, but now that he knew what drove his father, he couldn't fault him. He couldn't lose his only living relative.

His eyes screamed for me to understand.

I reached out and took his hand, squeezing it to convey that I understood and that I agreed with him.

"I'm not going to just leave you to the agency." Robby swiveled his gaze to his father.

"I didn't go through all this to have them cage or kill you. Now go." His father pointed toward town.

Robby shook his head and looked at me before jutting his chin at his father. "Compel him to come with us."

It wasn't a request either. I could feel Robby's alpha punch with it. Although he didn't need to do that, I understood. If I had any feelings that would cause me to hesitate, he wanted them overridden.

"Don't." His father's face turned almost feral.

"Come with us." I pushed my compelling power with the words, and his father's expression turned dark. Fury built behind his eyes, just the way it did when I compelled Robby. "He hates it too, but I only do it to keep those we care about safe."

"We can't go home," Robert Senior said through clenched teeth.

"I have no intention of going to our house." Robby looked at him as we started to walk back the way we came. "I have contingencies in place, too."

"You're not dragging anyone else into this," Robby's father snapped as he fell in line with us. Each of his steps were similar to the march of an angry toddler. If we had been inside a house, I was sure the pounding of each footfall would be felt all throughout the structure.

"She's apparently already involved." Robby glanced at his father. "Maddy's the one who practically begged me not to do anything rash."

His father's features smoothed in understanding. "We cannot involve her any more than we already have. And we should get as far from this place as possible. We do not want to bring the wrath of the agency here, not with the pack so vulnerable." Robert Senior's voice lowered as he glanced around. He frowned. "I may have already compromised the pack by coming here, but I knew you wouldn't be foolish enough to march into headquarters, demanding to see your dear old dad."

Robby gave him a side-eye. "You predicted I would come here?"

Robert Senior smiled and nodded. "You're smart, and although you can be pigheaded like me, you don't react to impulses." He glanced at me. "If you did, you would have taken her a long time ago." He chuckled. "I'll give you that much. Your self-restraint is far superior to mine. Fifteen years as her partner...I have no idea how you did it."

"They would have killed her. That's what kept my hands in my pockets and my pants on," Robby said. "And as far as the damn agency, I plan on bringing my wrath to them." Robby didn't turn back. "But we will need our things, and a car, and Sarah can't conjure a car just like that." He snapped his fingers. "As it is, she used her magic back at the cemetery, so her signature is here. So, I agree we have to get away, but we need wheels that are not associated with us."

"And then where are we going?" his father asked.

"The tattoo parlor," Robby said.

"Phillip?" I asked as I slowed. "We really shouldn't pull him into this mess." I didn't want anyone's blood on my hands.

Robby nodded. "He's already involved. And it's time to gather our troops to take down this behemoth."

I could see the neon sign for the diner poking out of the trees less than a mile away. It would take us no time to get there and grab our things. Getting a car would be more of a challenge.

His father plugged on in silence for a few minutes as he chewed on the side of his bottom lip, much like Robby did when he was deep in thought. "I don't have anyone on my side. I've played this close to the vest for a reason," his father finally said as the diner came into view.

Robby glanced at him. "Then it's good that Johnson had a few pack members on his side."

"I doubt he'll back us after what I did to his wife."

It was a valid point, and one we'd have to cross when everyone was face-to-face. "He'll want answers for that damn elixir you gave him first," I said.

Robby's father glanced at me with his eyebrows arched and his mouth popped open in a little O.

"Yeah, we know about that. Was that supposed to be meant for me?" Robby glared at him as his hostility reared its ugly head.

"It was. But *that* wasn't *my* brainchild. I just didn't put up the same roadblocks when it was Johnson in the alpha position as I had with you. I stalled for years, but I applied just enough pressure on you to meet Judy to keep Terrance happy. They wanted me to hold back the alpha position, to tie it up with the provision of getting married. That was one battle I won. I told them you had earned it, and if I held it up, there would be mutiny from the entire pack." He glanced at me and then back at Robby. "They wanted more leverage over me, and they were tired of my stalling."

"They didn't suspect anything about us?" Robby waved his finger between the two of us.

His father let out a full-bodied laugh that was an echo of his son's. "No fucking way. With your history, they just assumed you liked being a playboy. As far as you and I were concerned, I explained that we did not see eye-to-eye on anything. That we had a combative relationship at best, but you were still my blood.”

“Then why did they make us partners?” I asked.

“Because I told them to. I told them you were the strongest witch at the school and my son, the future alpha of my pack, needed to be partnered with the strongest of the candidates despite you being a girl.” He shrugged. “I thought it would be a harder sell, but because I had legacy status that transferred to my son, they didn’t squawk that bad. My partner-matching skills didn’t go unnoticed either. You turned out to be the best students at the academy. I wasn’t so sure after that incident your first semester.” He glanced at me. “But it was all bullshit. You see, I knew my son. If I hadn’t pulled something so unconventionally drastic, he would have done the same stupid thing I did. I also knew he would never put you in danger. If I hadn’t done what I did, the two of you would have been destroyed by the agency.”

Robby stopped before we reached the door and turned to his father. “That vampire asshole fucked me up to the point I have a gnarly case of PTSD.” He stared his father down. “And you knew that bastard had me.”

Oh, here we go. Robby’s cheeks turned red as he let his frustrations surface.

“That bastard informed me you died by her hand.” He hooked his thumb at me. “I lost my shit for a while, too.”

Robby narrowed his eyes. “Johnson said you almost immediately gave him the alpha spot and my fucking house in New York. You don't lose your shit. Ever."

His father let out the same sardonic laugh as Robby. "I could not bring myself to step inside your house. I went to Johnson's wedding and had to leave early because if I stayed too long, I'd rip Judy to shreds in front of everyone. You have no concept of what it's been like battling with you all these years and keeping up fucking pretenses so they wouldn't kill you. And when you came down those stairs, I nearly forgot my goal."

"But you still toed the same line. Didn't you?" Robby stepped closer to his father, almost chest to chest. His father was an inch shorter than Robby this close together, and he stared down his nose at the man. "You still handed us over."

"Yes. And now all vampires are wiped off the fucking planet."

"Not all." I smiled at him and let my teeth come out.

He blinked at me. "The compelling thing isn't the phoenix part of you?" His voice cracked, as if I had just let loose a vicious monster.

I retracted my teeth.

"No." I glanced at Robby, as though he would have the answer. "At least not that I am aware of."

"Vampires compel. That wasn't one of the phoenix's character traits they taught us in school," Robby said. "But she doesn't crave blood since we killed that bitch, and that reddish tint in her eyes is gone. It seems she just has the teeth at this point." His lips tilted into a smile of sorts. "But I have no idea. She withstands the daylight. She wasn't compelled by either her maker or the mother of vampires, and she can compel even with the agency charms on. So maybe it is the phoenix that drives her unique set of power.”

“Do you want me to move a table out here to the parking lot so the entire town can hear you?” Maddy asked from the doorway.

I hadn’t even heard the bell over the door and spun toward her in surprise. I could not let myself get that engrossed in conversation when we were being hunted. “We’re just going to get our things and be on our way,” I said.

She cocked an eyebrow at me. “You can go out the back.” She held the door open and waved us inside. It seemed a bit odd, but Robby’s father was the first to pass her.

“I don’t want to involve you,” he said softly and with such warmth that I immediately got the hint. There was more to the two of them than just pack members. A lot more.

“It’s a little late for that, don’t you think?” She ran her hand down his arm as he moved past her, and their fingers touched before he pulled away to let us inside.

Robby didn’t catch it. He just walked into the dim diner behind his father. I followed, and Maddy shut and locked the door, turning the sign to Closed.

She turned and met Robby’s gaze. “Thank you for giving him a chance to explain. I wasn’t sure I’d be able to handle another loss in my life.”

I smirked at her and pressed my lips together as Robby’s glance shot to his father and then to Maddy again.

“Did he lose his shit when he thought I was dead?” he asked.

I couldn't believe those were the first words out of his mouth. Especially with the ramifications of her words.

"Yes. He was more of a mess than I was when I lost my husband."

I gathered from her reference and Robby pulling back as if her words were a slap, he had been witness to her loss.

After a few blinks, Robby crossed his arms. "So, the bastard shed a tear?"

God. It seemed the man didn't know the first thing about forgiveness. "Don't be such an ass, Robby," I snapped at him.

"I'm sorry to say but that kind of does run in the family," his father said with a tilted grin.

"Seriously?" I looked at the two of them. "He's too caught up in his little hissy fit to realize what is going on here."

Robby's forehead crunched at me in his "I don't get what you're saying" look.

I started to laugh. "Maddy and your father." I waved toward the two who hadn't quite hugged, but they stood closer than normal people stand.

"No." Robby drew out the word but even as he said it, his gaze bounced between the two of them as if they had committed an atrocious sin. "But...Mom?"

"Has not been Mom since the day they locked her up, and today, you two set her free." He glanced at Maddy and took her hand in his. "Maddy always shot straight with me, even if I didn't like what she was saying. And after I thought I lost you, I went to the only person on earth who really knew what the hell was going on inside my head." He took a breath. "I shouldn't have confided in her and put her in danger, but I needed someone to lean on for a change."

I snorted. The look that passed between them was much more than just leaning on someone. It wasn't quite the same way Robby looked at me, but there was an underlying sexual tension between them.

"So, you formed an alliance, knowing I would go to her." Robby still didn't get it.

"Robby, your dad has found someone to share his life with." Sometimes the man could be denser than dirt.

"It's not like that," Maddy was quick to say, and the surprise on Robert Sr.'s face was more telling than words.

Robby's eyes widened as they bounced between the elders in the room. "You're sleeping together?" His voice cracked.

Maddy's cheeks reddened. "We are consenting adults. Besides, I want that damn agency taken down as much as he does." She looked at Robby's father. "And you need to get out of here before they show up to skin your hide." She reached into her pocket and pulled out a set of keys. "The truck is out back, all gassed up." She stepped closer and pressed her lips to his. "Don't go getting yourself killed, understand?"

"Yes, ma'am." Robert Sr. smiled and headed for the door that led to the kitchen. "You coming?" he asked when Robby and I just stared after him.

I grabbed our bags and followed, but before I passed Maddy, she grabbed my arm. "Keep them safe," she said without a trace of the humor she had shown Robby's father a moment before.

It was a tall order. "You know what we are going up against?"

She nodded.

"Then you know our odds. I'll do what I can, but no matter what, Robby and I are not getting locked up again. If they try, I will unleash hell despite the collateral damage."

She blinked and glanced at Robby's father with a slow nod. She understood the odds of all of us walking back into town was slim, but that didn't stop her from hoping, no matter how insane the chances seemed.

TAINTED MIND 5

WHEN WE STEPPPED OUT INTO the dark alley behind the restaurant, I stopped and stared at the old truck. It looked like an antique made of blue paint and rust, a tad beat up, but a classic all the same. Robby's father took the driver's side, and I slid onto the old Ford's bench seat, squished between the two men. Robby took the bags and slid them in the space behind the seat, which was barely big enough to ingest both duffels.

Robby's father glanced at me. "No more magic for a while, okay?"

I nodded. The agency could track that shit, and none of us wanted a showdown before we were ready. "Johnson may try to take you out," I said as we all waved at Maddy, standing backlit in the doorway.

"I'm aware." He pulled out onto the road.

We drove in silence, Robby brooding on one side of me with his arms crossed and his father looking as though he had a thousand thoughts running through his head but saying nothing.

"How did you get out here?" he asked as he pulled out on the highway.

"We bribed a cab driver," Robby said, still studying the scenery.

"And you don't think that cab driver will blab about it all over the place?" He barked the question, as if we had done the most asinine of things.

I sent a glare in his direction. "If anyone questions the cab driver, he will only remember a young single mother and her son whose car was stolen in the city."

He tilted his chin toward his chest as if he were admonishing himself for jumping to a conclusion before asking more questions. When he caught me still staring at him, he nodded.

"Mr. Young. Neither of us are idiots." Saying his surname felt weird on my tongue, but I could not bring myself to call him Robert. It was too close to Robby, and I knew I would confuse names at the most inopportune moment. "We may have enough scars to fuck us up for a long time, but we are good at covering our tracks."

He snorted at me with a sideways glare. "You walked out of that townhouse without any protections in place."

I opened my mouth and immediately closed it. He was right. Neither of us were thinking straight. We thought Johnson was dead. "How did you make Judy and Robby think Johnson was dead?"

His lip twerked into a partial smile. "If you remember, I had a very strong witch as a partner, and he was just as disgusted with the agency as I was. He taught me some interesting spells over the years. And one was the potion to break a mark and hide the person from the psychic connections to their mate, and the pack. It's a good way to get people out."

Robby glanced at him. "What do you mean, out?"

Robby's father stared out the window. "Out of the agency. Agents tagged for destruction. I've helped a few escape before the agency found them. If I hadn't, they would have ended up six feet under. I guess you could say it was a witness protection kind of thing." He glanced over at his son. "Chandler was very much against killing other agents, and after your mother, I wasn't inclined to give him any grief. I learned enough before he died to be able to do it a few times since then." He chewed his bottom lip. "Unfortunately, the agency always requires a body, so the ones they got were torn up beyond recognition."

"Johnson wanted out?" I asked.

"No. I needed him out of the game. And I needed a reason to see Judy. That sting wasn't approved by the agency, and Phillip wasn't supposed to be breathing. I gave him a pass when he told me Judy had brought a redheaded chick to the tattoo parlor." He wiped his face. "Only a handful of agents were involved. If I had pushed that up the chain, Terrance would have told me to turn a blind eye on it and figured out another way to take you two down that didn't involve his niece. The people I used were told Judy was aiding and abetting one of our most wanted criminals." His hands shifted on the wheel. "And I knew the vampires were looking for the one who killed that vampire douchebag. Which I surmised was you." He nodded his head toward me. "I was going to use Johnson as a poker chip to get you to kill the mother of vampires, but when I saw Robby, I almost lost sight of everything."

Robby snorted next to me. "You could have fooled me."

His father glanced at me. "And then you with your compelling shit. You almost ruined it all. But after seeing you two tranquilized on the street, I took you two and Judy in. I figured if you protected him before, you'd do it again."

"He died."

The truck swerved a little, and he glanced at me.

"I brought him back." I pointed toward the road. "Which is why he is fucking mammoth now."

"You turned him?"

"No, you asshole, phoenix tears," Robby said. "Don't you remember anything from the academy?"

"I must have been screwing around with your mother during that lesson." His cheeks turned a rosy color as he shifted in the seat and pressed harder on the gas pedal.

"We don't need a ticket," Robby muttered. "And really?"

His father dialed back the speed down to a reasonable amount over the limit but not high enough for a cop to pull out after us. "I am not that different than you are, Robert."

"It's Robby," he snapped.

The sigh that came from his father pulled a smirk to my lips.

"Look, can we ditch the attitude for a change?" Robert Senior asked.

Robby glowered in the seat next to me. "Fine," he mumbled after a moment. "But if Johnson wants to throw a punch, I'm not stopping him."

"Fair enough."

On the far side of the highway, a couple of speeding sedans caught our attention.

"That was a bit faster than I anticipated," his father said. "Thankfully, we aren't alone on the highway." He didn't have to say the rest. If we had been alone, it would have been easy to pick us back up on the flip side.

"Did you happen to pick up the gun?" He glanced at Robby.

Robby reached around to the small of his back and pulled out the revolver, showing it to his father before he stowed it in the glove compartment. "Maybe we should get off the highway."

"They would expect that. There's less traffic. This is better, with the few other cars traveling this late. It's not conspicuous."

"And it's faster," I added. I wanted to get where I felt reasonably safe and not like a sitting duck.

"It will be daylight before we reach the city." Robert Senior looked at me.

"Daywalker. Remember?" I put my hand up and then pointed to my chest.

"Sorry. It's been a few days since I slept."

"Maybe I should be driving." Robby glanced around me at his father.

His father tilted his head as he watched the road before us, as if he were weighing his exhaustion with the offer. "You can't park this car anywhere near the tattoo place or your apartment." He glanced at Robby.

"I'll park it in the Bronx, and we can clean out the glove box and leave it unlocked, with the keys in it." He grinned at his father. "And you can text Maddy to report it stolen."

"Sounds like a plan." His father navigated to the breakdown lane, and they did the switch. We were underway in less than a minute toward what could be certain disaster.

6

TAINTED MIND 6

WE ARRIVED AS THE SUN crested the horizon, painting the city in that yellow morning hue that made the buildings look as if they were on fire. I shifted in the seat at the sight, with a feeling of foreboding filling me. I didn't want to actually destroy New York City, but in my heart, I knew I might not have a choice.

Robby pulled off the highway and parked the truck in an alley. He wiped down the steering wheel with one of the shirts in the bag and did the same to the door handle before he leaned over and shook his father awake.

"Dad, we're here." When his father lifted his head and glanced around, Robby shoved the shirt at him. "Wipe off your prints and empty that glove box."

He groggily took the shirt and wiped down the dashboard and door before he used the cloth to open the glove compartment. He handed Robby the gun before he sifted through the paperwork and left only the vehicle's manual in there. He stuffed the rest into the bag with the money and stepped out of the vehicle.

When I slid to the open door, he offered me his hand to help me out of the truck. I didn't refuse. He slipped by me and wiped the seat before transferring the cloth back to Robby, who did the same.

Robert Senior used his elbow to close the door and Robby used the cloth before he shoved it in the bag with the rest of our stuff. With the key still hanging in the ignition, and the doors unlocked, we walked away from the truck.

"How long do you figure the truck will sit there?" I kept my voice low enough so it wouldn't echo off the walls.

Robby and his father exchanged a glance.

"I give it an hour," Robert Senior said.

Robby glanced at his watch. "That's probably right."

We spotted a subway station and climbed down to the platform and waited for the next train heading downtown toward Brooklyn to arrive. Thankfully it was early enough that the train was nearly empty when it arrived and remained sparsely populated for the entire ride. The stop we exited on was only a few blocks away from the tattoo parlor. Robert Senior led us down a maze of alleys and then stopped at a door. He knocked on the side door that my vampire father had bolted out of the night I first saw him in Phillip's tattoo chair. He knocked again, in the same light pattern as before.

A moment later, the door swung open. Phillip eyed Robby's father and then the two of us behind him before scowling at us and widening the opening for us to enter. As soon as the door was locked and secured behind us, Phillip spun to face us.

"You have no idea what a pain in the ass your friend has been," Phillip said to Robby's father and then he glanced at us, narrowing his eyes and clenching his jaw. "I thought you said all the vampires would be taken care of?"

"They were. She's not just a vampire."

"She fucking smells like one." Phillip glared at me.

I sighed. "I was the one who warned you to get out."

His brow furrowed.

I rolled my eyes, remembering I compelled him to forget us. "Remember everything," I commanded.

Phillip's eyelids fluttered as if he were short-circuiting, and I wondered whether that was what I looked like when Cassius commanded the same of me. Finally, his eyes widened. "The wolf tattoo," he whispered and then grinned. "And the meal that has left me satiated for much longer than anything I've ever tasted before."

Robert Senior's gaze snapped to me.

"I traded a pint for a week." I shrugged, not very proud of the trade, but it was necessary. "I needed blood and there was no way I was biting your son again. Phillip obliged."

Phillip's eyes narrowed. "Why would you alter my memories like that?" He blinked. "And how the hell could you compel me at all? I have the same tattoo as your friends."

"First, for your safety and ours, altering your memories was necessary." Robby answered the first question for me and bypassed the second. "Now, if you'll just bring me to Johnson." He waved his hand forward for Phillip to lead the way.

"Not until she answers my question." Phillip crossed his arms, jutting his chin at me.

"I am more than just a vampire. The agency charms never worked with me. Since I was turned, I could compel almost everyone."

"Almost?" He cocked an eyebrow.

"I couldn't compel my maker."

"Stop stalling and take us to Johnson," Robby's father interjected.

"I don't like your tone." Phillip turned away toward the tattoo parlor.

"I don't give a damn whether you like our tone or not. I want to see my beta. Now," Robby growled. His teeth appeared.

I reached out, touching his arm, and his teeth transformed back to normal. "Phillip, please. If someone hears us, we're all dead."

"Fine." He pointed toward the stairwell leading both upward and downward on the far wall. "He's downstairs."

"After you." Robert Senior waved him forward.

Phillip pressed his lips together and led the way.

"What's upstairs?" I asked as we followed.

"My apartment," Phillip said. "I own the building," he added.

"Nice." We once worked in the same building we slept in, and although the amount of people had been overwhelming, the commute was awesome. The basement of the building, however, was not as nice as one would think. It was oddly shaped, with one side where the stairs descended being full size and the other side tapered to a small crawl space. "What's up with this?" I waved at the narrowing space.

"Subway tunnels." Phillip gave me a shrug. "Your friend is in there." He pointed at a solid door with a small window. "He woke up and nearly tore the room apart, trying to get out."

I stepped up to the door and looked in. Johnson sat against the far wall, glaring at the floor. His knuckles were scabbed over, but the floor was sprayed with droplets and the walls were dented and smeared with blood. I knocked on the window, and his gaze shot to the glass. The irritation smoothed out as he stared at me. Johnson climbed to his feet and started for the door.

"Where's Judy?" he asked.

His voice was muffled in the hallway, even to my sensitive ears. I just shook my head, and he stopped walking. His eyes turned sad.

I tried the door, but the handle didn't budge. "Is there a key?" I glanced back at Phillip.

He reached in his pocket, pulled out a key, and handed it to me. I slid it in the keyhole and disengaged the lock. Without waiting for anyone to tell me it was okay, I pulled the door back and stepped inside, crossing to Johnson to give him a hug.

He clung to me much the same way Judy had when she thought he was dead, but no tears fell from his eyes.

"How?"

"I killed her," Robert Senior said from the hallway. "And it's just the start of retribution for my family." He stood tall, without an ounce of remorse in his eyes.

A growl rumbled in Johnson's throat, and he tried to break away from me, but I tightened my hug. "I'm sorry she's gone," I whispered in his ear.

Robby reacted. He jabbed a punch right into the side of his father's face. "That's for Judy," he said with enough venom in his voice for me to turn his way.

Robert Senior stumbled to the side and caught himself before he fell over. He didn't retaliate for the strike, even though I saw a flash of irritation pass over his face before he schooled his expression into that neutral look that always annoyed me. It was as if the man didn't know how to show emotion. I blinked at the thought and realized he had been suppressing so much for so long that he probably didn't know how to show it. What we had witnessed in the graveyard was a fluke.

Johnson struggled in my grip. He had become a lot stronger than he had been back at the academy and nearly broke my hold.

"The bastard drugged me to marry her and then killed her?" Johnson snarled, looking from Robby to his father as he continued to try to get me to let go without hurting me.

"I didn't drug you. Her parents did. I just went along with it." Robert Senior rubbed his cheek where Robby's fist had landed.

"Calm down," I whispered. It wasn't a request, and the glare I received in response made me feel as shitty as I had when I put him to sleep the night we came to this very tattoo parlor with Judy.

"I fucking hate you for doing that. He deserves to be beat to death for what he's done. I am the alpha of the pack, and he crossed the line," Johnson snarled.

"You are dead to the pack. I made sure the bonds you held were severed before I took care of Judy." Robert Senior's eyes were as cold as the basement chill penetrating my bones.

"What the fuck did you do to me?" Johnson growled.

"I kept you safe." He pointed at Johnson. "You would have paid the price for not taking out Phillip. I took that call and had to do a hell of a lot to cover that shit up. Based on the magical signatures and where they were found, I had a hunch you were helping Sarah, too, and at that time, I was still hell-bent on killing her for Robby. But I wasn't willing to see you die. You've been protecting Robby for as long as I've known you, and that made you as close to a son as anything. Judy would have walked, but you would have died for the transgression. So, I cast a spell that breaks all bonds. It's something I've used from time to time to get people out before the agency had a chance to kill them. And then I drugged you and asked Phillip to keep you locked up until I got back."

He blinked at Robby's father, and his eyebrows rose. "What?"

Robert Senior's lips formed into a cold smile. "I'm not loyal to the agency like I had you all believing. I've saved a few shifters and witches alike over the years."

He looked at Robby and waved to Robert Senior. "Did you know?"

Robby laughed and shook his head. "I've been in the dark, just like you. There seems to be only one other person in the pack who knew, but that's only because Cassius told him I was dead, and he needed a friend."

"Are you working with your father?" Johnson's voice cracked as he stared between the two of them.

Robby shrugged. "I'm still processing everything."

"After all he has done, you're trusting him?" he clarified.

"We are," I said before Robby could answer. "It's a long story, and if Phillip has any human food up in his apartment, I'll whip something up for us all while we catch you up to speed." I glanced at Phillip.

"You're in luck. I went shopping so I could feed this barbaric fool." He waved at Johnson. "You're going to have to do some repairs in here for me." He pointed to the state of the room. The furniture had been smashed. The mattress had been shredded to tiny bits, and I wasn't sure what the other items were, only that they were made of wood because splinters were everywhere.

"Fuck you," Johnson growled.

Phillip raised an eyebrow and licked his lips before he smiled. "If that's what you're into…"

"Jesus," Johnson muttered and stomped up the stairs. He kept going until he got to the top and then the sound of a door splintering filled the space.

Phillip's smile turned into a scowl.

"We'll fix it." I sailed past the three of them before Johnson decided to destroy Phillip's apartment.

7

TAINTED MIND 7

WE ALL POURED INTO PHILLIP'S apartment. It covered the entire second and third floor of the building in an open concept that reminded me a little of the apartment in the movie *Ghost*. Johnson had stripped on his way through the living room, leaving a trail of clothing dropped up the stairs all the way to the bathroom door. The shower went on, and I turned toward the others.

"Couldn't he have undressed in the bathroom?" Phillip's voice was filled with disgust as he picked up the clothing with only his pointer finger and thumb.

I was thoroughly amused as he piled the clothing in an open trash can near the stairs;

then he disappeared down the upper hall and came back, dumping a pair of sweatpants and a sweatshirt outside the bathroom door.

Phillip's expression seemed pained, and he glared at us as he descended the stairs. "I did not sign up for this shit." His hands found his waist, making him look more like an angry housewife rather than an ancient soul sucker. He looked at the sun streaking through the windows and then me standing in the direct light. His eyes narrowed. "What exactly are you?"

I faced the light, letting it bathe my face before I looked over my shoulders at him. "I am the last of my kind."

Phillip glanced at Robert Senior. "The last vampire?"

I held my hands out and let the fire come forth. It danced across my fingertips, and I played with it as if it were an extension of myself as I stared at him. "Technically, yes. But more importantly, I am the last phoenix."

Phillip stumbled to the nearest seat. He mumbled words in an ancient language that I had no idea what they meant. And then he slid off the cushion on to his knees and bowed his head as if I were some kind of royalty.

"Get up," I hissed.

Phillip's gaze snapped to mine, and he scrambled to his feet. "I-I'm sorry. I did not mean to anger you," he stuttered.

I wiped my face. "I'm not royalty. Please do not treat me that way."

The shower went off and the door opened. Johnson didn't step out; instead, his hand shot out, snatching the clothing on the floor before he slammed the door closed again. I wasn't sure that Phillip's clothing would fit Johnson. I mean, he was tall enough, but his shoulders were not the width of Johnson's.

When Johnson came out with only the sweatpants on, my lips twitched into a smirk.

"This doesn't fit." He tossed the sweatshirt to Phillip. His angry gaze locked on mine. "Think you could conjure me a shirt?"

"No," Robby and his father said in unison.

"No magic," Robby's father clarified. "It can be tracked."

Johnson sat down on the couch. "You going to cook while they fill me in?"

The cocky way he said it had me narrowing my eyes. "Maybe I'll just let you cook for us, since we both died yesterday."

He blinked and his jaw slowly dropped. He glanced at Robby for confirmation and got a nod in return.

"But all the other vampires walking the earth got toasted." I grinned at him.

"Manny?" he asked.

A lump formed in my throat. I hadn't considered Manny. I hope he embraced the freedom before he blinked out of existence.

"Yeah." Robby nodded. "And it seems my mother turned to ash, too."

Johnson's expression fell, and he glanced at Robby's father. "But..."

"She didn't die that night." Those words hung on the air like a dark cloud.

"She's been locked up this whole time?" His voice cracked.

"Yes." Robert Senior took a deep breath, studying his hands. "And I've had to do some atrocious things over the years to keep Robby and the pack safe." He looked up at Johnson. "Robby's the rightful alpha of our pack." He leaned back in his seat.

"You made me alpha." Johnson narrowed his gaze.

Robert Senior shrugged. "Neither of you can claim that position until we take down the agency. But this time, you'll have to fight for it."

Johnson let out a laugh. "I'm not fighting my best friend. Besides, have you seen his wolf?" He pointed his thumb toward Robby.

Robby quietly took all the conversation in. He hadn't commented on whether he wanted alpha rights back or not. But he was chewing his bottom lip, as if he were considering it. He met my gaze. "You want help in the kitchen?" he asked, avoiding this conversation altogether.

Phillip took us into the kitchen. "Pastas and sauces are in the cabinets near the sink. Meats in the freezer. Eggs and bacon in the refrigerator." He opened and closed each place for us to get a look at what he had available. "Pots and pans are under the stove. Plates and glasses are in the cabinet near the refrigerator."

I couldn't decide on what I wanted to eat and glanced at Phillip. "What would you like?"

He grinned and that twinkle found his eyes again. "I'd like another taste of you."

Robby growled low.

Phillip put his hands up. "She asked."

"Human food, Phillip." I rolled my eyes at him and waved at the cabinets.

"Since I don't have the ingredients for those delectable strawberry pancakes you conjured, I'll go for anything with bacon. Bacon burgers, eggs and bacon, steaks wrapped in bacon. Whatever you're in the mood for, my lady." He gave me a smile and a hint of a bow, but stopped when I scowled at him.

"Bacon. Got it." I waved him away and looked at the options. Three werewolves, one soul eater, and me. What was there that was going to satiate us enough at one time?

"BLTs?" Robby asked as he peered in the refrigerator from behind my shoulder.

"Eh." I wasn't all that into a bacon, lettuce, and tomato sandwich. I wanted something hardier. "I'm thinking a monster omelet." I took out the eggs, bacon, shredded cheese, tomatoes, and a pepper that I found in the refrigerator. I handed the vegetables to Robby. "Can you chop these up while I find a couple pans?"

"Sure." Robby rummaged through the drawers, looking for a knife and cutting board, and took the far counter to chop the tomato and pepper.

I found a bowl and cracked all twelve eggs into it, grabbed a fork out of the silverware drawer, and whisked it like it was my mortal enemy. I added a little water to the mix to fluff the beaten eggs up a little more.

While Robby chopped up the vegetables, I put the bacon, sandwiched between paper towels, into the microwave.

When Robby was done cutting the pepper, I added that to a large fry pan, sautéing them with butter. When they were soft, I poured the eggs into the pan and waited. I moved some of the edges in, tilting the pan so the loose egg would fill the gap until most of it was solid. I picked up the pan and moved it back and forth, watching as the omelet slid in the pan easily, and then I jerked the pan upward, and the omelet flipped up into the air. I caught it in the pan and smiled at Robby as the uncooked side sizzled.

I sprinkled the cheese all over the omelet and then added the tomatoes over half of the giant dish. Then I carefully folded it over and waited a minute to make sure the cheese had melted before transferring it to the largest plate I could find. I sliced it into five even chunks while Robby got the bacon and put it on the same serving plate.

The ease at which we worked together in the kitchen was a testament to our compatibility. We didn't stumble over each other at all. It was the perfect coordination of a meal, and I smiled at him as he grabbed five plates and forks. We headed back into the living room, where Robby's father had been reliving the last few days with Johnson and Phillip.

Outside of that one punch Robby delivered, no one else started anything physical. The tension in the room still made my skin itch, but I gave Johnson props for not trying to level Robert Senior at least once. But I had held him back during those pivotal moments of fury and ordered him to calm down.

I would have done much more than that had he not had that tape playing for us. I was ready to annihilate the man without hearing his side of things, despite what I told Maddy.

Everyone perked up when I set the platter on the table. No one spoke; we all just took a piece of the omelet and a stack of bacon, and settled in our seats to shovel the food into our mouths. When the last empty plate was stacked on the platter, I glanced around at everyone.

"What's the plan?" My gaze fell to Robert Senior because he seemed to have the most intel.

"Take it down. All of it. Every last agent, from the custodians all the way to Terrance and his benefactors."

"No." Johnson shook his head. "I have people who were ready to defy orders and go after the vampires. We need manpower."

"I don't think that's such a good idea," I said. "They'll try to kill us." I pointed between Robby and me. "We're on the most wanted list. Or have you forgotten?"

Phillip raised an eyebrow. "I know plenty of supernaturals who would love to see the agency burn to the ground." He smiled at me.

"Yeah, and they'd probably be just as likely to hand us over for the bounty on our heads," I said. "While I am not totally sure about you having my back, I trust Robby and Johnson explicitly."

"You can trust me," Phillip said.

"I don't expect your trust," Robert Senior said. "But I do expect your cooperation."

Robby laughed. "You are no longer the boss, with the agency backing." He pointed at his father and leaned forward. "I expect *your* cooperation."

"You've already used us as pawns in your game," Johnson added and then looked at me. "The people I'm talking about are pack members."

"Pack members still loyal to the idea of the agency. The only one I'll consider is anyone who allowed Phillip to stay alive. Basically, anyone who was an insider who got the same tattoo." Anyone who chose to get the tattoo instead of relying on the agency charms was bypassing the rules.

Johnson wiped his face. "No one else knows about the tattoos."

I bit my lip, thinking on everything that Robby's father had said since we decided not to annihilate him in the cemetery. "You said the vampires were by far the largest species running the agency. What else do we have to deal with?" My mind perused over the supernaturals we've brought in over the years.

Robert Senior stared at me. "There's only one who pulls all the strings, even that of the vampires." He wiped his face. "But there is nothing that will kill it." He stared at me. "Nothing except the fire of a phoenix, which is probably why the vampires were aggressively hunting you down. None of them liked to be ordered around. Neither do shifters, or witches, and humans are equally as annoyed by it."

"By what?" I couldn't think of anything beyond a high-ranking demon, but even that could be killed by certain ancient types of metals.

"Her name is Aellope. She's a harpyiai."

I cocked my head, trying to pull any information on what a harpyiai was from the archives in my brain. I came up empty. It wasn't anything we had been taught about at the academy or encountered in the streets. So, beyond what Robby's father told us, we were in the blind.

Phillip paled in a way that drew my attention.

"Phillip, what is it?"

His gaze jumped to mine. "Harpyiai tortures souls on the way to hell. They feed on pain and blood and fear, the way I feed on your essence. They are the reason civilizations have fallen, and nothing but righteous fire can destroy them. I've lived long enough to have seen one fall, but only after all those around them were destroyed in the battle. The only one left standing was a phoenix, and she burned that ugly bitch to ash."

Silence fell over the room.

"It was after the destruction of that particular harpy and her nest that the phoenix began to be hunted by the vampires." He looked at the knives on my hip. "Your blades will not work on them." He looked at Robby. "Your claws and teeth will only serve to irritate them." He shook his head and eyed me again. "Your magic won't work either. However, your phoenix is perfectly suited to destroy it. Although, I fear the firebomb you'll need to produce will likely take out a good portion of the city."

"How old are you?" Johnson asked.

For the first time since I met Phillip, he let his guard down, and I got a glimpse of the ancientness of the man.

"I've tasted the essence of Moses." His lips tipped into a smile. "I was the tattoo artist to many pharaohs." He winked at me. "They had eclectic tastes, just like you, my lady."

"You're over three thousand years old?" I gasped. My eyes widened as I looked him over, looking for any signs of that type of aging. But he looked somewhere around thirty years old.

"I am not human." He cocked an eyebrow.

"Still." I waved at him.

He smiled. "I'm one of the originals. You destroyed the original vampire, and she was older than I am. I shared your distaste of her."

"She looked like an alabaster statue," Robby said.

"What about the original shifter?" Johnson asked.

"Shifters didn't come until much later. Closer to the birth of Jesus." He glanced at us. "Do you know the story of how they came to be?"

"They teach it at the academy," Robby's father said. "But since you were actually there, why don't you tell us the real, unfiltered version."

"What is it that they teach you?" He leaned forward with his head cocked.

"A wolf and a mage were sworn enemies, and ended up battling to the death. When the wolf killed the mage, some of the magic bled into the animal, allowing it to turn from beast to man and back at will." Johnson gave the summary of the wolf origin story we all learned while at the academy.

Phillip leaned back and let out a laugh that shook the room. "That is such bullshit. They were not mortal enemies. It was an epic love story. A wolf and a very powerful witch named Oria fell in love. They were inseparable for years. But she had made enemies, one in particular who coveted her pet wolf as much as her magic. In an effort to steal the wolf, a battle between the mages sparked and ended when Oria sacrificed herself for her wolf.

Her injuries were more than she could repair. She made a desperate last wish to save her pet from being enslaved. She wished he could be transformed into a man of inhuman strength. One that wouldn't bend to the evil mage's wishes. As soon as her dying request fell from her lips, her magic seeped into the wolf, turning him into a brute of a man who dispensed of the evil mage easily. But Oria died before she could see the results of her magic and the wolf was now saddled with the curse of shifting.

"Rameus lived a solitary life for decades, mourning the loss of Oria. But eventually he found another who captured his heart. Daphne was a wisp of a woman who loved the outdoors as much as Rameus. She would run barefoot through the woods, laughing as her hair caught on the tree branches. Her spirit transformed him, and he appeared to her one day as a man. The two fell in love and their pure union transferred the magic to their offspring, bringing a new species to the world. One that held the wildness of the wolf with the refinement of the human soul. That magic has never left your species. It only has served to get stronger with each generation."

"That's why witches and wolves have a bond?" Robby asked. "One that the agency capitalizes on?"

"You said it. Not me, pal." Phillip glanced at his watch and sighed. "I have a customer coming in ten. You're welcome to hang up here until you have a plan." He started for the door and paused with his hand on the handle. "Do you want me to start pulling in those who would like to see the agency gone?"

Robert Senior glanced around at us. "Not yet. We have to have a solid plan. Although taking Terrance out is on my list, it won't change a thing. The agency is still controlled by that ancient bitch, and I have no idea how to pull her out of the woodwork."

Phillip shifted his weight from foot to foot. "You may have to use her as bait." He pointed at me.

While the room was still stunned by his words, Phillip slid out of the apartment, leaving us to deal with his parting comment.

"No." Robby shook his head. "We are not using Sarah as bait ever again."

I glanced at him. "What if it's the only way to take the agency down?"

"Nope. It's not going to happen. I'm not going through that again. We can walk away. Just let it go. Find an unpopulated area and raise a family there. I'm not risking losing you. Period."

Robby had that crazed look that screamed there was no reasoning with him and if we pushed it, he'd become completely unhinged.

But whether he liked it or not, if that was the only way to take that monster down, and topple the agency at the same time, I was willing to make that kind of sacrifice for our freedom.

8

TAINTED MIND 8

THE PLAN, IF YOU COULD call it that, was take down Terrance, and then we'd deal with the harpy and anyone else who popped up to take control. Basically, we spent all day arguing and now I was exhausted. Robby had dark circles under his eyes, and Johnson looked downright annoyed at the whole deal.

"How are we going to draw Terrance out?" I pinched the top of my nose to try to dull the headache that had formed.

As they debated, an idea formed in my mind, relieving the pounding in my head. "I got it!" I jumped up to my feet and started to pace the room as I turned it over in my head, letting it form into a solid plan. I spun to stare at the three of them as they silenced and just watched me pace.

"What if I called Terrance, demanding he hand over your father?" I met Robby's gaze. "He has no idea that you survived. Just like he doesn't know he is with us."

"Terrance wants you in a cage or dead," Robert Senior said.

"You and I know that, but if I tell him Robby was killed because you handed us over and I want your blood, won't he take that as the chance to capture me?"

Robert Senior leaned back in the seat, rubbing his chin as he thought about my proposal.

"That puts you in danger," Robby said. "Plus, you've never met Terrance, so who's to say he'll actually show up?"

I tapped my lips, thinking some more. "Was he in any of your wedding photos?" I glanced at Johnson.

"Probably, but we hadn't gotten the proofs yet."

"He wouldn't know that. Can you two draw him for me?" I looked at Johnson and Robert Senior.

"I can," Robby's dad said. "But I still don't know that he will show without serious backup." He met my gaze. "And I want to be the one who tears his heart from his chest."

"I'm not sure that will be possible. Wherever we meet, I will be alone. And I want you all a safe distance away. I'm talking miles away, because I will torch everything within sight of the meeting place."

"No." Robby crossed his arms and glared at me.

"Yes." I pointed at his father and Johnson. "I cannot keep them safe from my fire."

"Then I'm going with you."

"Oh, like that will go over well. Me showing up with the person I said I wanted vengeance for." I threw my hands in the air and turned away.

"Then I'll go in wolf form."

"And that's super inconspicuous." I rolled my eyes and collapsed into the chair, pinching my upper nose again as my headache roared back to life.

Robby's father barely suppressed his smirk, and Johnson outright snorted a laugh. He hadn't seen Robby since his last revival. But what he saw in the woods had been enough.

Robby turned on them, snarling. His alpha powers flared. "I'm going with you." His alpha influence rolled over me like an unwanted fleece jacket.

I slowly stood and peeled my lips back at him, letting my vampire teeth form as I stalked forward. "You want to muzzle that shit," I said, with the warning pulsing through my veins.

He stepped toe-to-toe with me as his anger surfaced. His fists clenched and he glared down at me. "No."

I tilted my head and narrowed my eyes. "Do I have to compel you?"

He moved fast, and within a blink, he had me pinned to the wall. "You will not do this alone." His eyes had turned the wild that reminded me of his PTSD episodes. And the anger that pulsed from him packed a punch with his alpha radiating with it.

I pushed against his chest and swept my foot, knocking him to the ground, but he held onto me, pulling me on top of him. I tried to roll away, but he gripped me tight with one arm around my waist and the other around my shoulders, trapping my arms between us.

"You will do as I say," he bellowed at me.

I hissed at him. "I will not hide in your shadow. I've never played this subservient game, and I don't intend to now."

He threw his head back and clenched his teeth so hard I thought they would break.

"Let me go." I pushed with my compelling voice.

Robby snapped his gaze to mine, and he narrowed his eyes. His muscles strained against the order. For the first time since I had been turned, he was able to deny a direct order for long enough to give me pause. And then his arms snapped open like a trap springing wide.

I climbed to my feet, keeping my gaze on him.

"Fuck you, Sarah," he snarled, climbed to his feet, and stomped off up the stairs and down the hall. A moment later, a door slammed closed.

Robby's father sat, wide-eyed, staring at me. He blinked a few times as though he had something to say, but he pressed his lips together, keeping his thoughts to himself.

"Do you think it will work?" I looked between Johnson and Robby's father.

"It's actually the best idea that any of us has come up with." Robert Senior went back to rubbing his chin.

"Grab some paper from the printer and start that drawing." Although I wanted to go to Robby, he needed some time to cool down before I drilled into him. For that matter, I needed to get hold of myself as well. I could almost feel the fire trying to come forth.

I watched as Robert Senior took a couple of sheets of paper and a pencil he found hanging on the refrigerator near a pad with a to-do list on it. He started to sketch. The soft sound of the pencil tracing lines on paper filled the room. Johnson came around to the back of the chair and looked on as Robert Senior drew what was now starting to look like a face.

"His chin is more square than rounded," he said.

Robert Senior stopped and glanced behind him. "Would you like to take over?" he asked with a voice so full of snark that Johnson reared back, bristling. "I didn't think so." He went back to drawing but to his credit, he did adjust the chin to not be so round.

The man he drew looked like an older version of Richard Gere at a quick glance. He wasn't hard on the eyes in the least, if Robby's father's drawing was accurate. I glanced up at Johnson. "That's Terrance Winters?"

Johnson nodded. "More or less."

"He looks like that actor from *Pretty Woman.*" I pointed at the picture. "Without the glasses."

Johnson cocked his head and let out a laugh. "He kind of does."

Robby's father looked up at me. "He does look quite a bit like that actor. The main difference is this scar near his right eye." He leaned over and began to craft a jagged scar that started a little below his right brow and zigged down to a point an inch below his eyes before it zagged across his cheekbone through his ear and into his hairline. "And his hair is as white as snow." He sat back and looked at the drawing.

"That's pretty damn good," Johnson said.

I stared at the picture for a moment and then nodded. "I'm going to go check on Robby now that he's had a chance to calm down." I left them in the living room, climbed the stairs, and headed down the hall, bypassing what looked like Phillip's bedroom to the closed door beyond. I didn't knock; I just turned the knob and stepped into the sparsely furnished spare bedroom.

Robby stood at the window, watching the midday traffic flowing in a steady stream. I didn't speak. I just crossed to him, wrapped my arms around his waist, and kissed his shoulder. He covered my hands with his.

"I have a bad feeling about your plan." He softly ran his thumbs over the back of my hands. "And it's not because it's dangerous." He glanced back and met my gaze. "I know you can handle danger." He shook his head and stared back at the street. "This is something more visceral that's making me react this way. Like, if we separate, the worst will happen."

I couldn't deny the feeling of foreboding, but I couldn't not act on this now that I'd formulated a plan. Even if it meant that plan went straight to hell.

9

TAINTED MIND 9

"SO, DID YOU ALL COME up with a plan?" Phillip asked as he entered the apartment. The sun had dipped on the horizon enough to give the city that fiery hue.

"I think we might have. But there's no telling how it will play out." I glanced at the picture Robby's father drew, memorizing the face.

"You know I have reservations about that." Robby sent a glare at me.

Phillip picked up the paper from the table and cocked his head. His eyes narrowed in a way that screamed familiarity…and not the pleasant kind. "I have encountered this asshole and his family a few times over the years." He looked up at Robby. "He's a sneaky fuck."

"He runs the agency," Johnson said.

Phillip laughed and tossed the paper on the table. "No wonder it's so fucking diabolical. It's run by a sociopath who wants to rule the world. Now that I know who is behind the slaughter of those powerful supernaturals who do not choose to follow the agency and their archaic rules, I insist on offering my network to assist in destroying this entity."

"As I said to Robby, I don't want anyone near me when I confront him." I pointed at the picture. "Because I'll end up toasting the entire area if he double-crosses me. And the only one I can protect from my fire is Robby. But he can't be there due to the reason I'm giving Terrance to meet me."

"And what reason is that?"

"That I want his father on a platter since he was the one who handed us over to the vampires, which resulted in Robby's death. Basically, I'm out for blood."

Phillip tapped his lips as he stared at the drawing. "It will be an ambush." He looked up at me. "As I said, this prick is a slippery bastard. He is devoid of honor."

I nodded. "I'm well aware of that, thus my need not to have anyone I care about near the meeting spot."

"And where were you thinking?"

I sighed. "Sheep Meadow is the only area that is open enough and not much is around."

"The ballfields might be better."

I shook my head. "The museum is too close. If I go nuclear, I'll take that out, and I'd rather not."

"There are too many trees that could hide someone with a tranquilizer rifle," Robby said.

"I agree with my son," Robert Senior said.

"My network can clear the area for you."

"And I'm coming with you," Robert Senior said. "Because I want to be the one to kill Terrance, and I'm not bending on that. I've waited too goddamned long to waive that right."

"No." I dismissed him and looked at Phillip. "I will need a communications jammer because Terrance will likely have comms with his team."

"What if I go with you?" Johnson asked. "I have just as much of a reason to kill Robby's dad as you do." He glared at Robert Senior.

I put my hands out as my patience ran dry. "Stop. No one is going with me." I glanced at Phillip. "And whatever help you enlist has to be gone by the time I meet Terrance midfield."

Robby crossed his arms and his jaw tightened. "It doesn't work that way. You and I are partners. We've never allowed the other to walk into an ambush alone." He glanced around the room. "And this is our team." He stared at me. "As much as we hate the agency, it did teach us the best rules of engagement. We know their strategy. We know the dangers. And we know what a suicide mission looks like."

"I can't guarantee I won't turn them to ash. If Terrance pulls something that we aren't expecting, I will annihilate him and whoever else is in the vicinity, whether they are part of the team or the enemy." I did not want to be responsible for my friends' deaths.

"I understand. You don't want to harm your friends. I don't want that either. But if the agency went to where those vampires had us, they will know I'm alive." Robby used his "let's be reasonable" voice as he spoke.

Damn it. He was right. But would they send someone there even if all the vampires fell? "It's a risk I'll have to take. If they know you're alive, they could conclude that I have no idea." I shrugged. "But that still doesn't address the firepocolypse I could cause."

"Look, we all know it's dangerous," Phillip started. "And although I don't know you all that well, I knew your ancestors, and you seem even fiercer and more loyal than they were. I also know the agency and although I've been leery of Robert and Johnson, they've never given me cause to think they were trying to double-cross me. And now that you've restored my memories, I have the fact you tried to warn me when you thought the agency was coming for me. Even though it wasn't in your best interest to do so." He glanced at both Robby and me. "I have never bowed down to anyone, ever. Strangely, I find myself wanting to pledge my loyalty to you." He smiled and then winked at me. "It was either tattooing your ass or tasting your essence that did it."

Robby let out a growl.

Phillip put his hand up. "I know. She's yours." He rolled his eyes and then met my gaze. "And you need to let us work with you."

"I do not want your deaths on my head!" It was my turn to stomp off and slam the door to the spare bedroom. Instead of standing before the window, I threw myself onto the bed face-first. This wasn't what I had in mind when I left the vampire nest. I was ready to burn down

Manhattan, but now, I did not want to hurt innocents. That would make me no better than the assholes we wanted to exterminate.

TAINTED MIND 10

ROBBY HAD LET ENOUGH TIME elapse for me to calm down before he came to the room. I wasn't sure whether he felt the turmoil subside in his mark or whether he just knew I needed to think things through, but either way, I loved him for giving me the space I needed. The alternative would spark my fire, and I really didn't want to burn our only true ally's home to the ground.

He closed the door behind him and then climbed onto the bed, pulling me to his chest. He kissed my forehead, but remained quiet. When I didn't speak, he sighed.

"We tried to think of another viable alternative to start this war, but the only other one was what you initially set out to do."

I glanced up at him.

"Burn the headquarters to the ground. But that doesn't guarantee we get Terrance or the harpy thing, or any of the others who will step in and take over when Terrance dies." He stared at me. "My dad thinks Terrance will bring one of the big guns with him disguised as him, but it won't be the harpy."

"So, kill two birds with one stone?" I grinned but Robby just stared at me in that "are you serious" kind of way that shut me down.

"It's likely to be far more than just two birds."

My smile faded.

"My dad still wants to plant the knife that kills Terrance. And Phillip still wants his network of soul suckers to clear the playing field for you." He let out a soft laugh.

I did not want potential casualties and was about to say just that when he continued.

"I learned something new about soul suckers that is quite frightening, and I'm not sure my father knew either because he looked just as shocked as I was."

My internal whining about having people around for the battle fizzled out. Robby had caught my full attention. "What's that?"

"Apparently, when they congregate in a group, they can combine their powers. When they do that, all they have to do is look at someone to kill them." He let out a nervous laugh. "Just a single glance and bam, they're dead."

"So, they could have taken out the agency at any time?" I sat up and stared at him, confused. If Phillip wanted the agency gone, all he'd have to do is get enough soul eaters outside of headquarters and pick off people as they exited the building.

Robby took a deep breath. "It's not that easy, but, yes, they could have done quite a bit of damage had they been motivated enough to gather. They don't gather in one place like that very often because if things do not go according to plan, there is usually a battle between the different soul eater clans." He rolled onto his back and stared at the ceiling. "Phillip said this only happened a handful of times over the course of his existence." He glanced at me. "The last time was taking down Hitler. Before that, it was Genghis Khan." His lip tilted into that half smile I adored, but it was so out of place in this conversation. "He said annihilating the last harpy is on par with those monsters. Especially with the bonus of disabling a corrupt agency being the lynchpin to getting the harpy to show itself."

As I digested this new information, Robby started to run his fingers through my hair. I closed my eyes at the slow cadence of his hand. "What big gun do you think Terrance will bring?"

"I don't know. But Phillip seems to think you riding in on me will give Terrance enough pause to give my dad the time to kill him. And then we dispatch whatever they bring."

I didn't want to argue with Robby. I didn't want to think about what needed to be done. I just wanted to lay in his arms and forget the world for a little while.

But this wasn't going to be about what I wanted. I came to that conclusion in the time he let me be. Robby had been right; a team like we had could be useful. And I trusted most of the members. I still had my reservations about Robby's father. He was blinded by his need for revenge, and that could get people killed.

Before I let my mate or anyone else walk into a trap, I needed some things and the only way to get them was magic.

"Can you ward the apartment?" I glanced at him. "Or at least this room so I can conjure things we may need?"

He sat up next to me and sucked his lower lip between his teeth as he glanced around the room. "Things like what?"

He was stalling, and I narrowed my eyes at him. "I need a burner phone, and a computer to change the triangulation of the call so we can't be tracked here."

He slowly nodded, still looking around the room. "I can probably ward this room. But it's been years since I did that to my house." His gaze came to rest on mine.

"And?" I put my hands up in a "what the hell's your problem" way.

"And I don't know if I can remember all the steps. I didn't do it alone. Heddie helped me." He flopped onto his back and ran his hand through his hair.

Shit. I didn't want him trying a spell that could end up being a beacon to our whereabouts. There was only one other viable alternative. "Burner and a coffee shop across town then?"

Robby laughed. "I'm not letting you cross this town after you make that call. It's bad enough we have to cross the city to get to Central Park."

Not this again. I opened my mouth to argue with him when a knock on the door interrupted us.

"Come in," I said, loud enough to be heard through the door but not loud enough to transmit my irritation. I might as well just use my damn magic to get what we needed, but I refrained.

Johnson opened the door. "Phillip's ordering Chinese. You want any?"

My stomach growled in an immediate response. Maybe my endless prickliness was due to being hungry. "Yeah." We climbed out of the bed and headed back downstairs to the living room. "Hot and spicy chicken with fried rice, please." I reached into my bag, pulling out a couple hundred dollars. I handed it toward Phillip. "I don't have anything smaller."

He plucked one bill out of my hand. "That's more than enough." He placed the call. Once he hung up, he looked me square in the eye. "We agreed that it would not be in your best interest to go to the park alone."

"So I understand. But there's an even more difficult hurdle to get over."

"What's that?" He cocked his head like an inquisitive puppy.

"Placing the call without them being able to trace it."

Phillip's slow smile made me want to wrap myself in a blanket. Impish light danced in his eyes. "Where do you want them to think you are?"

It was a question I hadn't considered, and I almost said, *Anywhere but here.* I inhaled, giving it some thought. I didn't want them to think I was close enough to do damage, but I also didn't want them thinking I was so far away that I couldn't follow through on a meeting. "I don't know. Maybe on one of the ferries? A moving target would be better than somewhere stationary." I narrowed my gaze. "What's going through your mind?"

"Have you ever heard of a party line?"

I shook my head. Robby and Johnson did the same. But Robby's father's brows rose at the phrase.

"It's not actually a party line, in the truest sense of the word. It's more like I have someone on that boat call you and then conference Terrance in. And I can have a few relays to muddy the waters as well."

"Really?" I glanced at him and then around the room. "Can we all have burners?" They were harder to trace, but not impossible.

His grin widened. "With your stash of money, you can have just about anything you want."

I took a breath. "Why does this just seem too easy?" I eyed Phillip suspiciously.

He crossed to me and took my hands. "I have been hiding in plain sight for lifetimes. And made it my business to learn the newest technologies to do just that. I am just as resourceful as your agency is. And I have been waiting for an opportunity to take it down so my kind can live in peace. And now that I am fully aware of what has been controlling the agency for all these years, I am inclined to offer you, the last phoenix, all my resources."

The bells of mistrust rang in my head, and I pulled my hands from his warm grip, leery of his total cooperation. "Why?"

"Because you are to be revered. Had I known what you were when I came to put that glorious tattoo on your ass, I would have never taken any part of your essence. That is an unforgiveable offense, and I apologize."

"And yet you take every opportunity to reference having another taste," Robby said from behind me. His voice dripped with disdain.

"Because I have what's called a sense of humor. You seemed to have lost yours a long time ago." He came back at Robby so quickly it almost gave me whiplash. "Besides, look at her. She is female perfection. Who wouldn't want a taste of her?"

Heat filled my cheeks at his compliment. Neither Johnson nor Robby's father were inclined to jump to Robby's defense, either. "This is not a subject I wish to continue discussing." I crossed my arms. "Again, tell me why you want to help us—without all the bullshit." I pushed my influence over Phillip because I wasn't sure I could trust him.

"Because I was once in love with a phoenix, the one who destroyed a harpy, as a matter of fact. I made a pledge to her to protect her kind. You remind me a little of her." He smiled warmly, but it turned bitter. "We were together for eons before that fateful day. She had a younger sister I watched over, but I failed her. A vampire found her and stripped her of her lives, trying to find a phoenix child who had been hidden from him. I still remember the bastard's name, too. Cassius."

His lips pulled back from his teeth as if just saying the name drew him into a feral rage.

My face grew cold at the mention of Cassius's name, and I glanced at Robby. His cheeks paled as well.

"When you wiped out all the vampires, you wiped him out, too. So, I am eternally grateful for a vengeance I wasn't personally able to deliver, but it was still satisfying to know that bastard was no more." He nodded his head in thanks.

"Cassius was the one who turned me," I said quietly.

Phillip blinked at me, and his mouth popped open. "That bloody fucking asshole," he said, appalled.

Oh, Phillip didn't know the half of it.

"I ripped Cassius Chase to fucking pieces," Robby said from behind me. "That bastard made me watch while he killed Sarah over and over in a bid to wipe her memory of me. But, as you can see, it didn't work." His hand landed softly on my shoulder, and he squeezed gently.

Phillip's gaze lifted to Robby. "Then I owe you a debt of gratitude, as well."

Robby gave him a curt nod. "So, when do we make this bad decision?" he asked.

"It's the best option we have, Robby," his father said from the chair.

We all looked at him. It was the first time he ever addressed his son the way Robby wanted.

"Who the fuck are you and what have you done with Robby's father?" Johnson asked from across the room. His eyes narrowed as they scanned Robby's father.

Robert Senior smirked. "I'm the same asshole you've always known. I'm just trying to make up for some of the crap I've put him through by calling him what he's asked me to call him for years."

Phillip's phone buzzed. He glanced at it. "We can discuss timing over dinner." He left the apartment.

"My preference is to get things rolling as soon as possible." I glanced back at Robby. "I know that doesn't thrill you, but the sooner we take those fuckers down, the sooner we can start a normal life. And I'm ready for that."

Robby tucked a hair behind my ear and then pulled me into a hug. Although, from the tense set of his muscles, I knew he wasn't comfortable with any of this.

Phillip came back in with a large bag of food, and he placed it on the coffee table, taking each of the cartons out and lining them up on the table before dumping out the sauces and chopsticks onto the table. He then lined up a row of waters for everyone. "Do you want me to get plates?" he asked as he grabbed one of the boxes and made himself comfortable on the couch with a pair of chopsticks.

"We're good," Robby's father said as he looked over the boxes and plucked what he had ordered from the array. Johnson grabbed his as well, leaving two containers each for me and Robby.

I plopped down on the floor, facing the table and the couch beyond it. Robby joined me, and we all dug in.

"I can get the phone call set up for tomorrow morning," Phillip said through a mouthful. "And I can get your backup together by sunset."

"We need comms and jammers and, and other things." I couldn't think of what else I would need, but I couldn't believe he could pull this off in a blink.

He looked around the apartment. "You've seen this building, right?"

I nodded.

"And does this apartment really fill up that space? Or the tattoo shop, for that matter?"

Everyone's brows creased as they looked around.

I surveyed the apartment. "It's not deep enough." Although the width covered the building, the first floor wasn't deep enough to cover the building's footprint. But the second floor went straight back from the open stairwell. "This looks as deep as your tattoo shop and storeroom downstairs." Which meant there was space as big as the bedrooms above that wasn't accounted for on two floors. "Show me."

"Eat first." He pointed his chopsticks.

I nearly inhaled the entire box of spicy chicken and at least half the rice. It was by far the most I've eaten since I was turned, and I leaned back. "I'm stuffed." I hadn't had an adverse reaction to the breakfast I ate this morning either. Maybe my latest rebirth reset my stomach.

I tried to cover a burp with my hand, but it was louder than I anticipated. Robby's dad looked over the edge of his container at me.

"Excuse me," I mumbled and wiped my mouth with a napkin before I took to the water and downed it.

Once everyone was done, we grabbed the remnants and threw them away in the garbage, neatening up the area. After we finished cleaning up the living room, Phillip stood, but his brow creased, and his lips pressed together as he stared at us all. He started to chew on his lower lip as he met my gaze.

I got it immediately. Trusting us could get him killed. "I put my trust in you the minute I gave you your memories back." I didn't know whether it would ease the conflict in him or not, but telling him I trusted him seemed to smooth out the harsh lines of his face.

He gave me a nod and then turned, heading toward the kitchen. He stepped into the pantry and pushed a group of boxes aside as we gathered around the doorway, peering inside. Behind the boxes was a keypad. Phillip took a breath, gave us a last glance over his shoulder, and punched in a six-digit code.

I didn't catch the numbers, but I think Robby and Johnson did as they gave each other a nod before glancing back at Phillip.

The wall swiveled, opening to a dark entry that Phillip stepped into. A moment later, banks of lights illuminated a room equal to the size of the apartment, and next to the entrance was a set of curling iron stairs that went down into the darkness below.

A half-dozen computers sat in the middle of the room, and the far wall showed at least a hundred monitors with different parts of the city.

In the corner of each, there was a street designation. The most interesting one was the lobby of agency headquarters.

I glanced over my shoulder at Robby's father. His eyebrows arched in appreciation at the amassment of technology in this room. And the fact they had a camera inside the agency was impressive.

Phillip waved at the monitors. "We are hacked into the city network and have successfully hacked into the lobby camera at the agency. The agency thinks it's the city and the city thinks it's the agency. Neither are concerned as their contact in the city is on our payroll and has made it known that they are aware of the agency's taps on their camera system and told them that the tap to their lobby is the price they have to pay to have this access."

"Slick," Robert Senior said.

"I did say I kept up with technology." Phillip turned toward the computers. "This is where I contact my network." He walked over to the keyboard and began to type. The center monitor changed to show his text.

"Looking for a phone relay for a party chat. Multiple points and the last one on the ferry. How quickly can we set it up?"

Six people immediately responded, and I stared at the 10:00 a.m. timeframe. I had a little over twelve hours to figure out exactly what I was going to say.

"Does that work?" Phillip looked over his shoulder at me.

I nodded.

Phillip confirmed it and saved the first number in the list. "I'll call this number at a little before ten and then we can get the chain on." He also typed that he would have the number for the final caller to use at the time we connected. He reminded them that all but the last caller on the ferry would need to be in a silent environment.

Six users typed that they understood.

"I am impressed." The response time was even better than the agency. "What do you have over them?"

Phillip straightened and turned to me with wide eyes. "I hold nothing over my contacts." The offense in his tone made me drop my gaze. "Don't assume that because your agency uses threats and coercion that all organizations do that."

"I'm sorry."

He took a breath. "My network is loyal because I am loyal to them. Although, they don't really know who I am, per se. They only know me as the skin artist." He shrugged. "Before the internet, it took longer to arrange these things. I have had the same distinct seal since the beginning of time, and they respond to it. It's on all my communications and has been since the very beginning. And we have a common cause."

"What's that?" Robby asked.

"Survival."

TAINTED MIND 11

ROBBY AND I SLID INTO the guest bedroom to get some rest, but the moment the door closed, he pinned me to the wall and his lips crushed down on mine.

"Robby." I pushed at his chest, and he pulled back far enough to meet my gaze. His eyes reflected a hunger that the food hadn't touched.

"If we're going to step into the line of fire tonight, I want to still feel the taste of you on my lips and the memory of ravaging you, so I don't lose sight of what I'm fighting for." He stared deep into my eyes. "Anger isn't enough of a reason, but this is." He didn't wait for me to answer; he captured my mouth with his, swiping his tongue across my lips.

I opened my mouth, allowing his tongue to explore and play with mine. Robby knew how to kiss, and it weakened my knees with the amount of heat it promised. He reached out and locked the door before he brought me to the bed and then removed my clothes without destroying them. It made me grin under the pressure of his lips.

He moved his mouth to my ear. "I figured you would appreciate having your kick-ass outfit intact."

I did, especially considering it would make an impression whenever I met with Terrance. But my mind totally forgot about what the next day or so would bring the moment Robby nipped my breast. His playful grin caught me by surprise. This was the old Robby, the one who broke the rules to be with me. The one who didn't shake with fear whenever I got too close to him. The one before Cassius damaged us.

He trailed kisses down my body, creating liquid pleasure in all the right places. I willed my mind to ignore the tender way he played with me—much more reminiscent of our first time—and he knew how to get me to that sexual high. I let out a low moan, unable to keep the pent-up desire inside any longer.

He stopped his tongue-lashing. "Shhh," he whispered.

"Don't stop," I hissed as my body cooled down enough to send a flare of irritation through me.

He flicked my clit with his tongue. "You mean that?" His teasing grin nearly made me scream and then his demeanor changed. "Beg," he said.

"For fuck's sake, Robby." I stared at him.

His grin was enough for me to want to slam him into the mattress and climb on top of him, tease him to the point of no return, and then stop. It was maddening, especially because I knew he wasn't going to relent. He had that stubborn gleam in his eyes.

I took a deep breath. "Please don't stop what you were doing." I sent him a sweet smile and batted my eyes.

"What exactly was I doing?" he teased, cocking his head to the side.

"Please play with my clit," I whispered breathlessly. Just his breath on me was enough to reignite the heat inside. "With your tongue," I added.

His smile reached his eyes, and he obliged. God, with the inferno he created inside me, it was a wonder I didn't spontaneously combust. The fact that I had to keep silent only heightened my reaction. When I came, I arched my back entirely off the bed and my toes curled so tight that they nearly cramped up.

He kissed his way up my body and then pushed in me insanely slow, inch by inch, as if going any faster would make him lose control. He closed his eyes.

"Sarah," he whispered, as if my name were a prayer of some sort. He opened his eyes and met my gaze. "You feel so incredible." His voice held the roughness of his hunger. His hips moved languidly enough to take me to another level.

I needed to feel the full length of him pounding into me like there was no tomorrow, and I tried moving my pelvis harder into him.

But he stopped moving, and his hands gripped my hips, holding me still.

"I'm in control here."

The warning growl in his voice had me stilling, but it did nothing for the need building inside me, the one I had to keep quiet. I tilted my head back and grabbed the sheets at my sides, pulling at the material so I didn't cry out. If I grabbed his shoulders, my fingers would claw him hard enough to draw blood.

His genuine smile made his eyes sparkle, and he resumed that slow cadence that revved my engine.

The friction of his slow movements and the grind of his hips brought me close to my next orgasm with each pass. But it was as if he knew and tempted me just enough to bring me to the brink, but then back off.

"You're driving me crazy," I gasped with his next pass.

He leaned down and pressed a gentle kiss as he held himself over me. "Good," he whispered.

When the vein in his forehead started to pulse, I knew he was nearing losing control. I twirled my hips, grinding into him just as slowly as he was moving. He groaned in response and then he captured my mouth in a demanding kiss. His hips moved faster, slamming into mine with the same ferocity that gripped me.

I came like a gunshot, moaning into Robby's mouth with the force of it. He rode me hard, heightening my orgasm and sparking one right after another. He groaned in my mouth, his tongue moving as frantically as his hips until he buried himself deep inside me and arched away from me with his eyes clamped shut. His muscles tightened with his release.

"Fuck," he whispered, drawing the word out the way I loved hearing him say it.

I reached up and pulled his lips back to mine. This time, the kiss was as languid as his initial lovemaking, drawing out my breath with its sweetness. When our after-tremors subsided, he rolled off and pulled me into his arms.

"I love you, Sarah. Remember that through all the bloodshed that's likely to come."

"I've said it before—I would die a thousand deaths and still come back to you." I turned and cupped his cheek. "I love you beyond time. Beyond death."

"Let's hope it doesn't come to that, again." He kissed my nose.

I cuddled into him. I prayed it didn't either.

TAINTED MIND 12

THE SUN SPLASHED ACROSS THE disheveled blankets, and I blinked at the unfamiliar room. I turned, to find Robby's back facing me. It was the first time since we escaped Cassius's place that I didn't wake up still in the clutches of his tight grip.

I traced his muscles with my fingers, and he stirred, stretched, and then rolled toward me.

"Sleep good?" he asked through a yawn.

The knock on the door interrupted any ideas Robby may have had in that waking moment. He rolled his eyes.

"What?" His voice radiated irritation.

His father cracked the door. "Are you decent?"

I pulled the sheet up to cover myself and tucked it under my arms.

"Yes," I said, and his father stepped into the room, closing the door behind him.

He glanced at us and then sighed. "I figured I'd coach you a little this morning before you get on the phone with Terrance."

"What time is it?" Robby grumbled.

"A little before nine."

"Give us a few minutes to get dressed and then we'll meet you in the living room." Robby sat up in the bed, leaving the sheet over his waist.

His father gave a nod and left us.

"Are you sure this is the right move?" Robby asked, with his back to me.

Even if I didn't have the doubt pounding in my mark, I would have known he wasn't happy with this choice just by the tone of his voice. I reached out, rubbing his back gently. "Yes."

"Okay." He leaned over and grabbed the clothing strewn over the floor and handed me my outfit before he pulled on his clothes.

I dressed and then straightened the bed before heading out of the bedroom. I made a pit stop at the bathroom to try to tame my hair and rinse my mouth before I addressed anyone. The minute I exited, Robby took my place, and I headed downstairs, where the smell of pancakes moved my feet a little faster.

Robert Senior looked up from the drawing he held and dropped it on the table. Neither Phillip nor Johnson were in the room with us, but Robert Senior waved at a plate of pancakes with a smile.

"They assumed you two would like breakfast before they disappeared into Phillip's control room to set everything up."

"Accurate assumption." I took a seat in the chair and picked up the plate, pouring syrup over the stack before I dug in. I could have eaten the entire stack, but I stopped at half just as Robby descended the stairs. I handed him the plate when he approached.

Robby didn't say anything. He just inhaled the rest of the breakfast and set the plate aside before he took a seat on the floor facing everyone.

His father glanced at the plate and then nodded toward the kitchen, raising an eye at his son. "And while you're in there, can you fix me a cup of coffee along with yours?"

Robby sighed and stood, collecting the plate and the syrup before he disappeared.

"When you talk to Terrance, you have to be seething mad." He put a hand up when I opened my mouth. "You have to demand he bring me to you. And you don't care what the price is. You want me alive so you can kill me slowly as payback for Robby."

"I'm not agreeing—"

"Yes. You are agreeing to anything he puts on the table."

"You want me to lie." I leaned back in the chair and crossed my arms.

"He knows what you are. And he knows you've been to our hometown, looking for me. Your magical signature was there. He may also know Robby is alive. But you have to be very clear of what you saw and that the only thing left in that room with the ancient vampire after you blew the vampires away was ash.”

“Okay,” I said.

“And if he doesn’t comply with your request, you will raze New York City and everyone within a hundred miles.”

“You think threatening him is going to work?”

He smiled in such a way that I shifted in my seat. “It’s the only way to get Terrance’s attention.” He leaned forward. “And then you have to make him understand that if he runs, you will find him, even if it means burning the world so there’s no place to hide.”

I stared at him.

“You need to let him know in no uncertain terms that only my blood will satisfy your revenge, and you will do anything to make that happen, including killing millions upon millions of people and supernaturals alike.”

“Do you think it will come to that?” I was angry with the agency, but I didn’t know whether I could articulate the kind of irrational fury that Robby’s dad outlined.

He inhaled and looked out at what we could see of the city from Phillip’s living room window. “I honestly don’t know. But he has no clue where I am, and he certainly won’t show that card to you. He’ll stall for time to figure out an alternative and a sure way to take you down, though.”

“So, give him a concrete time and place and if he’s not there, New York City will be no more. And if he decides to double-cross me, it will be the last thing he ever does.”

“Give him a time and lead him to the space. Tell him an open field in the city big enough to have a clear viewpoint for both of you. Something that likely clears out at night. There are only a couple areas that fall into that bucket and if he suggests something different than what you have in mind, pause and then offer your option. If necessary, you can switch to his option."

I nodded. "You know, all this is really unnecessary."

The way his lips twitched into almost a smirk irritated me. "It is necessary. This will make you focus and not wing it like the impulsive woman you are."

My brow furrowed at that, and the irritation of his smirk grew. "You don't know a damn thing about me. I don't take kindly to your assumption that I'm somehow not the sharpest tool in the shed." I snarled out the words.

He grinned. "Impulsive and passionate. Just like my son."

"You're going to get your ass kicked," Robby said from the doorway. "And she can take me down when she's mad." He walked out with two cups of coffee, setting his father's cup on the table in front of him on the couch and took the farthest seat away. "Keep pushing her and it'll be your funeral." He took a sip of his coffee and winked at me.

"She operates on emotion and always has, based upon her write-ups. This sting has to go flawlessly. Otherwise, we are all dead." Robby's father stared him down and then slid his narrowed gaze to me. "You understand the stakes. He will have sharpshooters all over those woods. But he won't take you down until you are close enough to see his fucking grin."

"He's that much of an asshole?" Robby asked. He had never met Terrance and had no frame of reference except some of the shit he'd heard through third-party sources like his father.

"He's a sadistic motherfucker. Everyone thought his father was the warped one, but he's just as bad as that asshole." He glanced at me and then Robby. "He despises werewolves. Although he is part werewolf, he has never been able to shift. He's just using us as his agency's muscle. He was put in this position after his father died, but he was not put in charge of the werewolf council, thus the bad blood between the two organizations. Terrance has found ways to pull packs in and get them to be loyal to the agency over the years. He did that with our pack long before I became the alpha, and when the agency rules didn't keep me in line, they found other ways of coercing me."

"Like keeping Mom locked up and a death sentence hanging over my head," Robby said.

His fury bit at my mark, sending my heart rate into a staccato drumbeat in my chest.

"Yes." He rubbed his face. "The man is smart and has seers with him, but they never predicted my duplicity, and they certainly couldn't see her." He nodded at me. "Otherwise, she would have been dead a long time ago. It's almost like we are in a predictive blind spot."

He gave me a tilted smile so much like Robby's apology smile that I blinked.

The door to the command center opened, and Phillip strolled in with a tight pair of jeans and a button-down black shirt that hung open, giving us all a view of his tattooed chest. I stared at the phoenix rising from the ashes. The colors nearly leapt from his skin they were so vibrant, and I could almost feel the heat from the fire. His gaze dropped to his open shirt and then his cheeks reddened as he quickly buttoned it.

"It's time," he said, avoiding my eyes.

"Your tattoo is stunning."

When his eyes rose, I caught the sadness in them. "If only she had risen like that." He tried to right his frown, but it didn't work. "Come, we only have a small window."

Robert Senior scribbled a number on a piece of paper and handed it to me. "That's the agency switchboard. If you call him directly, he'll know."

I took the paper.

"Be nice to the operator. Ask for Clara Hart. If you ask for Terrance, you won't get through. But if you ask for Clara, his secretary, you'll have a better chance to get to him. And you have to be nice and polite, but tell her that you have a message from me that you were told only to give to Terrance."

"Will that work?"

"I don't know. It's your best chance to get him on the line personally. And only tell him who you are. Make up a name for his secretary."

"Thank you," I said to his father and glanced at Robby, who remained in the chair.

"You've got this."

Why did I suddenly feel like this was too much? With all the doubts in the world clouding my mind, I followed Phillip into the darkened command center. "Where's Johnson?" I asked.

"He's in the bathroom. He'll be right out."

I gave him a nod and handed him the number. Phillip picked up the phone and waited.

"Are you ready?" he asked just as the phone buzzed. "Hello," he said into the phone. "Good. Here's the number." He read off the number and then handed the phone to me.

My heart thundered in my chest, and I took a deep breath, putting the phone to my ear. The phone connected and a ringing line echoed in my ear. I held my breath. *One ring, two ring...*

"Monster Defense Agency, how may I direct your call?" the friendly operator asked.

"Clara Hart, please," I asked, keeping my voice steady.

"Hold, please."

I met Phillip's gaze just as Johnson came out of the bathroom. He crossed to stand close enough to me to hear the voice on the phone. He knew Terrance's voice and that gave me an extra boost.

"This is Clara," a curt voice snapped into the phone line.

I closed my eyes and conjured my sweetest voice. "Hi, Clara. It's Holly Hudson. I need to speak with Terrance, please." Before she could balk at me, I added, "I am supposed to give him a message from Robert Young Senior." I licked my lips and opened my eyes.

"You can give me the message," she said, but there was a note of curiosity in her voice now that softened it.

I clutched the phone tighter and made myself not jump into the hostility that was rising inside me. "I'm sorry, but Robert was adamant that I only give this message to Terrance himself."

"It's okay—I won't tell him."

Nice. I have to be nice. "I can't. He said he would hurt my kids if I didn't do this right." I lowered my voice to almost a hushed whisper. "Please," I added, praying that playing the kids card would work with this frigid bitch.

The huff came through the line. "Hold, please."

I exhaled and met Phillip's gaze. He gave me a thumbs-up.

A moment later, a high-pitched male voice came on the line, reminding me of the weasel of a boss we used to have. "This is Terrance Winters. I understand you have a message for me?"

Johnson shook his head.

"Nice try. The message is for Terrance. If you don't get him on the line, I will end up losing one of my children, so please, get the real Terrance on the line."

Another huff, and then a ring came through the line.

"Terrance Winters," a deep, soothing voice purred over the line.

It was almost seductive, and I glanced at Johnson. He gave me a nod and stepped away.

"Terrance. It's a pleasure to finally speak to the head of the agency."

"Who is this?"

I smiled. "It's Sarah Stone. I want you to bring Robert Young to me so I can rip his ass to shreds. The bastard turned us over to the vampires and they killed Robby, so that asswipe has to pay. Just so you understand how serious I am about this, I will burn the entire city to the ground if you refuse."

The chill came through the line and in the background, I heard the creak of his chair. "What makes you think I'll make that kind of deal with someone like you?"

The stall. "Because I will kill anyone who gives that bastard safe haven. I just missed him in his hometown, and I figured he was back in the city now that the vampires were dead."

"Why aren't you dead?" he asked, still stalling.

"You fucking know damn well why I'm not dead. And you better take me seriously, because I'm out for blood." I let the growl come into my voice. "You think the mother of vampires was a hard-ass? You haven't seen anything yet."

"What are you willing to give me for Robert?"

"Your life." I figured that would be enough, but then he chuckled in a way that made me feel dirty.

"I'd rather have you back at the agency."

Okay. That was out of left field. "Why? You were hell-bent on killing me or caging me."

"That wasn't me, honey. That was all Robert. He didn't like the thought of a witch tainting his pack."

That answer was a little too close to home, and I looked at Phillip, second-guessing who I was putting my trust in. *Was I being played?* "What would you have me do at the agency?" I asked, giving my voice a cautious tone but one that wasn't negative.

"Since you will be taking my right hand, I will have a need to fill that spot."

Oh, he was good. Too bad that kind of power wasn't what I was looking for. And he didn't have anything concrete to hold over my head to keep me in line. I remained silent.

"Did I lose you on the ferry, honey?" he asked.

I took in a deep breath. We knew he would trace the call but hearing him identify where our connection was still unnerved me. "This is how this is going to go..."

"You don't have the upper hand. I will have that boat surrounded the moment it docks." His voice went from friendly to frigid in a millisecond.

"Then I'll burn down Manhattan," I said in just as cool of a tone as he used.

"Wait," he said, with a little panic surfacing. "Agree to work for me again, and I'll bring him to you."

He took the bait. Now it was my turn. "As I was saying before you so rudely interrupted, I'm not doing a daylight meet. There are just too many people wandering around the city when there's light. I am thinking somewhere there is enough of a view that I can see anything coming at me."

"Where were you thinking?"

"The ballfields in Central Park?" I offered. It was not my preferred spot, and I offered it up in hopes he would give me exactly where I wanted to meet.

"What about Sheep Meadow? It's farther inside the park and less likely to have people around," he offered.

I grinned. *Bingo!* I kept silent for more than a few beats and then exhaled loud into the line. "Fine. But know this—if you ambush me, I will burn this city down. Then I'll find wherever you've stashed your family and burn them to ash. I will raze the entire world if I have to. And if you come empty-handed, we will have an even bigger problem."

"Oh, I'll bring Robert to you, as long as you promise me on his son's grave that you'll work for me again."

My mouth tasted bitter as I swallowed. I didn't want to swear on Robby's grave. Lying did not agree with me, but I pressed on, crossing my fingers as I spoke. "He isn't buried, you asshole. He's ash, like the rest of those fucking vampires. But yes. I swear on his ashes that I will be at your beck and call, if, and only if, you give me his father and allow me to have my revenge."

A sigh came over the line. "I'm sorry to hear about your partner," he said with such sincerity that I glanced at Johnson. "I will meet you in the park at ten tonight with Robert."

"And *you* need to promise no funny stuff," I said before I agreed.

"I promise. As long as you keep your end of the bargain, I'll keep mine."

"Ten tonight it is." I hung up the phone just as the docking announcement came through the line. I prayed the rest of the team would disconnect, too.

Phillip hit a button and nodded. "Everyone has hung up." He sat down and started typing an all-bulletin message. A call to arms for his kind. Within minutes, at least one hundred responses came in, and he glanced over his shoulder at me. "We will be in the surrounding areas at nine, scouting it out for you and taking out their sharpshooters before you step into the field."

I needed a few minutes to collect my thoughts, so I walked to the wall of monitors and took a deep breath.

"We'll need comms," Johnson said.

"You're not going," Phillip said. "I need someone here to monitor the area and direct us to anything odd before we even let her near the park."

I spun around and stared at Phillip. "Excuse me?"

"You heard me. I'm not letting you near there if they use magic that will harm you." Phillip stared me down.

"That's the only way I'd allow this," Robby said as he entered the room.

Oh great. Just what I needed. An overprotective alpha. "And you can pull that off?" I glanced at Phillip.

"Sweetheart, I can pull off just about anything, except killing that harpy. That has to be you. But anything short of that, I'm your man." He gave me an exaggerated bow.

With this kind of support, what could possibly go wrong?

TAINTED MIND 13

ROBBY STOOD AT MY SIDE in the shadow of the trees. The comms in my ear echoed with the timed takedowns. But no noise filtered into the night. Across the open field, a man walked, dragging a hooded figure behind him.

"All clear. Comms jamming underway."

The earpiece became static, and I pulled it out, stomping it to bits so no one could trace it back to Phillip's organization. Robby took the cue and shifted, lowering to the ground so I could climb up on his back. No one had ever seen a wolf as big as he was. Nor one with gold shimmering at the edges of each piece of fur. I guess a phoenix had never cried tears on a wolf before, but he was spectacular because of it.

As soon as Terrance was dead center with his prisoner on his knees in front of him, I tapped my heels on Robby's sides. The spectacle of me riding a gold-painted wolf into the open would hopefully capture all of Terrance's attention.

We stepped out into the open, and even from this distance, his eyes widened significantly enough for me to see it. Robby growled, baring his teeth as we crossed the distance.

On silent feet behind Terrance, Robert Senior approached.

Muffled words came from under the hood, and then whoever Terrance brought to the fight with him dropped to the side, devoid of life courtesy of the soul eaters. A wisp of light flowed out of the body, sailing into the night, only to drop in the middle of the woods, where the soul eaters had planned to congregate.

Terrance muttered something and touched his ear, and then his eyes jumped to me.

"You didn't think I was stupid enough to come without my own precautions, did you?" I asked when we were a few yards from him.

Terrance stared at me as we stopped before him. I slid off Robby and put my hand on his massive shoulder.

"Is that the bastard?" I pointed at the still form on the ground.

He nodded dumbly. "You said if I brought him, you would be happy to work with me?" he asked, but his voice didn't have the certainty that it had on the phone.

I batted my eyes at him and smiled. "That was before you had at least a dozen sharpshooters aiming guns at me."

"Stand down!" he called out in a loud voice, holding his hands up. Thankfully, he didn't turn in a circle; otherwise, he would have seen Robert Senior only a few steps away.

"Oh, Terrance." I grinned. "Your team is already dead, as is this fool of a witch at your feet."

The ground started to quake, and Terrance smiled. "Not all of my team." He reached for the taser on his hip.

Robert Senior slammed a blade into Terrance's back before he could get out his weapon and shoot me. The silver tip glinted in the moonlight as it pierced through Terrance's fine threads.

"That was for my family. Know this—before the next moon, the agency and all its masters will be as dead as you are right now," Robert Senior whispered in Terrance's ear as he slowly twisted the knife.

Robby transitioned back to human form with a snarl, and I waved a hand to clothe his exposed skin.

Terrance tried to speak. Nothing came out but the whisper of a laugh. The tremors in the ground seemed to be getting worse.

Phillip trotted up next to Robby and inhaled like he was capturing the scent of a million chocolate chip cookies. Terrance's essence filtered out of his body and into Phillip. When the last morsel flowed out of Terrance, Robert Senior yanked the blade from his chest and stared at him in disgust as Terrance crumbled to the ground.

"That did not seem like the proper amount of torment." He leaned down, wiping the blade clean on Terrance's clothes. "Let's see who the poor bastard he brought with him is." He pulled the hood off the dead body and growled. An ancient warlock with dead eyes stared at the starlit night. "I've seen this bastard a few times, and death always follows him." He glanced around the park as if he were actually looking for a person.

The ground shook more violently, as if we were standing on a fault line. I grabbed hold of Robby. The four of us stared at one another, and then Phillip's eyes widened at a point to our left.

"Demons," he said. "Turn these bodies to ash so they don't have a vessel with latent magic still hanging around," he added, pointing at Terrance and the witch.

I didn't question him; instead, I pointed my palms to the ground and pushed out my fire. Two lasers of flame engulfed the bodies and within seconds, only ash and charred soil remained. "I think you better shift." I glanced at Robby and his father. "You'll do better fighting these bastards as wolves." As the horde scrambled toward us, Robby transformed into his massive wolf and Robby's father shifted. They flanked me and Phillip like a furry barrier.

I conjured swords made of pure steel carved with demon-killing sigils and handed one to Phillip.

"Just raze them with your fire." He waved toward the oncoming danger.

"I'm not that practiced with my fire, and if I lose control, you and Robby's father will pay the price, along with whoever is in the vicinity. I'd rather not if I don't have to."

He pointed at the charred ground. "You seemed to have control while dispatching the bodies."

I glanced at him and shrugged. "It's inconsistent. Besides, I'm in the mood to bathe in the blood of demons right now." I grinned and instead of waiting for the demons to reach us, I barreled forward, using my amped-up vampire speed to take on the group of demons.

Robby was at my side in a flash, and he seemed to have the same taste for violence roiling in my blood. The two of us worked in tandem like we always had, protecting each other while annihilating the enemy as if we hadn't been benched for almost eight months.

I kept an eye out for Robby's father and Phillip, drawing my blade back a few times to stop a potentially fatal blow from hitting the wrong target before I jumped back into the fray.

When the last demon lay in a bloody heap, I turned and surveyed my team. Robby had a gash on his leg, but that was it. Phillip seemed to be uninjured, and the least blood-soaked of us all. Robert Senior had a few more oozing cuts and the same wild wolf grin that Robby sported.

I glanced down at myself, taking stock. I didn't go unharmed, but none of my cuts and bruises were life threatening. But they would hurt like a bitch once my adrenaline faded.

Robby stepped forward and licked the length of my arm and then my face before he nuzzled against me, bloodying the areas that he had cleaned with the gore clinging to his fur.

I pushed his muzzle away. "Later," I whispered and met his gaze. "We need to get back and figure out our next move."

"The harpy."

I glanced at Phillip and nodded. "And with this much activity, this place will be crawling with agents soon." I started to walk toward the nearest subway station as Robby and his father shifted back to human form. Robby's hiss pulled me back around.

I waved a bandage around the cut on his leg and then reclothed us all in clean outfits. I couldn't do a thing about the blood covering our skin. We looked like a fresh set of zombies cast from *The Walking Dead*. Especially Robby, with his limping gait and his arm around his father's shoulders.

Unlike the early morning ride to the tattoo shop from the Bronx, this subway was a little more crowded. However, people shuffled away from us.

"None of you will remember us being here," I said loud enough to carry over the subway car. "Except you three." I touched Robby, Robert, and Phillip.

"Lady, you really are a wonder." Phillip chuckled under his breath.

"Are you hurt?" one of the passengers asked.

"No. We just came from a night shoot in Central Park. This is makeup." I waved at our appearances and smiled in the sweetest way I could.

I had to do the compulsion three more times before we reached our stop. Unfortunately, we did leave a blood mark where we stood, but no one on the train would remember us and hopefully over the next hour, the comings and goings of passengers would smudge our footprints enough to make it disappear. I conjured a mop and dragged it behind us as we walked, wiping up whatever trail we might be leaving behind us. I left it in an alcove near the stairwell, because I didn't dare use magic this close to the tattoo shop.

By the time we got to the tattoo parlor, there was no more trail behind us. And the moment Phillip reached for the door, Johnson tore it open, his eyes wide and darting at each of us before relief swept over him.

"You smell like dead demon," he said as soon as he closed the door behind us.

"Lots of dead demons." Phillip grinned. "You failed to tell me just how lethal she is with a sword." He pointed at me. "I think she took down double the count of your alpha, and he's vicious."

Johnson smiled back at Phillip. "They are a sight to behold when they fight together, and I'd imagine she is much more lethal than she was before she was turned."

"She is." Robby limped toward the stairs, glancing back at me. "We're taking the shower first. I need her to take a look at that cut. It might need stitches."

"I'm surprised you didn't run into any agents," Johnson said. "The alarms were going off and an all-hands-on deck call went out."

"Subway." I smiled. "Safer than a cab."

We disappeared upstairs, with Robby leading the way to the bathroom. As we peeled off the tacky clothing, I balled up the garments and dunked them into the garbage can. Leaving them on the floor seemed wrong as a guest and burning them would likely start a fire, so the garbage can was it.

Robby was already under the warm water, lathering soap in his hair. It rained red as his fingers ran over his scalp. He stared at me, and a hint of a smile tilted his lips. His cock stood at attention despite his bloodied leg.

"You were fucking amazing." He pulled me to him and crushed my lips.

He had told me seeing me in battle turned him on, but this was a whole new side of Robby as he hiked me onto his hips and pressed me against the wall, fucking me in the shower as if we hadn't just killed over fifty demons in a field and were still covered in gore.

His passion took my breath away, as did his kiss. It was demanding, and punishing, and possessive all mingled together, and battered my mouth the way his hips plowed into mine. He moved his lips to my throat. "Bite me," he whispered.

I pushed him away so he would look at me, and I shook my head. "I'm never doing that again."

His eyes sparkled. "What if I want you to?"

"Then you are truly fucked up."

He shrugged and leaned down to my shoulder where his mark stood out on my pale skin. His teeth penetrated my skin, superimposing on the mark, and I gasped, arching into him as both pain and pleasure ran through me. My mark flared with his emotions, and I found my gaze moving to the vein throbbing in his neck.

His hips kept their brutal pace and his teeth remained in my skin, like a silent dare.

His passion, laced with something darker, ran through me like a hot sword and before I could control myself, I sank my teeth into his throat. The reward of his blood gave me a high I thought I'd never feel again, and with it an orgasm that nearly made me scream out his name, but I was too busy pulling mouthfuls of blood from him as he groaned against my shoulder.

It only took a few gulps to realize what I was doing, and I pulled away, swiping my finger over the punctures with a gasp.

He lifted his head with a bloody smile and kissed me as his pace slowed, replaced by brutal aftershocks of pleasure. All I tasted was fire and ice and a passion beyond this world.

When he pulled away, I swatted his chest. "You made me break my promise," I hissed.

"Sorry." But he didn't look the least bit sorry. A smile toyed on his lips, and we uncoupled so we could clean the rest of the blood off.

"You aren't one bit sorry." I grabbed the shampoo off the shelf and dumped a healthy amount into my hair. Before I could start scrubbing, he turned me, so my back faced him, and began to massage the shampoo into my scalp and through my hair until the water ran clear. I soaped up my skin as he finished the last of my hair, and then I rinsed as he did a quick wash. He leaned over and licked my shoulder, closing up the bite as best as he could.

"I needed that. It was the last fear I had to break." He turned off the shower and then squeezed the water from my hair.

I glanced down at his leg. It still oozed a little, but it wasn't even close to needing stitches. "You'll just need a bandage, so pants don't irritate that cut."

He looked me over. "Yours are just flesh wounds, too." He cupped my face. "You scared me a little when you barreled into those demons."

I rolled my eyes. "I needed to slay. It's been too long."

He smiled and his eyes twinkled. "I get it. You're a badass."

I stepped out of the shower and wrapped myself in a towel. We hadn't grabbed the bag of our clothes on our way in, and I didn't feel like walking through the apartment in only a towel.

"Come on. I'm sure the others would like to clean up, too." Robby grabbed a towel from the small linen closet and stepped out of the bathroom, heading downstairs and into the living room. I stayed in the hallway, but I caught the smirk Johnson gave him. His father just stared out the window, but I could tell he knew what just happened in the bathroom by the pink hue in his visible cheek.

Without a word, Robby grabbed the bag and sauntered down the hall to the spare bedroom that we had claimed for ourselves, leaving the guest bathroom to his father to clean up.

As I pulled on one of the last pairs of clothing in the bag, I sighed. I wasn't looking forward to whatever battle lay ahead of us now. This one had gone without a loss, but my gut told me that it was only a matter of time before our luck ran out.

TAINTED MIND 14

A KNOCK SOUNDED ON THE bedroom door just as we finished dressing. Robby opened the door to find Phillip on the other side, with a brush in his hand. He held it out to me.

"We need to work on your ability to control your fire. Running into that crowd of demons was not a smart thing to do, young lady. All that should have been left in that field was ash." His eyebrow cocked with the admonishment.

My cheeks heated at the chiding of this ancient soul eater. "I needed to vent some of this fury that I've capped since we escaped Cassius's place."

"By putting your team at risk?" He crossed his arms. "And that's exactly what you did. You put the three of us at risk by your impulsive behavior."

"We've fought demons before, thus the blades." I tried to deflect, but deep down I knew he was right.

He leaned forward into my personal space, crowding me. "You still put us all at risk when you have the power to obliterate anything."

"When I'm pressured, I lose control. I go off like a fucking nuclear explosion. Would you have preferred to see half this city as ash?" My hands found my hips and attitude flowed from me like a skunk shooting off stink.

He closed the distance, staring down at me. "You need to learn to control your temper and your panic."

"No shit," I spat up at him. I wasn't too proud to admit I was a disaster where my fire was concerned. "But where the hell are we going to train with fire?" My eyes blazed with irritation.

Robby cleared his throat, and I realized I had broken out in flame.

I shook my head, claiming control and dousing the flames at the same time. I stepped back. "I'm aware I need training. I just don't know where I can train without burning whatever surrounds me to the ground." I avoided eye contact.

"How about we try the room Johnson was in when you arrived? We can staple fire-retardant blankets to the walls and ceiling, and you should be good to go."

I looked up at Phillip. He was risking a hell of a lot, allowing me to train in his home. "You will want to cover the floor, too."

"Fine. And the floor." He rolled his eyes, and Robby smirked. "Give me a few hours to clean up Johnson's mess, get some blankets and fire extinguishers, and then we can get started."

"Really? Don't you have to work today?"

"It's Sunday. I don't work on Sundays. It's usually my day to do all the things I need to or my day to just have a good time."

"So, you consider the possibility of this building going up in smoke fun?" I didn't comment on having a day off. We never seemed to. Even on vacations, anytime the agency called, we were expected to drop whatever we were doing and get to the office.

"No. It's a need-to-do kind of thing." He gave me a look that made me want to shrink in on myself.

Before I could think of a witty comeback, Phillip turned on his heel and sauntered out of the room. I turned to Robby and his infuriating smirk.

"What?" I snapped. I didn't like being wrong. And I certainly didn't like the fact that I put everyone at risk. I just wanted to let off steam and didn't think it through, which seemed to be a new pattern of mine.

"Maybe we should have let you kill all those demons by yourself. Then perhaps you'd be a little chill instead of still stressed."

I glared at him. "I'm stressed because I don't want to burn this place down." It was a half-assed excuse. I was stressed for more reasons than I could count. And the unsettled feeling in my stomach added to it all.

"Then don't."

Like my fire's control was a conscious decision. Me lighting up while arguing with Phillip should have given them all a clue at how not in control I was. "It's not that easy. You've seen me lose control."

"I have, and it's badass." He crossed and took me in his arms, grinning down at me as if he were ready to tear my clothes off again.

"I need food." My gaze lowered to where I had bitten him before traveling back to his face. His cheeks lost a little of their color and he tried to smile, but that skittishness was back.

"There is no rhyme or reason to PTSD." He closed his eyes and took a long, slow breath. "Let's go get some food. Maybe when we are done, Phillip will be ready to test the fire-retardant blankets." He placed a soft kiss on my forehead and then led me down to the kitchen to rummage for food.

IT WAS MORE LIKE HALF a day before Phillip sought me out. And now I stood at one end of the room with hands that itched to let go and nerves so raw, I doubted I could control my powers.

The room cleaned up well. All the debris had been cleared, and the walls, ceilings, and floors were covered with fireproof blankets as requested. These blankets were the kind they advertise for putting out grease fires and keeping people safe enough to escape from a burning building. But I was still skeptical. Under the blankets, items like drywall and wood frames were still flammable. And the last thing I wanted to do was burn down Phillip's building.

"Concentrate," Phillip said in my earpiece. He stood outside, with only the window to view inside.

I stared at the umpteenth candle. The last dozen tries to light just the wick had ended with a pile of wax on the metal table and, beyond that, the wall covering was marred black. This was different than cauterizing wounds, where I just blazed with my fingertip. Phillip wanted me to send a stream of fire at the wick and pull it back without melting the wax.

"I got it." I sent him a glare and then closed my eyes, taking a slow, deep breath to steady my irritation. Sweat dripped into my eye, and I swiped it away. After a few more steadying breaths, I reached my arm out, willing flame to the tips of my fingers. This was the easy part.

With my focus on the clean white wick sticking out of the blue tapered candle, I imagined my flame barreling out with all its fury, slowing as it neared the candle, lighting the wick, and then rolling back into my hand like a fiery boomerang. When I let my fire go, it did race forward, but there was no slowing this plowing beam. It vaporized the candle this time and caught the blanket on the far wall on fire.

I fisted my hand, dousing the flames. Phillip opened the door and hurried to the flaming blanket with a fire extinguisher in hand. He pointed the nozzle and depressed the trigger, sending white foam all over the fire, putting it out in seconds.

He turned to look at the table and sighed at the blackened steel. "At least you didn't melt the table." He smiled and waved at the nearly charred metal like that was a win.

I wiped my face and looked at what was left of the fireproof blanket. It hung in blackened tatters, and the material underneath carried a blackened hue. "Wasn't that supposed to be fireproof?" I pointed at the pieces.

He just shrugged.

"I've had enough for today."

This time, Phillip nodded, caving to my nervousness at ruining his livelihood. "You can juggle fireballs, but you can't aim and pull back very effectively."

"My aim is killer."

He laughed. "Yes, I suppose it is. But the pullback is just as important as the throw. Licking the wick. That's all you have to do to light the candle."

The way he said it was a little suggestive, and the gleam in his eye truly radiated his meaning.

I just rolled my eyes. "I'm with Robby." I glanced at the opening of the room. If Robby was anywhere within hearing range, he'd be down here in a millisecond to put Phillip in his place.

His cheeks turned pink. "The candle wick. Jesus. You have a dirty mind."

"Oh, like you didn't mean it that way," I teased. The more time I spent with Phillip, the more I liked the guy. He was entertaining and smart, but he was not Robby. He'd never be a part of me the way Robby was. Yet, I couldn't help but needle Phillip whenever he got close to the line of improprieties.

His lips tilted on one side, and he flicked a gaze in my direction. "Sorry. I just can't help it sometimes."

"It's okay. What's a little teasing between friends." I let him off the hook and glanced around the room. I waved toward the tattered blanket still hanging on the wall. "We're going to need more of those blankets if we're going to continue this insanity."

"Yes. We will. Which is why I'm letting you chill for the rest of the day. Having a structural fire here would be a disaster with the hidden half of the building." His smile faded as he sighed. "It may take a couple of days to get more."

"Has Robert found the harpy yet?" I headed out of the room, letting the question linger.

"Not that I am aware of." Phillip held the cellar door open for me.

Instead of heading up to the apartment, I made a beeline for the hidden half of the building he mentioned. I wanted to see what Johnson, Robby, and his father had found.

The command center was buzzing. Every screen flashed images, and the lobby of the Monster Defense Agency was complete pandemonium.

Robby's father stood in the center of the room with his arms crossed and the most haunting smirk on his face. He glanced at me. "This is what panic looks like. They don't know what happened at the park, only that there are a whole slew of dead agents and dead demons. And no one can find Terrance or his witch." He radiated a measure of glee as he spoke.

Robby glanced back at him. "Those were all good agents we killed." At least he had some sense of respect for those who were just following orders.

"And every single one of them had a gun pointed at your mate," Phillip said from beside me. "And not all of them were tranquilizers."

My head snapped to look at him.

He shrugged at me. "My contacts mentioned it. They took a couple of the guns for their arsenals."

Robby stared at him and whatever compassion he had displayed evaporated, and he glared back at the screen.

"They can't find me either," Robert Senior said. "And the vampires are gone. Not just one or two like they thought, but all of them." He glanced at me. "Well, all but one."

"It's been a few days since that happened, though."

He huffed. "Terrance must have kept that under wraps. He was too busy trying to find me after I killed his niece."

"Who is the next in charge after you?" Robby asked.

The known chain of command had been Terrance, then Robert. Then dozens of equally weighted senior managers, like Harrison had been, who were probably battling it out as to who was in charge while the entire organization went to shit.

"It depends on how many of those managers were out in those trees."

I had never considered that, and from Robby's raised eyebrows, he hadn't either.

Robert Senior laughed. "You don't really think he'd trust just any agent to back him up in that field? He'd only choose his most trusted advisers and those who were militantly loyal."

I glanced at Robby. Very few of us were militantly loyal to the agency. We followed orders but grumbled about it after. Obviously, Johnson struggled enough to let some people go, like Phillip. And I didn't recall any agents taking down other agents, but it had to have happened. One day they were there and the next day a tragic event had happened that took them out. It always left me cold. We all knew the agency was not loyal to us, so his father's comments felt true.

"So, there might not be any chain of command anymore."

"How much do you think the harpy knows?" Johnson asked as he began to type away on the keyboard in front of him.

Robert Senior chewed on his lower lip and then shrugged.

I approached him. "What if you were to return to the agency? If most of the agents don't know what went down, you could say you were at home, tending to pack business since Johnson and Terrance's niece had been put down for crossing the agency?"

He glanced at me and then back at the screens. The way his eyes dodged from screen to screen, and his hand slowly rubbed his chin, reminded me of his son. He was considering my question.

"You could flush out the harpy." Robby turned to his father.

Robert Senior nodded. "If shit goes sideways..." He locked his gaze on Robby's.

Robby slowly nodded. "They might ask you to talk with a seer to be sure."

His father raised an eyebrow. "Do you know how many seers I've snowed over the years?"

Robby's jaw dropped open. He blinked and then snapped his mouth closed. "How?"

"I was given a gift from a witch I saved. She put a spell into my blood that gives the seers whatever images I choose. And the only thing that could nullify it is being bled to death."

"And you couldn't have passed that to me?" Robby gawked. After all, it was his encounter with a seer after we slept together that put us both on the agency's hit list.

"I was still playing the game of bad father, so no. I couldn't offer this to you before I found Mindy a different identity."

Johnson turned away from the computer. "You saved witches?"

Robert Senior smiled. "A few of them, yes. I have some solid contacts in the werewolf council who have helped over the years for both the witches and wolves I've managed to get out."

"The werewolf council?"

"We had to give a yearly report to them regarding the agency's practices." He shrugged. "Terrance dragged me down there in the beginning and then let me go alone some years later after I proved I was the worst father on the planet. I found an ally early on. Their rules aren't as outlandish as Terrance made them out to be, and if they got wind of his affinity for using boiling silver, they would have had him taken out a long time ago."

"So, you weren't all that honest with them either," Robby said.

His father shook his head.

"Are you being honest with us now?" He shot back.

"Yes."

Robby looked at me, and I sighed as irritation scraped my skin like a sharp nail. I believed his father, but I got what he wanted me to do. "Are you being honest with us?" I asked, pushing my influence on him.

"Yes," he repeated and glared at me.

"There you go. We both know he isn't immune to my influence." I waved at his father and met Robby's gaze with a sharp, warning glare. I hated it when he asked me to use my influence just as much as he hated it when I controlled him.

"I needed to be sure," he said softly, his eyes pleading for me to understand.

"Really?" His father spread his hands out. "You still don't trust me?"

Robby glared at his father, and then closed his eyes and hung his head. "You've conditioned me not to."

The aggravation etched into his father's face smoothed out. "You're right." He sighed and looked back at me. "And the more I think about your idea, the more I like it. It is a risk because there could still be insiders who knew I betrayed Terrance, but maybe the harpy doesn't know that quite yet because Terrance moved fucking fast to try to stamp me out and get Sarah into custody. But if the harpy does know..." He trailed off and stared at the monitors before he cocked his head and nodded. "If the harpy knows, she'll probably use me as bait."

I winced as he said the words. He was bait either way we looked at it, just the way I had been in that field. Our odds of pulling this off without losing anyone lowered with each battle.

"How do we keep in touch?" Phillip asked.

"I'll contact you." Robert Senior glanced at his son and gave a nod.

He turned to head out, and I grabbed his arm. He glanced at my hand and then at me. "Family doesn't leave without a hug." I gave him a hug. My parents never let me leave without a hug. I didn't hug often because I hadn't had a true family in years, but the people in this room qualified. And if this somehow was goodbye, I wanted him to know I cared.

His arms slowly encircled me. "You know the drill," he whispered in my ear.

I pulled back. "Protect your son?" I raised my eyebrows. *That's a given.*

He smiled and nodded, giving me a soft peck on the cheek. "I'm glad he has someone like you."

My throat tightened, and I blinked the sudden wetness from my eyes and pointed toward Robby. "He needs a hug, too." My voice cracked with emotion. *What the hell was wrong with me?* I was never this emotional.

Robby rolled his eyes at me, but he met his father in the middle for a quick hug. Although his father held on a little longer while he whispered in Robby's ear. I didn't catch all the words, but it was something about being the rightful alpha of the pack.

Robby pulled away and glanced in Johnson's direction, but his father pointed his index finger right into Robby's chest. Nothing else was said, but I got the gist. Robert Senior gave Johnson and Phillip a two-finger wave and headed out of the control room.

We all stood in silence, digesting the last few minutes and staring at the monitors. My chest squeezed enough for me to grab a chair.

"Did we just send your father to his death?"

15

TAINTED MIND 15

THE MOMENT ROBBY'S FATHER WALKED into the agency on screen, he was surrounded by agents. Although we couldn't hear anything from the one camera Phillip had planted, we could almost feel the tension radiating off everyone. Some had guns drawn, but Robby's father spread his hands out slowly, palms facing those with the guns.

The gunmen's pinched faces smoothed and eventually they sheathed their guns and saluted Robby's father before starting to disperse. The panic of the entry that had been present earlier seemed to be completely gone by the appearance of Robert Senior. It was amazing to see the sudden relief on almost everyone's face now that one of the leaders of the agency had finally shown up.

Robert Senior pointed at one of them, and he followed as Robert walked toward the elevator. The gunman's hands were animated and he seemed to be explaining things in detail.

I wished I was a fly on the wall to hear the conversation. They stepped into the elevator, and Robert looked straight into the camera and gave us a slight nod. Things hadn't gone sideways. Yet.

I slumped in the chair and took a breath. I hadn't realized I had been holding it from the moment he entered the screen until the elevator doors closed. I glanced at Robby, and his gaze found mine, filled with the same relief loosening the tightness in my muscles.

"How'd training go?" he asked.

"I need more blankets." Phillip glanced at his watch. "So I'll be out for a little while." He bowed and rolled his hand in a grand gesture before he let himself out of the command center.

I glanced at Robby and Johnson. "What do we do now?"

The way Robby's smile tilted, and a single eyebrow rose, immediately started my engine.

"Oh, for the love of God!" Johnson stood up with a huff and stormed out of the room, leaving Robby and me staring at each other, both wearing the same knowing smirk.

Apparently, this morning hadn't been enough for my mate. "I'm tired." As if on cue, a yawn gripped me. I hadn't slept more than a few hours before we headed out to the park. "So, a little sleep is in order before you exhaust me further."

Robby pouted like a little boy as he stalked toward me. "You'll sleep much better after." He slung his arm around my waist, pulling me against him as he guided me back to the chair I had been sitting in and pushed me into the seat.

I landed and a puff of air left my chest as my gaze landed on the front of his pants. His hard form stood out against the jeans he wore, and I glanced up at him. He leaned down and placed his hands on the arms of the chair, and then kissed me softly.

"If you don't feel up to riding, how about putting your sweet mouth to good use." He straightened and glanced at his watch. "We probably have a half hour at best."

I leaned back in the chair and stared up at him, crossing my arms. "Is this the way you were with all your girlfriends?" I pursed my lips. Although I wasn't opposed to the idea, it was his assumption that irked me.

He blinked down at me as his hands stalled on the button of his jeans. "What do you mean?"

"If you can't get a fuck, you get a suck?"

He stepped back and dropped his hands. "No," he said, but it wasn't all that convincing.

I smirked at him. "Why are you the one who gets to be satisfied?" I challenged him with a cocked eyebrow.

He narrowed his eyes, and his hands landed on his hips. "Because you said you were tired, and for me it's a quick zip of the pants versus stripping you." He cocked his head. "But if that's what you'd like..." He waved for me to remove my pants.

I glanced around the room. The likelihood of either Johnson or Phillip walking in on us was pretty high. This was the command center and not a bedroom, and my aversion to voyeurism won out.

"Come here." I leaned forward, grabbing his hand. I pulled him between my legs and reached up to unbutton his pants.

He placed his hand over mine. "If you don't want to…"

I glared up at him. "If I didn't want to, I wouldn't. You should know that by now."

He laughed. "Were you just busting my balls?"

I unzipped his pants and smiled as I popped his cock free of the tight fabric. "Yes. You deserved it for assuming I would automatically take care of your needs."

He started to open his mouth to argue, but I slipped him in my mouth and a low groan escaped his lips instead. His hands threaded through my hair, keeping it out of my face, but he didn't take control from me. He let me play with him and suck him as deep as I was comfortable with while he said my name with such reverence, I got a little wet myself.

"Fuck," he whispered. His hands tightened in my hair, and then his hips pushed deeper as he thickened in my mouth.

A stream of hot cum shot down my throat, and I swallowed and swallowed until his grip on my hair loosened. I sucked as he pulled out, and he groaned, as if this were his idea of heaven. His hooded eyes found mine as he readjusted himself and zipped up.

Robby grabbed my hand and pulled me to his chest, capturing a hungry kiss as he spun around and took a seat, pulling me to his lap. I tried to break the kiss, but he held tighter. And then his hand slid between my legs, finding the spot that ached for him.

He ravaged my mouth while his fingers manipulated me through my jeans. He smiled when I gasped. His hand stopped long enough to unbutton my pants and then he slid his hand inside the tight confines. His fingers resumed their dance on my clit until my body tightened. His other hand held the back of my head in place as the kiss continued. He didn't allow me up for air, battling my tongue with his as he played me to my own release.

And when I let go, his finger slid into the wetness like the ultimate tease.

"You're fucking dripping," Robby said against my lips as he finally pulled away from my mouth. His eyes burned as they met mine. "You sure you don't want to lose the pants?"

I wasn't sure of anything as his finger continued to enter and exit me like a slow-motion plunge that just about had me tearing my clothing off.

The sound of the keypad buttons being pushed rang out, and Robby pulled his hand free. I scrambled to straighten myself out as Robby slid his finger into his mouth, sucking my juices off with a playful grin.

I stood and nearly fell on the floor from legs that had little strength left. I had the feeling I looked as wrecked as I felt. Robby stood and adjusted himself before the door swung open.

Phillip stepped into the room and took one look at us before his eyes widened. He stopped, his gaze bouncing between us and something on the screen.

We had been so consumed with each other that we hadn't looked up at the screens in a while.

A tall woman marched through the lobby. I blinked because her hair seemed long and black, but it looked overlaid by white. Her skin had the same type of overlay, but instead of smooth like I saw in my initial glance, her skin was wrinkled beyond human capacity, and it was a putrid gray color.

I swiveled my gaze to Phillip, and his lips were pulled back in a hateful sneer.

"It's the harpy, isn't it?" I asked in that breathy way I had after sex.

Phillip nodded and closed the door behind him. "I hope for your father's sake that she does not know of his duplicity."

Robby stiffened next to me and glanced between the screen and Phillip. "That's the harpy?" He pointed at the woman now facing us in the elevator.

I wasn't sure what he saw, but the image I was seeing had to be the same one that pulled a growling grunt from Phillip.

"She's not hideous," he said.

I spun to look at him like he was short half a deck. "Yes, she is."

"She wears a glamour. Otherwise, people would run screaming at the sight of her." Phillip crossed the room to stand closer to the monitors. His hands clenched and opened over and over.

"I've never seen her before," Robby said. "Why show up now without being contacted?"

"Because the chaos and fear that we saw running rampant suddenly calmed when your father arrived. She feeds off chaos and fear, and would have soaked it in for a lot longer before she stepped in to take over the agency with her diabolical orders." His hands still did their violent parade of opening and closing, as though he were trying not to completely lose his cool.

"Besides vampires, what other creatures does she have domain over?" I stared at the screen, wondering what type of monsters we would be encountering now that the apex predators were extinct.

He glanced at me and then back to the screen. "There is a faction of soul eaters she has at her disposal, but they are more demon than human, and loyal as fucking dogs." He ran his hand down his face and then looked at Robby. "And they don't need a mass of soul eaters together to kill on sight. I need the three of you in the tattoo parlor, now."

"Why?" I really wanted to catch some z's.

"Because there is a tattoo that can make you...resistant to soul eaters." He glanced at me with a measure of regret.

"Why would you do that?" *And why hadn't he given us the tattoo before we went into that field with Terrance?* I kept my mouth closed and waited for his answer.

He turned to me. "Because, frankly, I like you. All of you. And I'd rather not have what happened to those agents happen to you." His voice hissed with impatience. "I should have done it before we sent Robert back into the agency." He glanced at Robby. "I'll have to figure out a way to get a message to him, because if there is any forewarning of running into a phoenix, then that bitch will bring the big guns to try to kill us all."

16

TAINTED MIND 16

"WHO'S FIRST?" PHILLIP ASKED AS we stood in his tattoo parlor. His eyes lingered on me before passing to Robby and Johnson. "There is a specific location that the tattoo must go." He unbuttoned his shirt and pointed to the spot on the middle of his breast bone. Just below the start of the phoenix tattoo was a small ornate tattoo that looked as if it were made of gold, sapphires, and rubies. It shimmered and almost looked like the eye of Horus, but a much more ornate version. His gaze went from Robby to me and then back.

Robby's gaze narrowed, and he slowly shook his head. "You're not suggesting what I think you are."

"Oh, for Christ's sake. He saw my bare ass." I stepped forward and reached for the hem of my shirt.

Phillip splayed his hand out. "I have something similar to a hospital johnny for you to wear." He pointed to a curtained area as his cheeks reddened. He glanced at Robby. "It has to go there, or it does not work," he explained.

"How the fuck do you know that?" Robby growled.

"Trust me. I know."

I sent Robby a look warning him to stop being overprotective, and then slipped behind the screen and found a stack of exactly what Phillip described. The johnny that he described actually had a seam on each side that had a strip of adhesive and I followed the instructions next to the garment, peeling back the tape to reveal the sticky fabric that I pressed to my skin so I could have an iota of modesty. My skin warmed at the thought of the tattoo. It was almost as gorgeous as the one of Robby on my ass.

I stepped out a second later, and Robby glanced at the way I was covered and seemed to pull his alpha protectiveness back a notch or two.

"These are actually pretty cool." I waved at the open shirt I wore pasted to the inner curve of my breasts, leaving an opening straight down my middle.

Phillip smiled. "Better than just a pasty?" He winked at me.

"Much better."

He glanced at Robby. "If you or Johnson would like one, feel free." He waved at the screen and got an eye roll in response.

The minute I got into the chair, Phillip took a deep breath and met my gaze with one that showed a level of worry that made my skin ache.

"What is it?" I asked, and he glanced away.

"I did not always know the power of proper location for this symbol." His hand touched his chest. "I learned the hard way." His gaze flitted to Robby. "This will make you all impervious to a soul eater, much like the way your other tattoo made you impervious to a vampire's compulsion."

"Will it look like yours?" I asked, mesmerized by the way the jewel tones on his captured the light.

"As best as I can make it. But mine is made with precious metals. Yours will only be ink, but I can make that ink metallic. However, the minute I complete this tattoo, you will feel...discomfort until I complete the spell."

"Discomfort?"

He took a breath. "The spell is actually quite painful. It anchors your soul to your flesh."

I blinked at him as he continued to stare at me, trying to silently convey the meaning. But whatever he was trying to tell me was lost in translation.

"When the body dies..." He twirled his hand a couple of times, coaxing me to finish the sentence.

Then it all clicked together. "The soul dies?" I winced saying it.

He nodded. "And your phoenix abilities can't bring us back." He glanced at the three of us. "So, if anyone of us gets killed, you won't be able to use your magical tears to bring us back." He pointedly looked at Robby and then back at me. "It will protect you from a soul eater, but nothing else."

My heart dropped, and my cheeks cooled. If this ended like the last showdown, I would lose Robby. That could not happen.

"And what about Sarah? What if she gets killed?" Robby asked, ignoring my reaction.

I pointed at Robby. "I will always come back to you. I already told you that."

Phillip didn't say anything but the flash in his eyes was enough to make my mouth dry.

"You promise?" Robby asked. "Like, on *my life* promise?" His eyes begged in a way that I couldn't refuse.

I nodded. "I promise."

"Then protect her," he said to Phillip and pointed at me with no regard to what that meant if things turned south for him.

Phillip turned to his station and mixed three vials of paint. The first shimmered as gold as the adornments on my ass. The others looked like liquid jewels. He loaded the gold first, then leaned forward with the same concentration I saw from him when he tattooed Robby with the anti-compulsion tattoo.

The needle burned this time, being so close to the bone beneath. Phillip didn't notice my wince, but Robby did and took my hand in his.

Phillip muttered under his breath as he formed the tattoo. Magic filled the air around us so thick, I could barely draw a full breath. I couldn't see the tattoo, but every injection of ink felt as if he were using a butane torch instead of a tattoo gun. It felt like he was not only staining my skin, but my very soul.

I remained still, but I squeezed Robby's hand so hard that he grunted from my steel-like grip. To his credit, he didn't attempt to pull his hand away, but he did tighten his grip, too, to combat his hand being crushed.

I stared into the blue depths of his eyes, getting lost there as my body endured the pain. In Robby's eyes, I saw the promise of a future and that promise was something I was hell-bent on seeing come to fruition. I wanted a life with this man. I wanted children. A whole damn brood of them if I had my way. And I wanted a settled future, not a life on the run.

The same wants reflected in his eyes, and my promise to him embedded into the magic around us as much as whatever Phillip was conjuring.

Phillip paused, wiped the tattoo area, and changed out the gold ink for the metallic blue. Before he started again, he glanced at me. "You okay for me to continue?"

I nodded, not trusting my voice.

He went back to work and that soul-burning began again, along with his mumbling chants.

Sweat broke out on my forehead and upper lip. It dripped down the back of my skull like wet molasses by the time he switched to the red vial.

His gaze flicked to mine and then, without asking whether he should continue, he leaned down with the needle.

My ears buzzed louder than the ink gun, and I took measured breaths, concentrating as best I could through the agony. It was as if Phillip were tattooing my heart instead of my skin, and each beat sent pain spiraling to every nerve in my body, overloading me. At last, he turned the gun off, and my back bowed as he continued chanting. It was too big for me, and I clenched my teeth against a scream. But it came anyway.

My fire wanted to lash out, but I kept it in check.

As soon as the last word fell from his lips, the agony vanished, and silence settled on the room. Light poured from where he had been working and settled over the rest of my skin like a net sinking in until the glow faded.

I panted in the seat and closed my eyes now that the ordeal was over. Phillip looked just as frazzled as I felt. He leaned back in his seat as though doing the tattoo had taken a toll on him as well.

He reached for a wet rag and the antibacterial cleaner and went to work sanitizing and covering the tattoo before he looked up at me and gave me a weary smile.

Then Phillip looked at Robby and Johnson. "Who's next?"

17

TAINTED MIND 17

NEITHER ROBBY'S NOR JOHNSON'S SEEMED to have the same intensity as mine did, but their tattoos were just as stunning when he finished. Phillip looked wrecked when he put away his tattoo guns and cleaned the station. The black circles under his eyes stood out against his paler than normal skin.

He glanced at us. "I need to eat," he said, and then lowered his eyes.

"I can whip something up in the kitchen," I said. The way his gaze cut to mine, I suddenly understood. He needed his kind of nourishment. Whatever he had done to us left him at nearly empty. He needed a soul and from the looks of him, he needed a hell of a lot more than just a week's time.

"You can take a week from me again," I said.

His sad gaze found mine. "I'll never taste you again, ma cherie," he said with such a sad tone that my stomach cramped.

"Oh." I looked to Johnson and Robby for help.

Robby looked at the floor and nodded. "Just be sure it's a criminal who deserves it," he said with a heavy sigh, and looked at Phillip.

Phillip wiped his hands and buttoned his shirt back up. "I will." And then he walked out the door.

A moment later, I heard the door to the alley clang shut, and I glanced at Robby.

"You're condoning killing?" I asked. More like squawked.

"I wouldn't normally, but he just spent almost all his mojo on us, if you hadn't noticed. He needs to eat to sustain life. Just like we all do. It's just that his meals are a little more questionable." He shrugged and started toward the apartment. "I'm kind of glad my dad wasn't here. I don't think Phillip would have had the juice left to finish another one."

I started after them, but my legs felt like rubber now that I was on my feet. I had gone from the tattoo chair to another seat after Phillip finished with me. Robby had gotten my shirt and bra for me, but I was too sore to lift my arms to put the shirt over the johnny.

Robby slowed and looked back at me with his brow creased. He moved out of the way so Johnson could head up the stairs and then backtracked to me. Concern laced his gaze. "Are you okay?" he asked softly.

"I am exhausted." But it was more than that. I was almost as drained as Phillip had looked. After all, I had fought at least two dozen demons, sent his father into what looked like his possible death, and stripped one of my only friends of his energy. And we still had to worry about that damned harpy.

Robby leaned over and grabbed me behind the knees, effortlessly picking me up in his arms.

I didn't argue. I just leaned my head into his chest. I don't even remember us climbing the stairs. Darkness gripped me, yanking me completely under like a coffin closing.

* * *

STARTLED AWAKE, I BLINKED MY eyes open, trying to gain my bearings. Robby's snore rang in my ear, and remnants of my dreams flashed in my mind. But it wasn't his snore that woke me. Something else set off the alarms in my head.

Another set of timed clangs echoed, and I sat up. Robby's eyes blinked open, as well. Training and being on the run conditioned me to react, and react fast. The bangs repeated in that same pattern. The pattern his father had used when we first got here. I glanced at Robby, and then I jumped out of bed and out the bedroom door in a flash.

I swung open the door to the alley, and Robert pushed his way inside, slamming the door behind us just as quickly.

"Where is Phillip?" he said with a voice full of accusation.

The door to the tattoo shop opened, and Phillip stuck his head through the crack. "I've got a client. Do you mind?" His voice was low, and his warning clear. He didn't want his clientele to know we were here.

He looked a million times better than when we last saw him. "When did you get back?" I asked.

Phillip's gaze shot to mine with an expression that screamed "stop talking."

"How many, Phillip?" Robert Senior snarled.

"Half a dozen gangbangers who were taking turns with that woman." He raised an eyebrow in a silent challenge.

"Six?" I balked just as much as Robert Senior.

His gaze landed on me, and he nodded. "Maybe more. I was tired and the injustice of what they were doing pissed me the hell off, so yes. I relieved them all of their time here." He grimaced. "They tasted like pure evil, too, so it was the kind of meal I desperately needed." There wasn't an iota of regret in his tone. "And I have enough juice to ink you after I finish." He pointed at Robert and then disappeared back into his shop, closing the door behind him.

We could hear his apology for the interruption to his client and then the drone of the tattoo gun resumed.

"You let him?" Robert glared at me and then at Robby, who was on the stairs in sweatpants.

I glanced down because I hadn't looked at what I was wearing when I ran down here and was suddenly aware that I did not have anything covering my legs. A long T-shirt draped over me, reaching to nearly my knees. It wasn't one of Robby's, and I raised an eyebrow and waved at my attire.

"I rummaged through Phillip's closet." Robby shrugged and then looked at his father. "Phillip nearly used everything he had doing these to keep us safe from other soul eaters." He pointed at the ornate eye on the middle of his bare chest. "So, yes. We did allow him to hunt and re-energize. We need him."

"Well, he's now on the agency's radar." Robert Senior wiped his face and shook his head. "I recognized his scent. But I don't think anyone else did." He glanced at the door behind him. "I think Johnson was the only other one who could identify Phillip by his scent."

"Well, that's good," I said, although I thought *"need"* was a strong word. He was our friend, and I know I'd been willing to bend rules in the past for friends.

"What's happening with the harpy?" Robby crossed behind me to wrap his arms around me.

His father took a deep breath. "She's a fucking piece of work. Thankfully, none of her cronies have the power to break the spell I'm under. Otherwise, I would be dead. They did bring a seer in, to make sure my alliances were to the agency. Especially after telling them that I had gone home to mourn my son's true death and that's why I wasn't around for whatever the hell happened in the park. There was just enough truth in what I told them to reflect in what I projected to the seer. I also told her I did not know what you were when I handed you and my son over to the vampires for killing Cassius Chase."

"What's the plan?" Robby asked.

His father shrugged. "The harpy isn't as angry about the annihilation of the vampires as I thought she'd be. They had been her allies for a very long time, but they had competing desires and couldn't be controlled the way the werewolf population can." He moved his weight from foot to foot, and the scowl on his face grew darker. "She feels conquering the human race should be easy. She just needs that pesky phoenix who survived to be extinguished." His gaze pierced mine. "So, I've been tasked with finding you."

"Conquering the human race?" I was still caught up with her lofty goals. It seemed to be the same as the mother of vampires.

His smile turned truly bitter. "She wants them trembling in fear until they are no more. And then she will turn her sights on us." He glanced at Robby. "She wants to bring an army of demons to rule us all."

"And I'm in her way?" I crossed my arms.

"Your death is the key to opening the doors to the demons she wants flooding the fucking earth. And these aren't the lesser demons we've battled. They are hell spawn, and she has a couple with her from when she slaughtered a phoenix. I guess the door opened enough for them to slip through but slammed shut seconds later because you existed."

I stared at him. "Thus the hunt for me for who knows how many centuries."

He nodded. "And that's where the competing desires play out. Vampires wanted your power to rule the world, and so does the harpy."

"Fuck. And my fire is the only thing that kills this bitch."

No one replied to my statement, but all three of us traded glances. I looked at the door to the tattoo shop. I needed more details about the harpy who had been taken down. And Phillip was just the person to enlighten me.

TAINTED MIND 18

IT WAS A GOOD HOUR before Phillip came up to the apartment. Robby, his father, and I had escaped upstairs to raid the refrigerator while waiting for him to finish his late-night customer.

"I'm ready for you now." Phillip looked at Robby's dad.

Robert Senior just stared at him from the chair. "I'm not sure I can protect you from the agency," he said after the air between them nearly crackled with hostility.

"They weren't good people, Robert." Phillip leveled a glare at him. "And the woman was okay when I left. Confused as shit, but okay."

Robert Senior leaned forward. "You didn't hide your face."

Phillip blinked, and then his eyes widened in understanding. "How much time do you think we have?"

Robert Senior wiped his face with his hand. "Maybe twelve hours at best."

"Then get your ass downstairs so I can do this tattoo and then I'll clean house like I've up and moved, and we'll hide in the command center." He glanced at us. "There are a couple of cots we can take from the storage room." He shrugged and looked at Robert Senior again. "I don't have all night."

Robby jogged down to the room and gathered what we had of ours into our backpack and grabbed both the clothing pack and the money pack. If we needed to truly bug out, having cash wasn't a bad thing. And then we made our way to the command center, depositing our bags.

Johnson was studying communications and glanced up when we entered. "I saw your dad come by. Anything I need to know?"

"He's been tasked with finding Sarah," Robby said. "He's getting his tattoo right now. We're going to have a chat with Phillip after he's done. There's some things we need to know, and Phillip's the only one who's seen a harpy taken down."

Johnson nodded. "I'm going to keep watch. It seems Phillip may have not been as clandestine as he should have."

"Yeah. My father mentioned that as well. Phillip's going to clean out after he finishes to give the impression that he left fast, and we're going to hunker down here."

Johnson glanced at the command center and back. "Not exactly ideal, especially with no way out."

I didn't argue with Johnson's assessment. The idea of being locked in this location with the doors easily viewed in the apartment and the storage room had me unsettled now that the seed had been planted. But Phillip wouldn't cage us in on purpose, would he?

My chest itched in response, but I refrained from scratching the tattoo film covering my new ink. Instead, we left and made our way into the tattoo shop.

Phillip didn't even glance up at us. He was hard at work on Robert Senior's chest. It was the first time I ever saw his father without a shirt, and I blinked and looked at Robby. His father was just as cut as he was. But there were scars across his chest, as though he had been whipped or cut with silver. Those type of wounds don't fade away.

From the stunned expression on Robby's face, he hadn't ever seen those marks either.

"My back is worse," Robert Senior said from the chair. His glance moved to his son, and he gave a tilted smile. "When was the last time you saw me come out of a shift in front of you?"

Robby blinked and shrugged as his brow creased. "When I was a kid?"

"When your mother was alive." He waved to the scars. "These were courtesy of the agency. Your mother being turned, and your brother and sister's death, wasn't enough. They decided I needed a lasting reminder of who owned me."

"Jesus," Robby whispered.

"Terrance made sure I knew he could haul you in and do the same if I stepped out of line again. And at your age, he wasn't sure you'd survive this kind of beating."

Phillip paused and glanced at Robert Senior before looking at us. "There's a suitcase in my closet. Can you pack it and bring it down to the command center? Make it look like I left in a hurry?" He went to begin again and paused. "There's also some air sanitizers in the closet. Saturate the place on your way out so your scents are all wiped out. Even the storeroom."

I wanted to talk to him, but he went back to work, mumbling the same words he had when he did all of our tattoos, so we turned and did as he asked. I even stripped the bed in the guest room and threw a load of his dirty laundry in the washer with the sheets. I cleaned out the sink and grabbed anything that didn't need to be refrigerated and threw them in bags, carting them down to the command center before I went back to help Robby sanitize the place.

With the laundry machine and dishwasher running, we sprayed the hell out of every room in the apartment until my nose tickled with the scent of the air freshener. We sprayed behind us as we went, muting all traces of us. The cans were nearly empty as we turned to the command center entry.

We sprayed the keypad after punching in the numbers Phillip had given us and slipped inside to wait for them to finish. It didn't take long for Robby's father to come in with his shirt in hand and the same stunning artwork on his chest that all three of us had. He slipped on his shirt and took a seat, waiting for Phillip.

Phillip came in with a case of water and the same case he had brought to our house to do our tattoos. "I left some of the things in the tattoo parlor. And I transferred the clothes from the washer to the dryer. I don't want mold in my washing machine." He glanced at us. "You did a great job making it look like a quick escape. It's almost like you've become experts at it." He smirked at us and glanced around. "Hopefully this isn't our residence for a long time."

"What about the doors here? They're pretty visible."

He laughed. "Only to those I allow entry. Not even the most sophisticated witch can see through the charms this place has." He glanced at me. "Even if you do your magic here, it's warded, so no one will know."

"Now you tell me that?" I glared at Phillip. "I could have conjured clothes and what we needed like that?" I snapped my fingers. This spoon-feeding of just enough information was beginning to wear on me.

He just shrugged.

I refocused on the current situation. My irritation could wait. "Now that you've got the tattoo, what's the plan?" I asked, looking at Robert Senior.

He sighed and glanced at Phillip before meeting my gaze. "We can't face off in New York City." He scanned the monitors. "Too many people would die if you go off like you did on that rural road before Cassius grabbed you two."

"I expect to blow the harpy to bits like that, so I agree." I glanced at Phillip. "Tell me exactly what happened with the phoenix you saw take down the harpy."

Phillip bit his lower lip, and his gaze wandered to Robby. "They both died, not just the harpy. But a couple of things did get released before the harpy died."

"He already explained the higher demons who protect the harpy." I waved toward Robby's dad.

"Your external fire isn't enough to kill the harpy. It may stop the ritual of opening whatever gate of hell the harpy is looking to open, but it isn't enough to kill the harpy. As I said before, Erin, who I loved with all my heart, learned that external fire doesn't kill a harpy. She witnessed her mother's death, and the harpy survived the blast. Her mother hadn't waited, and died in her own inferno. She blew before the harpy could finish a critical piece of the ritual."

My skin grew cold, and Phillip wouldn't look at me. "What is the critical piece?"

"It's what Erin did. Killing the harpy involves...sacrifice." He looked down at his hands, avoiding everyone's gaze.

A chill worked its way up my back, and I actually shivered. "What sacrifice?"

His gaze finally met mine. "You need to let the harpy eat your heart before you ignite. It will burn her from the inside out. That's the only way to kill this thing."

I blinked a couple of times before my jaw slowly lowered open. Erin didn't survive the killing of the harpy. He had told me as much in the apartment, but I never connected those dots.

His lips moved into a sad smile. "You've got one advantage that Erin didn't have. You're a vampire. You won't die."

I let out a high-pitched laugh. "Do you know how many times Cassius killed me? I hate to inform you, but I can die."

His smile faltered. "But having your heart pulled out of your chest doesn't kill a vampire immediately. Erin held on when most would die on the spot, and it successfully killed that bitch of a thing."

"But she didn't survive, either."

He slowly shook his head. "No, she didn't rise from the ashes."

I stared at him. "And you didn't enlighten us to this before?"

Phillip looked at his hands and shook his head. "I did not believe we would ever locate the remaining harpy."

My tattoo itched again. I ran my hand over my chest. "And with this tattoo, you ensured I would die, didn't you?" I narrowed my eyes at him, remembering his words. When the body died, the soul died with it.

He shook his head. "I ensured the harpy's ritual would fail. That she would never be able to claim your soul."

"You bastard!" Robby launched at Phillip, but his father moved fast enough to get an arm around his waist, stopping him.

I glared at Phillip while Robby struggled in his father's grasp, roaring with his own fury. I couldn't comprehend this type of betrayal. Not from someone who I had gotten comfortable considering as a friend. "Explain," I demanded.

"You know angel powers transfer if you eat their hearts, right?" he asked.

I stared at him with a blank expression. The academy never mentioned angels. Although with the existence of demons, it made sense that angels exist, but I had no idea how they transferred powers. From the equally blank expressions surrounding me, I didn't think any of us had this type of knowledge.

Phillip wiped his face and took a breath. "Okay then. It seems the agency left out one of the more exceptional supernaturals." He let out a nervous laugh. "Angels exist, but they haven't been earthbound for a very long time." He stared at me. "Just like every other supernatural being, the original phoenix became so through a union of two very powerful beings. Sort of in the same vein as the werewolf, an angel fell in love with a fire witch. But that caused a holy war between heaven and hell. Neither condoned the union and when they finally tracked them down, the witch sustained a mortal wound, crippling her ability to defend against the attack. And the angel wasn't willing to lose her.

"He pulled his own heart from his chest and instructed her to eat it before he was struck down, too. As disgusting as that sounds, she did it, and the moment she swallowed the last morsel, he was struck down, but his powers had already transferred. Unfortunately, it was too late for her as well, and they both took their last breaths while reaching across the battlefield for each other."

He let out a soft laugh. "But angel grace is enough to resurrect the dead." His gaze moved back to mine. "That union. That grace. It created your kind. It melded together with the fire witch's natural powers and became something indestructible." He moved his gaze to the shifters in the room. "And just like the shifter magic, the phoenix's magic grew with each generation. The only caveat—a phoenix's human blood limits the number of times they can be resurrected."

He glanced back at me. "You've become something more with the vampire's curse. Still a phoenix, but a new breed, and although the heart ingestion is supposed to transfer your powers to whoever eats it, I've locked your soul in your flesh. It will not transfer to that heinous bitch. And as long as you are alive, you control your fire."

I stared at him and then touched my chest. "You put this tattoo on the phoenix you loved. On Erin."

He nodded.

I thought about his sacrifice and hers. "The harpy who died, how is it tied to the one we are battling now?"

"It's the sister of the one Erin killed." He sighed. "It's not going to be pleasant at all. And because I care about you in a way I cannot explain, this pains me almost as much as it pains your mate."

Robby growled as though Phillip had just crossed an uncrossable line.

Phillip's hand snapped up in a universal stop motion with his palm facing Robby and his fingers splayed out. Even without the word, the action shut Robby down. "I would never intentionally do anything to put her in harm's way. But this harpy will hunt her down as relentlessly as the vampires. And without the tattoo I put on each one of you, the harpy's soul eaters would end you like that just for standing in her way." He snapped his fingers and then returned his gaze to mine. "Your tattoo is a little different, but I doubt any of you noticed. It will prevent the soul eaters from sucking your soul out, but it also traps your soul in your body, and your powers are connected to your soul. It prevents that bitch from getting what she wants."

I took a breath. The idea of anyone ripping my heart from my body left me shivering, but I got what he was saying. I glanced at Robby, and his expression shut down into a hardness that reminded me of his father.

"Don't you dare consider it." His voice was feral. "I've seen you die too many times. And if you agree to this madness, it will break me."

I met his gaze. "Then we live on the run until we are caught."

"And make no mistake. The harpy will never stop hunting her, and I can only run so much interference before she catches on." Robby's father let his son go.

Robby looked between his father and me, and then his chin dipped to his chest. "I just can't." He turned away and found a quiet seat in the corner of the room and sat down.

I glanced at him and then sighed. I wasn't sure I could willingly either. "She's at headquarters right now?"

Robert Senior's eyes narrowed. "So are members from our pack."

"And you can't kill her with your fire," Phillip reminded me.

"But I could hurt her, right?" I met his gaze.

"You could, but you will also kill a slew of innocent people." He raised his eyebrows. "Pack members of your mate. That will hurt him, too."

"Not as much as seeing her die again," Robby piped in from across the room, and then met my gaze. "Take it down," he said with a nod.

I turned and looked at the screens. "I have to be within sight of the building to take it down."

"We aren't leaving here right now." Phillip pointed at Robert's father. "You need to boogie." He pointed at the cameras showing the street view and agency cars pulling up to the curb like some major FBI sting. Phillip grabbed Robert's arm and dragged him toward the wall of monitors. In the corner, he knelt and pulled back the carpet. Then the sound of a combination lock rang through the quiet room. A moment later, a metal floorboard swung up.

"Subway entrance. Just watch out for the trains," Phillip said while looking up at Robert Senior.

When Robby's father stepped behind the metal floorboard, Phillip said, "Wait." Phillip grabbed a burner phone and programmed a number into it before he handed Robby's dad the phone. "Call the pizza number with information when you can."

Robby's dad glanced at me and then his son. With a nod, he slipped down into the opening, out of view.

Phillip closed the floorboard and turned a knob, locking the opening before putting the carpet back in place.

The fact we weren't stuck like caged victims gave me a measure of relief, but it still didn't ease my nerves as the agents descended on Phillip's place.

19

TAINTED MIND 19

THEY PILLAGED SO MUCH OF the shop that Phillip actually bristled next to me. It wasn't until Robert walked in the front door that he seemed to relax.

His reaction made me wonder, and I leaned over to him. "Is there something else in your shop that I should know about?"

Phillip turned to look at me. "It's my equipment they're ruining." He waved at the callous way things were handled. "That shit's expensive."

"I'll buy you new stuff when this is all over with."

"I don't need your money. I just need them to respect the things they are touching." Even though his voice still held irritation, he did give me a partial smile and seemed to relax a little more.

We focused back on the monitor, and Phillip turned up the sound.

"I expect you to clean this place up before you leave. I don't want our subject to know we were here, understand?" He glanced around the room. "As for surveillance, set up a camera facing each of the doors and a long view of the shop."

"What about the apartment?"

"Are there multiple entrances to it?" he asked.

"No, just the stairwell in the storeroom."

"Then a camera inside the apartment would be a waste of time if we have one on the storeroom door, right?" His eyebrow cocked and his tone, although level, portrayed an impatience that I remember from our boss when he thought we were being stupid. Robert Senior played the part well.

"Yes, sir," the young agent said with a pout.

"This isn't our highest priority, but it's one we should monitor. I'll make sure I have someone on the surveillance transmissions on a twenty-four-hour loop." He gave a nod and then directed the staff as to where to put the cameras. None of them were anywhere near Phillip's surveillance spots, which was a good thing. I would have wanted to get the same angle Phillip had and likely would have run into the hardware in at least one of the rooms. But with Robby's dad directing things, that wasn't an issue.

"Your father is a good man." Phillip glanced at Robby.

Robby just sighed as he watched him work on the screen. "I haven't seen the side of him that you've seen until the morning we showed up at your alley door. So, you'll have to excuse me if I don't readily agree."

Phillip swung his chair toward Robby. "What would you do for your child?" He crossed his arms.

Robby stared at the screen and then looked at me. "Almost anything."

"Almost?" Phillip asked in a tone that was meant to needle.

Robby nodded. "Anything is too broad. Anything would include killing my mate to save my child's life. I am not sure I'd be able to do that. But anything else, including laying my life down for my child, is a no-brainer."

I glanced at my hands. I would kill anyone, including Robby, to save my child's life. I have a fierce protectiveness built into me and as much as I love Robby, he would land second to a child. I looked up at the screen as a level of understanding bloomed in my blood. All Robby's father had done to keep his son safe was forgivable. Every last damn thing.

"Would you have done what your father did?" I asked, still looking at the screen, because I knew how much it all fucked Robby up. But I needed to know his answer.

"If I was dealt his hand..." A heavy sigh followed.

I glanced over, and Robby was chewing his bottom lip and rubbing his chin. He and his father were so very much alike.

He finally nodded. "Yeah." It's all he said as his eyes tracked his father on screen.

In that moment, my mark tingled, and I actually felt all the hostility toward his father leave him and the space fill with forgiveness, lightening whatever burdens he carried. His gaze slid to mine and there in his eyes the weight he had been carrying lifted as a result.

Forgiveness was a powerful thing. But neither of us could find it in our hearts to forgive the agency for all they had done. Some things were just too evil.

Robby's father pulled out his phone—it wasn't the burner—and pressed a few keys. "I have some pack business to attend to. Can I grab the members of my pack for a quick meeting?" He closed his eyes and pinched the bridge of his nose. "No. This cannot wait. Besides, while I have them gathered, I can relay the orders to lean on every supernatural in the city to find Sarah Stone." He rolled his eyes and looked right into the camera. "I need to let them know I am taking alpha responsibilities over until everything settles down and we can elect a proper alpha." His face turned red. "No. I cannot do that in a fucking email."

The way he inhaled and closed his eyes, I could guess the shit coming over the phone line. He nodded. "It will only be an hour at most. I'm requesting they meet me at my son's prior residence here in the city." He looked into the camera. "Yes. I'll come back after the meeting so we can discuss strategy." He ended the call and then typed out a message on his phone, hit Send, and then headed out of the shop.

A moment later, Phillip's phone rang.

"Phil's Pizza, how can I help you?" Phillip answered with the phone on speaker.

"Can I have a dozen large pizzas delivered?" he asked and rattled off Robby's address in the city. "And can you put a rush on that?"

"Sure."

"Burn them," Robby's father said and hung up.

Phillip glanced at me. "You heard the man. It's time to cook that building."

I glanced at the screen, and at least a dozen shifters trotted out of the building with their phones in hand.

Johnson traded a glance with Robby and nodded. "That's all of them."

I pulled my hair into a ponytail and glanced at Phillip. "It's safe to do magic?"

He nodded. "If it isn't, we'll find out pretty damn quick." He pointed at the screens, where a half a dozen agents still milled about, straightening up the shop.

I willed a blonde wig and an oversized hoodie to cover my head even with the blonde hair. Next, a pair of sunglasses slid onto my face, and I glanced at Robby. He wasn't going to be as easy to hide with his size, so I turned to Phillip and manifested a black wig with a man bun for him, along with sunglasses and baggy clothing.

"You're coming with me." I pointed at him.

"I'm not..."

I pointed at Robby. "You are staying here."

Robby closed his eyes. "Please let me come."

"You are supposed to be dead. So is Johnson. If anyone recognizes you, this whole thing starts to unravel, and it puts all of us in danger." I blew a stream of air. "And I am not even sure I can do this. My attempts to light the candle were disastrous."

Robby stood and approached me, taking my hands. "Remember what I said about us being apart?"

I gave him a tilted smile and palmed his cheek. "All our worst shit went down when we were together. My chances going with Phillip are much better than going with you. I know it is hard for you. I get it, but I need to know you are here, keeping an eye on the streets for me. Warning me if I'm going to get blindsided. We may need a navigator to help with a quick escape."

Phillip moved to the floor, in the corner where Robby's father had escaped the control room. "I'm the only one who can get back in from the other side." He met Robby's gaze. "I will keep her safe. This is not the place for a standoff."

Robby sighed and nodded, letting go of my hands. "You're going to have to compel me to stay, because if I get freaked out, you know damn well I won't be able to stay here."

"I don't want to compel you."

"You need to. I can already feel the PTSD creeping in, and Johnson won't be able to settle me down."

I leaned up and kissed him. "Stay here," I commanded softly against his lips.

"Be safe," he whispered back. "And come back in one piece."

"I'll always come back to you."

"Promise?" He stared into my eyes.

"Always."

"I am going to hold you to that." He stepped away and waved me toward Phillip. "And, for the record, blonde doesn't do it for me."

I raised an eyebrow.

"I'm more partial to redheads." He grinned and winked.

I rolled my eyes and disappeared into the darkness below with Phillip. He followed me down the stairs, where there was barely enough room for us to stand together.

His watch lit up in the small space, and he put up a finger. My feet started to tingle and then the entire space seemed to tremble with the roar of the subway. And then it gradually subsided. Phillip opened the door and grabbed my hand, and pulled me along with him into the dark shaft. The light from a platform about a hundred yards down beckoned, and he moved us quickly out of the darkness. Thankfully, the ledge we were on was the same height as the platform, and he pulled me around the corner to a ramp that led upward to the turnstiles and then a stairwell to the street.

"He'll be okay, right?" Phillip asked as he dragged me along toward Midtown. Obviously, he knew where headquarters was, but he was bringing me to the backside of the building and not the front.

"Yes. Why the back?"

"Less traffic. Less chance of being noticed." He glanced at the buildings and then took me down another side street winding around from the east side to the west side, where headquarters sat between two other office buildings. Headquarters had their own corner, so I only had to worry about the office building right next door.

When we had a visual of the building, Phillip steered me into an open-ended alley between two buildings.

"Lick the wick," he whispered, looking at headquarters and not me.

"Like I did that so well back at your place. Besides, that's a big-ass building."

"Focus." He stood behind me, with his hands on my shoulders. "All the people responsible for where you are now are in that building."

He knew how to stoke the fires inside me.

"Turn it to ash," he said.

My mind wandered back over the years. All the slights. All the rules. All the killings that really did not need to happen. Vampires, sure, but the other creatures, like Phillip. We were hired killers. The agency made me a murderer and kept me from my mate.

"Start at the top and tear it down floor by floor, trapping the harpy inside."

I tilted my head back, staring at the spire at the top of our building. It wasn't the Chrysler Building, but it was pretty just the same. I gave Phillip a quick glance. "Here goes nothing," I mumbled and then concentrated. I lifted my hands up in the air, spreading my fingers as if reaching for the spire. When flames broke out on the building, my heart lurched in my chest, along with the power flowing through me. I brought my hands down fast, pulling the flames down like a tidal wave.

That's when the screams reached our ears and the flames hit the ground like a billowing ball of debris. I closed my hands and stumbled back into Phillip, pushing him down the alley. He didn't resist and we bolted, winding through the garbage. When we hit the far sidewalk, he grabbed my hand and darted across the busy street, dodging cars as he headed directly toward a subway entrance.

As we rounded the stairs, I had a quick glance at the black smoke billowing into the sky. I just prayed no one we knew had been in the building. Hopefully they were all out on jobs, but the lump in my throat still formed as I ducked into the subway. My breath labored and my hands shook as we wound through the station.

The train going downtown had to pass close to where the fire was and even this far below, the heat penetrated the subway enough so that passengers loosened their ties and unbuttoned their shirts. Sirens pierced the cab and then faded as we traveled away from the burning buildings.

When we reached a stop near Phillip's shop, he led me off the train and into one of the mazes of hallways until we were across from the original platform.

"We need to cross. Watch out for the electric rail." He jumped down and bolted across, jumping rails, and then climbed up on the other platform as I stood, panting.

He turned, looked both ways, and waved me to follow. I jumped down on shaky legs and made my way over cautiously. By the time I reached the other side, the ground rumbled beneath my feet.

I reached for the platform and Phillip damn near tore my arm from the socket as he yanked me up. He fell back on his ass with me in his arms just as a subway train barreled by at top speed.

"You should have been right behind me," he scolded as he lifted me to my feet and headed down the same path we came out of. There was no slowing down until we were in the little room, and he closed the door behind him just as the rumble of a train echoed through the room. He glared over at me. "What is wrong with you?" He took me by the shoulders and stared into my eyes.

My vision blurred, and I peeled the wig off. "I just killed hundreds of people in a few seconds." The beginnings of an all-out panic attack were blooming inside me, and I couldn't catch my breath.

His lips pinched together. "I know. I captured as many souls as I could before we started running." His eyes glowed in the darkness.

I gawked at him. A part of me wanted to end him, and my fingers itched to be free of my fists.

"Don't look at me like that. I just capitalized on the aftermath, okay?" He climbed up the stairs and put his hand on the panel. The gears moved and then he turned the handle, pushing the metal up and out of the way.

We entered the room, and Robby was by my side in an instant, pulling me into his arms as his wide-eyed gaze glanced from the screens to me. I caught the first view of my devastation via the local news channels. They were likening what happened to the Twin Towers falling, except there was very little debris. Just a thick coat of ash.

The office building next to headquarters still had flames licking some of the floors facing headquarters, and all the glass was gone. Large tankers aimed torrents of water at the areas still on fire.

But what my gaze fell to was the background behind the reporter. The pretty blonde who had escorted Robby's father into the elevator was pacing in front of the building like a rabid dog, waiting for something to rise from the ashes. And she was not accompanied by the pair of thugs who had been in the elevator with her. A smile formed on my lips. At least I took out her demon goons.

But the harpy didn't get out without injury. Under that pretty façade, the harpy was mostly burned and hissing. It was an odd dichotomy to see.

"You didn't get her." Johnson pointed.

"Well, it depends on what you're seeing. The harpy underneath the glamour is burnt to shit, and she looks pissed," I said.

"You can see the real thing?" Johnson asked.

"Yes. Before she was ugly. Now she's fucking hideous," I said. "Did you notice the absence of her demons?"

Phillip laughed, nodded, and glanced at the screen. "You did damage."

"But not enough." I peeled out of Robby's arms just as a slew of off-duty or on-assignment agents started to flood the area. Robby's father, along with the rest of the pack, tumbled out of cabs and were let under the police barrier to the scene. Robert Senior's face showed the same level of shock as everyone else.

"I count thirty agents." Johnson let out a low whistle. "The pack members may never forgive us." He glanced at Robby. "Most of their partners were in the building since a pack meeting was called."

Robby nodded acknowledgment. "Some were elsewhere." He waved as a few more people stumbled into the fray. All agents had their badges visible, so it was easy to tell who was left.

The harpy marched up to Robby's father and grabbed him by the shirt. His gaze ripped from the scene before him to the harpy, with the blaze reflected in his eyes. I smiled as it was all caught on the local television stations.

His lips moved and his hand waved at the building. I could almost read what he was saying: "What the hell happened here?"

The harpy shook him and then stopped as she glanced around at the cameras pointing at them. She smoothed his shirt and gave him what looked like an apology before gathering the troops far enough away from the cameras to have a moment.

The cameras turned back to the building as the reporter droned on.

Phillip reached over and clicked the sound off. He didn't acknowledge what happened in the subway tunnel either. My mind couldn't wrap around the number of people missing and presumed dead displayed on the screen. I caused that. I killed people I knew. People I had worked alongside for years.

My stomach cramped, and I sat in the nearest chair. I couldn't catch my breath, and sweat rolled down my back as if it were a hundred and ten degrees in this room. Robby knelt beside me.

"Head between your knees," he said, from what seemed like far away.

His hand on my back felt like it was hotter than I was. "I caused that." I pointed without looking. Before it had only been woods and monsters. This time it was people, some of them innocent.

"There's always collateral damage, hon," he said, trying to absolve me of the pain gripping me at the results of my actions. "And from what they said, whoever was in that building didn't know what hit them."

"It's true," Phillip said. "The souls I was able to collect didn't even know they were dead." He typed away at one of the computer stations.

"That still doesn't make me feel good about what I did." I glanced at the number. I decreased the agency force by nearly a thousand agents and technical assets who were in the building. And a couple dozen who had offices on the same side of the building next door. Wiping out vampires was different. That saved lives. But killing witches, werewolves, fae, and humans was not something I could get behind.

"You didn't blow a path a mile wide," Robby said, pulling my gaze back to him.

He was just trying to be helpful, but it did not wipe out my crime. Until this point, I had kept my promise to not take out innocents. But this just crushed it to hell.

He must have felt the devastation still present in my bones. "They would have gladly hunted us down and put a bullet in our brains."

I glanced at the ash that still filtered through the air. "They'll never be able to identify them." The building was no more. The card entry records were torched. Everything that would have been used was gone.

A picture of the storeroom looped on a camera over and over, and an outside view of the door did the same. "What are you doing?" I asked Phillip.

"Interrupting the feed from the agency's cameras and putting a view on loop."

"No one's looking at those transmissions anymore." I waved at the monitors.

He glanced at me. "There are still at least thirty agents in the city and thousands more across the continent. I'm not taking a chance." He continued to type commands under the looping video.

"Most of the remaining agents live outside of the agency," Johnson said, still studying the muted news transmissions.

Phillip's phone pinged, and he pulled it out just as the agents gathered dispersed. He picked up the burner. "Phillip's Pizza. How can I help you?"

It floored me that he could still keep in character after what went down.

"I need to cancel those pizzas," Robby's father said, and gave his name and address. "Unless you deliver to the Pennsylvania Amish country," he added with a little chuckle.

"Unfortunately, we don't. But my brother owns a pizza joint out that way. If you give me the address, I'll see if it's within his delivery area."

Robby's father paused and then read off an address. "It's in farm country."

Phillip sighed. "That isn't in his delivery zone, either. I'll cancel your order." He covered the handset. "Put a hold on order number 37." He glanced at us. "Your order has been canceled, sir."

"Thank you. Charge my card anyway. I think I remember a couple of homeless people hanging around your shop. If they're there, give the pies to them."

"Will do, sir." Phillip disconnected the call. "I think he was telling us she has a couple more bodyguards out there." Phillip brought the address up on Google Maps and leaned back in the chair.

"We're going to need some wheels," he said.

The image showed a network of farms, and the address that he entered stood out as a blue dot in the middle of them. It was southwest of the popular Amish village that tourists flocked to. I had even seen ads for bus tours down there. My brain pinged, and I looked at the distance between the tourist trap and that little blue dot.

We had walked farther than that before.

"Why don't we just sign up for one of those bus tours?" I sat back up. The cramping in my chest and abdomen abated as I went into planning mode.

Phillip turned in the seat and gave me an appreciative nod. "And I assume we walk from there?"

"Sounds like a plan." I wanted out of the city and the cloud of guilt pressing down on me. And even though I knew what awaited me at the end of the trip, I wasn't as stressed about it as I should be. Not with what I had done.

Perhaps a brutal death was what was in the cards for me after all.

TAINTED MIND 20

I WAS QUIET ON THE bus, sitting at the window and looking out as the road passed by. Robby held my hand as if I could be snatched right out of the side of the bus. His anxiety rubbed against me like a blanket made of sandpaper. Johnson and Phillip sat across from us, and they both closed their eyes for the ride, trying to reserve their energy.

"I wish we were at my apartment," Robby whispered to me.

"Why?"

"Then I could properly remind you of what you have here."

I turned and stared into his blue eyes, getting lost in their depths, and nodded. I couldn't quite muster up a smile. I didn't know whether any of us would survive this. I rubbed my chest and looked back out the window.

"Promise me," he whispered in my ear.

I inhaled and returned my gaze to his and palmed his cheek. "Even if I die a thousand deaths, I will always come back to you." I pressed my lips to his, trying to believe that silly mantra.

"I'm holding you to that," he said against my mouth, and then kissed me as if I were his last breath.

My chest squeezed with the intensity of it. I would do everything within my power to be in his arms again after all this went down, but somehow, I doubted that would happen. At least, not where we were headed.

The bus stopped at what looked like a souvenir shop and announced we had arrived. We climbed out onto the blacktop of the parking lot and glanced around. The tour guide waved us all toward the town, but we hung back, scanning the store.

I pointed toward the restroom side on the building, and we headed that way. Everyone outside of the tourists had old-fashioned clothing on. As we got closer to the bathrooms, I looked at our attire. We would stand out like a sore thumb in jeans and T-shirts.

I shooed them into the men's room and waved my hand at them, changing their clothing to match the men I had seen, and then I waved at my attire, changing it from form-fitting jeans and a tight T-shirt to a long-sleeve maxi dress in a neutral color. The loafers I changed to were actually comfortable but not nearly in the kick-ass realm of my boots. The thing is, in the mirror, my red hair stood out even more against the beige. I sighed and marched outside.

"Why..." Robby started and then his gaze went to the people surrounding us. "Never mind." He turned to Phillip, who had his phone out with the directions.

He pointed at the road that stretched out behind the store. "That way." And he pocketed the phone. "We want to boogie because her magical signature is now here, and if they are looking for it, you just lit up their radar."

We started by foot, which did not seem unusual. Either people walked or had horse-drawn buggies. I felt as if we had just stepped into the 1800s and we looked the part. No one gave us any mind as we traveled the roads, checking coordinates every now and then to make sure we were heading in the right direction.

The tour bus had long since headed back to the city by the time we reached what looked like the halfway point between the town and the farm where the harpy was located. We weren't in a hurry, and we had no real plan as to what we were going to do once we got to the property. We didn't even know how many agents would be there.

"We don't have a plan beyond storming the castle," I said as the sun set.

No one responded, but we kept walking down this long, desolate country road surrounded by farmland as far as the eye could see. It was the ideal spot to have whatever showdown we were about to engage in. But whatever these poor saps were growing would be torched when I fried the harpy.

"I'm not looking forward to this."

Robby grunted his agreement and squeezed my hand.

The closer we got to the destination on Phillip's phone, the more my skin itched. I stopped on the road and glanced around at the farms surrounding us, turning in a circle. As I faced away from the direction we were headed, the itching subsided, but the minute I turned back in the direction that the little arrow indicated, it was as if a thousand ants marched across my skin.

"I don't like this."

"No kidding," Phillip said.

"Does your map show the property lines?"

He played around with his phone and typed in the town we were in, looking for property maps. It took him a few minutes, but he finally showed me the map.

We were close to one of the edges of her property. She had to have some major voodoo protecting her property for me to feel like I was being attacked by insects. I glanced at Robby; his eyes scanned the fields around us and his nose crinkled when he faced the harpy's property.

"I don't think we can just sneak in and surprise her," Johnson said with the same expression as Robby. "The magic on the property is too strong."

Robby and I traded a glance. Neutralizing magic spells wasn't as hard as one might think, but I wasn't sure whether saying those words while off property would change anything.

Still...

"Frange vincula," Robby said.

The air didn't even crackle, and that itch persisted.

"I think you have to be inside the barrier."

A low growl escaped him. He didn't want to get any closer either. But we had no choice.

Hoofs hitting the pavement pulled my attention down the road. It was just another buggy, but it was coming from the direction we were heading. Although, like several other buggies we saw on our walk, the occupants wore similar garb. We exchanged a friendly wave, and they continued on their way.

Phillip's phone rang, and he answered. "Hello?"

The sound of the phone shuffled despite a growl in the background. "Let me speak to the phoenix." A female voice came over the line.

"I'm sorry, but I think you have the wrong number." Phillip went to press the End button.

"Then your friend dies."

He paused and met my gaze. "I'm sorry, ma'am, but this is a pizza shop, and I was just closing up." He called her bluff.

A grunt sounded in the background. "Then I guess you are not standing on the road with two wolves and a phoenix less than a few hundred yards out from my drive?" The phone dinged and a picture of us waving came through the line. "And one of those wolves looks just like the one I'm about to fillet."

I snatched the phone. "What do you want?" It was a stupid question, but I wasn't going to listen as she gutted Robby's father.

"You, my dear. If you stride right up the drive without your posse, I will let this wolf walk. If not, I will slaughter all of you."

"Don't—" His father's warning was cut off by a smack, followed by the sound of a body falling hard.

"And don't get cute with your fire the way you did back at headquarters. You can't kill me, but you can piss me off enough to make you watch as I slowly strip your friends of their skin, then their muscles, then crush bones one by one until all they are is a gelatinous mess. And then maybe I'll kill them to put them out of their misery. But you will not be able to save them."

My gaze moved to Robby's. He shook his head, but we both knew that I had to walk this path. I had to sacrifice a life to rid the earth of this bitch.

"If I do this, will you guarantee my friends' safety? That no matter what happens, they live free of you and your reach?"

Now everyone was shaking their heads. I put my hand up, stopping them.

"Robert Young included?"

"If you walk up my drive alone, yes."

"Fine. I expect to see him walking toward the road by the time I get to your driveway."

An evil cackle filled the line, and I shivered. *Why did I feel as though I just signed everyone's death warrant?* I pressed End and handed Phillip the phone. The minute it was in his hand, I turned and ran toward the road. If I didn't, I would have chickened out. Their feet followed. The moment I turned onto the driveway, I nearly choked from the magic.

The three of them followed me, and I spun, splaying my fingers and jamming my palm at them. "Stay," I commanded.

They skidded to a halt, and Robby snarled at me, struggling against my invisible bonds I placed around them. I prayed it was enough to keep them safe.

"You can run back the way you came, but you cannot take another step forward toward where I am going." I crossed to Robby and leaned up to give him a kiss. He turned away, giving me his cheek instead. The wild look in his eyes was enough. His pain coursed through my mark. "Keep them safe." I nodded at Phillip and Johnson, and pressed my lips to his cheek anyway.

I turned back toward the house. The fields surrounding us swayed in the wind and the harpy stepped out, dragging Robert Senior with her. Silver glinted against his throat. Even from this distance, I knew he wasn't okay.

The scrape of magic went from just an itch to a burning sensation on my skin the closer I got. The harpy wasn't alone either. Two towering demons flanked her, and on the steps of the house stood a witch. I willed knives into my palms as well as Johnson, Robby, and Phillip behind me. I couldn't leave them unarmed, not with the monster before me.

Halfway down the driveway, I slowed to a stop. "Let him go."

She dragged him along the dirt path toward me. Her demons and witch followed. Something glinted in the light from the front porch. I took a closer look at the demons. Their clawed hands were covered, and it took me a second to realize the demons had hands that looked as though they were dipped in silver.

Shit. How long had Robert been here before we arrived? I swallowed hard, thinking of how rough that had to have been. He bled from several welts, including one that traversed his chest.

I met Robert's gaze as he stumbled beside the hag. His eyes held fear like I had never seen from the man, and his gaze moved from me to where Robby was and back.

"They won't come any closer," I said softly, trying to reassure him, but it didn't seem to make any difference.

I launched a knife at one of the demons. It landed true, cutting right through his chest. He roared and then stumbled to his knees, falling backward as my charmed blade did its magic. The witch hissed and the harpy turned, losing a grip on Robert.

He took advantage of the breach and lumbered toward me. Two more demons came out of the crops on both sides of the driveway. Instead of heading toward Robby at the end of the driveway, they headed toward me.

Robert was near me, but the other demon raced forward. I launched my second knife, but he knocked it away. I pulled on my fire, but before I could, the witch uttered four words that layered over the land around me, nullifying my blaze.

The demon backhanded me, sending me on my back, and then launched at Robert, dragging his claws down the man's back. Burnt skin filled the air, along with a howl of pain. The two demons who came out of the fields grabbed me, dragging me forward as the other demon slashed Robert to pieces before my very eyes.

Robby howled as he struggled against my command. Even from this distance, his eyes were wild, and his muscles strained. Witnessing his father's death was hard, but the night wasn't over yet...and I knew the next death might very well send him over the edge.

When the demon finally finished with Robby's father, his head snapped up and he glared at the group at the end of the road, baring his teeth in a feral snarl.

I struggled in the grip of the demons, but they were too strong for me. It was as if they were fueled by magic. *The damned witch.*

"I will let you and your brothers take care of them just as soon as I finish this ritual," the harpy said.

The demon who killed Robby's father turned back toward us like an obedient slave. "You promised."

The harpy laughed and pointed to a spot at the side of the driveway. "Bring her here. Into the circle."

I glanced at the circle on the ground, and then the stench hit my nose. *Blood.* I looked at what was left of Robby's dad. They had used his blood to draw the circle.

"The blood of an animal." She smiled. "He was the closest thing I could find in a pinch." She cackled as the demons dragged me into the center.

I cast a glance at Robby. Even from this distance, I could see the panic in his eyes. I wished I could tell him it would be all right, but I had no idea. Then I sent a prayer to whoever was listening to not let me screw this up.

TAINTED MIND 21

I STOOD WITH EACH OF my arms trapped in the demon's grasp. The harpy approached, and she dropped her glamour.

"You have got to be the ugliest creature I have ever seen," I said as I studied her wrinkled gray skin. Her hair seemed to shudder in the wind. Her beady white eyes stared at me and when she smiled, her razor-like teeth gleamed in the moonlight.

My muscles seized with the heat of panic. I struggled against the demons, but they didn't budge. The damn witch did this, and I wanted to spit in her eye before I torched her. My fire snaked inside my skin, fighting against the invisible barrier she created with that spell.

I took a breath, calming my nerves, willing my fire to churn and gather strength. It was not time to utter the words that would kill the spells surrounding us. Whatever happened, I had to stay alive long enough to set off my explosion, and I couldn't worry about Johnson and Phillip. I had to trust that Robby would protect them. I needed the full force of my phoenix to take out this bitch.

The harpy raised her hand in a claw formation and shot it toward my chest. Her nails dug into my skin, burning like poison. I gasped as she crashed through my ribs and clawed at my heart. And then she yanked.

I didn't even have time to scream. It was so sudden, but now my nerve endings recognized the pain. If I hadn't been a vampire, I would surely have died the moment my heart was ripped from my body. My breath wheezed in my ears and time slowed. The harpy grinned and stared at the beating appendage in her hand, mumbling words I didn't recognize. My body burned beneath the skin as every cell reached the point of explosion.

My blood dripped from her clawed hand.

Robby screamed, a wail of a sound that was hauntingly like a howl that hung on the air.

Darkness threatened, but I held on. Watching. Waiting for the perfect moment. The harpy gobbled my heart in one slurping bite. As soon as she swallowed and the lump in her throat moved down her neck, I smiled and tilted my head.

I clucked my tongue at the harpy.

The harpy blinked at me.

"Frange vincula," hissed from my laboring lungs. The magic around us crackled as those two words nullified all the spells and wards placed on the property.

My fire was at its ignition point, and I willed my heart to burn. I pushed my fire outward from every part of my body, allowing it to engulf me in pure light. "You thought you could end me? News flash—I'm here to end you, you evil bitch."

The harpy screamed and started ripping at her chest as I burned her from the inside out. The demons holding me turned to ash, and the fucking witch blew to pieces like a human bomb before she could utter another spell. Her blood sprayed, covering the harpy before it turned to ash.

The harpy's wail rang through the air as my flame devoured her. The evil surrounding this place needed to be cleansed, and my fire thirsted to purify. It consumed me, bursting from my body in a light brighter than an atomic bomb.

Protect my mate. My last coherent thought blasted through me as I let go. All pain disappeared, followed by my promise to Robby.

I would return to him.

One way or another, I was destined to be his.

TAINTED MIND 22

ROBBY
Jesus, she's going to blow.
All my panic at seeing her heart ripped from her chest evaporated, and a new terror set in. I would probably survive her fire, but it would surely annihilate Johnson and Phillip.

I had no time to deal with anything else; I willed my shift and in a blink, my wolf form towered over Johnson and Phillip. I threw them to the ground underneath me and laid down on top of them, covering them completely. Hopefully I didn't suffocate them, but I tucked my snout under me and covered my eyes with my paws just as the heat hit. I curled up over them as best I could.

The connection to Sarah and my mark on her broke like a twig snapped by a boulder. I whined as every cell in my body flared with pain. My heart squeezed, as if a thousand knives stabbed me at once. This was the same pain I had dealt with every time Cassius killed Sarah. My soul crushed, shriveling into a dark husk. And I waited for my mark to start tingling again, as it had so many times before, like a blossom of life. But it remained silent.

The heat dissipated enough for me to lift my head.

A perfect circle of destruction surrounded us, but the grass my head had been on was still green. I slowly stood, glancing down at Johnson and Phillip staring around in awe from underneath me.

I started toward where Sarah had been, but the moment my paw hit the blackened ground, it sizzled, and I pulled back with a yelp. Nothing remained but ash. I couldn't even see the form of her body.

I shifted back to human form at the sound of a helicopter in the distance.

Phillip and Johnson stood.

"Thanks." Johnson reached into one of his pockets and pulled out a pair of gym shorts, handing them to me. The fact he had come prepared humbled me.

I pulled on the scant clothing, still surveying the landscape and looking for movement of any kind. I didn't know what the casualty count was, but Sarah blew a distance around her of at least a mile. The woods at the edges of her blaze radius burned unchecked. Thankfully, the harpy had chosen a spot outside the city for this final battle.

If this had occurred in Manhattan...

I closed my eyes at that thought and wiped a hand down my face. Her loss pummeled every muscle, and my legs gave out. I collapsed to my knees. "Please tell me you feel her somewhere." I glanced at Phillip, clinging desperately to hope.

His sad eyes met mine, and he slowly shook his head. A single tear escaped and slid down his cheek as he surveyed the damage. "I had hoped..." He pressed his lips together and hung his head in something akin to defeat.

"She promised," I whispered as the sounds of sirens filled the air.

I leaned my head back and screamed my anger and sorrow until my throat was so raw I could no longer speak. Then I put my head on the ground and let my tears of pain flow, mourning her loss and wishing it had been me instead.

TAINTED MIND 23

SARAH

Darkness surrounded me. This place felt familiar, as if I had been here before. I blinked and stared at the blankness blanketing everything. My shoulder tingled, and I lifted my hand to Robby's mark. Relief flooded through me. He had survived.

A flame appeared in the distance, coming closer with each passing second. The flaming bird landed before me, forming a woman I recognized. Her eyes matched mine, and she smiled in such a sad way that my throat closed.

"I am proud of you." Her gaze drifted down to my stomach and then back up to me. Her eyes widened in a way that I didn't understand. She reached out and wrapped her arms around me. "You have no more lives left," she said in my ear.

I pushed away from her. "I promised Robby that I would return to him." I wasn't going to let death stop me.

Her sad smile burned.

"You cannot hold me here. I promised him!" My voice rose to almost a screech as her words burned me from the inside out. I wished for a sword and cool metal graced my palm. Even in the ethereal realm, I had my magic. I pointed it at her chest. "Release me."

"Your time has come to pass." She stood, with the tip of my sword digging into the center of her chest.

"I will give up everything to go back."

Her gaze lowered again. "You would give up your child?"

I stepped back, blinking as I lowered the sword. "Didn't I already give that up when that vampire bitch killed me?" My voice cracked. I had just assumed the child couldn't survive my death.

"No. Your child survived. But she is not destined to be born in your world. Just like you were not destined to be born in my world."

I swallowed hard and ran my hand over my flat stomach. "I promised my mate." Tears choked me and blurred my vision. "Besides, I am done with destiny. It has screwed me my entire life, and I will not let it screw me out of finally finding happiness with my mate." I shook my head and let my fire burn bright inside me. "I can light this place up just like I did that field," I warned as my teeth elongated into deadly fangs.

The gods could go fuck themselves for all I cared. I was returning to Robby with my child, even if I had to destroy the heavens to do so.

My mother's eyes widened at the threat and at my light illuminating the darkness around us. It dwarfed her own flame.

"You tell the powers that be either they let me go back fully intact, with my child, or their reign is over." I wasn't bluffing, either. Power fed into me like I was a charging battery, and I would use every ounce of it to wipe heaven and hell off the map.

A part of me knew this was irrational, but the fear in my mother's eyes told me it wasn't pure bullshit.

She cocked her head, as if someone were whispering to her. Then she refocused on me with eyes as hard as I've ever seen. "So be it."

She splayed out her fingers, and her hand darted toward me so quickly I didn't have time to react. The heel of her palm connected with my chest, sending pain through my entire form. I flew away from her like a bullet from a gun, spiraling into the darkness until it consumed me the way my fire had consumed the harpy.

TAINTED MIND 24

I INHALED, CHOKING ON ASHES. Coughing it out was just as bad as inhaling it. Black soot permeated every orifice, and I attempted to shift my weight, but my movements were restricted by the sheer volume covering me. I wished for a shovel or even an oxygen mask. I didn't even know whether I was facing the sky or the ground, but I forced my hands in opposite directions. One stopped immediately on the gravel below me, and my other pushed through the hot ash above me. I ignored the prickling heat.

The heaviness gave way and coolness licked the skin of my hand. Now all I had to do was sit up and climb to my feet, which was almost laughable, but I pushed down with the hand still pinned by my side. I needed to do this fast because my breath was locked in all this ash. If I didn't free myself, I would die.

Both of us would die.

That strange thought gave me almost inhuman strength, and I sat up, coughing in the ash-laden air. I wheezed and shook my head. Ash cascaded down around me. I blinked madly, trying to dislodge the soot covering my eyes. My hands were equally grimy, so I couldn't wipe away the dirt to see clearer.

Slowly, I climbed to my feet. My mind could not process what I saw. The ground was as black as coal, singeing out from where I stood. All of it was black except for a section that remained green, although the outer edges looked scalded. It was another strange phenomenon. Outside of that anomaly, everything as far as the eye could see was black.

It looked like a bomb went off.

Steam lifted into the air at the edges of the blast zone, but I couldn't make out the fire trucks that had to be tackling the flames I caught here and there in the surrounding woods.

I was at the epicenter of whatever the hell had happened. My heart jumped in my chest, sending a wave of adrenaline through me. My shoulder tingled.

I took a tentative step, and the ash crunched under my bare foot. Latent heat rose from beneath the crusty surface, as if the fires of hell burned below the ash, but I had no alternatives. I needed to reach people to find out what happened.

I paused. Not only that, but I needed to know why I was here. My eyes widened. Hell, I didn't know anything more than waking up in the ashes.

Who the hell was I?

My hand searched out my belly, and I stared down at the imperceptible roundness where my child grew. My condition was the only other thing I knew about myself. Everything else was a complete blank. Terror surfaced.

What if I had caused this?

That one thought chilled me to the point I couldn't move another foot.

A sound to my right spun me that way, and my heart stopped. A giant wolf—and when I say giant, I mean the size of a house giant—galloped toward me. I screamed and my brain told my feet to move, but my legs tangled, and I tripped, hitting the ash face-first. I rolled and tried to crab walk backward away from the beast coming to finish me off.

The wolf slowed, as if sensing my utter panic. Its blue eyes widened as he sniffed the air and stopped a few yards away. Black fur tipped with gold waved in the wind, and then the wolf blinked out of existence and a naked man stood where the wolf had been.

I let out a sharp keen of fear and scrambled to my feet as he strode forward. "Stay back," I yelped as I blinked to dislodge more ash that had flown up into my face when I fell. My brain could not wrap around what the hell I just witnessed, but my body was rooted firmly in the flight response. I stepped backward, away from him.

He stopped and put his hands out. "It's okay, Sarah. I'm here."

My shoulder tingled as he spoke. Even though my heart felt like a caged bird trying to escape, his voice seemed to calm me. I was still afraid of what he was, but I couldn't put a name to it. An itch in my brain started, like I should know, but it was all just a big blank.

"What happened?" I asked and then went into a coughing fit, spewing black dust from my lungs. My stomach cramped, and I turned away, vomiting on the spot just in front of my feet.

"You don't remember?" he asked cautiously but remained a few feet away.

I spit and then shook my head, inching away from the puddle sinking into the ash. The woods behind him came to life as a battalion of soldiers aiming weapons in our direction stepped onto the blackened field.

"Mr. Young," one of the soldiers called.

The man put his hands up in the air so they could see them, but he didn't turn away from me. "It's okay," he said to me, but from the irritation etched into his features, I gathered it really wasn't okay.

His blue eyes seemed pained as they traveled over my form. I guess I must be a sight to behold, blackened by ash from head to toe.

"You don't even remember me?" he asked, so softly I almost missed it.

Something stung my leg before I could answer, and I glanced down. A dart stuck out of my thigh. I blinked again and looked up into the man's concerned blue eyes. The world spun, and he lurched forward, catching me before all went black.

"I'M TELLING YOU, HER MIND'S been wiped," a male voice said just outside of the darkness gripping me.

That voice soothed me, just like the man's voice had in that field. I wondered whether it was him, and my heart fluttered with both anticipation and a little fear. He was a shifter, after all. I jerked as the name for what he was struck my consciousness.

"And she smells like she did back at the academy." The same voice sighed.

"Caramel and lemons," another said.

A sensation of warmth covered my hand, followed by the wetness of a soft kiss on my knuckles. My shoulder tingled in response.

A creak interrupted. "You all should not be in here." A female voice rang out over the room. "She needs her rest. Scoot."

"I'm not leaving. And if you try to cart me out of here again, my wolf will not allow it. Understand?" That voice again, but this time it was hard and unyielding as an iron wall.

The warmth on my hand increased, along with pressure.

"Look, Mr. Young, she needs rest to get that tranquilizer out of her. We are hydrating her and giving her nutrients and vitamins to help both her and her child, so please do not test me. I will get the military police in here if you do."

"Excuse me?" His voice cracked. "What did you just say?"

"She needs rest."

"She's pregnant?" another voice piped in.

It sounded familiar, too, but I could not place the names that belonged to these voices.

"Yes. Now she needs rest while her body combats the tranquilizer."

Silence and then shuffling feet, but the pressure on my hand remained. And after another beat or two of my heart, that voice spoke again.

"I am staying. She's my partner and she's carrying my child, so you can call the entire company. I am not leaving her side."

My free arm was lifted, and something clipped on my index finger.

A thumb slowly caressed my other hand. And when my arm was gently replaced next to me, the man's voice asked, "Are they both okay?" This time it was tentative and carried worry to it, which tingled in my shoulder like an echo of his emotions.

"Yes, Mr. Young. They both will be just fine after some more hydration and rest."

"She didn't remember me."

I could just about see the sadness in his voice, and I realized this was someone who was very important to me.

"And neither of us had any clue she was pregnant." The thumb continued to rub my hand.

"Whatever happened out in that field must have been horrific enough to give her amnesia. But with most trauma, victim's memories eventually return." Her voice sounded as if she were giving the man a smile of reassurance.

And then footfalls, followed by the door creaking and then clicking closed.

I waited a few minutes. I don't know what I expected. Maybe for the man to release my hand, but I did not expect the emotional words that tumbled from his lips.

"Please come back to me, Sarah. I need you."

I gulped the lump in my throat down and blinked my eyes open. Light pierced my eyes like picks slamming through my skull, and I groaned, squeezing them shut again. A fresh wave of dizziness hit, and my stomach rolled. I gagged, but clamped my teeth closed against the burn of acid in my throat.

"Easy." That deep timbre soothed the nerves jumping all through me.

Something touched my lips, and I pulled back.

"Ginger ale. It will help with the stomach rolls."

I took a sip and nearly moaned as my stomach decided whether to keep or reject the liquid. Coolness covered my forehead, and I looked between my lashes.

Dark disheveled hair, almost the color of the wolf's coat, hung around his face. His eyes reminded me of the afternoon sky, and lips, even sporting a frown, were full enough to kiss. His strong chin seemed to tremble with emotion, and he sniffed his perfect nose. The symmetry of his face screamed perfection and the way he was looking at me was something between love and loss.

"What happened?" I whispered, trying not to make my head crack open.

"You were tranquilized."

I let that settle. Something about the term rang a distant bell, but I still couldn't reach through the wall holding my memories at bay. "Why?"

"Because they didn't know if you were dangerous or not."

"Who are they?" I squinted and brought my hand up to cover the glare from the lights.

His soft laugh layered over me like a weighted blanket. "They. Another organization, if you will. The United States military. What you set off was the equivalent of a small nuke. Except without the radiation."

I narrowed my eyes. "I set off a bomb?"

He blinked at me and then settled back into the seat. "You remember nothing?"

My hand moved to my belly. "I remember that I'm pregnant."

Something shifted in his eyes, like a privacy curtain drawing across a room. "You knew that before we went to the farm?" The tightness in his body echoed in my shoulder.

I rubbed the spot on my shoulder and stared at him before I shrugged. "I knew when I woke in the ash." I blinked at him, trying to think beyond the pain cradling my head.

He glanced at the ceiling and closed his eyes, as if trying to reconcile things himself.

"Who am I?"

His gaze shot down to mine. "You are Sarah Stone."

"And who are you?"

His eyes swam in a sheen of tears. "I'm Robby Young. Your mate." He looked at my stomach. "The father of your child." He covered my stomach with his hand.

I blinked at him. "Mate? Am I a shifter, too?"

The question caught him off guard. He chuckled and shook his head, giving me a side-eye full of mirth. "You were something altogether different, hon."

"Were?"

He nodded. "I think you might be back to being just the badass you were back at the academy."

"I was a badass?"

"You were the fiercest witch to ever grace those halls."

"A witch? Is that what happened? A spell gone bad?" I started to sit up but thought twice about it when the spin came back. I settled into the pillow again.

"It's a long story, and I'd rather not get you worked up. That's a surefire way to get myself kicked out of this room." He picked up my hand and brought it to his lips. "We have time."

<hr>

THE DOOR TO THE HOSPITAL room creaked open, and I glanced over at a tall, thin form that slid into the room. He approached while watching Robby snore away in the chair.

"Hi, Sarah. Do you remember me?" He sat in the chair opposite Robby.

I studied his face. It was kind but there was something in his eyes, as if he were much older than his appearance. The dark shadows of the room seemed to hide him. I finally shook my head.

"I'm Phillip. I am the one who put that tattoo on your chest and on your backside."

"So, you are a tattoo artist?"

"I am a friend." He didn't reach for me, but his smile was warm enough. "I honestly didn't think I'd ever see you again." Now his voice hitched, but he shook it off. "I felt you go." His chin trembled, and his eyes cast downward. "God help me, I felt you die and not the temporary death of a phoenix, but like death actually came to claim you for good." A tear slipped down his cheek, and he nodded toward Robby. "He was inconsolable. And when he said his mark was tingling, I thought he was having a psychotic break."

I remained quiet. I had nothing to offer to this conversation except a big black canvas of nothing.

He sniffled and wiped his face. "But here you are, with your vibrant life force thriving as if none of this happened. Snapped right back to the true innocent that you are." He took my hand and put his forehead against it. "I'm sorry I failed you."

Robby turned his head. "How did you fail her?"

Phillip looked at Robby. "You can't feel the absence of her power?" he asked as he looked up.

Robby glanced at me and then at Phillip. "I just assumed it was dormant, like the memory thing."

Phillip shook his head. "No. It's gone. She carries no signature of magic of any form." His gaze moved to my stomach. "But I can't say the same about your child."

When he looked back at me, I shivered under the stare.

What in God's name was I carrying?

TAINTED MIND 25

BEING THE SUBJECT OF A military tribunal is as fun as getting teeth pulled without novocaine. Especially when I didn't know who I really was, much less anything about my life before that field.

But at least they let us live in the barracks together instead of locking us up in cells. However, military life was not easy. They expected us to get up at the crack of dawn and do all the normal things, like run ten miles with a pack on our backs and scrub floors and work in the mess tent, making meals that didn't appeal to me at all.

I kept Robby at arm's length. I couldn't just step into a romantic relationship when I had no idea who I was. And getting to know him was like savoring a good dessert. So, although we were all in the same room, my bunk was on the opposite side of the three men.

The only thing that unnerved me about Robby were his night terrors. He grunted and growled in his dreams, tossing from side to side most nights, and called out my name at least once during sleeping hours.

And all the while, my shoulder ached in some weird echo of his emotions.

Tonight was no different, except he was whining like a hurt puppy.

Neither Johnson nor Phillip stirred, and I stared at the ceiling.

I sighed and got up, crossing to his cot. I sat on the edge and put my hand on his chest, right over the Egyptian eye tattoo. His eyes shot open, and he stared at me with both horror and sadness in his eyes.

His hand snaked up behind my head and he pulled me down, meeting me in the middle, and before I could pull away, his mouth claimed mine. It was our first kiss since I woke in that field.

An electrical current surged through me, and I gasped at the intensity of it. The way this man kissed me was all-consuming. Every muscle melted in his arms, and he sat up, pulling me against his chest. The kiss deepened until I gasped for air.

He moved his kisses to my throat. "You're mine," he whispered in my ear, and then lowered his mouth to my shoulder. It pulsed with the energy filling me. I didn't even notice when he moved the material away. And then the pleasure flared with pain as his teeth sunk into my flesh.

My breath locked in my chest and then every memory locked in my brain flooded through me like a tidal wave, mixing with the agony in my shoulder. He kept his teeth embedded in my flesh and held me close, whining softly through the entire memory dump as if he were reliving every moment with me.

Tears flowed from my eyes as I fought to catch my breath, clinging to him as if he were life itself.

Finally, the barrage ended, and his teeth retracted. He pressed his head to my shoulder, shaking in my arms. I was shaking just as hard as he was.

When he finally looked up, his gaze held awe. "You threatened to burn all of heaven out of existence?"

I smiled down at him and shuffled through my more recent memories. "I told you, I'd die a thousand deaths and still come back to you."

Epilogue

TAINTED MIND
EPIOGUE

I SAT IN THE SWING, letting it slowly rock under the deck of our home as I rubbed my large belly. I had gotten used to the quiet of the countryside, and I loved our new life amid the pack. We claimed Robby's father's house and updated it to our tastes. Although Robby was the true alpha of the pack, he let Johnson run the business side of the pack because he couldn't bring himself to strip his beta of the alpha title.

Johnson kept Robby in the loop even though he really didn't need to, and any critical pack decisions always included Robby. And Phillip

848

decided to relocate outside of the city as well. He started up a tattoo shop in town and lived right down the road. I guess he got kind of attached to us and wanted some peace and quiet for a change. He still charged a certain fee for the tattoos, but since he fed on my essence, his appetite had diminished greatly, as if my phoenix had given him the same power to resist feeding the way it had for me.

Laughter rang out in the yard, and I focused on my daughter dancing around with her father, trying to tag him. Her auburn hair blew in the breeze, blocking her blue eyes. She was a true mix of both of us. When he evaded her touch, she let out a laugh, followed by a frustrated growl. Robby turned and scooped her up in his arms. His blue eyes sparkled with joy, even from this distance.

Our little two-year-old seemed normal, but we knew better. She was one of a kind—a hybrid werewolf with witch, phoenix, and vampire blood running through her. She had already shown some tendencies of each, much to our chagrin, but Robby's alpha kept her in control.

For now.

Who knew how long he'd be able to keep her in line. If she was anything like her mother, we were in deep shit.

My stomach cramped, and I folded over as liquid gushed from between my legs.

"Um, honey, I think it's time," I called as I tried to breathe through the contraction. They said the second child came faster, which had my pulse racing right now. Erica had been delivered after a couple of hours of labor. Too fast to have any medications.

As if on cue, Phillip ran out of the house with my hospital bag in his hands and the car keys in the other. He traded the items for Erica. "We are going to have such fun, aren't we, my little queen." He fricken' doted on our daughter, like she was queen of all things.

I gave her a kiss and moved quickly to the car. "Don't try teaching her control again." I pointed at Phillip before I folded into the car. "We don't need another fire."

"Cross my heart." He glanced at Erica's pouting face. "I will behave," he added.

I closed the door and glanced at Robby as the next contraction hit. "We better go unless you want to deliver your son here in the car." I huffed my breath as he peeled out.

Robby sent a wave to Phillip, and then took my hand, bringing it to his lips. "Breathe."

His eyes glowed with excitement, and my mark echoed the purest joy this side of heaven.

"I love you, Sarah Young." He winked at me as he took the next turn like we were on rails.

"I love you, too." I puffed through each word as I concentrated on breathing through the contraction.

We barely made it to the hospital, and as they were rolling the gurney down the hall, our boy's head crowned. By the time we made it to the delivery room, I had my son in my arms.

"What's his name?" the nurse asked as she smiled down at the swaddled baby.

Robby and I exchanged glances.

"Robert William Young the Third," Robby said. We had agreed to carry on his name in honor of his father's sacrifice. But we also agreed that we would call our son by his middle name because, honestly, I couldn't handle two Roberts under the same roof. "We'll call him Will."

Robby smiled with tears in his eyes, and he leaned over, gently pressing his lips to mine. "Maybe next time, we should have a midwife at the house."

"Oh, you think there's going to be a next time?" I cocked an eyebrow at him.

He grinned. "A next, and a next, and a next."

I let out an exasperated laugh and shoved him away. "We'll see," I said as I stared down at our little boy nestled against my chest. My heart filled with the rightness of this moment.

Even though a small part of me missed the thrill of the hunt, creating life was so much more satisfying than being an agent of death.

My eyes blurred with a sudden sheen of tears as realization set in.

We finally had everything we had ever dreamed, and so much more.

The End

If you enjoyed the Shades of Night series, please consider leaving a review!

About J.E. Taylor

J.E. Taylor is a USA Today bestselling author, a publisher, an editor, a manuscript formatter, a mother, a wife, a business analyst, and a Supernatural fangirl, not necessarily in that order. She first sat down to seriously write in February of 2007 after her daughter asked:

"Mom, if you could do anything, what would you do?"

From that moment on, she hasn't looked back.

Besides being co-owner of Novel Concept Publishing, Ms. Taylor also moonlights as a Senior Editor of Allegory E-zine, an online venue for Science Fiction, Fantasy and Horror, and co-host of the popular YouTube talk show Spilling Ink.

She lives in New Hampshire with her husband and during the summer months enjoys her weekends on the shore in southern Maine.

Visit her at www.jetaylor75.com to check out her other titles.

Look for Erica's story in a Shades of Night
Sequel - Pack Magic

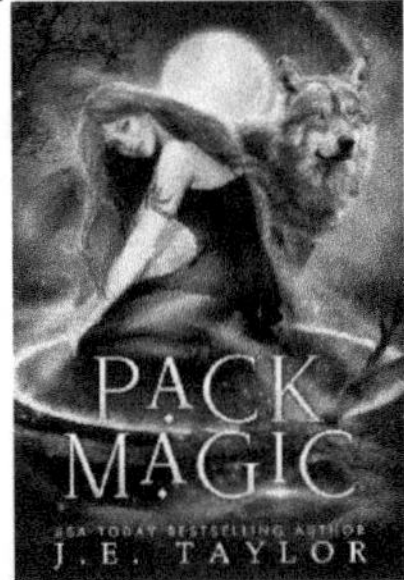

PACK MAGIC

Destinies collide when two alphas aim for the role of leader of the pack.

Daughter of a tribrid and a flame-touched alpha werewolf, Erica Young's course in life should be set. Except no one wants a phoenix-werewolf with a taste for blood to be their alpha.

When the head of the werewolf council shows up with a possible candidate to take her place in the pack, sparks fly.

Logan Blaez, the prodigal son of the council head, is willing to challenge Erica for the role of alpha, even if that means a fight to the death. Until he lays eyes on her.

Now he wants to claim Erica as his mate and rule as her alpha.

Too bad Erica isn't willing to submit, or give up her birthright.

www.ingramcontent.com/pod-product-compliance
Lightning Source LLC
Chambersburg PA
CBHW070828020826
48982CB00015B/809